John Lubbock

# The origin of civilisation and the primitive condition of man

## Mental and social condition of savages

John Lubbock

**The origin of civilisation and the primitive condition of man**
*Mental and social condition of savages*

ISBN/EAN: 9783742830920

Manufactured in Europe, USA, Canada, Australia, Japa

Cover: Foto ©Andreas Hilbeck / pixelio.de

Manufactured and distributed by brebook publishing software
(www.brebook.com)

John Lubbock

**The origin of civilisation and the primitive condition of man**

VIEW OF STONEHENGE

# THE
# ORIGIN OF CIVILISATION
### AND THE
# PRIMITIVE CONDITION OF MAN.

---

## MENTAL AND SOCIAL CONDITION OF SAVAGES.

---

BY

## SIR JOHN LUBBOCK, Bart., M.P., F.R.S.

VICE-CHANCELLOR OF THE UNIVERSITY OF LONDON;
AUTHOR OF 'PREHISTORIC TIMES' ETC.; HONORARY SECRETARY OF THE LONDON BANKERS;
FELLOW OF THE LINNEAN, GEOLOGICAL, ENTOMOLOGICAL, AND OTHER SOCIETIES.

THIRD EDITION, WITH NUMEROUS ADDITIONS

# PREFACE.

IN my work on 'Prehistoric Times' I have devoted
several chapters to the description of modern
savages, because the weapons and implements now used
by the lower races of men throw much light on the signification and use of those discovered in ancient tumuli,
or in the drift gravels; and because a knowledge of
modern savages and their modes of life enables us more
accurately to picture, and more vividly to conceive,
the manners and customs of our ancestors in bygone
ages.

In the present volume, which is founded on a course
of lectures delivered at the Royal Institution in the
spring of 1868, I propose more particularly to describe
the social and mental condition of savages, their art,
their systems of marriage and of relationship, their religions, language, moral character, and laws. Subsequently I shall hope to publish those portions of my
lectures which have reference to their houses, dress,
boats, arms, implements, &c. From the very nature of
the subjects dealt with in the present volume, I shall
have to record many actions and ideas very abhorrent to

us; so many, in fact, that if I pass them without comment or condemnation, it is because I am reluctant to fatigue the reader by a wearisome iteration of disapproval. In the chapters on Marriage and Religion more especially, though I have endeavoured to avoid everything that was needlessly offensive, still it was impossible not to mention some facts which are very repugnant to our feelings. Yet were I to express my sentiments in some cases, silence in others might be held to imply indifference, if not approval.

Montesquieu[1] commences with an apology that portion of his great work which is devoted to Religion. As, he says, 'on peut juger parmi les ténèbres celles qui sont les moins épaisses, et parmi les abimes ceux qui sont les moins profonds, ainsi l'on peut chercher entre les religions fausses celles qui sont les plus conformes au bien de la société; celles qui, quoiqu'elles n'aient pas l'effet de mener les hommes aux félicités de l'autre vie, peuvent le plus contribuer à leur bonheur dans celle-ci. Je n'examinerai donc les diverses religions du monde que par rapport au bien que l'on en tire dans l'état civil, soit que je parle de celle qui a sa racine dans le ciel, ou bien de celles qui ont la leur sur la terre.' The difficulty which I have felt has taken a different form, but I deem it necessary to say these few words of explanation, lest I should be supposed to approve that which I do not expressly condemn.

Klemm, in his 'Allgemeine Culturgeschichte der

---

[1] 'Esprit des Lois,' liv. xxiv. ch. 1.

Menschen,' and recently Mr. Wood, in a more popular manner ('Natural History of Man'), have described the various races of man consecutively; a system which has its advantages, but which does not well bring out the general stages of progress in civilisation.

Various other works, amongst which I must specially mention Müller's 'Geschichte der American-ischen Urreligionen,' M'Lennan's 'Primitive Marriage,' and Bachofen's 'Das Mutterrecht,' deal with particular portions of the subject. Maine's interesting work on 'Ancient Law,' again, considers man in a more advanced stage than that which is the special subject of my work.

The plan pursued by Tylor in his remarkable work on the 'Early History of Mankind' more nearly re-sembles that which I have sketched out for myself, but the subject is one which no two minds would view in the same manner, and is so vast that I am sure my friend will not regard me as intruding upon a field which he has done so much to make his own.

Nor must I omit to mention Lord Kames' 'History of Man,' and Montesquieu's 'Esprit des Lois,' both of them works of great interest, although written at a time when our knowledge of savage races was even more imperfect than it is now.

Yet the materials for such a work as the present are immense, and are daily increasing. Those who take an interest in the subject become every year more and more numerous; and while none of my readers can be

more sensible of my deficiencies than I am myself, yet
after ten years of study, I have been anxious to publish
this portion of my work, in the hope that it may contribute something towards the progress of a science
which is in itself of the deepest interest, and which has
a peculiar importance to an Empire such as ours, comprising races in every stage of civilisation yet attained
by man.

HIGH ELMS, DOWN, KENT :
*February*, 1870.

# CONTENTS.

## CHAPTER VI.

### RELIGION (*continued*).

## CHAPTER VII.

### RELIGION (*concluded*).

## CHAPTER VIII.

### CHARACTER AND MORALS.

## CHAPTER IX.

### LANGUAGE.

## CHAPTER X.

### LAWS.

# APPENDIX.

## PART I.

## PART II.

# ILLUSTRATIONS.

## DESCRIPTION OF THE PLATES.

# LIST OF THE PRINCIPAL WORKS QUOTED IN THIS VOLUME.

Adelung. Mithridates.
Arago, Narrative of a Voyage round the World.
Arbousset and Daumas. Tour at the Cape of Good Hope.
Asiatic Researches.
Astley, Collection of Voyages.
Athinson, Oriental and Western Siberia.
  „ Upper and Lower Amoor.
Azara, Voyages dans l'Amérique Meridionale.

Bachofen, Das Mutterrecht.
Baikie, Exploring Voyage up the rivers Kwora and Binua.
Bain, Mental and Moral Science.
Baker, Albert Nyanza.
  „ Nile Tributaries of Abyssinia.
Barth, Travels in Central Africa.
Battel, The strange Adventures of (Pinkerton's Voyages and Travels).
Beechey, Narrative of a Voyage to the Pacific.
Bosman, Description of Guinea (Pinkerton's Voyages and Travels).
Brett, Indian Tribes of Guiana.
Brooke, Lapland.
Bruce, Travels in Abyssinia.
Burchell, Travels in Southern Africa.
Burton, Lake Regions of Africa.
  „ First Footsteps in Africa.
  „ Abbeokuta and the Cameroon Mountains.
  „ City of the Saints.
  „ Mission to the King of Dahoma.

Caillié, Travels to Timbuctoo.
Callaway, Religious System of the Amazulu.
Campbell, Tales of the West Highlands.
  „ Wild Tribes of Khondistan.
Carver, Travels in North America.
Casalis, The Basutos.
Catlin, North American Indians.
Chapman, Travels in S. Africa.
Charlevoix, History of Paraguay.
Clarke, Travels.
Collins, English Colony in New South Wales.
Cook, Voyage round the World. (In Hawkesworth's Voyages.)
  „ Second Voyage towards the South Pole.
  „ Third Voyage to the Pacific Ocean.
Cox, Manual of Mythology.
Crantz, History of Greenland.

Dalton, Descriptive Ethnology of Bengal.
Darwin, Animals and Plants under Domestication.
  „ Origin of Species.
  „ Researches in Geology and Natural History.
Davis, Dr. J. B., Thesaurus Craniorum.
Davis, The Chinese.
Davy, Account of Ceylon.
Deane, Worship of the Serpent traced throughout the World.
De Brosses, Du Culte des Dieux fétiches.

De Hell, Steppes of the Caspian Sea.
Denham, Travels in Africa.
Depons, Travels in South America.
Dias, Diccionario da Lingua Tupy.
Dieffenbach, New Zealand.
Dobrizhoffer, History of the Abipones.
Drury, Adventures in Madagascar.
Dubois, Description of the People of India.
Dunn, The Oregon Territory.
Dulaure, Histoire abrégée des différents Cultes.
D'Urville, Voyage au Pôle sud,

Earle, Residence in New Zealand.
Egede, Greenland.
Ellis, Three Visits to Madagascar.
  „ Polynesian Researches.
Erman, Travels in Siberia.
Erskine, Western Pacific.
Eyre, Discoveries in Central Australia.

Farrar, Origin of Language.
Fergusson, Tree and Serpent Worship
Fitzroy, Voyage of the 'Adventure' and 'Beagle.'
Forbes Leslie, Early Races of Scotland.
Forster, Observations made during a Voyage round the World.
Forsyth, Highlands of Central India.
Franklin, Journey to the Shores of the Polar Sea.
Fraser, Travels in Koordistan and Mesopotamia.
  „ Tour to the Himalaya Mountains.
Freycinet, Voyage autour du Monde.

Gaius, Commentaries on Roman Law.
Gama, Descripcion histórica y cronológica de las Pedras de Mexico.
Garcilasso de la Vega, Commentaries of the Yncas.
Gardner, Faiths of the World.
Galton, Tropical South Africa.
Gibbs, H. H., Romance of the Chevelere Assigne.
Girard-Teulon, La Mère chez certains Peuples de l'Antiquité.
Gladstone, Juventus Mundi.
Goguet, De l'Origine des Lois, des Arts et des Sciences.

Graah, Voyage to Greenland.
Gray, Travels in Western Africa.
Grey, Sir G., Polynesian Mythology.
  „ Journal of two Expeditions of Discovery in North-West and Western Australia.

Hale, Ethnology of the United States Exploring Expedition.
  „ Ethnology and Philology.
Hallam, History of England.
Hamilton, Account of the Kingdom of Nepaul.
Hanway, Travels in Persia.
Hayes, Open Polar Sea.
Hawkesworth, Voyages of Discovery in the Southern Hemisphere.
Hearne, Voyage to the Northern Ocean.
Herodotus.
Hooper, Tents of the Tuski.
Humboldt, Personal Researches.
Hunter, Comparative Dictionary of the Non-Aryan Languages of India and High Asia.
  „ The Annals of Rural Bengal.
Hume, Essays.
  „ History of England.

Inman, Ancient Faiths in Ancient Names.

James, Expedition to the Rocky Mountains.
Jones, Antiquities of the Southern Indians.
Journal of the Royal Institution.
Jukes, Voyage of the 'Fly.'

Kames, History of Man.
Kenrick, Phoenicia.
Keppel, Visit to the Indian Archipelago.
  „ Expedition to Borneo.
Klemm, Allgemeine Culturgeschichte der Menschheit.
  „ Werkzeuge und Waffen.
Koelle, Polyglotta Africana.
Kolben, History of the Cape of Good Hope.
Kolff, Voyage of the 'Doorga.'
Kotzebue, Voyage round the World.

Lalat, Voyage aux Iles de l'Amérique.

Labillardière, Voyage in search of La Perouse.

Laflan Murure des Sauvages américains.

Laird, Expedition into the Interior of Africa.

Lander (R. and J.), Niger Expedition.

Lang, Aborigines of Australia.

Latham, Descriptive Ethnology.

Lecky, History of Rationalism.

Lewin, Hill Tracts of Chittagong.

Lichtenstein, Travels in South Africa.

Livingstone, Missionary Travels and Researches in South Africa.

„ Expedition to the Zambesi.

Locke, On the Human Understanding.

Lubbock, Prehistoric Times.

Lyon, Journal during the Voyage of Captain Parry.


McGillivray, Voyage of the 'Rattle-snake.'

MacLean, Compendium of Kaffir Laws and Customs.

M'Lennan, Primitive Marriage.

Maine, Ancient Law.

Marco Polo, Travels of.

Marsden, History of Sumatra.

Mariner, Tonga Islands.

Martius, Von dem Rechtszustande unter den Ureinwohnern Brasiliens.

Merolla, Voyage to Congo (Pinkerton's Voyages and Travels).

Metz, Tribes of the Neilgherries.

Metlahkatlah, published by the Church Missionary Society.

Middendorf, Sibirische Reise.

Mollhausen, Journey to the Pacific.

Monboddo, Origin and Progress of Language.

Montesquieu, Esprit des Lois.

Moser, The Caucasus and its People.

Moor, Notices of the Indian Archipelago.

Morgan, Proc. Acad. Nat. Sci. Philadelphia.

Mouhot, Travels in the Central Parts of Indo-China.

Müller (Max), Chips from a German Workshop.

Müller (Max), Lectures on Language, First Series.

„ Lectures on Language, Second Series.

Müller (F. G.), Geschichte der Amerikanischen Urreligionen.

Müller (C. O.), Scientific Mythology.

„ (C. S.), Description de toutes les Nations de l'Empire de Russe.

Nilsson, On the Stone Age.

Olaus Magnus.

Ortolan, Justinian.

Pallas, Voyages en différentes Provinces de l'Empire de Russie.

„ Voyages entrepris dans les Gouvernements méridionaux de l'Empire de Russie.

Park, Travels.

Parkyns, Life in Abyssinia.

Perouse, La, Voyage autour du Monde.

Pliny, Natural History.

Prescott, History of Peru.

„ History of Mexico.

Prichard, Natural History of Man.

Proceedings of the American Academy of Arts and Sciences.

Proceedings of the Boston Society of Natural History.

Proyart, History of Loango (Pinkerton's Voyages and Travels).

Raffles, History of Java.

Report of Committee of Legislative Council of Victoria on the Aborigines.

Reade, Savage Africa.

Renan, Origine du Langage.

Richardson, Journal of a Boat Journey.

Robertson, History of America.

Ross, Voyage to Baffin's Bay.

Rutimeyer, Beitr. zur Kenntnis der fossilen Pferde.

Scherzer, Voyage of the 'Novara.'

Schoolcraft, Indian Tribes.

Seemann, A Mission to Viti.

Shortland, Traditions and Superstitions of the New Zealanders.

Smith A., Theory of Moral Sentiments, and Dissertation on the Origin of Languages.
  „ G. (Bishop of Victoria). Ten Weeks in Japan.
  „ J. History of Virginia.
  „ W., Voyage to Guinea.
Smithsonian Reports.
Snowden and Prall, Grammar of the Mpongwe Language. New York.
Speke, Discovery of the Source of the Nile.
Spencer's Principles of Biology.
Spiers, Life in Ancient India.
Spix and Martius, Travels in Brazil.
Sproat, Scenes and Studies of Savage Life.
Squiers, Serpent Symbol in America.
Stephens, South Australia.
Stevenson, Travels in North America.
Strahlenberg, Description of Russia, Siberia, and Great Tartary.
Systems of Land Tenure. Published by the Cobden Club.

Tacitus.
Tanner, Narrative of a Captivity among the North American Indians.
Taylor, New Zealand and its Inhabitants.
Tertre, History of the Caribby Islands.
Tindall, Grammar and Dictionary of the Namaqua (Hottentot) Language.
Transactions of the Americ. Antiq. Soc.
Transactions of the Ethnological Society.

Transactions of the R. S. of Victoria.
Tuckey, Expedition to Explore River Zaire.
Turner, Nineteen Years in Polynesia.
Tylor, Anahuac.
  „ Early History of Man.

Upham, History and Doctrine of Buddhism in Ceylon.

Vancouver, Voyage of Discovery.
Vogt, Lectures on Man.

Waitz, Anthropologie der Naturvölker.
Wake, Chapters on Man.
Wallace, Travels in the Amazons and Rio Negro.
Wallace, Malay Archipelago.
Watson and Kaye, The People of India.
Wedgwood, Introduction to the Dictionary of the English Language.
  „ Origin of Language.
Whately (Archbishop of Dublin), Political Economy.
Whipple, Report on the Indian Tribes.
Wilkes, United States Exploring Expedition.
Williams, Fiji and the Fijians.
Wood, Natural History of Man.
Wrangel, Siberia and the Polar Sea.
Wright, Superstitions of England.
Wuttke, Die ersten Stufen der Gesch. der Menschheit.

Yate, New Zealand.

---

*Erratum.*

P. 317, line 10, *for* 'Umklanga' *read* 'Uthlanga.'

# THE ORIGIN OF CIVILISATION

*&c.*

## CHAPTER I.

### INTRODUCTION.

THE study of the lower races of men, apart from the
direct importance which it possesses in an empire
like ours, is of great interest from three points of view.
In the first place, the condition and habits of existing
savages resemble in many ways, though not in all, those
of our own ancestors in a period now long gone by:[1]
in the second, they illustrate much of what is passing among ourselves, many customs which have evidently no relation to present circumstances; and even
some ideas which are rooted in our minds, as fossils are
imbedded in the soil : while, thirdly, we can even, by
means of them, penetrate some of that mist which
separates the present from the future.

In fact, the lower races of men in various parts of

---

[1] I am very glad to find that so
able and cautious a critic as Mr.
Bagehot has expressed his assent to
the line of argument here used, and
the general conclusions at which I
have arrived. See his Physics and
Politics, 1872, especially the excellent chapter on 'Nation-making.'

the world present us with illustrations of a social condition
ruder, and more archaic, than any which history records
as having ever existed among the more advanced races.
Even among civilised peoples, however, we find traces
of former barbarism.  Not only is language in this respect very instructive ; but the laws and customs are
often of very ancient origin, and contain symbols which
are the relics of former realities.  Thus the use of stone
knives in certain Egyptian ceremonies points to a time
when that people habitually used stone implements.
Again, the form of marriage by coemptio among the
Romans indicates a period in their history when they
habitually bought wives, as so many savage tribes do
now.  So also the form of capture in weddings can only
be explained by the hypothesis that the capture of wives
was once a stern reality.  In such cases as these the
sequence is obvious.  The use of stone knives in certain ceremonies is evidently a case of survival, not of
invention ; and in the same way the form of capture in
weddings would naturally survive the actual reality,
while we cannot suppose that the reality would rise out
of the symbol.

It must not be supposed, however, that the condition
of primitive man is correctly represented by even the
lowest of existing races.  The very fact that the latter
have remained stationary, that their manners, habits,
and mode of life have continued almost unaltered for
generations, has created a strict, and often complicated, system of customs, from which the former was
necessarily free, but which has in some cases gradually
acquired even more than the force of law.  In order,
then, to arrive at a clear idea of this primitive con-

dition of the human race, we must eliminate these customs from our conception of that condition ; and this we are best enabled to do by a comparison of savage tribes belonging to different families of the human race.

Although the differences of race, of geographical position, and of their general surroundings, have necessarily led to considerable divergencies in the social and mental development of different tribes, still I have endeavoured to show that, in the main, the development of higher and better ideas as to Marriage, Relationships, Law, Religion, &c., has followed in its earlier stages a very similar course even in the most distinct races of man; and when we find customs and ideas which to us seem absurd or illogical, reappearing in distinct families of mankind at the same stage of development, we may safely conclude that, however absurd they may appear to us, they are founded on the innate characteristics of humanity, and are no unmeaning or insignificant accidents. It has been said by some writers that savages are merely the degenerate descendants of more civilised ancestors, and I am far from denying that there are cases of retrogression. But, in the first place, a tribe which had sunk from civilisation into barbarism would by no means exhibit the same features, as one which had risen into barbarism from savagery. And, what is even more important, races which fall back in civilisation, diminish in numbers. The whole history of man shows how the stronger and progressive, increase in numbers and drive out the weaker and lower races. I have endeavoured, for instance, to show that the ideas on the subject of re-

lationships which are prevalent among the less advanced
races, would naturally arise in the course of progress,
but are inconsistent with the theory of degradation. So,
again, a people who trusted in luck would have no
chance in the struggle for existence against one which
believed in law: if we find a belief in fetichism interwoven with the religion of even the highest races, it is
because these races were Fetichists before they became
Buddhist, Mahometan, or Christian.   A tribe in which
the feeling of relationship was weak and ill-defined would,
*cæteris paribus*, have no chance in a struggle with one
in which the family feeling was strong and well-organ-
ised.   Hence, although we are very far as yet from
having arrived at such a result, I believe it will be possible for us to realise to ourselves a condition through
which our ancestors must have passed in pre-historic
times—one far more primitive than any of which we
have at present an actual example.

At any rate it cannot be doubted that the careful
study of manners and customs, traditions and superstitions, will eventually solve many difficult problems
of Ethnology.   This mode of research, however, requires
to be used with great caution, and has in fact led to
many erroneous conclusions.   For instance, in more
than one case savage races have been regarded as descendants of the Ten Tribes, because their customs
offer some singular points of resemblance with those recorded in the Pentateuch.   In these cases, more profound acquaintance with the manners and customs of
savage races would have shown that these coincidences,
so far from being, as supposed, peculiar to these tribes,
were, in fact, common to several, if not to all, the prin-

cipal races of mankind. Much careful study will, therefore, be required before this class of evidence can be used with safety, though I doubt not that eventually it will be found most instructive.

The study of savage life is, moreover, of peculiar importance to us, forming, as we do, part of a great empire, with colonies in every part of the world, and fellow-citizens in every stage of civilisation. Of this our Indian possessions afford us a good illustration. ' We have ' studied the lowland population,' says Mr. Hunter,[1] ' as ' no conquerors ever studied or understood a subject ' race. Their history, their habits, their requirements, ' their very weaknesses and prejudices are known, and ' furnish a basis for those political inductions which, ' under the titles of administrative foresight and timely ' reform, meet popular movements half-way. The East ' India Company grudged neither honours nor solid re-' wards to any meritorious effort to illustrate the peoples ' whom it ruled.' . . . . . . .

' The practical result now appears. English admi-' nistrators understand the Aryan, and are almost totally ' ignorant of the non-Aryan, population of India. They ' know with remarkable precision how a measure will be ' received by the higher or purely Aryan ranks of the ' community ; they can foresee with less certainty its ' effect upon the lower or semi-Aryan classes, but they ' neither know nor venture to predict the results of any ' line of action among the non-Aryan tribes. Political ' calculations are impossible without a knowledge of the ' people. But the evil does not stop here. In the void

---

[1] Non-Aryan Languages of India, p. 2.

' left by ignorance, prejudice has taken up its seat, and
' the calamity of the non-Aryan races is not merely that
' they are not understood, but that they are misrepre-
' sented.'

Well, therefore, has it been observed by Sir Henry
Maine, in his excellent work on 'Ancient Law,' that, 'even
' if they gave more trouble than they do, no pains would
' be wasted in ascertaining the germs out of which has
' assuredly been unfolded every form of moral restraint
' which controls our actions and shapes our conduct at
' the present moment. The rudiments of the social
' state,' he adds, ' so far as they are known to us at all,
' are known through testimony of three sorts—accounts
' by contemporary observers of civilisations less advanced
' than their own, the records which particular races have
' preserved concerning their primitive history, and
' ancient law. The first kind of evidence is the best we
' could have expected. As societies do not advance
' concurrently, but at different rates of progress, there
' have been epochs at which men trained to habits of
' methodical observation have really been in a position
' to watch and describe the infancy of mankind.' [1] He
refers particularly to Tacitus, whom he praises for having ' made the most of such an opportunity ;' adding,
however, 'but the "Germany," unlike most celebrated
' classical books, has not induced others to follow the
' excellent example set by its author, and the amount of
' this sort of testimony which we possess is exceedingly
' small.'

This is, however, I think, far from being really

[1] Maine's Ancient Law, p. 120.

the case. At all epochs some ' men trained to habits
' of methodical observation have really been in a posi-
' tion to watch and describe the infancy of mankind,' and
the testimony of our modern travellers is of the same
nature as that for which we are indebted to Tacitus.

It must, however, be admitted that our information
with reference to the social and moral condition of the
lower races of man is certainly very far from being
satisfactory, either in extent or in accuracy. Travellers
naturally find it far easier to describe the houses,
boats, food, dress, weapons, and implements of savages,
than to understand their thoughts and feelings. The
whole mental condition of a savage is so different
from ours, that it is often very difficult to follow what
is passing in his mind, or to understand the motives
by which he is influenced. Many things appear natural
and almost self-evident to him, which produce a very
different impression on us. ' What!' said a negro to
Burton, ' am I to starve, while my sister has children
' whom she can sell?'

Though savages always have a reason, such as it is,
for what they do and what they believe, their reasons
often are very absurd. Moreover, the difficulty of
ascertaining what is passing in their minds is of course
much enhanced by the difficulty of communicating
with them. This has produced many laughable mistakes. Thus, when Labillardière enquired of the
Friendly Islanders the word for 1,000,000, they seem
to have thought the question absurd, and answered him
by a word which apparently has no meaning ; when he
asked for 10,000,000, they said ' laoalai,' which I will

leave unexplained ; for 100,000,000, 'laonnoua,' that is to say, 'nonsense ; ' while for the higher numbers they gave him certain coarse expressions, which he has gravely published in his table of numerals.

A mistake made by Dampier led to more serious results. He had met some Australians, and apprehending an attack, he says :—'I discharged my gun to 'scare them, but avoided shooting any of them ; till 'finding the young man in great danger from them, 'and myself in some, and that though the gun had a 'little frightened them at first, yet *they had soon learnt* 'to despise it, tossing up their hands, and crying "Pooh, '"pooh, pooh!" and coming on afresh with a great noise, 'I thought it high time to charge again, and shoot one 'of them, which I did. The rest, seeing him fall, made 'a stand again, and my young man took the opportunity 'to disengage himself, and come off to me ; my other 'man also was with me, who had done nothing all this 'while, having come out unarmed ; and I returned 'back with my men, designing to attempt the natives 'no farther, being very sorry for what had happened 'already.'[1]   'Pooh, pooh,' however, or 'puff, puff,' is the name which savages, like children, naturally apply to guns.

Another source of error is, that savages are often reluctant to contradict what is said to them. Livingstone calls special attention to this as a characteristic of the natives of Africa.[2]   Mr. Oldfield,[3] again, speaking of the Australians, tells us :—'I have found

[1] Pinkerton's Voyages, vol. xi. p. 473.
[2] Expedition to the Zambesi, p. 309.
[3] Trans. Ethn. Soc., N.S., vol. iii. p. 255.

'this habit of non-contradiction to stand very much
'in my way when making enquiries of them, for, as
'my knowledge of their language was only sufficient
'to enable me to seek information on some points by
'putting suggestive questions, in which they im-
'mediately concurred, I was frequently driven nearly
'to my wits' end to arrive at the truth. A native once
'brought me in some specimens of a species of euca-
'lyptus, and being desirous of ascertaining the habit of
'the plant, I asked, "A tall tree?" to which his ready
'answer was in the affirmative. Not feeling quite
'satisfied, I again demanded, "A low bush?" to which
'"Yes," was also the response.'

Again, the mind of the savage, like that of the child,
is easily fatigued, and he will then give random answers,
to spare himself the trouble of thought. Speaking of
the Ahts (N.W. America), Mr. Sproat[1] says :—'The
'native mind, to an educated man, seems generally to
'be asleep ; and if you suddenly ask a novel question,
'you have to repeat it while the mind of the savage is
'awaking, and to speak with emphasis until he has
'quite got your meaning. This may partly arise from
'the questioner's imperfect knowledge of the language ;
'still, I think, not entirely, as the savage may be
'observed occasionally to become forgetful when volun-
'tarily communicating information. On his attention
'being fully aroused, he often shows much quickness
'in reply and ingenuity in argument. But a short
'conversation wearies him, particularly if questions are
'asked that require efforts of thought or memory on

[1] Scenes and Studies of Savage Life, p. 120.

'his part. The mind of the savage then appears to
'rock to and fro out of mere weakness, and he tells lies
'and talks nonsense.'

'I frequently enquired of the negroes,' says Park,
'what became of the sun during the night, and whether
'we should see the same sun, or a different one, in the
'morning; but I found that they considered the ques-
'tion as very childish. The subject appeared to them
'as placed beyond the reach of human investigation;
'they had never indulged a conjecture, nor formed any
'hypothesis, about the matter.' [1]

Such ideas are, in fact, entirely beyond the mental
range of the lower savages, whose extreme mental in-
feriority we have much difficulty in realising.

Speaking of the wild men in the interior of Borneo,
Mr. Dalton [2] says that they are found living 'absolutely
'in a state of nature, who neither cultivate the ground
'nor live in huts; who neither eat rice nor salt, and who
'do not associate with each other, but rove about some
'woods, like wild beasts; the sexes meet in the jungle,
'or the man carries away a woman from some campong.
'When the children are old enough to shift for them-
'selves, they usually separate, neither one afterwards
'thinking of the other. At night they sleep under some
'large tree, the branches of which hang low; on these
'they fasten the children in a kind of swing; around
'the tree they make a fire to keep off the wild beasts
'and snakes. They cover themselves with a piece of
'bark, and in this also they wrap their children; it is
'soft and warm, but will not keep out the rain. The

[1] Park's Travels, vol. I. p. 205.        Archipelago, p. 40. See also Keppel's
[2] Moor's Notices of the Indian        Expedition to Borneo, vol. ii. p. 10.

' poor creatures are looked on and treated by the other
' Dyaks as wild beasts.'

Lichtenstein describes a Bushman as presenting 'the
' true physiognomy of the small blue ape of Caffraria.
' What gives the more verity to such a comparison was
' the vivacity of his eyes, and the flexibility of his eye-
' brows. . . . Even his nostrils and the corners of
' his mouth, nay his very ears, moved involuntarily.
' . . . There was not, on the contrary, a single
' feature in his countenance that evinced a consciousness
' of mental powers.' [1]

Under these circumstances it cannot be wondered at
that we have most contradictory accounts as to the character and mental condition of savages. Nevertheless, by
comparing together the accounts of different travellers,
we can to a great extent avoid these sources of error;
and we are very much aided in this by the remarkable
similarity between different races. So striking, indeed, is
this, that different races in similar stages of development
often present more features of resemblance to one
another than the same race does to itself in different
stages of its history.

Some ideas, indeed, which seem to us at first inexplicable and fantastic, are yet very widely distributed.
Thus among many races a woman is absolutely forbidden
to speak to her son-in-law. Franklin [2] tells us that
among the American Indians of the far North ' it is
' considered extremely improper for a mother-in-law to
' speak or even look at him; and when she has a com-
' munication to make to him it is the etiquette that she

---

[1] Lichtenstein, vol. ii. p. 224.
[2] Journey to the Shores of the Polar Sea, vol. i. p. 137.

' should turn her back upon him, and address him only
' through the medium of a third person.'

Further south, among the Omahaws, ' neither the
' father-in-law nor mother-in-law will hold any direct
' communication with their son-in-law; nor will he, on
' any occasion, or under any consideration, converse im-
' mediately with them, although no ill-will exists between
' them; they will not, on any account, mention each
' other's name in company, nor look in each other's faces;
' any conversation that passes between them is conducted
' through the medium of some other person.'[1]

Harmon says that among the Indians east of the
Rocky Mountains the same rule prevails.

Baegert[2] mentions that among the Indians of California ' the son-in-law was not allowed, for some time, to
' look into the face of his mother-in-law, or his wife's
' nearest relations, but had to step on one side, or to
' hide himself when these women were present.'

Lafitau,[3] indeed, makes the same statements as regards the North American Indians generally.  We find
it among the Crees and Dacotahs, and again in Florida.
Rochefort mentions it among the Caribs, and in South
America it recurs among the Arawaks.

In Asia, among the Mongols and Kalmucks, a woman
must not speak to her father-in-law nor sit down in his
presence.  Among the Ostiaks of Siberia,[4] ' une fille

[1] James's Expedition to the
Rocky Mountains, vol. i. p. 232.

[2] Account of California, 1773.
Translated by C. Rau, in Smithsonian Rep. for 1863-4, p. 394.

[3] Mœurs des Sauvages Américains, vol. I. p. 576.

[4] Pallas, vol. iv. pp. 71, 577.
He makes the same statement with
reference to the Samoyedes, loc. cit.
p. 99.  See also Müller, Description
de toutes les Nations de l'Empire de
Russie, pt. I. pp. 191-203; pt. II.
p. 104.

' mariée évite autant qu'il lui est possible la présence du
' père de son mari, tant qu'elle n'a pas d'enfant ; et le
' mari, pendant ce temps, n'ose pas paroitre devant la mère
' de sa femme. S'ils se rencontrent par hasard, le mari
' lui tourne le dos, et la femme se couvre le visage. On ne
' donne point de nom aux filles ostiakes; lorsqu'elles sont
' mariées, les hommes les nomment *Imi*, femmes. Les
' femmes, par respect pour leurs maris, ne les appellent
' pas par leur nom ; elles se servent du mot de *Tahé*,
' hommes.'

Dubois mentions that in certain districts of Hindostan a woman ' is not permitted to speak to her mother-
' in-law. When any task is prescribed to her, she shows
' her acquiescence only by signs ;' a contrivance, he
sarcastically adds, ' well adapted for securing domestic
' tranquillity.'[1]

In China, according to Duhalde, the father-in-law,
after the wedding-day, 'never sees the face of his
' daughter-in-law again ; he never visits her,' and if they
chance to meet he hides himself.[2] A similar custom
prevails in Borneo and in the Fiji Islands. In Australia,
also, Eyre states that a man must not pronounce the
name of his father-in-law, his mother-in-law, or his son-
in-law.

In Central Africa, Caillié[3] observes that, ' from this
' moment the lover is not to see the father and mother
' of his future bride: he takes the greatest care to avoid
' them, and if by chance they perceive him they cover
' their faces, as if all ties of friendship were broken. I

---

[1] On the People of India, p. 235.
[2] Astley's Collection of Voyages, vol. iv. p. 91.
[3] Caillié's Travels to Timbuctoo vol. i. p. 94.

' tried in vain to discover the origin of this whimsical
' custom; the only answer I could obtain was, " It's our
' " way."   The custom extends beyond the relations: if
' the lover is of a different camp, he avoids all the in-
' habitants of the lady's camp, except a few intimate
' friends whom he is permitted to visit.   A little tent is
' generally set up for him, under which he remains all
' day, and if he is obliged to come out, or to cross the
' camp, he covers his face.   He is not allowed to see his
' intended during the day, but, when everybody is at
' rest, he creeps into her tent and remains with her till
' daybreak.'   Among the Kaffirs' a married woman ' is
' required to " hlonipa" her father-in-law and all her
' husband's male relations in the ascending line—that
' is, to be cut off from all intercourse with them.   She
' is not allowed to pronounce their names, even mentally;
' and whenever the emphatic syllable of either of their
' names occurs in any other word, she must avoid it, by
' either substituting an entirely new word, or at least
' another syllable, in its place.   The son-in-law is placed
' under certain restrictions towards his mother-in-law.
' He cannot enjoy her society, or remain in the same
' hut with her; nor can he pronounce her name.'   Among
the Bushmen in the far South, Chapman recounts
exactly the same thing, yet none of these observers had
any idea how general the custom is.

In Australia, among the aborigines of Victoria, ' it
' is compulsory on the mothers-in-law to avoid the sight
' of their sons-in-law, by making the mothers-in-law
' take a very circuitous route on all occasions to avoid

---

' Kaffir Laws and Customs, pp. 55, 56.

'being seen, and they hide the face and figure with the
'rug which the female carries about her.'[1] So strict is
this rule, that if married men are jealous of any one,
they sometimes promise to give him a daughter in
marriage. This places the wife, according to custom,
in the position of a mother-in-law, and renders any
communication between her and her future son-in-law
a capital crime[2]

Mr. Tylor, who has some very interesting remarks
on these customs in his 'Early History of Man,' observes
that 'it is hard even to guess what state of things can
'have brought them into existence,' nor, so far as I
am aware, has any one else attempted to explain
them. In the Chapter on Marriage I shall, however,
point out the manner in which I conceive that they
have arisen.

Another curious custom is that known in Béarn
under the name of La Couvade. Probably every Englishman who had not studied other races would assume,
as a matter of course, that on the birth of a child the
mother would everywhere be put to bed and nursed.
But this is not the case. In many races the father, and
not the mother, is doctored when a baby is born.

Yet, though this custom seems so ludicrous to us, it
is very widely distributed. Commencing with South
America, Dobritzhoffer tells us that 'no sooner do you
'hear that a woman has borne a child, than you see the
'husband lying in bed, huddled up with mats and skins,
'lest some ruder breath of air should touch him, fasting,
'kept in private, and for a number of days abstaining

---

[1] Report of Select Committee on Aborigines, Victoria, 1859, p. 73.
[2] *Loc. cit.* p. 78.

'religiously from certain viands: you would swear it
'was he who had had the child. . . . I had read
'about this in old times, and laughed at it, never think-
'ing I could believe such madness, and I used to
'suspect that this barbarian custom was related more
'in jest than in earnest; but at last I saw it with my
'own eyes among the Abipones.'

In Brazil, among the Coroados, Martius tells us that
'as soon as the woman is evidently pregnant, or has
'been delivered, the man withdraws.   A strict regimen
'is observed before the birth; the man and the woman
'refrain for a time from the flesh of certain animals, and
'live chiefly on fish and fruits.'[1]

Further, north in Guiana, Mr. Brett[2] observes that
'some of the men of the Acawoio and Caribi nations,
'when they have reason to expect an increase of their
'families, consider themselves bound to abstain from
'certain kinds of meat, lest the expected child should, in
'some very mysterious way, be injured by their partaking
'of it.  The *Acouri* (or Agouti) is thus tabooed, lest, like
'that little animal, the child should be meagre; the
'*Haimara*, also, lest it should be blind—the outer coating
'of the eye of that fish suggesting film or cataract; the
'*Labba*, lest the infant's mouth should protrude like the
'labba's, or lest it be spotted like the labba, which spots
'would ultimately become ulcers.  The *Marudi* is also
'forbidden, lest the infant be stillborn, the screeching
'of that bird being considered ominous of death.'  And
again:—'On the birth of a child, the ancient Indian
'etiquette requires the father to take to his hammock,

---

[1] Spix's and Martius's Travels in      [2] Brett's Indian Tribes of Guiana,
Brazil, vol. ii. p. 247.                 p. 355.

' where he remains some days as if he were sick, and
' receives the congratulations and condolence of his
' friends. An instance of this custom came under my
' own observation, where the man, in robust health
' and excellent condition, without a single bodily
' ailment, was lying in his hammock in the most
' provoking manner, and carefully and respectfully at-
' tended by the women, while the mother of the new-
' born infant was cooking—none apparently regarding
' her !' [1]

Similar statements have been made by various other
travellers, including De Tertre, Giliz, Biet, Fermin, and
in fact almost all who have written on the natives of
South America.

In North America, Rémy mentions that among the
Shoshonès, when a woman is in labour, the husband
' also is bound to remain in seclusion, away from every
' one, even from his wife.' [2] In Greenland, after a
woman is confined, the ' husband must forbear working
' for some weeks, neither must they drive any trade
' during that time;' [3] in Kamskatka, for some time before
the birth of a baby, the husband must do no hard work.
In South India, according to Mr. Tylor, [4] Mr. F. W.
Jennings states that among natives of the higher
castes about Madras, Seringapatam, and on the
Malabar Coast ' a man, at the birth of his first son
' or daughter by the chief wife, or for any son after-
' wards, will retire to bed for a lunar month, living
' principally on a rice diet, abstaining from exciting

[1] Brott, *loc. cit.* p. 101.   City, p. 120.
[2] Egede's Greenland, p. 196.   [4] Tylor's Early History of Man,
[3] Journey to the Great Salt Lake   2nd ed., p. 301.

'food and from smoking.' Similar notions occur among
the Chinese of West Yunnan, among the Dyaks of
Borneo, among the Kaffirs, in the north of Spain, in
Corsica, and in the south of France, where it is called
'faire la couvade.' While, however, I regard this
curious custom as of much ethnological interest, I
cannot agree with Mr. Tylor in regarding it as evidence that the races by whom it is practised belong to
one variety of the human species.[1] On the contrary, I
believe that it originated independently, in several distinct parts of the world.

It is of course evident that a custom so ancient, and
so widely spread, must have its origin in some idea which
satisfies the savage mind. Several explanations have been
suggested. Professor Max Müller,[2] in his 'Chips from
'a German Workshop,' says :—'It is clear that the
'poor husband was at first tyrannised over by his female
'relations, and afterwards frightened into superstition.
'He then began to make a martyr of himself till he made
'himself really ill, or took to his bed in self-defence.
'Strange and absurd as the couvade appears at first
'sight, there is something in it with which, we believe,
'most mothers-in-law can sympathise.' Lafitau[3] regards it as arising from a dim recollection of original
sin; rejecting the Carib and Abipon explanation, which
I have little doubt is the correct one, that they do it
because they believe that if the father engaged in
any rough work, or was careless in his diet, 'cela feroit
'mal à l'enfant, et que cet enfant participeroit à tous

[1] *Loc. cit.* p. 206.
[2] Chips from a German Workshop, vol. ii. p. 261.

[3] Mœurs des Sauvages Américains, vol. i. p. 259.

' les défauts naturels des animaux dont le père auroit
' mangé.'

This idea—namely, that a person imbibes the characteristics of an animal which he eats—is very widely
distributed. In India, Forsyth mentions that Mahouts
often give their elephant 'a piece of a tiger's liver to make
' him courageous, and the eyes of the brown horned
' owl to make him see well at night.'[1] The Malays at
Singapore also give a large price for the flesh of the tiger,
not because they like it, but because they believe that
the man who eats tiger ' acquires the sagacity as well as
' the courage of that animal,'[2] an idea which occurs
among several of the Indian hill tribes.[3]

' The Dyaks of Borneo have a prejudice against the
' flesh of deer, which the men may not eat, but which
' is allowed to women and children. The reason given
' for this is, that if the warriors eat the flesh of deer
' they become as faint-hearted as that animal.'[4]

' In ancient times those who wished for children used
' to eat frogs, because that animal lays so many eggs.'[5]

The Caribs will not eat the flesh of pigs or of tortoises, lest their eyes should become as small as those
of these animals.[6] The Dacotahs eat the liver of the
dog, in order to possess the sagacity and courage of
that animal.[7] The Arabs also impute the passionate
and revengeful character of their countrymen to the

[1] Forsyth's Highlands of Central India, p. 462.
[2] Keppel's Visit to the Indian Archipelago, p. 13.
[3] Dalton's Des. Ethn. of Bengal, p. 33.
[4] Keppel's Expedition to Borneo, vol. i. p. 231.
[5] Inman's Ancient Faiths in An-
cient Names, p. 383.
[6] Müller's Geschichte der Americanischen Urreligionen, p. 221.
[7] Schoolcraft's Indian Tribes, vol. ii. p. 60.

use of camel's flesh.[1]  In Siberia the bear is eaten under
the idea that its flesh 'gives a zest for the chase, and
' renders them proof against fear.'[2]  The Kaffirs also
prepare a powder 'made of the dried flesh of various
' wild beasts—leopard, lion, elephant, snakes, &c.—the
' natives intending by the administering of this com-
' pound to impart to the men the qualities of the several
' animals.'[3]

Tylor[4] mentions that 'an English merchant in Shang-
' hai, at the time of the Taeping attack, met his Chinese
' servant carrying home a heart, and asked him what he
' had got there.  He said it was the heart of a rebel,
' and that he was going to take it home and eat it to
' make him brave.'  The New Zealanders, after baptis-
ing an infant, used to make it swallow pebbles, so that
its heart might be hard and incapable of pity.[5]

Even cannibalism is sometimes due to this idea, and
the New Zealanders eat their most formidable enemies
partly for this reason.  It is from the same kind of
idea that 'eyebright,' because the flower somewhat
resembles an eye, was supposed to be good for ocular
complaints.

To us the idea seems absurd.  Not so to children.  I
have myself heard a little girl say to her brother, 'If
' you eat so much goose you will be quite silly;' and
there are perhaps few children to whom the induction
would not seem perfectly legitimate.

From the same notion, the Esquimaux, ' to render

[1] Astley's Collection of Voyages, vol. ii. p. 143.

[2] Atkinson's Upper and Lower Amoor, p. 402.

[3] Callaway's ReligiousSystem of the Amazulu, pt. iv. p. 438.

[4] Early History of Man, p. 131.

[5] Yate's New Zealand, p. 82.

' barren women fertile or teeming, take old pieces of the
' soles of our shoes to hang about them ; for, as they
' take our nation to be more fertile, and of a stronger
' disposition of body than theirs, they fancy the virtue
' of our body communicates itself to our clothing.'[1]

In fact, savages do not act without reason, any more
than we do, though their reasons may often be bad ones
and seem to us singularly absurd. Thus they have a
great dread of having their portraits taken. The better
the likeness, the worse they think for the sitter ; so
much life could not be put into the copy, except at the
expense of the original. Once, when a good deal annoyed by some Indians, Kane got rid of them instantly
by threatening to draw them if they remained. Catlin
tells an amusing, but melancholy, anecdote in reference
to this feeling. On one occasion he was drawing a
chief named Mahtocheega, in profile. This, when observed, excited much commotion among the Indians :
' Why was half his face left out?' they asked ; ' Mah-
' tocheega was never ashamed to look a white in the
' face.' Mahtocheega himself does not seem to have
taken any offence, but Shonka, ' the Dog,' took advantage of the idea to taunt him. ' The Englishman knows,'
he said, ' that you are but half a man ; he has painted
' but one-half of your face, and knows that the rest is
' good for nothing.' This view of the case led to a
fight, in which poor Mahtocheega was shot ; and as ill
luck would have it, the bullet by which he was killed
tore away just that part of the face which had been
omitted in the drawing.

[1] Egede's Greenland, p. 108.

This was very unfortunate for Mr. Catlin, who had great difficulty in making his escape, and lived some months after in fear for his life; nor was the matter settled until both Shonka and his brother had been killed in revenge for the death of Mahtocheega.

Franklin also mentions that the North American Indians 'prize pictures very highly, and esteem any 'they can get, however badly executed, as efficient 'charms.'[1]

The natives of Bornou had a similar horror of being 'written;' they said 'that they did not like it; that 'the Sheik did not like it; that it was a sin; and I am 'quite sure, from the impression, that we had much 'better never have produced the book at all.'[2] The Fetich women in Dahome, says Burton, 'were easily 'dispersed by their likenesses being sketched.'[3] In his Travels in Lapland, Sir A. de C. Brooke says:—'I 'could clearly perceive[4] that many of them imagined 'the magical art to be connected with what I was doing, 'and on this account showed signs of uneasiness, till 'reassured by some of the merchants. An instance of 'this happened one morning, when a Laplander knocked 'at the door of my chamber, and entered it, as they 'usually did, without further ceremony. Having come 'from Alten to Hammerfest on some business, curiosity 'had induced him, previously to his return, to pay the 'Englishman a visit. After a dram he seemed quite at 'his ease; and, producing my pencil, I proceeded, as he 'stood, to sketch his portrait. His countenance now

[1] Voyage to the Polar Seas, ii. 6.
[2] Denham's Travels in Africa, vol. i. p. 275.
[3] Mission to the King of Dahome, i, 278.
[4] Brooke's Lapland, p. 354.

' immediately changed, and, taking up his cap, he was
' on the point of making an abrupt exit, without my
' being able to conjecture the cause.   As he spoke only
' his own tongue, I was obliged to have recourse to as-
' sistance ; when I found that his alarm was occasioned
' by my employment, which he at once comprehended,
' but suspected that, by obtaining a likeness of him, I
' should acquire over him a certain power and influence
' that might be prejudicial.   He therefore refused to
' allow it, and expressed a wish, before any other steps
' were taken, to return to Alten, and ask the permission
' of his master.'   Mr. Ellis mentions the existence of a
similar feeling in Madagascar.[1]

We can hardly wonder that writing should seem to
savages even more magical than drawing.   Carver, for
instance, allowed the North American Indians to open
a book as often as and wherever they pleased, and then
told them the number of leaves.   'The only way they
' could account,' he says, 'for my knowledge, was by
' concluding that the book was a spirit, and whispered
' me answers to whatever I demanded of it.'[2]

Father Baegert mentions[3] that 'a certain missionary
' sent a native to one of his colleagues, with some loaves
' of bread and a letter stating their number.   The mes-
' senger ate a part of the bread, and the theft was con-
' sequently discovered.   Another time when he had to
' deliver four loaves, he ate two of them, but hid the
' accompanying letter under a stone while he was thus
' engaged, believing that his conduct would not be

[1] Three Visits to Madagascar, p. 358.
[2] Travels, p. 255.
[3] Smithsonian Report, 1864, 370.

' revealed this time, as the letter had not seen him in
' the act of eating the loaves.'

Further north, the Minatarrees, seeing Catlin intent
over a copy of the ' New York Commercial Advertiser,'
were much puzzled, but at length came to the conclusion that it was a medicine-cloth for sore eyes. One of
them eventually bought it for a high price.[1]

This use of writing as a medicine prevails largely in
Africa, where the priests or wizards write a prayer on a
piece of board, wash it off and make the patient drink
it. Caillié[2] met with a man who had a great reputation
for sanctity, and who made his living by writing prayers
on a board, washing them off, and then selling the
water, which was sprinkled over various objects, and
supposed to improve or protect them.

Mungo Park on one occasion profited by this idea.
' A Bambarran having,' he says, ' heard that I was a
' Christian, immediately thought of procuring a saphie;
' and for this purpose brought out his *walha* or writing-
' board, assuring me that he would dress me a supper
' of rice, if I would write him a saphie to protect him
' from wicked men. The proposal was of too great con-
' sequence to me to be refused: I therefore wrote the
' board full from top to bottom on both sides; and my
' landlord, to be certain of having the whole force of
' the charm, washed the writing from the board into a
' calabash with a little water, and, having said a few
' prayers over it, drank this powerful draught; after
' which, lest a single word should escape, he licked the
' board until it was quite dry.'[3]

[1] American Indians, vol. ii. p. 92.    See also p. 50. Caillié's Travels to
[2] Travels, vol. i. p. 202.      Timbuctoo, vol. i. p. 370.
[3] Park's Travels, vol. i. p. 367.

In Africa, the prayers written as medicine or as amulets are generally taken from the Koran. It is admitted that they are no protection from firearms; but this does not the least weaken the faith in them, because, as guns were not invented in Mahomet's time, he naturally provided no specific against them.[1]

Among the Kirghiz, also, Atkinson tells us that the Mullas sell similar amulets, 'at the rate of a sheep ' for each scrap of paper;'[2] and similar charms are ' in great request among the Turkomans,[3] and in Afghanistan.'[4]

The science of medicine, indeed, like that of astronomy, and like religion, assumes among savages very much the character of witchcraft.

Ignorant as they are of the processes by which life is maintained, of anatomy and of physiology, the true nature of disease does not occur to them. Thus the negroes universally believe that diseases are caused by evil spirits:[5] among the Kaffirs, 'diseases are all attributed ' to three causes—either to being enchanted by an ' enemy, to the anger of certain beings whose abode ' appears to be in the rivers, or to the power of evil ' spirits.'[6] So, again, in Guinea, the native doctors paint their patients different colours in honour of the spirit which is supposed to have caused the disease.[7]

Similar theories on the origin and nature of disease

[1] Astley's Collection of Voyages, vol. ii. p. 37.

[2] Siberia, p. 310.

[3] Vambery's Travels in Central Asia, p. 60.

[4] Masson's Travels in Baluchistan, Afghanistan, &c., vol. i. pp. 74, 90, 312; vol. ii. pp. 127, 302.

[5] Pritchard's Natural History of Man, vol. ii. p. 701.

[6] Lichtenstein, vol. i. p. 255. Maclean's Kaffir Laws and Customs, p. 86.

[7] Astley's Collection of Voyages, vol. ii. p. 439.

occur in various parts of the world, as, for instance, in Siberia, among the Kalmucks, the Kirghiz, and Bashkirs;[1] in many of the Indian tribes, as the Abors, Kacharis, Kols, &c.;[2] in the Andamans; in the Samoan and other Pacific Islands;[3] in Madagascar, among the Caribs,[4] &c. The consequence of this is that cures are effected by ejecting or exorcising the evil spirit. Among the Kalmucks, this is the business of the so-called 'Priests,' who induce the evil spirit to quit the body of the patient and enter some other object. If a chief is ill, some other person is induced to take his name, and thus, as is supposed, 'the evil spirit passes into his body.'[5] In Rome there was an altar dedicated to the Goddess Fever.[6] Certain forms of disease, indeed, are now, and, as we know, have long been regarded, even among the more advanced nations of the East, as caused by the presence of evil spirits. 'The Assyrians and Baby'lonians,' says the Rev. A. H. Sayce, 'like the Jews of 'the Talmud, believed that the world was swarming 'with obnoxious spirits who produced the various 'diseases to which man is liable.'[7]

Many savage races do not believe in natural death, and if a man, however old, dies without being wounded, conclude that he must have been the victim of magic. Thus, then, when a savage is ill, he naturally attributes

---

[1] Müller's Des. de toutes les Nations de l'Empire de Russie, part I. pp. 123, 142.

[2] Dalton's Des. Ethnology of Bengal, pp. 25, 85.

[3] Turner's Nineteen Years in Polynesia, p. 224. Gerland's Cont. of Waitz's Anthrop., vol. vi. p. 682.

[4] Tylor's Primitive Culture, vol.

ii. p. 134.

[5] Du Hell's Steppes of the Caspian Sea, p. 250.

[6] Epictetus, trs. by Mrs. Carter, vol. i. pp. 91, 104.

[7] Records of the Past, pub. by the Society of Biblical Literature, vol. i. p. 131.

his sufferings to some enemy within him, or to some
foreign object, and the result is a peculiar system of
treatment, curious both for its simplicity and universality.

'It is remarkable in the Abiponian (Paraguay) phy-
'sicians,' says Father Dobritzhoffer,[1] 'that they cure
'every kind of disease with one and the same medicine.
'Let us examine this method of healing. They apply
'their lips to the part affected, and suck it, spitting
'after every suction. At intervals they draw up their
'breath from the very bottom of their breast, and blow
'upon that part of the body which is in pain. That
'blowing and sucking are alternately repeated. . . .
'This method of healing is in use amongst all the
'savages of Paraguay and Brazil that I am acquainted
'with, and, according to Father Jean Grillet, amongst
'the Galibe Indians. . . . The Abipones, still more
'irrational, expect sucking and blowing to rid the body
'of whatever causes pain or inconvenience. This belief
'is constantly fostered by the jugglers with fresh
'artifices; for when they prepare to suck the sick
'man, they secretly put thorns, beetles, worms, &c.
'into their mouths, and spitting them out, after having
'sucked for some time, say to him, pointing to the
'worm or thorn, "See here the cause of your disorder."
'At this sight the sick man revives, when he thinks the
'enemy that has tormented him is at length expelled.'

At first one might almost be disposed to think that
some one had been amusing himself at the expense of
the worthy father, but we shall find the very same mode

[1] History of the Abipones, vol. ii. l'Amér. Mérid., vol. ii. pp. 25, 117,
p. 240. See also Azara, Voy. dans 140, 142.

of treatment among other races.  Martius tells us that
the cures of the Guaycurus (Brazil) 'are very simple,
' and consist principally in fumigating or in sucking
' the part affected, on which the Payé spits into a pit,
' as if he would give back the evil principle which he
' has sucked out to the earth and bury it.'[1]

In British Guiana, Mr. Brett mentions that, 'if the
' patient be strong enough to endure the disease, the
' excitement, the noise, and the fumes of tobacco in
' which he is at times enveloped, and the sorcerer
' observes signs of recovery, he will pretend to extract
' the cause of the complaint by sucking the part
' affected.   After many ceremonies, he will produce
' from his mouth some strange substance, such as a
' thorn or gravel-stone, a fish bone or bird's claw, a
' snake's tooth or a piece of wire, which some malicious
' yauhahn is supposed to have inserted in the affected
' part.'[2]

Father Baegert mentions that the Californian sorcerers blow upon and suck those who are ill, and finally
show them some small object, assuring them that it had
been extracted, and that it was the cause of the pain.
Wilkes thus describes a scene at Wallawalla, on the
Columbia River :—' The doctor, who was a woman,
' bending over the body, began to suck his neck and
' chest in different parts, in order more effectually to
' extract the bad spirit.   She would every now and then
' seem to obtain some of the disease, and then faint
' away.   On the next morning she was still found suck-
' ing the boy's chest. . . . So powerful was the influence

[1] Travels in Brazil, vol. ii. p. 77.
[2] Brett's Indian Tribes of Guiana, p. 304.

' operated on the boy that he indeed seemed better. . . .
' The last time Mr. Drayton visited the doctress, she
' exhibited a stone, about the size of a goose's egg, say-
' ing that she had taken the disease of the boy out of
' him.'[1]

Among the Prairie Indians, also, all diseases are
treated alike, being referred to one cause, viz. the
presence of an evil spirit, which must be expelled.
This the medicine-man ' attempts, in the first place, by
' certain incantations and ceremonies, intended to secure
' the aid of the spirit or spirits he worships, and then
' by all kinds of frightful noises and gestures, and suck-
' ing over the seat of pain with his mouth.'[2]  Speaking
of the Hudson's Bay Indians, Hearne says :—' Here it is
' necessary to remark that they use no medicine either
' for internal or external complaints, but perform all
' their cures by charms—in ordinary cases sucking the
' part affected, blowing and singing.'[3]

Again, in the extreme North, Crantz tells us that
among the Esquimaux old women are accustomed ' to
' extract from a swollen leg a parcel of hair or scraps of
' leather ; they do it by sucking with their mouth,
' which they had before crammed full of such stuff.'[4]
Passing now to the Laplanders, we are told that if any
one among them is ill, a wizard sucks his forehead and
blows in his face, thinking thus to cure him.

In South Africa, Chapman thus describes a similar
custom :—A man having been injured, he says, ' our

---

[1] United States Exploring Expe-
dition, vol. iv. p. 400. See also
Jones's Antiquities of the Southern
Indians, pp. 29, 30.

[2] Schoolcraft's Indian Tribes, vol.
i. p. 250.

[3] Voyage to the Northern Ocean,
p. 189.

[4] History of Greenland, vol. i. p.
214.

' friend sucked at the wound, and then . . . extracted
' from his mouth a lump of some substance, which was
' supposed to be the disease.' [1]

In Australia, we are told by ex-Governor Eyre, in
his interesting work, that, ' as all internal pains are at-
' tributed to witchcraft, sorcerers possess the power of
' relieving or curing them. Sometimes the mouth is ap-
' plied to the surface where the pain is seated, the blood
' is sucked out, and a bunch of green leaves applied to
' the part. Besides the blood, which is derived from the
' gums of the sorcerer, a bone is sometimes put out of
' the mouth, and declared to have been procured from
' the diseased part. On other occasions the disease is
' drawn out in an invisible form, and burnt in the fire
' or thrown into the water.' [2]

Thus, then, we find all over the world this primitive
cure by sucking out the evil, which perhaps even with
ourselves lingers among nurses and children in the
universal nursery remedy of ' Kiss it and make it
' well.'

These misconceptions of the true nature of disease
lead to many other singular modes of treatment. Thus,
among the Kukis, the doctor, not the patient, takes the
remedies. Consequently, food is generally prescribed,
and in cases of severe illness a buffalo is sacrificed, and
the doctor gives a feast. [3]

Another curious remedy practised by the Australians
is to tie a line round the forehead or neck of the patient,

[1] Travels in Africa, vol. ii. p. 45.
See also Livingstone's Travels in
South Africa, p. 130.

[2] Discoveries in Central Australia,
vol. ii. p. 300. See also Oldfield,

Trans. Ethn. Soc., N.S., vol. iii. p.
245.

[3] Dalton's Des. Ethn. of Bengal,
p. 40.

while some kind friend rubs her lips with the 'other
'end of the string until they bleed freely; this blood is
'supposed to come from the patient, passing along the
'string.'[1]

A dislike of twins is widely distributed. In the
Island of Bali[2] (near Java), the natives 'have the sin-
'gular idea, when a woman is brought to bed of twins,
'that it is an unlucky omen; and immediately on its
'being known, the woman, with her husband and chil-
'dren, is obliged to go and live on the seashore or
'among the tombs for the space of a month, to purify
'themselves, after which they may return into the
'village, upon a suitable sacrifice being made.' This
idea is, however, far from being peculiar to that island.

Among the Khasias of Hindostan,[3] 'in the case of
'twins being born, one used frequently to be killed; it
'is considered unlucky, and also degrading, to have
'twins, as they consider that it assimilates them with
'the lower animals.'

Among some of the Siberian tribes, twins are attributed to the influence of evil spirits.[4]

Among the Ainos of Japan,[5] when twins are born,
one is always destroyed. Among some of the South
African tribes one of two twins is killed.[6] At Arebo, in
Guinea, Smith and Bosman[7] tell us that when twins are
born, both they and the mother are killed. 'In Dahome

[1] English Colony in New South
Wales, pp. 343, 382.

[2] Moor's Notices of the Indian
Archipelago, p. 90.

[3] Steel, Trans. Ethn. Soc., N.S.,
vol. vii. p. 308.

[4] Müller's Des. de toutes les Nations de l'Emp. de Russie, vol. iii.
p. 134.

[5] Bickmore, Proc. Bost. Soc. of
Nat. His. 1867.

[6] Livingstone's Travels in South
Africa, p. 577.

[7] Voyage to Guinea, p. 239. Pinkerton, vol. xv. p. 520. Elsewhere
in Guinea twins are welcomed.

' and iu Nguru, one of the sister provinces to Unyan-
' yembé, twins are ordered to be killed and thrown into
' the water the moment they are born, lest droughts
' and famines or floods should oppress the land. Should
' any one attempt to conceal twins, the whole family
' would be murdered.'[1]

In Peru, Garcilasso de la Vega tells us that some
tribes welcomed twins, as an evidence of fertility, while
others ' held such births to be a bad omen.'[2]

The Australians[3] and the North American Indians,[4]
on the birth of twins killed one; perhaps merely under
the idea that one strong child was better than two weak
ones.

This is not, however, I think, the general cause of
the prejudice against twins. I should rather account
for it by the idea indicated in the following passage from
the introduction to the curious old Chevalier Assigne,
or Knight of the Swan (the king and queen are sitting
on the wall together):—

> The kynge loked adowne, and byhelde onder,
> And seygh a pore womman, at the yate sytte,
> Withe two chyldewen her byfore, were borne at a byrthe ;
> And he turned him thenne, and torre lette he falle.
> Sythen sykede he on hyghe, and to the qwene sayde,
> So yo the yonder poor womman. Now that she is pyned
> With twynlenges two, and that dare I my hedde wolde.
> The qwene nykked him with nay, and seyde it is not to lere ;
> Oon manne for oon chylde, and two wymmen for tweyne ;
> Or ellis hit were unsemelye thynge, as me wolde thenke,
> But eche chylde hadde a fader, how-manye so ther were.[5]

---

[1] Speke's Discovery of the Source of the Nile, pp. 511, 542.
[2] Royal Commentaries of the Incas. Hakluyt Society, vol. i. p. 110.
[3] Waitz, Anthropologie, vol. vi. p. 779.
[4] Lafitau, vol. i. p. 592.
[5] The Romance of the Chevalier Assigne, edited by H. H. Gibbs, Esq. Trübner, 1868.

Since reading this I have found that the very same idea occurs in Guinea.[1]

Some curious ideas prevalent among savages arise from the fact that as their own actions are due to life, so they attribute life even to inanimate objects. Even Plato assumed that everything which moves itself must have a soul, and hence that the world must have a soul. Hearne tells us that the North American Indians prefer a hook that has caught a big fish to a handful that have never been tried; and that they never put two nets together for fear they should be jealous.[2]

The Esquimaux thought that Captain Lyons's musical box was the child of his small hand-organ.[3]

The Bushmen thought Chapman's big waggon was the mother of his smaller ones ; they ' despise an arrow ' that has once failed of its mark; and on the contrary ' consider one that has hit as of double value. They ' will, therefore, rather make new arrows, how much ' time and trouble soever it may cost them, than collect ' those that have missed, and use them again.'[4]

The natives of Tahiti sowed some iron nails given them by Captain Cook, hoping thus to obtain young ones. They also believe that ' not only all animals, but ' trees, fruit, and even stones, have souls, which at death, ' or upon being consumed or broken, ascend to the di- ' vinity, with whom they first mix, and afterwards pass ' into the mansion allotted to each.'

[1] Astley's Collection of Voyages, vol. iii. p. 83. At p. 364, in the same vol., we find a curious variation of this idea among the Hottentots. See also Burton's Dahome, vol. ii. p. 145.

[2] *Loc. cit.*, p. 330.
[3] Lyons's Journal, p. 140.
[4] Lichtenstein's Travels in South Africa, vol. ii. p. 271.

The Tongans were of opinion that ' if an animal dies,[1]
' its soul immediately goes to Bolotoo ; if a stone or any
' other substance is broken, immortality is equally its
' reward ; nay, artificial bodies have equal good luck
' with men, and hogs, and yams.  If an axe or a chisel
' is worn out or broken up, away flies its soul for the
' service of the gods.  If a house is taken down or any
' way destroyed, its immortal part will find a situation
' on the plains of Bolotoo.'  Hence probably the custom
of breaking the implements, &c. buried with the dead.
This was not done to render them useless, for the savage
would not dream of violating the tomb, bringing on
himself the wrath of its occupant; but because the implements required to be ' killed,' so that their spirits,
like those of the wives and slaves, might accompany
their master to the land of shadows.

Lichtenstein relates that the king of the Coussa
Kaffirs, having broken off a piece of the anchor of a
stranded ship, died soon afterwards ; upon which all the
Kaffirs made a point of saluting the anchor very respectfully whenever they passed near it, regarding it as a
vindictive being.

Some similar accident probably gave rise to the ancient Mohawk notion that some great misfortune would
happen if any one spoke on Saratoga Lake.  A strong-
minded Englishwoman, on one occasion, while being
ferried over, insisted on talking, and, as she got across
safely, rallied her boatman on his superstition; but I
think he had the best of it after all, for he at once replied, ' The Great Spirit is merciful, and knows that a
' white woman cannot hold her tongue.'[2]

[1] Mariner's Tonga Islands, vol.          [2] Burton's Abbeokuta, vol. i. p.
ii. p. 137.                                       108.

The forms of salutation among savages are sometimes very curious, and their modes of showing their feelings quite unlike ours. Kissing appears to us to be the natural language of affection. 'It is certain,' says Steele, 'that nature was its author, and it began with 'the first courtship;' but this seems to be quite a mistake. In fact, it was unknown to the Australians, the New Zealanders, the Papouans, and the Esquimaux; the African negroes, we are told, do not like it, otherwise I should have thought that, when once discovered, it would have been universally popular. The New Zealanders, according to Shortland, did not know how to whistle;[1] the West Africans do not shake hands;[2] the Batonga (one of the tribes residing on the Zambesi) salute their friends by throwing themselves on their backs on the ground, rolling from side to side, and slapping their thighs with their hands.[3] In the same country the Bakaa have a peculiar prejudice against children who cut the upper front teeth before the lower ones; and 'you cut your top teeth first' is one of the bitterest insults a man can receive.[4]

The Polynesians and the Malays always sit down when speaking to a superior; a Chinaman puts on his hat instead of taking it off. Cook asserts that the people of Mallicollo show their admiration by hissing, and the same is the case, according to Casalis, among the Kaffirs.[5] In some of the Pacific Islands, in parts of Hindostan[6] and some parts of Africa, it is considered

[1] Traditions of the New Zealanders, p. 131.

[2] Burton's Mission to Dahome, vol. i. p. 36.

[3] Livingstone's Travels in South Africa, p. 551.

[4] Livingstone, *loc. cit.*, p. 577.

[5] The Basutos, by the Rev. E. Casalis, p. 234.

[6] Dubois, &c. *cit.*, p. 210.

respectful to turn your back to a superior.    The Todas
of the Neilgherry Hills are said to show respect by
' raising the open right hand to the brow, resting the
' thumb on the nose ; ' on the upper Nile, Dr. Schweinfurth tells us,[1] that the mode of showing admiration is
to open the mouth wide, and then cover it with
the open hand; and it has been asserted that in one
tribe of Esquimaux it is customary to pull a person's
nose as a compliment, though it is but right to say that
Dr. Rae thinks there was some mistake on the point ;
on the other hand, Dr. Blackmore mentions that ' the
' sign of the Arapahoes, and from which they derive
' their name,' consists in seizing the nose with the
thumb and forefinger.[2]

It is asserted that in China a coffin is regarded as an
appropriate present for an aged relative, especially if he
be in bad health.

[1] Heart of Africa, vol. ii. p. 77.
[2] Trans. Ethn. Soc. 1869, p. 310.

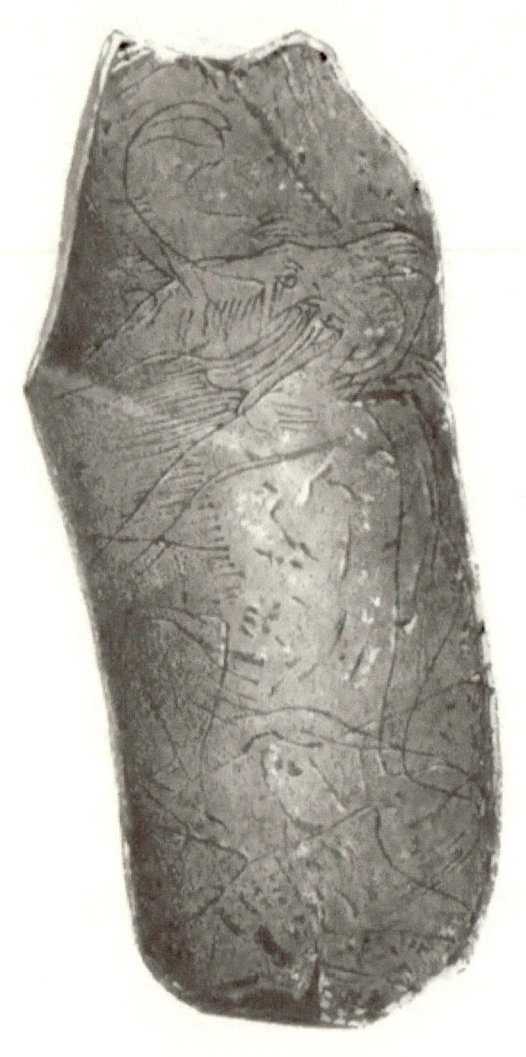

# CHAPTER II.

## ART AND ORNAMENTS.

THE earliest traces of art yet discovered belong to the
Stone Age—to a time so remote that the reindeer
was abundant in the south of France, and that probably,
though on this point there is some doubt, even the
mammoth had not entirely disappeared. These works
of art are sometimes sculptures, if one may say so, and
sometimes drawings or etchings made on bone or horn
with the point of a flint.

They are of peculiar interest, both as being the earliest works of art known to us—older than any Egyptian statues, or any of the Assyrian monuments—and
also because, though so ancient, they show really considerable skill. There is, for instance, a certain spirit
about the subjoined group of reindeer (fig. 1), copied
from a specimen in the collection of the Marquis de
Vibraye. The mammoth (Pl. I.) represented on the
opposite page, though less artistic, is perhaps even more
interesting. It is scratched on a piece of mammoth's
tusk, and was found in the cave of La Madeleine in the
Dordogne.

It is somewhat remarkable that while even in the
Stone Period we find very fair drawings of animals, yet
in the latest part of the Stone Age, and throughout that
of Bronze, they are almost entirely wanting, and the

ornamentation is confined to various combinations of straight and curved lines and geometrical patterns. This, I believe, will eventually be found to imply a difference of race between the population of Western

Fig. 1.

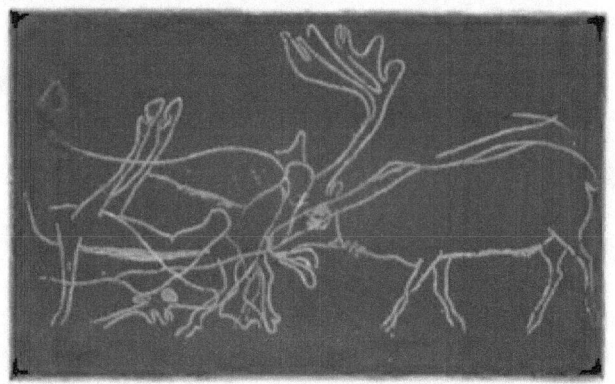

GROUP OF REINDEER.

Europe at these different periods. Thus at present the Esquimaux (see figs. 2–4) are very fair draughtsmen, while the Polynesians, though much more advanced in many ways, and though skilful in ornamenting both themselves and their weapons, have very little idea indeed of representing animals or plants. Their tattooings, for instance, and the patterns on their weapons, are, like the ornaments of the Bronze Age, almost invariably of a geometrical character. Representations of animals and plants are not, indeed, entirely wanting; but, whether attempted in drawing or in sculpture, they are always rude and grotesque. With the Esquimaux the very reverse is the case: among them we find none of those graceful spirals, and other geometrical patterns,

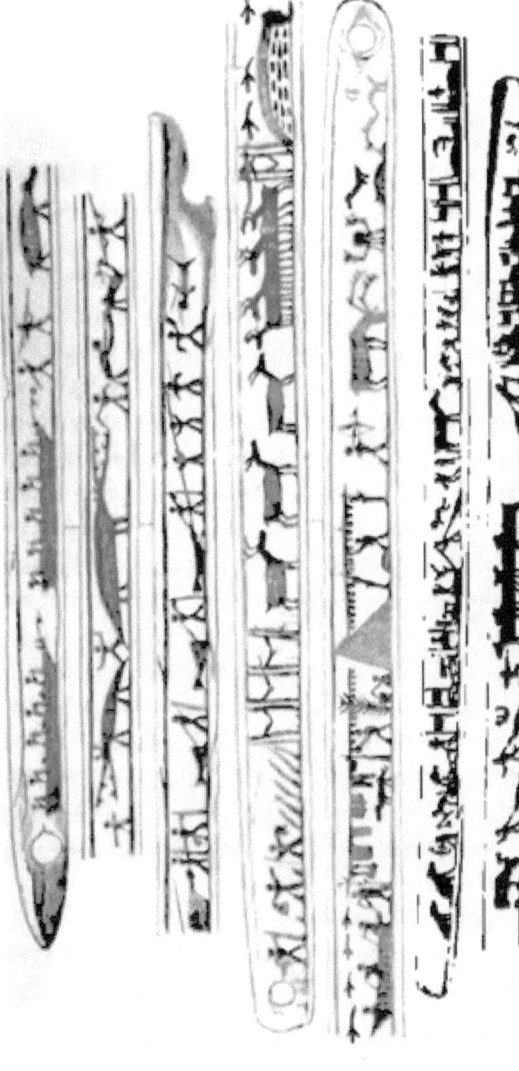

Fig. 2-4.

ETCHINGS ON ESQUIMAUX INSTRUMENTS.

so characteristic of Polynesia; but, on the other hand,
their weapons are often covered with representations
of animals and hunting scenes.  Thus Beechey,[1] describing the weapons of the Esquimaux at Hotham's
Inlet, says :—

'On the outside of this and other instruments there
' were etched a variety of figures of men, beasts, birds,
' &c., with a truth and a character which showed the
' art to be common among them.  The reindeer were
' generally in herds; in one picture they were pursued
' by a man in a stooping posture, in snow-shoes ; in
' another he had approached nearer to his game, and
' was in the act of drawing his bow.  A third repre-
' sented the manner of taking seals with an inflated skin
' of the same animal as a decoy; it was placed upon the
' ice, and not far from it was a man lying upon his
' belly, with a harpoon ready to strike the animal when
' it should make its appearance.  Another was dragging
' a seal home upon a small sledge ; and several baidars
' were employed harpooning whales which had been
' previously shot with arrows ; and thus, by comparing
' one with another, a little history was obtained which
' gave us a better insight into their habits than could be
' elicited from any signs or intimations.'  Some of these
drawings are represented in figs. 2–4, which are taken
from specimens presented by Captain Beechey to the
Ashmolean Museum at Oxford.

Hooper[2] also mentions drawings among the Tuski,
especially 'a sealskin tanned and bleached perfectly
' white, ornamented all over in painting and staining

---

[1] Narrative of a Voyage to the Pacific, vol. i. p. 251.
[2] Tents of the Tuski, p. 85.

' with figures of men, boats, animals, and delineations of
' whale-fishing, &c.—a valuable curiosity.'

In the same way we may, I think, fairly hope eventually to obtain from the ancient drawings of the bone
caves a better insight into the habits of our predecessors
in Western Europe; to ascertain, for instance, whether
their reindeer were domesticated or wild. As yet,
however, mere representations of animals have been
met with, and nothing has been found to supplement
in any way the evidence derivable from the implements, &c.

But though we thus find art—simple, indeed, but
by no means contemptible—in very ancient times, and
among very savage tribes, there are also other races who
are singularly deficient in it.

Thus, though some Australians are capable of making rude drawings of animals, &c., others, on the contrary, as Oldfield[1] tells us, 'seem quite unable to
' realise the most vivid artistic representations. On
' being shown a large coloured engraving of an abo-
' riginal New Hollander, one declared it to be a ship,
' another a kangaroo, and so on; not one of a dozen
' identifying the portrait as having any connection with
' himself. A rude drawing, with all the lesser parts
' much exaggerated, they can realise. Thus, to give
' them an idea of a man, the head must be drawn dis-
' proportionately large.'

Dr. Collingwood,[2] speaking of the Kibalans of Formosa, to whom he showed a copy of the ' Illustrated
' London News,' tells us that he found it ' impossible

[1] Trans. Ethn. Soc., N.S., vol. iii. p. 227.
[2] Ibid., vol. vi. p. 139.

' to interest them by pointing out the most striking
' illustrations, which they did not appear to com-
' prehend.'

Denham, in his ' Travels in Central Africa,' says that
Bookhaloom, a man otherwise of considerable intelligence, though he readily recognised figures, could not
understand a landscape. ' I could not,' he says, ' make
' him understand the intention of the print of the sand-
' wind in the desert, which is really so well described
' by Captain Lyons's drawing ; he would look at it up-
' side down ; and when I twice reversed it for him he ex-
' claimed, " Why ! why ! it is all the same." A camel or
' a human figure was all I could make him understand,
' and at these he was all agitation and delight—" Gieb !
' " gieb ! "—Wonderful ! wonderful ! The eyes first took
' his attention, then the other features ; at the sight of
' the sword he exclaimed, " Allah ! Allah ! " and, on
' discovering the guns, instantly exclaimed, " Where is
' " the powder ? " ' [1]

So also the Kaffir has great difficulty in understanding drawings, and perspective is altogether beyond him.
Central and Southern Africa seem, indeed, to be very
backward in matters of art. Still the negroes are not
altogether deficient in the idea. Their idols cannot be
called, indeed, works of art, but they often not only
represent men, but give some of the African characte-
teristics with grotesque fidelity.

The Kaffirs also can carve fair representations of
animals and plants, and are fond of doing so. The
handles of their spoons are often shaped into unmistake-
able likenesses of giraffes, ostriches, and other animals.

[1] Denham's Travels in Africa, vol. i. p. 167.

As to the Bushmen, we have rather different accounts. It has been stated by some that they have no idea of perspective, nor of how a curved surface can possibly be represented on a flat piece of paper; while, on the contrary, other travellers assert that they readily recognise drawings of animals or flowers. The Chinese, although so advanced in many ways, are, we know, very deficient in the idea of perspective.

Probably no race of men in the Stone Age had attained the art of communicating facts by means of letters, or even by the far ruder system of picture-writing; nor does anything, perhaps, surprise the savage more than to find that Europeans can communicate with one another by means of a few black scratches on a piece of paper.

Even the Peruvians had no better means of recording events than the Quippu or Quipu, which was a cord about two feet long, to which a number of different coloured threads were attached in the form of a fringe. These threads were tied into knots, whence the name Quippu, meaning a knot. These knots served as cyphers, and the various threads had also conventional meanings attached to them, indicated by the various colours. This singular and apparently very cumbersome mode of assisting the memory reappears in China and in Africa. Thus, 'As to' the original of the Chinese characters, 'before the commencement of the monarchy, little cords 'with sliding knots, each of which had its particular 'signification, were used in transacting business. These 'are represented in two tables by the *Chinese*, called 'Hotû, and *Lo-shu*. The first colonies who inhabited

---

[1] Astley's Collection of Voyages, vol. iv. p. 104.

'*Sechuen* had no other literature besides some arith-
'metical sets of counters made with little knotted cords,
'in imitation of a string of round beads, with which
'they calculated and made up all their accounts in com-
'merce.'    Again, in West Africa, we are told that the
people of Ardrah[1] 'can neither write nor read.  They
'use small cords tied, the knots of which have their
'signification.  These are also used by several savage
'nations in America.'  It seems not impossible that
tying a knot in a pocket-handkerchief may be the direct
lineal representative of this ancient and widely-extended
mode of assisting the memory.

The so-called picture-writing is, however, a great
advance.  Yet from representations of hunts in general,
such as those of the Esquimaux (see figs. 2–4), it is
indeed but a step to record pictorially some particular
hunt.  Again, the Esquimaux almost always places his
mark on his arrows, but I am not aware that any Polynesian ever conceived the idea of doing so.  Thus we
get among the Esquimaux a double commencement, as
it were, for the representation of ideas by means of
signs.

This art of pictorial writing was still more advanced
among the Red Skins.

Thus Carver tells us that on one occasion his Chipéway guide, fearing that the Naudowessies, a hostile tribe,
might accidentally fall in with and attack them, 'peeled
'the bark from a large tree near the entrance of a river,
'and with wood-coal mixed with bear's grease, their
'usual substitute for ink, made in an uncouth but ex-
'pressive manner the figure of the town of the Otta-

[1] Astley's Collection of Voyages, vol. iii. p. 71.

'gaumies. He then formed to the left a man dressed
'in skins, by which he intended to represent a Nau-
'dowessie, with a line drawn from his mouth to that of
'a deer, the symbol of the Chipéways. After this he
'depicted still farther to the left a canoe as proceeding
'up the river, in which he placed a man sitting with
'a hat on ; this figure was designed to represent an
'Englishman, or myself, and my Frenchman was drawn
'with a handkerchief tied round his head, and rowing
'the canoe ; to these he added several other significant
'emblems, among which the pipe of peace appeared
'painted on the prow of the canoe. The meaning he
'intended to convey to the Naudowessies, and which I
'doubt not appeared perfectly intelligible to them, was
'that one of the Chipéway chiefs had received a speech
'from some Naudowessie chiefs at the town of the Otta-
'gaumies, desiring him to conduct the Englishman, who
'had lately been among them, up the Chipéway river ;
'and that they thereby required that the Chipéway,
'notwithstanding he was an avowed enemy, should not
'be molested by them on his passage, as he had the
'care of a person whom they esteemed as one of their
'nation.' [1]

An excellent account of the Red Skin pictorial art
is given by Schoolcraft in his 'History of the Indian
'Tribes in the United States.'

Fig. 5 represents the census-roll of an Indian band
at Mille Lac, in the territory of Minnesota, sent in to
the United States agent by Nago-nabe, a Chipéway
Indian, during the progress of the annuity payments in
1849. The Indians generally denote themselves by their

[1] Carver's Travels, p. 418.

FIG. 5.

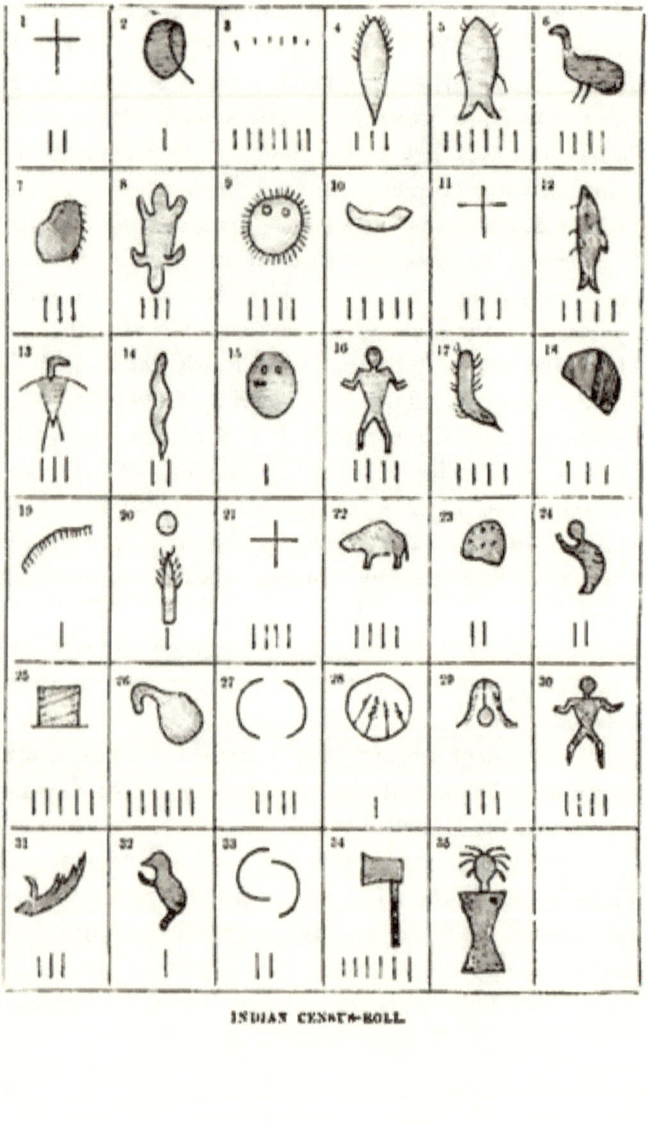

' totem,' or family sign ; but in this case, as they all had
the same totem, he had designated each family by a sign
denoting the common name of the chief. Thus number
5 denotes a catfish, and the six strokes indicate that
the Catfish's family consisted of six individuals ; 8 is a
beaver skin, 9 a sun, 13 an eagle, 14 a snake, 22 a
buffalo, 34 an axe, 35 the medicine-man, and so on.

FIG. 6.                    FIG. 7.

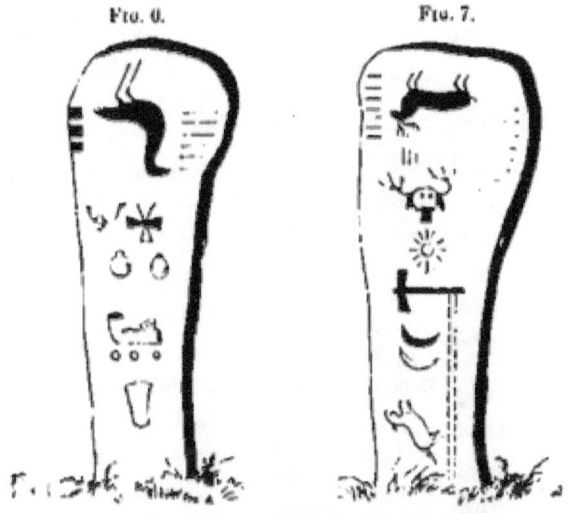

INDIAN GRAVE-POSTS. (Schoolcraft, vol. i. pl. 60.)

Fig. 6 is the record of a noted chief of the St. Mary's
band, called Shin-ga-ba-was-sin, or the Image-stone, who
died on Lake Superior in 1828. He was of the totem
of the crane, as indicated by the figure. The six strokes
on the right, and the three on the left, are marks of
honour. The latter represent three important general
treaties of peace in which he had taken part at various
times.[1]    Among the former marks are included his

[1] Schoolcraft, Indian Tribes, vol. i. p. 357.

presence under Tecumseh, at the battle of Moravian-
town, where he lost a brother.

Fig. 7 represents the adjedatig, or tomb-board, of

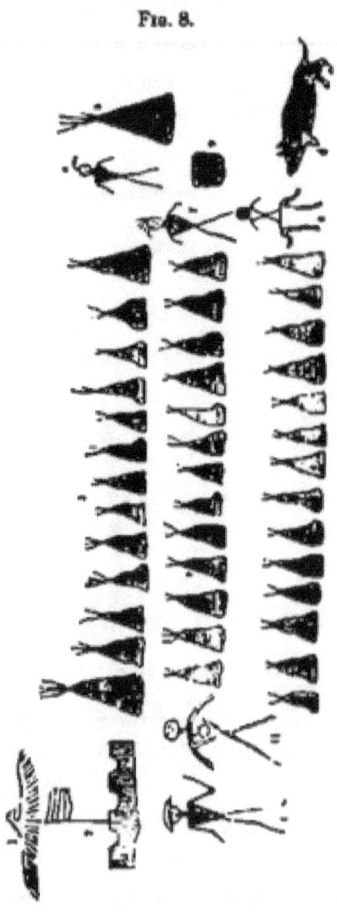

FIG. 8.

INDIAN BARK LETTER.

Wabojeeg, a celebrated
war-chief, who died on
Lake Superior, about
1793. He was of the
family or clan of the
reindeer. This fact is
symbolised by the
figure of the deer.
The reverse position
denotes death. His
own personal name,
which was the White
Fisher, is not noticed.
The seven marks on
the left denote that
he had led seven war
parties. The three
perpendicular lines be-
low the totem repre-
sent three wounds re-
ceived in battle. The
figure of a moose's
head relates to a des-
perate conflict with an
enraged animal of this
kind. Fig. 8 is copied
from a bark letter
which was found above St. Anthony's Falls, in 1820.
' It consisted of white birch bark, and the figures had

'been carefully drawn. No. 1 denotes the flag of
'the Union: No. 2 the cantonment, then recently
'established, at Cold Spring, on the western side of
'the cliffs, above the influx of the St. Peters: No. 4
'is the symbol of the commanding officer (Colonel
'H. Leavenworth), under whose authority a mission
'of peace had been sent into the Chippewa country:
'No. 11 is the symbol of Chakope, or the Six, the
'leading Sioux chief, under whose orders the party
'moved : No. 8 is the second chief, called Wabedatunka,
'or the Black Dog. The symbol of his name is No. 10;
'he has fourteen lodges. No. 7 is a chief, subordinate
'to Chakope, with thirteen lodges, and a bale of goods
'(No. 9), which was devoted by the Government to the
'objects of the peace. The name of No. 6, whose
'wigwam is No. 5, with thirteen subordinate lodges,
'was not given.'[1]

This was intended to imply that a party of Sioux,
headed by Chakope, and accompanied or at least coun-
tenanced by Colonel Leavenworth, had come to this spot
in the hope of meeting the Chippewa hunters and concluding a peace. The Chippewa chief, Babesacundabee,
who found this letter, read off its meaning without
doubt or hesitation.

On one occasion a party of explorers, with two
Indian guides, saw, one morning, just as they were
about to start, a pole stuck in the direction they were
going, and holding at the top a piece of bark, covered
with drawings, intended for the information of any other
Indians who might pass that way. This is represented
in fig. 9.

[1] Schoolcraft's Indian Tribes, vol. i. pp. 352, 353.

E

No. 1 represents the subaltern officer in command of the party. He is drawn with a sword to denote his rank. No. 2 denotes the secretary. He is represented as holding a book, the Indians having understood him to be an attorney. No. 3 represents the geologist, appropriately indicated by a hammer. Nos. 4 and 5 are attaches; No. 6 the interpreter. The group of figures marked 9 represents seven infantry soldiers, each of whom, as shown in group No. 10, was armed with a musket. No. 15 denotes that they had a separate fire,

Fig. 9.

INDIAN BARK LETTER.

and constituted a separate mess. Figs. 7 and 8 represent the two Chippewa guides. These are the only human figures drawn without the distinguishing symbol of a hat. This was the characteristic seized on by them, and generally employed by the Indians, to distinguish the *Red* from the *White* race. Figs. 11 and 12 represent a prairie hen and a green tortoise, which constituted the sum of the preceding day's chase, and were eaten at the encampment. The inclination of the pole was designed to show the course pursued, and there were three hacks in it below the scroll of bark, to indicate the estimated length of this part of the journey, computing from water to water. The following figure (fig. 10) gives

the biography of Wingemund, a noted chief of the Delawares. 1 shows that it belonged to the oldest branch
of the tribe, which use the tortoise on their symbol; 2
is his totem or symbol ; 3 is the sun, and the ten strokes
represent ten war parties in which he was engaged.
Those figures on the left represent the captives which
he made in each of his excursions, the men being distin-

Fig. 10.

INDIAN BARK LETTER.

guished from the women, and the captives being denoted
by having heads, while a man without his head is of
course a dead man. The central figures represent three
forts which he attacked; 8 one on Lake Erie, 9 that of
Detroit, and 10 Fort Pitt, at the junction of the Alleg-
hany and the Monongahela. The sloping strokes denote
the number of his followers.[1]

Fig. 11 represents a petition presented to the President of the United States for the right to certain lakes
(8) in the neighbourhood of Lake Superior (10).

[1] Schoolcraft, vol. i. p. 353.

E 2

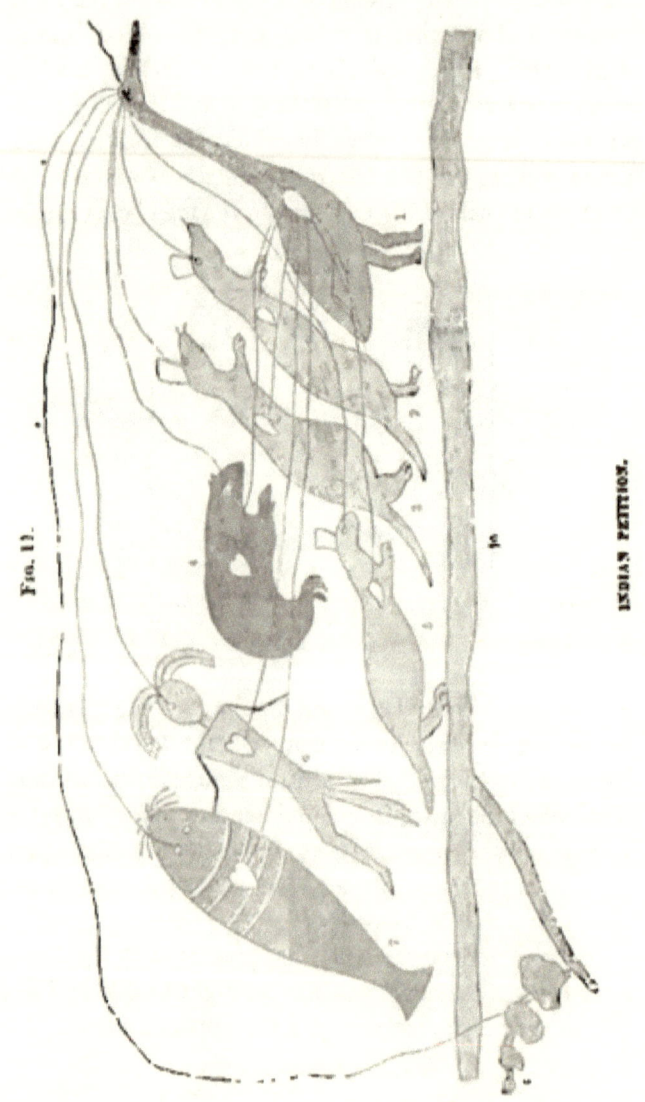

FIG. 11.

INDIAN PETITION.

No. 1 represents Osheabawis, the leader, who is of the Crane clan. The eyes of his followers are all connected with his to symbolise unity of views, and their hearts to denote unity of feeling. No. 2 is Wai-mit-tig-oazh, whose totem is a marten; No. 3 is Ogemageezhig, also a marten; 4 is another marten, Muk-o-mis-ud-ains, the Little Tortoise; 5 is O-mush-kose, the Little Elk, belonging, however, to the Bear totem; 6 belongs to the Manfish totem, and 7 to the Catfish. The eye of the leader has a line directed forwards to the President, and another backwards to the lakes (8).

In some places of Western Europe, rock sculptures have been discovered, to which we cannot yet safely ascribe any meaning, but on which perhaps the more complete study of the picture-writing of modern savages may eventually throw some light.

We will now pass to art as applied to the purposes of personal decoration. Savages are passionately fond of ornaments. In some of the very lowest races, indeed, the women are almost undecorated, but that is only because the men keep all the ornaments themselves. As a general rule, we may say that Southerners ornament themselves, Northerners their clothes. In fact, all savage races who leave much of their skin uncovered delight in painting themselves in the most brilliant colours they can obtain. Black, white, red, and yellow are the favourite, or rather, perhaps, the commonest colours. Although perfectly naked, the Australians of Botany Bay were by no means without ornaments. They painted themselves with red ochre, white clay, and charcoal; the red was laid on in broad patches, the white generally in stripes, or on the face in spots, often

with a circle round each eye; [1] through the septum of
the nose they wore a bone as thick as a man's finger and
five or six inches long. This was of course very awk-
ward, as it prevented them from breathing freely through
the nose, but they submitted cheerfully to the inconvenience for the sake of appearance.

They had also necklaces made of shells, neatly cut
and strung together; earrings, bracelets of small cord,
and strings of plaited human hair, which they wound
round their waists. Some also had gorgets of large
shells hanging from the neck across the breast. On all
these things they placed a high value.

Spix and Martius [2] thus describe the ornaments of a
Coronado woman:—' On the cheek she had a circle, and
' over that two strokes; under the nose several marks
' resembling an M; from the corners of the mouth to
' the middle of the cheek were two parallel lines, and
' below them on both sides many straight stripes;
' below and between her breasts there were some con-
' nected segments of circles, and down her arms the
' figure of a snake was depicted. This beauty wore no
' ornaments, except a necklace of monkeys' teeth.'

In Tanna ' one would have the one-half of his face
' smeared with red clay, and the other the plain dark
' copper skin; another would have the brow and cheeks
' red; another would have the brow red and cheeks
' black; another all the face red, and a round, black,
' glittering spot on the forehead; and another would have
' his face black all over. The black all over, by the way,
' was the sign of mourning.' [3]

[1] Hawkesworth's Voyages, vol.
iii. p. 635.　　　　　[2] Travels in Brazil, vol. ii. p. 224.
[3] Turner's Nineteen Years in
Polynesia, p. 5.

The savage also wears necklaces and rings, bracelets and anklets, armlets and leglets—even, if I may say so, bodylets. Round their bodies, round their necks, round their arms and legs, their fingers, and even their toes, they wear ornaments of all kinds. From their number and weight these must sometimes be very inconvenient. Lichtenstein saw the wife of a Bechuan chief wearing no less than seventy-two brass rings.

A South African chieftainess, visited by Livingstone,[1] wore 'eighteen solid brass rings, as thick as 'one's finger, on each leg, and three of copper under 'each knee; nineteen brass rings on her left arm, and 'eight of brass and copper on her right; also a large 'ivory ring above each elbow. She had a pretty bead 'necklace, and a bead sash encircled her waist.'

Nor are they particular as to the material: copper, brass, or iron, leather or ivory, stones, shells, glass, bits of wood, seeds, or teeth—nothing comes amiss. In South East Island, one of the Louisiade Archipelago, M'Gillivray even saw several bracelets made each of a lower human jaw, crossed by a collar-bone; and other travellers have seen brass curtain rings, the brass plates for keyholes, the lids of sardine cases, and other such incongruous objects worn with much gravity and pride.

The Felatah ladies in Central Africa spend several hours a day over their toilet. In fact they begin overnight by carefully wrapping their fingers and toes in henna leaves, so that by morning they are a rich purple. The teeth are stained alternately blue, yellow, and purple, one here and there being left of its natural colour, as a contrast. About the eyelids they are very

[1] Exp. to the Zambesi, p. 284.

particular; pencilling them with sulphuret of antimony. The hair is coloured carefully with indigo. Studs and other jewellery are worn in great profusion.[1]

Not content with hanging things round their necks, arms, ancles, and in fact wherever nature has enabled them to do so, savages also cut holes in themselves for the purpose.

The Esquimaux from Mackenzie River westward make two openings in their cheeks, one on each side, which they gradually enlarge, and in which they wear an ornament of stone resembling in form a large stud, and which may therefore be called a cheek stud. Brenchley saw the natives of the Solomon Islands decorated by crabs' claws stuck in the cartilage of the nose.[2]

Throughout a great part of Western America, and again in Africa, we also find the custom of wearing a piece of wood through the central part of the lower lip. A small hole is made in the lip during infancy, and it is then extended by degrees until it is sometimes as much as two inches long.

Some races extend the lobe of the ear until it reaches the shoulder ; others file the teeth in various manners.

Thus, among the Rejangs of Sumatra, 'both sexes ' have the extraordinary custom of filing and otherwise ' disfiguring their teeth, which are naturally very white ' and beautiful, from the simplicity of their food.  For ' files they make use of small whetstones of different ' degrees of fineness, and the patients lie on their backs

[1] Laird's Expedition into the Interior of Africa, vol. ii. p. 94.
[2] Cruise of the 'Curacoa,' p. 370.

' during the operation. Many, particularly women of
' the Lampong country, have their teeth rubbed down
' quite even with the gums; others have them formed
' in points, and some file off no more than the outer
' coat and extremities, in order that they may the
' better receive and retain the jetty blackness with
' which they almost universally adorn them.'[1]

Dr. J. B. Davis has a Dyak skull in which the six
front teeth have each been carefully pierced with a
small hole, into which a pin with a spherical brass head
has been driven. In this way, the upper lip being
raised, the shining knob on each tooth would be displayed.[2] Some of the African tribes also chip their
teeth in various manners, each community having a
fashion of its own.

Ornamentation of the skin is almost universal among
the lower races of men. In some cases every individual
follows his own fancy; in others, each clan has a special
pattern. Thus, speaking of Abeokuta, Captain Burton[3]
says :—' There was a vast variety of tattoos and orna-
' mentation, rendering them a serious difficulty to
' strangers. The skin patterns were of every variety,
' from the diminutive prick to the great gash and the
' large boil-like lumps. They affected various figures—
' tortoises, alligators, and the favourite lizard, stars,
' concentric circles, lozenges, right lines, welts, gouts of
' gore, marble or button-like knobs of flesh, and ele-
' vated scars, resembling scalds, which are opened for
' the introduction of fetish medicines, and to expel evil

[1] Marsden's History of Sumatra, p. 52.
[2] Thesaurus Craniorum, p. 289.
[3] Abeokuta, vol. I. p. 104.

' influences. In this country every tribe, sub-tribe, and
' even family, has its blazon,[1] whose infinite diversifica-
' tions may be compared with the lines and ordinaries
' of European heraldry.'

In South Africa the Nyambanas are characterised by
a row of pimples or warts, about the size of a pea, and
extending from the upper part of the forehead to the
tip of the nose. Among the Bachapin Kaffirs, those who
have distinguished themselves in battle are allowed the
privilege of marking their thigh with a long scar, which
is rendered indelible and of a bluish colour by rubbing
ashes into the fresh wound.

The tribal mark of the Bunns[2] (Africa) consists of
three slashes from the crown of the head down the
face towards the mouth; the ridges of flesh stand out
in bold relief. This painful operation is performed by
cutting the skin, and taking out a strip of flesh; palm
oil and wood ashes are then rubbed into the wound,
thus causing a thick ridge.

The Bornouese in Central Africa have twenty cuts
or lines on each side of the face, which are drawn from
the corners of the mouth towards the angles of the
lower jaw and cheekbone. They have also one cut in
the centre of the forehead, six on each arm, six on each
leg, four on each breast, and nine on each side, just
above the hips. This makes 91 large cuts, and the
process is said to be extremely painful on account of
the heat and flies.[3]

The islanders of Torres Straits ornament themselves

[1] See also Baikie's Exploring
Voyage, pp. 77, 204, 330, and especially 450.

[2] Trans. Ethn. Soc., vol. v. p. 80.
[3] Denham, vol. iii. p. 175.

by a large oval scar, slightly raised and neatly made.
It is situated on the right shoulder, but some of them
have a second on the left. At Cape York many of the
natives also had two or three long transverse scars on
the chest. Many had also a two-horned mark on each
breast, but these differences seemed to depend on the
taste of the individual.

The custom of tattooing is found almost all over
the world, though, as might be expected, it is most
developed in hot countries. In Siberia, however, the
Ostiak women tattoo the backs of the hands, the forearm, and the front of the leg. The men only tattoo,
on the wrist, the mark or sign which stands as their
signature.[1]

Among the Tuski[2] 'the faces of the women are tat-
'tooed on the chin in diverging lines ; men only make
'a permanent mark on the face for an act of prowess
'or success, such as killing a bear, capturing a whale,
'&c., and possibly also, in war time, for the death of
'an enemy.'

Among the Arabs[3] 'the Aenezi women puncture
'their lips and dye them blue ; the Serhhan women
'puncture their cheeks, breasts, and arms, and the
'Ammour women their ancles.'

The Aleutian Islanders decorate their hands and
faces with figures of quadrupeds, birds, flowers, &c.
Among the Tunguses the patterns are generally formed
by straight and curved lines.[4]

---

[1] Pallas, vol. iv. p. 50.
[2] Hooper. The Tents of the Tuski, p. 37.
[3] Burckhardt. Notes on the Bedouins and Wahabys, vol. i. p. 51.
[4] Muller. Des. de toutes les Nat. de l'Emp. de Russe, Pt. III. p. 68, 112.

The Malagasy do not generally tattoo, but the women of the Bétsiléo tribes, according to Mr. Campbell,[1] have their arms 'tattooed all over, some of them 'having also a kind of open-work collar tattooed round 'their necks. The breasts of the men were ornamented 'after the same fashion.'

Many of the hill tribes of India tattoo.[2] Among the Abors, for instance, the men have a cross on the forehead: the women a smaller one on the upper lip just below the nose, and seven stripes under the mouth. The Khyens are more extensively tattooed, with figures of animals, &c.; they admit that it is not ornamental, but allege that they were driven to it because their women were naturally so beautiful that they were constantly carried off by neighbouring tribes. The Oraon women have three marks on the brow and two on the temple, while the men burn marks on their forearm.

The women of Bruner Island, on the south coast of New Guinea, were tattooed on the face, arms, and front of the body, but generally not on the back, in vertical stripes less than an inch apart, and connected by zigzag markings. On the face these were more complicated, and on the forearm and wrist they were frequently so elaborate as to resemble lace-work.[3] The men were more rarely tattooed, and then only with a few lines or stars on the right breast. Sometimes, however, the markings consisted of a double series of large stars and dots stretching from the shoulder to the pit of the stomach.

[1] Sibree. Madagascar and its  p. 27, 114, 251.
People, p. 221.                            [3] M'Gillivray's Voyage of the
[2] Dalton. Des. Ethn. of Bengal,  'Rattlesnake,' vol. i. p. 262.

Not content with the paint already mentioned, the inhabitants of Tanna have on their arms and chests elevated scars, representing plants, flowers, stars, and various other figures. 'The inhabitants of Tazovan, 'or Formosa, by a very painful operation, impress on 'their naked skins various figures of trees, flowers, 'and animals. The great men in Guinea have their 'skin flowered like damask; and in Decan the women 'likewise have flowers cut into their flesh on the fore- 'head, the arms, and the breast, and the elevated scars 'are painted in colours, and exhibit the appearance of 'flowered damask.'[1]

In the Tonga Islands 'the men are tattooed from 'the middle of the thigh to above the hips. The women 'are only tattooed on the arms and fingers, and there 'very slightly.'[2] In the Feejee Islands, on the con- trary, the women are tattooed and not the men.

In the Gambier Islands, Beechey says,[3] 'tattooing is 'so universally practised, that it is rare to meet a man 'without it; and it is carried to such an extent that 'the figure is sometimes covered with small checkered 'lines from the neck to the ancles, though the breast is 'generally exempt, or only ornamented with a single 'device. In some, generally elderly men, the face is 'covered below the eyes, in which case the lines or net- 'work are more open than on other parts of the body, 'probably on account of the pain of the operation, and 'terminate at the upper part in a straight line from ear 'to ear, passing over the bridge of the nose. With

[1] Forster's Observations made during a Voyage Round the World, p. 588.
[2] Cook's Voyage towards the South Pole, vol. i. p. 218.
[3] Beechey, vol. i. p. 138.

'these exceptions, to which we may add the fashion,
'with some few, of blue lines, resembling stockings,
'from the middle of the thigh to the ancle, the effect is
'becoming, and in a great measure destroys the appear-
'ance of nakedness. The patterns which most improve
'the shape, and which appear to me peculiar to this
'group, are those which extend from the armpits to
'the hips, and are drawn forward with a curve which
'seems to contract the waist, and at a short distance
'gives the figure an elegance and outline, not unlike
'that of the figures seen on the walls of the Egyptian
'tombs.'

Fig. 12 represents a Caroline Islander, after Freycinet, and gives an idea of the tattooing, though it
cannot be taken as representing the form or features
characteristic of those islanders.

The tattooing of the Sandwich Islanders is less
ornamental, the devices being, according to Arago,
'unmeaning and whimsical, without taste, and in general
'badly executed.'[1] Perhaps, however, the most beautiful of all was that of the New Zealanders (see figs.
13 and 14), who were generally tattooed in curved or
spiral lines. The process is extremely painful, particularly on the lips; but to shrink from it, or even to
show any signs of suffering while under the operation,
would be thought very unmanly. The natives used
the 'Moko' or pattern of their tattooing as a kind of
signature. The women have their lips tattooed with
horizontal lines. To have red lips is thought to be a
great reproach.[2]

[1] Arago's Letters, Pt. II. p. 147.
[2] For details of Polynesian tattooing see Hale's United States
Exploring Expedition: Ethnography, p. 40.

When tastefully executed, tattooing has been regarded by many travellers as a real ornament. Thus
Laird says that some of the tattooing in West Africa
'in the absence of clothing gives a finish to the skin.'[1]

Fig. 12.

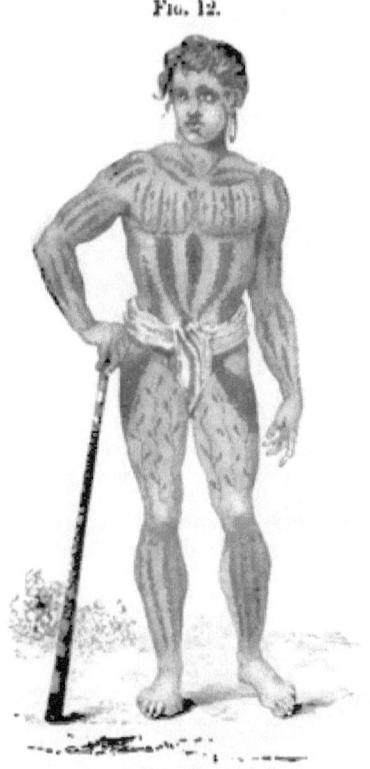

CAROLINE ISLANDER.

Many similar cases might be given in which savages
ornament themselves, as they suppose, in a manner which

[1] Narrative of an Expedition into the Interior of Africa, vol. I. p. 291.

must be very painful.   Perhaps none is more remarkable
than the practice which we find in several parts of the
world of modifying the human form by means of tight
bandages.   The small size of the Chinese ladies' feet is
a well-known case, but is scarcely less mischievous than
the compression of the waist as practised in Europe.
The Samoans[1] and some of the American tribes even
modified the form of the head.   One would have sup-

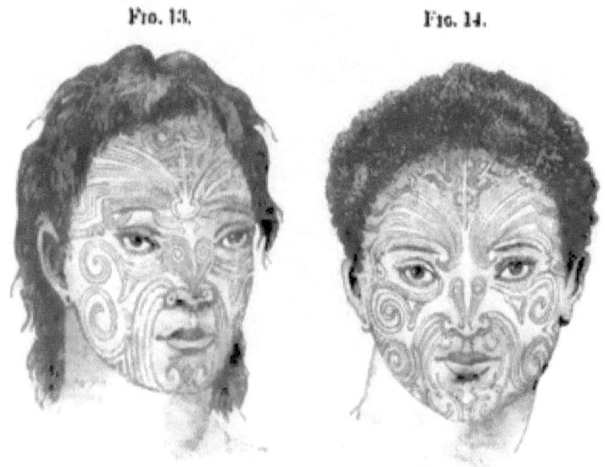

Fig. 13.                              Fig. 14.

HEAD OF NEW ZEALANDER.     HEAD OF NEW ZEALANDER.

posed that any such compression would have exercised
a very prejudicial effect on the intellect, but, as far as
the existing evidence goes, it does not appear to do so.

The mode of dealing with the hair varies very much
in different races.   Some races remove it almost entirely,
some leave a ridge along the top of the head ; the Kaffir
wears a round ring of hair ; the North American Indian

[1] Turner's Nineteen Years in Polynesia, p. 175.

Pl. II.

FEEJEEAN MODES OF DRESSING THE HAIR.

regards it as a point of honour to leave one tuft, in case he ever has the misfortune of being defeated, for it would be mean to cheat his victor of the scalp, the recognised emblem of conquest.

The Islanders of Torres Straits twist their hair into long pipe-like ringlets, and also wear a kind of wig prepared in the same fashion. Sometimes they shave the head, leaving a transverse crest of hair. At Cape York the hair is almost always kept short.[1] In Tanna the women wear it short, but have it all laid out in a forest of little erect curls, about an inch and a half long. The men wear it twelve and eighteen inches long, and have it divided into some six or seven hundred little locks or tresses. Beginning at the roots, every one of these is carefully wound round by the thin rind of a creeping plant, giving it the appearance of a piece of twine. The ends are left exposed for about two inches, and oiled and curled.[2]

The Feejeeans give a great deal of time and attention to their hair, as is shown in Pl. II. Most of the chiefs have a special hairdresser, to whom they sometimes devote several hours a day. Their heads of hair are often more than three feet in circumference, and Mr. Williams measured one which was nearly five feet round. This forces them to sleep on narrow wooden pillows or neck-rests, which must be very uncomfortable. They also dye the hair. Black is the natural and favourite colour, but some prefer white, flaxen, or bright red.

'On one head,' says Mr. Williams,[3] 'all the hair is

[1] McGillivray's Voyage of the Rattlesnake, pp. 11, 13.
[2] Turner's Nineteen Years in Polynesia, p. 77.
[3] Fiji and the Fijians, vol. L p. 158.

'of a uniform height; but one-third in front is ashy or
' sandy, and the rest black, a sharply defined separation
' dividing the two colours.  Not a few are so ingeniously
' grotesque as to appear as if done purposely to excite
' laughter.  One has a large knot of fiery hair on his
' crown, all the rest of his head being bald.  Another
' has the most of his hair cut away, leaving three or four
' rows of small clusters, as if his head were planted with
' small paint-brushes.  A third has his head bare except
' where a large patch projects over each temple.  One,
' two, or three cords of twisted hair often fall from the
' right temple, a foot or eighteen inches long.  Some
' men wear a number of these braids, so as to form a
' curtain at the back of the neck, reaching from one ear
' to the other.  A mode that requires great care has
' the hair brought into distinct locks radiating from the
' head.  Each lock is a perfect cone about seven inches
' long, having the base outwards; so that the surface of
' the hair is marked out into a great number of small
' circles, the ends being turned in in each lock, towards
' the centre of the cone.'[1]  In some of the Pacific
Islands the natives wear wigs, or tresses of hair, in
addition to their own.[2]

Schweinfurth describes a dandy, belonging to the
Dinkas, a negro tribe of the Soudan, whose hair was
dyed red, and trained up into points like tongues of
flame, standing stiffly up, all round his head.

In fact, the passion for self-ornamentation seems to
prevail amongst the lowest as much as, if not more than,
among the more civilised races of man.

[1] See, for many further particulars, Darwin's Descent of Man,
p. 328, et seq.

[2] Hale's United States Expl.
Exp.: Ethnography, p. 12.

# CHAPTER III.

## MARRIAGE AND RELATIONSHIP.

NOTHING, perhaps, gives a more instructive insight into the true condition of savages than their ideas on the subject of relationship and marriage; nor can the great advantages of civilisation be more conclusively proved than by the improvement which it has already effected in the relation between the two sexes.

Marriage, and the relationship of a child to its father and mother, seem to us so natural and obvious, that we are apt to look on them as aboriginal and general to the human race. This, however, is very far from being the case. The lowest races have no institution of marriage; true love is almost unknown among them; and marriage, in its lowest phases, is by no means a matter of affection and companionship.

The Hottentots, says Kolben,[1] 'are so cold and in- 'different to one another that you would think there 'was no such thing as love between them.' Among the Koussa Kaffirs, Lichtenstein asserts that there is 'no 'feeling of love in marriage.'[2] In North America, the Tinné Indians had no word for 'dear' or 'beloved;' and the Algonquin language is stated to have contained no verb meaning 'to love;' so that when the Bible was

[1] Kolben's Hist. of the Cape of Good Hope, vol. L p. 162.    [2] Travels in South Africa, vol. L p. 201.

translated by the missionaries into that language it was necessary to invent a word for the purpose.

'In his native state,' says Mr. Morgan,[1] ' the (North 'American) Indian is below the passion of love. It is 'entirely unknown among them, with the exception, to 'a limited extent, of the village Indians.' He mentions elsewhere a case of an Alabuelin woman named 'Ethabe,' who had been married for three years to a Blackfoot Indian, yet there was no common articulate language which they both understood. They communicated entirely by signs, neither of them having taken the trouble to learn the other's language.[2]

Though the songs of savages are generally devoted to the chase, war, or women, they can very rarely be called love songs. Dr. Mitchell, for instance, who was for several years chairman of the United States Senate Committee on Indian Affairs, mentions that 'neither 'among the Osages nor the Cherokees could there be 'found a single poetical or musical sentiment, founded 'on the tender passion between the sexes. Though 'often asked, they produced no songs of love.'[3]

In Yariba (Central Africa),[4] says Lander, 'marriage 'is celebrated by the natives as unconcernedly as 'possible : a man thinks as little of taking a wife as of 'cutting an ear of corn—affection is altogether out of 'the question.' The King of Boussa,[5] he tells us in another place, 'when he is not engaged in public affairs, 'usually employs all his leisure hours in superintending

---

[1] Systems of Consanguinity and Affinity of the Human Family, p. 207.

[2] *Loc. cit.*, p. 227.

[3] Archæol. Americanas, vol. i. p. 317.

[4] R. and J. Lander's Niger Expedition, vol. i. p. 161.

[5] *Ibid.*, vol. ii. p. 100. See also p. 107.

' the occupations of his household, and making his own
' clothes. The Midiki (queen) and he have distinct
' establishments, divided fortunes, and separate in-
' terests; indeed, they appear to have nothing in
' common with each other, and yet we have never seen
' so friendly a couple since leaving our native country.'
On the Gold Coast, 'not even the appearance of
' affection exists between husband and wife.'[1] Among
the Mandingoes marriage is merely a form of regulated
slavery. Husband and wife 'never laugh or joke to-
' gether.' 'I asked Baba,' says Caillié, 'why he did not
' sometimes make merry with his wives. He replied
' that if he did he should not be able to manage them,
' for they would laugh at him when he ordered them to
' do anything.'[2]

In India, the Hill tribes of Chittagong, says Captain
Lewin, regard marriage 'as a mere animal and con-
' venient connection;' as the 'means of getting their
' dinner cooked. They have no idea of tenderness, nor
' of chivalrous devotion.'[3]

Among the Samoyedes[4] of Siberia the husbands
show little affection for their wives, and, according to
Pallas, 'daignent à peine leur dire une parole de
' douceur.' Further East, in the Aleutian Islands, the
marriages, according to Müller,[5] 'méritent à peine le
' nom;' and the facts he mentions go far to justify this
statement.

Among the Guyacurus of Paraguay 'the bonds of
' matrimony are so very slight, that when the parties do

[1] Barton's Mission to the King of Dahomey, vol. ii. p. 100.
[2] Travels, vol. I. p. 350.
[3] Hill Tracts of Chittagong, p. 116.
[4] Pallas's Voyages, vol. iv. p. 94.
[5] Des. de toutes les Nat. de l'Empire de Russe, Part III., p. 120.

' not like each other they separate without any further
' ceremony. In other respects they do not appear to
' have the most distant notions of that bashfulness so
' natural to the rest of mankind.'[1]   The Guaranis seem
to have been in a very similar condition.[2]

In North America the marriage tie was by no means
regarded as of a religious character.[3]

In Australia ' little real affection exists between
' husbands and wives: and young men value a wife
' principally for her services as a slave ; in fact, when
' asked why they are anxious to obtain wives, their
' usual reply is, that they may get wood, water, and
' food for them, and carry whatever property they
' possess.'[4]   The position of women in Australia seems
indeed to be wretched in the extreme. They are
treated with the utmost brutality, beaten and speared in
the limbs on the most trivial provocation. Few women,
says Eyre, ' will be found, upon examination, to be free
' from frightful scars upon the head, or the marks of
' spear wounds about the body. I have seen a young
' woman who, from the number of these marks, appeared
' to have been almost riddled with spear wounds. If
' at all good-looking, their position is, if possible, even
' worse than otherwise.'

Again, our family system, which regards a child as
equally related to his father and his mother, seems so
natural that we experience a feeling of surprise on
meeting with any other system. Yet we shall find, I
think, reason for concluding that a man was first re-

[1] Charlevoix, Hist. of Paraguay,
vol. i. p. 91.
[2] Loc. cit., p. 352. See also
Azara, vol. ii. p. 60.
[3] Jones, Antiquities of the
Southern Indians, p. 67.
[4] Eyre's Discoveries, vol. ii. p.
321.  See note.

garded as merely related to his tribe ; then to his
mother but not to his father; then to his father and
not to his mother; and only at last to both father and
mother. Even among the Romans the family was
based, not on marriage or on relationship, but on power;[1]
' le lien seul,' says Ortolan, ' de la parenté naturelle, de
' la parenté de sang, n'est rien chez les Romains ;' and
a man's wife and children only formed a part of his
family, not because they were his relatives, but because
they were subject to his control ; so that a son who was
emancipated—that is to say, made free—had no share
in the inheritance, having ceased to belong to the
family. We shall, however, be better able to understand this part of the question when we have considered the various phases which marriage presents; for
it is by no means of an uniform character, but takes
almost every possible form. In some cases nothing of
the sort appears to exist at all; in others it is essentially
temporary, and exists only till the birth of the child,
when both man and woman are free to mate themselves
afresh. In others, the man buys the woman, who
becomes as much his property as his horse or his dog.

In Sumatra there were formerly three perfectly distinct kinds of marriage: the ' Jugur,' in which the man
purchased the woman ; the ' Ambel-anak,' in which the
woman purchased the man ; and the ' Semando,' in
which they joined on terms of equality. In the mode of
marriage by Ambel-anak, says Marsden,[2] ' the father
' of a virgin makes choice of some young man for her

---

[1] Ortolan's Expl. His. des Institute de l'Emp. Justinien, vol. i. pp.
126, 128, 130, 416.

[2] Marsden's Hist. of Sumatra, p.
262.

' husband, generally from an inferior family, which re-
' nounces all further right to, or interest in, him ; and
' he is taken into the house of his father-iu-law, who
' kills a buffalo on the occasion, and receives twenty
' dollars from his son's relations. After this, the buruk
' baik' nia (the good and bad of him) is invested in the
' wife's family. If he murders or robs, they pay the
' bañgun, or fine. If he is murdered, they receive the
' bañgun. They are liable to any debts he may con-
' tract in marriage; those prior to it remaining with
' his parents. He lives in the family, in a state between
' that of a son and a debtor. He partakes as a son of
' what the house affords, but has no property in himself.
' His rice plantation, the produce of his pepper garden,
' with everything that he can gain or earn, belongs to
' the family. He is liable to be divorced at their
' pleasure, and though he has children, must leave all,
' and return naked as he came.'

    ' The Semando¹ is a regular treaty between the
' parties, on the footing of equality. The adat paid to
' the girl's friends has usually been twelve dollars.
' The agreement stipulates that all effects, gains, or
' earnings are to be equally the property of both ; and,
' in case of divorce by mutual consent, the stock, debts,
' and credits are to be equally divided. If the man only
' insists on the divorce, he gives the woman her half of
' the effects, and loses the twelve dollars he has paid.
' If the woman only claims the divorce, she forfeits her
' right to the proportion of the effects, but is entitled
' to keep her tikar, bantal, and dandan (paraphernalia),

¹ Marsden's Hist. of Sumatra, p. 263.

'and her relations are liable to pay back the twelve
'dollars; but it is seldom demanded. This mode,
'doubtless the most conformable to our ideas of con-
'jugal right and felicity, is that which the chiefs of the
'Rejang country have formally consented to establish
'throughout their jurisdiction, and to their orders the
'influence of the Malayan priests will contribute to
'give efficacy.'

In the Jugur marriage the woman became the property of the man.

The Hassaniyeh Arabs have a very curious form
of marriage, which may be called 'three-quarter'
marriage; that is to say, the woman is legally married
for three days out of four, remaining perfectly free for
the fourth.

In Ceylon there were two kinds of marriage—the
Deega marriage, and the Beena marriage. In the
former the woman went to her husband's hut; in the
latter the man transferred himself to that of the woman.
Moreover, according to Davy, marriages in Ceylon
were provisional for the first fortnight, at the expiration of which they were either annulled or confirmed.[1]

In Japan, among the higher classes, it is said that
the eldest son brings his bride to the paternal home;
but, on the other hand, the eldest daughter does the
same, and retains her name, which is assumed by the
bridegroom. Thus the wife of an eldest son joins her
husband's family; but, on the other hand, the husband
of an eldest daughter enters into that of his wife.

[1] Davy's Ceylon, p. 280.

Hence the eldest son of one family cannot marry the eldest daughter of another. As regards the younger children, if the husband's father provides the house, the wife takes her husband's name; while if the bride's father does so, the bridegroom assumes that of his wife.[1]

Among the Reddies[2] of Southern India a very singular custom prevails:—' A young woman of sixteen ' or twenty years of age may be married to a boy of five ' or six years! She, however, lives with some other ' adult male—perhaps a maternal uncle or cousin—but ' is not allowed to form a connection with the father's ' relatives; occasionally it may be the boy-husband's ' father himself—that is, the woman's father-in-law! ' Should there be children from these liaisons, they are ' fathered on the boy-husband. When the boy grows ' up the wife is either old or past child-bearing, when ' he in his turn takes up with some other " boy's " wife ' in a manner precisely similar to his own, and pro- ' creates children for the boy-husband.'

Polyandry, or the marriage of one woman to several men at once, is more common than is generally supposed, though much less so than polygamy, which is almost universally permitted among the lower races of men. One reason—though I do not say the only one— for this, is obvious when pointed out. Long after our children are weaned, milk remains an important and necessary part of their food. We supply this want with cow's milk; but among people who have no domesti-

---

[1] Morgan's System of Consanguinity and Affinity of the Human Family, p. 428.

[2] Shortt, Trans. Ethn. Soc., New Series, vol. vii. p. 194.

cated animals this cannot, of course, be done, and consequently the children are not weaned until they are
two, three, or even four years old, during all which period
the husband and wife generally remain apart. Thus,
in Feejee ' the relatives of a woman take it as a public
' insult if any child should be born before the customary
' three or four years have elapsed, and they consider
' themselves in duty bound to avenge it in an equally
' public manner.' [1]

It seems to us natural and proper that husband and
wife should enjoy as much as possible the society of one
another; but, among the Turkomans, according to
Fraser, for six months or a year, or even sometimes two
years, after a marriage, the husband was only allowed
to visit his wife by stealth. 'After the wedding,' says
Burnes, 'the bride returns to the house of her parents,
' and passes a year in preparing the carpets and clothes,
' which are necessary for a Toorkmun tent; and on the
' anniversary of her elopement, she is finally transferred
' to the arms and house of her gallant lover.' [2]

Klemm states that the same is the case among the
Circassians until the first child is born. Among the
Feejeeans, husbands and wives do not usually spend the
night together, except as it were by stealth. It is
quite contrary to Feejeean ideas of delicacy that they
should sleep under the same roof. A man spends his
day with his family, but absents himself on the approach of night.[3] In Chittagong (India), although,

[1] Seemann, A Mission to Fiji, p. 101.

[2] Burnes' Travels in Bokhara, vol. ii. p. 56. See also Vambery's Travels in Central Asia, p. 323.

[3] Seemann's Mission to Viti, p. 101.

' according to European ideas, the standard of morality
' among the Kyoungtha is low,' yet husband and wife
are on no account permitted to sleep together until
seven days after marriage.[1]

Burckhardt[2] states, that in Arabia, after the wedding,
if it can be called so, the bride returns to her mother's
tent, but again runs away in the evening, and repeats
these flights several times, till she finally returns to her
tent.   She does not go to live in her husband's tent for
some months, perhaps not even till a full year, from the
wedding-day.   Among the Votyaks, some weeks after
the wedding the bride returns to her father's tent, and
lives there for two or three months, sometimes even for
a year, during which time she dresses and behaves like
a girl, and after which she returns to her husband ;
making, however, even on the second occasion, a show
of resistance.[3]

Lafitau informs us that among the North American
Indians the husband only visits the wife as it were by
stealth :—' ils n'osent aller dans les cabanes particulières,
' où habitent leurs épouses, que durant l'obscurité de la
' nuit . . . . ce serait une action extraordinaire de s'y
' présenter le jour.'[4]

In Futa, one of the West African kingdoms, it is
said that no husband is allowed to see his wife's face
until he has been three years married.

In Sparta, and in Crete, according to Xenophon and
Strabo, married people were for some time after the

[1] Lowin's Hill Tracts of Chittagong, p. 61.
[2] Burckhardt's Notes, vol. ii. p.
200, quoted in M'Lennan's Primitive
Marriage, p. 302.

[3] Müller's Des. de toutes les
Nations de l'Emp. de Russe, Part
II., p. 71.
[4] Loc. cit., vol. i. p. 576.

wedding only allowed to see one another as it were clandestinely; and a similar custom is said to have existed among the Lycians. So far as I am aware, no satisfactory explanation of this custom has yet been given. I shall, however, presently venture to suggest one.

There are many cases in which savages have no such thing as any ceremony of marriage. 'I have said nothing,' says Metz, 'about the marriage ceremonies of the Bada-'gas (Hindostan), because they can scarcely be said to 'have any.' The Kurumbas, another tribe of the Neil-gherry Hills, 'have no marriage ceremony.'[1] According to Colonel Dalton,[2] the Keriahs of Central India 'have no 'word for marriage in their own language, and the only 'ceremony used appears to be little more than a sort of 'public recognition of the fact.' It is very singular, he adds elsewhere, 'that of the many intelligent observers 'who have visited and written on Butan, not one has 'been able to tell us that they have such an institution 'as a marriage ceremony.' The tie between man and woman seems to be very slight, and to be a mere matter of servitude. 'From my own observation,' he continues, 'I believe the Butias to be utterly indifferent on the 'subject of the honour of their women.'[3] So also the Spanish missionaries found no word for marriage, nor any marriage ceremony, among the Indians of Califor-nia.[4] Farther north, among the Kutchin Indians, 'there is no ceremony observed at marriage or birth.'[5]

---

[1] Trans. Ethn. Soc., vol. vii. p. 270.
[2] *Ibid.*, vol. vi. p. 25.
[3] Des. Ethn. of Bengal, p. 97.
[4] Bagaert, Smithsonian Report, 1863, p. 368.
[5] Smithsonian Report, 1866, p. 320.

The marital rite, says Schoolcraft, 'among our tribes'
(i.e. the Redskins of the United States) ' is nothing more
' than the personal consent of the parties, without re-
' quiring any concurrent act of a priesthood, a magistracy,
' or witnesses; the act is assumed by the parties, without
' the necessity of any extraneous sanction.'[1]

According to Brett, there is no marriage ceremony
among the Arawaks of South America.[2] Martius makes
the same assertion with reference to the Brazilian tribes
generally,[3] and it is also the case with some of the
Australian tribes.[4]

There is, says Bruce, ' no such thing as marriage in
' Abyssinia, unless that which is contracted by mutual
' consent, without other form, subsisting only till· dis-
' solved by dissent of one or other, and to be renewed
' or repeated as often as it is agreeable to both parties,
' who, when they please, live together again as man and
' wife, after having been divorced, had children by others,
' or whether they have been married, or had children
' with others or not.  I remember to have once been at
' Koscam in presence of the Iteghe (the queen), when,
' in the circle, there was a woman of great quality, and
' seven men who had all been her husbands, none of
' whom was the happy spouse at that time.[5]  And yet
' there is no country in the world where there are so
' many churches.'[6]  Among the Bedouin Arabs there is
a marriage ceremony in the case of a girl, but the re-
marriage of a widow is not thought sufficiently im-

[1] Indian Tribes, pp. 248, 132.    319.
[2] Guiana, p. 101.              [5] Bruce's Travels, vol. iv. p. 487.
[3] Luc. cit., p. 51.           [6] Ibid., vol. v. p. 1.
[4] Eyre's Discoveries, vol. ii. p.

portant to deserve one. Speke says, 'there are no such 'things as marriages in Uganda.'[1]

Of the Mandingoes (West Africa), Caillié[2] says that husband and wife are not united by any ceremony; and Hutton[3] makes the same statement as regards the Ashantees. In Congo and Angola[4] 'they use no peculiar 'ceremonies in marriage, nor scarce trouble themselves 'for consent of friends.' Le Vaillant says that there are no marriage ceremonies among the Hottentots;[5] and the Bushmen, according to Mr. Wood, had in their language no means of distinguishing an unmarried from a married girl.[6]

Yet we must not assume that marriage is necessarily and always lightly regarded, where it is unaccompanied by ceremonial. Thus, 'marriage in this island (Tahiti) 'as appeared to us,' says Cook, 'is nothing more than 'an agreement between the man and woman, with which 'the priest has no concern. Where it is contracted it 'appears to be pretty well kept, though sometimes 'the parties separate by mutual consent, and in that 'case a divorce takes place with as little trouble as 'the marriage. But though the priesthood has laid 'the people under no tax for a nuptial benediction, 'there are two operations which it has appropriated, 'and from which it derives considerable advantages. 'One is tattooing, and the other circumcision.'[7] Yet

[1] Journal, p. 361.

[2] Loc. cit., vol. i. p. 350.

[3] Klemm, Cultur d. Menschen, vol. iii. p. 280.

[4] Astley's Coll. of Voyages, vol. iii. pp. 221, 227.

[5] Voyage, vol. ii. p. 58.

[6] Natural History of Man, vol. i. p. 209.

[7] Cook's Voyage Round the World. Hawkesworth's Voyages, vol. ii. p. 240. For Caroline Islands, see Klemm, loc. cit., vol. iv. p. 290

he elsewhere informs us that married women in Tahiti
are as faithful to their husbands as in any other part of
the world.

We must bear in mind that there is a great distinction
between what may be called 'lax' and 'brittle' marriages. In some countries the marriage tie may be
broken with the greatest ease, and yet, as long as it lasts,
is strictly respected; while in other countries the very
reverse is the case.

Perhaps on the whole any marriage ceremony is better
than none at all, but some races have practices at marriage which are extremely objectionable. Some, also,
are very curious, and no doubt symbolical. At Banabe,
one of the Micronesian Pacific Islands, the wife is
tattooed with the marks standing for the names of her
husband's ancestors.[1] One portion of the marriage
ceremony among the Mundaris, one of the Bengal Hill
tribes, is very suggestive. The bride walks in front of
the bridegroom with a pitcher of water on her head,
supported by one arm. The bridegroom walks behind,
and through the pretty loop-hole thus formed he shoots
an arrow. The girl walks on to where the arrow falls,
picks it up with her foot, takes it into her hand, and respectfully returns it to her husband.[2] In many parts of
India, bride and bridegroom are marked with one
another's blood, probably to signify the intimate union
which has taken place between them. This is the
custom, for instance, among the Birhors. Col. Dalton
believes this to be 'the origin of the custom now so

---

[1] Hale's United States Explor.        [2] Dalton's Des. Ethn. of Bengal,
Exped.: Ethnography, p. 70.        p. 195.

' universal of marking with red lead.'[1]  In other cases
the idea symbolised is less obvious.  Among some of the
Hindoo tribes the bride and bridegroom are respectively
married to trees in the first instance, and subsequently
to one another.  Thus a Kurmi bridegroom is married
to a mango, his bride to a malwa tree.[2]  The idea un-
derlying this I take to be that they are thus devoted to
the deities of the Mango and Malwa, and having thus
become respectively tabooed to other men and women,
are, with the consent of the deities, espoused to one
another.

Among the Canadian Indians, Carver[3] says that
when the chief has pronounced the pair to be married,
' the bridegroom turns round, and, bending his body,
' takes his wife on his back, in which manner he carries
' her, amidst the acclamations of the spectators, to his
' tent.'  Bruce, in Abyssinia, observed an identical
custom.  When the ceremony is over, he says, ' the
' bridegroom takes his lady on his shoulders, and carries
' her off to his house.  If it be at a distance he does
' the same thing, but only goes entirely round about the
' bride's house.'[4]

In China, when the bridal procession reaches the
bridegroom's house, the bride is carried into the house
by a matron, and ' lifted over a pan of charcoal at the
' door.'[5]

We shall presently see that these are no isolated cases,
nor is the act of lifting the bride over the bridegroom's

[1] Dalton's Des. Ethn. of Bengal,
pp. 2:0, 310.
[2] Ibid., p. 310.
[3] Travels, p. 374.
[4] Vol. vii. p. 97.
[5] Davis. The Chinese, vol. i. p.
285.

threshold an act without a meaning. I shall shortly mention many allied customs, to the importance and significance of which our attention has recently been called by Mr. M'Lennan, in his masterly work on ' Primitive Marriage.'

I will now attempt to trace up the custom of marriage in its gradual development. There is strong evidence that the lowest races of men live, or did live, in a state of what may perhaps be called ' Communal Marriage.' In the Andaman Islands,[1] Sir Edward Belcher states that the custom is for the man and woman to remain together until the child is weaned, when they separate as a matter of course, and each seeks a new partner. The Bushmen of South Africa are stated to be entirely without marriage. Among the Nairs (India), as Buchanan tells us, ' no one knows his father, and every man looks ' on his sister's children as his heirs.' The Teehurs of Oude ' live together almost indiscriminately in large ' communities, and even when two people are regarded ' as married the tie is but nominal.'[2]

In China, communal marriage is stated to have prevailed down to the time of Fouhi,[3] and in Greece to that of Cecrops. The Messagetæ,[4] and the Auses,[5] an Ethiopian tribe, had, according to Herodotus, no marriage—a statement which is confirmed by Strabo as regards the former. Strabo and Solinus make the same statement as regards the Garamantes, another Ethiopian tribe.

[1] Trans. Ethn. Soc., vol. v. p. 45.
[2] The People of India, by J. F. Watson and J. W. Kaye, published by the Indian Government, vol. ii. pl. 85.
[3] Goguet, L'Origine des Lois, des Arts et des Sciences, vol. iii. p. 328.
[4] Clio, vol. l. p. 216.
[5] Melpomene, vol. iv. 180.

In California, according to Baegert,[1] the sexes met without any formalities, and their vocabulary did not even contain the words ' to marry.' Garcilasso de la Vega asserts that among some of the Peruvian tribes, before the time of the Incas, men had no special wives.[2]

Speaking of the natives of Queen Charlotte Island, Mr. Poole says,[3] ' among these simple and primitive ' tribes, the institution of marriage is altogether un- ' known.' The women appear to consider almost all the men of their own tribe in the light of husbands. They are, on the contrary, very circumspect in their behaviour with other men.

The backwardness (until lately) of the Sandwich Islanders in their social relations, is manifested in their language. This is shown from the following table extracted from a longer one, given by Mr. Morgan in a most interesting work on the Origin of the Classificatory System of Relationship.[4]

| *Hawaian* | *English* |
|---|---|
| Kupuna signifies | Great grandfather |
| | Great great uncle |
| | Great grandmother |
| | Great grandaunt |
| | Grandfather |
| | Granduncle |
| | Grandmother |
| | Grandaunt |

[1] *Loc. cit.*, p. 308.
[2] Commentaries of the Incas, trans. by C. R. Markham, vol. ii. p. 443.
[3] Queen Charlotte Islands, p. 312.
[4] Proc. of the Amer. Acad. of Arts and Sciences, 1868.

| Hawaiian | | English |
|---|---|---|
| Makua kana | = | Father<br>Father's brother<br>Father's brother-in-law<br>Mother's brother<br>Mother's brother-in-law<br>Grandfather's brother's son. |
| Makua waheena | = | Mother<br>Mother's sister<br>Mother's sister-in-law<br>Father's sister<br>Father's sister-in-law. |
| Kaikee kana | = | Son<br>Sister's son<br>Brother's son<br>Brother's son's son<br>Brother's daughter's son<br>Sister's son's son<br>Sister's daughter's son<br>Mother's sister's son's son<br>Mother's brother's son's son. |
| Hunona | = | Brother's son's wife<br>Brother's daughter's husband<br>Sister's son's wife<br>Sister's daughter's husband. |
| Waheena | = | Wife<br>Wife's sister<br>Brother's wife<br>Wife's brother's wife<br>Father's brother's son's wife<br>Father's sister's son's wife<br>Mother's sister's son's wife<br>Mother's brother's son's wife. |

| *Hawaiian* | | *English* |
|---|---|---|
| Kana | = | Husband<br>Husband's brother<br>Sister's husband. |
| Panalua | = | Wife's sister's husband (brother-in-law). |
| Kaikoaka | = | Wife's brother. |

The key of this Hawaian or Sandwich Island [1] system is the idea conveyed in the word waheena (woman). Thus—

| Waheena | = | Wife<br>Wife's sister<br>Brother's wife<br>Wife's brother's wife. |
|---|---|---|

All these are equally related to each husband. Hence the word—

Kaikee = Child, also signifies the brother's wife's child;

and no doubt the wife's sister's child, and the wife's brother's wife's child. So also, as the sister is wife to the brother-in-law (though not to her brother), and as the brother-in-law is husband to his brother's wife, he is consequently a father to his brother's children. Hence 'Kaikee' also means 'sister's son' and 'brother's son.' In fact 'Kaikee' and 'Waheena' correspond to our words 'child' and 'woman,' and there are apparently no words answering to 'son,' 'daughter,' 'wife,' or 'husband.' That this does not arise from poverty of language is evident, because the same system discriminates between other relationships which we do not distinguish.

[1] Morgan, Proceedings of the American Association, 1858.

Perhaps the contrast is most clearly shown in the terms for brother-in-law and sister-in-law.

Thus, when a woman is speaking—

Sister-in-law = husband's brother's wife = punalua.
Sister-in-law = husband's sister = kaikoaka.
But brother-in-law, whether sister's husband or husband's brother } = kana, i.e. husband.

When, on the contrary, a man is speaking—

Sister-in-law = wife's sister = waheena, i.e. wife.
Sister-in-law = brother's wife = waheena, i.e. wife.

And so—

Brother-in-law = wife's brother = kaikoaka.
Brother-in-law = wife's sister's husband = punalua.

Thus a woman has husbands and sisters-in-law, but no brothers-in-law ; a man, on the contrary, has wives and brothers-in-law, but no sisters-in-law.  The same idea runs through all other relationships: cousins, for instance, are called brothers and sisters.

So again, while the Romans distinguished between the

Father's brother = patruus, and the mother's brother = avunculus,
Father's sister = amita, and the mother's sister = matertera ;

the first two in Hawaiian are makua kana, which also signifies father ; and the last two are makua waheena, which also means mother.

In the next chapter I shall enter more at length

into the subject of Relationships, but the above will suffice to show that the idea of marriage does not, in fact, enter into the Hawaian system. Uncleship, auntship, cousinship, are ignored ; and we have only—

> Grandparents
> Parents
> Brothers and sisters
> Children and
> Grandchildren.

Here it is clear that the child is related to the group. It is not specially related either to its father or its mother, who stand in the same relation as mere uncles and aunts ; so that every child has several fathers and several mothers.

There are, I think, reasons in the social habits of these islanders which go far to explain the persistence of this archaic nomenclature. From the mildness of the climate and the abundance of food, children soon become independent ; the prevalence of large houses, used as mere dormitories, and the curious prejudice against eating in common, must also have greatly tended to retard the development of special family feelings. Yet the system of nomenclature above mentioned did not correspond with the actual state of society as found by Captain Cook and other early voyagers.

Among the Todas of the Neilgherry Hills, however, when a man marries a girl she becomes the wife of all his brothers as they successively reach manhood, and they also become the husbands of all her sisters as they become old enough to marry. In this case ' the first-

'born child is fathered upon the eldest brother, the
'next-born on the second, and so on throughout the
'series. Notwithstanding this unnatural system, the
'Todas, it must be confessed, exhibit much fondness
'and attachment towards their offspring, more so than
'their practice of mixed intercourse would seem to
'foster.'[1]

In the Tottiyars of India, also, we have a case in
which it is actually recorded that 'brothers, uncles,
'and nephews hold their wives in common.'[2]  So also,
according to Nicolaus,[3] the Galactophagi had communal marriage, 'where they called all old men fathers,
'young men sons, and those of equal age brothers.'
'Among the Sioux and some other North American
'tribes the custom is to buy the eldest of the chief's
'daughters ; then the others all belong to him, and are
'taken to wife at such times as the husband sees fit.'[4]

Such social conditions as these tend to explain the
frequency of adoption among the lower races of men,
and the fact that it is often considered to be as close a
connection as real parentage.  Among the Esquimaux,
Captain Lyon tells us that 'this curious connection
'binds the parties as firmly together as the ties of
'blood ; and an adopted son, if senior to one by nature,
'is the heir to all the family riches.'[5]

In Central Africa, Denham states that 'the practice
'of adopting children is very prevalent among the
'Felatahs, and, though they have sons and daughters of
'their own, the adopted child generally becomes heir

[1] Shortt, Trans. Ethn. Soc., N.S.
vol. vii. p. 240.
[2] Dubois' Description of the People of India, p. 9.
[3] Bachofen, Das Mutterrecht, p.
21.
[4] Ethn. Journal, 1869, p. 280.
[5] Journal, p. 353.  See 305.

'to the whole property.'[1] In Madagascar[2] also 'the
'adoption of other children, generally those of relatives,
'is of frequent occurrence. These children are regarded
'in every respect as if they were born of their adopted
'parents, and their real father and mother give up all
'claim to them.'

'It is a custom,' says Mariner,[3] 'in the Tonga
'Islands, for women to be what they call mothers to
'children or grown-up young persons who are not their
'own, for the purpose of providing them, or seeing that
'they are provided, with all the conveniences of life;'
this is often done even if the natural mother be still
living, in which case the adopted mother 'is regarded
'the same as the natural mother.' The same custom
also existed in Samoa,[4] the Marquesas, and other Pacific
Islands.[5] Among the Romans, also, adoption was an
important feature, and was effected by the symbol of a
mock birth, without which it was not regarded as complete. This custom seems to have continued down to
the time of Nerva, who, in adopting Trajan, transferred
the ceremony from the marriage-bed to the temple of
Jupiter.[6] Diodorus[7] gives a very curious account of
the same custom as it existed among the Greeks, mentioning that Juno adopted Hercules by going through
a ceremony of mock birth.

In other cases the symbol of adoption represented
not the birth, but the milk-tie. Thus, in Circassia, the

[1] Denham's Travels in Africa, vol. iv. p. 131.
[2] Sibree's Madagascar and its People, p. 107.
[3] Mariner's Tonga Islands, vol. ii. p. 98.
[4] Nineteen Years in Polynesia, p. 170.
[5] Gerland, Waitz' Anthropologie, vol. vi. p. 210.
[6] Muller, Das Mutterrecht, p. 254.
[7] IV. 39. See Notes.

woman offered her breast to the person she was
adopting. In Abyssinia, Parkyn tells us that 'if a man
' wishes to be adopted as the son of one of superior
' station or influence, he takes his hand, and, sucking
' one of his fingers, declares himself to be his "child by
' "adoption," and his new father is bound to assist him
' as far as he can.'[1]

The same idea underlies, perhaps, the curious Esquimaux habit of licking anything which is presented
to them, apparently in token of ownership.[2]

Dieffenbach[3] also mentions the practice of licking a
present in New Zealand ; here, however, it is the donor
who does so. In the Tonga Islands, Captain Cook tells
us that the natives 'have a singular custom of putting
' everything you give them to their heads, by way of
' thanks, as we conjectured.'[4] Labillardière observed
the same practice in Tasmania.[5]

Assuming, then, that the communal marriage system
shown in the preceding pages to prevail, or have prevailed, so widely among races in a low stage of civilisation, represents the primitive and earliest social condition of man, we now come to consider the various
ways in which it may have been broken up and replaced
by individual marriage.

Montesquieu lays it down almost as an axiom, that
' l'obligation naturelle qu'a le père de nourrir ses
' enfants a fait établir le mariage, qui déclare celui qui
' doit remplir cette obligation.'[6] Elsewhere he states

[1] Parkyn's Abyssinia, p. 108.
[2] Franklin's Journeys, 1819-22, vol. l. p. 34.
[3] New Zealand, vol. ii. p. 104.
[4] Voyage towards the South Pole, vol. l. p. 221.
[5] Gerland. Waitz' Anthropologie, vol. vi. p. 812.
[6] Esprit des Lois, vol. ii. p. 180.

that ' il est arrivé dans tous les pays et dans tous les 'temps que la religion s'est mêlée des mariages.'[1] How far these assertions are from the truth will be conclusively shown in the following pages.

Bachofen,[2] M'Lennan,[3] and Morgan, the most recent authors who have studied this subject, all agree that the primitive condition of man, socially, was one in which marriage did not exist,[4] or, as we may perhaps for convenience call it, of communal marriage, where all the men and women in a small community were regarded as equally married to one another.

Bachofen considers that after a while the women, shocked and scandalised by such a state of things, revolted against it, and established a system of marriage with female supremacy, the husband being subject to the wife, property and descent being considered to go in the female line, and women enjoying the principal share of political power. The first period he calls that of ' Hetairism,' the second of ' Mutterrecht,' or ' mother- ' right.'

In the third stage he considers that the ethereal influence of the father prevailed over the more material idea of motherhood. Men claimed pre-eminence, property and descent were traced in the male line, sun worship superseded moon worship, and many other changes in social organisation took place—mainly because it came to be recognised that the creative influence of the father was more important than the material tie of motherhood. The father, in fact, was the author of life, the mother a mere nurse.

[1] *Loc cit.*, p. 209.  [3] Primitive Marriage.
[2] *Das Mutterrecht.*  [4] *Ibid.*, xviii. xix.

Thus he regards the first stage as lawless, the second
as material, the third as spiritual.  I believe, however,
that communities in which women have exercised the
supreme power are rare and exceptional, if indeed they
ever existed at all.  We do not find in history, as a
matter of fact, that women do assert their rights, and
savage women would, I think, be peculiarly unlikely to
uphold their dignity in the manner supposed.  On the
contrary, among the lowest races of men, as, for
instance, in Australia, the position of the women is one
of complete subjection ; and it seems to me perfectly
clear that the idea of marriage is founded on the rights,
not of the woman, but of the man, being an illustration of

> the good old plan,
> That he should take who has the power,
> And he should keep who can.

Among low races the wife is indeed literally the
property of the husband.  As Petruchio says of
Catherine:

> I will be master of what is mine own.
> She is my goods, my chattels ; she is my house,
> My household stuff, my field, my barn,
> My horse, my ox, my ass, my anything.

So thoroughly is this the case, that a Roman's
'family' originally, and indeed throughout classical
times, meant his slaves, and the children only formed
part of the family because they were his slaves; so that
if a father freed his son, the latter ceased to be one of
the family, and had no part in the inheritance.

'The mere tie of blood relationship,' says Ortolan,

'was of no account among the Romans. . . . . . The
'most general expression and the most comprehensive
'term indicating relationship in Roman Law is *cognatio*
' —the cognation, that is to say, the tie between persons
'who are united by the same blood, or those reputed
'by the law as such (*cognati; quasi una communiter
' nati*). But cognation alone, whether it proceeds from
'legal marriage or any other union, does not place
'the individual within the family, nor does it give any
'right of family.'[1] Even at the present day, in some
parts of Africa, a man's property goes, not to his children, as such, but to his slaves.

The fact that the wife is regarded literally as the
property of the husband explains those cases which seem
to us so remarkable, in which great laxity of conduct
before, is combined with the utmost strictness after,
marriage. Hence, also, the custom, so prevalent among
the lower races of men, that on the death of the elder
brother the wives belong to the second.

This complete subjection of the woman in marriage
also explains those cases in which women of rank were
considered too great to marry. Livingstone distinctly
states this in the case of Mamochisâne, daughter of
Sebituane, chief of the Bechuanas. Sebituane 'could
' not look upon the husband except as the woman's
' lord, so he told her all the men were hers, she might
' take any one, but ought to keep none.'[2]

Hearne tells us, that among the Hudson's Bay
Indians 'it has ever been the custom for the men to

[1] Ortolan's History of Roman Law, tr. by Prichard and Nasmith, p. 129.
[2] Travels in South Africa, p.

170. See also Burton's Dahomey, vol. I. pp. 107, 308, vol. ii. p. 72. Tuckey's Exp. to the River Zaire p. 140.

' wrestle for any woman to whom they are attached;
' and, of course, the strongest party always carries off
' the prize. A weak man, unless he be a good hunter
' and well-beloved, is seldom permitted to keep a wife
' that a stronger man thinks worth his notice. . . . .
' This custom prevails throughout all their tribes, and
' causes a great spirit of emulation among their youth,
' who are upon all occasions, from their childhood, trying
' their strength and skill in wrestling.'[1] Franklin also
says that the Copper Indians hold women in the same
low estimation as the Chipewyans do, ' looking upon
' them as a kind of property, which the stronger may
' take from the weaker ;'[2] and Richardson[3] ' more than
' once saw a stronger man assert his right to take the
' wife of a weaker countryman. Anyone may challenge
' another to wrestle, and, if he overcomes, may carry off
' the wife as the prize.' Yet the women never dream
of protesting against this, which, indeed, seems to them
perfectly natural. The theory, therefore, of Dr. Bachofen, and the sequence of social customs suggested by
him, although supported with much learning, cannot, I
think, be regarded as correct.[4]

M'Lennan, like Bachofen and Morgan, starts with a
stage of Hetairism or communal marriage. The next
stage was, in his opinion, that form of polyandry in
which brothers had their wives in common; afterwards
came that of the *levirate*, i.e. the system under which,
when an elder brother died, his second brother married
the widow, and so on with the others in succession.

[1] Hearne, p. 104.
[2] Journey to the Shores of the Polar Seas, vol. viii. p. 43.
[3] Richardson's Boat Journey, vol. ii. p. 24.
[4] See, for instance, Lewin's Hill Tracts of Chittagong, pp. 47, 77, 80, 83, 98, 101.

Thence he considers that some tribes branched off into endogamy, others into exogamy;[1] that is to say, some forbade marriage out of, others within, the tribe. If either of these two systems was older than the other, he considers that exogamy must have been the most ancient. Exogamy was based on infanticide,[2] and led to the practice of marriage by capture.[3]

In a further stage the idea of female descent, producing as it would a division in the tribe, obviated the necessity of capture as a reality and reduced it to a symbol.

In support of this view Mr. M'Lennan has certainly brought forward many striking facts; but, while admitting that it probably represents the succession of events in some cases, I cannot but think that these are exceptional. Fully admitting the prevalence of infanticide among savages, it will, I think, be found that among the lowest races boys were killed as frequently as girls. Eyre expressly states that this was the case in Australia.[4] In fact, the distinction between the sexes implies an amount of forethought and prudence which the lower races of men do not possess.

For reasons to be given shortly, I believe that communal marriage was gradually superseded by individual marriage founded on capture, and that this led firstly to exogamy and then to female infanticide; thus reversing M'Lennan's order of sequence. Endogamy and regulated polyandry, though frequent, I regard as exceptional, and as not entering into the normal progress of development.

---

[1] *Loc. cit.*, p. 145.
[2] *Loc. cit.*, p. 138.
[3] *Loc. cit.*, p. 140.
[4] *Discoveries, &c.*, vol. ii. p. 324.

With M'Lennan, Bachofen, and Morgan, I believe that our present social relations have arisen from an initial stage of Hetairism or communal marriage. It is obvious, however, that even under communal marriage, a warrior who had captured a beautiful girl in some marauding expedition would claim a peculiar right to her, and, when possible, would set custom at defiance. We have already seen that there are other cases of the existence of marriage under two forms side by side in one country; and there is, therefore, no real difficulty in assuming the co-existence of communal and individual marriage. It is true that under a communal marriage system no man could appropriate a girl entirely to himself without infringing the rights of the whole tribe. Such an act would naturally be looked on with jealousy, and only regarded as justifiable under peculiar circumstances. A war-captive, however, was in a peculiar position: the tribe had no right to her; her capturer might have killed her if he chose; if he preferred to keep her alive he was at liberty to do so; he did as he liked, and the tribe was no sufferer.

M'Lennan,[1] indeed, says that ' it is impossible to ' believe that the mere lawlessness of savages should be ' consecrated into a legal symbol, or to assign a reason ' —could this be believed—why a similar symbol should ' not appear in transferences of other kinds of property.' The symbol of capture, however, was not one of law-lessness, but, on the other hand, of—according to the ideas of the time—lawful possession. It did not refer to those from whom the captive was taken, but was

---

[1] *Loc. cit.*, p. 44.

intended to bar the rights of the tribe into which she was introduced. Individual marriage was, in fact, an infringement of communal rights; the man retaining to himself, or the man and woman mutually appropriating to each other, that which should have belonged to the whole tribe. Thus, among the Andamaners, any woman who attempted to resist the marital privileges claimed by any member of the tribe was liable to severe punishment.[1]

Nor is it, I think, difficult to understand why the symbol of capture does not appear in transferences of other kinds of property. Every generation requires fresh wives; the actual capture, or at any rate the symbol, needed therefore repetition. This, however, does not apply to land; when once the idea of landed property arose, the same land descended from owner to owner. In other kinds of property, again, there is an important, though different kind of, distinction. A man made his own bow and arrows, his own hut, his own arms; hence the necessity of capture did not exist, and the symbol would not arise.

M'Lennan supposes that savages were driven by female infanticide, and the consequent absence or paucity of women, into exogamy, and marriage by capture. I shall presently give my reasons for rejecting this explanation.

He also considers that marriage by capture followed, and arose from, that remarkable custom of marrying always out of the tribe, for which he has proposed the appropriate name of exogamy. On the con-

[1] Trans. Ethn. Soc., N.S., vol. ii. p. 35.

H

trary, I believe that exogamy arose from marriage by capture, not marriage by capture from exogamy ; that capture, and capture alone, could originally give a man the right to monopolise a woman, to the exclusion of his fellow-clansmen ; and that hence, even after all necessity for actual capture had long ceased, the symbol remained ; capture having, by long habit, come to be received as a necessary preliminary to marriage.

That marriage by capture has not arisen from female modesty is, I think, evident, not only because we have no reason to suppose that such a feeling prevails specially among the lower races of man, but also, firstly, because it cannot explain the mock resistance of the relatives ; and, secondly, because the very question to be solved is why it became so generally the custom to win the female not by persuasion but by force.

Mr. M'Lennan's view throws no light on the remarkable ceremonies of expiation for marriage, to which I shall presently call attention.

I will, however, first proceed to show how widely ' capture,' either actual or symbolical, enters into the idea of marriage. Mr. M'Lennan was, I believe, the first to appreciate its importance. I have taken some of the following instances from his valuable work, adding, however, many additional cases.

It requires, no doubt, strong evidence, which, however, exists in abundance, to satisfy us that the origin of marriage was independent of all sacred and social considerations ; that it had nothing to do with mutual affection or sympathy ; that it was invalidated by any appearance of consent ; and that it was symbolised, not by any demonstration of warm affection on the one side and tender devotion on the other, but by brutal violence and unwilling submission.

Yet, as already mentioned, the evidence is overwhelming. So completely, for instance, did the Caribs supply themselves with wives from the neighbouring races, and so little communication did they hold with them, that the men and women actually spoke different languages. So, again, in Australia the men, says Oldfield, ' are in excess of the other sex, and, consequently, ' many men of every tribe are unprovided with that ' especial necessary to their comfortable subsistence, a ' wife; who is a slave in the strictest sense of the word, ' being a beast of burden, a provider of food, and a ' ready object on which to vent those passions that the ' men do not dare to vent on each other. Hence, for ' those coveting such a luxury, arises the necessity of ' stealing the women of some other tribe; and, in their ' expeditions to effect so laudable a design, they will ' cheerfully undergo privations and dangers equal to ' those they incur when in search of blood-revenge. ' When, on such an errand, they discover an unprotected ' female, their proceedings are not of the most gentle ' nature. Stunning her by a blow from the dowak (to ' make her love them, perhaps), they drag her by the ' hair to the nearest thicket to await her recovery. ' When she comes to her senses they force her to ' accompany them; and as at worst it is but the ex-' change of one brutal lord for another, she generally ' enters into the spirit of the affair, and takes as much ' pains to escape as though it were a matter of her own ' free choice.'[1]

[1] Trans. Ethn. Soc., vol. iii. p. 250.

Collins thus describes the manner in which the natives about Sydney used to procure wives :—' The poor
' wretch is stolen upon in the absence of her protectors.
' Being first stupefied with blows, inflicted with clubs
' or wooden swords, on the head, back, and shoulders,
' every one of which is followed by a stream of blood,
' she is then dragged through the woods by one arm,
' with a perseverance and violence that it might be sup-
' posed would displace it from its socket. The lover,
' or rather the ravisher, is regardless of the stones or
' broken pieces of trees which may lie in his route,
' being anxious only to convey his prize in safety to his
' own party, when a scene ensues too shocking to relate.
' This outrage is not resented by the relations of the
' female, who only retaliate by a similar outrage when
' they find an opportunity. This is so constantly the
' practice among them that even the children make it a
' play-game, or exercise.' [1]

In Bali also,[2] one of the islands between Java and New Guinea, it is stated to be the practice that girls
' are stolen away by their brutal lovers, who sometimes
' surprise them alone, or overpower them by the way,
' and carry them off with dishevelled hair and tattered
' garments to the woods. When brought back from
' thence, and reconciliation is effected with enraged
' friends, the poor female becomes the slave of her rough
' lover, by a certain compensation-price being paid to
' her relatives.'

So deeply rooted is the feeling of a connection between force and marriage, that we find the former

[1] Collins's English Colony in New South Wales, p. 362.

[2] Notices of the Indian Archipelago, p. 00.

used as a form long after all necessity for it had ceased ;
and it is very interesting to trace, as Mr. M'Lennan
has done, the gradual stages through which a stern
reality softens down into a mere symbol.

It is easy to see that if we assume the case of a
country in which there are four neighbouring tribes,
who have the custom of exogamy, and who trace pedi-
grees through the mother, and not through the father
—a custom which, as we shall presently find, is so
common that it may be said to be the usual one among
the lower races—after a certain time the result would
be that each tribe would consist of four septs or clans,
representing the four original tribes, and hence we
should find communities in which each tribe is divided
into clans, and a man must always marry a woman of a
different clan.   But as communities became larger and
more civilised, the actual ' capture ' would become
inconvenient, and at last impossible.

Gradually therefore it came to be more and more a
mock ceremony, forming, however, a necessary part of
the marriage ceremony.   Of this many cases might be
given.

Speaking of the Khonds of Orissa, Major-General
Campbell says that on one occasion he ' heard loud cries
' proceeding from a village close at hand.   Fearing some
' quarrel, I rode to the spot, and there I saw a man
' bearing away upon his back something enveloped in
' an ample covering of scarlet cloth ; he was surrounded
' by twenty or thirty young fellows, and by them pro-
' tected from the desperate attacks made upon him by
' a party of young women.   On seeking an explanation
' of this novel scene, I was told that the man had just

' been married, and his precious burden was his bloom-
' ing bride, whom he was conveying to his own village.
' Her youthful friends (as it appears is the custom)
' were seeking to regain possession of her, and hurled
' stones and bamboos at the head of the devoted bride-
' groom, until he reached the confines of his own vil-
' lage.' [1]

Dalton mentions that among the Kols of Central
India, when the price of a girl has been arranged, ' the
' bridegroom and a large party of his friends of both
' sexes enter with much singing and dancing, and *sham*
' *fighting* in the village of the bride, where they meet
' the bride's party, and are hospitably entertained.' [2]

Sir W. Elliot also mentions that not only amongst
the Khonds, but also in ' several other tribes of Central
' India, the bridegroom seizes his bride by force, either
' affected or real ;' [3] and the same was customary
among the Badagas of the Neilgherry Hills, the Mun-
dahs, Hos, Garos, Oraons, Ghonds, and other Hill tribes. [4]

Among the Garos a young man and woman who
wish to marry, take some provisions and retire to the
Hills for a few days. The girl goes first, and the lover
follows after, well knowing of course where she will be
found. In a few days they return to the village, when
the marriage is publicly announced and solemnised, a
mock fight taking place, though in this case the pretended reluctance is on the part of the bridegroom. [5]

[1] Quoted in M'Lennan's Primitive Marriage, p. 28.
[2] Trans. Ethn. Soc., vol. vi. p. 24.
See also p. 27 ; the Tribes of India,
vol. i. p. 15 ; and Dalton's Des.
Ethnology of Bengal, pp. 61, 80,
163, 252, 278, 310.

[3] Trans. Ethn. Soc. 1869, p. 125.
[4] Meta. The tribes of the Neilgherries, p. 74. See also Lewin's
Hill Tracts of Chittagong, pp. 30,
80.
[5] Dalton's Des. Ethn. of Bengal,
p. 64.

In this tribe the girls propose to the men, as is also said to be the case among the Bhinyas.[1]

M. Bourien[2] thus describes the marriage ceremony among the wild tribes of the Malay Peninsula:—'When 'all are assembled, and all ready, the bride and bride-'groom are led by one of the old men of the tribe 'towards a circle more or less great, according to the 'presumed strength of the intended pair; the girl 'runs round first, and the young man pursues a short 'distance behind; if he succeed in reaching her and 'retaining her, she becomes his wife; if not, he loses 'all claim to her. At other times, a larger field is 'appointed for the trial, and they pursue one another 'in the forest. The race, according to the words of the 'chronicle, "is not to the swift nor the battle to the '"strong," but to the young man who has had the good 'fortune to please the intended bride.'

Among the Kalmucks, De Hell tells us that, after the price of the girl has been duly agreed on, when the bridegroom comes with his friends to carry off his bride, 'a sham resistance is always made by the people 'of her camp, in spite of which she fails not to be borne 'away on a richly caparisoned horse, with loud shouts 'and feu de joie.'[3]

Dr. Clarke[4] gives a charmingly romantic account of the ceremony. 'The girl,' he says, 'is first mounted, 'who rides off at full speed. Her lover pursues; if he 'overtakes her, she becomes his wife, and the marriage

[1] *Loc. cit.*, p. 142.
[2] Trans. Ethn. Soc. 1865, p. 81.
[3] Steppes of the Caspian, p. 260. Quoted in M'Lennan's Primitive Marriage, p. 30.

[4] Travels, vol. I. p. 332. See also Vambéry's Travels in Central Asia, p. 323. Burnes' Travels in Bokhara, pp. 11, 50.

'is consummated on the spot; after this she returns
'with him to his tent.  But it sometimes happens that
'the woman does not wish to marry the person by
'whom she is pursued; in this case, she will not suffer
'him to overtake her.  We were assured that no in-
'stance occurs of a Kalmuck girl being thus caught,
'unless she have a partiality to the pursuer.  If she
'dislikes him, she rides, to use the language of English
'sportsmen, "neck or nought," until she has completely
'effected her escape, or until her pursuer's horse
'becomes exhausted, leaving her at liberty to return,
'and to be afterwards chased by some more favoured
'admirer.'

'Among the Tunguses and Kamchadales,' says
Erman,[1] 'a matrimonial engagement is not definitely
'arranged and concluded until the suitor has got the
'better of his beloved by force, and has torn her
'clothes.'  Attacks on women are not allowed to be
avenged by blood unless they take place within the
yourt or house.  The man is not regarded as to blame,
if the woman 'has ventured to leave her natural place,
'the sacred and protecting hearth.'  Pallas observes
that in his time 'marriage by capture prevailed also
'among the Samoyedes.'[2]

Among the Mongols,[3] when a marriage is arranged,
the girl 'flies to some relations to hide herself.  The
'bridegroom coming to demand his wife, the father-in-
'law says, "My daughter is yours; go, take her wher-

[1] Travels in Siberia, vol. ii. p. 412.  See also Kames' History of Man, vol. ii. p. 58.
[2] Vol. iv. p. 97.  See also Astley's Collections of Voyages, vol. iv. p. 575.
[3] Astley, vol. iv. p. 77.

' " ever you can find her." Having thus obtained his
' warrant, he, with his friends, runs about searching,
' and having found her, seizes her as his property, and
' carries her home as it were by force.' Marriage by
capture, indeed, prevails throughout Siberia. In Kamskatka, says Müller, 'attraper une fille est leur ex-
' pression pour dire marier.'[1]

'In the Korea, when a man marries, he mounts on
' horseback, attended by his friends, and, having ridden
' about the town, stops at the bride's door, where he is
' received by her relations, who then carry her to his
' house, and the ceremony is complete.'[2] Traces of the
custom also occur in Japan.[3]

Among the Esquimaux of Cape York (Smith Sound),
according to Dr. Hayes,[4] ' there is no marriage cere-
' mony further than that the boy is required to carry
' off his bride by main force; for, even among these
' blubber-eating people, the woman only saves her
' modesty by a sham resistance, although she knows
' years beforehand that her destiny is sealed, and that
' she is to become the wife of the man from whose
' embraces, when the nuptial day comes, she is obliged
' by the inexorable law of public opinion to free herself
' if possible, by kicking and screaming with might and
' main, until she is safely landed in the hut of her future
' lord, when she gives up the combat very cheerfully
' and takes possession of her new abode.'

In Greenland, according to Egede, ' when a young

---

[1] Des. de toutes les Nations de l'Empire de Russe, Pt. II. p. 80. See also Pt. I. p. 170; Pt. III. pp. 36, 71.

[2] Ibid., p. 342.
[3] Le Japon Illustré, vol. ii. p. 130.
[4] Open Polar Sea, p. 432.

' man likes a maiden he commonly proposes it to their
' parents and relations on both sides ; and after he has
' obtained their consent, he gets two or more old women
' to fetch the bride (and if he is a stout fellow he will
' fetch her himself).     They go to the place where
' the young woman is, and carry her away by force.'[1]

We have already seen (p. 93) that marriage by
capture exists in full force among the Northern Redskins.

The Aborigines of the Amazon Valley, says
Wallace,[2] ' have no particular ceremony at their mar-
' riages, except that of always carrying away the girl
' by force, or making a show of doing so, even when
' she and her parents are quite willing.'

M. Bardel, in the notes to D'Urville's Voyage, mentions that among the Indians round Conception, in
South America, after a man has agreed on the price of
a girl with her parents, he surprises her, and carries
her off to the woods for a few days, after which the
happy couple return home.[3]

In Tierra del Fuego, as Admiral Fitzroy tells us,[4]
as soon ' as a youth is able to maintain a wife by his
' exertions in fishing or bird-catching, he obtains the
' consent of her relations, and . . . . having built or
' stolen a canoe for himself, he watches for an oppor-
' tunity, and carries off his bride.    If she is unwilling
' she hides herself in the woods until her admirer is
' heartily tired of looking for her, and gives up the
' pursuit ; but this seldom happens.'

[1] History of Greenland, p. 143.          [4] Voyage of the 'Adventure' and
[2] Travels in the Amazons, p. 497.       'Beagle,' vol. ii. p. 182.
[3] Vol. iii. pp. 277 and 22.

Williams mentions that among the Feejeeans the custom prevails ' of seizing upon a woman by apparent ' or actual force, in order to make her a wife. On ' reaching the home of her abductor, should she not ' approve of the match, she runs to some one who can ' protect her : if, however, she is satisfied, the matter is ' settled forthwith; a feast is given to her friends the ' next morning, and the couple are thenceforward con- ' sidered as man and wife.'[1]

Earle[2] gives the following account of marriage in New Zealand, which he regards as ' most extraordinary,' while in reality it is, as we now see, nothing of the sort:—' The New Zealand method of courtship and ' matrimony is,' he says, ' most extraordinary; so much ' so that an observer could never imagine any affection ' existed between the parties. A man sees a woman ' whom he fancies he should like for a wife; he asks the ' consent of her father, or, if an orphan, of her nearest ' relation; which, if he obtains, he carries his " intended" ' off by force, she resisting with all her strength; and, ' as the New Zealand girls are generally pretty robust, ' sometimes a dreadful struggle takes place; both are ' soon stripped to the skin ; and it is sometimes the ' work of hours to remove the fair prize a hundred ' yards. If she breaks away she instantly flies from her ' antagonist, and he has his labour to commence again. ' We may suppose that if the lady feels any wish to be ' united to her would-be spouse she will not make too ' violent an opposition; but it sometimes happens that ' she secures her retreat into her father's house, and the

[1] Fiji and the Fijians, vol. i. p. 174.   [2] Residence in New Zealand, p. 244.

'lover loses all chance of ever obtaining her; whereas,
'if he can manage to carry her in triumph into his own,
'she immediately becomes his wife.'

Even after a marriage, it is customary in New Zealand to have a mock scuffle. Mr. Yate[1] gives a good illustration. There was, he says, 'a little opposition to
'the wedding, but not till it was over, as is always the
'custom here. The bride's mother came to me the
'preceding afternoon, and said she was well pleased in
'her heart that her daughter was going to be married
'to Pahau; but that she must be angry about it with
'her mouth in the presence of her tribe, lest the natives
'should come and take away all her possessions, and
'destroy her crops. This is customary on all occasions.
'If a chief meets with an accident he is stripped, as a
'mark of respect; if he marries a wife he has to lose
'all his property; and this is done out of respect—not
'from disrespect, as it was once printed, inadvertently,
'in an official publication. A chief would think himself
'slighted if his food and garments were not taken away
'from him upon many occasions. To prevent this,
'Manga, the old mother, acted with policy. As I was
'returning, therefore, from the church with the bride-
'groom and bride, she met the procession and began
'to assail us all furiously. She put on a most terrific
'countenance, threw her garments about, and tore her
'hair like a fury; then said to me, "Ah! you white
'"missionary, you are worse than the devil: you first
'"make a slave-lad your son by redeeming him from
'"his master, and then marry him to my daughter,
'"who is a lady. I will tear your eyes out! I will

' " tear your eyes out ! "  The old woman, suiting the
' action to the word, feigned a scratch at my face, at
' the same time saying in an under tone that it was " all
' " mouth," and that she did not mean what she said.
' I told her I should stop her mouth with a blanket.
' " Ha, ha, ha ! " she replied ; " that was all I wanted :
' " I only wanted to get a blanket, and therefore I
' " made this noise."  The whole affair went off after
' this remarkably well ; all seemed to enjoy themselves ;
' and everyone was satisfied.'  It is evident, however,
that Yate did not thoroughly understand the meaning
of the scene.

Among the Ahitas of the Philippine Islands, when
a man wishes to marry a girl, her parents send her
before sunrise into the woods.  She has an hour's start,
after which the lover goes to seek her.  If he finds her
and brings her back before sunset, the marriage is
acknowledged ; if not, he must abandon all claim to
her.[1]  The natives of New Guinea also have a very
similar custom.[2]

Among the Kaffirs marriage is an affair of purchase,
notwithstanding which 'the bridegroom is required to
' carry off his bride by force, after the preliminaries are
' completed.  This is attempted by the help of all the
' friends and relatives that the man can muster, and
' resisted by the friends and relatives of the woman ;
' and the contest now and then terminates in the dis-
' comfiture of the unlucky husband, who is reduced to
' the necessity of waylaying his wife, when she may
' be alone in the fields or fetching water from the well.'[3]

[1] Earl's Native Races of the
Indian Archipelago, p. 133.
[2] Gerland's Waitz' Anthropologie, vol. i. p. 133.
[3] Pritchard's Nat. His. of Man,
ii. 403.  See also Arbousset's Tour

In the West African kingdom of Futa,[1] after all
other preliminaries are arranged, 'one difficulty yet
' remains, viz., how the young man shall get his wife
' home ; for the women-cousins and relations take on
' mightily, and guard the door of the house to prevent
' her being carried away. At last, by the bridegroom's
' presents and generosity, their grief is assuaged. He
' then provides a friend, well mounted, to carry her off;
' but as soon as she is on horseback the women renew
' their lamentations, and rush in to dismount her.
' However, the man is generally successful, and rides
' off with his prize to the house prepared for her.'

Gray mentions[2] that a Mandingo (West Africa)
wishing to marry a young girl at Kayaye, applied to
her mother, who 'consented to his obtaining her in any
' way he could. Accordingly, when the poor girl was
' employed preparing some rice for supper, she was
' seized by her intended husband, assisted by three or
' four of his companions, and carried off by force. She
' made much resistance, by biting, scratching, kicking,
' and roaring most bitterly. Many, both men and
' women, some of them her own relations, who wit-
' nessed the affair, only laughed at the farce, and con-
' soled her by saying that she would soon be reconciled
' to her situation.' Evidently therefore this was not,
as Gray seems to have supposed, a mere act of lawless
violence, but a recognised custom, which called for no
interference on the part of spectators. Denham,[3] describing a marriage at Sockna (North Africa), says that

to the North-east of the Cape of
Good Hope, p. 249; and Maclean's
Kaffir Laws and Customs, p. 52.
  [1] Astley's Collection of Voyages,

vol. ii. p. 240.
  [2] Gray's Travels in Western
Africa, p. 50.
  [3] Loc. cit., vol. i. p. 30.

the bride is taken on a camel to the bridegroom's house,
' upon which it is necessary for her to appear greatly
' surprised, and refuse to dismount; the women scream,
' the men shout, and she is at length persuaded to enter.'

Among the Arabs of Sinai, when a marriage has
been arranged, the girl is waylaid by her lover 'and
' a couple of his friends, and carried off by force to his
' father's tent. If she entertains any suspicion of their
' designs, she defends herself with stones, and often
' inflicts wounds on the young men, even though she
' does not dislike the lover.'[1]

In Circassia weddings are accompanied by a feast,
' in the midst of which the bridegroom has to rush in,
' and, with the help of a few daring young men, carry
' off the lady by force ; and by this process she becomes
' the lawful wife.'[2] According to Spencer, another important part of the ceremony consists in the bridegroom
drawing his dagger and cutting open the bride's corset.

As regards Europe, Plutarch[3] tells us that in Sparta
the bridegroom usually carried off his bride by force,
evidently, however, of a friendly character. I would
venture to suggest that the character of Helen, as
portrayed in the 'Iliad,' can only be understood by
regarding her marriage with Paris as a case of marriage
by capture.[4] 'Les premiers Romains,' says Ortolan,[5] 'ont
' été obligés de recourir à la surprise et à la force pour en-
'lever leurs premières femmes,'and he points out that long
after any actual violence had ceased, it was customary to

[1] Burckhardt's Notes on the Bedouins and Wahabys, vol. i. p. 263.
See also pp. 108, 231.

[2] Moser, The Caucasus and its
People, p. 31 ; quoted by M'Louran

loc. cit., p. 36.

[3] See also Herodotus, vi. 65.

[4] See Appendix.

[5] Exp. His. des Ins. de l'Emp.
Justinian, pp. 81, 82.

pass a lance over the head of the bride, 'en signe de la
' puissance que va acquérir le mari.' Hence also while
a man might be married in his absence, this was not
the case as regards the woman.  A man might capture
a bride for his friend, but the woman could not be
captured unless really present.[1]  In North Friesland,
' a young fellow called the bride-lifter lifts the bride
' and her two bridesmaids upon the waggon in which
' the married couple are to travel to their home.'[2]
M'Lennan states that in some parts of France, down to
the seventeenth century, it was customary for the bride
to feign reluctance to enter the bridegroom's house.

In Poland, Lithuania, Russia, and parts of Prussia,
according to Seignior Gaya,[3] young men used to carry
off their sweethearts by force, and then apply to the
parents for their consent.

Lord Kames,[4] in his ' Sketches of the History of
' Man,' mentions that the following marriage ceremony
was, in his day, or at least had till shortly before, been
customary among the Welsh:—' On the morning of the
' wedding-day the bridegroom, accompanied by his
' friends on horseback, demands the bride.  Her friends,
' who are likewise on horseback, give a positive refusal,
' on which a mock scuffle ensues.  The bride, mounted
' behind her nearest kinsman, is carried off, and is pur-
' sued by the bridegroom and his friends, with loud
' shouts.  It is not uncommon on such an occasion to
' see 200 or 300 sturdy Cambro-Britons riding at full
' speed, crossing and jostling, to the no small amuse-
' ment of the spectators.  When they have fatigued

[1] Loc. cit., p 127.                     See also Olaus Magnus, vol. xiv.
[2] M'Lennan, loc. cit., p. 32.      chapter 9.
[3] Marriage Ceremonies, p. 35.         [4] History of Man, vol. ii. p. 59.

' themselves and their horses, the bridegroom is suffered
' to overtake his bride.  He leads her away in triumph,
' and the scene is concluded with feasting and festivity.'

In European Turkey Mr. Tozer tells us that ' the
' Mirdites never intermarry ; but when any of them,
' from the highest to the lowest, wants a wife, he carries
' off a Mahometan woman from one of the neighbouring
' tribes, baptizes her, and marries her.  The parents,
' we were told, do not usually feel much aggrieved, as
' it is well understood that a sum of money will be paid
' in return.' [1]

Thus, then, we see that marriage by capture, either
as a stern reality or as an important ceremony, pre-
vails in Australia, among the Malays, in Hindostan,
Central Asia, Siberia, and Kamskatka ; among the
Esquimaux, the Northern Redskins, the Aborigines of
Brazil, in Chili, and Tierra del Fuego, in the Pacific
Islands, both among the Polynesians and the Feejeeans,
in the Philippines, among the Kaffirs, Arabs, and
Negroes, in Circassia, and, until recently, throughout a
great part of Europe.

I have already referred to the custom of lifting the
bride over the doorstep, which we find in such distinct and
distant races as the Romans, the Redskins of Canada,
the Chinese, and the Abyssinians.  Hence, also, perhaps
our honeymoon, during which the bridegroom keeps
his bride away from her relatives and friends ; hence
even, perhaps, as Mr. M'Lennan supposes, the slipper
is, in mock anger, thrown after the departing bride and
bridegroom.

The curious custom which forbids the father and

[1] The Highlands of Turkey, vol. i. p. 318.

mother-in-law to speak to their son-in-law, and *vice versâ*, which I have already shown (p. 15) to be very widely distributed, but for which no satisfactory explanation has yet been given, seems to me a natural consequence of marriage by capture. When the capture was a reality, the indignation of the parents would also be real; when it became a mere symbol, the parental anger would be symbolised also, and would be continued even after its origin was forgotten.

The separation of husband and wife, to which also I have referred (p. 75), may also arise from the same custom. It is very remarkable, indeed, how persistent are all customs and ceremonies connected with marriage. Thus our 'bride cake,' which so invariably accompanies a wedding, and *which must always be cut by the bride*, may be traced back to the old Roman form of marriage by 'confarreatio,' or eating together. So also among the Iroquois, bride and bridegroom used to partake together of a cake of 'sagamité,'[1] which the bride offered to her husband. The Feejee Islanders[2] have a very similar custom. The marriage ceremony in Samoa, says Turner, 'reminds us of the Roman confarreatio.'[3] Again, among the Tipperahs, one of the Hill tribes of Chittagong, the bride prepares some drink, 'sits on her 'lover's knee, drinks half, and gives him the other half; 'they afterwards crook together their little fingers.'[4] In one form or another a similar custom is found among most of the Hill tribes of India. A very similar custom

[1] Lafitau, vol. i. pp. 606, 671.    p. 180.
[2] Fiji and the Fijians, vol. i. p. 170.    [4] Lewin's Hill Tracts of Chittagong, pp. 71, 80.  Dalton's Des.
[3] Nineteen Years in Polynesia,    Ethn. of Bengal, p. 183.

occurs in New Guinea,[1] and in Madagascar also, part of the marriage ceremony consists in the bride and bridegroom eating out of one dish.[2]

Mr. M'Lennan conceives that marriage by capture arose from the custom of exogamy, that is to say, from the custom which forbade marriage within the tribe. Exogamy, again, he considers to have arisen from the practice of female infanticide. I have already indicated the reasons which prevent me from accepting this explanation, and which induce me to regard exogamy as arising from marriage by capture, not marriage by capture from exogamy. Mr. M'Lennan's theory seems to me quite inconsistent with the existence of tribes which have marriage by capture and yet are endogamous. The Bedouins, for instance, have marriage by capture, and yet the man has a recognised right to marry his cousin, if only he be willing to give the price demanded for her.[3]

Mr. M'Lennan, indeed, feels the difficulty which would be presented by such cases, the existence of which he seems, however, to doubt; adding, that if the symbol of capture be ever found in the marriage ceremonies of an endogamous tribe, we may be sure that it is a relic of an early time at which the tribe was organised on another principle than that of exogamy.[4]

That marriage by capture has not arisen merely from female coyness is, I think, evident, as already mentioned, firstly, because it does not account for the

[1] Gerland's Con. of Waitz' Anthrop., vol. vi. p. 633.
[2] Sibree's Madagascar and its People, p. 118.
[3] Klemm, Allg. Culturg. d. Mensch. vol. iv. p. 140.
[4] *Loc. cit.*, p. 53.

resistance of the relatives ; secondly, because it is contrary to all experience that feminine delicacy diminishes with civilisation; and thirdly, because the very question to be solved is why it has become so generally the custom to win the wife by force rather than by persuasion.

The explanation which I have suggested derives additional probability from the evidence of a general feeling that marriage was an act for which some compensation was due to those whose rights were invaded.

The nature of the ceremonies by which this was effected makes me reluctant to enter into this part of the subject at length ; and I will here therefore merely indicate in general terms the character of the evidence.

I will firstly refer to certain details given by Dulaure [1] in his chapter on the worship of Venus, of which he regards these customs merely as one illustration, although they have. I cannot but think, a signification deeper than, and different from, that which he attributes to them.

We must remember that the better known savage races have, in most cases, now arrived at the stage in which paternal rights are recognised, and hence that fathers can and do sell their daughters into matrimony. The price of a wife is of course regulated by the circumstances of the tribe, and every, or nearly every, industrious young man is enabled to buy one for himself. As long, however, as communal marriage rights were in force this would be almost impossible. That special marriage was an infringement of these communal rights, for which some compensation was due, seems to me the true explanation of the offerings which

[1] Hist. abrégée des diff. Cultes.

virgins were so generally compelled to make before being permitted to marry.

In many cases the exclusive possession of a wife could only be legally acquired by a temporary recognition of the pre-existing communal rights. See, for instance, the account given by Herodotus,[1] of the custom existing in Babylonia. According to Strabo, there was a very similar law in Armenia.[2] In some parts of Cyprus also, among the Nasamones,[3] and other Ethiopian tribes, he tells us that the same custom existed; and Dulaure asserts that it occurred also at Carthage, and in several parts of Greece, as also, according to Hamilton,[4] in Hindostan. The account which Herodotus gives of the Lydians, though not so clear, seems to indicate a similar law.

The customs of the Thracians, as described by Herodotus,[5] point to a similar feeling. Among races somewhat more advanced, the symbol supersedes the reality of this custom, and St. Augustine found it necessary to protest against that which prevailed, even in his time, in Italy.[6]

Diodorus Siculus mentions that in the Balearic Islands, Majorca, Minorca, and Ivica, the bride was for one night considered as the common property of all the guests present; after which she belonged exclusively to her husband.[7] Garcilasso de la Vega records the existence of a similar custom among the

---

[1] Clio, 199.
[2] Strabo, lib. 2.
[3] Melpomene, 172.
[4] Account of the East Indies. Pinkerton's Voyages, vol. viii. p. 574.
[5] Terpsichore, v. 6.
[6] Dulaure, *loc. cit.*, vol. ii. p. 199. See App.
[7] Diodorus, v. 18.

Mantas, a Peruvian tribe,[1] as also does Langsdorf,[2] in Nukahiva.

In India,[3] and particularly in the valleys of the Ganges, virgins were compelled before marriage to present themselves in the temples dedicated to Juggernaut, and the same is said to have been customary in Pondicherry and at Goa.[4]

Among the Sonthals, one of the aboriginal Indian tribes, the marriages take place once a year, mostly in January. 'For six days all the candidates for 'matrimony live together;' after which only are the separate couples regarded as having established their right to marry.[5]

Carver mentions[6] that while among the Naudowessies, he observed that they paid uncommon respect to one of their women, and found that she was considered to be a person of high distinction, because on one occasion she invited forty of the principal warriors to her tent, provided them with a feast, and treated them in every respect as husbands. On enquiry he was informed that this was an old custom, but had fallen into abeyance, and 'scarcely once in an age any of the 'females are hardy enough to make this feast, notwith-'standing a husband of the first rank awaits as a sure 'reward the successful giver of it.'

Speaking of the Greenland Esquimaux, Egede expressly states that 'those are reputed the best and

[1] Royal Commentaries of the Incas, vol. ii. p. 442.

[2] Wuttke's Die ersten Stufen der Geschichte der Menschheit, vol. i. p. 177.

[3] Histoire abrégée des Cultes, vol. i. p. 431.

[4] *Ibid.*, vol. ii. p. 108.

[5] The People of India, by J. F. Watson and J. W. Kaye, vol. i. p. 2.

[6] Travels in North America, p. 245. See also Note.

' noblest tempered who, without any pain or reluctancy,
' will lend their friends their wives.' [1]

The same feeling, probably, gave rise to the curious
custom existing, according to Strabo,[2] among the (Par-
thian) Tapyrians, that when a man had had two or three
children by one wife, he was obliged to leave her, so that
she might marry some one else. There is some reason
to suppose that a similar custom once prevailed among
the Romans; thus Cato, who was proverbially austere
in his morals, did not think it right permanently to
retain his wife Martia, whom his friend Hortensius
wished to marry. This he accordingly permitted, and
Martia lived with Hortensius until his death, when she
returned to her first husband. The high character
of Cato is sufficient proof that he would not have
permitted this, if he had regarded it as wrong; and
Plutarch expressly states that the custom of lending
wives existed among the Romans. Akin to this feeling
is that which induces so many savage tribes [3] to provide
their guests with temporary wives. To omit this would
be regarded as quite inhospitable. The practice, moreover, seems to recognise the existence of a right inherent in every member of the community, and to
visitors as temporary members; which, in the case of
the latter, could not be abrogated by arrangements
made before their arrival, and, consequently, without
their concurrence. The prevalence of this custom
brings home to us forcibly the difference existing

[1] History of Greenland, p. 142.
[2] Strabo, ii. pp. 515, 520.
[3] For instance, the Esquimaux, North and South American Indians, Polynesians, Australians, Eastern and Western Negroes, Arabs, Abyssinians, Kaffirs, Mongols, Tutski, &c.

between the savage and the civilised modes of regarding the relation of the sexes to one another.

Perhaps the most striking case of all is that afforded by some of the Brazilian tribes. The captives taken by them in war used to be kept for some time and fatted up; after which they were killed and eaten. Yet even here, during the time that they had to live, the poor wretches were always provided with a temporary wife.[1]

This view also throws some light on the remarkable subordination of the wife to the husband, which is so characteristic of marriage, and so curiously inconsistent with all our avowed ideas; moreover it tends to explain those curious cases in which Hetairæ were held in greater estimation than those women who were, as we should consider, properly and respectably married to a single husband.[2] The former were originally fellow-countrywomen and relations; the latter captives and slaves. And even when this ceased to be the case, the idea would long survive the circumstances which gave rise to it.

We know that in Athens courtesans were highly respected. ' The daily conversation they listened to,' says Lord Kames,[3] ' on philosophy, politics, poetry, en-' lightened their understanding and improved their taste. ' Their houses became agreeable schools, where every-' one might be instructed in his own art. Socrates and ' Pericles met frequently at the house of Aspasia, for ' from her they acquired delicacy of taste, and, in ' return, procured to her public respect and reputation.

[1] Lafitau, Mœurs des Sauv. Amér., vol. II. p. 294.
[2] Bachofen, Das Mutterrecht,
pp. xix. 125. Burton's Lake Regions of Africa, vol. I. p. 194.
[3] History of Man, vol. II. p. 60.

'Greece at that time was governed by orators, over
'whom some celebrated courtesans had great influence,
'and by that means entered deep into the government.'

So also it was an essential of the model Platonic
Republic that 'among the guardians, at least, the
'sexual arrangements should be under public regu-
'lation, and the monopoly of one woman by one man
'forbidden.'[1]

In Java, we are told that courtesans are by no
means despised, and in some parts of Western Africa
the negroes are stated to look on them with respect;
while, on the other hand, oddly enough, they have a
strong feeling against musicians, who are looked on as
'infamous, but necessary tools for their pleasure.' They
did not even permit them to be buried, lest they should
pollute the earth.[2] In India, again, various occupations
which we regard as useful[3] and innocent, if humble, are
considered to be degrading in the highest degree. On
the other hand, in the famous Indian city of Vesali,
'marriage was forbidden, and high rank attached to the
'lady who held office as Chief of the Courtesans.'
When the Holy Buddha (Sakyamuni), in his old age,
visited Vesali, 'he was lodged in a garden belonging to
'the Chief of the Courtesans, and received a visit from
'this grand lady, who drove out to see him, attended
'by her suite in stately carriages. Having approached
'and bowed down, she took her seat on one side of him
'and listened to a discourse on Dharma. . . . . . On
'entering the town she met the rulers of Vesali, gor-
'geously apparelled; but their equipages made way for

[1] Bain's Mental and Moral Science.
[2] Waits' Anthropology, p. 317.
[3] Astley, vol. ii. p. 270.

'her.   They asked her to resign to them the honour of
'entertaining Sakyamuni; but she refused, and the
'great man himself, when solicited by the rulers in per-
'son, also refused to break his engagement with the
'lady.'[1]

Until recently the courtesans were the only educated
women in India.[2]   Even now many of the great Hindoo
temples have bands of women attached to them, and it
seems at first sight a strange anomaly that, while a
woman born of, or adopted into, one of these families
is not held to pursue a shameless vocation, other women
who have fallen from good repute are esteemed disgrace-
ful.[3]   There is, in reality, however, nothing anomalous
in this.   The former continue an old custom of the
country, under solemn religious sanction; the latter, on
the contrary, have given way to lawless inclinations,
have outraged public feelings, and brought disgrace on
their families.   In Ancient Egypt, again, it would
appear that illegitimate children were, under certain
circumstances, preferred over those born in wedlock.[4]

When the special wife was a stranger and a slave,
while the communal wife was a relative and a free-
woman, such feelings would naturally arise, and would,
in some cases, long survive the social condition to which
they owed their origin.

I now pass to the curious custom, for which
M'Lennan has proposed the convenient term 'exo-
'gamy'—that, namely, of necessarily marrying out or

[1] Mrs. Spier's Life in Ancient India, p. 281.
[2] Dubois' People of India, pp. 217, 402.
[3] The People of India, by J. F. Watson and J. W. Kaye, vol. iii. p. 105.
[4] Bachofen, Das Mutterrecht, p. 127.

the tribe. Tylor, who also called particular attention
to this custom in his interesting work on 'The Early
'History of Man,' which was published in the very
same year as M'Lennan's 'Primitive Marriage,' thought
that ' the evils of marrying near relatives might be the
'main ground of this series of restrictions.' Morgan[1]
also considers exogamy as ' explainable, and only ex-
'plainable, as a reformatory movement to break up the
'intermarriage of blood relations,' and which could only
be effected by exogamy because all in the tribe were
regarded as related. In fact, however, exogamy afforded
little protection against the marriage of relatives, and,
wherever it was systematised, it permitted marriage
even between half brothers and sisters, either on the
father's or mother's side. Where an objection to the
intermarriage of relatives existed, exogamy was unnecessary ; where it did not exist, exogamy, if this view
was correct, could not arise.

M'Lennan says, ' I believe this restriction on mar-
'riage to be connected with the practice in early times
'of female infanticide, which, rendering women scarce,
'led at once to polyandry within the tribe, and the cap-
'turing of women from without.'[2] He has not alluded
to the natural preponderance of men over women. Thus,
throughout Europe, the proportion of boys to girls is as
106 to 100.[3] Here, therefore, even without infanticide
we see that there is no exact balance between the
sexes. In many savage races, in various parts of the
world, it has been observed the men are much more

[1] Proc. Amer. Acad. of Arts and Science, 1800.
[2] *Loc. cit.*, p. 138.
[3] Waitz' Anthropology, p. 111.

numerous, but it is difficult to ascertain how far this is
due to an original difference, and how far to other
causes.

It is conceivable that the difference between endogamous and exogamous tribes may have been due to
the different proportion of the sexes: those races tending to become exogamous where boys prevail; those, on
the other hand, endogamous where the reverse is the
case.[1] I am not, however, aware that we have any
statistics which enable us to determine this point, nor
do I believe that it is the true explanation of the
custom.

Infanticide is, no doubt, very prevalent among
savages. As long, indeed, as men were few in number,
enemies were scarce and game was tame. Under these
circumstances, there was no temptation to infanticide.
There were some things which women could do better
than men—some occupations which pride and laziness,
or both, induced them to leave to the women. As
soon, however, as in any country population became
even slightly more dense, neighbours became a nuisance.
They invaded the hunting grounds, and disturbed the
game. Hence, if for no other reason, wars would arise.
Once begun, they would continually break out again
and again, under one pretence or another. Men for
slaves, women for wives, and the thirst for glory, made
a weak tribe always a temptation to a strong one.
Under these circumstances, female children became a
source of weakness in several ways. They ate, and did
not hunt. They weakened their mothers when young,

---

[1] See Das Mutterrecht, p. 109.

and. when grown-up, were a temptation to surrounding tribes. Hence female infanticide is very prevalent, and easily accounted for. Yet I cannot regard it as the true cause of exogamy. On the other hand, we must remember that under the communal system the women of the tribe were all common property. No one could appropriate one of them to himself without infringing on the general rights of the tribe. Women taken in war were, on the contrary, in a different position. The tribe, as a tribe, had no right to them, and men surely would reserve to themselves exclusively their own prizes. These captives then would naturally become the wives in our sense of the term.

Several causes would tend to increase the importance of the separate, and decrease that of communal, marriage. The impulse which it would give to, and receive back from, the development of the affections; the convenience with reference to domestic arrangements; the natural wishes of the wife herself; and last, not least, the inferior energy of the children sprung from ' in ' and in ' marriages, would all tend to increase the importance of individual marriage.

Even were there no other cause, the advantage of crossing, so well known to breeders of stock, would soon give a marked preponderance to those races by whom exogamy was largely practised, and for several reasons therefore we need not be surprised to find exogamy very prevalent among the lower races of man. When this state of things had gone on for some time, usage, as M'Lennan well observes, would ' establish a ' prejudice among the tribes observing it—a prejudice ' strong as a principle of religion, as every prejudice

' relating to marriage is apt to be—against marrying
' women of their stock.' [1]

We should not, perhaps, have *à priori* expected to
find among savages any such remarkable restriction, yet
it is very widely distributed; and from this point of
view we can, I think, clearly see how it arose.

In Australia, where the same family names are common almost over the whole continent, no man may
marry a woman whose family name is the same as his
own, and who belongs therefore to the same tribe.[2]
' No man,' says Mr. Lang, ' can marry a woman of the
' same clan, though the parties be no way related ac-
' cording to our ideas.' [3]

In many parts there are four male and four female
names in each tribe.    Thus:—

The Kimilaroi natives, near Sydney, are divided into
four families,[4] in which the males are known as ippai,
murri, kubbi, and kumbo; the females, ippata, mata,
kapota, and buta.

' I. Ippai may marry an ippata (of another family)
' or any kapota.

' II. Murri may marry only buta.

' III. Kubbi may marry only ippata.

' IV. Kumbo may marry only mata.

' Any attempt to infringe these rules would be
' unanimously resisted, even to bloodshed ; but it seems
' they never dream of attempting to transgress them.

[1] *Loc. cit.*, p. 140.

[2] Eyre's Discoveries in Australia,
vol. ii. p. 320.  Grey's Journal, p.
242.

[3] The Aborigines of Australia,
p. 10.

[4] Prichard's Nat. His. of Man,
vol. ii. p. 491.   Ridley's Jour.
Anthr. Inst. 1872, p. 263.  Lang's
Queensland, p. 283.

'I. The children of ippai by ippata are all kumbo
' and buta.

'II. The children of ippai by kapota are all murri
' or baia and mata.

'III. The children of murri or baia are all ippai
' and ippata.

'IV. The children of kubbi are all kumbo and
' buta.

'V. The children of kumbo are all kubbi and
' kapota.'

In Eastern Africa, Burton[1] says that ' some clans of
' the Somal will not marry one of the same, or even of
' a consanguineous family;' and the Bakalari have the
same rule.[2]

Du Chaillu,[3] speaking of Western Equatorial Africa,
says, 'the law of marriages among the tribes I have
' visited is peculiar; each tribe is divided into clans;
' the children in most of the tribes belong to the clan of
' the mother, and these cannot by any possible laws
' marry among themselves, however removed in degree
' they may have been connected: it is considered an
' abomination among them. But there exists no ob-
' jection to possessing a father's or brother's wife. I
' could not but be struck with the healthful influence
' of such regulations against blood marriages among
' them.'

In India the Khasias,[4] Juangs,[5] and Waralis are
divided into sections, and no man may marry a woman
belonging to his own section. In the Magar tribes

[1] First Footsteps, p. 120.
[2] Trans. Ethn. Soc., N. S., vol. L
p. 321.
[3] *Ibid.*, p. 307.

[4] Godwin Austen, Jour. Anthrop.
Inst., 1871, p. 131.
[5] Dalton's Des. Ethn. of Bengal,
p. 158.

these sections are called Thums, and the same rule prevails.   Col. Dalton tells us that 'the Hos, Moondahs,
' and Oraons are divided into clans or keelis, and may
' not take to wife a girl of the same keeli.'   Again, the
Garrows are divided into ' maharis,' and a man may not
marry a girl of his own ' mahari.'

The Munnieporees and other tribes inhabiting the
hills round Munniepore—the Koupooees, Mows, Mu-
rams, and Murrings, as M'Lennan points out on the
authority of M'Culloch—' are each and all divided into
' four families: Koomrul, Looang, Angom, and Ning-
' thaja.   A member of any of these families may marry
' a member of any other, but the intermarriage of
' members of the same family is strictly prohibited.'[1]
On the contrary, the Todas, says Metz,[2] 'are divided into
' five distinct classes, known by the names Peiky,
' Pekkan, Kuttan, Kennae, and Tody; of which the
' first is regarded as the most aristocratic.   These classes
' do not even intermarry with each other, and can there-
' fore never lose their distinctive characteristics.'   The
Khonds, as we are informed by General Campbell, ' re-
' gard it as degrading to bestow their daughters in
' marriage on men of their own tribe; and consider it
' more manly to seek their wives in a distant country.'[3]
Major M'Pherson also tells us that they consider marriage between people of the same tribe as wicked, and
punishable with death.   The mountain tribes of Nepaul,
before the advent of the Rajpoots, are said to have consisted of twelve Thums or clans, and no man was per-

[1] Account of the Valley of Munniepore, 1850, pp. 40, 63.

[2] Tribes of the Neilgherry Hills,
p. 21.

[3] Campbell, p. 142.

mitted to marry a woman of the same Thum.[1] The Kalmucks, according to De Hell, are divided into hordes, and no man can marry a woman of the same horde. The bride, says Bergman, speaking of the same people, is always chosen from another stock; 'among the Derbets, for instance, from the Torgot 'stock, and among the Torgots from the Derbet 'stock.'

The same custom prevails among the Circassians and the Samoyedes.[2] The Ostyaks regard it as a crime to marry a woman of the same family or even of the same name.[3]

When a Jakut (Siberia) wishes to marry, he must, says Middendorf,[4] choose a girl from another clan. No one is permitted to marry a woman from his own. In China, says Davis,[5] 'marriage between all persons of 'the same surname being unlawful, this rule must of 'course include all descendants of the male branch for 'ever; and as, in so vast a population, there are not a 'great many more than one hundred surnames through-'out the empire, the embarrassments that arise from so 'strict a law must be considerable.'

Amongst the Tinné Indians of North-west America, 'a Chit-sangh cannot, by their rules,[6] marry a Chit-'sangh, although the rule is set at nought occasionally; 'but when it does take place the persons are ridiculed 'and laughed at. The man is said to have married his

[1] Hamilton's Account of the Kingdom of Nepaul, p. 27.
[2] Pallas, vol. iv. p. 90.
[3] Ibid., vol. iv. p. 90.
[4] Sibirische Reise, p. 72. See also Müller's Des. de toutes les Races de l'Emp. Russe, Pt. II. p. 53.
[5] The Chinese, vol. i. p. 282.
[6] Notes on the Tinneh. Hardisty. Smithsonian Report, 1866, p. 315.

E

' sister, even though she may be from another tribe,
' and there be not the slightest connection by blood
' between them.  The same way with the other two
' divisions.  The children are of the same colour as
' their mother.  They receive caste from their mother ;
' if a male Chit-saugh marry a Nah-tsingh woman, the
' children are Nah-tsingh, and if a male Nah-tsingh
' marry a Chit-sangh woman, the children are Chit-
' sangh, so that the divisions are always changing.  As
' the fathers die out the country inhabited by the
' Chit-sangh becomes occupied by the Nah-tsingh, and
' so *vice versâ*.  They are continually changing coun-
' tries, as it were.'

Among the Kenaiyers (N.W. America), 'it was the
' custom that the men of one stock should choose their
' wives from another, and the offspring belonged to the
' race of the mother.  This custom has fallen into
' disuse, and marriages in the same tribe occur; but the
' old people say that mortality among the Kenaiyers has
' arisen from the neglect of the ancient usage.  A man's
' nearest heirs in this tribe are his sister's children.'[1]
The Tsimshoean Indians of British Columbia[2] are
similarly divided into tribes and totems, or 'crests,
' which are common to all the tribes.  The crests are
' the whale, the porpoise, the eagle, the coon, the wolf,
' and the frog.  In connection with these crests, several
' very important points of Indian character and law are
' seen.  The relationship existing between persons of
' the same crest is nearer than that between members

---

[1] Richardson's Boat Journey,
vol. i. p. 400.  See also Smithsonian
Report, 1866, p. 320.

[2] Metlahkatlah, published by the
Church Missionary Society, 1869,
p. 6.

' of the same tribe, which is seen in this, that members
' of the same tribe may marry, but those of the same
' crest are not allowed to do so under any circumstances;
' that is, a whale may not marry a whale, but a whale
' may marry a frog, &c.'

Indeed, as regards the Northern Redskins generally,
it is stated,[1] in the Archæologia Americana that 'every
' nation was divided into a number of clans, varying in
' the several nations from three to eight or ten, the
' members of which respectively were dispersed indis-
' criminately throughout the whole nation. It has been
' fully ascertained that the inviolable regulations by
' which these clans were perpetuated amongst the
' southern nations were, first, that no man could marry
' in his own clan; secondly, that every child should
' belong to his or her mother's clan.'

The Indians of Guiana,[2] ' are divided into families,
' each of which has a distinct name, as the *Siwidi,*
' *Karuafudi, Onisidi,* &c. Unlike our families, these all
' descend in the female line, and no individual of either
' sex is allowed to marry another of the same family
' name. Thus, a woman of the Siwidi family bears the
' same name as her mother, but neither her father nor
' her husband can be of that family. Her children and
' the children of her daughters will also be called Siwidi,
' but both her sons and daughters are prohibited from
' an alliance with any individual bearing the same name;
' though they may marry into the family of their father
' if they choose. These customs are strictly observed,

[1] Gallatin, *loc. cit.*, vol. xi. p. 109. [2] Brett's Indian Tribes of Guiana,
Lafitau, vol. i. p. 558. Tanner's p. 98.
Narrative, p. 313.

' and any breach of them would be considered as
' wicked.'

Lastly, the Brazilian races, according to Martius,
differ greatly in their marriage regulations.  In some of
the very scattered tribes, who live in small families far
remote from one another, the nearest relatives often
intermarry.  In more populous districts, on the contrary,
the tribes are divided into families, and a strict system
of exogamy prevails.[1]

Thus, then, we see that this remarkable custom of
exogamy prevails throughout Western and Eastern
Africa, in Circassia, Hindostan, Tartary, Siberia,
China, and Australia, as well as in North and South
America.

The relations existing between husband and wife in
the lower races of man, as indicated in the preceding
pages, are sufficient to remove all surprise at the prevalence of polygamy.  There are, however, other causes,
not less powerful, though perhaps less prominent, to
which much influence must be ascribed.  Thus in all
tropical regions girls become marriageable very young;
their beauty is acquired early, and soon fades, while
men, on the contrary, retain their full powers much
longer.  Hence, when love depends, not on similarity of
tastes, pursuits, or sympathies, but entirely on external
attractions, we cannot wonder that every man who is
able to do so, provides himself with a succession of
favourites, even when the first wife remains not only
nominally the head, but really his confidant and adviser.
Another cause has no doubt exercised great influence.

[1] *Loc. cit.*, p. 63.

Milk is necessary for children, and in the absence of domestic animals it consequently follows that they are not weaned until they are several years old. The effect of this on the social relations has been already referred to (*ante* p. 74).

Polyandry, on the contrary, is far less common, though more frequent than is generally supposed. M'Lennan and Morgan, indeed, both regard it as a phase through which human progress has necessarily passed. If, however, we define it as the condition in which one woman is married to several men, but (as distinguished from communal marriage) to them exclusively, then I am rather disposed to regard it as an exceptional phenomenon, arising from the paucity of females.

M'Lennan, indeed,[1] gives a long list of tribes which he regards as polyandrous, namely, those of Thibet, Cashmeer, and the Himalayan regions, the Todas, Coorgs, Nairs, and various other races in India, in Ceylon, in New Zealand,[2] and one or two other Pacific islands, in the Aleutian Archipelago, among the Koryaks, the Saporogian Cossacks, on the Orinoco, in parts of Africa, and in Lancerote. He also mentions the ancient Britons, some of the Median cantons, the Picts, and the Getes, while traces of it occurred among the ancient Germans. On the other hand, to the instances quoted by M'Lennan we may add that of some families among the Australians,[3] Nukehivans,[4] and Iroquois.

---

[1] *loc. cit.*, p. 180.
[2] Lafitau, *loc. cit.*, vol. i. p. 555.
[3] Gerland's 'Waitz' Anthropologie, vol. vi. p. 774.
[4] Gerland's 'Waitz' Anthropologie, vol. vi. p. 128.

If we examine the above instances, some of them will, I think, prove irrelevant. The passage referred to in Tacitus [1] does not appear to me to justify us in regarding the Germans as having been polyandrous.

Erman is correctly referred to by Mr. M‘Lennan as mentioning the existence of ‘lawful polyandry in the ‘Aleutian Islands.’ He does not, however, give his authority for the statement. The account he gives of the Koryaks by no means, I think, proves that polyandry occurs among them. The case of the Kalmucks, to judge from the account given by Clarke, [2] is certainly one in which brothers, but brothers only, have a wife in common.

For Polynesia, M‘Lennan relies on the Legend of Rupe, as told by Sir G. Grey. [3] Here, however, it is merely stated that two brothers named Ihuatamai and Ihuwareware, having found Hinauri, when she was thrown by the surf on the coast at Wairarawa, ‘looked ‘upon her with pleasure, and took her as a wife between ‘them both.’ This seems to me rather a case of communal marriage than of polyandry, especially when the rest of the legend is borne in mind. Neither is the evidence as regards Africa at all satisfactory. The custom referred to by Mr. M‘Lennan [4] probably originates in the subjection of the woman which is there implied by marriage, and which may be regarded as inconsistent with high rank.

Several of the above cases are, indeed, I think, merely instances of communal marriage. Indeed, it is evident that where our information is incomplete, it

---

[1] Germania, xx.
[2] Travels, vol. i. p. 241.
[3] Polynesian Mythology, p. 81.
[4] Reade's Savage Africa, p. 43.

must often be far from easy to distinguish between communal marriage and true polyandry.

Polyandry is no doubt widely distributed in Ceylon, India, and Thibet, and among some of the Hill tribes of India. A very pretty Dophla girl once came into the station of Luckimpur, threw herself at Colonel Dalton's feet, ' and in most poetical language asked me ' to give her my protection.' She was promised by her father to a man whom she did not love, and had ' eloped with her beloved. This was interesting and ' romantic.' Colonel Dalton sent for the beloved, and, he says, ' the romance was dispelled. She had eloped with ' two young men.'[1] In Ceylon the joint husbands are always brothers,[2] and this is also the case among the tribes residing at the foot of the Himalaya[3] Mountains. But, on the whole, lawful polyandry (as opposed to mere laxness of morality) seems to be an exceptional system, generally intended to avoid the evils arising from monogamy where the number of women is less than that of men.

The system of Levirate, under which, at a man's death, his wife or wives pass to his brother, is, I think, more intimately connected with the rights of property than with polyandry. This custom is widely distributed. It is found, for instance, among the Mongols[4] and Kaffirs.[5] When an elder brother dies, says Livingstone,[6] ' the same thing occurs in

[1] Des. Ethn. of Bengal, p. 30.
[2] Davy's Ceylon, p. 284.
[3] Fraser's Tour to the Himala Mountains, pp. 70, 208.
[4] Wuttke's Ges. der Menschheit, vol. i. p. 223.
[5] Arbousset's Tour to the N.E. of the Cape of Good Hope, pp. 34, 154.
[6] Travels in South Africa, p. 185.

' respect of his wives; the brother next in age takes
' them, as among the Jews, and the children that may
' be born of those women he calls his brothers also.'

In India, among the Mars, ' a man always takes to
' wife, by the custom called Sagai, his elder brother's
' widow.' [1]　Among the Pacific Islands, Mr. Brenchley
mentions that in Erromango ' the wives of deceased
' brothers fall to the eldest surviving brother.' [2]

Passing on now to the custom of endogamy,
M'Lennan remarks that ' the separate endogamous
' tribes are nearly as numerous, and they are in some
' respects as rude, as the separate exogamous tribes.' [3]

So far as my knowledge goes, on the contrary,
endogamy is much less prevalent than exogamy, and it
seems to me to have arisen from a feeling of race-pride,
as for instance, in Peru,[4] and a disdain of surrounding
tribes which were either really or hypothetically in a
lower condition.

Thus, among the Ahts of N.W. America, as mentioned by Sproat, ' though the different tribes of the
' Aht nation are frequently at war with one another,
' women are not captured from other tribes for marriage,
' but only to be kept as slaves. The idea of slavery
' connected with capture is so common, that a free-born
' Aht would hesitate to marry a woman taken in war,
' whatever her rank had been in her own tribe.' [5]

Some of the Indian races, as the Abors,[6] Kocchs,
and Hos, are forbidden to marry excepting within the

[1] Dalton's Des. Ethn. of Bengal, p. 138.
[2] Cruise of the 'Curacoa,' p. 310.
[3] *Loc. cit.,* p. 145.
[4] Wuttke, Ges. der Menschheit,

vol. i. pp. 325, 331.
[5] Sproat, Scenes and Studies of Savage Life, p. 98.
[6] Dalton's Des. Ethn. of Bengal, p. 28.

tribe. The latter at least, however, are not truly
endogamous, for, as already mentioned, they are divided
into 'keelis' or clans, and 'may not take to wife a girl
'of their own keeli.'[1] Thus they are in fact exogamous, and it is possible that some of the other cases of
endogamy might, if we were better acquainted with
them, present the same duplex phenomenon.

Among the Yerkalas[2] of Southern India ' a custom
' prevails by which the first two daughters of a family
' may be claimed by the maternal uncle as wives for his
' sons. The value of a wife is fixed at twenty pagodas.
' The maternal uncle's right to the first two daughters
' is valued at eight out of twenty pagodas, and is carried
' out thus : if he urges his preferential claim, and
' marries his own sons to his nieces, he pays for each
' only twelve pagodas ; and, similarly, if he, from not
' having sons, or any other cause, forego his claim,
' he receives eight pagodas of the twenty paid to
' the girls' parents by anybody else who may marry
' them.'

The Doingnaks, a branch of the Chukmas, appear
also to have been endogamous, and Captain Lewin
mentions that they ' abandoned the parent stem during
' the chiefship of Jaunbux Khan, about 1782. The
' reason of this split was a disagreement on the subject
' of marriages. The chief passed an order that the
' Doingnaks should intermarry with the tribe in general.
' This was contrary to ancient custom, and caused dis-
' content and eventually a break in the tribe.'[3] This

---

[1] *Antl,* p. 115.

[2] Shortt, Trans. Ethn. Soc., N.S.,
vol. vii. p. 187.

[3] Lewin's Hill Tracts of Chittagong, p. 65.

is one of the very few cases where we have evidence of a change in this respect.

The Kalangs of Java are also endogamous, and when a man asks a girl in marriage he must prove his descent from their peculiar stock.[1]  The Mantchu Tartars forbid marriages between those whose family names are different.[2]  Among the Bedouins, 'a man has an exclusive right to the hand ' of his cousin,'[3] and it is the custom of the Karens that 'marriages ' must always be contracted by relations.'[4]  Livingstone also mentions that in South Africa the women of the Akombwi 'never intermarry with any other ' tribe.'[5]  In Guam brothers and sisters used to intermarry, and it is even stated that such unions were preferred as being most natural and proper.[6]  Endogamy would seem to have prevailed in the Sandwich Islands,[7] and in New Zealand, where, as Yate mentions, 'great opposition is made to anyone taking, except ' for some political purpose, a wife from another tribe, ' so that such intermarriages seldom occur.'[8]  On the whole, however, endogamy seems a far less common custom than exogamy.

The idea of relationship as existing amongst us, founded on marriage, and implying equal connection of a child to its father and mother, seems so natural and obvious that there are, perhaps, many to whom the

[1] Raffles' History of Java, vol. i. p. 328.

[2] M'Lennan, loc. cit., p. 146.

[3] Burckhardt's Notes on the Bedouins and Wahabys, vol. i. pp. 113, 272.

[4] Morgan. Sys. of Cons. and Aff.

of the Human Family, p. 444.

[5] Exp. to the Zambesi, p. 39.

[6] Arago's Letters  Freycinet's Voyage, vol. ii. p. 17.

[7] Ibid., p. 114.

[8] New Zealand, p. 99.

possibility of any other has not occurred. The facts already recorded will, however, have prepared us for the existence of peculiar ideas on the subject of relationship. The strength of the foster-feeling—the milk-tie —among the Scotch Highlanders is a familiar instance of a mode of regarding relationship very different from that prevalent amongst us.

We have also seen that, under the custom of communal marriage, a child was regarded as related to the tribe, but not specially to any particular father or mother. Such a state of things, indeed, is only possible in very small communities. It is evident that under communal marriage—and little less so wherever polygamy prevailed, and men had many wives—the tie between father and son must have been very slight. Among agricultural tribes, and under settled forms of government, the chiefs often have very large harems, and their importance even is measured by the number of their wives, as in other cases by that of their cows or horses.

This state of things is in many ways very prejudicial. It checks, of course, the natural affection and friendly intercourse between man and wife. The King of Ashantee, for instance, always has **3,333** wives, but no man can love so many women, nor can so many women cherish any personal affection for one man.

Even among hunting races, though men were unable to maintain so many wives, still, as changes are of frequent occurrence, the tie between a mother and child is much stronger than that which binds a child to its father. Hence we find that among many of the lower races relationship through females is the prevalent custom, and we are thus able to understand the curious practice that a man's heirs are not his own, but his sister's children.

By some it has been regarded as indicating the high respect paid to women. Thus Plutarch tells us that 'when Bellerophon slew a certain wild boar, which 'destroyed the cattle and fruits in the province of the 'Xanthians, and received no due reward of his services, 'he prayed to Neptune for vengeance, and obtained 'that all the fields should cast forth a salt dew and be 'universally corrupted, which continued till he, con- 'descendingly regarding the women suppliants, prayed 'to Neptune and removed his wrath from them. Hence 'there was a law among the Xanthians, that they should 'derive their names in future, not from the fathers, but 'from the mothers.' [1]

Montesquieu[2] regarded relationship through females as intended to prevent the accumulation of landed pro- perty in few hands—an explanation manifestly in- applicable to many, nay, the majority, of cases in which the custom exists—and the explanation above suggested is, I have no doubt, the correct one.

Thus, when a rich man dies in Guinea, his property, excepting the armour, descended to the sister's son, expressly, according to Smith, on the ground that he must certainly be a relative.[3] Battel mentions that the town of Longo (Loango) 'is governed by four chiefs,

---

[1] Plutarch. Concerning the Vir- tues of Women.

[2] Esprit des Lois, vol. i. p. 70.

[3] Smith's Voyage to Guinea, p. 143. See also Pinkerton's Voyages, vol. xv. pp. 417, 421, 528. Astley's Collection of Voyages, vol. ii. pp. 63, 250.

'which are sons of the king's sisters; for the king's
'sons never come to be kings.'[1]   Quatremère mentions
that 'Chez les Nubiens, dit Abou Selah, lorsqu'un roi
'vient à mourir et qu'il laisse un fils et un neveu du
'côté de sa sœur, celui monte sur le trône de pré-
'férence à l'héritier naturel.'[2]

In Central Africa, Caillié[3] says that 'the sovereignty
'remains always in the same family, but the son never
'succeeds his father; they choose in preference a son of
'the king's sister, conceiving that by this method the
'sovereign power is more sure to be transmitted to one
'of the blood royal; a precaution which shows how
'little faith is put in the virtue of the women of this
'country.'   In South Africa, among the Bangalas of the
Cassange valley, 'the sons of a sister belong to her
'brother; and he often sells his nephews to pay his
'debts;'[4] the Banyai 'choose the son of the deceased
'chief's sister in preference to his own offspring.'   In
Northern Africa we find the same custom among the
Berbers;[5] Burton records it as existing in the North-
East; and on the Congo, according to Tuckey, the
chieftainships 'are hereditary, through the female line, as
'a precaution to make certain of the blood royal in the
'succession.'[6]   Sibree mentions that the same is the case
in Madagascar, where the custom is defended expressly
on the ground 'that the descent can be proved from the

[1] Pinkerton's Voyages, vol. xvi. p. 331.
[2] Mém. Géogr. sur l'Égypte et sur quelques contrées voisines, Paris, 1811. Quoted in Bachofen's Mutterrecht, p. 108.
[3] Caillié's Travels, vol. i. p. 153.
Barth's Travels, vol. i. p. 397.
[4] Livingstone's Travels in South Africa, pp. 431, 617.
[5] La Mère chez certains peuples de l'Antiquité, p. 45.
[6] Tuckey's Exp. to the River Zaire, p. 385.

'mother, while it is often impossible to know the paternity of a child.'[1]

Herodotus[2] supposed that this custom was peculiar to the Lycians : they have, he says, ' one custom peculiar ' to themselves, in which they differ from all other ' nations; for they take their name from their mothers, ' and not from their fathers ; so that if anyone asks ' another who he is, he will describe himself by his ' mother's side, and reckon up his maternal ancestry in ' the female line.' Polybius makes the same statement as regards the Locrians ; and on Etruscan tombs descent is stated in the female line.

In Athens, also, relationship through females prevailed down to the time of Cecrops.

Tacitus,[3] speaking of the Germans, says, 'Children ' are regarded with equal affection by their maternal ' uncles as by their fathers ; some even consider this as ' the more sacred bond of consanguinity, and prefer it ' in the requisition of hostages.' He adds, ' a person's ' own children, however, are his heirs and successors ; ' no wills are made.' From this it would appear as if female inheritance had been recently and not universally abandoned. Again, ' In the Pictish Kingdom, until the ' close of the eighth century, no son is recorded to have ' succeeded his father.'[4]

In India the Kasias, the Koechs, and the Nairs have the system of female kinship. Buchanan[5] tells us that among the Bantar in Tulava a man's property does not descend to his own children, but to those of his sister.

---

[1] Madagascar and its People, p. 192.
[2] Clio, 173.
[3] De Mor. Germ., xx.
[4] Crania Britannica.
[5] Vol. iii. p. 10.

Sir W. Elliot states that the people of Malabar 'all
' agree in one remarkable usage—that of transmitting
' property through females only.'[1]  He adds, on the
authority of Lieutenant Conner, that the same is the
case in Travancore, among all the castes except the
Ponans and the Namburi Brahmans.

As Latham states, 'no Nair son knows his own
' father ; and, *vice versâ*, no Nair father knows his own
' son.  What becomes of the property of the husband?
' It descends to the children of his sister.'[2]

Among the Limboos (India), a tribe near Darjeeling,[3] the boys become the property of the father on his
paying the mother a small sum of money, when the child
is named and enters his father's tribe: girls remain with
the mother, and belong to her tribe.

Marsden tells us,[4] that among the Battas of Sumatra
' the succession to the chiefships does not go, in the
' first instance, to the son of the deceased, but to the
' nephew by a sister ; and that the same extraordinary
' rule, with respect to the property in general, prevails
' also amongst the Malays of that part of the island,
' and even in the neighbourhood of Padang.  The
' authorities for this are various and unconnected
' with each other, but not sufficiently circumstantial
' to induce me to admit it as a generally established
' practice.'

Among the Kenaiyers at Cook's Inlet, according to
Sir John Richardson, property descends, not to a man's

[1] Trans. Ethn. Soc., 1869, p. 110.  N. S., vol. vii. p. 155.
[2] Descriptive Ethnology, vol. ii.  [4] Marsden's History of Sumatra,
p. 451.  p. 376.
[3] Campbell, Trans. Ethn. Soc.,

own children, but to those of his sister.[1]   The same is the case with the Kutchin.[2]

Carver[3] mentions that among the Hudson's Bay Indians the children ' are always distinguished by the ' name of the mother ; and if a woman marries several ' husbands, and has issue by each of them, they are all ' called after her.   The reason they give for this is, that ' as their offspring are indebted to the father for their ' souls, the invisible part of their essence, and to the ' mother for their corporeal and apparent part, it is ' more rational that they should be distinguished by the ' name of the latter, from whom they indubitably derive ' their being, than by that of the father, to which a ' doubt might sometimes arise whether they are justly ' entitled.' ' Descent amongst the Iroquois is in the ' female line, both as to the tribe and as to nationality. ' The children are of the tribe of the mother.   If a ' Cayuga marries a Delaware woman, for example, his ' children are Delawares and aliens, unless formally ' naturalised with the forms of adoption ; but if a Dela- ' ware marries a Cayuga woman, her children are ' Cayugas, and of her tribe of the Cayugas.   It is the ' same if she marries a Seneca.'[4]

In fact, among the North American Indians gene- rally, as we shall see more particularly in the next chapter, the relationship of the uncle, that is to say, the mother's brother, is more important than any other. He is practically the head of his sister's family.   Among

[1] Boat Journey, vol. i. p. 400.
[2] Smithsonian Report, 1866, p. 326.
[3] Carver, p. 378.   See also p. 259; also *ante*, p. 96.

[4] Morgan's Sys. of Cons. and Aff. of the Human Family, p. 167. Hunter's Captivity among the North American Indians, p. 240.

the Choctas, for instance, even now, if a boy is to be placed at school, his uncle, and not his father, takes him to the mission and makes the arrangement.[1] A similar rule prevailed in Haiti and Mexico.[2]

As regards Polynesia, Mariner states that in the Friendly or Tonga Islands 'nobility descends by the 'female line, for when the mother is not a noble, the 'children are not nobles.'[3] The same custom, or traces of it, exist throughout Polynesia, but it would seem that these islanders were passing the stage of relationship through females to that through males. The existence of inheritance through females is clearly indicated in the Feejeean custom known as Vasu. In some of the Carolines and Mariannes the highest honour passed in the female line.[4]

So, also, in Western Australia, 'children of either 'sex always take the family name of their mother.'[5]

Among the ancient Jews, Abraham married his half-sister, Nahor married his brother's daughter, and Amram his father's sister; this was permitted because they were not regarded as relations. Tamar also evidently might have married Amnon, though they were both children of David: 'Speak unto the king,' she said, 'for he will not withhold me from thee;' for, as their mothers were not the same, they were no relations in the eye of the law.

[1] Morgan, *loc. cit.*, p. 158.
[2] Müller, Gesch. d. American. Urreligionen, pp. 167, 530.
[3] Tonga Islands, vol. ii. pp. 80, 91.
[4] Hale, United States Ex. Exp., p. 83. Gerland, Con. of Waitz' Anthr., vol. v. pt. ii. pp. 108, 114, 117.
[5] Eyre, *loc. cit.*, p. 330. Ridley, Journal Anthrop. Institute, 1872, p. 204.

Solon also permitted marriage with sisters on the father's side, but not on the mother's.

Here, therefore, we have abundant evidence of the second stage, in which the child is related to the mother, and not to the father; whence a man's heir is his nephew on the sister's side—not his own child, who is in some cases regarded as no relation to him at all.

When, however, marriage became more respected, and the family affections stronger, it is easy to see that the rule under which a man's property went to his sister's children would become unpopular, both with the father, who would naturally wish his children to inherit his property, and not less so with the children themselves.

M. Girard Teulon, indeed, to whom we are indebted for a very interesting memoir on this subject,[1] regards the first recognition of his parental relationship as an act of noble self-devotion on the part of some great genius in ancient times. 'Le premier,' he says, 'qui 'consentit à se reconnaître père fut un homme de génie 'et de cœur, un des grands bienfaiteurs de l'humanité. 'Prouve en effet que l'enfant t'appartient. Es-tu sûr 'qu'il est un autre toi-même ton fruit? que tu l'as 'enfanté? ou bien, à l'aide d'une généreuse et volon-'taire crédulité, marches-tu, noble inventeur, à la con-'quête d'un but supérieur?'[2]

Bachofen also, while characterising the change from male to female relationship as the 'wichtigsten Wende-'punkt in der Geschichte des Geschlechts-verhältnisses,'

---

[1] La Mère chez certains peuples de l'Antiquité.
[2] Loc. cit., p. 52.

explains it, as I cannot but think, in an altogether erroneous manner. He regards it as a liberation of the spirit from the deceptive appearances of nature, an elevation of human existence above the laws of mere matter; as a recognition that the creative power is the most important; and, in short, as a subordination of the material to the spiritual part of our nature. By this step, he says, 'Man durchbricht die bänder des Tellur'ismus und erhebt seinen Blick zu den höhern regionen 'des Kosmos.'[1]

These seem to me, I confess, very curious notions, and I cannot at all agree with them. The recognition of paternal responsibility grew up, I believe, gradually and from the force of circumstances, aided by the impulses of natural affection. On the other hand, the adoption of relationship through the father's line, instead of through the mother's, was probably effected by the natural wish which every one would feel that his property should go to his own children. It is true that we have very few cases like that of Athens, in which there is a record of this change; but as it is easy to see how it might have been brought about, and difficult to suppose that the opposite step can ever have been made; as, moreover, we find relationship through the father very general, not to say universal, in civilised races, while the opposite system is very common among savages, it is evident that this change must frequently have been effected.

Taking all these facts, then, into consideration, whenever we find relationship through females only, I think

---

[1] Bachofen, Das Mutterrecht, p. 27.

we may safely look upon it as the relic of an ancient barbarism.

As soon as the change was made, the father would take the place held previously by the mother, and he, instead of she, would be regarded as the parent. Hence, on the birth of a child, the father would naturally be very careful what he did, and what he ate, for fear the child be injured. Thus, I believe, arises the curious custom of the Couvade to which I referred in my first chapter.

Relationship to the father at first excludes that to the mother, and, from having been regarded as no relation to the former, children came to be looked on as none to the latter.

In some parts of South America, where it is customary to treat captives well in every respect for a certain time, giving them clothes, food, a wife, &c., and then to kill and eat them, any children they may have are killed and eaten also.[1]  As a general rule inheritance and relationship go together, but in some parts of Australia, while the old rule of tracing descent through the mother still exists, property is inherited in the male line,[2] though it appears that the division is made during the father's life.

How completely the idea of relationship through the father, when once recognised, might replace that through the mother we may see in the very curious trial of Orestes.  Agamemnon, having been murdered by his wife Clytemnestra, was avenged by their son Orestes, who killed his mother for the murder of his

---

[1] Lafitau, vol. ii. p. 307.
[2] Grey's Australia, vol. ii. p. 226, 230.

father. For this act he was prosecuted before the tribunal of the gods by the Erinnyes, whose function it was to punish those who shed the blood of relatives. In his defence, Orestes asks them why they did not punish Clytemnestra for the murder of Agamemnon; and when they reply that marriage does not constitute blood relationship,—'She was not the kindred of the 'man whom she slew,'—he pleads that by the same rule they cannot touch *him*, because a man is a relation to his father, but not to his mother. This view, which seems to us so unnatural, was supported by Apollo and Minerva, and being adopted by the majority of the gods, led to the acquittal of Orestes.

Hence we see that the views prevalent on relationship—views by which the whole social organisation is so profoundly affected—are by no means the same among different races, nor uniform at the same historical period. We ourselves still confuse affinity and consanguinity; but into this part of the question it is not my intention to enter: the evidence brought forward in the preceding pages is, however, I think sufficient to show that children were not in the earliest times regarded as related equally to their father and their mother, but that the natural progress of ideas is, first, that a child is related to his tribe generally; secondly, to his mother, and not to his father; thirdly, to his father, and not to his mother; lastly, and lastly only, that he is related to both.

# CHAPTER IV.

## ON THE DEVELOPMENT OF RELATIONSHIPS.

In the previous chapter I have discussed the question of marriage as it exists among the lower races of men, and the relation of children to their parents. In the present I propose to discuss the question of relationships in general, and to endeavour to trace up the ideas on this subject from their rudest form to the more advanced condition in which they exist amongst more civilised races.

For the facts on which this chapter is based we are mainly indebted to Mr. Morgan, who has collected a great mass of information on the subject, which has recently been published by the Smithsonian Institution. Though I dissent from Mr. Morgan's main conclusions, his work appears to me to be one of the most valuable contributions to ethnological science which has appeared for many years.[1] It contains schedules, most of which are very complete, giving the systems of relationships of no less than 139 races or tribes ; and we have, therefore (though there are still many lamentable deficiencies—the Siberians, South Americans, and true Negroes, being, for instance, as yet unrepresented), a great body

[1] Systems of Consanguinity and Affinity of the Human Family, by L. H. Morgan, 1870.

of evidence illustrating the ideas on the subject of relationships which prevail among different races of men.

Our own system of relationships naturally follows from the marriage of single pairs; and it is, in its general nomenclature, so mere a description of the actual facts, that most persons tacitly regard it as necessarily general to the human race, with, of course, verbal and unimportant differences in detail. Hence but little information can be extracted from dictionaries and vocabularies. They generally, for instance, give words for uncle, aunt, and cousin; but an uncle may be either a father's brother or a mother's brother, and an aunt may be either a father's sister or a mother's sister; a first cousin, again, may be the child of any one of these four uncles and aunts; but practically, as we shall see, these cases are in many races distinguished from one another; and I may add, in passing, it is by no means clear that we are right in regarding them as identical and equivalent. Travellers have, on various occasions, noticed with surprise some special peculiarity of nomenclature which came under their notice; but Mr. Morgan was the first to collect complete schedules of relationships. The special points which have been observed have, indeed, been generally regarded as mere eccentricities; but this is evidently not the case, because the principle or principles to which they are due are consistently carried out, and the nomenclature is reciprocal generally, though not quite without exceptions. Thus, if the Mohawks call a father's brother, not an uncle, but a father, they not only call his son a brother and his grandson a son, but these descendants also use the correlative terms.

We must remember that our ideas of relationships are founded on our social system, and that, as other races have very different habits and ideas on this subject, it is natural to expect that their systems of relationship would also differ from ours. I have in the previous chapter pointed out that the ideas and customs with reference to marriage are very dissimilar in different races, and we may say, as a general rule, that, as we descend in the scale of civilisation, the family diminishes, and the tribe increases, in importance. Words have a profound influence over thought, and true family-names prevail principally among the highest races of men. Even in the less advanced portions of our own country, we know that collective names were those of the tribe, rather than the family.

I have already mentioned that among the Romans the 'family' was not a natural family in our sense of the term. It was founded,[1] not on marriage, but on power. The family of a chief consisted, not of those allied to him by blood, but of those over whom he exercised control. Hence, an emancipated son ceased to be one of the family, and did not, except by will, take any share in his father's property; on the other hand, the wife introduced into the family by marriage, or the stranger converted into a son by adoption, became regularly recognised members of the family, though no blood tie existed.

Marriage, again, in Rome, was symbolised by cap-

---

[1] See Ortolan's Justinian, p. 120, *et seq.*

ture or purchase, as among so many of the lower races
at the present day. In fact, the idea of marriage
among the lower races of men generally is essentially
of a different character from ours; it is material, not
spiritual; it is founded on force, not on love; the wife
is not united with, but enslaved to, her husband. Of
such a system, traces, and more than traces, still exist in
our own country : our customs, indeed, are more advanced, and wives enjoy a very different status in
reality, to that which they occupy in law. Among the
Redskins, however, the wife is a mere servant to her
husband, and there are cases on record, in which husband and wife, belonging originally to different tribes,
have lived together for years without either caring to
acquire the other's language, satisfied to communicate
with one another entirely by signs.

It must, however, be observed that, though the
Redskin family is constituted in a manner very unlike
ours, still the nomenclature of relationships is founded
upon it, such as it is, and has no relation to the tribal
system, as will presently be shown.

Mr. Morgan divides the systems of relationship into
two great classes, the descriptive and the classificatory.
The first, he says (p. 12), ' which is that of the Aryan,
' Semitic, and Uralian families, rejecting the classifica-
' tion of kindred, except so far as it is in accordance
' with the numerical system, describes collateral con-
' sanguinei, for the most part, by an augmentation or
' combination of the primary terms of relationship.
' These terms, which are those for husband and wife,
' father and mother, brother and sister, and son and
' daughter, to which must be added, in such languages

'as possess them, grandfather and grandmother, and
'grandson and granddaughter, are thus restricted to
'the primary sense in which they are here employed.
'All other terms are secondary. Each relationship is
'thus made independent and distinct from every other.
'But the second, which is that of the Turanian,
'American Indian, and Malayan families, rejecting
'descriptive phrases in every instance, and reducing
'consanguinei to great classes by a series of apparently
'arbitrary generalisations, applies the same terms to all
'the members of the same class. It thus confounds
'relationships, which, under the descriptive system, are
'distinct, and enlarges the signification both of the
'primary and secondary terms beyond their seemingly
'appropriate sense.'

While, however, I fully admit the radical difference
between, say, our English system and that of the Kingsmill Islanders, as shown in Table I.[1] opposite, they
seem to me to be rather the extremes of a series than
founded on different ideals.

Mr. Morgan admits that systems of relationships
have undergone a gradual development, following that
of the social condition; but he also attributes to them
great value in the determination of ethnological affinities. I am not sure that I exactly understand his
views, as to the precise bearing of these two conclusions
in relation to one another; and I have elsewhere given
my reasons for dissenting from his interpretation of the

---

[1] I have constructed this table
from Mr. Morgan's schedules, select-
ing the relationships which are the
most significant, and arranging them
in a manner which seems to me
more instructive than that adopted
by Mr. Morgan.

| ) | 11 |
|---|---|
| ...MAN | TONGAN |
| | Uncle |
| | Cousin |
| | ? |
| | ? |
| u. | ? |
| | Aunt |
| | Cousin |
| | ? |
| | ? |
| u. | — |
| | Father |
| B. or T. | Brother |
| | Son |
| | Boy |
| u. | Grandson |
| | Mother |
| B. or T. | Brother |
| | Son |
| | Boy |
| u. | — |
| ...ther | Grandfather |
| ...ather | Grandmoth... |
| | Son |
| | Nephew |
| | Nephew |
| | Boy |
| u. | Grandson |
| u. | Grandson |

...ed Canarese substant...

| 9 | |
|---|---|
| CHEROKEE | |
| Uncle | Mo... |
| Child | Cou... |
| Grandchild | Son... |
| Grandchild | |
| Grandchild | Ne... |
| Grandchild | Ne... |
| Grandchild | Un... |
| Aunt | Au... |
| Father | Cou... |
| Father | Net... |
| Father | Son... |
| Father | Ne... |
| Father | Son... |

facts in reference to social relations. I shall, therefore,
now confine myself to the question of the bearing of
systems of relationships on questions of ethnological
affinity, and to a consideration of the manner in which
the various systems have arisen. As might naturally
have been expected, Mr. Morgan's information is most
full and complete with reference to the North American
Indians. Of these, he gives the terms for no less than
268 relationships in about seventy different tribes. Of
these relationships, some are, for our present purposes
much more important than others. The most significant are the following:—

1. Brother's son and daughter.
2. Sister's son and daughter.
3. Mother's brother.
4. Mother's brother's son.
5. Father's sister.
6. Father's sister's son.
7. Father's brother.
8. Father's brother's son.
9. Mother's sister.
10. Mother's sister's son.
11. Grandfather's brother.
12. Brothers' and sisters' grandchildren.

Now let me call attention to the Wyandot system as
shown in column 8 of Table I. It will be observed
that a mother's brother is called an uncle; his son a
cousin; his grandson a son when a male is speaking, a
nephew when a female is speaking; his great-grandson
a grandson. A father's sister is termed an aunt; her
son a cousin; her grandson a son; her great-grandson a
grandson. A father's brother is a father; his son a

brother, distinguished, however, by different terms, according as he is older or younger than the speaker; his grandson a son; his great-grandson a grandson. A mother's sister is a mother;[1] her son is a brother, distinguished as before; her grandson a son when a male is speaking, a nephew when a female is speaking. A grandfather's brother is a grandfather; and a grandfather's sister is a grandmother. A brother's son is a son when a male is speaking, but a nephew when a female is speaking; while a sister's son is a nephew when a male is speaking, but a son when a female is speaking. Lastly, brothers' grandchildren, and sisters' grandchildren, are called grandchildren.

This system, at first, strikes one as illogical and inconsistent. How can a person have more than one mother? How can a brother's son be a son, or an uncle's great-grandson a grandson? Again, while classing together several relationships which we justly separate, it distinguishes between elder and younger brothers and sisters; and in several cases the relationship depends on the sex of the speaker. Since, however, a similar system prevails over a very wide area, it cannot be dismissed as a mere arbitrary or accidental arrangement. The system is, moreover, far from being merely theoretical, in every-day use. Every member of the tribe knows his exact relationship to each other, according to

[1] In Madagascar 'first cousins 'are usually termed brother and 'sister, and uncles and aunts father 'and mother respectively; and it is 'only by asking distinctly of persons 'whether they are "of one father" 'or are "uterine brother and sister," 'that we learn the exact degree of 'relationship. These secondary fathers and mothers seem often to be 'regarded with little less affection 'than the actual parents.'—*Sibree's Madagascar and its People*, p. 192.

this system ; and this knowledge is kept up by the habit, general among the American tribes, and occurring also elsewhere—as, for instance, among the Esquimaux, the Tamils, Telugus, Chinese, Japanese, Feejeeans, &c.—of addressing a person, not by his name, but by his relationship. Among the Telugus and Tamils an elder may address a younger by name, but a younger must always use the term for relationship in speaking to an elder. This custom is, probably, connected with the curious superstitions about names; but, however it may have arisen, the result is that an Indian addresses his neighbour as 'my father,' 'my son,' or 'my brother,' as the case may be: if not related, he says, ' my friend.'

Thus the system is kept up by daily use; nor is it a mere mode of expression. Although, in many respects, opposed to the existing customs and ideas, it is, in some, entirely consonant with them: thus, among many of the Redskin tribes, if a man marries the eldest girl in a family, he can claim in marriage all the others as they successively come to maturity; this custom exists among the Shyennes, Omahas, Iowas, Kaws, Osages, Blackfeet, Crees, Minnitarees, Crows, and other tribes. I have already mentioned that among the Redskins, generally, the mother's brother exercises a more than paternal authority over his sister's children. I shall have occasion to refer again to this remarkable exaggeration of avuncular authority.

Mr. Morgan was much surprised to find that a system, more or less like that of the Wyandots, was very general among the Redskins of North America; but he was still more astonished to find that the Tamil races of India have one almost identical. A comparison of

columns 8 and 9 in Table I., will show that this is the case,
and the similarity is even more striking in Mr. Morgan's
tables, where a larger number of relationships is given.

How, then, did this system arise? How is it to be
accounted for? It is by no means consonant, in all
respects, to the present social conditions of the races in
question; nor does it agree with tribal affinities. The
American Indians generally follow the custom of
exogamy, as it has been called by Mr. M'Lennan, that
is to say, no one is permitted to marry within the clan;
and, as descent goes in the female line, a man's brother's
son, though called his son, belongs to a different clan;
while his sister's son does belong to the clan, though he
is regarded as a nephew, and consequently as less
closely connected. Hence, a man's nephew belongs
to his clan, but his son belongs to a different clan.

Mr. Morgan, from several passages, appears to regard
the system as arbitrary, artificial, and intentional.[1] He
discusses, at some length, the conclusions to be drawn
from its wide extension over the American continent,
and its presence also in India. ' The several hypotheses,'
he says, ' of accidental concurrent invention, of borrow-
' ing from each other, and of spontaneous growth, are
' entirely inadequate.'[2]  With reference to the hypothesis of independent development in disconnected
areas, he observes that it possesses ' both plausibility
' and force.' It has, therefore, he adds, ' been made a
' subject of not less careful study and reflection than the
' system itself. Not until after a patient analysis and

[1] See pp. 157, 392, 394, 421, 450, etc.
[2] Loc. cit., p. 495.

'comparison of its several forms upon the extended
'scale in which they are given in the tables, and not
'until after a careful consideration of the functions of
'the system, as a domestic institution, and of the evi-
'dence of its mode of propagation from age to age, did
'these doubts finally give way, and the insufficiency of
'this hypothesis to account for the origin of the system
'many times over, or even a second time, became fully
'apparent.'

And again, 'if the two families—i.e., the Redskin
'and the Tamil—commenced on separate continents in
'a state of promiscuous intercourse, having such a
'system of consanguinity as this state would beget, of
'the character of which no conception can be formed,
'it would be little less than a miracle if both should
'develop the same system of relationship.'[1]  He concludes, then, that it must be due to 'transmission with
'the blood from a common original source.  If the four
'hypotheses named cover and exhaust the subject, and
'the first three are incapable of explaining the present
'existence of the system in the two families, then the
'fourth and last, if capable of accounting for its
'transmission, becomes transformed into an established
'conclusion.'[2]

That there is any near alliance between the Redskin
and Tamil races would be an ethnological conclusion of
great importance.  It does not, however, seem to me to
be borne out by the evidence.  The Feejeean system,
with which the Tongan is almost identical, is very
instructive in this respect, and scarcely seems to have

[1] *Loc. cit.*, p. 505.
[2] *Ibid.*  See also p. 407.

received from Mr. Morgan the consideration which it merits. Now, columns 9, 10, and 11 of Table I. show that the Feejeean and Tongan systems are identical with the Tamil. If, then, this similarity is, in the case of the Tamil, proof of close ethnological affinity between that race and the Redskin, it must equally be so in reference to the Feejeeans and the Tongans. It is, however, well known that these races belong to very distinct divisions of mankind, and any facts which prove similarity between these races, however interesting and important they may be as proofs of identity in human character and history, can obviously have no bearing on special ethnological affinities. Moreover, it seems clear, as I shall attempt presently to show, that the Tongans have not used their present system ever since their ancestors first landed on the Pacific Islands, but that it has subsequently developed itself from a far ruder system, which is still in existence in many of the surrounding islands.

I may also observe that the Two-Mountain Iroquois, whose close ethnological affinity with the Wyandots no one will question, actually agree, as shown by columns 3 and 4 of Table I., more nearly with this ruder Pacific, or, as Morgan calls it, ' Malayan' system, than they do with that of the neighbouring American tribes.

For these and other reasons, I think it impossible to adopt Mr. Morgan's views, either on the causes which have led to the existence of the Tamil system, or as to the ethnological conclusions which follow from it.

How, then, have these systems arisen, and how can we account for such remarkable similarities between races so distinct, and so distant, as the Wyandots, Tamils,

Feejeeans, and Tongans? In illustration of my views on this subject, I have constructed the preceding table (Table I.), in which I have given the translation of the native words, and, following Morgan, when one word is used for several relationships, have translated it by the simplest. Thus, in Feejeean, the word 'Tamanngu'—literally 'Tama my,' the suffix 'nngu,' meaning 'my' —is applied, not only to a father, but to a father's brother; hence, as the father is the more important, we say that they call a father's brother a father.

In many cases the origins of the terms for relationships are undeterminable; I shall discuss some in a subsequent chapter. Others, however, have so far withstood the wear and tear of daily use as to be still traceable.

Thus, in Polish, the word for my great-uncle is, literally, 'my cold grandfather;' the word for 'wife' among the Crees is 'part of myself;' that for husband, among the Choctas, is 'he who leads me;' a daughter-in-law among the Delawares is called 'Nah-hum,' literally, 'my cook;' for which ungracious expression, however, they make amends by their word for husband or wife, 'Wee-chaa-oke,' which is, literally, 'my aid ' through life.'

It might, *à priori*, be supposed that the nomenclature of relationships would be greatly affected by the question of male or female descent. This, however, does not appear to be the case. Under a system of female descent, combined with exogamy, a man must marry out of his tribe; and, as his children belong to their mother's tribe, it follows that a man's children do not belong to his tribe. On the other hand, a woman's children, whomsoever she may marry, belong to her tribe. Hence, while neither a man's nor his brother's children belong to the same tribe as himself, his sister's children must do so, and are, in consequence, often regarded as his heirs. In fact, for all practical purposes, among many of the Redskin and other tribes, a man's sister's sons are regarded as his children.

As we have already seen, this remarkable custom prevails, not only among the Redskins, but also in various other parts of the world. As regards the native tribes of North America, it may almost be laid down as a general proposition that the mother's brother exercises a more than paternal authority over his sister's children. He has a recognised right to any property they may acquire, if he choose to exercise it; he can give orders which a true father would not venture to issue; he arranges the marriages of his nieces, and is entitled to share in the price paid for them. The same custom prevails even among the semi-civilised races; for instance, among the Choctas the uncle, not the father, sends a boy to school.

Yet among these very tribes a man's sister's son is called his nephew, while his brother's son is called his son.

Thus, although a man's mother's brother is called an uncle, he has, in reality, more power and responsibility than the true father. The true father is classed with the father's brother and the mother's sister; but the mother's brother stands by himself, and, although he is called an uncle, he exercises the real parental power, and on him rests the parental responsibility. In fact, while the names of relationships follow the marriage customs, the ideas are guided by the tribal organisation. Hence we see that not only do the ideas of the several relationships, among the lower races of men, differ from ours; but the idea of relationship, as a whole, is, so to say, embryonic, and subsidiary to that of the tribe.

In fact, the idea of relationship, like that of marriage, was founded, not upon duty, but upon power. Only with the gradual elevation of the race has the latter been subordinated to the former.

I have endeavoured to illustrate the various systems of relationship by Table I. (opposite p. 154), which begins with the Hawaiian, or Sandwich Island system.

The Hawaiian language is rich in terms for relationships. A grandparent is 'Kupuna,' a parent is 'Makua,' a child 'Kaikee,' a son-in-law, or daughter-law, is 'Hunona,' a grand-child 'Moopuna;' brothers in the plural are 'Hoahanau;' a brother-in-law, or sister-in-law, is addressed as 'Kaikoeke;' there are special words for brother and sister according to age and sex; thus, a boy speaking of an elder brother, and a girl speaking of an elder sister, use the term 'Kai-kuuana;' a boy speaking of a younger brother, or a girl of a younger sister, uses the word 'Kaikaina;' a boy speaking of a sister calls her Kaikuwahine, while a sister calls a brother, whether older or younger, 'Kai-kuaana.' They also recognise some relationships for which we have no special terms; thus, an adopted son is 'Hunai;' the parents of a son-in-law, or daughter-in-law, are 'Puliena;' a man addresses his brother-in-law, and a woman her sister-law, as 'Punalon;' lastly, the word 'Kolai' has no corresponding term in English.

It will be observed that these relationships are conceived in a manner entirely unlike ours ; we make no difference between an elder brother and a younger brother, nor does the term used depend on the sex of the speaker. The contrast between the two systems is, however, much more striking when we come to consider the deficiencies of the Hawaiian system, as indicated in the nomenclature. Thus, there is no word for cousin, none for uncle or aunt, nephew or niece, son or daughter ; nay, while there is a word indicating parent, there is said to be none for father or even for mother.

The principal features of this remarkable system, so elaborate, yet so rude, are indicated in the second column of Table I. I have already mentioned that there is no word for father or mother ; for the latter they say ' parent female,' for the former, ' parent male ;' but the term ' parent male ' is not confined to the true parent, but is applied equally to the father's brother and mother's brother ; while the term ' parent female ' denotes also father's sister and mother's sister. Thus, uncleships and auntships are ignored, and a child may have several fathers and several mothers. In the succeeding generation, as a man calls his brother's and sister's children his children, so do they regard him as their father. Again, as a mother's brother and a father's brother are termed ' parents male,' a mother's sister and father's sister, ' parents female,' their sons are regarded as brothers, and their daughters as sisters. Again, a man calls the children of these constructive brothers and sisters, equally with those of true brothers and sisters, his children ; and their children, his grandchildren.

The term 'parent male,' then, denotes not only a man's father,

|        |                  |
|--------|------------------|
| but also his | father's brother |
| and | mother's brother, |

while the term 'parent female' in the same way denotes not only a man's mother,

|        |                  |
|--------|------------------|
| but also his | mother's sister |
| and | father's sister. |

There are, in fact, six classes of parents: three on the male side, and three on the female.

The term, my elder brother, or younger brother, as the case may be,[1] stands also for my

Mother's brother's son,

Mother's sister's son,

Father's brother's son,

Father's sister's son,

while their children, again, are all my grandchildren. Here there is a succession of generations, but no family. We find here no true fathers and mothers, uncles or aunts, nephews or nieces, but only

Grandparents,

Parents,

Brothers and sisters,

Children, and

Grandchildren.

This nomenclature is actually in use, and, so far from having become obsolete, being in Feejee combined with inheritance through females, and the custom of imme-

---

[1] Among the Australians, near Sydney, 'brothers and sisters speak of one another by titles that indicate relative age; that is, their words for brother and sister always involve the distinction of elder or younger.' —Ridley, Jour. Anthr. Inst., vol. xxvi. p. 260,

diate inheritance, gives a nephew the right to take his
mother's brother's property : a right which is frequently exercised, and never questioned, although apparently moderated by custom.   It will very likely
be said that though the word 'son,' for instance, is used
to include many who are really not sons, it by no
means follows that a man should regard himself as
equally related to all his so-called 'sons.'   And this
is true, but not in the manner which might have been
*à priori* expected.   For, as many among the lower races
of men have the system of inheritance through females,
it follows that they consider their sister's children to be in
reality more nearly related to them, not only than their
brother's children, but even than  their very own
children.   Hence we see that these terms, son, father,
mother, &c., which to us imply relationship, have not
strictly, in all cases, this significance, but rather imply
the relative position in the tribe.

Additional evidence of this is afforded by the restrictions on marriage which follow the tribe, and not
the terms.   Thus the customs of a tribe may, and constantly do, forbid marriage with one set of constructive
sisters or brothers, but not with another.

The system shown in column 2 is not apparently
confined to the Sandwich Islands, but occurs also in
other islands of the Pacific.   Thus, the Kingsmill
system, as shown in column 3, is essentially similar,
though they have made one step in advance, having
devised words for father and mother.   Still, however,
the same term is applied to a father's brother and a
mother's brother as to a father; and to a father's sister
and a mother's sister as to a mother: consequently,

first cousins are still called brothers and sisters, and their children and grandchildren are called children and grandchildren.

The habits of the South Sea Islanders, the entire absence of privacy in their houses, their objection to sociable meals, and other points in their mode of life, have probably favoured the survival of this very rude system, which is by no means in accordance with their present social and family relations, but indicates a time when these were less developed than at present. We know as yet no other part of the world where the nomenclature of relationships is so primitive.

Yet a near approach is made by the system of the Two-Mountain Iroquois, which is, perhaps, the lowest yet observed in America. In this tribe a brother's children are still regarded as sons, and a woman calls her sister's children her sons; a man, however, does not regard his sister's children as his children, but distinguishes them by a special term; they become his nephews. This distinction between relationships, which we regard as identical, has its basis in, and is in accordance with, American marriage customs. Unfortunately, I have no means of ascertaining whether these rules prevail among the tribe in question, but they are so general among the Indians of North America that in all probability it is the case. One of these customs is that if a man marries a girl who has younger sisters, he thereby acquires a right to those younger sisters as they successively arrive at maturity.[1] This right is widely recognised, and frequently acted upon. The

[1] Archæol. Amer., vol. ii. p. 100.

first wife makes no objection, for the work which fell
heavily on her is divided with another, and it is easy to
see that, when polygamy prevails, it would be uncomplimentary to refuse a wife who legally belonged to you.
Hence a woman regards her sister's sons as her sons;
they may be, in fact, the sons of her husband: any
other hypothesis is uncomplimentary to the sister.
Throughout the North American races, therefore, we
shall find that a woman calls her sister's children her
children; in no case does she term them nephews or
nieces, though in some few tribes she distinguishes
them from her own children by calling them step-
children.

Another general rule in America, as elsewhere, is
that no one may marry within his own clan or family.
It has been shown in the previous chapter that this rule
is not only general in North America, but widely prevalent elsewhere.   The result is, that as a woman and her
brother belong to one family, her husband must be
chosen from another.   Hence while a man's father's
brother and sister belong to his clan, and his mother's
sister, being one of his father's wives, is a member of
the family—one of the fire-circle, if I may so say—the
mother's brother is necessarily neither a member of
the fire-circle nor even of the clan.   Hence, while a
father's sister and mother's sister are called mother,
and a father's brother father, in most of the Redskin
tribes the marriage rules exclude the mother's brother,
who is accordingly distinguished by a special term, and
in fact is recognised as uncle.   Thus we can understand
how it is that of the six classes of parents mentioned
above, the mother's brother is the first to be distin-

guished from the rest by a special name. It will, however, be seen by the table that among the Two-Mountain
Iroquois a mother's brother's son is called brother, his
grandson son, and so on. This shows that he also was
once called 'father,' as in Polynesia, for in no other manner can such a system of nomenclature be accounted
for. All the other relationships, as given in the table,
are, it will be seen, identical with those recognised in
the Hawaiian and Kingsmill system. Thus, in two respects only, and two, moreover, which can be satisfac-
torily explained by their marriage regulations, do the
Two-Mountain Iroquois differ from the Pacific system.
It is true that these two points of difference involve
some others not shown in the table. Thus, while a
woman's father's sister's daughter's son is her son, a
man's father's sister's daughter's son is his nephew,
because his father's sister's daughter is his sister, and
his sister's son, as already explained, is his nephew.
It should also be added that the Two-Mountain Iroquois show an advance, as compared with the Hawaiian system, in the terms relating to relationships by
marriage.

The Micmac system, as shown in column 5, is in
three points an advance on that of the Two-Mountain
Iroquois. Not only does a man call his sister's son his
nephew, but a woman applies the same term to her
brother's son. Thus, men term their brother's sons
'sons,' and their sister's sons 'nephews;' while women,
on the contrary, call their brother's sons 'nephews,'
and their sister's sons 'sons;' obviously because there
was a time when, though brothers and sisters could not
marry, brothers might have their wives in common,

while sisters, as we know, habitually married the same
man.   It is remarkable also that a father's brother and
a mother's sister are also distinguished from the true
father and mother.   In this respect the Micmac system
is superior to that prevailing in most other Redskin
races.   For the same reason, not only is a mother's
brother termed an uncle, but the father's sister is no
longer called a mother, being distinguished by a special
term, and thus becomes an aunt.   The social habits of
the Redskins, which have already been briefly alluded
to, sufficiently explain why the father's sister is thus
distinguished, while the father's brother and mother's
sister are still called respectively father and mother.
Moreover, as we found among the Two-Mountain Iroquois that although the mother's brother is recognised
as an uncle, his son is still called brother, thus pointing
back to a time when the father's brother was still called
father; so here we see that though the father's sister is
called aunt, her son is still regarded as a brother;
indicating the existence of a time when, among the Micmacs, as among the Two-Mountain Iroquois, a father's
sister was termed a mother.   It follows as a consequence
that, as a father's brother's son, a mother's brother's
son, a father's sister's son, and a mother's sister's son,
are considered to be brothers, their children are termed
sons by the males; but as a woman calls her brother's
son a nephew, so she applies the same term to the sons
of the so-called brothers.

If the system of relationship be subject to gradual
growth, and approach step by step towards perfection, we
should naturally expect that, from differences of habits
and customs, the various advances would not among

all races follow one another in precisely the same order. Of this the Micmacs and Wyandots afford us an illustration. While the latter have, on the whole, made most progress, the former are in advance on one point; for though the Micmacs have distinguished a father's brother from a father, he is among the Wyandots still termed a father; on the other hand, the Wyandots call a mother's brother's son a cousin, while among the Micmacs he is still termed a brother.

Here we may conveniently consider two Asiatic nations—the Burmese and the Japanese—which, though on the whole considerably more advanced in civilisation than any of the foregoing races, yet appear to be singularly backward in their systems of family nomenclature. I will commence with the Burmese. A mother's brother is called either father (great or little) or uncle; his son is regarded as a brother; his grandson as a nephew; his great-grandson as a grandson. A father's sister is an aunt; but her son is a brother, her grandson is a son, and her great-grandson a grandson. A father's brother is still a father (great or little); his son is a brother; his grandson a nephew; and his great-grandson a grandson. A mother's sister is a mother (great or little); her son is a brother; her grandson a nephew; and her great-grandson a grandson. Grandfathers' brothers and sisters are grandfathers and grandmothers. Brothers' and sisters' sons and daughters are recognised as nephews and nieces, whether the speaker is a male or female; but their children again are still classed as grandchildren.

Among the Japanese a mother's brother is called a 'second little father;' a father's sister a 'little mother'

or 'aunt;' a father's brother a 'little father' or 'uncle;'
and a mother's sister a 'little mother' or 'aunt.'  The
other relationships shown in the table are the same
as among the Burmese.

The Wyandots, descendants of the ancient Hurons,
are illustrated in the eighth column.  Their system is
somewhat more advanced than that of the Micmacs.
While, among the latter, a mother's brother's son, and
a father's sister's son, are called brothers, among the
Wyandots they are recognised as cousins.  The children
of these cousins, however, are still called sons by males,
thus reminding us that there was a time when these
cousins were still regarded as brothers.  A second
mark of progress is, that women regard their mother's
brother's grandsons as nephews, and not as sons, though
the great-grandsons of uncles and aunts are still, in all
cases, termed grandsons.

I crave particular attention to this system, which
may be regarded as the typical system of the Redskins,[1]
although, as we have seen, some tribes have a ruder
nomenclature, and we shall presently allude to others
which are rather more advanced.  A mother's brother
is termed uncle; his son is a cousin; his grandson is
termed nephew when a woman is speaking, son in the
case of a male.  In either case, his grandson is termed
grandson.  A father's sister is an aunt, and her son a
cousin; but her grandson and great-grandson are termed,
respectively, son and grandson, thus reminding us that

---

[1] The Peruvian system appears, from the vocabularies given in Mr. Clements Markham's Quichua Grammar and Dictionary, to have been very similar, in some of it most essential features, to that of the Wyandots.

there was a time when a father's sister was regarded as a mother. A father's brother is called father; his son brother; his grandson, son; and his great-grandson, grandson.

A mother's sister is a mother, her son is a brother, her grandson is called nephew by a female, son by a male; her great-grandson is, in either case, called grandson. A grandfather's brother and sister are called grandfather and grandmother respectively.

A brother's son is called son by a male, and nephew by a female, while a sister's son is called nephew by a male, and son by a female, the reasons for which have been already explained.

Lastly, brothers' son's sons and daughters, sisters' son's sons and daughters, are all called grandsons and granddaughters. Thus we see that in every case the third generation returns to the direct line.

The two following columns represent the Tamil and Feejeean system, with which also that of the Tonga Islands very closely agrees. I have already called attention to this, and given my reasons for being unable to adopt the explanation suggested by Mr. Morgan.

It will be observed that the only differences shown in the table between the system of these races and that of the Wyandots, are, firstly, that the mother's brother's grandson is regarded among the Wyandots as a nephew by males, and as a son by females; while in the Tamil and Feejeean system the reverse is said to be the case, and he is termed son by males, and nephew by females. Secondly, that the father's sister's grandson is regarded as a son among the Wyandots, while in the Tamil and Feejeean system he is, when an uncle is speaking,

recognised as a nephew.  The latter difference merely
indicates that the Tamil and Feejeean systems are
slightly more advanced than the Wyandot.  The other
difference is more difficult to understand.

But though the Redskin, Tamil, and Feejeean systems, differing as they do from ours in many ways,
which at first seem altogether arbitrary and unaccountable, agree so remarkably with one another, we
find, also, in some cases, remarkable differences among
the Redskin races themselves.  These differences affect
principally the lines of the mother's brother and father's
sister.  This is natural.  They are the first to be distinguished from true parents, and new means have,
therefore, to be adopted to distinguish the relationships
thus recognised.  In several cases other old terms were
tried, with very comical results.  These modes of over-
coming the difficulty were so unsatisfactory, that, by
the time a father's sister's son was recognised as a
cousin, the necessity for the creation of new terms
seems to have been generally felt.

Table II. shows, as regards fourteen tribes, the result
of the attempt to distinguish these relationships.
Taking, for instance, the line which gives the terms
in use for a mother's brother's grandson, we find the
following, viz. son, stepbrother, grandson, and grandchild, stepson, and uncle; in the case of a father's
sister's grandson (male speaking), we have grandchild,
son, stepson, brother, and father; when a female is
speaking, grandchild, son, nephew, brother, and father.
Thus, for this single relationship we find six terms in
use, and a difference of three generations, viz., from
grandfather to son.  At first the use of such terms

seems altogether arbitrary, but a further examination will show that this is by no means the case.

Column 2 gives the system of the Redknives, one of the most backward tribes on the American continent as regards their nomenclature of relationships. Here, though a mother's brother and a father's sister are, respectively, uncle and aunt, their children are regarded as brothers, their grandchildren as sons, and their great-grandchildren as grandsons. The Munsee system shows a slight advance. Here, though the women call their sister's sons their sons, the males, on the contrary, term them nephews, and, consequently, apply the same term to their mother's brother's daughter's son, and their father's sister's daughter's son; because, as in the preceding case, mother's brother's daughters, and father's sister's daughters, are termed sisters. The Micmacs (column 3) show another step in advance. Here, not only does a man call his sister's son nephew, but, in addition, a woman applies the same term to her brother's son's; consequently, not only a mother's brother's daughter's sons, if a male is speaking, but a mother's brother's son's son, if a female is speaking, and the corresponding relations, on the side of the father's sister, are termed nephews.

Among the Delawares a mother's brother's son, and father's sister's son, are distinguished from true brothers by a term corresponding to 'stepbrother.' They appear to have also felt the necessity of distinguishing a step-brother's son from a true son; but, having no special term, they retain the same word, thus calling a step-brother's son a stepbrother. This principle, as we shall see, is followed by several other tribes, and has produced

the most striking inconsistencies shown in the table.
We find it again among the Crows, where a father's
sister is called mother, her daughter again, mother; but
as her son cannot of course be a mother, he is called
'father.' The same system is followed by the Pawnees,
as shown in columns 7 and 8; and the Grand Pawnee
carry it a generation lower, and call their father's
sister's grandson on the male side 'father;' a father's
sister's daughter's son is, however, called a brother.
Among the Cherokees we find this principle most
thoroughly carried out, and a father's sister's grandson
is also called a father. This case is the more interesting,
because the circumstance which produced the system is
no longer in existence; for, as will be seen, a father's
sister is called an aunt. It is not at first obvious that
a father's sister being called a mother would account
for her son being called a father; but, with the Crow
and Pawnee systems before us, we see that the Cherokees could not call their father's sister's sons 'fathers,'
unless there had been a time when a father's sister was
regarded as a mother.

The Hare Indians supply us with a case in which
mother's brothers and father's sisters being distinguished
from fathers and mothers, their children are no longer
termed brothers, but are distinguished as cousins; while
their grandchildren and great-grandchildren, on the
contrary, are still termed sons and grandsons.

So far as the relationships shown in the table are
concerned, the system of the Omahas, and of the Sawks
and Foxes, is identical. A mother's brother is an
uncle, and, for the reason already pointed out, in the
case of the Delawares, his sons and son's sons, and even
son's grandsons, are also termed grandsons. His

daughter's sons, on the contrary, retain the old name of brother. A father's sister is an aunt, her children are nephews, and the descendants of these nephews are grandchildren.

Among the Oneidas, a father's brother is an uncle, and his son is a cousin; his son's sons, however, are still sons. His daughter's son is a son, when a female is speaking; but, for the reason already explained in the case of the Munsees, males term them nephews. The relationships connected with a father's sister are dealt with in a similar manner, except that a father's sister is still called mother.

The Otawa system resembles the Micmac, and is formed on the same plan, being, however, somewhat more advanced, inasmuch as the children of uncles and aunts are recognised as cousins, and a man calls his cousin's son, not his son, but his stepson. The Ojibwa system is the same, except that a woman also calls her mother's brother's daughter's son, and father's sister's daughter's son, her stepson, instead of her son. In some of the relationships by marriage the same causes have led to even more striking differences. Thus, a woman generally calls her father's sister's daughter's husband her brother-in-law; but among the Missouri and Mississippi nations, her son-in-law; among the Minnitarees, the Crows, and some of the Choctа clans, her father; among the Cherokees, her stepparent; the Republican Pawnees, and some of the Choctas, her grandfather; and among the Tukuthes, her grandson! 

Having thus pointed out the curious results to which some of the lower races have been led in their attempts to distinguish relationships, and endeavoured

N

to explain those shown in Table II., I will now return
to the main argument.

The Kaffir (Amazulu) system is given in column
12, Table I. Here, for the first time, we find the
father's brother regarded as an uncle, and the mother's
sister as an aunt. In other respects, however, the
system is not more advanced than the Tamil, Feejeean,
or Wyandot. The mother's brother is called uncle;[1]
his son, cousin; his grandson, son; and his great-grandson, grandchild. A father's sister, quaintly enough, is
called father, the Kaffir word for which, ubaba, closely
resembles ours. His son, however, is called brother;
his grandson, accordingly, son; his great-grandson,
grandchild. A father's brother, as already mentioned,
is uncle; but, as before, his son is called brother; his
grandson, son; and his great-grandson, grandson. So,
also, a mother's sister is an aunt, but her son is a
brother; her grandson, a son; and her great-grandson,
a grandson. As in all the preceding cases, grandfather's brothers and sisters are considered as, respectively, grandfathers and grandmothers. Brothers'
sons and sisters' sons are called sons, and, lastly, their
sons again are grandsons.

Excepting in the case of nephews, this system,
therefore, closely resembles the Tamil, Feejeean, and
Wyandot; the other principal differences being, oddly
enough, a more correct nomenclature of uncles and
aunts.

Column 13, Table I.,[1] exhibits the nomenclature in
use among the Mohegans, whose name signifies 'sea-

---

[1] It is, however, significant that he calls his sister's sons 'sons,' and
not nephews.

side people,' from their geographical position on the
Hudson and the Connecticut. They belong to the
great Algonkin stock. Here, for the first time, a distinction is introduced between a father and a father's
brother. The latter, however, is not recognised as an
uncle; that is to say, a father's brother and a mother's
brother are not regarded as equivalent relationships,
but the former is termed stepfather. This distinguishing prefix is the characteristic feature; and, as will be
seen, we find the terms, stepmother, stepbrother, and
stepchild (to the exclusion of cousin), as natural consequences of the stepfathership. Still, the mother's
sister remains a mother, and her son a brother; and the
derivation of this system from one similar to those
already considered is, moreover, indicated by the fact
that the members of the third generation are still
regarded as grandchildren.

The Crees and Ojibwas, or Chippewas (of Lake
Michigan), who also belong to the great Algonkin
stock, resemble the Mohegan in the use, though with
some minor differences, of the prefix 'step-', a device
which occurs also in a more complicated form among
the Chinese. In some points, however, they are rather
more advanced, and, in fact, these tribes possess the
highest system of relationship yet recorded among the
Redskins of North America. A mother's brother is an
uncle, and his son is a cousin; as regards his grandson,
the tendency to the use of different terms, according as
the speaker is a male or female, shows itself in the use
by the former of the term stepson, where the latter say
nephew, as in some of the ruder tribes. In both cases,
mothers' brothers' great grandchildren are called grand-

children. A father's sister is an aunt, and the nomenclature with reference to her descendants is the same as in the case of the mother's brother. A father's brother is a stepbrother; his son is still called a brother by males among the Crees, but is called stepson by the Ojibwas; the other relationships in this line being the same as in the case of the mother's brother and father's sister.

No Redskin regards his mother's sister as an aunt, but the Crees and Ojibwas distinguish her from a true mother by the term stepmother, and her descendants are addressed by the same terms as those of the father's brother. The grandfather's brothers and sisters are called grandfathers and grandmothers. As before, brothers' sons, when a female is speaking, and sisters' sons, when a male is speaking, are called nephews; while brothers' sons, when a male is speaking, and sisters' sons, when a female is speaking, are no longer regarded as true sons, but are distinguished as stepsons. The grandchildren of these nephews and stepsons are, however, all termed grandchildren.

If, now, we compare this system with that of the Two-Mountain Iroquois, we find that out of twenty-eight relationships given in the table, only ten have remained the same. Of these, two are indicative of progress made by the Two-Mountain Iroquois, namely, the term for mother's brother and sister's son; the other eight are marks of imperfection still remaining in the Ojibwa nomenclature: points, moreover, not by any means characteristic of American races, but common, also, as we have seen, to the Hawaiian, Kingsmill, Burmese, Japanese, Tongan, Feejeean, Kaffir, and

Tamil systems; as we shall also find, to the Hindi, Karen, and Esquimaux; in fact, to almost all, if not all barbarous peoples, and to some of the most advanced races.

Column 14 (Table I.) shows the system of nomenclature as it exists in Hindi, and it may be added that the Benguli, Marathi, and Gujerathi are essentially the same, although the words differ. All these languages are said to be Sanskrit as regards their words; aboriginal, on the contrary, in their grammar. Hindi contains 90% of Sanskrit words, Guzerathi as much as 95%. With three or four exceptions, it appears that the terms for relationships may be all of Sanskrit origin.

Here, for the first time, we find that a brother's son and a sister's son are termed nephews, whether the speaker is a male or a female. Yet nephews' children are still termed grandchildren. Again, for the first time, the mother's brother, father's brother, mother's sister, and father's sister are regarded as equivalent, and the terms for their descendants are similar. The two former—i.e., mother's brother and father's brother, are termed 'uncles;' the two latter—i.e., mother's sister and father's sister, are called aunts. Yet, as regards the next generations, the system is less advanced than the Ojibwa, for uncles' sons and aunts' sons are termed brothers; their grandsons, nephews; and their great grandsons, grandsons. It should, however, be observed that, in the first three languages, viz. the Hindi, Bengali, and Marathi, besides the simple term 'brother,' the terms 'brother through paternal uncle,' 'brother through paternal aunt,' 'brother through maternal uncle,' and 'brother through maternal aunt,' are also in

use, and are less cumbersome than our English literal
translation would indicate.   The system, therefore, is
transitional on this point.   Lastly, a grandfather's
brother is called 'grandfather ;' a grandfather's sister,
' grandmother.'

The Karens are a rude, but peaceable and teachable
race, inhabiting parts of Tenasserim, Burmah, Siam,
and extending into the southern parts of China.   They
have been encroached upon and subjected by more
powerful races, and are now divided into different
tribes, speaking distinct dialects, of which three are
given in Mr. Morgan's tables.   Though rude and
savage in their mode of life, they are described as
extremely moral in their social relations—praise which
seems to be fully borne out by their system of relationships, as shown in column 17, Table I.

Column 18 shows the system of another rude
people, belonging to a distinct family of the human
race, and inhabiting a distant and very different part of
the world.   Like the Karens, the Esquimaux are a
rude people, but, like them, they are a quiet, peaceable,
and moral race.   No doubt, on some points their ideas
differ from ours; their condition does not admit of much
refinement—of any great advance in science or art.
They cannot be said to have any religion worthy of the
name, yet there is perhaps no more moral people on the
face of the earth; none among whom there is less crime ;
and it is, perhaps, not going too far to say that there is,
as far as I can judge, no race of men which has more
fully availed itself of its opportunities.

It is most remarkable to find these two races of
men, so distinct, so distant, so dissimilar in their modes

of life, without a word in common, yet using systems of relationship which, in their essential features, are identical, although by no means in harmony with the existing social condition: in both, uncles and aunts are correctly recognised, and their children regarded as cousins; their grandchildren, however, are termed nephews, and the children of these so-called nephews are classed, as in all the previous cases, as grandchildren. Thus, out of the twenty-eight relationships indicated in the table, the Karens and Esquimaux agree with us in twelve, and differ in sixteen. As regards every one, however, of these sixteen they agree with one another, while in eight they follow the same system as every other race which we have been considering.

These facts cannot be the result of chance; there is one way, and as it seems to me, one way only, of accounting for them, and that is by regarding them as the outcome of a progressive development, such as that which I have endeavoured to sketch. An examination of the several cases will, I think, confirm this view.

The Karen-Esquimaux system is inconsistent with itself in three respects, and precisely where it differs from ours. The children of cousins are termed nephews, which they are not; the children of nephews are regarded as grandchildren, and a grandfather's brothers and sisters are termed, respectively, grandfathers and grandmothers.

The first fact, namely, that a mother's brother's grandsons, and a mother's sister's grandsons; a father's sister's grandsons, and a father's brother's grandsons, are all termed 'nephews,' clearly points to the existence of a time when a mother's brother and a father's brother

were regarded as fathers, a mother's sister and a father's
sister as mothers, and their children, consequently, as
brothers.   The second, namely, that the great-grandchildren of uncles and aunts are regarded as grandchildren, similarly points to a time when nephews and
nieces were termed, and regarded as, sons and daughters,
and their children, consequently, as grandchildren.
Lastly, why should grandfathers' brothers and grandfathers' sisters be called grandfathers and grandmothers,
unless there was a time when fathers' brothers and sisters
were respectively called 'fathers' and 'mothers :' unless
the Karens and Esquimaux once had a system of relationship similar to that which still prevails among so
many barbarous tribes, and which, to all appearance,
has been gradually modified?   Hence, though the
Karens and Esquimaux have now a far more correct
system of nomenclature than that of many other races,
we find, even in this, clear traces of a time when these
peoples had not advanced in this respect beyond the
lowest stage.

As already mentioned, the European nations follow,
almost without exception, a strictly descriptive system,
founded on the marriage of single pairs.   The principle
is, however, departed from in a few very rare cases, and
in them we find an approach to the Karen-Esquimaux
system.   Thus, in Spanish, a brother's great-grandson
is called 'grandson.'   Again, in Bulgarian, a brother's
grandson and sister's grandson are called ' Mal vnook
mi,' literally 'little grandson my.'   A father's father's
sister is termed a grandmother, and a father's father's
brother a grandfather, as is also the case in Russian.
The French and Sanskrit, alone, so far as I know,

among the Aryan languages, have special words for
elder and younger brother. Among Aryan races the
Romans and the Germans alone developed a term for
cousin,[1] and we, ourselves, have, even now, no word for
a cousin's son. The history of the term 'nephew' is
also instructive. The word 'nepos,' says Morgan,[2]
' among the Romans, as late as the fourth century, was
' applied to a nephew as well as a grandson, although
' both "avus" and "avunculus" had come into use.
' Eutropius, in speaking of Octavianus, calls him the
' nephew of Cæsar, "Cæsaris nepos." (Lib. vii. c. i.)
' Suetonius speaks of him as "sororis nepos" (Cæsar,
' c. lxxxiii), and afterwards (Octavianus, c. vii.) describes
' Cæsar as his greater uncle, "major avunculus," in
' which he contradicts himself. When "nepos" was
' finally restricted to grandson, and thus became a
' strict correlative of "avus," the Latin language was
' without a term for nephew, whence the descriptive
' phrase, "Fratris vel sororis filius." In English,
' "nephew" was applied to grandson, as well as
' nephew, as late as 1611, the period of King James's
' translation of the Bible. Niece is so used by Shak-
' speare in his will, in which he describes his grand-
' daughter, Susannah Hall, as "my niece." '

So that even among the most advanced races we find
some lingering confusion about nephews, nieces, and
grandchildren.

Thus, then, we have traced these systems of relationships from the simple and rude nomenclature of the

---

[1] So that of many nations it may be said, literally as well as figura-
tively, that ' les nations n'ont pas de cousins.'

[2] *Loc. cit.*, p. 35.

Sandwich Islanders up to the far purer and more correct terminology of the Karens and Esquimaux. I have endeavoured to show that the systems indicated are explicable only on the theory of a gradual improvement and elevation, and are incompatible with degradation; that as the valves indicate the course of the blood in our veins, so do the terms applied to relationships point out the course of past history. In the first place, the moral condition of the lower races, wherever we can ascertain it, is actually higher than that indicated by the phraseology in use; and, secondly, the systems themselves are, in almost all cases, inexplicable, except on the hypothesis that they were themselves preceded by still ruder ones.

Take, for instance, the case of the Two-Mountain Iroquois: they call a mother's brother an uncle, but his son they regard as a brother. This is no accident, for the idea is carried out in the other relationships, and occurs also in other races. On the theory of progress it is easily accounted for: if a father's brother was previously called a father, his son would, of course, be a brother; and when the father's brother came to be distinguished as an uncle, some time would, no doubt, often elapse before the other changes, consequent on this step, would be effected. But how could such a system be accounted for on the opposite theory? How could a father's brother's son come to be regarded as a brother, if a father's brother had always been termed an uncle? The sequence of terms for the relationships connected with a father's sister, on the two hypotheses of progress on the one hand, and degradation on the other, may be illustrated as in the Table III. (p. 192).

In the first, or lowest stage, the sequence is mother, brother, son, grandson, as in the Sandwich and Two-Mountain Iroquois system. In the next stage, the mother's sister being recognised as an aunt, and the other relationships remaining the same, we have the sequence, aunt, brother, son, grandson, as among the Micmacs. When a brother's son becomes a nephew, we have aunt, brother, nephew, grandson, as in the Burmese, Japanese, and Hindi systems. In the next stage, an aunt's son being distinguished as a cousin, we have aunt, cousin, nephew, grandson, as among the Tamils and Feejees. The last two stages would be aunt, cousin, aunt's grandson, grandson; and, lastly, aunt, cousin, aunt's grandson, aunt's great-grandson. Thus, out of these six stages, five at least actually exist.

On the other hand, on the theory of retrogression, we should commence with the highest system; namely, aunt, cousin, aunt's grandson, and aunt's great-grandson. The second stage would be, mother, cousin, aunt's grandson, aunt's great-grandson. The third, mother, brother, aunt's grandson, aunt's great-grandson. The fourth, mother, brother, nephew, aunt's great-grandson. The fifth, mother, brother, son, aunt's great-grandson. And the last, mother, brother, son, grandson. Thus, it will be observed that, except, of course, the first and last, they have not a stage in common; and, though there may be some doubt whether the sequence suggested on the second hypothesis is the one which would be followed, it cannot be maintained that we could ever have the systems which would occur in the case of progress, as shown in Table III., and the first four of which are actually in existence.

Whenever, then, the son or daughter of an uncle, or aunt, is termed a brother, as in the case of seven of the races referred to in the table, we may be sure that there was once a time when that uncle, or aunt, was termed a father or mother; whenever a cousin's son is termed a son, as again in seven races, we must infer, not only that those cousins were once regarded as brothers, but that brothers' sons were once termed sons. Again, when great-uncles and aunts are termed grandfathers and grandmothers—when great-nephews and nieces are termed grandchildren, as in the case of all the races we have been considering—we have, I submit, good reason to infer that those races must once have had a system of nomenclature as rude as that of the Hawaiians or Kingsmill Islanders.

But it may be asked: admitting that the seventeen races, illustrated in Table I., are really advancing, are there not cases of the contrary? The answer is clear: out of the 139 races whose systems of relationship are more or less completely given by Mr. Morgan, there is not one in which evidence of degradation is thus indicated. To show this clearly and concisely, I have prepared the following table (p. 189). It will be seen that, taking merely the relation of uncles and aunts with reference to their children, there are 207 cases indicating progress. On the other hand, there are four cases, the Cayuga, Onondaga, Oneida, and Mohawks, among whom, while a father's sister is called a mother, her son is called a cousin. These cases, however, are neutralised by the fact that the sons of these cousins are called sons. We have, therefore, a very large body of evidence indicating progress, and collected among very different

| Relationship | No. | | No. | | No. |
|---|---|---|---|---|---|
| PROGRESS. Mother's brother, called uncle, With Mother's brother's son, called brother. | 14 | Do, do, Mother's brother's grandson – son. | 23 | Do, do, Do, do, great-grandson – grandson. | 64 |
| DEGRADATION. Mother's brother, called father, With Mother's brother's son, called cousin. | 0 | Do, do, Do, do, grandson – cousin. | 0 | Do, do, Do, do, great-grandson – cousin. – nephew. | 0 / 0 |
| PROGRESS. Father's sister – aunt, With Father's sister's son – brother. | 11 | Do, do, Do, do, grandson – son. | 21 | Do, do, Do, do, do., do. – grandson. | 02 |
| DEGRADATION. Father's sister – mother, With Father's sister's son – cousin. | 4 | Do, do, Do, do, grandson – cousin. | 0 | Do, do, Do, do, do., do. – cousin. – nephew. | 0 / 7 |
| PROGRESS. Father's brother – uncle, With Father's brother's son – brother. | 4 | Do, do, Do, do, grandson – son. | 0 | Do, do, Do, do, do. – grandson. | 0 |
| DEGRADATION. Father's brother – father, With Father's brother's son – cousin. | 0 | Do, do, Do, do, grandson – cousin. | 0 | Do, do, Do, do, do., do. – cousin. – nephew. | 0 / 7 |
| PROGRESS. Mother's sister – aunt, With Mother's sister's son – brother. | 4 | Do, do, Do, do, grandson – son. | 0 | Do, do, Do, do, do. – grandson. | 0 |
| DEGRADATION. Mother's sister – mother, With Mother's sister's son – cousin. | 0 | Do, do, Do, do, grandson – cousin. | 0 | Do, do, Do, do, do., do. – cousin. – nephew. | 0 / 0 |
| Totals. | 53 – 4 = 3? | | 44 | | 130 |

Grand total . . . 207 indicating progress.

races of men, while there appear to be none which favour the opposite hypothesis.

In the preceding chapter, I have endeavoured to show that relationship is, at first, a matter, not of blood, but of tribal organisation; that it is, in the second place, traced through the mother; in the third, through the father; and that only in the fourth stage is the idea of family constituted as amongst ourselves. To obtain clear and correct ideas on this subject, it is necessary to know the laws and customs of various races. The nomenclature alone, would, in many cases, lead us into error, and, in fact, has often done so. When checked by a knowledge of the tribal rules and customs, it is, however, most interesting and instructive. From this point of view especially, Mr. Morgan's work is of great value. It has been seen, however, that I differ greatly from him as to the conclusions to be drawn from the facts which he has so diligently collected.

Of course, I do not deny that these facts may, in some cases, indicate ethnological affinities; but they have not, I think, so great an importance in solving questions of ethnological relationships as he supposes. I do not, however, in any way, undervalue their importance; they afford a striking evidence in favour of the doctrine of development, and are thus a very interesting and important contribution to the great problem of human history.

From the materials which he has so laboriously collected, and for which ethnologists owe him an immense debt of gratitude, I have endeavoured to show:

Firstly, that the terms for, what we call, relationships, are, among the lower races of men, mere expressions for the results of marriage customs, and do not comprise the idea of relationship as we understand it; that, in fact, the connection of individuals *inter se*, their duties to one another, their rights, and the descent of their property, are all regulated more by the relation to the tribe than by that to the family; that when the two conflict, the latter must give way.

Secondly, that the nomenclature of relationships is, in all the cases yet collected, explainable in a clear and simple manner on the hypothesis of progress.

Thirdly, that while two races in the same state of social condition, but of which the one has risen from the lowest known system, the other sunk from the highest, would, necessarily, have a totally different system of nomenclature for relationships, we have not a single instance of such a system as would result from the latter hypothesis.

Fourthly, that some of those races which approximate most nearly to our European system differ from it upon points only explainable on the hypothesis that they were once in a much lower social condition than they are at present.

## TABLE III.—SYSTEMS OF RELATIONSHIP UPON THEORY OF PROGRESS.

| | First Stage* | Second Stage† | Third Stage‡ | Fourth Stage§ | Fifth Stage‖ | Sixth Stage¶ |
|---|---|---|---|---|---|---|
| Father's sister | Mother. | Aunt. | Aunt. | Aunt. | Aunt. | Aunt. |
| „ „ son | Brother. | Brother. | Brother. | Cousin. | Cousin. | Cousin. |
| „ „ „ son | Son. | Son. | Nephew. | Nephew. | Aunt's grandson. | Aunt's grandson. |
| „ „ „ „ son | Grandson. | Grandson. | Grandson. | Grandson. | Grandson. | Aunt's great-grandson. |

* This is the system of the Sandwich Islands, Kingsmill Islands, Two-Mountain Iroquois, &c.
† System of the Micmacs.
‡ This is the system of the Burmese, Japanese, Hindi.
§ This is the Tamil and Feejeean systems.
‖ Our system.

## SYSTEMS OF RELATIONSHIP UPON THEORY OF DEGRADATION.

| | First Stage* | Second Stage | Third Stage | Fourth Stage | Fifth Stage | Sixth Stage |
|---|---|---|---|---|---|---|
| Father's sister | Aunt. | Mother. | Mother. | Mother. | Mother. | Mother. |
| „ „ son | Cousin. | Cousin. | Brother. | Brother. | Brother. | Brother. |
| „ „ „ son | Aunt's grandson. | Aunt's grandson. | Aunt's grandson. | Nephew. | Son. | Son. |
| „ „ „ „ son | Aunt's great-grandson. | Aunt's great-grandson. | Aunt's great-grandson. | Aunt's great-grandson. | Aunt's grandson. | Grandson. |

Excepting of course the first and last, none of these systems exist so far as I am aware.

# CHAPTER V.

## RELIGION.

THE religion of savages, though of peculiar interest, is in many respects, perhaps, the most difficult part of my whole subject. I shall endeavour to avoid, as far as possible, anything which might justly give pain to any of my readers. Many ideas, however, which have been, or are, prevalent on religious matters, are so utterly opposed to our own that it is impossible to discuss the subject without mentioning some things which are very repugnant to our feelings. Yet, while savages show us a melancholy spectacle of gross superstitions and ferocious forms of worship, the religious mind cannot but feel a peculiar satisfaction in tracing up the gradual evolution of more correct ideas and of nobler creeds.

M. Arbrousset quotes the following touching remarks made to him by Sekesa, a very respectable Kaffir:[1] 'Your tidings,' he said, 'are what I want; and 'I was seeking before I knew you, as you shall hear 'and judge for yourselves. Twelve years ago I went 'to feed my flocks. The weather was hazy. I sat 'down upon a rock and asked myself sorrowful ques- 'tions; yes, sorrowful, because I was unable to answer

[1] Tour at the Cape of Good Hope, p. 120.

'them. "Who has touched the stars with his hands?
'"On what pillars do they rest?" I asked myself.
'"The waters are never weary: they know no other
'"law than to flow, without ceasing, from morning till
'"night, and from night till morning; but where do
'"they stop? and who makes them flow thus? The
'"clouds also come and go, and burst in water over
'"the earth. Whence come they? Who sends them?
'"The diviners certainly do not give us rain, for how
'"could they do it? and why do I not see them with
'"my own eyes when they go up to heaven to fetch it?
'"I cannot see the wind, but what is it? Who brings
'"it, makes it blow, and roar and terrify us? Do I
'"know how the corn sprouts? Yesterday there was
'"not a blade in my field; to-day I returned to the
'"field and found some. Who can have given to the
'"earth the wisdom and the power to produce it?"
'Then I buried my face in both my hands.'

This, however, was an exceptional case. As a
general rule savages do not set themselves to think out
such questions, but adopt the ideas which suggest themselves most naturally; so that, as I shall attempt to
show, races in a similar state of mental development,
however distinct their origin may be, and however
distant the regions they inhabit, have very similar
religious conceptions. Most of those who have endeavoured to account for the various superstitions of
savage races have done so by crediting them with a
much more elaborate system of ideas than they in
reality possess. Thus Lafitau supposes that fire was
worshipped because it so well represents 'cette suprême
'intelligence dégagée de la nature, dont la puissance est

' toujours active.' [1]   Again, with reference to idols, he
' observes[2] that 'La dépendance que nous avons de
' l'imagination et des sens ne nous permettant pas de
' voir Dieu autrement qu'en énigme, comme parle Saint
' Paul, a causé une espèce de nécessité de nous le
' montrer sous des images sensibles, lesquelles fussent
' autant de symboles, qui nous élevassent jusqu'à lui,
' comme le portrait nous remet dans l'idée de celui
' dont il est la peinture.' Plutarch, again, supposed that
the crocodile was worshipped by Egypt because, having
no tongue, it was a type of the Deity who made laws
for nature by his mere will ! Explanations, however,
such as these are radically wrong.

I have felt doubtful whether this chapter should not
be entitled 'the superstitions' rather than 'the re-
'ligion' of savages ; but have preferred the latter,
partly because many of the superstitious ideas pass
gradually into nobler conceptions, and partly from a
reluctance to condemn any honest belief, however
absurd and imperfect it may be.  It must, however, be
admitted that religion, as understood by the lower
savage races, differs essentially from ours ; nay, it is
not only different, but even opposite.  Thus, their
deities are evil, not good ; they may be forced into
compliance with the wishes of man ; they require
bloody, and rejoice in human, sacrifices ; they are
mortal, not immortal ; a part, not the author, of
nature ; they are to be approached by dances rather
than by prayers ; and often approve what we call vice,
rather than what we esteem as virtue.

[1] Mœurs des Sauvages Américains, vol. I. p. 152.
[2] Loc. cit., p. 121.

In fact, the so-called religion of the lower races bears somewhat the same relation to religion in its higher forms that astrology does to astronomy, or alchemy to chemistry.    Astronomy is derived from astrology, yet their spirit is in entire opposition ; and we shall find the same difference between the religions of backward and of advanced races.    We regard the Deity as good; they look upon him as evil ; we submit ourselves to him ; they endeavour to obtain the control of him ; we feel the necessity of accounting for the blessings by which we are surrounded ; they think the blessings come of themselves, and attribute all evil to the interference of malignant beings.

These characteristics are not exceptional and rare. On the contrary, I shall attempt to show that, though the religions of the lower races have received different names, they agree in their general characteristics, and are but phases of one sequence, having the same origin, and passing through similar, if not identical, stages. This will explain the great similarities which occur in the most distinct and distant races, which have puzzled many ethnologists, and in some cases led them to utterly untenable theories.    Thus, even Robertson, though in many respects he held very correct views as to the religious condition of savages, remarks that Sun-worship prevailed among the Natchez and the Persians, and observes:[1] 'This surprising coincidence in senti-'ment between two nations in such different states of 'improvement is one of the many singular and unac-'countable circumstances which occur in the history of 'human affairs.'

[1] History of America, book iv. p. 127.

Although, however, we find the most remarkable coincidences between the religions of distinct races, one of the peculiar difficulties in the study of religion arises from the fact that, while each nation has generally but one language, we may almost say that in religious matters, *quot homines tot sententiæ;* no two men having exactly the same views, however much they may wish to agree.

Many travellers have pointed out this difficulty. Thus, Captain Cook, speaking of the South Sea Islanders,[1] says: 'Of the religion of these people we 'were not able to acquire any clear and consistent 'knowledge; we found it like the religion of most other 'countries—involved in mystery and perplexed with 'apparent inconsistencies.' Many also of those to whom we are indebted for information on the subject, fully expecting to find among savages ideas like our own, obscured only by errors and superstition, have put leading questions, and thus got misleading answers. We constantly hear, for instance, of a Devil; but, in fact, no spiritual being in the mythology of any savage races possesses the characteristics of Satan. Again, it is often very difficult to determine in what sense an object is worshipped. A mountain, or a river, for instance, may be held sacred either as an actual Deity or merely as his abode; and in the same way a statue may be actually worshipped as a god, or merely reverenced as representing the Divinity.

To a great extent, moreover, these difficulties arise from the fact that when man, either by natural progress or the influence of a more advanced race, rises to the

---

[1] Hawkesworth's Voyages, vol. ii. p. 237.

conception of a higher religion, he still retains his old beliefs, which long linger on, side by side with, and yet in utter opposition to, the higher creed. The new and more powerful Spirit is an addition to the old Pantheon, and diminishes the importance of the older deities; gradually the worship of the latter sinks in the social scale, and becomes confined to the ignorant and the young. Thus, a belief in witchcraft still flourishes among our agricultural labourers and the lowest classes in our great cities; and the deities of our ancestors survive in the nursery tales of our children. We must therefore expect to find in each race traces—nay, more than traces—of lower religions. Even if this were not the case, we should still be met by the difficulty that there are few really sharp lines in religious systems. It might be supposed that a belief in the immortality of the soul, or in the efficacy of sacrifices, would give us good lines of division; but it is not so: these and many other ideas rise gradually, and even often appear at first in a form very different from that which they ultimately assume.

Hitherto it has been usual to classify religions according to the nature of the object worshipped: Fetichism, for instance, being the worship of inanimate objects, Sabæism that of the heavenly bodies. The true test, however, seems to me to be the estimate in which the Deity is held. The first great stages in religious thought may, I think, be regarded as—

*Atheism*; understanding by this term not a denial of the existence of a Deity, but an absence of any definite ideas on the subject.

*Fetichism*; the stage in which man supposes he can force the deities to comply with his desires.

*Nature-worship*, or *Totemism*; in which natural objects, trees, lakes, stones, animals, &c., are worshipped.

*Shamanism*; in which the superior deities are far more powerful than man, and of a different nature. Their place of abode also is far away, and accessible only to Shamans.

*Idolatry*, or *Anthropomorphism*; in which the gods take still more completely the nature of men, being, however, more powerful. They are still amenable to persuasion; they are a part of nature, and not creators. They are represented by images or idols.

In the next stage the Deity is regarded as the author, not merely a part, of nature. He becomes for the first time a really supernatural being.

The last stage to which I will refer is that in which morality is associated with religion.

Since the above was written, my attention was called by De Brosse's ' Culte des Dieux fétiches ' to a passage in Sanchoniatho, quoted by Eusebius. From his description of the first thirteen generations of men I extract the following passages :—

*Generation* 1.—The ' first men consecrated the ' plants shooting out of the earth, and judged them ' gods, and worshipped them, upon whom they them- ' selves lived.'

*Gen.* 2.—The second generation of men ' were called ' Genus and Genea, and dwelt in Phœnicia; but when ' great droughts came, they stretched their hands up to

' heaven towards the Sun, for him they thought the only
' Lord of Heaven.'

*Gen.* 3.—Afterwards other mortal issue was begotten,
whose names were Phôs, Pur, and Phlox (*i.e.* Light,
Fire, and Flame). These found out the way of gene-
rating fire by the rubbing of pieces of wood against each
other, and taught men the use thereof.

*Gen.* 4.—The fourth generation consists of giants.

*Gen.* 5.—With reference to the fifth he mentions
the existence of communal marriage, and that Usous
' consecrated *two pillars* to Fire and Wind, and bowed
' down to them, and poured out to them the blood of
' such wild beasts as had been caught in hunting.'

*Gen.* 6.—Hunting and fishing are invented; which
seems rather inconsistent with the preceding statement.

*Gen.* 7.—Chrysor, whom he affirms to be Vulcan,
discovered iron and the art of forging. ' Wherefore he
' also was worshipped after his death for a god, and they
' called him Diamichius (or Zeus Michius).'

*Gen.* 8.—Pottery was discovered.

*Gen.* 9.—Now comes Agrus, 'who had a much-
' worshipped statue, and a temple carried about by one
' or more yoke of oxen in Phœnicia.'

*Gen.* 10.—Villages were formed, and men kept
flocks.

*Gen.* 11.—Salt was discovered.

*Gen.* 12.—Taautus or Hermes discovered letters.
The Cabiri belong to this generation.

Thus, then, we find mentioned in order the worship
of plants, heavenly bodies, pillars, and men; later still
comes Idolatry coupled with Temples. It will be

observed that Sanchoniatho makes no special mention of Shamanism, and that he regards the worship of plants as aboriginal.

The opinion that religion is general and universal has been entertained by many high authorities. Yet it is opposed to the evidence of numerous trustworthy observers. Sailors, traders, and philosophers, Roman Catholic priests and Protestant missionaries, in ancient and in modern times, in every part of the globe, have concurred in stating that there are races of men altogether devoid of religion. The case is the stronger because in several instances the fact has greatly surprised him who records it, and has been entirely in opposition to all his preconceived views. On the other hand, it must be confessed that in some cases travellers denied the existence of religion merely because the tenets were unlike ours. The question as to the general existence of religion among men is, indeed, to a great extent a matter of definition. If the mere sensation of fear, and the recognition that there are probably other beings more powerful than oneself, are sufficient alone to constitute a religion, then we must, I think, admit that religion is general to the human race. But when a child dreads the darkness, and shrinks from a lightless room, we never regard that as an evidence of religion. Moreover, if this definition be adopted, we cannot longer regard religion as peculiar to man. We must admit that the feeling of a dog or a horse towards its master is of the same character; and the baying of a dog to the moon is as much an act of worship as some ceremonies which have been so described by travellers.

In 'Prehistoric Times,'[1] I have quoted the following writers as witnesses to the existence of tribes without religion. For some of the Esquimaux tribes, Captain Ross;[2] for some of the Canadians, Hearne; for the Californians, Baegert, who lived among them seventeen years, and La Perouse; for many of the Brazilian tribes, Spix and Martius, Bates and Wallace; for Paraguay, Dobritzhoffer ; for some of the Polynesians, Williams's Missionary Enterprises, the Voyage of the Novara, and Dieffenbach; for Damood Island (North of Australia), Jukes (Voyage of the Fly) ; for the Pellew Islands, Wilson ; for the Aru Islands, Wallace; for the Andamaners, Mouatt; for certain tribes of Hindostan, Hooker and Shortt; for some of the Eastern African nations, Burton and Grant ; for the Bachapin Kaffirs, Burchell; and for the Hottentots, Le Vaillant. I will here only give a few additional instances.

The natives of Queensland, says Mr. Lang. 'have no 'idea of a Supreme Divinity, the creator and governor 'of the world, the witness of their actions, and their 'future judge. They have no object of worship, even 'of a subordinate and inferior rank. They have no 'idols, no temples, no sacrifices. In short, they have 'nothing whatever of the character of religion, or of 'religious observance, to distinguish them from the 'beasts that perish. They live "without God in the '"world."'[3] He quotes, also, in support of this, the opinion of Mr. Schmidt, who lived as a missionary among the natives of Moreton Bay for seven years, and was well acquainted with their language.

---

[1] Prehistoric Times, 3rd edition, p. 570.
[2] See also Franklin's Journey to the Polar Sea, vol. ii. p. 205.
[3] Lang's Queensland, p. 374.

'It is evident,' says M. Bik,[1] 'that the Arafuras of
'Vorkay (one of the Southern Arus) possess no religion
'whatever. . . . Of the immortality of the soul they
'have not the least conception. To all my enquiries on
'this subject they answered, "No Arafura has ever
'"returned to us after death, therefore we know
'"nothing of a future state, and this is the first time
'"we have heard of it." Their idea was Mati, Mati
'sudah (When you are dead there is an end of you).
'Neither have they any notion of the creation of the
'world. To convince myself more fully respecting
'their want of knowledge of a Supreme Being, I
'demanded of them on whom they called for help in
'their need, when their vessels were overtaken by
'violent tempests. The eldest among them, after
'having consulted the others, answered that they
'knew not on whom they could call for assistance,
'but begged me, if I knew, to be so good as to inform
'them.'

'The wilder Bedouins,'[2] says Burton, 'will inquire
'where Allah is to be found: when asked the object of
'the question, they reply, "If the Eesa could but catch
'"him they would spear him upon the spot; who but
'"he lays waste their homes and kills their cattle and
'"wives?"' He also considers that atheism is 'the
'natural condition of the savage and uninstructed mind,
'the night of spiritual existence, which disappears
'before the dawn of a belief in things unseen. A
'Creator is to creation what the cause of any event
'in life is to its effect; those familiar to the sequence

[1] Quoted in Kolff's Voyages of
the Dourga, p. 160.

[2] First Footsteps in East Africa,
p. 52.

'will hardly credit its absence from the minds of
'others.'[1]

Among the Koossa Kaffirs, Lichtenstein[2] affirms
that 'there is no appearance of any religious worship
'whatever.'

'It might be the proper time now,' says Father
Baegert, 'to speak of the form of government and the
'religion of the Californians previous to their conver-
'sion to Christianity; but neither the one nor the
'other existed among them. They had no magistrates,
'no police, and no laws; idols, temples, religious
'worship or ceremonies, were unknown to them, and
'they neither believed in the true and only God, nor
'adored false deities. . . . I made diligent en-
'quiries, among those with whom I lived, to ascertain
'whether they had any conception of God, a future life,
'and their own souls, but I never could discover the
'slightest trace of such a knowledge. Their language
'has no words for "God" and "soul."'[3] Indeed, the
missionaries found no word which they could use for
'God' in any of the Oregon languages.[4]

Although, as Captain John Smith[5] quaintly puts it,
there was 'in Virginia no place discovered to be so
'savage in which they had not a religion, Deere, and
'bows and arrows,' still the ruder tribes in the far
North, according to the testimony of Hearne, who knew
them intimately, had no religion.

Several tribes, says Robertson,[6] 'have been dis-

[1] Abeokuta, vol. i. p. 170.
[2] Lichtenstein, vol. i. p. 253.
[3] Baegert. Smithsonian trans., 1863–4, p. 390.
[4] Hale's Ethnography of the U. S. Expl. Exped., p. 200.
[5] Voyages in Virginia, p. 138.
[6] History of America, book iv. p. 122. See also Pritchard's Nat. History of Man, vol. ii. p. 608.

' covered in America, which have no idea whatever of a
' Supreme Being, and no rites of religious worship. . . .
' Some rude tribes have not in their language any name
' for the Deity, nor have the most accurate observers
' been able to discover any practice or institution which
' seemed to imply that they recognised his authority,
' or were solicitous to obtain his favour.'

In the face of such a crowd of witnesses it may at
first sight seem extraordinary that there can still be
any difference of opinion on the subject. This, however, arises partly from the fact that the term ' Religion ' has not always been used in the same sense,
and partly from a belief that, as has no doubt happened
in several cases, travellers may, from ignorance of the
language, or from shortness of residence, have overlooked a religion which really existed.

For instance, the first describers of Tahiti asserted
that the natives had no religion, which subsequently
proved to be a complete mistake ; and several other
similar cases might be quoted. As regards the lowest
races of men, however, it seems to me, even *à priori,*
very difficult to suppose that a people so backward as
to be unable to count their own fingers should be sufficiently advanced in their intellectual conceptions as to
have any system of belief worthy of the name of a
religion.

We shall, however, obtain a clearer view of the
question if we consider the superstitions of those races
which have a rudimentary religion, and endeavour to
trace these ideas up into a more developed condition.

Here, again, we shall perhaps be met by the doubt
whether travellers have correctly understood the ac-

counts given to them. In many cases, however, when the narrator had lived for months, or years, among those whom he was describing, we need certainly feel no suspicion, and in others we shall obtain a satisfactory result by comparing together the statements of different observers and using them as a check one upon the other.

The religious theories of savages are certainly not the result of deep thought, nor must they be regarded as constituting any elaborate or continuous theory. A Zulu candidly said to Mr. Callaway:[1] 'Our knowledge ' does not urge us to search out the roots of it ; we do ' not try to see them; if any one thinks ever so little, ' he soon gives it up, and passes on to what he sees ' with his eyes ; and he does not understand the real ' state of even what he sees.' Dulaure[2] truly observes, that the savage 'aime mieux soumettre sa raison, ' souvent révoltée, à ce que ses institutions ont de plus ' absurde, que de se livrer à l'examen, parce que ce ' travail est toujours pénible pour celui qui ne s'y est ' point exercé.' With this statement I entirely concur, and I believe that through all the various religious systems of the lower races may be traced a natural and unconscious process of development.

The ideas of religion among the lower races of man are intimately associated with, if indeed they have not originated from, the condition of man during sleep, and especially from dreams. Sleep and death have always been regarded as nearly related to one another. Thus, in classical mythology, Somnus, the god of sleep, and

---

[1] The Religious System of the Amazulu, p. 22.     [2] Histoire des Cultes, vol. i. p. 22.

Mors, the god of death, were both fabled to have been the children of Nox, the goddess of night. So, also, the savage would naturally look on death as a kind of sleep, and would expect—hoping on even against hope —to see his friend awake from the one as he had so often done from the other.

Hence, probably, one reason for the great import- ance ascribed to the treatment of the body after death. But what happens to the spirit during sleep ? The body lies lifeless, and the savage not unnaturally con- cludes that the spirit has left it. In this he is con- firmed by the phenomena of dreams, which conse- quently to the savage have a reality and an importance which we can scarcely appreciate. During sleep the spirit seems to desert the body; and as in dreams we visit other localities and even other worlds, living, as it were, a separate and different life, the two phenomena are not unnaturally regarded as the complements of one another. Hence the savage considers the events in his dreams to be as real as those of his waking hours, and hence he naturally feels that he has a spirit which can quit the body. 'Dreams,' says Burton, 'ac- ' cording to the Yorubans (West African) and to many ' of our fetichists, are not an irregular action and ' partial activity of the brain, but so many revelations ' brought by the manes of the departed.'[1] So strong was the North American faith in dreams that on one occasion, when an Indian dreamt he was taken captive, he induced his friends to make a mock attack on him, to bind him and treat him as a captive, actually sub- mitting to a considerable amount of torture, in the hope

[1] Abeokuta, vol. i. p. 204.

thus to fulfil his dream.[1] The Greenlanders[2] also
believe in the reality of dreams, and think that at night
they go hunting, visiting, courting, and so on. It is of
course obvious that the body takes no part in these
nocturnal adventures, and hence it is natural to conclude that they have a spirit which can quit the body.

In Madagascar[3] 'the people throughout the whole
'island pay a religious regard to dreams, and imagine
'that their good demons (for I cannot tell what other
'name to give their inferior deities, which, as they say,
'attend on their owleys,) tell them in their dreams
'what ought to be done, or warn them of what ought
'to be avoided.'

Lastly, when they dream of their departed friends
or relatives, savages firmly believe themselves to be
visited by their spirits, and hence believe, not indeed
in the immortality of the soul, but in its survival of the
body. Thus the Veddahs of Ceylon believe in spirits,
because their deceased relatives visit them in dreams,[4]
and the Manganjas (South Africa) expressly ground
their belief in a future life on the same fact. 'Persons
'who are pursued in their sleep by the image of a
'deceased relation, are often known to sacrifice a vic-
'tim on the tomb of the defunct, in order, as they say,
'to calm his disquietude.'[5] Again:[6] 'If during sleep
'you dream of returning to your people from whom
'you separated a long time ago; and see that so-and-so

---

[1] Lafitau, loc. cit., vol. i. p. 380.
[2] Cranz, loc. cit., vol. i. p. 200.
[3] The Adventures of Robert
Drury, p. 171. See also pp. 178,
272.
[4] Bailey, in Trans. Eth. Soc. N.S.

vol. ii. p. 301.
[5] The Basutos, Rev. E. Casalis,
p. 245.
[6] Uskulunkulu; or, the Tradition
of Creation as existing among the
Amazulu, p. 228.

' and so-and-so are unhappy; and when you wake your
' body is unstrung; you know that the Itongo has
' taken you to your people, that you might see the
' trouble in which they are; and that if you go to them
' you will find out the cause of their unhappiness.'
Indeed, the whole chapter on dreams in Dean Callaway's
treatise on the religion of the Kaffirs is most interesting
and instructive.

Speaking of the Peruvians, Garcilasso de la Vega
says,[1] ' for ordinary omens they made use of dreams.'
The Tongans thought that the souls of chiefs—for those
of the common people were considered to die with their
bodies—' had the power of returning to Tonga to inspire
' priests, relations, or others, or to appear in dreams.[2]
The Feejeeans[3] also believe ' that the spirit of a man
' who still lives will leave the body to trouble other
' people whenasleep. When anyone faints or dies, their
' spirit, it is said, may sometimes be brought back by
' calling after it.' Herodotus, speaking of the Nasamones,
says that when they wish to divine, they go ' to the
' tombs of their ancestors, and after having prayed,
' they lie down to sleep, and whatever dream they have,
' this they avail themselves of.'[4]

Again, savages are rarely ill; their sufferings generally
arise from wounds; their deaths are generally violent.
As an external injury received in war causes pain, so
when they suffer internally they attribute it to some internal enemy. Hence when the Australian, perhaps after
too heavy a meal, has his slumbers disturbed, he never

---

[1] The Royal Commentaries of
the Incas, vol. i. p. 183. See also
Wuttke, *loc. cit.*, vol. i. p. 310.

[2] Mariner's Tonga Islands, vol. ii.

p. 138.

[3] Williams' Fiji and the Fijians,
vol. i. p. 242.

[4] Melpomene, p. 172.

P

doubts the reality of what is passing, but considers that he is attacked by some being whom his companions cannot see.

This is well illustrated in the following passage from the 'United States Exploring Expedition:'[1] 'Some-'times, when the Australians are asleep, Koin makes 'his appearance, seizes upon one of them and carries 'him off. The person seized endeavours in vain to cry 'out, being almost strangled. At daylight, however, 'he disappears, and the man finds himself conveyed 'safely to his own fireside. From this it would appear 'that the demon is here a sort of personification of the 'nightmare—a visitation to which the natives, from 'their habits of gorging themselves to the utmost when 'they obtain a supply of food, must be very subject.'

Speaking of the North-Western Americans, Mr. Sproat says:[2] 'The apparition of ghosts is especially an 'occasion on which the services of the sorcerers, the 'old women, and all the friends of the ghost-seer are 'in great request. Owing to the quantity of indiges-'tible food eaten by the natives, they often dream that 'they are visited by ghosts. After a supper of blubber, 'followed by one of the long talks about departed 'friends, which take place round the fire, some nervous 'and timid person may fancy, in the night-time, that 'he sees a ghost.'

In some cases the belief that man possesses a spirit seems to have been suggested by the shadow. Thus, among the Feejeeans,[3] 'some speak of man as having 'two spirits. His shadow is called "the dark spirit,"

---

[1] *Loc. cit.*, vol. vi. p. 110.
[2] Scenes and Studies of Savage Life, p. 172.
[3] Williams' Fiji and the Fijians, vol. i. p. 241.

' which they say goes to Hades. The other is his like-
' ness reflected in water or a looking-glass, and is sup-
' posed to stay near the place in which a man dies.
' Probably this doctrine of shadows has to do with the
' notion of inanimate objects having spirits. I once
' placed a good-looking native suddenly before a mirror.
' He stood delighted. "Now," said he, softly, "I can
' " see into the world of spirits." '

The North American Indians also consider a man's
shadow as his soul or life. 'I have,' says Tanner,
' heard them reproach a sick person for what they
' considered imprudent exposure in convalescence, tell-
' ing him that his shadow was not well settled down in
' him.'[1]

The natives of Benin ' call a man's shadow his pass-
' adoor, or conductor, and believe it will witness if he
' lived well or ill. If well, he is raised to great happi-
' ness and dignity in the place before mentioned; if ill,
' he is to perish with hunger and poverty.'[2] They are
indeed a most superstitious race; and Lander mentions
a case in which an echo was taken for the voice of a
Fetich.[3] The Basutos when walking along a river are
very careful not to let their shadow fall on the water.
The crocodile, they think, ' has the power of seizing the
' shadow of a man passing by, and by it dragging him
' into the river, where it will certainly kill him, though
' it will not eat a morsel of his flesh.' In Micronesia
the usual word for soul 'tamune' or 'tamre,' means

[1] Tanner's Captivity, p. 201.
[2] Astley's Collection of Voyages,
vol. iii. p. 99. Pinkerton, vol. xvi.
p. 531. See also Callaway on the

Religious System of the Amazulu,
p. 91.
[3] Niger Expedition, vol. iii. p.
242.

properly shadow,[1] and the same was the case in Tasmania.[2]

Thunder, also, was often regarded either as an actual deity or as a heavenly voice. 'One night,' says Tanner, ' Picheto (a North American chief), becoming ' much alarmed at the violence of the storm, got up and ' offered some tobacco to the thunder, entreating it to ' stop.'[3]

I have already mentioned that savages almost always regard spirits as evil beings. We can, I think, easily understand why this should be. Amongst the very lowest races every other man—amongst those slightly more advanced, every man—of a different tribe is regarded as naturally, and almost necessarily hostile. A stranger is synonymous with an enemy, and a spirit is but a member of an invisible tribe.

The Hottentots, according to Thunberg, have very vague ideas about a good Deity. 'They have much ' clearer notions about an evil spirit, whom they fear, ' believing him to be the occasion of sickness, death, ' thunder, and every calamity that befalls them.'[4] The Bechuanas attribute all evil to an invisible god, whom they call Murimo, and ' never hesitate to show their ' indignation at any ill experienced, or any wish unac- ' complished, by the most bitter curses. They have no ' religious worship, and could never be persuaded by ' the missionaries that this was a thing displeasing to ' God.'[5]

[1] Hale's Ethnography of the United States Expl. Exp., p. 96.
[2] Bonwick's Daily Life of the Tasmanians, p. 182.
[3] Tanner's Narrative of a Cap-

tivity among the Indians, p. 123.
[4] Thunberg. Pinkerton's Voyages, vol. xv. p. 142. Astley, &c. cit., p. 353.
[5] Lichtenstein, vol. ii. p. 332.

Among the Bongos of Central Africa 'good spirits
' are quite unrecognised, and, according to the gene-
' ral negro idea, no benefit can ever come from a
' spirit.'[1]

The Abipones of South America, so well described
by Dobritzhoffer, had some vague notions of an evil
spirit, but none of a good one.[2] The Coroados[3] of
Brazil ' acknowledge no cause of good, or no God, but
' only an evil principle, which . . . . leads him astray,
' vexes him, brings him into difficulty and danger, and
' even kills him.'

In Virginia and Florida the evil spirit was worshipped and not the good, because the former might be
propitiated, while the latter was sure to do all the good
he could.[4] So also the 'Cemis' of the West Indian
Islands were regarded as evil, and ' reputed to be the
' authors of every calamity that affects the human
' race.'[5] The Redskin, says Carver,[6] ' lives in continual
' apprehension of the unkind attacks of spirits, and to
' avert them has recourse to charms, to the fantastic
' ceremonies of his priest, or the powerful influence of
' his manitous. Fear has of course a greater share in
' his devotions than gratitude, and he pays more atten-
' tion to deprecating the wrath of the evil than securing
' the favour of the good beings.' The Tartars of Kats-
chiutzi also considered the evil spirit to be more powerful
than the good.[7] The West Coast negroes, according to

---

[1] Schweinfurth's Heart of Africa, vol. i. p. 300.

[2] Dobritzhoffer, loc. cit., vol. ii. pp. 35, 64.

[3] Spix and Martius, vol. ii. p. 242.

[4] Müller's Gesch. d. American. Urreligionen, p. 151.

[5] Robertson's America, book iv. p. 124.

[6] Travels, p. 388.

[7] Pallas, vol. iii. p. 433.

Artus,' represent their deities as ' black and mischievous,
' delighting to torment them in various ways.' They said
' that the Europeans' God was very good, who gave them
' such blessings, and treated them like his children.
' Others asked, murmuring, why God was not as kind to
' them?  Why did not he supply them with woollen
' and linen cloth, iron, brass, and such things, as well as
' the Dutch?  The Dutch answered, that God had not
' neglected them, since he had sent them gold, palm-
' wine, fruits, corn, oxen, goats, hens, and many other
' things necessary to life, as tokens of his bounty.  But
' there was no persuading them these things came from
' God.  They said the earth, and not God, gave them
' gold, which was dug out of its bowels; that the earth
' yielded them maize and rice, and that not without
' the help of their own labour ; that for fruits they were
' obliged to the Portuguese, who had planted the trees ;
' that their cattle brought them young ones, and the
' sea furnished them with fish; that, however, in all
' these their own industry and labour were required,
' without which they must starve ; so that they could
' not see how they were obliged to God for any of those
' benefits.'  When Burton spoke to the Eastern negroes
about the Deity, they eagerly asked where he was to be
found, in order that they might kill him ; for they said,
' Who but he lays waste our homes, and kills our wives
' and cattle?'  The following expression of Eesa feelings,
overheard by Burton, gives a dreadful illustration of
this idea.  An old woman, belonging to that Arab tribe,
having a toothache, offered up the following prayer :
' Oh, Allah, may thy teeth ache like mine!  Oh, Allah,

¹ Astley's Collection of Voyages, vol. ii. p. 604.

'may thy gums be as sore as mine!' Can this be called 'religion'? Surely in spirit it is the very reverse.

Dr. Nixon, first Bishop of Tasmania, tells[1] us that among the natives of that country 'no trace can be 'found of the existence of any religious usage, or even 'sentiment amongst them; unless, indeed, we may call by 'that name the dread of a malignant and destructive 'spirit, which seems to have been their predominant, if 'not their only, feeling on the subject.'

In New Zealand,[2] each disease was regarded as being caused by a particular god; thus 'Tonga was the god 'who caused headache and sickness: he took up his 'abode in the forehead. Mako-Tiki, a lizard god, was 'the source of all pains in the breast; Tu-tangata-kino 'was the god of the stomach; Titi-hai occasioned pains 'in the ancles and feet; Rongomai and Tuparitapu 'were the gods of consumption; Koro-kio presided over 'childbirth.'

In North America, among the Carolina tribes, 'the 'theory was that all distempers were caused by evil 'spirits.'[3]

'Sickness,' says Yate,[4] 'is brought on by the '"Atua," who, when he is angry, comes to them in the 'form of a lizard, enters their inside, and preys upon 'their vitals till they die. Hence they use incantations 'over the sick, with the expectation of either pro-'pitiating the angry deity or of driving him away; for 'the latter of which purposes they make use of the

[1] Bonwick's Daily Life of the Tasmanians, p. 172.
[2] Taylor's New Zealand and its Inhabitants, p. 34. Shortland, loc. cit., p. 114.
[3] Jones's Antiquities of the Southern Indians, p. 31.
[4] Yate's New Zealand, p. 141.

'most threatening and outrageous language.' The
Stiens of Cambodia believe 'in an evil genius, and
'attribute all disease to him. If anyone be suffering
'from illness, they say it is the demon tormenting
'him; and, with this idea, make, night and day, an
'insupportable noise around the patient.'[1]

The Koussa Kaffirs,[2] says Lichtenstein, ascribe all
their diseases 'to one of three causes: either to being
'enchanted by an enemy; to the anger of certain beings,
'whose abode appears to be in the rivers; or to the
'power of evil spirits.' Among the Kols of Nagpore,
as Colonel E. T. Dalton tells us, 'all disease in men
'and in cattle is attributed to one of two causes: the
'wrath of some evil spirit who has to be appeased, or
'the spell of some witch or sorcerer.'[3] The same, indeed, is the case with the aboriginal races of India
generally. 'Of a supreme and beneficent God,' says
Hunter,[4] 'the Santal has no conception. His religion
'is a religion of terror and degradation. Hunted and
'driven from country to country by a superior race, he
'cannot understand how a Being can be more powerful
'than himself without wishing to harm him.' The
Circassians[5] and some of the Chinese[6] have also the
same belief.

Hence it is that mad people are in many countries
looked on with so much reverence, since they are regarded as the special abode of some deity.[7] Savages

[1] Mouhot's Travels in the Central Parts of Indo-China, vol. i. p.
250.
[2] Lichtenstein, vol. ii. p. 257.
[3] Trans. Ethn. Soc., N.S., 1868,
p. 30.
[4] Annals of Rural Bengal, p. 181.
[5] Klemm, Allg. Cult. d. Mensch.,
vol. iv. p. 30.
[6] Trans. Ethn. Soc. 1870, p.
21.
[7] See Cook, Voyage to the
Pacific, vol. ii. p. 18.

who believe that diseases are owing to magic naturally
conclude that death is so too. Far from having realised
to themselves the idea of a future life, they have not even
learnt that death is the natural end of this one. We
find a very general conviction among savages that there
is no such thing as natural death, and that when a man
dies without being wounded he must be the victim of
magic.

Thus Mr. Lang, [1] speaking of the Australians, says
that whenever a native dies, 'no matter how evident it
' may be that death has been the result of natural
' causes, it is at once set down that the defunct was
' bewitched by the sorcerers of some neighbouring tribe.'
Among the natives of Southern Africa no one is supposed to die naturally.[2]  The Bechuanas, says Philip,
' and all the Kaffir tribes, have no idea of any man
' dying except from hunger, violence, or witchcraft.
' If a man die even at the age of ninety, if he do not die
' of hunger or by violence, his death is imputed to
' sorcery or to witchcraft, and blood is required to
' expiate or avenge it.'[3]  So also Battel tells us that
on the Guinea Coast 'none on any account dieth,
' but that some other has bewitched them to death.'[4]
Dobritzhoffer[5] mentions that, 'even if an Abipon die
' from being pierced with many wounds, or from having
' his bones broken, or his strength exhausted by ex-
' treme old age, his countrymen all deny that wounds

[1] Lecture on the Aborigines of Australia, p. 14. See also Oldfield's Trans. Ethn. Soc., N.S., vol. iii. p. 230.

[2] Chapman's Travels in Africa, vol. i. p. 47.

[3] Philip's South Africa, vol. i. p. 118.

[4] Adventures of Andrew Battel, Pinkerton, vol. xvi. p. 331. See also Astley, vol. ii. p. 300.

[5] Loc. cit., vol. ii. p. 84.

'or weakness occasioned his death, and anxiously try to
'discover by which of the jugglers, and for what reason,
'he was killed.'    Stevenson[1] states that in South
America 'the Indians never believe that death is
'owing to natural causes, but that it is the effect of
'sorcery and witchcraft.    Thus on the death of an in-
'dividual one or more diviners are consulted, who
'generally name the enchanter, and are so implicitly
'believed, that the unfortunate object of their caprice
'or malice is certain to fall a sacrifice.'    Wallace[2] found
the same idea among the tribes of the Amazons; Müller[3]
mentions it as prevalent among the Dacotahs; Hearne[4]
among the Hudson's Bay Indians.

But though spirits are naturally much to be dreaded
on various accounts, it by no means follows that they
should be conceived as necessarily wiser or more powerful than men.    Of this our table-turners and spirit-
rappers give a modern illustration.    So also the natives
of the Nicobar Islands were in the habit of putting up
scarecrows to frighten the 'Eewees' away from their
villages.[5]    The inhabitants of Kamtschatka, according
to Kotzebue,[6] insult their deities if their wishes are
unfulfilled.    They even feel a contempt for them.    If
Kutka, they say, had not been so stupid, would he
have made inaccessible rocks, and too rapid rivers?[7]
The Lapps, according to Klemm, made idols for their
deities, and placed each in a separate box, on which

[1] Travels in South America, vol. i. p. 60.

[2] Loc. cit., p. 500.

[3] Amer. Urreligionen, p. 82.

[4] Loc. cit., p. 338.

[5] Voyage of the Novara, vol. ii. p. 60.

[6] Loc. cit., vol. ii. p. 13.

[7] Klemm, Cult. d. Menschen, vol. ii. p. 318. Müller's Des. de toutes les Nations de l'Empire Russe, pt. iii. p. 92.

they indicated the name of the deity, so that each might know its own box.[1]

Vancouver[2] mentions that the inhabitants of Owhyhee were seriously offended with their deity for permitting the death of a popular young chief named Whokaa. Yate observes[3] that the New Zealanders, attributing certain diseases to the attacks of the Atua, endeavour either to propitiate or drive him away; in the latter case ' they make use of the most threatening ' and outrageous language, sometimes telling their deity ' that they will kill and eat him.'

In India the seven great ' Rishis ' or penitents are described in some of the popular tales as even superior to the gods. One of them is said to have ' paid a visit ' to each of the three principal divinities of India, and ' began his interview by giving each of them a kick! ' His object was to know how they would demean them-' selves, and to find out their temper, by the conduct ' which they would adopt upon such a salutation. The ' penitents always maintained a kind of superiority over ' the gods, and punished them severely when they found ' them in fault.' [4]

The negro of Guinea beats his Fetich if his wishes are not complied with, and hides him in his waist-cloth, if about to do anything of which he is ashamed, so that the Fetich may not be able to see what is going on.[5]

During a storm the Bechuanas cursed the Deity for

---

[1] *Loc. cit.,* vol. iii. p. 81.

[2] Voyage of Discovery, vol. iii. p. 14.

[3] Account of New Zealand, p. 141. D'Urville's Voyage de l'Astro-labe, vol. iii. pp. 245, 440, 470.

[4] Dubois, *loc. cit.,* p. 301.

[5] Astley's Collection of Voyages, vol. ii. p. 608. Tuckey's Exp. to the Zaire, p. 377.

sending thunder;[1] the Mincopies[2] and the Namaquas
shot poisoned arrows at storms to drive them away.[3]
When the Basuto (Kaffir) is on a marauding expedition
he 'gives utterance to those cries and hisses in which
'cattle-drivers indulge when they drive a herd before
'them; thinking in this manner to persuade the poor
'divinities (of the country they are attacking) that he
'is bringing cattle to their worshippers, instead of
'coming to take it from them.'[4]

According to Thomson,[5] the natives of Cambodia
assumed that the Deity did not understand foreign
languages. Franklin[6] says that the Cree Indians treat
their deity, whom they call Kepoochikawn, 'with con-
'siderable familiarity, interlarding their most solemn
'speeches with expostulations and threats of neglect if
'he fails in complying with their requests.' The North
Australian native[7] will not go near graves 'at night by
'himself; but when they are obliged to pass them they
'carry a fire-stick to keep off the spirit of darkness.'

The Kyoungtha of Chittagong are Buddhists. Their
village temples contain a small stand of bells and an
image of Boodh, which the villagers generally worship
morning and evening, 'first ringing the bells to let him
'know that they are there.'[8] The Sinto temples of the
Sun Goddess in Japan also contain a bell, 'intended to
'arouse the goddess and to awaken her attention to the

[1] Chapman's Travels in Africa, vol. i. p. 45.
[2] Day, p. 172.
[3] Wood's Natural History of Man, vol. i. p. 307.
[4] Casalis' Basutos, p. 253.
[5] Trans. Ethn. Soc., vol. vi. p. 230.
[6] Visit to the Polar Seas, vol. iv. p. 181.
[7] Keppel's Visit to the Indian Archipelago, vol. ii. p. 182.
[8] Lewin's Hill Tracts of Chittagong, p. 30.

'prayers of her worshippers.'[1]    According to the Brahmans,[2] 'two things are indispensably necessary 'to the sacrificer in performing the ceremony : several 'lighted lamps and a bell.'

The Shamans among the Tonguses and Buraets, according to Müller, 'font résonner le tambour magique 'pour convoquer les Dieux, les Diables, et les Esprits, 'et pour leurs rendre attentifs.'[3]  The Tartars of the Altai picture to themselves the Deity as an old man, with a long beard, and dressed in the uniform of a Russian officer of dragoons.[4]

Even the Greeks and Romans believed stories very derogatory, not only to the moral character but to the intellect and power of their deities.  Thus they were liable to defeat from mortals ; Mars, though the God of War, was wounded by Diomed and fled away howling with pain.  They had little or no power over the elements ; they had no foreknowledge, and were often represented as inferior, both morally and mentally, to men.  Even Homer does not seem to have embraced the idea of omnipotence.[5]

Again, Diomed not only wounds Venus in the hand but addresses her in most insulting terms : —

> Daughter of Jove, from battle fields retire ;
> Enough for thee weak women to delude ;
> If war thou seek'st, the lesson thou shalt learn
> Shall cause thee shudder but to hear it named.[6]

---

[1] Smith's Ten Weeks in Japan, p. 40.  See also Gutzlaff's Three Voyages to China, p. 273.

[2] Dubois, The People of India, p. 400.

[3] Des. de toutes les Nations de l'Empire Russe, pt. iii. p. 139.

[4] Müller's Des. de toutes les Nat. de l'Emp. Russe, pt. iii. p. 142.

[5] Gladstone's Juventus Mundi, pp. 108, 228.  See also Müller's Sci. System of Mythology, p. 202.

[6] Iliad, Lord Derby's translation, v. 397.

Venus flies to Dione, who says :—

> Have patience, dearest child; though much enforced,
> Restrain thine anger; we, in heaven who dwell,
> Have much to bear from mortals; and ourselves
> Too oft upon each other sufferings lay.
> Mars had his sufferings; by Alœus' sons,
> Otus and Ephialtes, strongly bound,
> He thirteen months in brazen fetters lay :
> And there had pined away the God of War,
> Insatiate Mars, had not their stepmother,
> The beauteous Eribœa, sought the aid
> Of Hermes; he by stealth released the god,
> Sore worn and wasted by his galling chains.
> Juno too suffered, when Amphitryon's son
> Through her right breast a three-barbed arrow sent.
> Dire, and unheard of, were the pangs she bore.
> Great Pluto's self the stinging arrow felt,
> When that same son of œgis-bearing Jove
> Assailed him in the very gates of hell,
> And wrought him keenest anguish; pierced with pain
> To high Olympus, to the courts of Jove,
> Groaning, he came; the bitter shaft remained
> Deep in his shoulder fixed, and grieved his soul;
> But Pæon's hand with soothing anodynes
> (For death on him was powerless) healed the wound.

In fact, it may truly be said that the savage has a
much greater respect for his chief than for his god.[1]
This low estimate of spirits is shown in a very striking
manner by the behaviour of savages during eclipses. All
over the world we find races of men who believe that
the sun and moon are alive, and who consider that
during eclipses they are either quarrelling with each
other, or attacked by the evil spirits of the air. Hence
it naturally follows, although to us it seems absurd,
that the savage endeavours to assist the sun or moon.
The Greenlanders[2] regard the sun and moon as sister
and brother; the former being the female, and being

---

[1] See Burton's Abbeokuta, vol. i. p. 180.  Dubois, loc. cit., pp. 304, 430.
[2] Crantz, vol. i. p. 232.

constantly pursued by the latter. During an eclipse they think the moon 'goes about among the houses to 'pilfer their skins and eatables, and even to kill those 'people that have not duly observed the rules of absti-'nence. At such times they hide away everything, and 'the men carry chests and kettles on the top of the 'house, and rattle and beat upon them to frighten away 'the moon, and make him return to his place. At an 'eclipse of the sun the women pinch the dogs by the 'ears; if they cry, 'tis a sign that the end of the world 'is not yet come.'

The Iroquois, says Dr. Mitchill,[1] believe that eclipses are caused by a bad spirit, 'who mischievously 'intercepts the light intended to be shed upon the earth 'and its inhabitants. Upon such occasions the greatest 'solicitude exists. All the individuals of the tribe feel 'a strong desire to drive away the demon, and to re-'move thereby the impediment to the transmission of 'luminous rays. For this purpose they go forth, and, 'by crying, shouting, drumming, and the firing of guns, 'endeavour to frighten him. They never fail in their 'object; for by courage and perseverance, they infal-'libly drive him off. His retreat is succeeded by a re-'turn of the obstructed light.'

The Caribs, says Lafitau, accounted for eclipses by supposing either that the moon was ill, or that she was attacked by enemies; these they endeavoured to drive away by dances, by cries, and by the sacred rattle.[2] The Chiquito Indians,[3] according to Dobritzhoffer, think

[1] Archæol. Americana, vol. i. p. 351.
[2] Lafitau, vol. i. pp. 248, 252. Terise, History of the Caribby Islands, p. 272. Depons' Trav. in S. America, vol. i. p. 107.
[3] Loc. cit., vol. ii. p. 84.

that the sun and moon during eclipses are ' cruelly torn
' by dogs, with which they think that the air abounds,
' when they see their light fail; attributing their blood-
' red colour to the bites of these animals.    Accordingly,
' to defend their dear planets from those aërial mastiffs,
' they send a shower of arrows up into the sky, amid
' loud vociferations, at the time of the eclipse.'    When
the Guaycurus, says Charlevoix, ' think themselves
' threatened with a storm, they sally out of their towns,
' the men armed with their maneanns, and the women
' and children howling with all their might; for they
' believe that, by so doing, they put to flight the devil
' that intended to excite it.'[1]    The ancient Peruvians,
also, during eclipses of the moon, used to beat their
dogs in order that by their howlings they might awaken
her out of the swoon into which she was supposed to
have fallen.[2]

The Chinese of Kiatka thought that eclipses were
caused by the evil spirit placing his hand on the moon,
in whose defence they immediately made as much noise
as possible.[3]    The Stiens of Cambodia,[4] like the Cam-
bodians themselves, account for eclipses by the hypothesis ' that some being has swallowed up the sun
' and the moon; and, in order to deliver them, they
' made a frightful noise, beat the tam-tam, uttered
' savage cries, and shot arrows into the air, until the
' sun reappeared.'

During an eclipse the Sumatrans [5] also ' make a loud

[1] History of Paraguay, vol. i. p.
92. See also p. 203.

[2] G. de la Vega, vol. i. p. 181;
Martius, &c. cit., p. 32.

[3] Pallas, vol. iv. p. 220.

[4] Mouhot's Travels in Indo-
China, vol. i. p. 252.

[5] Marsden's History of Sumatra,
p. 194.    Anderson's Mission to
Sumatra, p. 70.

'noise with sounding instruments, to prevent one
'luminary from devouring the other, as the Chinese, to
'frighten away the dragon; a superstition that has its
'source in the ancient systems of astronomy (particu-
'larly the Hindu), where the nodes of the moon are
'identified with the dragon's head and tail. They tell
'of a man in the moon who is continually employed in
'spinning cotton, but that every night a rat gnaws his
'thread, and obliges him to begin his work afresh.'

' In Eastern Africa,' Speke[1] mentions that on one
occasion, ' as there was a partial eclipse of the moon, all
' the Wanguana marched up and down from Rumanika's
' to Nnanagi's huts, singing and beating our tin cook-
' ing-pots to frighten off the spirit of the sun from con-
' suming entirely the chief object of reverence, the
' moon.' Lander[2] mentions that at Boussa, in Central
Africa, an eclipse was attributed to an attack made by
the sun on the moon. During the whole time the
eclipse lasted the natives made as much noise as possible, ' in the hope of being able to frighten away the sun
' to his proper sphere, and leave the moon to enlighten
' the world as at other times.'

I was myself at Darhoot, in Upper Egypt, last year,
during an eclipse of the moon, and the natives fired
guns, either to frighten away the moon's assailants, or,
as some said, out of joy at her escape from danger,
though it may be observed that the firing began during
the eclipse.

I reserve to a future chapter the consideration of
the ideas which prevail among the lower races on the

[1] Speke, p. 243.
[2] R. and I. Landers' Niger Expedition, vol. ii. pp. 180, 181.

Q

subject of the soul; but I must here remark that one of
the difficulties in arriving at any clear conception of the
religious system of the lower races arises from a confusion between a belief in ghosts and that in an immortal
spirit. Yet the two are essentially distinct; and the
spirit is not necessarily regarded as immortal, because
it does not perish with the body. The negroes, for instance, says one of our keenest observers, Captain
Burton, ' believe in a ghost, but not in a spirit; in a
' present immaterial, but not in a future.'[1] Counting
on nothing after the present life, there is for them
no hope beyond the grave. They wail and sorrow
with a burden of despair. 'Amekwisha'—'he is
' finished'—is the East African's last word concerning parent or friend. 'All is done for ever,' sing the
West Africans. The least allusion to loss of life makes
their black skins pale. 'Ah!' they exclaim, 'it is bad
' to die; to leave house and home, wife and children;
' no more to wear soft cloth, nor eat meat, nor smoke
' tobacco.' The Bongos of Soudan have, says Schweinfurth,[2] not the remotest conception of immortality.
They have no more idea of the transmigration of souls,
or any doctrine of the kind, than they have of the
existence of an ocean. The Hudson's Bay Indians,
according to Hearne,[3] a good observer, and one who had
ample means of judging, had no idea of any life after
death.

In other cases the spirit is supposed to survive the
body for a certain time, and to linger about its old

---

[1] Burton, Trans. Ethn. Soc.,    [3] *Loc. cit.*, p. 344. See also
N.S., vol. i. p. 323.        *ante*, p. 140.
[2] Heart of Africa, vol. i. p. 304.

abode. Ask the negro, says M. Du Chaillu,[1] 'where is
' the spirit of his great-grandfather? he says he does
' not know; it is done. Ask him about the spirit of his
' father or brother who died yesterday, then he is full
' of fear and terror; he believes it to be generally near
' the place where the body has been buried, and among
' many tribes the village is removed immediately after
' the death of one of the inhabitants.' The same belief
prevails among the Amazulu Kaffirs, as has been well
shown by Mr. Callaway.[2] They believe that the spirits
of their deceased fathers and brothers still live, because
they appear in dreams; by inverse reasoning, however,
grandfathers are generally regarded as having ceased to
exist.

Bosman mentions that on the Guinea Coast, when
' any considerable person dies, they perplex one another
' with horrid fears, proceeding from an opinion that he
' appears for several nights successively near his late
' dwelling.'[8] Thus it seems that the power of a ghost
after death bears some relation to that which the man
possessed when alive.

For the dead, also, the prospect is cheerless enough.
For instance, according to Livingstone, the natives of
Angola fancy that when dead they will be 'completely
' in the power of the disembodied spirits, and look upon
' the prospect of following them as the greatest of mis-
' fortunes.'[4]

Other negroes think that after death they become
white men[5]—a curious idea, which also occurs in Aus-

[1] Trans. Ethn. Soc., N.S., vol. i.
p. 309.
[2] The Religious System of the
Amazulu, 1869.
[8] Bosman, *loc. cit.*, p. 402.
[4] Travels in S. Africa, p. 440.
[5] Bosman, *loc. cit.*, p. 401.

tralia,[1] in Tasmania,[2] in Tanna,[3] New Guinea,[4] and New Caledonia,[5] that is to say, in at least four of the most distinct human races. Among the Tipperahs of Chittagong, if a man dies away from home, his relatives stretch a thread over all the intermediate streams, so that the spirit of the dead man may return to his own village; it being supposed that 'without assistance 'spirits are unable to cross running water; therefore 'the stream here had been bridged in the manner afore-'said.'[6] We know that a somewhat similar idea existed in Europe, and it occurs also in the Feejee Islands.

Again, some modes of death are supposed to kill not only the body, but the spirit also. Thus a Bushman, having put to death a woman, who was a magician, dashed the head of the corpse to pieces with large stones, buried her, and made a large fire over the grave, for fear, as he explained to Lichtenstein, lest she should rise again and 'trouble him.'[7] Even the New Zealanders believed that a man who was eaten was destroyed, both body and spirit. The same idea evidently influenced the Californian who, as recorded by Mr. Gibbs, did not dispute the immortality of the whites who buried their dead, but could not believe the same of his own people, because they were in the habit of burning them.[8]

In these cases it will be observed that the existence

[1] Lang's Queensland, pp. 346, 354.

[2] Bonwick's Daily Life of the Tasmanians, p. 184.

[3] Turner's Nineteen Years in Polynesia, p. 424.

[4] Gill, Journ. R. Geog. Soc. 1873, p. 33.

[5] Brenchley's Cruise of the 'Curaçoa,' p. 312. See also Burton's Dahome, vol. ii. p. 165.

[6] Lewin's Hill Tracts of Chittagong, p. 84.

[7] Lichtenstein, vol. ii. p. 61.

[8] Schoolcraft's Indian Tribes, Pt. III. p. 107.

of the ghost depends upon the manner of death, and the mode of burial. This is no doubt absurd, but it is not illogical. The savage's idea of a spirit is something ethereal indeed, but not altogether immaterial, and consequently it may be injured by violence. Some races believe in ghosts of the living, as well as of the dead. For instance, the Feejeeans[1] believe 'that the spirit of 'a man who still lives will leave the body to trouble 'other people when asleep. When anyone faints or 'dies, their spirit, it is said, may sometimes be brought 'back by calling after it.'

Even when the ideas of a soul and of future life are more developed, they are far from always taking the direction of our beliefs. Thus the Caribs and Redskins believe that a man has more than one soul; to this they are probably led by the pulsation of the heart and the arteries, which they regard as evidences of independent life. Thus also they account for inconsistencies of behaviour.

The belief in ghosts, then, is essentially different from our notions of a future life. Ghosts are mortal, they haunt burial-grounds and hover round their own graves. Even when a higher stage has been gained, the place of departed souls is not a heaven, but merely a better earth.

Divination and sorcery are so widely distributed that they may almost be said to be universal. Their characteristics are so well known and so similar all over the world, that I shall only give a few suggestive illustrations.

[1] Fiji and the Fijians, vol. i. p. 242.

Whipple[1] thus describes a scene of divination among
the Cherokees. The priest, having concluded an elo-
quent address, took ‘ a curiously wrought bowl, alleged
‘ to be of great antiquity; he filled it with water and
‘ placed the black substance within, causing it to move
‘ from one side to the other, and from bottom to top,
‘ by a word. Alluding, then, to danger and foes, the
‘ enchanted mineral fled from the point of his knife;
‘ but as he began to speak of peace and security, it
‘ turned toward and clung to it, till lifted entirely from
‘ the water. The priest finally interpreted the omen by
‘ informing the people that peace was in the ascendant,
‘ no enemy being near.’ In West Africa[2] they have a
mode of divination with nuts, ‘ which they pretend to
‘ take up by guess, and let fall again ; after which they
‘ tell them, and form their answers according as the
‘ numbers are even or odd.’ The negroes of Egba[3]
consult Shango by ‘ throwing sixteen pierced cowries :
‘ if eight fall upwards and eight downwards, it is peace;
‘ if all are upwards, it is also a good sign; and *vice
‘ versâ*, if all fall with their teeth to the ground, it
‘ is war.’

The Lapps have a curious mode of divination. They
put a shoulder-blade in the fire, and then foretell the
future by the arrangement of the cracks (figs. 15–17).
The same custom exists among the Mongols[4] and Tonguses[5] of Siberia, the Affghans,[6] the Bedouins, and even

[1] Report on the Indian Tribes, p.
35.
[2] Astley’s Collection of Voyages,
vol. ii. p. 674.
[3] Abbeokuta, vol. i. p. 188.
[4] Klemm, Cult. der Mensch., vol.

iii. p. 100.
[5] Müller’s Des. de toutes les
Nat. de l’Emp. Russe, Pt. III. p.
103.
[6] Masson’s Journeys in Beloo-
chistan, vol. iii. p. 334.

in our own country.[1]   The lines vary of course greatly,
still there are certain principal cracks which usually
occur.   The following figures of Kalmuck specimens
are copied from Klemm, who explains, after Pallas, the
meaning of the various lines.

FIG. 15.

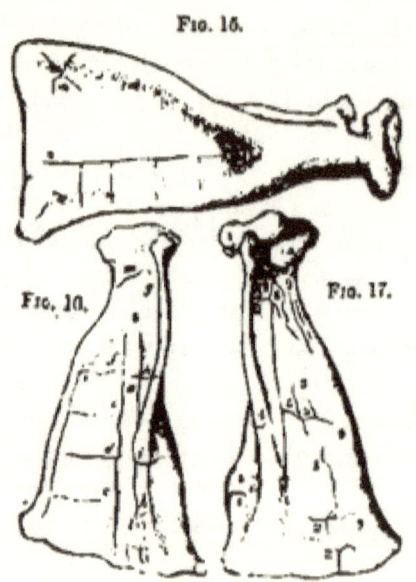

FIG. 16.                    FIG. 17.

SHOULDER-BLADES PREPARED FOR DIVINATION.   (Klemm, Culturg. der
Menschheit, vol. iii, p. 200.)

Other Yakuts profess to foretell the future by the
lines of the palm of the hand.[2]

The Chipewyans of North America also make their
magic drawings on shoulder-blades, which they then

[1] Tylor's Primitive Culture, vol.     de l'Empire de Russe, Pt. III. p.
ii. p. 113.                                          163.
[2] Müller's Des. de tout. les Nat.

throw into the fire.[1] Williams[2] describes various modes of divination practised in Feejee.

Canon Callaway gives an interesting account of divination as practised among the Zulus, and mentions one case in which the persons enquiring of the magician gave him no clue to the answer they expected, upon which he gravely told them that 'they did not know 'how to enquire of a diviner,' so he would send his servant to hear their case, and put the enquiries for them. An amusing illustration of the manner in which people allow themselves to be deceived.[3]

Dr. Anderson mentions a similar illustration from West Yunan.[4] 'Three men had gone to the Kakhyen 'hills, and a report having reached their families that 'one of them had died, the old hags·were deciding 'upon the truth of the rumour, and determining which 'of the men it was who had passed into Nâtland. To 'arrive at this, they had taken, for each of the men 'whose fates were to be determined, a small piece of 'cotton-wool, and strung it through the eye of a needle; 'and giving to each a special mark and the name of a 'man, they had let the needles gently into the water in 'which they were suspended by the cotton float. It 'takes some time before the cotton is so thoroughly 'wetted as to sink, but the needle which first drops to 'the bottom consigns the unfortunate whose name it 'bears to the land of forgetfulness.'

In New Zealand, before a warlike expedition is

[1] Tanner's Narrative, p. 102.
[2] Fiji and the Fijians, vol. 1. p. 228. See also Mariner's Tonga Islands, vol. ii. p. 239.
[3] Religious System of the Amazulu, Pt. III. p. 328.
[4] Exped. to Western Yunan, p. 230.

undertaken, the natives sometimes plant sticks in the
ground in two rows, one of which denotes their own
party, the other that of the enemy.  If the wind blows
the enemy's sticks backwards, they will be defeated ;
if forwards, they will be victorious; if obliquely, the
expedition will be indecisive.  The same criterion is
applied to their own sticks.[1]

This is a case of divination, but from it to sorcery is
a short and obvious step.  When once it is granted
that the fall of a stick certainly preludes that of the
person it represents, it follows that by upsetting the
stick his death can be caused.

We find a very similar idea in the Western Highlands of Scotland.  In the 'Sea Maiden' a mermaid
appears to a fisherman, and gives him three seeds,
which are to produce three trees, which ' will be a sign,
' when one of the sons dies, one of the trees will
' wither ;' and this accordingly took place.[2]  A supposed prophet of the Shawnees (North America) sent
word to Tanner that the fire in his lodge was intimately connected with his life.  ' Henceforth,' said he,
' the fire must  never be suffered to go out in
' your lodge.  Summer and winter, day and night, in
' the storm, or when it is calm, you must remember
' that the life in your body and the fire in your lodge
' are the same.  If you suffer your fire to be extin-
' guished, at that moment your life will be at an end.'[3]

When the Zulu soldiers go to battle, their wives
hang up against the walls of their huts ' a simple mat
' of rushes which they have themselves plaited.  As

[1] Yate's New Zealand, p. 91.        Highlands, vol. i. p. 71.
[2] Campbell's Tales of the West      [3] Tanner's Narrative, p. 156.

'long as that casts a little shade upon the wall, the
'credulous woman believes that her husband is safe;
'but when it ceases to do so the sight of it is produc-
'tive only of grief.'[1]

Father Merolla mentions a case in which a Congo
(negro) witch tried to destroy him. With this object
she dug a hole in the ground, 'and I resolved,' says the
worthy Father,[2] 'not to stand long in one place, thereby
'to avoid the design she had upon me to bewitch me
'to death, that having been the reason of her making a
'hole in the earth. It seems their custom is, that when
'they have a mind to bewitch anyone mortally, they
'put a certain herb or plant into the hole they have so
'dug; which, as it perishes or decays, so the vigour
'and spirits of the person they have a design upon
'will fail and decay.' In Feejee[3] 'one mode of operat-
'ing is to bury a cocoa-nut, with the eye upwards,
'beneath the temple hearth, on which a fire is kept
'constantly burning; and as the life of the nut is
'destroyed, so the health of the person it represents
'will fail, till death ensues. At Matuku there is a
'grove sacred to the god Tokalau, the wind. The
'priest promises the destruction of any hated person in
'four days if those who wish his death bring a portion
'of his hair, dress, or food which he has left. This
'priest keeps a fire burning, and approaches the place
'on his hands and knees. If the victim bathe before
'the fourth day the spell is broken. The most common
'method, however, is the Vakadranikau, or compound-

---

[1] Arbousset's Tour to the Cape
of Good Hope, p. 146.

[2] Pinkerton, vol. xvi. p. 200.

[3] Fiji and the Fijians, vol. i. p.
248.

'ing of certain leaves supposed to possess a magical
'power, and which are wrapped in other leaves, or put
'into a small bamboo case, and buried in the garden
'of the person to be bewitched, or hidden in the thatch
'of his house.  The native imagination is so absolutely
'under the control of the fear of these charms, that
'persons, hearing that they were the objects of such
'spells, have lain down on their mats, and died through
'fear.  Those who have reason to suspect others of
'plotting against them avoid eating in their presence,
'or are careful to leave no fragment of food behind ;
'they also dispose their garments so that no part can
'be removed.  Most natives on cutting their hair hide
'what is cut off in the thatch of their own houses.
'Some build themselves a small house, and surround
'it with a moat, believing that a little water will
'neutralise the charms which are directed against them.'
In North America, to ensure a successful war, courtship, or hunt, the Indians make a rude drawing, or a
little image to represent the man, woman, or animal;
then medicine is applied to it; or, if the design is to
cause death, the heart is pierced.[1]  The Romans, when
sacrifices were forbidden, used as a substitute to throw
dolls into the Tiber, and in India the magicians make
small figures of mud, on the breasts of which they
write the names of those whom they wish to annoy.
They then 'pierce the images with thorns, or mutilate
'them, so as to communicate a corresponding injury
'to the person represented.'[2]

In other cases, the possession of a person's name is

[1] Tanner's Narrative, p. 174.
[2] Dubois, The People of India, p. 347.

sufficient; and, indeed, all over the world we find more or less confusion between a thing or a person, and its' or his name. Hence the importance attached in North America, Polynesia, and South Africa to an exchange of names. Hence, as for instance among the Negroes[1] and Australians,[2] we often find a person's real name concealed, lest a knowledge of it should give a power over the person.

In one of the despatches intercepted during our war with Nepaul, Gouree Sah sent orders to 'find out the 'name of the Commander of the British Army; write 'it upon a piece of paper; take it, and some rice and 'turmeric, say the great incantation three times; 'having said it, send for some plum-tree wood and 'therewith burn it.'[3]

Even the Romans, when they besieged a town, had a curious ceremony founded on the same idea. They invoked the tutelar deity of the city, and tempted him by the offer of rewards and sacrifices 'to betray his friends and votaries. In that cere-'mony the name of the tutelar deity was thought of 'importance, and for that reason the tutelar deity of 'Rome was a profound secret.'[4] Valerius Soranus is 'said to have been put to death for daring to di-'vulge it.'[5]

Sumatra gives us a curious instance of long survival of this idea in a somewhat advanced community. 'A 'Sumatran[6] ever scrupulously abstains from pronounc-

[1] Burton's Dahome, vol. ii. p. 244.

[2] Prichard's Nat. His. of Man, vol. ii. p. 492.

[3] Fraser's Tour to the Himalas, p. 530.

[4] Lord Kames' History of Man, vol. iv. p. 220. Ortolan's Justinian, vol. i. p. 8.

[5] Pliny, Bk. III. ch. ix.

[6] Marsden's History of Sumatra, p. 286.

' ing his own name ; not, as I understand, from any
' motive of superstition, but merely as a punctilio in
' manners. It occasions him infinite embarrassment
' when a stranger, unacquainted with their customs,
' requires it of him. As soon as he recovers from his
' confusion he solicits the interposition of his neigh-
' bour. He is never addressed, except in the case of a
' superior dictating to his dependant, in the second
' person, but always in the third ; using his name or
' title instead of the pronoun ; and when these are un-
' known, a general title of respect is substituted, and
' they say, for instance, "apa orang kaya punia suka,"
' " what is his honour's pleasure," for "what is your,
' " or your honour's pleasure." When criminals or
' other ignominious persons are spoken to, use is made
' of the pronoun personal kau (a contraction of angkau),
' particularly expressive of contempt.'

Generally, however, it was considered indispensable
that the sorcerer should possess ' something connected
' with the body of the object of vengeance. The parings
' of the nails, a lock of the hair, the saliva from the
' mouth, or other secretions from the body, or else a
' portion of the food which the person was to eat. This
' was considered as the vehicle by which the demon
' entered the person, who afterwards became possessed.
' It was called the tubu, growing or causing to grow.
' When procured, the tars was performed; the sorcerer
' took the hair, saliva, or other substance that had
' belonged to his victim to his house, or marae, performed
' his incantations over it, and offered his prayers ; the
' demon was then supposed to enter the tubu, and through
' it the individual, who afterwards became possessed.' [1]

[1] Williams' Polynesian Researches, vol. ii. p. 228.

Speaking of New Zealand, Taylor[1] says that a ' per-
' son who wished to bewitch another sought to obtain
' something belonging to him—a lock of hair, a portion
' of his garment, or even some of his food; this being
' possessed, he uttered certain karakias over it, and then
' buried it; as the article decayed, the individual also
' was supposed to waste away. This was sure to be
' the case if the victim heard of it; fear quickly accom-
' plishing his enemy's wish.    The person who be-
' witched another remained three days without eating;
' on the fourth he ate, and his victim died.'

So also Seemann[2] tells us that ' if a Feejeean wishes
' to cause the destruction of an individual by other
' means than open violence or secret poison, the case is
' put in the hands of one of these sorcerers, care being
' taken to let this fact be generally and widely known.
' The sorcerer now proceeds to obtain any article that
' has once been in the possession of the person to be
' operated upon.    These articles are then burnt with
' certain leaves, and if the reputation of the sorcerer be
' sufficiently powerful, in nine cases out of ten the
' nervous fears of the individual to be punished will
' bring on disease, if not death: a similar process is
' applied to discover thieves.'

Mr. Turner gives a very similar account of disease-
making as practised in Tanna.[3]  Sir G. Grey thus describes a scene of witchcraft in New Zealand: ' The
' priests [4] then dug a long pit, termed the pit of wrath,

---

[1] New Zealand and its Inhabitants, pp. 80, 167.  See also Shortland's Traditions of the New Zealanders, p. 117.

[2] A Mission to Viti, p. 189.
[3] Nineteen Years in Polynesia,
p. 90.
[4] Polynesian Mythology, p. 108.

' into which by their long enchantments they might
' bring the spirits of their enemies, and hang them and
' destroy them there; and when they had dug the pit,
' muttering the necessary incantations, they took large
' shells in their hands to scrape the spirits of their
' enemies into the pit with, whilst they muttered en-
' chantments; and when they had done this they
' scraped the earth into the pit again to cover them up,
' and beat down the earth with their hands, and crossed
' the pit with enchanted cloths, and wove baskets of
' flax-leaves to hold the spirits of the foes which they
' had thus destroyed, and each of these acts they
' accompanied with proper spells.'

The Tasmanians [1] ' procured something belonging to
' the unfortunate object of their wrath, wrapped it in
' fat, placed it before the fire, and expected that as the
' fat dissolved before the heat, so would the health of
' the party decline.'

In North America, also, 'a hair from the head of
' the victim ' is supposed to increase greatly the efficacy
of charms, and the same idea occurs at the Cape thus
Livingstone tells [2] us that among the Makololo ' when a
' man has his hair cut, he is careful to burn it, or bury
' it secretly, lest, falling into the hands of one who has
' an evil eye, or is a witch, it should be used as a charm
to afflict him with headache;' indeed, no one can read
a book of African travels without being struck by the
great dread of witchcraft felt by the natives of that
continent.

We cannot wonder that savages believe in witch-

[1] Bonwick's Daily Life of the
Tasmanians, p. 178.

[2] Expedition to the Zambesi, p.
46.

craft, since even the most civilised races have not long,
nor entirely, ceased to do so.

Like our spirit-rappers and table-turners, the Chinese
magicians,[1] 'though they have never seen the person
'who consults them, tell his name, and all the cir-
'cumstances of his family; in what manner his house is
'situated, how many children he has, their names and
'age; with a hundred other particulars, which may be
'naturally enough supposed known to the demons, and
'are strangely surprising to weak and credulous minds
'among the vulgar.

'Some of these conjurors, after invoking the demons,
'cause the figures of the chief of their sect, and of their
'idols, to appear in the air. Formerly they could make
'a pencil write of itself, without anybody touching it,
'upon paper or sand, the answers to questions. They
'likewise cause all people of any house to pass in review
'in a large vessel of water; wherein they also show the
'changes that shall happen in the empire, and the ima-
'ginary dignities to which those shall be advanced who
'embrace their sect.'

In all parts of India, says De Faira,' 'there are pro-
'digious wizards. When Vasco de Gama was sailing
'upon that discovery, some of them at Kalekût showed
'people, in basins of water, the three ships he had with
'him. When Don Francisco de Almeyda, the first
'viceroy of India, was returning to Portugal, some
'witches of Kochin told him he should not pass the
'Cape of Good Hope; and there he was buried.' (This
is strained a little; for he did pass the Cape, and was

[1] Astley's Collection of Voyages,          [2] Quoted in Astley's Collection
vol. iv. p. 205.                              of Voyages, vol. i. p. 68.

buried at the bay of Saldanna, some leagues beyond, as will be seen hereafter.) 'What follows is still more ' extraordinary. At Maskat there are such sorcerers ' that they eat the inside of a thing, only fixing their ' eyes upon it. With their sight they draw out the ' entrails of any human body, and so kill many people. ' One of these fascinators, fixing his eyes on a bateka, ' or water-melon, sucked out the inside; for, being cut ' open to try the experiment, it was found empty; and ' the wizard, to satisfy the spectators, vomited it up ' again.'

Father Merolla,[1] a Capuchin 'missioner,' tells quite gravely the following story. The army of Sogno having captured a neighbouring town, found in it a large cock with a ring of iron round one leg. This they killed, cut in pieces, and put into a pot to boil; when, however, they thought to eat it, 'the boiled pieces of the cock, ' though sodden, and near dissolved, began to move ' about, and unite into the form they were in before, ' and being so united, the restored cock immediately ' raised himself up, and jumped out of the platter upon ' the ground, where he walked about as well as when he ' was first taken. Afterwards he leaped upon an ad-' joining wall, where he became new-feathered all of a ' sudden, and then took his flight to a tree hard by, ' where, fixing himself, he, after three claps of his wings, ' made a most hideous noise, and then disappeared. ' Everyone may easily imagine what a terrible fright ' the spectators were in at this sight, who, leaping with ' a thousand Ave-Marias in their mouths from the place

---

[1] Voyage to Congo, Pinkerton, vol. xv. p. 220.

' where this had happened, were contented to observe
' most of the particulars at a distance.'

To doubt the reality of witchcraft, says Lafitau,[1]
' est une industrie des athées, et un effet de cet esprit
' d'irréligion qui fait aujourd'hui des progrès si sensibles
' dans le monde, d'avoir détruit en quelque sorte dans
' l'idée de ceux mêmes qui se piquent d'avoir de la
' religion, qu'il se trouve des hommes qui ayent com-
' merce avec les démons par la voye des enchantemens
' et de la magie.  On a attaché à cette opinion une
' certaine faiblesse d'esprit à la croire, qui fait qu'on ne
' la tolère plus que dans les femmelettes et dans le bas
' peuple, ou dans les prêtres et dans les religieux, qu'on
' suppose avoir intérêt à entretenir ces visions popu-
' laires qu'un homme de sens auroit honte d'avouer.
' Pour établir cependant cet esprit d'incrédulité, il faut
' que ces prétendus esprits forts veuillent s'aveugler au
' milieu de la lumière, qu'ils renversent l'Ancien et le
' Nouveau Testament, qu'ils contredisent toute l'anti-
' quité, l'histoire sacrée et la profane.  On trouve par-
' tout des témoignages de ce commerce des hommes
' avec les divinités du paganisme, ou pour mieux dire
' avec les démons.'

Lafitau does not, indeed, deny that some wizards were
impostors, but he maintains that ' ce seroit rendre le
' monde trop sot, que de vouloir le supposer pendant
' plusieurs siècles la dupe de quelques misérables joueurs
' de gobelets.'  Nay, he even maintained[2] that America
was, for some mysterious reason, handed over to the
devil, and accounted for the remarkable similarity
between some of the religious ceremonies, &c., in the

new and old worlds, by the hypothesis that ' le démon,
' jaloux de la gloire de Dieu, et du bonheur de l'homme,
' a toujours été attentif à dérober à l'un le culte qui lui
' est dû, et à perdre l'autre, en le rendant son adorateur.
' Pour cela il a érigé autel contre autel, et a affecté de
' maintenir le culte qu'il vouloit se faire rendre par les
' effets d'une puissance surhumaine, qui imposassent par
' le merveilleux, et qui fussent imités et copiés d'après
' ceux dont Dieu donnoit à son peuple des témoignages
' si authentiques par l'evidence des miracles qu'il faisoit
' en sa faveur.'

Father Labat [1] also observes, ' Qu'on exagère souvent
' dans ce qu'on en dit ; mais je crois qu'il faut convenir
' que tout ce qu'on dit n'est pas entièrement faux, quoi-
' qu'il ne soit peut-être pas entièrement vrai. Je suis
' aussi persuadé qu'il y a des faits d'une vérité très-con-
' stante ;' and after mentioning four of these supposed
facts, he concludes, ' Il me semble que ces quatre faits
' suffisent pour prouver qu'il y a véritablement des gens
' qui ont commerce avec le diable, et qui se servent de
' lui en bien des choses.'

Even among our recent missionaries some, according
to Williams, believed that the Polynesian wizards really
possessed supernatural powers, and were ' agents of the
' infernal powers.' [2] Nay, Williams himself thought it
' not impossible.'

We may well be surprised that Europeans should
believe in such things, and missionaries so credulous
and ignorant ought, one might suppose, rather to learn
than to teach ; on the other hand, it is not surprising

---

[1] Voyage aux Iles de l'Amérique,      [2] Polynesian Researches, vol. ii.
vol. ii. p. 57.      p. 226.

that savages should believe in witchcraft, nor even that the wizards should believe in themselves.

We must indeed by no means suppose that sorcerers are always, or indeed generally, impostors.

The Shamans of Siberia are, says Wrangel,[1] by no means 'ordinary deceivers, but a pyschological pheno-
' menon, well deserving of attention. Whenever I have
' seen them operate they have left me with a long-con-
' tinued and gloomy impression. The wild look, the
' bloodshot eyes, the labouring breast and convulsive
' utterance, the seemingly involuntary distortion of the
' face and the whole body, the streaming hair, even the
' hollow sound of the drum, all contributed to the effect;
' and I can well understand that the whole should ap-
' pear to the uncivilised spectator as the work of evil
' spirits.'

Speaking of the Ahts, in North-West America, it is undoubtedly a fact, says Mr. Sproat,[2] 'that many of
' the sorcerers themselves thoroughly believe in their
' own supernatural powers, and are able, in their pre-
' parations and practices, to endure excessive fatigue,
' want of food, and intense prolonged mental excite-
' ment.'

Dobritzhoffer also concludes that the sorcerers of the Abipones[3] themselves 'imagine that they are gifted
' with superior wisdom;' and Müller also is convinced that they honestly believe in themselves.[4]

We should, says Martius,[5] 'do them an injustice if
' we regarded the Brazilian sorcerers as mere impostors,'

[1] Siberia, p. 124.
[2] Scenes and Studies of Savage Life, p. 170.
[3] Loc. cit., vol. ii. p. 68.
[4] Gesch. d. Amer. Urrelig. p. 80.
[5] Von d. Rechtszus. unter den Ur. Brasiliens, p. 30.

though, he adds, 'they do not scruple to cheat where they can.'

Williams, also, who was by no means disposed to take a favourable view of the native sorcerers, admits that they believed in themselves, a fact which it is only fair to bear in mind.[1] Turner also says the same of the sorcerers in Tanna.[2]

This self-deception was much facilitated by, if not mainly due to, the very general practice of fasting by those who aspired to the position of wizards. The Greenlander, says Cranz,[3] who would be an angekok, 'must retire from all mankind for a while into some 'solitary recess or hermitage, must spend the time in 'profound meditation, and call upon Torngarsuk to 'send him a torngak. At length, by abandoning the 'converse of men, by fasting and emaciating the body, 'and by a strenuous intenseness of thought, the man's 'imagination grows distracted, so that blended images 'of men, beasts, and monsters appear before him. He 'readily thinks these are real spirits, because his 'thoughts are full of spirits, and this throws his body 'into great irregularities and convulsions, which he 'labours to cherish and augment.'

Among the North American Indians,[4] when a boy reaches maturity, he leaves home and absents himself for some days, during which he eats nothing, but lies on the ground thinking. When at length he falls asleep, the first animal about which he dreams is, he thinks,

[1] Polynesian Researches, vol. ii. p. 220.
[2] Nineteen Years in Polynesia, p. 81.
[3] History of Greenland, vol. i. p. 210.
[4] Catlin's North American Indians, vol. i. p. 36.

ordained to be his special protector through life.[1]   The
dream itself he looks on as a revelation.   Indeed, the
Redskins fast before any great expedition, thinking that
during their dreams they receive indications as to the
course of action which they should pursue.[2]   Among
the Cherokees also fasting is very prevalent, 'and an
'abstinence of seven days renders the devotee famous.'[3]
The Flatheads of Oregon have a very similar custom.
Here, however, a number of youths retire together.
'They spend three days and nights in the performance
'of these rites, without eating or drinking.  By the
'languor of the body and the high excitement of the
'imagination produced during this time, their sleep
'must be broken and visited by visions adapted to
'their views.'[4]   These, therefore, they not unnaturally
look on as the visits of spirits.

Those who by continued fasts have thus purified
and cleared their minds from gross ideas, are supposed to be capable of a clearer insight into the future
than that which is accorded to ordinary men, and
were called 'Saiotkatta' by the Hurons, and 'Agotsin-
'nachen' by the Iroquois, terms which mean literally
'seers.'[5]

In Brazil, a young man who wished to be a pajé
went alone to some mountain, or to some lone place, and
fasted for two years, after which he was admitted with
certain ceremonies into the order of pajés.[6]   Among

[1] Lafitau, loc. cit., vol. i. pp. 207,
200, 231, and especially pp. 336 and
370.  Prichard's Nat. Hist. of Man,
vol. ii. p. 672.
  [2] Carver's Travels, p. 285.
  [3] Whipple's Report on Indian
Tribes, p. 36.
  [4] Dunn's Oregon, p. 320.
  [5] Lafitau, vol. i. p. 371.
  [6] Martius, Recht. unter d. Ur.
Bras. p. 30.

the Abipones[1] and Caribs[2] those who aspired to be
'keebet' proceeded in a similar manner. Among the
South American Indians of the Rio de la Plata the
Medicine-men were prepared for their office by a long
fast.[3] Among the Lapps, also, would-be wizards prepare themselves by a strict fast.[4]

At first sight the introduction of the 'dance' may
seem out of place here. Among savages, however, it is
no mere amusement. It is, says Robertson,[5] 'a serious
'and important occupation, which mingles in every
'occurrence of public or private life. If any intercourse
'be necessary between two American tribes the ambas-
'sadors of the one approach in a solemn dance and
'present the calumet or emblem of peace; the sachems
'of the other receive it with the same ceremony. If
'war is denounced against an enemy, it is by a dance,
'expressive of the resentment which they feel, and of
'the vengeance which they meditate. If the wrath of
'their gods is to be appeased, or their beneficence to be
'celebrated—if they rejoice at the birth of a child, or
'mourn the death of a friend—they have dances appro-
'priated to each of these situations, and suited to the
'different sentiments with which they are then ani-
'mated. If a person is indisposed a dance is prescribed
'as the most effectual means to restore him to health;
'and if he himself cannot endure the fatigue of such an
'exercise, the physician or conjuror performs it in his

[1] Dobritzhoffer, vol. ii. p. 07.
[2] Du Tertre, History of the Caribby Islands, p. 342.
[3] Latitau, vol. i. p. 335.
[4] Klemm, Cult. der Mens., vol. iii. p. 85.
[5] Robertson's America, bk. iv. p. 133. See also Schoolcraft, loc. cit., vol. iii. p. 488, on the Sacred Dances of the Redskins.

Fig. 12.

A DANCE. (From Lafitau's 'Mœurs des Sauvages.')

' name, as if the virtue of his activity could be trans-
' ferred to his patient.'

Among the Kols of Nagpore Colonel Dalton[1] describes several dances which, he says, 'are all more or
' less connected with some religious ceremony.'

The Ostyaks also perform sacred sword dances in
honour of their god Yelan.[2]

Fig. 18 represents a sacred dance as practised by the
natives of Virginia. It is very interesting to see here
a circle of upright stones, which, except that they are
rudely carved at the upper end into the form of a head,
exactly resemble our so-called Druidical temples.

In Brazil, again, ' some of the tribes had no other
' worship than dancing to the sound of very noisy
' instruments.'[3] Bonwick, speaking of the Tasmanians,
tells us that 'among their superstitious rites dancing
was conspicuous.'[4]

The idea is by no means confined to mere savages.
Even Socrates[5] regarded the dance as a part of religion,
and David, we know, did so too.[6]

As sacrificial feasts so generally enter into religious
ceremonials, we need not wonder that smoking is
throughout America closely connected with all religious
ceremonies, just as incense is used for the same purpose
in the Old World.[7]

The Zulus also, when sacrificing, burn incense,

[1] Trans. Ethn. Soc., vol. vi. p. 30.
[2] Erman, vol. ii. p. 52.
[3] Depons, Tr. in S. America, vol. I. p. 108. See also Zeit. f. Ethnologie, 1870, p 270.
[4] Daily Life of the Tasmanians, p. 180.
[5] Soc. apud Athen. lib. 14. p. 628. Quoted in Lafitau, vol. i. p. 200.
[6] 2 Sam. vi. 14, 22.
[7] Lafitau, vol. ii. p. 133.

thinking that 'they are giving the spirits of their people a sweet savour.' [1]

Among the Sonthals, one of the aboriginal tribes of India, the whole of their religious observances 'are 'generally performed and attended to by the votaries 'whilst in a state of intoxication; a custom which re-'minds us of the worship of Bacchus among the Greeks 'and Romans.' [2]

[1] Callaway's Religious System of the Amazulu, p. 141.
[2] The People of India, by J. F. Watson and J. W. Kaye, vol. I. p. 1.

# CHAPTER VI.

## RELIGION (*continued*).

I HAVE already observed that any rational classification of religions should be founded, not so much on the nature of the object worshipped, as on the conception formed of the nature of the Deity. In support of this view I will now quote some illustrations to show how widely distributed is the worship of various material objects, and how much they are interwoven with one another.

How ready savages are to deify objects, both animate and inanimate, is well shown in the following story from Lander's ' Niger Expedition.'

In most African towns and villages, says Lander,[1] ' I was treated as a demigod.' He mentions that on one occasion, having landed at a village which white men had never visited before, his party caused great astonishment and terror. When at length they succeeded in establishing a communication with the natives, the chief of the village gave the following account of what had taken place. ' A few minutes,'[2] he said, ' after ' you first landed, one of my people came to me and ' said, that a number of strange people had arrived at

[1] R. and J. Lander's Niger Expedition, vol. iii. p. 108.
[2] *Loc. cit.*, vol. iii. p. 78.

'the market-place. I sent him back again to get as near
'to you as he could, to hear what you intended doing.
'He soon after returned to me and said that you spoke
'a language which he could not understand. Not
'doubting it was your intention to attack my village at
'night and carry off my people, I desired them to get
'ready to fight. . . . . But when you came to
'meet us unarmed, and we saw your white faces, we
'were all so frightened that we could not pull our
'bows, nor move hand or foot; and when you drew
'near me, and extended your hands towards me, I felt
'my heart faint within me, and believed that you were
'"children of Heaven," and had dropped from the
'skies.'

The worship of animals is very prevalent among
races of men in a somewhat higher stage of civilisation
than that characterised by Fetichism.[1]    Plutarch, long
ago, suggested that it arose from the custom of representing animals upon standards ; and it is possible that
some few cases may be due to this cause, though it is
manifestly inapplicable to the majority, because, in the
scale of human development, animal-worship much pre-
cedes the use of standards, which, for instance, do not
appear to have been used in the Trojan war.[2]    Diodorus
explains it by the myth that the gods, being at one
time hard pressed by the giants, concealed themselves
for a while under the form of animals, which in consequence became sacred, and were worshipped by men.

Another ancient suggestion was that the Egyptian

---

[1] Since the last edition of this book, Mr. McLennan has published a series of excellent papers on Animal-Worship, in the Fortnightly Review, 1869–70.

[2] Gognet, *loc. cit.*, vol. ii. p. 364.'

chiefs wore helmets in the form of animals' heads, and that hence these animals were worshipped. This theory, however, will not apply generally, because the other races which worship animals do not use such helmets, and even in Egypt there can be little doubt that the worship of animals preceded the use of helmets.

Plutarch, as already mentioned, supposed that the crocodile was worshipped because, having no tongue, it was a type of the Deity, who makes laws for nature by his mere will! This far-fetched explanation shows an entire misconception of savage nature.

The worship of animals is, however, susceptible of a very simple explanation, and perhaps, as I have ventured to suggest,[1] may have originated from the practice of naming, first individuals, and then their families, after particular animals. A family, for instance, which was called after the bear, would come to look on that animal first with interest, then with respect, and at length with a sort of awe.

The habit of calling children after some animal or plant is very common, which amongst the lowest races might naturally be expected from the poverty of their language. The Issinese of Guinea named their children 'after some beast, tree, or fruit, according to ' their fancy. Sometimes they call it after their fetich or ' some white, who is a Mingo ; that is, friend to them.'[2]

The Hottentots also generally named their children after some animal.[3] In Congo[4] 'some form of food ' is forbidden to everyone : in some it is a fish, in others

[1] Prehistoric Times, 1869, p. 608.    [2] *Ibid.*, vol. iii. p. 357.
[3] Astley's Collection of Voyages,    [4] *Ibid.*, p. 262.
vol. ii. p. 430.

'a bird, and so on.   This is not, however, expressly
'stated to be connected with the totem.'

In Southern Africa the Bechuanas are subdivided
into men of the crocodile, men of the fish, of the monkey, of the buffalo, of the elephant, porcupine, lion,
vine, and so on.   No one dares to eat the flesh or wear
the skin of the animal to the tribe of which he belongs ;
and although in this case the totems are not worshipped,[1] each tribe has a superstitious dread of the
animal after which it is named.

In China also the name is frequently 'that of a
'flower, animal, or such-like thing.'[2]   In Australia we
seem to find the totem, or, as it is there called, kobong,
almost in the very moment of deification.  Each family,
says Sir G. Grey,[3] 'adopts some animal or vegetable,
'as their crest or sign, or kobong, as they call it.   I
'imagine it more likely that these have been named
'after the families, than that the families have been
'named after them.'   This, however, does not seem to
me at all probable.

'A certain mysterious connection exists between
'the family and its kobong, so that a member of the
'family will never kill an animal of the species to which
'his kobong belongs, should he find it asleep; indeed,
'he always kills it reluctantly, and never without afford-
'ing it a chance of escape.   This arises from the family
'belief, that some one individual of the species is their
'nearest friend, to kill whom would be a great crime,

[1] The Basutos, Rev. E. Casalis,    vol. iv. p. 91.
p. 211.  Livingstone's Travels in S.    [2] Two Expeditions in Australia,
Africa, p. 13.                          vol. ii. p. 228.
[3] Astley's Collection of Voyages,

'and to be carefully avoided. Similarly a native who
'has a vegetable for his kobong, may not gather it
'under certain circumstances, and at a particular period
'of the year.'

Here we see a certain feeling for the kobong or
totem, though it does not amount to worship, and is
apparently confined to certain districts.[1] In America,
on the other hand, it has developed into a veritable
religion.

The totem of the Redskins, says Schoolcraft,[2] 'is a
'symbol of the name of the progenitor—generally some
'quadruped, or bird, or other object in the animal
'kingdom, which stands, if we may so express it, as
'the surname of the family. It is always some animated
'object, and seldom or never derived from the inani-
'mate class of nature. Its significant importance is
'derived from the fact that individuals unhesitatingly
'trace their lineage from it. By whatever names they
'may be called during their lifetime, it is the totem,
'and not their personal name, that is recorded on the
'tomb, or adjedatig, that makes the place of burial.
'Families are thus traced when expanded into bands or
'tribes, the multiplication of which, in North America,
'has been very great, and has increased, in like ratio,
'the labours of the ethnologist. The turtle, the bear,
'and the wolf appear to have been primary and honoured
'totems in most of the tribes, and bear a significant
'rank to the traditions of the Iroquois and Lenapis, or
'Delawares; and they are believed to have more or less
'prominency in the genealogies of all the tribes who

[1] See Eyre, vol. ii. p. 328.    vol. ii. p. 40. See also Laßtau, vol.
[2] Schoolcraft's Indian Tribes,    i. pp. 404, 407.

'are organised on the totemic principle.'  The Osages [1]
believe themselves to be descended from a beaver, and
consequently will not kill that animal.   In Peru, again,
many of the Indian families believed themselves to be
descended from animals. [2]  So, also, among the Khonds
of India, the different tribes 'take their designation
'from various animals, as the bear tribe, owl tribe, deer
'tribe,' &c., &c. [3]

The Kols of Nagpore also are divided into 'keelis'
or clans, generally called after animals, which, in consequence, they do not eat.   Thus the eel, hawk, and heron
tribe abstain respectively from the flesh of these animals. [4]  The Oraons also are divided into tribes, usually
named after some animal or plant, which is not eaten
by the tribe after which it is named. [5]

Among the Samoans, 'one saw his god in the eel,
'another in the shark, another in the turtle, another in
'the dog, another in the owl, another in the lizard, and
'so on. . . . A man would eat freely of what was
'regarded as the incarnation of the god of another man,
'but the incarnation of his own particular god he
'would consider it death to injure or to eat.' [6]   In
Northern Asia, among the Yakuts, 'each tribe looks
'on some particular animal as sacred, and abstains
'from eating it.' [7]

If, moreover, we bear in mind that the deity of a

[1] Schoolcraft, vol. i. p. 320.
[2] Garcilasso de la Vega, vol. i.
p. 75.
[3] Early Races of Scotland, vol. ii.
p. 405.
[4] Dalton, Trans. Ethn. Soc., N.S.,
vol. vi. p. 30.

[4] Dalton's Des. Ethn. of Bengal,
p. 254.  See also Campbell's Wild
Tribes of Khondistan, p. 20.
[6] Turner's Nineteen Years in
Polynesia, p. 234.
[7] Latham, Des. Ethnol., vol. i.
p. 304.

savage is merely a being of a slightly different nature from—though generally somewhat more powerful than—himself, we shall at once see that many animals, such as the bear or elephant, fulfil in a great measure his conception of a deity.

This is still more completely the case with nocturnal animals, such as the lion and tiger, where the effect is heightened by a certain amount of mystery. As the savage, crouching at night by his camp-fire, listens to the cries and roars of the animals prowling about, or watches them stealing like shadows round and round among the trees, what wonder if he weaves mysterious stories about them? And if in his estimate of animals he errs in one direction, we perhaps have fallen into the opposite extreme.

As an object of worship, however, the serpent is pre-eminent among animals.[1] Not only is it malevolent and mysterious, but its bite—so trifling in appearance and yet so deadly, producing fatal effects rapidly, and apparently by no adequate means—suggests to the savage almost irresistibly the notion of something divine, according to his notions of divinity. There were also some lower, but powerful, considerations which tended greatly to the development of serpent-worship. The animal is long-lived and easily kept in captivity; hence the same individual might be preserved for a long time, and easily exhibited at intervals to the multitude. In other respects, the serpent is a convenient god. Thus in Guinea, where the sea and the serpent were the principal deities, the priests, as Bosman expressly tells us, encouraged offerings to the serpent rather than to the

<hr>

[1] Deane's Worship of the Serpent traced throughout the World.

8

sen, because, in the latter case, 'there happens no 'remainder to be left for them.'[1]

Mr. Fergusson, in his work on Tree and Serpent-worship, has suggested that the beauty of the serpent, or the brilliancy of its eye, had a part among the causes of its original deification. I cannot, however, agree with him in this. Nor do I believe that serpent-worship is to be traced up to any common local origin; but, on the contrary, that it sprang up spontaneously in many places, and at very different times. In considering the wide distribution of serpent-worship, we must remember that in the case of the serpent we apply one name to a whole order of animals; and that serpents occur all over the world, except in very cold regions. On the contrary, the lion, the bear, the bull, have less extensive areas, and consequently their worship could never be so general. If, however, we compare, as we ought, serpent-worship with quadruped-worship, or bird-worship, or sun-worship, we shall find that it has no exceptionally wide area.

Mr. Fergusson, like previous writers, is surprised to find that the serpent-god is frequently regarded as a beneficent being. Müller, in his Scientific Mythology, has endeavoured to account for this by the statement that the serpent typified not only barren, impure nature, but also youth and health. This is not, I think, the true explanation. It may be that the serpent-god commenced as a malevolent being, who was flattered, as cruel rulers always are, and that, in process of time, this flattery, which was at first the mere expression

---

[1] Pinkerton, vol. xvi. p. 600.

of fear, came to be an article of faith. If, however, the totemic origin of serpent-worship, as above suggested, be the correct one, the serpent, like other totemic deities, would, from its origin, have a benevolent character.

As mentioned in Mr. Fergusson's work, the serpent was worshipped anciently in Egypt,[1] in India,[2] Phœnicia,[3] Babylonia,[4] Greece,[5] as well as in Italy,[6] where, however, it seems not to have prevailed much. Among the Lithuanians ' every family entertained a real serpent ' as a household god.'[7]

Passing on to those cases in which the serpent is even now worshipped, or was so until lately, we find in Asia evidence of serpent-worship, in Persia,[8] Cashmere,[9] Cambodia, Thibet,[10] India,[11] China (traces),[12] Ceylon,[13] and among the Kalmucks.[14]

In Africa the serpent was worshipped in some parts of Upper Egypt,[15] and in Abyssinia.[16] Among the negroes on the Guinea Coast it used to be the principal

[1] Herodotus, Euterpe, p. 74.

[2] Tertullian, de Præscript. Hereticorum, c. xlvii. Epiphanius, lib. 1, Heres, xxxvii. p. 207, et seq.

[3] Eusebius, Præ. Evan., vol. i. p. 0. Maurice, Ind. Antiq., vol. vi. p. 273.

[4] Bell and Dragon, v. 23.

[5] Pausanias, vol. ii. pp. 137, 175. Ælian de Animal. xvi. 39. Herodotus, viii. p. 41.

[6] Ælian, Var. Hist., ix. p. 10. Propertius, Eleg. viii. p. 4. Deane, loc. cit., p. 253.

[7] Lord Kames' History of Man, vol. iv. p. 103. Deane, loc. cit., p. 246.

[8] Mogruil, 15ff, Windischmann, 37; Shah Nameh, Atkinson's translation, p. 14.

[9] Asiatic Res., vol. xv. pp. 24, 25. Ayeen Akbaree, Gladwin's trans., p. 137.

[10] Hiouen-Thsang, vol. i. p. 4.

[11] Fergusson's Tree and Serpent Worship, p. 50.

[12] Ibid., p. 61.

[13] History and Doctrine of Buddhism in Ceylon, Upham.

[14] Klemm, Cult. der Mens., vol. iii. p. 202.

[15] Pococke, Pinkerton's Voyages, vol. xv. p. 269.

[16] Dillmann in Zeitsch. der Morgenlandischen Gesells., vol. vii p. 338. Ludolf. Comment. vol. iii. p. 281; Bruce's Travels, vol. iv. p. 35.

deity.[1]  Smith, in his Voyage to Guinea,[2] says that
the natives 'are all pagans, and worship three sorts of
' deities.   The first is a large, beautiful kind of snake,
' which is inoffensive in its nature.   These are kept in
' fittish-houses, or churches, built for that purpose in a
' grove, to whom they sacrifice great store of hogs,
' sheep, fowls, and goats, &c., and if not devoured by
' the snake, are sure to be taken care of by the fetish-
' men or pagan priests.'   From Liberia to Benzuela, if
not farther, the serpent was the principal deity,[3] and,
as elsewhere, is regarded as being on the whole beneficent.   To it the natives resort in times of drought and
sickness, or other calamities.   No negro would intention-
ally injure a serpent, and anyone doing so by accident
would assuredly be put to death.   All over the country
are small huts, built on purpose for the snakes,[4] which
are attended and fed by old women.   These snakes are
frequently consulted as oracles.

In addition to those small huts were temples, which,
judged by a negro standard, were of considerable magnificence,[5] with large courts, spacious apartments, and
numerous attendants.   Each of these temples had a
special snake.   That of Whydah was supposed to have
appeared to the army during an attack on Ardra.   It
was regarded as a presage of victory, which so encouraged the soldiers that they were perfectly successful.
Hence this fetich was reverenced beyond all others,

[1] Astley's Voyages, vol. iii. p.
480; Burton, vol. ii. p. 139; Smith,
loc. cit. p. 195, Burton's Dahome,
vol. i. p. 94.

[2] Smith's Voyage to Guinea, p.
195.  See also Bosman, Pinkerton's

Voyages, vol. xvi. p. 184, et seq.

[3] Bosman, loc. cit., pp. 404–405,
Smith, loc. cit., p. 195.

[4] Astley, loc. cit., pp. 27, 32.

[5] Ibid., p. 29.

and an annual pilgrimage was made to its temple with much ceremony. It is rather suspicious that any

Fig. 10.

AGOYE, AN IDOL OF WHYDAH. (Astley's Collection of Voyages.)

young women who may be ill are taken off to the snake's house to be cured. For this questionable service the attendants charge a high price to the parents.

It is observable that the harmless snakes only are thus worshipped. 'Agoye,' the fetich of Whydah, which has serpents and lizards coming out of its head [1] (fig. 19), presents a remarkable similarity to some of the Hindoo idols.

Snakes, says Schweinfurth, 'are the only creatures 'to which either Dinka or Shillooks (Upper Nile Re- 'gion) pay any sort of reverence.' [2]

The Kaffirs of South Africa have a general belief that the spirits of their ancestors appear to them in the form of serpents. [3]

Ellis mentions that in Madagascar the natives regard serpents ' with a sort of superstition.' [4]

In Feejee, 'the god' most generally known is ' Ndengei, who seems to be an impersonation of the ' abstract idea of eternal existence. He is the subject ' of no emotion or sensation, nor any appetite except ' hunger. The serpent—the world-wide symbol of ' eternity—is his adopted shrine. Some traditions ' represent him with the head and part of the body of ' that reptile, the rest of his form being stone, emblem- ' atic of everlasting and unchangeable duration. He ' passes a monotonous existence in a gloomy cavern; ' evincing no interest in anyone but his attendant, Uto, ' and giving no signs of life beyond eating, answering ' his priest, and changing his position from one side to ' the other.'

[1] Astley, loc. cit., vol. iii. p. 50.
[2] Heart of Africa, vol. i. p. 158.
[3] Casalis' Basutos, p. 240. Chap- man's Travels, vol. i. p. 195. Calla- way's Religious System of the Ama- zulu. Arbousset, &c. cit., p. 138.

Livingstone's Exp to the Zambesi, p. 46.
[4] Three Visits to Madagascar, p. 143.
[5] Fiji and the Fijians, vol. ii. p. 217.

In the Friendly Islands the water snake was much respected.[1]

In America serpents were worshipped by the Aztecs,[2] Peruvians,[3] Natchez,[4] Caribs,[5] Monitarris,[6] Mandans,[7] Pueblo Indians,[8] &c.

Alvarez, during his attempt to reach Peru from Paraguay, is reported[9] to have seen the 'temple and 'residence of a monstrous serpent, whom the inhabit- 'ants had chosen for their divinity, and fed with 'human flesh. He was as thick as an ox, and seven- 'and-twenty feet long, with a very large head, and 'very fierce though small eyes. His jaws, when ex- 'tended, displayed two ranks of crooked fangs. The 'whole body, except the tail, which was smooth, was 'covered with round scales of a great thickness. The 'Spaniards, though they could not be persuaded by 'the Indians that this monster delivered oracles, were 'exceedingly terrified at the first sight of him ; and 'their terror was greatly increased, when, on one of 'them having fired a blunderbuss at him, he gave a 'roar like that of a lion, and with a stroke of his tail 'shook the whole tower.'

The worship of serpents being so widely distributed, and presenting so many similar features, we cannot wonder that it has been regarded as something special,

[1] Mariner, vol. ii. p. 100.
[2] Squier's Serpent Symbol in America, p. 162. Gama, Descripcion Historica y Cronologica de las Pedras de Mexico, 1832, p. 39; Bernal Diaz, p. 125.
[3] Müller, Ges. d. Amer. Urreligionen, p. 300. Garcilasso de la Vega, v. i. p. 48.
[4] Ibid., p. 62.
[5] Ibid., p. 221.
[6] Klemm, vol. ii. p. 162.
[7] Ibid., p. 163.
[8] Möllhausen, Tour to the Pacific, vol. i. p. 204.
[9] Charlevoix's History of Paraguay, vol. i. p. 110.

that attempts have been made to trace it up to one source, and that it has been regarded by some as the primitive religion of man.

I will now, however, proceed to mention other cases of zoolatry.

Animal-worship was very prevalent in America.[1] The Redskins reverenced the bear,[2] the bison, the hare,[3] and the wolf,[4] and some species of birds.[5] The jaguar was worshipped in some parts of Brazil, and especially in La Plata.[6] In South America birds and jaguars seem to have been the specially sacred animals. The owl in Mexico was regarded as an evil spirit;[7] in South America toads,[8] eagles, and goatsuckers were much venerated.[9] The Abipones[10] think that certain little ducks ' which fly about at night, uttering a mourn- ' ful hiss, are the souls of the departed.'

In Yucatan it was customary to leave an infant alone in a place sprinkled with ashes. Next morning the ashes were examined, and if the footprints of any animals were found on them, that animal was chosen as the deity of the infant.[11]

The semi-civilised races of Mexico[12] and Peru were more advanced in their religious conceptions. In the latter the sun was the great deity.[13]  Yet in Peru,[14]

[1] Müller, Am. Urr., p. 60, et seq.
[2] Ibid., p. 61.
[3] Schoolcraft, vol. i. p. 310.
[4] Müller, loc. cit., p. 267.
[5] Ibid., p. 191. Klemm, loc. cit., vol. ii. p. 164.
[6] Müller, loc. cit., p. 258.
[7] Prescott, vol. i. p. 48.
[8] Depons, Tr. in South America, vol. i. p. 108.

[9] Müller, Amer. Urr., p. 237.
[10] Dobritzhoffer, Hist. of the Abipones, vol. ii. p. 74.
[11] De Brosses, Du Culte des Dieux Fétiches, p. 48.
[12] Müller, loc. cit., p. 481.
[13] Prescott's History of Peru, p. 88.
[14] Müller, p. 300. Garcilasso de la Vega, vol. i. pp. 47, 104.

even at the time of the conquest, many species of
animals were still much reverenced, including the fox,
dog, llama, condor, eagle, and puma, besides the serpent,
and various species of fish. From these animals the
various families of Indians were considered to be
descended,[1] and each species was supposed to have a
representative, or archetype, in heaven.[2] In Mexico a
similar feeling prevailed, but neither here nor in
Peru can it truly be said that animals at the time
of the conquest were nationally regarded as actual
deities.

The Polynesians, also, had generally advanced beyond the stage of totemism. The heavenly bodies
were not worshipped, and, when animals were regarded
with veneration, it was rather as representatives of the
deities, than with the idea that they were really deities.
Still the Tahitians[3] had a superstitious reverence for
various kinds of fish and birds, such as the heron,
kingfisher, and woodpecker; the latter apparently
because they frequented the temples.

The Sandwich Islanders[4] seem to have regarded the
raven as sacred,[5] and the New Zealanders, according to
Forster, regarded a species of tree-creeper as the 'bird
'of the divinity.'[6] The Tongans considered that the
deities 'sometimes come into the living bodies of lizards,
'porpoises, and a species of water-snake; hence these

[1] Garcilasso de la Vega, vol. I.
p. 75.
[2] Prescott's History of Peru, p.
87. Garcilasso de la Vega, vol. L p.
176.
[3] Polynesian Researches, vol. ii.
p. 202.

[4] Cook's Third Voyage, vol. iii.
p. 160.
[5] Cook's Voyage to the Pacific,
vol. iii. p. 161.
[6] Voyage round the World, vol.
i. p. 519.

'animals are much respected.'[1]   The Kingsmill Islanders also worshipped certain kinds of fish.[2]

The Bishop of Wellington informs us that 'spiders
'were special objects of reverence to Maoris; and, as the
'priests further told them that the souls of the faithful
'went to heaven on gossamer threads, they were very
'careful not to break any spiders' webs, or gossamers.
'Lizards were also supposed to be chosen by the Maori
'gods as favourite abodes.'[3]

In the Feejee Islands,[4] besides the serpent, 'certain
'birds, fish, and plants, and some men, are supposed to
'have deities closely connected with or residing in
'them.   At Lakemba, Tui Lakemba, and on Vanua
'Levu, Ravuravu, claim the hawk as their abode;
'Viavia, and other gods, the shark.   One is supposed to
'inhabit the eel, and another the common fowl, and so
'on, until nearly every animal becomes the shrine of
'some deity.   He who worships the god dwelling in
'the eel must never eat of that fish, and thus of the
'rest ; so that some are tabu from eating human flesh,
'because the shrine of their god is a man.'

In Siberia Erman mentions that ' the Polar bear, as
'the strongest of God's creatures, and that which seems
'to come nearest to the human being, is as much vene-
'rated by the Samoyedes as his black congener by the
'Ostyaks.   They even swear by the throat of this
'strong animal, whom they kill and eat; but when it is

---

[1] Mariner, *loc. cit.*, vol. ii. p. 100.
[2] Hale, Ethn. of the U. S.
Expl. Exp., p. 97.
[3] Trans. Ethn. Soc., 1870, p. 367.

[4] Williams' Fiji and the Fijians,
vol. i. p. 210.  Seemann, Mission to
Viti, p. 392.

' once killed, they show their respect for it in various
' ways.'[1]

Each tribe of the Jakuts 'look on some particular
' creature as sacred, *e.g.* a swan, goose, raven, &c., and
' such is not eaten by that tribe, though the others may
' eat it.'[2]  The same feeling extends even to plants; and
in China, when the sacred apricot tree is broken to
make the spirit-pen, it is customary to write an apology
on the bark.[3]

The Hindus, says Dubois,[4] 'in all things extrava-
' gant, pay honour and worship, less or more solemn, to
' almost every living creature, whether quadruped, bird,
' or reptile.'  The cow, the ape, the eagle (known as
garuda), and the serpent, receive the highest honours;
but the tiger, elephant, horse, stag, sheep, hog, dog, cat,
rat, peacock, cock, chameleon, lizard, tortoise, fish, and
even insects, have been made objects of worship.  The
ox is held especially sacred throughout most of India
and Ceylon.  Among the Todas[5] the 'buffaloes and bell
' are fused into an incomprehensible mystic whole, or
' unity, and constitute their prime object of adoration
' and worship.' . . . . 'Towards evening the herd is
' driven back to the tuel, when such of the male and
' female members of the family as are present assemble,
' and make obeisance to the animals.'

Dr. Anderson found the worship of the horse and
the snake interwoven with the Buddhism of the Shans

---

[1] Erman, vol. ii. p. 55.  Müller,
Des. de toutes les Nat. de l'Emp.
Russe, Pt. I. p. 107.
[2] Strahlenberg, p. 383.
[3] Tylor, Roy. Inst. Journ., vol. v.

p. 527.
[4] *Loc. cit.*, p. 445.
[5] Trans. Ethn. Soc., N.S., vol.
vii. pp. 250, 251.  See also Ethn.
Journ., 1869, p. 97.

of West Yunan.[1]  The goose is worshipped in Ceylon,[2] and the alligator in the Philippines.

The ancient Egyptians were greatly addicted to animal-worship, and even now Sir S. Baker states that on the White Nile the natives will not eat the ox.[3] The common fowl also is connected with superstitious ceremonies among the Obbo and other Nile tribes.[4]

The King of Ardra, on the Guinea Coast, had certain black birds for his fetiches,[5] and the negroes of Benin also reverence several kinds of birds. The negroes of Guinea regard[6] 'the sword-fish and the 'bonito as deities, and such is their veneration for them 'that they never catch either sort designedly. If a 'sword-fish happen to be taken by chance, they will 'not eat it till the sword be cut off, which, when dried, 'they regard as a *fetisso.*'  They also regard the crocodile as a deity.  On the Guinea Coast, says Bosman, 'a 'great part of the negroes believe that man was made 'by Anansie; that is, a great spider.'[7]  In South Africa the Malekutus and some Baperis worship the porcupine, while other Baperis regard a monkey as their tutelary deity.[8]

In Madagascar, Ellis[9] tells us that the natives regard crocodiles 'as possessed of supernatural power, invoke 'their forbearance with prayers, or seek protection by 'charms, rather than attack them; even the shaking of

[1] Expedition to Western Yuan rid Bhamô, p. 115.
[2] Tennent's Ceylon, vol. i. p. 481.
[3] Albert N'yanza, vol. i. p. 63.
[4] Baker, loc. cit., vol. i. p. 327.
[5] Astley's Collection of Voyages, vol. iii. pp. 72, 90.
[6] Astley, vol. ii. p. 607. Burton's Dahome, v. ii. pp. 145, 148.
[7] Pinkerton, loc. cit., vol. xvi. p. 300.
[8] Arbousset, loc. cit., p. 170.
[9] Three Visits to Madagascar, p. 207. See also Sibree, loc. cit., p. 103.

' a spear over the waters would be regarded as an act
' of sacrilegious insult to the sovereign of the flood, im-
' perilling the life of the offender the next time he
' should venture on the water.'

The nations of Southern Europe had for the most
part advanced beyond animal-worship even in the
earliest historical times. The extraordinary sanctity
attributed, in the Twelfth Odyssey, to the oxen of the
sun, stands almost alone in Greek mythology, and is
regarded by Mr. Gladstone as of Phœnician origin. It
is true that the horse is spoken of with mysterious
respect, and that deities on several occasions assumed
the form of birds; but this does not amount to actual
worship.

The deification of animals explains probably the
curious fact that various savage races habitually apolo-
gise to the animals which they kill in the chase; thus,
the Vogulitzi[1] of Siberia, when they have killed a bear,
address it formally, and maintain ' that the blame is to
' be laid on the arrows and iron, which were made and
' forged by the Russians.' The same custom exists
among the Ostyaks,[2] the Samoyeds,[3] and the Ainos of
Yesso.[4] Schoolcraft[5] mentions a case of an Indian on
the shores of Lake Superior begging pardon of a bear
which he had shot.

Before engaging in a hunt the Chippeways have a
' medicine ' dance in order to propitiate the spirits of
the bears or other game.[6] So also in British Columbia,[7]

[1] Strahlenberg's Voyage to Siberia, p. 97.

[2] Voyages, vol. iv. p. 85.

[3] De Brosses, Dieux Fetiches, p.
61.

[4] Trans. Ethn. Soc., N.S., vol. iv.
p. 30.

[5] Schoolcraft's Indian Tribes,
vol. iii. p. 229.

[6] Catlin's Amer. Ind., vol. ii. p.
248.

[7] Metlahkatlah, p. 90.

when the fishing season commences, and the fish begin coming up the rivers, the Indians used to meet them, and 'speak to them. They paid court to them, and ' would address them thus: " You fish, you fish; you ' " are all chiefs, you are; you are all chiefs." '

The Koussa Kaffirs[1] had a very similar custom. ' Before a party goes out hunting, a very odd ceremony ' or sport takes place, which they consider as absolutely ' necessary to ensure success to the undertaking. One ' of them takes a handful of grass into his mouth, and ' crawls about upon all-fours to represent some sort of ' game. The rest advance as if they would run him ' through with their spears, raising the hunting cry, till ' at length he falls upon the ground as if dead. If this ' man afterwards kills a head of game, he hangs a claw ' upon his arm as a trophy, but the animal must be ' shared with the rest.' Lichtenstein also mentions that 'if an elephant is killed after a very long and ' wearisome chase, as is commonly the case, they seek ' to exculpate themselves towards the dead animal, by ' declaring to him solemnly, that the thing happened ' entirely by accident, not by design.'[2] To make the apology more complete, they cut off the trunk and bury it carefully with much flattery.

Speaking of a Mandingo who had killed a lion, Gray says:[3] ' As I was not a little surprised at seeing the ' man, whom I conceived ought to be rewarded for ' having first so disabled the animal as to prevent it ' from attacking us, thus treated, I requested an ex-

[1] Lichtenstein's Travels, vol. i. p. 260.
[2] *Ibid.* p. 254.
[3] Gray's Travels in Western Africa, p. 119.

' planation; and was informed that, being a subject
' only, he was guilty of a great crime in killing or
' shooting a sovereign, and must suffer this punishment
' until released by the chiefs of the village, who, know-
' ing the deceased to have been their enemy, would not
' only do so immediately, but commend the man for his
' good conduct. I endeavoured to no purpose to find
' out the origin of this extraordinary mock ceremony,
' but could only gain the answer, frequently given
' by an African, "that his forefathers had always
' "done so."'

The Steins of Cambodia[1] believe that ' animals also
' have souls which wander about after their death; thus,
' when they have killed one, fearing lest its soul should
' come and torment them, they ask pardon for the evil
' they have done to it, and offer sacrifices proportioned
' to the strength and size of the animal.'

The Sumatrans speak of tigers[2] with a degree of
' awe, and hesitate to call them by their common name
' (rimau or machang), terming them respectfully satwa
' (the wild animals), or even nenek (ancestors); as
' really believing them such, or by way of soothing and
' coaxing them. When an European procures traps to
' be set, by means of persons less superstitious, the
' inhabitants of the neighbourhood have been known to
' go at night to the place, and practise some forms, in
' order to persuade the animals that it was not laid by
' them, or with their consent.'

The deification of inanimate objects seems at first

[1] Mouhot's Travels in the Central Parts of Indo-China, vol. i. p.
252.

[2] Marsden's Hist. of Sumatra,
p. 292. See also Depons, Travels in
S. America, vol. i. p. 100.

somewhat more difficult to understand than that of animals. The names of individuals, however, would be taken not only from animals, but also from inanimate objects, and would thus, as suggested at p. 253, lead to the worship of the latter as well as of the former. Some, moreover, are singularly lifelike. No one, I think, can wonder that rivers should have been regarded as living. The constant movement, the ripples and eddies on their surface, vibrations of the reeds and other water plants, the murmuring and gurgling sounds, the clearness and transparency of the water, combine to produce a singular effect on the mind even of civilised man.

Seneca long ago observed, that ' if you walk in a ' grove, thick planted with ancient trees of unusual ' growth, the interwoven boughs of which exclude the ' light of heaven; the vast height of the wood, the ' retired secrecy of the place, the deep unbroken gloom ' of shade, impress your mind with the conviction of a ' present deity.'

The savage also is susceptible to such influences, and is naturally prone to personify not only rivers but also other inanimate objects.

Who can wonder at that worship of the sun, moon, and stars, which has been regarded as a special form of religion, and is known as Sabæism? It does not, however, in its original form, essentially differ from mountain or river worship. To us, with our knowledge of astronomy, the sun-worship naturally seems a more sublime form of religion, but we must remember that the lower races who worship the heavenly bodies have no idea of their distance nor, consequently, of their magnitude. Nay, the very distance and magnitude of the

sun, combined with the regularity of its course, rendered
it the less likely to be selected by the lowest races of
men as an object of worship. Religion is not with them
a deep feeling of the soul, but a profound fear of
some immediate evil, a desire for some immediate
good. Hence the savage worships something which is
close to him, something which he can see and hear; and
the lawless, turbulent action of the sea gives him more
the impression of life and energy than the regular and
steady movements of the heavenly bodies. Even when
these are worshipped, it is in entire ignorance of their
real magnitude and grandeur. The people of Chincha,
in Peru, worshipped the sea rather than the sun, ' which
' did them no good at all, but rather annoyed them by
' its excessive heat.'[1] Hence the curious ideas with
reference to eclipses which I have already mentioned
(p. 223). Again, in illustration of the same fact, the
New Zealanders believed that Mawe, their ancestor,
caught the sun in a noose, and wounded it so severely
that its movements have been slower, and the days consequently longer, ever since.[2] According to another
account, Mawe ' tied a string to the sun and fastened
' it to the moon, that as the former went down, the
' other, being pulled after it by the superior power of
' the sun, may rise and give light during his absence.'[3]
A very similar story also occurs in Samoa.[4]

We must always bear in mind that the savage
notion of a deity is essentially different from that entertained by higher races. Instead of being supernatural, he

---

[1] Garcilasso de la Vega, vol. l.
p. 140.
[2] Polynesian Mythology, p. 35.
[3] Yate, *loc. cit.*, p. 149.
[4] Turner's Nineteen Years in
Polynesia, p. 248.

is merely a part of nature. This goes far to explain the tendency to deification which at first seems so strange.

A good illustration, and one which shows how easily deities are created by men in this frame of mind, is mentioned by Lichtenstein. The king of the Koussa Kaffirs having broken off a piece of a stranded anchor, died soon afterwards, upon which all the Kaffirs looked upon the anchor as alive, and saluted it respectfully whenever they passed near it.[1] Again, the natives near Sydney made it an invariable rule never to whistle when beneath a particular cliff, because on one occasion a rock fell from it, and crushed some natives who were whistling underneath it.[2]

A very interesting case is recorded by Mr. Fergusson.[3] 'The following instance of tree-worship,' he says, ' which I myself witnessed, is amusing, even if not ' instructive. While residing in Tessore, I observed at ' one time considerable crowds passing near the factory ' I then had charge of. As it might be merely an ordi- ' nary fair they were going to attend, I took no notice; ' but as the crowd grew daily larger, and assumed a ' more religious character, I inquired, and was told that ' a god had appeared in a tree at a place about six miles ' off. Next morning I rode over, and found a large ' space cleared in a village I knew well, in the centre of ' which stood an old decayed date tree, hung with gar- ' lands and offerings. Around it houses were erected ' for the attendant Brahmins, and a great deal of busi- ' ness was going on in offerings and Pûjâ. On my

[1] Travels, vol. i. p. 254.  [2] Tree and Serpent Worship, p.
[3] Collins' English Colony in   74.
N.S. Wales, p. 382.

' inquiring how the god manifested his presence, I was
' informed that soon after the sun rose in the morning
' the tree raised its head to welcome him, and bowed it
' down again when he departed.  As this was a miracle
' easily tested, I returned at noon and found it was so!
' After a little study and investigation, the mystery did
' not seem difficult of explanation.  The tree had
' originally grown across the principal pathway through
' the village, but at last hung so low, that in order to
' enable people to pass under it, it had been turned
' aside and fastened parallel to the road.  In the opera-
' tion the bundle of fibres which composed the root had
' become twisted like the strands of a rope.  When the
' morning sun struck on the upper surface of these, they
' contracted in drying, and hence a tendency to un-
' twist, which raised the head of the tree.  With the
' evening dews they relaxed, and the head of the tree
' declined, thus proving to the man of science as to the
' credulous Hindu that it was due to the direct action
' of the Sun God.'

The savage, indeed, accounts for all movement by
life.  Hence the wind is a living being.  Nay, even
motionless objects are regarded in a particular stage of
mental progress as possessing spirits.  The chief of
Teah could hardly be persuaded but that Lander's
watch was alive and had the power of moving.[1]  It is
probably for this reason that in most languages inanimate objects are distinguished by genders, being at first
regarded as either male or female.  Hence also the
practice of breaking or burning the weapons, &c., buried

---

[1] Niger Expedition, vol. II. p. 220.

with the dead.[1]  It has been generally supposed that
this was merely to prevent them from being a temptation to robbers.   This is not so, however ; savages do
not invade the sanctity of the tomb.   Just, however, as
they kill a man's wives and slaves, his favourite horse
or dog, that they may accompany him to the other
world, so do they 'kill' the weapons, that the spirits
of the bows, &c., may also go with their master, and
that he may enter the other world armed as a chief
should be.   Thus the Tahitians[2] believed 'that not
'only all other animals, but trees, fruit, and even
'stones, have souls which at death, or upon being con-
'sumed or broken, ascend to the divinity, with whom
'they first mix, and afterwards pass into the mansion
'allotted to each.'

The Feejeeans[3] considered that 'if an animal or a
'plant die, its soul immediately goes to Bolotoo ; if a
'stone or any other substance is broken, immortality is
'equally its reward ; nay, artificial bodies have equal
'good luck with men, and hogs, and yams.  If an axe
'or a chisel is worn out or broken up, away flies its
'soul for the service of the gods.  If a house is taken
'down, or any way destroyed, its immortal part will
find ' a situation on the plains of Bolotoo.'

The Finns believed that all inanimate objects had
their 'haltia,' or soul.[4]

Sproat,[5] speaking of N. W. America, says that

[1] Livingstone's Zambesi, p. 522
St. John's Hill Tribes of Armen. J.
Anthrop. Inst., vol. ii. p. 238.

[2] Cook's Third Voyage, vol. ii.
p. 108.

[3] Mariner, loc. cit., vol. ii. p. 137.

Seemann's Mission to Viti, pp. 302,
304.

[4] Castren. Finn. Myth., pp. 170,
182.

[5] Sproat's Scenes and Studies of
Savage Life, p. 213.

'when the dead are buried, the friends often burn
'blankets with them, for by destroying the blankets in
'this upper world, they send them also with the de-
'parted soul to the world below.'

Among the Hill tribes of India the Garos break the
objects buried with the dead, who 'would not benefit
'by them if they were given unbroken.'[1]

In China,[2] 'if the dead man was a person of note,
'the Bonzes make great processions; the mourners
'following them with candles and perfumes burning in
'their hands. They offer sacrifices at certain distances,
'and perform the obsequies; in which they burn statues
'of men, women, horses, saddles, and other things, and
'abundance of paper money; all which, they believe, in
'the next life, are converted into real ones, for the
'use of the party deceased, or in some cases forwarded,
'in his care, to friends who had gone before.'[3]

Thus, then, by man in this stage of progress everything was regarded as having life, and being more or
less a deity.

'Africans, as a rule,' says Captain Burton, 'wor-
'ship everything except the Creator.'[4]

In India, says Dubois,[5] 'a woman adores the basket
'which serves to bring or to hold her necessaries, and
'offers sacrifices to it; as well as to the rice-mill, and
'other implements that assist her in her household
'labours. A carpenter does the like homage to his
'hatchet, his adze, and other tools; and likewise offers
'sacrifices to them. A Brahman does so to the style

[1] Dalton's Des. Ethn. of Bengal, p. 07.
[2] Astley, vol. iv. p. 04.
[3] Primitive Culture, vol. i. p. 443.
[4] Burton's Dahome, vol. ii. p. 134.
[5] People of India, p. 373. See also pp. 383, 380.

'with which he is going to write ; a soldier to the arms
'he is to use in the field; a mason to his trowel, and a
'labourer to his plough.'

The popular religion of the Andean people, says
Mr. Clement Markham,[1] 'consisted in the belief that
'all things in nature had an ideal or soul which ruled
'and guided them, and to which men might pray for
'help.'

Sir S. Baker[2] says : 'Should the present history of
'the country be written by an Arab scribe, the style of
'the description would be purely that of the Old Tes-
'tament, and the various calamities or the good fortunes
'that have in the course of nature befallen both the
'tribes and the individuals would be recounted either
'as special visitations of Divine wrath, or blessings for
'good deeds performed. If in a dream a particular
'course of action is suggested, the Arab believes that
'God has *spoken* and directed him. The Arab scribe
'or historian would describe the event as the "*voice* of
'"the Lord" (Kallam el Allah) having spoken unto
'the person; or, that God appeared to him in a dream
'and "*said*, &c." Thus, much allowance would be
'necessary, on the part of a European reader, for the
'figurative ideas and expressions of the people.'

Mr. Fergusson, indeed, regards tree-worship in association with serpent-worship as the primitive faith of
mankind. Mr. Wake[3] also says : 'How are we to ac-
'count for the Polynesians also affixing a sacred charac-
'ter to a species of the banyan, called by them the ava
'tree, and for the same phenomenon being found among

[1] Rites and Laws of the Incas, p. 11.
[2] The Nile Tributaries of Abys- sinia, by Sir. S. W. Baker, p. 139.
[3] Chapters on Man, p. 260.

' the African tribes on the Zambesi and the Shire,
' among the negroes of Western equatorial Africa, and
' even in Northern Australia ?  Such a fact as this can-
' not be accounted for as a mere coincidence.'

Since, however, tree-worship equally prevails in
America, we cannot regard it as any ' evidence of the
' common origin of the various races which practise ' it.
It is, however, one among many illustrations that the
human mind, in its upward progress, everywhere passes
through the same or very similar phases.

Tree-worship formerly existed in Assyria, Greece,[1]
Poland,[2] and France.  In Persia the Homa or Soma
worship was perhaps a case in point; Tacitus[3] mentions the sacred groves of Germany, and those of
England are familiar to everyone.  In the eighth century, St. Boniface found it necessary to cut down a
sacred oak; even recently an oak copse at Loch Siant,
in the Isle of Skye, was held so sacred that no person
would venture to cut the smallest branch from it;[4] and
it is said that oak-worship is still practised in Livonia.[5]

Trees were worshipped by the ancient Celts, and
De Brosses[6] even derives the word kirk, now softened
into church, from *quercus*, an oak; that species being peculiarly sacred.  The Lapps also used to worship trees.[7]

At the present day tree-worship prevails throughout
Central Africa, south of Egypt, and the Sahara.  The
Shangallas in Bruce's time worshipped ' trees, serpents,
' the moon, planets, and stars.'[8]

[1] Baum cultus der Hellenen, Bottlcher. 1856.
[2] Olaus Magnus, Bk. III. ch. i.
[3] Tacitus, Germania, ix.
[4] Early Races of Scotland, vol. i. p. 171.
[5] Jour. Anthr. Inst., 1873, p. 275.
[6] Loc. cit., p. 176.
[7] De Brosses, loc. cit., p. 169.
[8] Travels, vol. iv. p. 35. See also vol. vi. p. 344.

The date tree, says Burckhardt, ' was worshipped by
' the tribe Khozaa; and the Beni Thckyf adored the
' rock called El Lat; a large tree, called Zat Arowat,
' was revered by the Koreysh."[1]

The negroes of Guinea[2] worshipped three deities,
—serpents, trees, and the sea. Park[3] observed a tree
on the confines of Bondou hung with innumerable
offerings, principally rags. 'It had,' he says, 'a very
' singular appearance, being decorated with innumerable
' rags or strips of cloth, which persons travelling across
' the wilderness had tied to the branches.'

The negroes of Congo[4] 'adored a sacred tree called
' "Mirrone." One is generally planted near the houses,
' as if it were the tutelar god of the dwelling, the
' Gentiles adoring it as one of their idols.' They place
calabashes of palm wine at the feet of these trees, in
case they should be thirsty. Bosman also states that
along the Guinea Coast almost every village has its
sacred grove.[5] At Adducoodah, Oldfield[6] saw a 'gi-
' gantic tree, twelve yards and eight inches in circum-
' ference. I soon found it was considered sacred, and
' had several arrows stuck in it, from which were sus-
' pended fowls, several sorts of birds, and many other
' things, which had been offered by the natives to it as
' a deity.'

---

[1] Travels in Arabia, vol. i. p.
209.

[2] Voyage to Guinea, p. 106.
Bosman, Pinkerton's Voyages, vol.
xvi. p. 404. Merolla, Pinkerton's
Voyages, vol. xvi. p. 236.

[3] Travels, 1817, vol. i. pp. 64,
100. See also Caillié, vol. i. p.
150.

[4] Merolla's Voyage to Congo.
Pinkerton, vol. xvi. p. 236. Astley's
Collection of Voyages, vol. II. pp.
95, 97.

[5] Loc. cit., p. 809. See also Astley's Collection of Voyages, vol. ii.
p. 20. Tuckey's Narrative, p. 181.
Livingstone's South Africa, p. 405.

[6] Expedition, vol. ii. p. 117.

Chapman mentions a sacred tree among the Kaffirs, which was hung with numerous offerings.[1]

The Bo tree is much worshipped in India[2] and Ceylon.[3] 'The planting of the Rájâyatana tree by 'Buddha,' says Fergusson, 'has already been alluded 'to, but the history of the transference of a branch of 'the Bo tree from the Buddh-gyâ to Anurâdhapura is 'as authentic and as important as any event recorded 'in the Ceylonese annals. Sent by Asóka (250 B.C.), 'it was received with the utmost reverence by Devanam-'piyatisso, and planted in the most conspicuous spot in 'the centre of his capital. There it has been reverenced 'as the chief and most important "numen" of Ceylon 'for more than 2,000 years, and it, or its lineal de-'scendant, sprung at least from the old root, is there 'worshipped at this hour. The city is in ruins; its 'great dagobas have fallen to decay; its monasteries 'have disappeared; but the great Bo tree still 'flourishes according to the legend—ever green, never 'growing or decreasing, but living on for ever for the 'delight and worship of mankind. Annually thou-'sands repair to the sacred precincts within which 'it stands, to do it honour, and to offer up those 'prayers for health and prosperity which are more 'likely to be answered if uttered in its presence. There 'is probably no older idol in the world, certainly none 'more venerated.'

Some of the Chittagong Hill tribes worship the

[1] Travels, vol. ii. p. 50. Klemm quotes also Villault, Rel. des Costes d'Afrique S., pp. 203, 207. Arbous-set, *loc. cit.*, p. 104.

[2] Tree and Serpent Worship, p. 50, *et seq.*
[3] *Ibid.*, p. 50.

bamboo,[1] and in the Simla Hills *Cupressus torulosa* is regarded as a sacred tree.[2]

In Beerbhoom, tree-worship is very general, and 'once a year the whole capital repairs to a shrine in 'the jungle.'[3] This shrine consists of three trees, but it would appear that they are now venerated rather as the abodes of deities, than as the actual deities themselves. The Khyens also worship a thick bushy tree called Subri.[4]

In Siberia the Jakuts have sacred trees on which they 'hang all manner of nicknacks, as iron, brass, 'copper, &c.'[5] The Ostyaks also, as Pallas informs us, used to worship trees.[6] 'There was pointed out to us,' says Erman,[7] 'as an important monument of an early 'epoch in the history of Beresov, a larch about fifty 'feet high, and now, through age, flourishing only at 'the top, which has been preserved in the churchyard. 'In former times, when the Ostyak rulers dwelt in 'Beresov, this tree was the particular object of their 'adoration. In this, as in many other instances, ob'served by the Russians, the peculiar sacredness of the 'tree was due to the singularity of its form and growth, 'for about six feet from the ground the trunk separated 'into two equal parts, and again united. It was the 'custom of the superstitious natives to place costly 'offerings of every kind in the opening of the trunk;

[1] Lewin's Hill Tracts of Chittagong, p. 10. Dalton's Trans. Etho. Soc., vol. vi. p. 34.

[2] Thomson's Travels in W. Himalaya, p. 10.

[3] Hunter's Annals of Rural Bengal, 1868, p. 191.

[4] Dalton's Des. Ethn. of Bengal,

p. 115.

[5] Strahlenberg's Travels in Siberia, p. 381.

[6] *Loc. cit.*, vol. iv. p. 70.

[7] Erman's Travels in Siberia, vol. i. p. 464. See also Des. de toutes les Nat. de l'Emp. Russe, Pt. XI. p. 49.

'nor have they yet abandoned the usage; a fact well
'known to the enlightened Kosaks, who enrich them-
'selves by carrying off secretly the sacrificial gifts.'
Hanway,[1] in his Travels in Persia, mentions a tree 'to
'which were affixed a number of rags left there as
'health-offerings by persons afflicted with ague. This
'was beside a desolate caravanserai where the traveller
'found nothing but water.'

In some parts[2] of Sumatra likewise 'they super-
'stitiously believe that certain trees, particularly those
'of venerable appearance (as an old jawi-jawi, or banian
'tree), are the residence, or rather the material frame
'of spirits of the woods; an opinion which exactly
'answers to the idea entertained by the ancients of the
'dryades and hamadryades. At Benkunat, in the Lam-
'pong country, there is a long stone, standing on a flat
'one, supposed by the people to possess extraordinary
'power of virtue. It is reported to have been once
'thrown down into the water, and to have raised itself
'again into its original position, agitating the elements
'at the same time with a prodigious storm. To ap-
'proach it without respect they believe to be the source
'of misfortune to the offender.'

Among the natives of the Philippines also we find
the worship of trees.[3] They 'believed that the world
'at first consisted only of sky and water, and between
'these two a glede; which, weary with flying about,
'and finding no place to rest, set the water at variance
'with the sky, which, in order to keep it in bounds,

[1] Quoted in the Early Races of Scotland, vol. i. p. 103. See also De Brosses, *loc. cit.*, pp. 144, 145.

[2] Marsden's History of Sumatra, p. 301.

[3] *Ibid.*, p. 303.

' and that it should not get uppermost, loaded the water
' with a number of islands, in which the glede might
' settle and leave them at peace. Mankind, they said,
' sprang out of a large cane with two joints; that floating
' about in the water was at length thrown by the waves
' against the feet of the glede, as it stood on shore,
' which opened it with its bill; the man came out of one
' joint, the woman out of the other. These were soon
' after married by the consent of their god, Bathala
' Meycapal, which caused the first trembling of the
' earth; and from thence are descended the different
' nations of the world.'

The Feejeeans also worshipped certain plants.[1]
Tree-worship was less prevalent in America. Trees
and plants were worshipped by the Mandans and
Monitarees.[2] A large ash was venerated by the Indians
of Lake Superior.[3]

In North America, Franklin[4] describes a sacred tree
on which the Crees ' had hung strips of buffalo flesh
' and pieces of cloth.' They complained to him of some
' Stone Indians, who, two nights before, had stripped
' their revered tree of many of its offerings.' In Mexico
Mr. Tylor[5] observed an ancient cypress of remarkable
size: ' all over its branches were fastened votive offer-
' ings of the Indians, hundreds of locks of coarse black
' hair, teeth, bits of coloured cloth, rags and morsels of
' ribbon. The tree was many centuries old, and had
' probably had some mysterious influence ascribed to it,

---

[1] Fiji and the Fijians, vol. i. p. 210.

[2] Müller, Amer. Urrel., p. 59.

[3] Müller, loc. cit., p. 125.

[4] Journeys to the Polar Sea, vol. i. p. 221.

[5] Anahuac, p. 215. He mentions a second case of the same sort on p. 204.

' and been decorated with such simple offerings long
' before the discovery of America.' In Nicaragua, not
only large trees, but even maize and beans, were worshipped.' Maize was also worshipped in the Peruvian
province of Huanca.[2]

In Patagonia, Mr. Darwin[3] mentions a sacred tree
' which the Indians reverence as the altar of Wallecchu.
' It is situated on a high part of the plain, and hence is
' a landmark visible at a great distance.  As soon as a
' tribe of Indians come in sight of it they offer their
' adorations by loud shouts. . . . . It stands by itself
' without any neighbour, and was indeed the first tree
' we saw; afterwards we met with a few others of the
' same kind, but they were far from common.  Being
' winter, the tree had no leaves, but in their place num-
' berless threads, by which the various offerings, such as
' cigars, bread, meat, pieces of cloth, &c., had been sus-
' pended.  Poor people, not having anything better, only
' pulled a thread out of their ponchoo, and fastened it
' to the tree.  The Indians, moreover, were accustomed
' to pour spirits and maté into a certain hole, and like-
' wise to smoke upwards, thinking thus to afford all
' possible gratification to Wallecchu.  To complete the
' scene, the tree was surrounded by the bleached bones
' of the horses which had been slaughtered as sacrifices.
' All Indians, of every age and sex, made their offerings;
' they then thought that their horses would not tire,
' and that they themselves should be prosperous.  The

---

' Müller, *loc. cit.*, p. 404.  See
also p. 401.
    [2] Martius, *loc. cit.*, p. 80.  G. de
la Vega, Commen. of the Incas, vol.

i. pp. 47, 331.
    [3] Researches in Geology and
Natural History, p. 70.

' Gaucho who told me this said that in the time of peace
' he had witnessed this scene, and that he and others
' used to wait till the Indians had passed by, for the
' sake of stealing their offerings from Walleechu.  The
' Gauchos think that the Indians consider the tree as
' the god itself; but it seems far more probable that
' they regard it as the altar '—a distinction, however,
which a Patagonian Indian would hardly perceive.

The Abenaquis also had a sacred tree.[1]

Thus, then, this form of religion can be shown to be
general to most of the great races of men at a certain
stage of mental development.[2]

We will now pass to the worship of lakes, rivers,
and springs, which we shall find to have been not less
widely distributed.  It was at one time very prevalent
in Western Europe.  Herodotus mentions the existence of sacred lakes among the Libyans.[3]  According
to Cicero, Justin, and Strabo, there was a lake near
Toulouse in which the neighbouring tribes used to de-
posit offerings of gold and silver.  Tacitus, Pliny, and
Virgil also allude to sacred lakes.  In the sixth century,
Gregory of Tours mentions a sacred lake on Mount
Helanus.

In Brittany there is the celebrated well of St. Anne
of Auray, and the sacred fountain at Lanmeur, in the
crypt of the church of St. Melars, to which crowds of
pilgrims still resort.[4]

In our own country traces of water-worship are
also abundant.  It is expressly mentioned by Gildas,[5]

[1] De Brosses, Du Culte des
Dieux Fétiches, p. 61.  Lafitau, vol.
i. p. 140.
[2] Early Races of Scotland, vol.
i. p. 168.
[3] Melpomene, clvlii. clxxxi.
[4] Mon. Hist. Brit. vii.

and is said to be denounced in a Saxon homily preserved in Cambridge.[1] ' At St. Fillan's [2] well, at Comrie,
' in Perthshire, numbers of persons in search of health,
' so late as 1791, came or were brought to drink of the
' waters and bathe in it. All these walked or were
' carried three times deasil (sunwise) round the well.
' They also threw each a white stone on an adjacent
' cairn, and left behind a scrap of their clothing as an
' offering to the genius of the place.' In the Scotch
islands also are many sacred wells, and I have myself
seen the holy well in one of the islands of Loch Maree,
surrounded by the little offerings of the peasantry, con-
sisting principally of rags and halfpence.

Colonel Forbes Leslie [3] observes that in Scotland
' there are few parishes without a holy well;' nor was
it much less general in Ireland. The kelpie, or spirit
of the waters, assumed various forms, that of a man,
woman, horse, or bull being the most common. Scotland and Ireland are full of legends about this spirit, a
firm belief in the existence of which was general in the
last century, and is even now far from abandoned.

Of river-worship we have many cases recorded in
Greek history.[4] Peleus dedicated a lock of Achilles'
hair to the river Spercheios. The Pulians sacrificed a
bull to Alpheios; Themis summoned the rivers to the
great Olympian assembly. Okeanos the Ocean, and
various fountains, were regarded as divinities. Water-
worship in the time of Homer was, however, gradually

[1] Wright's Superstitions of England.
[2] Early Races of Scotland, vol. i.
p. 150.
[3] See Forbes Leslie's Early
Races of Scotland, vol. i. p. 145.
Campbell's Tales of the West Highlands.
[4] Juventus Mundi, p. 100.

ebbing away; and belonged rather, I think, to an earlier
stage in development, than, as Mr. Gladstone believes,
to a different race.[1]

In Northern Asia, the Tunguses[2] and Votyaks[3]
worship various springs. De Brosses mentions that the
'River Sogd was worshipped at Samarcand.[4] In[5] the
'tenth century a schism took place in Persia among
'the Armenians, one party being accused of despising
'the holy well of Vagarschichat.'

The Bouriats also, though Buddhists, have sacred
lakes. Atkinson thus describes one. In an after-dinner
ramble, he says,[6] 'I came upon the small and pictu-
'resque lake of Ikeougoun, which lies in the mountains
'to the north of San-ghin-dalai, and is held in venera-
'tion. They have erected a small wooden temple on
'the shore, and here they come to sacrifice, offering up
'milk, butter, and the fat of the animals, which they
'burn on the little altars. The large rock in the lake
'is with them a sacred stone, on which some rude
'figures are traced; and on the bank opposite they
'place rods with small silk flags, having inscriptions
'printed on them.' Lake Ahoosh also is accounted
sacred among the Baskhirs.[7]

The divinity of water, says Dubois, is recognised by
'all the people of India.'[8] Besides the well-known
worship of the holy Ganges, the tribes of the Neilgherry
Hills[9] worship rivers under the name of Gangamma,

[1] Juventus Mundi, pp. 177, 187.
[2] Pallas, vol. iv. p. 641.
[3] Des. de toutes les Nat. de
l'Emp. Russe, Pt. II. p. 80.
[4] Loc. cit., p. 140.
[5] Whipple, Report on the Indian
Tribes, p. 44.

[6] Siberia, p. 445.
[7] Atkinson's Oriental and Western Siberia, p. 141.
[8] The People of India, p. 125.
See also pp. 376, 410.
[9] The Tribes of the Neilgherry
Hills, p. 68.

and in crossing them it is usual to drop a coin into the
water as an offering, and the price of a safe passage.
In the Deccan and in Ceylon trees and bushes near
springs may often be seen covered with votive offerings.[1]
The worship of rivers also prevails among many of the
Hill tribes, as, for instance, the Karrias, Santhals,
Khonds, &c.[2]  The people of Sumatra 'are said to pay
' a kind of adoration to the sea, and to make it an
' offering of cakes and sweetmeats on their beholding
' it for the first time, deprecating its power of doing
' them harm.'[3]

In the Ashantee country, Bosman mentions 'the
' Chamascian river, or Rio de San Juan, called by the
' negroes Bossum Pra, which they adore as a god, as
' the word Bossum signifies.'[4]  The Eufrates, the principal river of Whydah, is also looked on as sacred, and
a yearly procession is made to it.[5]  Phillips[6] mentions,
that on one occasion, in 1693, when the sea was un-
usually rough, the Kaboshcers complained to the king,
who ' desired them to be easy, and he would make the
' sea quiet next day.  Accordingly he sent his *fetish-*
' *man* with a jar of palm oil, a bag of rice and corn, a
' jar of *pitto*, a bottle of brandy, a piece of painted calico,
' and several other things to present to the sea.  Being
' come to the seaside (as the author was informed by
' his men, who saw the ceremony), he made a speech to
' it, assuring it that his king was its friend, and loved

[1] Early Races of Scotland, vol.
I. p. 163.
[2] Ibid, vol. ii. p. 407.  Dalton's
Des. Eths. of Bengal, p. 150.
[3] Marsden, loc. cit., p. 301.
[4] Loc. cit., p. 348.  See also p.
404.  Smith's Voyage to Guinea, p.
197.
[5] Astley, loc. cit., p. 20.
[6] Astley's Collection of Voyages,
vol. ii. p. 411.

' the white men; that they were honest fellows, and
' came to trade with him for what he wanted; and that
' he requested the sea not to be angry, nor hinder them
' to land their goods; he told it, that if it wanted palm
' oil, his king had sent it some; and so threw the jar
' with the oil into the sea, as he did, with the same
' compliment, the rice, corn, *pitto*, brandy, calico, &c.'
Again, Villault[1] mentions that lakes, rivers, and ponds
come in also for their share of worship. He was present
at a singular ceremony near Akkra. A great number
of blacks assembled about a pond, bringing with them a
sheep and some gallipots, which they offered to the
pond, M. Villault being informed 'that this lake, or
' pond, being one of their deities, and the common
' messenger of all the rivers of their country, they threw
' in the gallipots with these ceremonies to implore his
' assistance; and to beg him to carry immediately that
' pot, in their name, to the other rivers and lakes to buy
' water for them, and hoped, at his return, he would
' pour the pot-full on their corn, that they might have
' a good crop.'

Some of the negroes on the Guinea Coast[2] 'looked
' on the whites as the gods of the sea; that the mast
' was a divinity that made the ship walk, and the pump
' was a miracle, since it could make water rise up, whose
' natural property is to descend.'

Mr. Creswick, in his description of the Veys, says,[3]
' there is a dangerous rock in the Mafa river, which is
' never passed without giving tribute, either a leaf of

[1] Astley's Collection of Voyages,
p. 608.
[3] Astley, vol. ii. p. 106.

[2] Trans. Etho. Soc., vol. vi. p.
350.

' tobacco, a handful of rice, or drink of rum, as a peace-
' offering to the spirit of the flood.'

On the Zambési, the natives place offerings on the
rocks in dangerous places, to propitiate the spirits of
the waters.[1]

In North America the Dacotahs[2] worship a god of
the waters under the name of Unktahe. They say that
' this god and its associates are seen in their dreams. It
' is the master-spirit of all their juggling and supersti-
' tious belief. From it the medicine-men obtain their
' supernatural powers, and a great part of their religion
' springs from this god.' Franklin[3] mentions that, the
wife of one of his Indian guides being ill, her husband
' made an offering to the water-spirits, whose wrath he
' apprehended to be the cause of her malady. It con-
' sisted of a knife, a piece of tobacco, and some other
' trifling articles, which were tied up in a small bundle,
' and committed to the rapid.' Carver[4] observes that
when the Redskins ' arrive on the borders of Lake
' Superior, on the banks of the Mississippi, or any other
' great body of water, they present to the spirit who
' resides there some kind of offering, as the prince of
' the Winnebagoes did when he attended me to the Falls
' of St. Anthony.' Tanner also gives instances of this
custom.[5] On one occasion a Redskin, addressing the
spirit of the waters, ' told him that he had come a long
' way to pay his adorations to him, and now would
' make him the best offerings in his power. He

[1] Livingstone's Zambesi, p. 41.
[2] Schoolcraft's Indian Tribes, Pt. III. p. 445.
[3] Journey to the Shores of the Polar Sea, 1819-22, vol. ii. p. 245.
[4] Carver's Travels, p. 383.
[5] Narrative of the Captivity of John Tanner, p. 40.

' accordingly first threw his pipe into the stream; then
' the roll that contained his tobacco; after these, the
' bracelets he wore on his arms and wrists; next an
' ornament that encircled his neck, composed of beads
' and wires; and at last the earrings from his ears; in
' short, he presented to his god every part of his dress
' that was valuable.'[1]

The Mandans also were in the habit of sacrificing to
the spirit of the waters.[2]

In North Mexico, near the 35th Parallel, Lieutenant
Whipple found a sacred spring which from time imme-
morial 'had been held sacred to the rain-god.'[3] No
animal may drink of its waters. It must be annually
cleansed with ancient vases, which, having been transmitted from generation to generation by the caciques,
are then placed upon the walls, never to be removed.
The frog, the tortoise, and the rattlesnake, represented
upon them, are sacred to Montezuma, the patron of the
place, who would consume by lightning any sacrilegious
hand that should dare to take the relics away. In Nicaragua rain was worshipped under the name of
Quintcot. The principal water-god of Mexico, however, was Tlaloc, who was worshipped by the Toltecs,
Chichimecs, and Aztecs.[4] In New Mexico, not far from
Zuni, Dr. Bell[5] describes a sacred spring 'about eight
' feet in diameter, walled round with stones, of which
' neither cattle nor men may drink: the animals sacred
' to water (frogs, tortoises, and snakes) alone must

[1] Narrative of the Captivity of
John Tanner, p. 87.
[2] Catlin's North American Indians, vol. i. p. 160.
[3] Report on the Indian Tribes, p.
40.
[4] Müller, Amer. Urrel., p. 490.
[5] Ethn. Journ., 1863, p. 227.

' enter the pool. Once a year the cacique and his
' attendants perform certain religious rites at the
' spring : it is thoroughly cleared out ; water-pots are
' brought as an offering to the spirit of Montezuma, and
' are placed bottom upwards on the top of the wall of
' stones. Many of these have been removed ; but some
' still remain, while the ground around is strewn with
' fragments of vases which have crumbled into decay
' from age.' In Peru the sea, under the name of Mama
Cocha, was the principal deity of the Chinchas.[1] The
Indians of the Coast, says Garcilasso de la Vega, ' from
' Truxillo to Tarapaca, which are at the northern and
' southern extremities of Peru, worshipped the sea in
' the shape of a fish.'[2] One branch of the Collas deduced their origin from a river, the others from a
spring;[3] there was also a special rain-goddess. In
Paraguay[4] also the rivers are propitiated by offerings
of tobacco.

We will now pass to the worship of stones and
mountains, a form of religion not less general than
those already described.

M. Dulaure, in his ' Histoire Abrégée des Cultes,'
explains the origin of stone-worship as arising from the
respect paid to boundary-stones. I do not doubt that
the worship of some particular stones may thus have
originated. Hermes, or Termes, was evidently of this
character, and hence we may perhaps explain the peculiar characteristics of Hermes, or Mercury, whose symbol
was an upright stone.

[1] Müller, Amer. Urrel., p. 308.   p. 168.
[2] Loc. cit., p. 146.   [4] Loc. cit., p. 252.
[3] Garcilasso de la Vega, vol. i.

Mercury, or Hermes, says Lemprière, 'was the mes-
' senger of the gods.   He was the patron of travellers
' and shepherds; he conducted the souls of the dead
' into the infernal regions, and not only presided over
' orators, merchants, and declaimers, but he was also the
' god of thieves, pickpockets, and all dishonest persons.'
He invented letters and the lyre, and was the originator
of arts and sciences.

It is difficult at first to see the connection between
these various offices, characterised as they are by such
opposite peculiarities.   Yet they all follow, I think, from
the custom of marking boundaries by upright stones.
Hence the name Hermes, or Termes, the boundary.   In
the troublous times of old, it was usual, in order to avoid
disputes, to leave a tract of neutral territory between
the possessions of different nations.   These were called
marches ; hence the title of Marquis, which means an
officer appointed to watch the frontier or ' march.'
These marches, not being cultivated, served as grazing
grounds.    To them came merchants in order to exchange on neutral ground the products of their respective countries ; here also for the same reason treaties
were negotiated.   Here again international games and
sports were held.   Upright stones were used to indicate places of burial ; and lastly, on them were engraved
laws and decrees, records of remarkable events, and the
praises of the deceased.

Hence Mercury, represented by a plain upright
stone, was the god of travellers, because he was a landmark ; of shepherds, as presiding over the pastures ; he
conducted the souls of the dead into the infernal regions,
because even in very early days upright stones were

used as tombstones; he was the god of merchants, because commerce was carried on principally at the frontiers; and of thieves, out of sarcasm. He was the messenger of the gods, because ambassadors met at the frontiers; and of eloquence for the same reason. He invented the lyre, and presided over games, because contests in music, &c. were held on neutral ground; and he was regarded as the author of letters, because inscriptions were engraved on upright pillars.

Stone-worship, however, in its simpler forms has, I think, a different origin from this, and is merely a form of that indiscriminate worship which characterises the human mind in a particular phase of development.

Pallas states that the Ostyaks[1] and Tunguses worship mountains,[2] and the Tartars stones.[3] Near Lake Baikal[4] is a sacred rock which is regarded as the special abode of an evil spirit, and is consequently much feared by the natives. In India stone-worship is very prevalent, especially among the aboriginal tribes. The Asagas of Mysore ' worship a god called Bhuma Devam, ' who is represented by a shapeless stone.'[5] 'One ' thing is certain,' says Mr. Hislop, ' the worship (of ' stones) is spread over all parts of the country, from ' Berar to the extreme east of Bustar, and that not ' merely among the Hinduised aborigines, who had ' begun to honour Khandova, &c., but among the rudest ' and most savage tribes. He is generally adored in ' the form of an unshapely stone covered with ver-

[1] Voyages de Pallas, vol. iv. p. 70.

[2] Ibid, pp. 434, 648.

[3] Ibid., pp. 514, 588.

[4] Hill's Travels in Siberia, vol.

ii. p. 142.

[5] Buchanan's Journey, vol. i. p. 338. Quoted in Ethnol. Journ., vol. viii. p. 90.

' milion.' [1]　' Two rude slave castes in Tulava (Southern
' India), the Bakadaru and Betadâra, worship a benevo-
' lent deity named Buta, represented by a stone kept
' in every house.' [2]　Indeed, 'in every part of Southern
' India, four or five stones may often be seen in the
' ryots' field, placed in a row and daubed with red paint,
' which they consider as guardians of the field and call
' the five Pandus.' [3]　Colonel Forbes Leslie supposes
that this red paint is intended to represent blood. [4]
The god of each Khond village is represented by three
stones. [5]　Pl. III. represents a group of sacred stones,
near Delgaum, in the Dekkan, from a figure given by
Colonel Forbes Leslie in his interesting work. [6]　The
three largest stood ' in front of the centre of two straight
' lines, each of which consisted of thirteen stones.
' These lines were close together, and the edges of the
' stones were placed as near to each other as it was
' possible to do with slabs which, although selected, had
' never been artificially shaped.　The stone in the
' centre of each line was nearly as high as the highest
' of the three that stood in front; but the others gradually
' decreased in size from the centre, until those at the
' ends were less than a foot above the ground, into
' which they were all secured.　Three stones, not fixed,
' were placed in front of the centre of the group; they
' occupied the same position, and were intended for the
' same purposes, as those in the circular temple just
' described.　All the stones had been selected of an

[1] Aboriginal Tribes, p. 10.
Quoted in Ethnol. Journ., vol. viii.
p. 181.
[2] Journ. Ethnol. Soc., vol. viii.
p. 115.

[3] Ibid., vol. ix. p. 125.
[4] Early Races of Scotland, vol.
ii. p. 402.
[5] Loc. cit., vol. ii. p. 407.
[6] Loc. cit., vol. ii. p. 404.

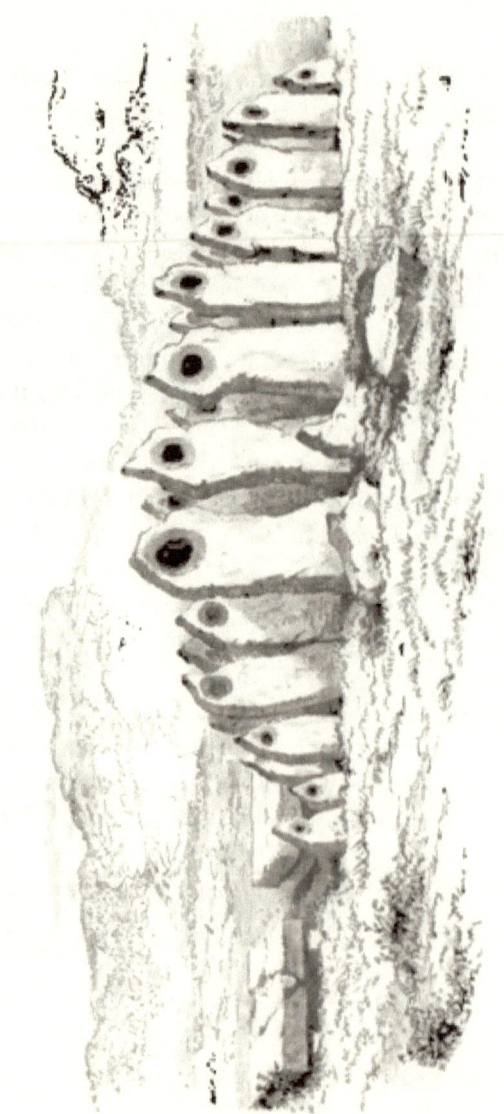

INDIAN SACRED STONES

' angular shape, with somewhat of an obelisk form in
' general appearance. The central group and double
' lines faced nearly east, and on that side were white-
' washed. On the white, near, although not reaching
' quite to the apex of each stone, nor extending alto-
' gether to the sides, was a large spot of red paint,
' two-thirds of which from the centre were blacked over,
' leaving only a circular external belt of red. This
' gave, as I believe it was intended to do, a good repre-
' sentation of a large spot of blood.'

In connection with these painted stones it is remarkable that in New Zealand red is a sacred colour, and
' the way of rendering anything tapu was by making it
' red. When a person died, his house was thus painted;
' when the tapu was laid on anything, the chief erected
' a post and painted it with the kura; wherever a corpse
' rested, some memorial was set up; oftentimes the
' nearest stone, rock, or tree served as a monument;
' but whatever object was selected, it was sure to be
' painted red. If the corpse was conveyed by water,
' wherever they landed a similar token was left; and
' when it reached its destination, the canoe was dragged
' on shore, painted red, and abandoned. When the
' hahunga took place, the scraped bones of the chief
' thus ornamented, and wrapped in a red-stained mat,
' were deposited in a box or bowl smeared with the
' sacred colour, and placed in a painted tomb. Near
' his final resting-place a lofty and elaborately carved
' monument was erected to his memory; this was called
' the tiki, which was also thus coloured.'[1] Red was
also a sacred colour in Congo.[2]

[1] Taylor's New Zealand and the New Zealanders, p. 115.

[2] Merolla, Pinkerton, vol. xvi p. 273.

Colonel Dalton describes[1] a ceremony which curiously resembles the well-known scene in the life of Elijah, when he met the Priests of Baal on the top of Carmel, showed his superior power, and recalled Israel to the old faith. The Southals of Central Hindostan worship a conspicuous hill called 'Marang Boroo.' In times of drought they go to the top of this sacred mountain, and offer their sacrifices on a large flat stone, playing on drums and beseeching their god for rain. 'They shake their heads violently, till they work them-'selves into a phrensy, and the movement becomes 'involuntary. They go on thus wildly gesticulating, 'till a "little cloud like a man's hand" is seen. Then 'they arise, take up the drums, and dance the kurrun 'on the rock, till Marang Boroo's response to their 'prayer is heard in the distant rumbling of thunder, 'and they go home rejoicing. They must go " fasting '" to the mount," and stay there till "there is a sound '" of abundance of rain," when they get them down to 'eat and drink. My informant tells me it always 'comes before evening.'

The Arabians, down to the time of Mahomet, worshipped a black stone. 'The Beni Thekyf adored the 'rock called El Lat.'[2] The Phœnicians also worshipped a deity under the form of an unshapen stone.[3] The god Heliogabulus was merely a black stone of a conical form. Upright stones were worshipped by the Romans and the Greeks, under the name of Hermes, or Mercury. The Thespians had a rude stone, which they regarded

---

[1] Trans. Ethn. Soc., N.S., vol.     vol. i. p. 290.
vi. p. 35.                          [2] Kenrick's Phœnicia, p. 323.
[3] Burckhardt's Tr. in Arabia,

as a deity, and the Bœotians worshipped Hercules under the same form.[1] The Laplanders also had sacred mountains and rocks.[2]

In Western Europe during the middle ages we meet with several denunciations of stone-worship, proving its strong hold on the people. Thus[3] 'the worship of ' stones was condemned by Theodoric, Archbishop of ' Canterbury, in the seventh century, and is among the ' acts of heathenism forbidden by King Edgar in the ' tenth, and by Cnut in the eleventh century. In a ' council held at Tours in A.D. 567 priests were admon- ' ished to shut the doors of their churches against all ' persons worshipping upright stones, and Mahé states ' that a manuscript record of the proceedings of a ' council held at Nantes in the seventh century makes ' mention of the stone-worship of the Armoricans.'

' Les Français,' says Dulaure,[4] ' adorèrent des pierres ' plusieurs siècles après l'établissement du christianisme ' parmi eux. Diverses lois civiles et religieuses attestent ' l'existence de ce culte. Un capitulaire de Charle- ' magne, et le concile de Leptine, de l'an 743, défendent ' les cérémonies superstitieuses qui se pratiquent auprès ' des pierres et auprès des Fans consacrés à Mercure et ' à Jupiter. Le concile de Nantes, cité par Réginon, ' fait la même défense. Il nous apprend que ces pierres ' étaient situées dans des lieux agrestes, et que le peuple, ' dupe des tromperies des démons, y apportait ses vœux ' et ses offrandes. Les conciles d'Arles, de Tours, le ' capitulaire d'Aix-la-Chapelle, de l'an 789, et plusieurs ' synodes, renouvellent ces prohibitions.'

[1] See De Brosses, *loc. cit.*, p. 155.    p. 250.
[2] Dulaure, *loc. cit.*, p. 541.    [4] Dulaure, *loc. cit.*, vol. i. p. 304.
[3] Forbes Leslie, *loc. cit.*, vol. i.

In Ireland, in the fifth century, King Laoghaire worshipped a stone pillar called the Crom-Cruach, which was overthrown by St. Patrick. Another stone at Clogher was worshipped by the Irish under the name of Kermand-Kelstach.[1] There was a sacred stone in Jura[2] round which the people used to move 'deasil,' i.e. sunwise. 'In some of the Hebrides[3] the people 'attributed oracular power to a large black stone.' In the island of Skye 'in every district there is to be met 'with a rude stone consecrated to Grungach, or Apollo. 'The Rev. Mr. McQueen of Skye says that in almost 'every village the sun, called Grugach, or the Fair-'haired, is represented by a rude stone; and he further 'states that libations of milk were poured on the gruaich-'stones.' 'Finn Magnusen,' says Prof. Nilsson, 'relates 'that the peasants in certain mountain districts in Nor-'way, even as late as the close of the last century, used 'to preserve stones of a round form, and reverence them 'in the same manner as their pagan ancestors used to 'worship their idols. They washed them every Thurs-'day evening, smeared them before the fire with butter, 'or some other grease, then dried them and laid them in 'the seat of honour upon fresh straw; at certain times of 'the year they were steeped in ale, and all this under 'the supposition that they would bring luck and com-'fort to the house.'[4]

Passing to Africa, Caillié observed near the negro village of N'pal a sacred stone, on which everyone as he passed threw a thread out of his 'pagne,' or breech-

[1] Dr. Todd's St. Patrick, p. 127.   257.
[2] Martin's Western Isles, p. 241.      [4] Nilsson on the Stone Age, p.
[3] Forbes Leslie, loc. cit., vol. i. p.   241.

cloth, as a sort of offering. The natives firmly believe that when any danger threatens the village this stone leaves its place and ' moves thrice round it in the pre- ' ceding night, by way of warning.'[1]

Bruce observes that the pagan Abyssinians ' worship ' a tree, and likewise a stone.'[2]

The Tahitians believed in two principal gods ; ' the ' Supreme Deity, one of these two first beings, they call ' Taroataihetoomoo, and the other, whom they suppose ' to have been a rock, Tepapa.'[3] The volcanic moun- tain Tongariro was ' held in traditional veneration by ' the New Zealanders.'[4]

In the Feejee [5] Islands ' rude consecrated stones (fig. ' 20) are to be seen near Vuna, where offerings of food ' are sometimes made. Another stands on a reef near ' Naloa, to which the natives *tama* ; and one near Tho- ' kova, Na Fiti Levu, named Lovekaveka, is regarded ' as the abode of a goddess, for whom food is provided. ' This, as seen in the engraving, is like a round black ' milestone, slightly inclined, and having a liku (girdle) ' tied round the middle. The shrine of O Rewau is a ' large stone, which, like the one near Naloa, hates mos- ' quitoes, and keeps them from collecting near where he ' rules ; he has also two large stones for his wives, one ' of whom came from Yandua, and the other from ' Yasawa. Although no one pretends to know the ' origin of Ndengei, it is said that his mother, in the ' form of two great stones, lies at the bottom of a moat.

[1] Caillié, vol. i. p. 26.
[2] Bruce's Travels, vol. vi. p. 343.
[3] Hawkesworth's Voyages, vol. ii. p. 238.
[4] Dieffenbach's New Zealand, vol. i. p. 347.
[5] Williams' Fiji and the Fijians, vol. i. p. 220.

' Stones are also used to denote the locality of some
' other gods, and the occasional resting-places of others.
· On the southern beaches of Vanua Levu a large stone
· is seen which has fallen upon a smaller one. These,
' it is said, represent the gods of two towns on that coast
' fighting, and their quarrel has for years been adopted
' by those towns.' On one of these sacred stones in the

Fig. 20.

SACRED STONES. (Feejee Islands.)

same neighbourhood are circular marks, closely resembling those on some of our European menhirs, &c.

In Micronesia, in the groups of Apamama and
Tarawa, 'Tabueriki is worshipped under the form of a
' flat coral stone, of irregular shape, about three feet
' long by eighteen inches wide, set up on one end in the
' open air.'[1] The Tannese also venerate stones, and

[1] Hale's Ethn. of the U.S. Ex. Exp., p. 97.

the principal deity of Tokalau was supposed to be embodied in a stone, which is carefully wrapped up in fine
mats.[1] The Sumatrans also, as already mentioned (anté,
p. 283), had sacred stones.

Prescott[2] says, that a Dacotah Indian ' will pick up
' a round stone, of any kind, and paint it, and go a few
' rods from his lodge, and clear away the grass, say
' from one to two feet in diameter, and there place his
' stone, or god, as he would term it, and make an
' offering of some tobacco and some feathers, and pray
' to the stone to deliver him from some danger that he
' has probably dreamed of, or from imagination.'

The Monitarris also before any great undertaking
were in the habit of making offerings to a sacred stone
named Mih Choppenish.[3] In Florida a mountain called
Olaimi was worshipped, and among the Natchez of
Louisiana a conical stone.[4]

In South America the Peruvians kept ' stones in
' their houses, treating them as gods, and sacrificing
' human flesh and blood to them.'[5]

Fire-worship is so widely distributed as to be almost
universal. Since the introduction of lucifer matches we
can hardly appreciate the difficulty which a savage has
in obtaining a light, especially in damp weather. It is
said, however, that some Australian tribes did not know
how to do so, and that others, if their fire went out,
would go many miles to borrow a spark from another
tribe, rather than attempt to produce a new one for

[1] Turner's Nineteen Years in Polynesia, pp. 88, 527.

[2] Schoolcraft's Indian Tribes, vol. ii. p. 220. Lafitau, vol. ii. p. 321.

[3] Klemm, Culturgeschichte, vol. ii. p. 178.

[4] Lafitau, vol. i. p. 140.

[5] Garcilasso de la Vega, vol. ii. p. 138. See also vol. i. p. 47.

themselves. Hence in several very widely separated parts of the world we find it has been customary to tell off one or more persons, whose sole duty it should be to keep up a continual fire. Hence, no doubt, the origin of the Vestal Virgins; and hence also the idea of the sacredness of fire would naturally arise.

According to Lafitau,[1] M. Huet, in a work which I have not been able to see, 'fait une longue énumération
' des peuples qui entretenoient ce feu sacré, et il cite
' partout ses autorités, de sorte qu'il paroit qu'il n'y
' avoit point de partie du monde cannu, où ce culte ne
' fût universellement répandu. Dans l'Asie, outre les
' Juifs et les Chaldéens dont nous venons de parler,
' outre les peuples de Phrygie, de Lycie, et de l'Asie-
' Mineure, il étoit encore chez les Perses, les Mèdes, les
' Scythes, les Sarmates, chez toutes les nations du Ponte
' et de la Cappadoce, chez toutes celles des Indes, où
' l'on se faisoit un devoir de se jeter dans les flammes,
' et de s'y consumer en holocauste, et chez toutes celles
' des deux Arabies, où chaque jour à certaines heures
' on faisoit un sacrifice au feu, dans lequel plusieurs
' personnes se dévouoient. Dans l'Afrique il étoit non-
' seulement chez les Égyptiens, qui entretenoient ce feu
' immortel dans chaque temple, ainsi que l'assure
' Porphyre, mais encore dans l'Éthiopie, dans la Lybie,
' dans le temple de Jupiter Ammon, et chez les Atlan-
' tiques, où Hiarbas, roy des Garamantes et des Getules,
' avoit dressé cent autels, et consacré autant de feux,
' que Virgile appelle des feux vigilans et les gardes
' éternelles des dieux. Dans l'Europe le culte de Vesta

---

[1] Garcilasso de la Vega, p. 153.

' étoit si bien établi, que, sans parler de Rome et de
' l'Italie, il n'y avoit point de ville de la Grèce qui n'eut
' un temple, un prytanée, et un feu éternel, ainsi que le
' remarque Casaubon dans ses "Notes sur Athénée."
' Les temples célèbres d'Hercule dans les Espagnes et
' dans les Gaules, celui de Vulcain au Mont Ethna, de
' Vénus Érycine, avoient tous leurs pyrèthes ou feux
' sacrés.  On peut citer de semblables témoignages des
' nations les plus reculées dans le nord, qui étoient
' toutes originaires des Scythes et des Sarmates.  Enfin
' M. Huet prétend qu'il n'y a pas encore long-temps que
' ce culte a été aboli dans l'Hybernie et dans la Moscovie,
' qu'il est encore aujourd'hui, non-seulement chez les
' Gaures, mais encore chez les Tartares, les Chinois, et
' dans l'Amérique chez les Mexiquains.  Il pouvoit
' encore en ajouter d'autres.'

Among the ancient Prussians a perpetual fire was
kept up in honour of the god Potrimpos, and if it
was allowed to go out, the priest in charge was burnt to
death.[1]

The Ainos of Yesso ' have many gods; but *fire*, not
' the sun, the moon, or the stars, is the principal one, and
' they are accustomed to pray to it, in general terms, for
' all they may need.'[2]  'Many Tunguz, Mongol, and
' Turk tribes,' says Tylor, 'sacrifice to fire, and some
' clans will not eat meat without first throwing a morsel
' upon the hearth.'[3]

The Natchez and Cherokees[4] had a temple in which

[1] Voigt, Gesch. Preussens, vol.
i. p. 592. Schwenk, Die Mythol.
der Slawen, p. 55.

[2] Bickmore, Trans. Ethn. Soc.,
vol. vii. p. 20.

[3] Tylor's Primitive Culture, vol.
ii. p. 254.

[4] Prichard's Nat. Hist. of Man,
1855, vol. ii. p. 535.

x

they kept up a perpetual fire.[1] The Ojibwas[2] maintained ' a continual fire as a symbol of their nationality.
' They maintained also a civil polity, which, however,
' was much mixed up with their religious and medicinal
' beliefs.' In Mexico also we find the same idea of
sacred fire. Colonel McLeod has seen the sacred fire
still kept burning in some of the valleys of South
Mexico.[3] At the great festival of Xiuhmolpia, the
priests and people went in procession to the mountain
of Huixachtecatl; then an unfortunate victim was
stretched on the ' stone of sacrifice,' and killed by a
priest with a knife of obsidian; the dish made use of to
kindle the new fire was then placed on the wound, and
fire was obtained by friction.[4]

In Peru [5] ' the sacred flame was entrusted to the care
' of the Virgins of the Sun; and if, by any neglect, it was
' suffered to go out in the course of the year, the event
' was regarded as a calamity that boded some strange
' disaster to the monarchy.'

Fire is also regarded as sacred in Congo, and in
Dahome Zo is the fire fetich. A pot is placed in a
room and sacrifice is offered to it, that fire may ' live '
there.[6]

No one can wonder that the worship of sun, moon,
and stars is very widely distributed. It can, however,
scarcely be regarded as of a higher character than the

[1] Lafitau, vol. l. p. 107.
[2] Warren in Schoolcraft's Indian Tribes, vol. ii. p. 134. See also Whipple's Report on Indian Tribes, p. 30.
[3] Jour. Ethn. Soc., 1869, p. 226. See also p. 240.
[4] Humboldt's Researches, Lon-
don, 1824, vol. i. pp. 225, 382. See also Lafitau, vol. i. p. 170. Garcilasso de la Vega, vol. ii. p. 162.
[5] Prescott, vol. l. p. 99. Wuttke, Ges. der Mensch., vol. i. p. 270.
[6] Burton's Dahome, vol. ii. p. 148.

preceding forms of Totemism; it is unknown in Australia, and almost so in Polynesia.

In hot countries the sun is generally regarded as an evil, and in cold as a beneficent, being. It was the chief object of religious worship among the Natchez,[1] and was also worshipped by the Navajos, and other allied tribes in North America.[2] Among the Comanches of Texas ' the sun, moon, and earth are the principal ' objects of worship.'[3] Lafitau observes that the American Redskins did not worship the stars and planets, but only the sun.[4] In North-West America, however, the Ahts worship both the sun and moon, but especially the latter. They regard the sun as feminine and the moon as masculine, being, moreover, the husband of the sun.[5] The Kaniagmioutes consider them to be brother and sister[6] It has been said that the Esquimaux of Greenland used to worship the sun. This, however, seems more than doubtful, and Crantz[7] expressly denies the statement.

The Peruvians worshipped the sun, making to it offerings of drink in a vessel of gold, and declaring ' that ' what appeared to be gone had been drunk by the sun, ' and they said truly, for the sun's heat had evaporated ' the liquor.'[8] We are told, however, that the Ynca Huayna Capac questioned this, asking if it was likely

[1] Robertson's America, bk. iv. p. 120.

[2] Whipple's Report on Indian Tribes, p. 36. Lafitau, vol. ii. p. 180. Tertre's History of the Caribby Islands, p. 230.

[3] Neighbors, in Schoolcraft's Indian Tribes, vol. ii. p. 127.

[4] Loc. cit., vol. i. p. 140.

[5] Sproat's Scenes and Studies of Savage Life, p. 206.

[6] Pinart, Revue d'Anthropologie, 1873, p. 678.

[7] Loc. cit., vol. i. p. 103. See Grank's Voyage to Greenland, p. 124.

[8] Garcilasso de la Vega, vol. ii. pp. 60, 131., vol. i. p. 271.

that the sun, if a god, would go over the same course
day after day. 'If he were supreme Lord he would
' occasionally go aside from his course, or rest for his
' pleasure, even though he might have no necessity what-
' ever for doing so.'[1] The moon was held to be the sister
and wife of the sun. Garcilasso states that she had no
separate temple, and that no sacrifices were offered to
her.[2] They also worshipped several of the stars, which
they regarded as attendants on the moon.[3]

In Brazil the Coroados worship the sun and moon,
the moon being the more powerful.[4] The Abipones[5]
thought that they were descended from the Pleiades;
and ' as that constellation disappears at certain periods
' from the sky of South America, upon such occasions
' they suppose that their grandfather is sick, and are
' under a yearly apprehension that he is going to die;
' but as soon as those seven stars are again visible in
' the month of May, they welcome their grandfather, as
' if returned and restored from sickness, with joyful
' shouts, and the festive sound of pipes and trumpets,
' congratulating him on the recovery of his health.'

In Central India sun-worship prevails among many
of the Hill tribes. ' The worship of the sun as the
' Supreme Deity is the foundation of the religion of the
' Hos and Oraons as well as of the Moondahs. By the
' former he is invoked as Dhurmi, the Holy One. He
' is the Creator and the Preserver; and, with reference
' to his purity, white animals are offered to him by his

[1] Loc. cit., p. 440. Molina, Fables and Rites of the Incas, p. 11.
[2] Loc. cit., vol. i. pp. 103, 275.
[3] Loc. cit., pp. 275, 183, 170.

[4] Spix and Martius, vol. ii. p.
243.
[5] Dobritzhoffer, loc. cit., vol. ii.
p. 65.

' votaries.' [1]    The sun and moon are both regarded as
deities by the Korkus,[2] Khonds,[3] Tunguses,[4] and
Burnets.[5]   In Northern Asia the Samoyedes are said to
have worshipped the sun.

In Western Africa moon-worship is very prevalent.
' At the appearance of every new moon,' says Merolla,[6]
' these people fall on their knees, or else cry out, stand-
' ing and clapping their hands, " So may I renew my
' " life as thou art renewed." '   They do not, however,
appear to venerate either the sun or the stars.   Bruce
also mentions moon-worship as occurring among the
Shangallas.[7]

Further South the Bechuanas ' watch most eagerly
' for the first glimpse of the new moon, and when they
' perceive the faint outline after the sun has set deep
' in the west, they utter a loud shout of " Kua ! " and
' vociferate prayers to it." [8]   Herodotus[9] mentions that
the Atarantes used to curse the sun as he passed over
their heads.

It is remarkable that the heavenly bodies do not
appear to be worshipped by the Polynesians.

The natives of Erromango, according to Mr. Brenchley, worship the moon, having stone images of the form
of new and full moons.[10]   According to Lord Kames,

[1] Colonel Dalton, Trans. Ethn. Soc., vol. vi. p. 33.

[2] Forsyth's Highlands of Central India, p. 146.

[3] Forbes Leslie's Early Races of Scotland, vol. ii. p. 490.  Campbell, Wild Tribes of Khondistan, p. 120.

[4] Bell's Travels from St. Peters-burg, vol. i. p. 274.

[5] Klemm, Cult. d. Mensch., v. iii. pp. 101, 109.  Müller, Des. de toutes les Nat. de l'Empire Russe, Pt. III. p. 25.

[6] Voyage to Congo, Pinkerton, vol. xv. p. 273.

[7] Travels, vol. iv. p. 35, vol. vi. p. 344.

[8] Livingstone's Journeys in South Africa, p. 235.

[9] Herodotus, iv. 184.

[10] Cruise of the 'Curaçoa,' p. 320.

'the inhabitants of Celebes formerly acknowledged no
'gods but the sun and moon.'[1]   The people of Borneo
are said to have done the same.

The worship of ancestors is a natural development
of the dread of ghosts, and is another widely distributed
form of religious belief; which, however, I shall not
enter into here, as it may be more conveniently considered when we come to deal with Idolatry.

These are the principal deities of man in this stage
of his religious development.   They are, however, as
already mentioned, by no means the only ones.

The heavens and earth, thunder, lightning, and
winds were regarded as deities in various parts of the
world.   The Scythians worshipped an iron scimetar as a
symbol of the war-god; 'to this scimetar they bring
'yearly sacrifices of cattle and horses; and to these
'scimetars they offer more sacrifices than to the rest of
'their gods.'[2]   In the Sagas many of the swords have
special names, and are treated with the greatest respect.
Similarly the Feejeeans regarded 'certain clubs with
'superstitious respect;'[3] and the negroes of Irawo, a
town in Western Yoruba, worshipped an iron bar with
very expensive ceremonies.[4]   The New Zealanders,
some of the Melanesians, and the Dahomans worshipped
the rainbow.[5]

When Mr. Williams was murdered at Dillon's Bay,
a piece of red sealing-wax which they found in his

---

[1] History of Man, vol. iv. p. 252.
[2] Her., iv. 62. See also Klemm, Werkzeuge und Waffen, p. 225.
[3] Fiji and the Fijians, vol. i. p. 210.

[4] Burton's Abbeokuta, vol. i. p. 192.
[5] Burton's Mission to Dahome, vol. ii. p. 148. Trans. Ethn. Soc. 1870, p. 307.

pocket ' was supposed by the natives to be some port-
' able god, and was carefully buried.' [1]

In Central India, as mentioned in p. 277, a great
variety of inanimate objects are treated as deities. The
Todas are said to worship a buffalo-bell.[2] The Kotas
worship two silver plates, which they regard as husband
and wife; ' they have no other deity.'[3] The Kurumbas
worship stones, trees, and anthills.[4] The Toreas,
another Neilgherry Hill tribe worship especially a
' gold nose-ring, which probably once belonged to one
' of their women.'[5] According to Nonnius, the sacred
lyre sang the victory of Jupiter over the Titans, without being touched.[6] Many other inanimate objects
have also been worshipped. De Brosses even mentions an instance of a king of hearts being made into a
deity.[7]

According to some of the earlier travellers in
America, even the rattle was regarded as a deity.[8]

Thus, then, I have attempted to show that animals
and plants, water, mountains and stones, fire and the
heavenly bodies, are, or have been, all very extensively
and often simultaneously worshipped, so that they do
not form the basis of a natural classification of religions.

[1] Turner's Nineteen Years in Polynesia, p. 487.
[2] The Tribes of the Neilgherries, p. 15.
[3] Ibid., p. 114.
[4] Trans. Ethn. Soc., vol. vii. p. 278.
[5] The Tribes of the Neilgherries, p. 67.
[6] Lafitau, vol. i. p. 205.
[7] Loc. cit., p. 52.
[8] Ibid., p. 211.

## CHAPTER VII.

### RELIGION (*concluded*).

HAVING thus given my reasons for regarding as unsatisfactory the classifications of religions which have been adopted hitherto, I will now endeavour to trace up the gradual evolution of religious beliefs, beginning with the Australians, who possess merely certain vague ideas as to the existence of evil spirits, and a general dread of witchcraft. This belief cannot be said to influence them by day, but it renders them very unwilling to quit the camp-fire by night, or to sleep near a grave. They have no idea of creation, nor do they use prayers; they have no religious forms, ceremonies, or worship. They do not believe in the existence of a Deity,[1] nor is morality in any way connected with their religion, if such it can be called. The words ' good ' or ' bad ' had reference to taste or bodily comfort, and did not convey any idea of right or wrong.[2] Another curious notion of the Australians is, that while men are blacks, who have risen from the dead. This notion was found among the natives north of Sydney as early as 1795, and can scarcely, therefore, be of missionary orgin.[3] It occurs also among the negroes of

[1] Report of the Committee of the Legislative Council on Aborigines, Victoria, 1850, pp. 9, 60, 77.

[2] Eyre's Discoveries in Central Australia, vol. II. pp. 354, 355, 356.

[3] Collins' English Colony in N.S. Wales, p. 303.

Guinea and elsewhere.[1] The ideas of the Australians on this point, however, seem to have been very various and confused. They had certainly no general and definite view on the subject.

As regards the North Australians we have trustworthy accounts given by a Scotchwoman, Mrs. Thomson, who was wrecked on the Eastern Prince of Wales Island. Her husband and the rest of the crew were drowned, but she was saved by the natives, and lived with them nearly five years, until the visit of the 'Rattlesnake,' when she escaped with some difficulty. On the whole she was kindly treated by the men, though the women were long jealous of her, and behaved towards her with much cruelty. These people had no idea of a Supreme Being.[2] They did not believe in the immortality of the soul, but held that they are 'after death changed into white people or 'Europeans, and as such pass the second and final period 'of their existence; nor is it any part of their creed that 'future rewards and punishments are awarded.'[3]

Mrs. Thomson was supposed to be the ghost of Giom, a daughter of a man named Piaquai, and when she was teased by children, the men would often tell them to leave her alone, saying, 'Poor thing! she is nothing— 'only a ghost.' This, however, did not prevent a man named Boroto making her his wife, which shows how little is actually implied in the statement that Australians believe in spirits. They really do no more than believe in the existence of men somewhat different from, and a

---

[1] Smith's Guinea, p. 216. Bosman, Pinkerton's Voyages, vol. xvi. p. 401.

[2] Macgillivray's Voyage of the 'Rattlesnake,' vol. ii. p. 29.

[3] *Loc. cit.*, p. 29.

little more powerful than themselves. The South Australians, as described by Stephens, had no religious rites, ceremonies, or worship; no idea of a Supreme Being, but a vague dread of evil spirits.[1]

The Veddahs of Ceylon, according to Davy, believe in evil beings, but ' have no idea of a supreme and bene- ' ficent God, or of a state of future existence, or of a ' system of rewards and punishments; and, in conse- ' quence, they are of opinion that it signifies little ' whether they do good or evil.'[2]

The Indians of California have been well described by Father Baegert, a Jesuit missionary, who lived among them no less than seventeen years.[3] As to government or religion, he says,[4] ' neither the one nor ' the other existed among them. They had no magis- ' trates, no police, and no laws; idols, temples, religious ' worship, or ceremonies were unknown to them, and ' they neither believed in the true and only God nor ' adored false deities. They were all equals, and every- ' one did as he pleased, without asking his neighbour or ' caring for his opinion, and thus all vices and misdeeds ' remained unpunished, excepting such cases in which ' the offended individual or his relations took the law ' into their own hands and revenged themselves on the ' guilty party. The different tribes represented by no ' means communities of rational beings, who submit to ' laws and regulations and obey their superiors, but ' resembled far more herds of wild swine, which run

---

[1] Stephens' South Australia, p. 78.

[2] Davy's Ceylon, p. 118.

[3] Nachrichten von der Amer. Halb. Californie, 1773. Translated in Smithsonian Reports, 1863–4.

[4] Smithsonian Reports, 1864, p. 300.

' about according to their own liking, being together
' to-day and scattered to-morrow, till they meet again
' by accident at some future time.

' In one word, the Californians lived, *salva venia*, as
' though they had been freethinkers and materialists.

' I made diligent inquiries among those with whom
' I lived, to ascertain whether they had any conception
' of God, a future life, and their own souls, but I never
' could discover the slightest trace of such a knowledge.
' Their language has no words for "God" and "soul,"
' for which reason the missionaries were compelled to
' use in their sermons and religious instructions the
' Spanish words *Dios* and *alma*. It could hardly be
' otherwise with people who thought of nothing but
' eating and merry-making, and never reflected on
' serious matters, but dismissed everything that lay be-
' yond the narrow compass of their conceptions with the
' phrase aipekériri, which means, "Who knows that?"
' I often asked them whether they had never put to
' themselves the question who might be the Creator
' and Preserver of the sun, moon, stars, and other
' objects of nature, but was always sent home with a
' vára, which means "no" in their language.' They
had, however, certain sorcerers, whom they believed
to possess power over diseases, to bring small-pox,
famine, &c., and of whom, therefore, they were in
much fear.

Mr. Gibbs, speaking of the Indians living in the
valleys drained by the Sacramento and the San Joaquin,
says: 'One of this tribe, who had been for three or four
' years among the whites, and accompanied the expedi-
' tion, on being questioned as to his own belief in a

'Deity, acknowledged his entire ignorance on the sub-
'ject.    As regarded a future state of any kind, he was
'equally uninformed and indifferent; in fact, did not
'believe in any for himself.    As a reason why his
'people did not go to another country after death,
'while the whites might, he assigned that the Indians
'burned their dead, and he supposed there was an end
'of them.'[1].

The religion of the Bachapins, a Kaffir tribe, has
been described by Burchell.  They had no outward
worship, nor, so far as he could learn, any private
devotion; indeed, they had no belief in a beneficent
Deity, though they feared an evil being called 'Mu-
'leemo,' or 'Murimo.'  They had no idea of creation.
Even when Burchell suggested it to them, they did not
attribute it to Muleemo, but 'asserted that everything
'made itself, and that trees and herbage grew by their
'own will.'[2]   They believed in sorcery, and in the
efficacy of amulets.

Dr. Vanderkemp, the first missionary to the Kaffirs,
'never could perceive that they had any religion, or any
'idea of the existence of God.'   Mr. Moffat also, who
lived in South Africa as a missionary for many years,
says that they were utterly destitute of theological
ideas; and Dr. Gardner, in his 'Faiths of the World,'
concludes as follows:[3] 'From all that can be ascertained
'on the religion of the Kaffirs, it seems that those of
'them who are still in their heathen state have no idea,
'(1) of a Supreme Intelligent Ruler of the universe;
'(2) of a Sabbath; (3) of a day of judgment; (4) of

[1] Schoolcraft's Indian Tribes, vol.        [2] Travels, vol. ii. p. 550.
iii. p. 107.                                 [3] Loc. cit., p. 200.

'the guilt and pollution of sin; (5) of a Saviour to
'deliver them from the wrath to come.'

The Rev. Canon Callaway has recently published a
very interesting memoir on 'The Religious System of
'the Amazulu,' who are somewhat more advanced in
their religious conceptions. The first portion is entitled
'Unkulunkulu, or the Tradition of Creation.' It does
not, however, appear that Unkulunkulu is regarded as
a Creator, or even as a deity at all. It is simply the
first man, the Zulu Adam. Some complication arises
from the fact that not only the ancestor of all mankind,
but also the first of each tribe, is called Unkulunkulu,
so that there are many Onkulunkulu, or Unkulunkulus.
None of them, however, have any of the characters of
Deity; no prayers or sacrifices are offered to them;[1]
indeed, they no longer exist, having been long dead.[2]
Unkulunkulu was in no sense a Creator,[3] nor, indeed, is
any special power attributed to him.[4] He, *i.e.* man,
arose from 'Umklangla,' that is 'a bed of reeds,' but
how he did so no one knew.[5] Mr. Callaway agrees
with Casalis, that 'it never entered the heads of the
'Zulus that the earth and sky might be the work of an
'invisible being.'[6] One native thought the white men
made the world.[7] They had, indeed, no idea of or
name for God.[8] When Moffat endeavoured to explain
to a chief about God he exclaimed, 'Would that I could
'catch it! I would transfix it with my spear;' yet this
was a man 'whose judgment on other subjects would
'command attention.'[9]

---

[1] *Loc. cit.*, pp. 9, 25, 34, 75.  
[2] *Loc. cit.*, pp. 15, 33, 62.  
[3] *Loc. cit.*, p. 137.  
[4] *Loc. cit.*, p. 48.  
[5] *Loc. cit.*, pp. 9, 40.  
[6] *Loc. cit.*, pp. 64, 108.  
[7] *Loc. cit.*, p. 55.  
[8] *Loc. cit.*, pp. 107, 113, 136.  
[9] *Loc. cit.*, p. 111.

Yet they are not without a belief in invisible beings. This is founded partly on the shadow, but principally on the dream. They regard the shadow as in some way the spirit which accompanies the body (reminding us of the similar idea among the Greeks), and they have a curious notion that a dead body casts no shadow.[1]

Still more important has been the influence of dreams. When a dead father or brother appears to a man in his sleep he does not doubt the reality of the occurrence, and hence concludes that their spirits still live. As, however, they rarely dream about their grandfathers, they suppose them to be dead.[2]

Diseases are regarded as being often caused by the spirits of discontented relatives.

In Samoa it was supposed that the spirits of the departed 'had power to return and cause disease and 'death in other members of the family. Hence, all were 'anxious as a person drew near the close of life to part 'on good terms with him, feeling assured that, if he 'died with angry feelings towards any one, he would 'certainly return, and bring some calamity upon that 'very person or some one closely allied to him.'[3]

In other respects these spirits are not regarded as possessing any special powers; though prayed to, it is not in such a manner as to indicate a belief that they have any supernatural influence, and they are clearly not regarded as immortal. In some cases departed spirits are regarded as reappearing in the form of snakes,[4] which may be known from ordinary snakes by certain

---

[1] Loc. cit., p. 91.          Polynesia, p. 220.
[2] Loc. cit., p. 15.          [4] L. c. cit., p. 8.
[3] Turner's Nineteen Years in

signs,[1] such as their frequenting huts, not eating mice, and showing no fear of man. Sometimes a snake is recognised as the representative of a given man by some peculiar mark or scar, the absence of an eye, or some other similar point of resemblance.

In such cases sacrifices are sometimes offered to the snake, and, when a bullock is killed, part is put away for the use of the dead, or Amatongo, who are specially invited to the feast, whose assistance is requested, and wrath deprecated. Yet this can hardly be called 'ancestor-worship.' The dead have, it is true, the advantage of invisibility, but they are not regarded as omnipresent, omnipotent, or immortal. There are even means by which troublesome spirits may be destroyed or 'laid.'[2] In such cases as these, then, we see religion in a very low phase; that in which it consists merely of belief in the existence of evil beings, less material than we are, but mortal like ourselves, and if more powerful than man in some respects, even less so in others.

## FETICHISM.

In the Fetichism of the negro, Religion, if it can be so called, is systematised, and greatly raised in importance. Nevertheless from another point of view Fetichism may almost be regarded as an anti-religion. It has hitherto been defined as the worship of material substances. This does not seem to me to be its true characteristic. Fetichism is not truly a form of 'worship' at all. For the negro believes that by means

---

[1] *Loc. cit.,* pp. 108, 109.    [2] *Loc. cit.,* p. 160.

of the fetich he can coerce and control his deity. In fact,
Fetichism is mere witchcraft. We have already seen
(ante, p. 237) that magicians all over the world think
that if they can obtain a part of an enemy the possession
of it gives them a power over him. Even a bit of his
clothing will answer the purpose, or, if this cannot be
got, it seems to them natural that an injury even to his
image would affect the original. That is to say, a man
who can destroy or torture the image thus inflicts pain
on the original, and this, being magical, is independent
of the power of that original. Even in Europe, and in
the eleventh century, some unfortunate Jews were accused of having murdered a certain Bishop Eberhard
in this way. They made a wax image of him, had it
baptised, and then burnt it, and so the bishop died.

Lord Kames says that at the time of Catherine de
Medicis 'it was common to take the resemblance of
' enemies in wax, in order to torment them by roasting
' the figure at a slow fire, and pricking it with needles.'[1]

In India, says Dubois,[2] 'a quantity of mud is
' moulded into small figures, on the breasts of which
' they write the name of the persons whom they mean
' to annoy. . . . . They pierce the images with
' thorns, or mutilate them, so as to communicate a cor-
' responding injury to the person represented.'

Now, it seems to me that Fetichism is an extension
of this belief. The negro supposes that the possession
of a fetich representing a spirit makes that spirit his
servant. We know that the negroes beat their fetich
if their prayers are unanswered, and I believe they

[1] Lord Kames' History of Man, vol. iv. p. 201.
[2] Lo. cit., p. 347.

seriously think they thus inflict suffering on the actual
Deity. Thus the fetich cannot fairly be called an idol.
The same image or object may indeed be a fetich to one
man and an idol to another; yet the two are essentially
different in their nature. An idol is, indeed, an object
of worship, while, on the contrary, a fetich is intended
to bring the Deity within the control of man—an attempt
which is less absurd than it at first sight appears, when
considered in connection with their low religious ideas.
If, then, witchcraft be not confused with religion, as
I think it ought not to be, Fetichism can hardly be
called a religion; to the true spirit of which it is indeed
entirely opposed.

Anything will do for a fetich; it need not represent
the human figure, though it may do so. Even an ear
of maize will answer the purpose. If, said an intelligent
negro to Bosman,[1] any of us is 'resolved to undertake
' anything of importance, we first of all search out a god
' to prosper our designed undertaking; and, going out
' of doors with this design, take the first creature that
' presents itself to our eyes, whether dog, cat, or the
' most contemptible animal in the world, for our god;
' or, perhaps, instead of that, any inanimate object that
' falls in our way, whether a stone, or piece of wood, or
' anything else of the same nature. This new-chosen
' god is immediately presented with an offering, which
' is accompanied with a solemn vow, that if he pleaseth
' to prosper our undertakings, for the future we will
' always worship and esteem him as a god. If our de-
' sign prove successful, we have discovered a new and

[1] Bosman's Guinea, Pinkerton's       Loyer (1701), Astley's Collection,
Voyages, vol xvi. p. 403. See also     vol. ii. p. 440.

'assisting god, which is daily presented with fresh
'offerings; but if the contrary happen, the new god is
'rejected as a useless tool, and consequently returns to
'his primitive estate. We make and break our gods
'daily, and consequently are the masters and inventors
'of what we sacrifice to.'

The term Fetichism is generally connected with the
negro race, but a corresponding state of mind exists in
many other parts of the world. In fact, it may almost
be said to be universal, since it is nothing more nor less
than witchcraft; and in the most advanced countries—
even in our own—the belief in witchcraft has scarcely
been entirely eradicated.

The Badagas (Hindostan), according to Metz, are
still in a 'condition little above Fetichism. Anything
'with them may become an object of adoration, if the
'head man or the village priest should take a fancy to
'deify it. As a necessary consequence, however, of this
'state of things, no real respect is entertained towards
'their deities, and it is not an uncommon thing to hear
'the people call them liars, and use opprobrious epithets
'respecting them.'[2] Again, speaking of the Chota Nagpore tribes of Central India, Colonel Dalton observes
that certain 'peculiarities in the paganism of the Oraon,
'and only practised by Moondahs who lived in the same
'village with them, appear to me to savour thoroughly
'of Fetichism.'[2]

In Jeypore[3] the body of a small musk-rat is regarded as a powerful talisman. 'The body of this

---

[1] The Tribes of the Neilgherries, p. 33.
p. 60.
[2] Trans. Ethn. Soc., N.S., vol. vi.
[3] Shortt, Trans., Ethn. Soc., vol. vi. p. 278.

' animal, dried, is enclosed in a case of brass, silver,
' or gold, according to the means of the individual, and
' is slung around the neck, or tied to the arm, to render
' the individual proof against all evil, not excepting
' sword and other cuts, musket-shot, &c.'

The Abors of Bengal worship trees, and if misfortunes occur, ' they retaliate on the spirits by cutting
' down trees.' [1]

In all these cases the tribes seem to me to be
naturally in the state of Fetichism, disguised, however,
and modified by fragments of the higher Hindoo religions, which they have adopted without understanding.

Though the Redskins of North America have reached
a higher state of religious development, they still retain
fetiches in the form of ' medicine-bags.' ' Every Indian,'
says Catlin,[2] ' in his primitive state, carries his medicine-
' bag in some form or other,' and to it he looks for protection and safety. The nature of the medicine-bag is
thus determined:—At fourteen or fifteen years of age
the boy wanders away alone upon the prairie, where he
remains two, three, four, or even five days, lying on the
ground musing and fasting. He remains awake as long
as he can, but when he sleeps the first animal of which
he dreams becomes his ' medicine.' As soon as possible
he shoots an animal of the species in question, and
makes a medicine-bag of the skin. To this he looks for
protection, to this he sacrifices; unlike the fickle negro,
however, the Redskin never changes his fetich. To
him it becomes an emblem of success, like the shield of

[1] Dalton, Des. Ethn. of Bengal, p. 26.
[2] American Indians, vol. i. p. 30.

the Greek, or the more modern sword, and to lose it is disgrace.

The Columbian Indians have small figures in the form of a quadruped, bird, or fish. These, though called idols, are rather fetiches, because, as all disease is attributed to them, when any one is ill they are beaten together, and the first which loses a tooth or claw is supposed to be the culprit.[1]

In China,[2] also, the lower people, 'if, after long 'praying to their images, they do not obtain what they 'desire, as it often happens, they turn them off as im-'potent gods; others use them in a most reproachful 'manner, loading them with hard names, and sometimes 'with blows. "How now, dog of a spirit!" say they 'to them; "we give you a lodging in a magnificent '"temple, we gild you handsomely, feed you well, and '"offer incense to you; yet, after all this care, you are '"so ungrateful as to refuse us what we ask of you." 'Hereupon they tie this image with cords, pluck him 'down, and drag him along the streets, through all the 'mud and dunghills, to punish him for the expense of 'perfume which they have thrown away upon him. If 'in the meantime it happens that they obtain their re-'quest, then, with a great deal of ceremony, they wash 'him clean, carry him back, and place him in his niche 'again; where they fall down to him, and make ex-'cuses for what they have done. "In a truth," say 'they, "we were a little too hasty, as well as you were '"somewhat too long in your grant. Why should you '"bring this beating on yourself? But what is done

[1] Dunn's Oregon, p. 125.
[2] Astley's Collection of Voyages, vol. iv. p. 218.

' " cannot be now undone; let us not therefore think of
' " it any more. If you will forget what is past, we will
' " gild you over again." '

Pallas, speaking of the Ostiaks, states that, ' Malgré
' la vénération et le respect qu'ils ont pour leurs idoles,
' malheur à elles lorsqu'il arrive un malheur à l'Ostiak,
' et que l'idole n'y remédie pas. Il la jette alors par
' terre, la frappe, la maltraite, et la brise en morceaux.
' Cette correction arrive fréquemment. Cette colère est
' commune à tous les peuples idolâtres de la Sibérie.' [1]
Müller also [2] makes very similar statements. Dr. Gerland, in the continuation of Waitz' Anthropologie,
mentions several cases of Fetichism in Polynesia.[3]

In Madagascar a small basket was in every house
hung against the northern roof-post, and in it was
placed the fetich, which was sometimes a stone, sometimes a leaf, a flower, or a piece of wood. This 'is the
' household " sampy," or charm, which is trusted in and
' prayed to as a protection from evil.' [4]

In Whydah (Western Africa), and I believe generally the negroes will not eat the animal or plant which
they have chosen for their fetich.[5] In Issini, on the
contrary, ' eating the fetich' is a solemn ceremony
on taking an oath, or as a token of friendship.[6]

Fetichism, strictly speaking, has no temples, idols,
priests, sacrifices, or prayer. It involves no belief in
creation or in a future life, and *à fortiori* none in a state
of rewards and punishments. It is entirely indepen-

---

[1] Pallas' Voyages, vol. iv. p. 70.
[2] Des. de toutes les Nat. de l'Emp. Russe, Pt. III. p. 151.
[3] *Loc. cit.*, vol. vi., pp. 322, 341.
[4] Sibree's Madagascar and its People, p. 204.
[5] Phillips, 1693. Astley, vol. ii. p. 417.
[6] Loyer, 1701, *loc. cit.*, p. 436.

dent of morality. In most, however, of the powerful
negro monarchies, religion has made some progress in
organisation; but though we find both sacred buildings
and priests, the religion itself shows little, if any, intellectual improvement.

## TOTEMISM.

The next stage in religious progress is that which
may be called Totemism. The savage does not abandon
his belief in Fetichism, from which, indeed, no race of
men has yet entirely freed itself; but he superinduces
on it a belief in beings of a higher and less material
nature. In this stage everything may be worshipped
—trees, stones, rivers, mountains, the heavenly bodies,
and animals; but the higher deities are no longer regarded as liable to be controlled by witchcraft. Still
they are not regarded as Creators; they do not reward
virtue, or punish vice. The spirits of the departed have
before them a weary and dangerous journey, and many
perish by the way; heaven, however, seems to be
merely a distant part of the earth.

Even the deities still inhabit this earth; they are
part of nature, not supernatural; in fact, we may say
that in Fetichism the deities are non-human, in Totemism superhuman, but do not become supernatural
until a still further stage of mental development.

Again, Totemism is a deification of classes; the
fetich is an individual. The negro who has, let us say,
an ear of maize as a fetich, values that particular ear,
more or less as the case may be, but has no feeling for
maize as a species. On the contrary, the Redskin who

regards the bear, or the wolf, as his totem, feels that he is in intimate, though mysterious, association with the whole species.

The name 'Totemism' is of North American origin, and is primarily used to denote the form of religion widely prevalent among the Redskins of that continent, but similar religious views are held in various other parts of the world.

In order to realise clearly the essential characteristics of the religions of different races, we must bear in mind that at the stage at which we have now arrived in the course of our enquiry, the modifications of which a religion is susceptible may be divided into two classes, viz., developmental and adaptational, or adaptive. I use the term 'developmental' to signify those changes which arise from the intellectual progress of the race. Thus a more elevated idea of the Deity is a developmental change. On the other hand, a Northern people is apt to look on the sun as a beneficent deity, while to a tropical race it would suggest drought and destruction. Again, hunters tend to worship the moon, agriculturists the sun. These I call adaptational modifications. They are changes produced, not by difference of race or of civilisation, but by physical causes.

In some cases the character of the language has probably exercised much influence over that of religion. No one, for instance, can fail to be struck by the differences existing between the Aryan and Semitic religions. All Aryan races have a complicated mythology, which is not the case with the Semitic races. Moreover, the character of the gods is quite different. The latter have El, Strong; Bel or Baal, Lord; Adonis, Lord; Shet,

Master; Moloch, King; Rain and Rimmon, the Exalted;
and other similar names for their deities. The Aryans,
on the contrary, Zeus, the sky; Phœbus Apollo, the
sun; Neptune, the sea; Mars, war; Venus, beauty, &c.
Max Müller [1] has very ingeniously endeavoured to explain this difference by the different character of the
language in these two races.

As a general rule nations in whose languages the
division of the nouns into classes has no reference to the
distinctions of sex, possess no mythology; and though
there are some apparent exceptions, it is probable, as
Dr. Bleek has suggested,[2] that in such cases the ' lan-
' guages, if not at the present day sex-denoting, may
' formerly have been so,' and that thus the presence of
inherited mythological ideas in a nation may give evidence of a former state of its language, a state of which
all other evidence may have now disappeared.

Again, in Semitic words the root remains always
distinct and unmistakable. In Aryan, on the contrary,
it soon becomes altered and disguised. Hence Semitic
dictionaries are mostly arranged according to the roots,
a method which in Aryan languages would be most
inconvenient, the root being often obscure, and in many
cases doubtful. Now, take such an expression as ' the
' sky thunders.' In any Semitic tongue the word ' sky '
would remain unaltered, and so clear in its meaning,
that it would with difficulty come to be thought of as
a proper name. But among the Aryans the case was
different, and we find in the earlier Vedic poetry that

---

[1] See Müller's Chips from a German Workshop, vol. i. p. 363.
[2] On Resemblances in Bushman
and Australian Mythology, Cape
Monthly Magazine, February 1874.

the names of the Greek gods stand as mere words denoting natural objects. Thus the Sanskrit Dyaus, the sky, became the Greek Zeus, and when the Greek said Ζεὺς βροντᾷ his idea was not 'the sky thunders,' but 'Zeus thunders.' When the gods were thus once created, the mythology follows as a matter of course. Some of the statements may be obscure, but when we are told that Hupnos, the god of sleep, was the father of Morpheus, the god of dreams ; or that Venus, married to Vulcan, lost her heart to Mars, and that the intrigue was made known to Vulcan by Apollo, the sun, we can clearly see how such myths might have arisen.

The attitude of the ancients towards them is very interesting. Homer and Hesiod relate them, apparently without suspicion, and we may be sure that the uneducated public received them without a doubt. Socrates, however, explains the story that Boreas carried off Oreithyia from the Ilissos, to mean that Oreithyia was blown off the rocks by the north wind. Ovid also says that under the name of Vesta, mere fire is to be understood. We can hardly doubt that many others also must have clearly perceived the origin of at any rate a portion of these myths, but they were probably restrained from expressing their opinion by the dread of incurring the odium of heterodoxy.

One great charm of this explanation is that we thus remove some of the revolting features of ancient myths. Thus, as the sun destroys the darkness from which it springs, and at evening disappears in the twilight, so Œdipus was fabled to have killed his father, and then married his mother. In this way the whole of that terrible story may be explained as arising, not from the

depravity of the human heart, but from a mistaken application of the statement that the sun destroys the
darkness, and ultimately marries, as it were, the twilight
from which it sprang.

But although poetry may thus throw much light on
the origin of the myths which formed the religion of
Greece and Rome, it cannot explain the origin or character of religion among the lower savages, because a
mythology such as that of Greece and Rome can only
arise amongst a people which have already made considerable progress.   True, myths do not occur among
the lowest races.   Even in Madagascar, according to a
good authority,[1] 'there is nothing corresponding to a
' mythology, or any fables of gods or goddesses, amongst
' the Malagasy.'   Tempting, therefore, as it may be to
seek in the nature of language and the use of poetical
expressions an explanation of the religious systems of
the lower races, and fully admitting the influence which
these causes have exercised, we must look deeper for
the origin of religion, and can be satisfied only by an
explanation which is applicable to the lowest races possessing any religious opinions.   In the preceding chapters
I have attempted to do this, and to show how certain
phenomena, as for instance sleep and dreams, pain,
disease, and death, have naturally created in the savage
mind a belief in the existence of mysterious and invisible
beings.

[1] Sibree's Madagascar and its People, p. 290.

## SHAMANISM.

As Totemism overlies Fetichism, so does Shamanism overlie Totemism. The word is derived from the name used in Siberia, where the 'Shamans' work themselves up into a fury, supposing or pretending that in this condition they are inspired by the Spirit in whose name they speak, and through whose inspiration they are enabled to answer questions and to foretell the future. In the phases of religion hitherto considered the deities (if indeed they deserve the name), are regarded as visible to all, and present amongst us. Shamanism is a considerable advance, inasmuch as it presents us with a higher conception of religion. Although the name is Siberian, the phase of thought is widely distributed, and seems to be a necessary stage in the progress of religious development. Those who are disposed to adopt the view advocated in this work will not be surprised to find that 'Shamanism' is no definite system of theology. Wrangel, however, regarding Shamanism as a religion in the ordinary sense, was astonished at this. 'It is re- 'markable,' he says, ' that Shamanism has no dogmas 'of any kind; it is not a system taught or handed down 'from one to another; though it is so widely spread, it 'seems to originate with each individual separately, as 'the fruit of a highly excited imagination, acted upon 'by external impressions, which closely resemble each 'other, throughout the deserts of Northern Siberia.' [1]

It is far from easy in practice always to distinguish Shamanism from Totemism on the one hand, and

[1] Siberia and Polar Sea, p. 123.

Idolatry on the other.   The main difference lies in the
conception of the Deity.   In Totemism the deities inhabit our earth; in Shamanism they live generally in a
world of their own, and trouble themselves little about
what is passing here.   The Shaman, however, is occasionally honoured by the presence of Deity, or is
allowed to visit the heavenly regions.

   Among the Esquimaux the 'Angekok' answers
precisely to the Shaman.   Graah thus describes a scene
in Greenland.   The angekok came in the evening, and
' the lamps' being extinguished, and skins hung before
' the windows (for such arts, for evident reasons, are
' best practised in the dark), took his station on the
' floor, close by a well-dried seal-skin there suspended,
' and commenced rattling it, beating the tambourine and
' singing, in which last he was seconded by all present.
' From time to time his chant was interrupted by a cry
' of " Goie, Goie, Goie, Goie, Goie, Goie! " the meaning
' of which I did not comprehend, coming first from one
' corner of the hut, and then from the other.   Presently
' all was quiet, nothing being heard but the angekok
' puffing and blowing as if struggling with something
' superior to him in strength, and then again a sound
' resembling somewhat that of castanets, whereupon
' commenced once more the same song as before, and
' the same cry of " Goie, Goie, Goie! "   In this way a
' whole hour elapsed before the wizard could make the
' torngak, or spirit, obey his summons.   Come he did,
' however, at last, and his approach was announced by
' a strange rushing sound, very like the sound of a large

   ¹ Graah's Voyage to Greenland, p. 123.   See also Egede's Greenland,
p. 189, and Lyon's Journ., p. 350.

‘ bird flying beneath the roof.  The angekok, still chant-
‘ ing, now proposed his questions, which were replied
‘ to in a voice quite strange to my ears, but which
‘ seemed to me to proceed from the entrance passage,
‘ near which the angekok had taken his station.’

The account given by Cranz agrees with the above
in all essential particulars.[1]

Williams[2] gives the following very similar account
of a scene in Feejee:—‘ Unbroken silence follows; the
‘ priest becomes absorbed in thought, and all eyes watch
‘ him with unblinking steadiness.  In a few minutes he
‘ trembles; slight distortions are seen in his face, and
‘ twitching movements in his limbs.  These increase to
‘ a violent muscular action, which spreads until the
‘ whole frame is strongly convulsed, and the man shivers
‘ as with a strong ague fit.  In some instances this is
‘ accompanied with murmurs and sobs, the veins are
‘ greatly enlarged, and the circulation of the blood
‘ quickened.  The priest is now possessed by his god,
‘ and all his words and actions are considered as no
‘ longer his own, but those of the deity who has entered
‘ into him.  Shrill cries of “ Koi au, Koi au! ” “ It is I,
‘ “ It is I! ” fill the air, and the god is supposed thus
‘ to notify his approach.  While giving the answer the
‘ priest’s eyes stand out and roll as in a frenzy; his
‘ voice is unnatural, his face pale, his lips livid, his
‘ breathing depressed, and his entire appearance like that
‘ of a furious madman; the sweat runs from every pore,
‘ and tears start from his strained eyes; after which the
‘ symptoms gradually disappear.  The priest looks round

[1] History of Greenland, vol. i. p. 210.   [2] Fiji and the Fijians, vol. i. p. 224.

' with a vacant stare, and, as the god says, " I depart,"
' announces his actual departure by violently flinging
' himself down on the mat, or by suddenly striking the
' ground with his club.   The convulsive movements do
' not entirely disappear for some time.'   The process
described by Dobritzhoffer[1] as occurring among the
Abipones is also somewhat similar.

Among the negroes of W. Africa, Brue[2] mentions a
' prophet' who pretended ' to be inspired by the Deity
' in such a manner as to know the most hidden secrets ;
' and go invisible wherever he pleased, as well as to
' make his voice be heard at the greatest distance.   His
' disciples and accomplices attested the truth of what he
' said by a thousand fabulous relations ; so that the
' common people, always credulous and fond of novelty,
' readily gave in to the cheat.'   Burton mentions the
same thing in Dahome.[3]

Colonel Dalton states that ' the paganism of the
' Ho and Moondah in all essential features is Sha-
' manistic.[4]

Among the Karens,[5] the ' wee,' or prophet, ' works
' himself into the state in which he can see departed
' spirits, visit their distant home, and even recall them
' to the body, thus raising the dead ; these wees are
' nervous excitable men, such as would become me-
' diums, and in giving oracles they go into actual con-
' vulsions.'

[1] History of the Abipones, vol.
ii. p. 73.

[2] Astley's Collection of Voyages,
vol. ii. p. 83.

[3] Mission to Dahome, vol. ii. p.
158.

[4] Trans. Ethn. Soc., 1868, p. 32.

[5] Tylor's Primitive Culture, vol.
ii. p. 120.

## IDOLATRY.

The worship of Idols characterises a somewhat higher stage of human development. We find no traces of it among the lowest races of men; and Lafitau [1] says truly, 'On peut dire en général que le grand nombre ' des peuples sauvages n'a point d'idoles.' The error of regarding Idolatry as the general religion of low races has no doubt mainly arisen from confusing the Idol and the Fetich. Fetichism, however, is an attack on the Deity, Idolatry is an act of submission to him ; rude, no doubt, but yet humble. Hence, Fetichism and Idolatry are not only different, but opposite, so that the one could not be developed directly out of the other. We must therefore expect to find between them, as indeed we do, a stage of religion without either the one or the other.

Captain Lyon states that the Esquimaux have no idols.[2] 'Neither among the Esquimaux nor the Tinne,' says Richardson, 'did I observe any image or visible ' object of worship.'[3]

Carver states that the Canadian Indians had no idols;[4] and this seems to have been true of the North American Indians generally. Lafitau mentions as an exception the existence of an idol named Oki in Virginia.[5]

In Eastern Africa Burton states that he knows 'but ' one people, the Wanyika, who have certain statuettes

[1] Mœurs des Sauvages Américaines, vol. i. p. 151.
[2] Journal, p. 372.
[3] Boat Journey, vol. ii. p. 44.
[4] Travels, p. 387.
[5] Vol. i. p. 168.

'called Kisukas.' Prichard, however, quotes a commu-
nication from Dr. Krapf, in which it is stated that 'the
'Wanika are pagans, though they have no images.'[1]
Neither the Kaffirs nor the Bechuanas have idols.[2]

Nor do the West African negroes worship idols.[3] It
is true that some writers mention idols, but the context
almost always shows that fetiches are really meant. In
the kingdom of Whydah 'Agoye' was represented
under the form of a deformed black man, from whose
head proceed lizards and snakes,[4] offering a striking
similarity to some of the Indian idols. This, is however, an exceptional case. Battel only mentions particularly two idols;[5] and Bosman[6] expressly says that
'on the Gold Coast the natives are not in the least
'acquainted with image-worship;' adding, 'but at
'Ardra there are thousands of idols,' *i.e.* fetiches. At
Loango there was a small black image named Chikokke,
which was placed in a little house close to the port.[7]
These, however, were merely fetiches in human form.
For instance, we are told by the same author that in
Kakongo, the kingdom which lies to the south of Loango,
the natives during the plague 'burnt their idols, saying,
' " *If they will not help us in such a misfortune as this,*
' " *when can we expect they should?"* '[8] Thus, appa-
rently doubting not so much their power as their will.
Again, in Congo the so-called idols are placed in fields

[1] Prichard's Nat. Hist. of Man,
vol. ii. p. 388.

[2] Livingstone's Travels in South
Africa, p. 154. Maclean's Comp. of
Kaffir Laws and Customs, p. 78.

[3] Astley's Collection of Voyages,
vol. ii. p. 240, for Futa, and for
Guinea, as far as Ardrah, p. 630.

[4] Astley's Collection of Voyages,
pp. 20, 60.

[5] Adventures of A. Battel. Pinkerton, vol. xvi. p. 331.

[6] Bosman's Guinea. Pinkerton,
loc. cit., p. 403.

[7] Astley, loc. cit., p. 210.

[8] Ibid, p. 217.

to protect the growing crops.[1] This is clearly the function of a fetich, not of a true idol.

In Madagascar, though of late years certain idols were treated with great respect, yet there seems reason to suppose that this 'idolatrous system is of compara-'tively modern date.'[2] The Australians and Tas-manians had no idols.

Idolatry, says Williams, of the Feejeean, 'he seems 'never to have known; for he makes no attempt to 'fashion material representations of his gods.'[3] As regards the New Zealanders, Yate[4] says, that 'though 'remarkably superstitious, they have no gods that they 'worship; nor have they anything to represent a being 'which they call God.' Dieffenbach also observes that in New Zealand 'there is no worship of idols, or of 'bodily representations of the Atoua.'[5]

The same may be said of the Tongans, while, on the other hand, the reverse seems to have been the case with the Society Islanders. The Tanuese had no idols,[6] and according to Hale this is true with the Micronesians generally.[7]

Speaking of the Singè Dyaks,[8] Sir James Brooke says, 'Religion they have none; and although they 'know the name for a god' (which is probably taken from the Hindoos), 'they have no priests nor idols, say 'no prayers, offer no offerings.' He subsequently modi-

[1] Astley, *loc. cit.*, vol. iii. p. 220. Livingstone, Expedition to the Zambesi, p. 523.

[2] Sibree, Madagascar and its People, p. 300.

[3] Fiji and the Fijians, vol. i. p. 210. Seeman's Mission to Viti, p. 104.

[4] *Loc. cit.*, p. 141.

[5] *Loc. cit.*, vol. ii. p. 118.

[6] Turner, Nineteen Years in Polynesia, p. 88.

[7] Ethno. of the United States Exp. Exp., pp. 77, 81.

[8] Keppel's Expedition to Borneo, vol. i. p. 231.

fied this opinion on some points, but as regards the absence of idols it seems to be correct.

In India the Khasias have no temples or idols.[1] The Kols of Central India worship the sun; ' material ' idol worship they have none.'[2]    Originally, says Dubois, the Hindoos did not resort ' to images of stone ' or other materials . . . . but when the people of ' India had deified their heroes or other mortals, they ' began then, and not before, to have recourse to statues ' and images.'[3]  In China ' it is observable' that there ' is not to be found, in the canonical books, the least ' footstep of idolatrous worship till the image of Fo was ' brought into China, several ages after Confucius.'

The Ostyaks never made an image of their god ' Torum,'[5] and some other Siberian tribes were without idols.[6]  In fact, idols do not occur until we arrive at the stage of the highest Polynesian Islanders.  Even then they are often, as Ellis expressly tells us,[7] mere shapeless pieces of wood; thus leaving much to the imagination.  It may, I think, be laid down almost as a constant rule, that mankind arrives at the stage of monarchy in government before he reaches idolatry in religion.

The idol usually assumes the human form, and idolatry is closely connected with that form of religion which consists in the worship of ancestors.  We have already seen how imperfectly uncivilised man realises

[1] Dalton, Des. Etha. of Bengal, p. 57. Jour. Anthr. Ins. 1871, p. 130.
[2] Dalton, Trans. Etha. Soc., N.S., vol. vi. p. 32.
[3] Dubois, The People of India, p. 370

[4] Astley, vol. iv. p. 203.
[5] Erman, loc. cit., vol. ii. p. 50.
[6] Müller, Des de toutes les Nat. de l'Empire Russe, pt. i. pp. 54, 64.
[7] Polynesian Researches, vol. ii. p. 220.

the conception of death; and we cannot wonder that death and sleep should long have been intimately connected together in the human mind. The savage, however, knows well that in sleep the spirit lives, even though the body appears to be dead. Morning after morning he wakes himself, and sees others rise, from sleep. Naturally, therefore, he endeavours to rouse the dead. Nor can we wonder at the very general custom of providing food and other necessaries for the use of the dead. Among races leading a settled and quiet life this habit would tend to continue longer and longer. Prayers to the dead would reasonably follow from such customs, for even without attributing a greater power to the dead than to the living, they might yet, from their different sphere and nature, exercise a considerable power, whether for good or evil. But it is impossible to distinguish a request to an invisible being from prayer; or a powerful spirit from a demigod.

The Kaffirs also sacrifice and pray to their deceased relatives, although ' it would perhaps be asserting too ' much to say absolutely that they believe in the exist-' ence and the immortality of the soul.' [1] In fact, their belief seems to go no further than this, that the ghosts of the dead haunt for a certain time their previous dwelling-places, and either assist or plague the living. No special powers are attributed to them, and it would be a misnomer to call them ' Deities.'

In uncivilised societies, when there were no great differences of rank, deceased spirits would, indeed,

---

[1] The Basutos; Casalis, p. 243. See also Callaway's Religious System of the Amazulu. Livingstone, Zambesi, p. 46.

scarcely rise beyond the dignity of ghosts; but under a more settled government, the ghosts of the great would tend to become gods. Thus it appears that in Polynesia,[1] the worship of ancestors has tended to replace that of the earlier deities.

The nations of Mysore at the new moon 'observe a 'feast in honour of deceased parents.'[2] The Kurumbars of the Deccan also 'sacrifice to the spirits of ancestors,' and the same is the case with the Santals.[3] Indeed the worship of ancestors appears to be more or less prevalent among all the aboriginal tribes of Central India.

Burton[4] considers that some of the Egba deities are 'palpably men and women of note in their day.'

'The gods whom the New Zealanders fear,' says Shortland, 'are the spirits of the dead, who are believed 'to be constantly watching over the living with jealous 'eyes.'[5] I have already indeed mentioned that throughout Polynesia the worship of ancestors seems to have been gaining ground over the older forms of religion; and Hale says broadly[6] that the religion of the Micronesians 'is the worship of the spirits of their ancestors.' In Peru, the deceased Yncas were worshipped as gods,[7] and in Mexico Quetzalcoatl was doubtless, says Prescott, 'one of those benefactors of their species, who have 'been deified by the gratitude of posterity.'[8] In Tanna

[1] Gerland's Cont. of Waitz's Anthropologie, vol. vi. p. 330.

[2] Buchanan, quoted in Trans. Ethn. Soc., N.S., vol. viii. p. 96.

[3] Elliott, Trans. Ethn. Soc., N.S., vol. viii. pp. 104, 106.

[4] Abeokuta, vol. i. p. 181.

[5] Traditions of the New Zealanders, p. 81.

[6] U.S. Expl. Expedition, p. 77.

[7] Garcilasso de la Vega, vol. 1. p. 93. Markham, Rites and Laws of the Yncas, p. 12.

[8] Hist. of Mexico, vol. i, p. 40. See also Wüttke, Ges. der Menschh. vol. i. p. 202.

and other neighbouring islands they worship the spirits of their ancestors.' There can be little doubt, says Hale,[2] speaking of the Micronesians, 'that the deities ' worshipped in the Southern clusters were only deified ' chiefs, the memory of whose existence has been lost in ' the lapse of time;' in many cases, at any rate, worship is avowedly paid to the spirits of their ancestors.

Other races endeavour to preserve the memory of the dead by rude statues. Thus, ancestor worship is very prevalent in Siberia, and Pallas[3] mentions that the Ostyaks of Siberia 'rendent aussi un culte à leurs ' morts. Ils sculptent des figures de bois pour repré- ' senter les Ostiaks célèbres. Dans les repas de commé- ' moration on place devant ces figures une partie des ' mets. Les femmes qui ont chéri leurs maris ont de ' pareilles figures, les couchent avec elles, les parent, et ' ne mangent point sans leur présenter une partie de ' leur portion.' Erman[4] also mentions that when a man dies 'the relatives form a rude wooden image ' representing, and in honour of, the deceased, which is ' set up in their yurt, and receives divine honours' for a certain time. 'At every meal they set an offering of ' food before the image; and should this represent a ' deceased husband, the widow embraces it from time ' to time, and lavishes on it every sign of attachment.' In ordinary cases this semi-worship only lasts a few years, after which the image is buried. 'But when a ' Shaman dies, this custom changes, in his favour, into a ' complete and decided canonisation; for it is not ' thought enough that, in this case, the dressed block of

[1] Turner, Nineteen Years in Polynesia, pp. 88, 304, 411.
[2] Ethn. of the U.S. Expl. Exp.
p. 97.
[3] Pallas' Voyages, vol. iv. p. 79.
[4] Erman, &c. ed., vol. ii. p. 51.

'wood which represents the deceased should receive
'homage for a limited period, but the priest's descend-
'ants do their best to keep him in vogue from genera-
'tion to generation; and by well-contrived oracles and
'other arts they manage to procure offerings for these
'their families' penates, as abundant as those laid on
'the altars of the universally acknowledged gods.   But
'that these latter also have an historical origin, that
'they were originally monuments of distinguished men,
'to which prescription and the interest of the Shamans
'gave by degrees an arbitrary meaning and importance,
'seems to me not liable to doubt; and this is, further-
'more, corroborated by the circumstance that of all the
'sacred yurts dedicated to these saints, which have been
'numerous from the earliest times in the vicinity of the
'river, only one has been seen (near Samarovo) con-
'taining the image of a woman.'

It seems to me that in other countries also, statues
have in this manner come to be worshipped as deities.

The writer of the 'Wisdom of Solomon,'[1] long ago,
observed truly of idols that

'13. Neither were they from the beginning, neither
'shall they be for ever.

'14. For by the vain glory of men they entered
'into the world, and therefore shall they come shortly
'to an end.

'15. For a father afflicted with untimely mourning,
'when he hath made an image of his child soon taken
'away, now honoured him as a god, which was then
'a dead man, and delivered to those that were under
'him ceremonies and sacrifices.

[1] Wisdom, ch. xiv. p. 12.

' 16. Thus, in process of time, an ungodly custom
' grown strong was kept as a law, and graven images
' were worshipped by the commandments of kings:

' 17. Whom men could not honour in presence, be-
' cause they dwelt far off, they took the counterfeit of
' the visage from far, and make an express image of a
' king whom they honoured, to the end that by this their
' forwardness, they might flatter him that was absent as
' if he were present.

' 18. Also the singular diligence of the artificer did
' help to set forward the ignorant to more superstition.

' 19. For he, peradventure willing to please one in
' authority, forced all his skill to make the resemblance
' of the best fashion.

' 20. And so the multitude, allured by the grace of
' the work, took him now for a god, which a little before
' was but honoured as a man.'

The idol is by no means regarded as a mere emblem.
In India,[1] when the offerings of the people have been
less profuse than usual, the Brahmans sometimes ' put
' the idols in irons, chaining their hands and feet.
' They exhibit them to the people in this humiliating
' state, into which they tell them they have been
' brought by rigorous creditors, from whom their gods
' had been obliged, in times of trouble, to borrow money
' to supply their wants. They declare that the in-
' exorable creditors refuse to set the god at liberty,
' until the whole sum, with interest, shall have been
' paid. The people come forward, alarmed at the sight
' of their divinity in irons ; and thinking it the most
' meritorious of all good works to contribute to his

[1] Dubois, The People of India, p. 407.

'deliverance, they raise the sum required by the
'Brahmans for that purpose.'

'A statue of Hercules' was worshipped at Tyre, not
'as a representative of the Deity but as the Deity him-
'self; and accordingly when Tyre was besieged by
'Alexander, the Deity was fast bound in chains, to
'prevent him from deserting to the enemy.'

It is hard for us to appreciate the difficulty which an
undeveloped mind finds in raising itself to any elevated
conception. Thus Campbell mentions that a High-
lander, wishing to describe a castle of the utmost possible magnificence, ended with this climax: 'That was
'the beautiful castle! There was not a shadow of a
'thing that was for the use of a castle that was not
'in it, even to a herd for the geese.' As, however,
civilisation progresses, and the chiefs, becoming more
despotic, exact more and more respect, the people are
introduced to conceptions of power and magnificence
higher than any which they had previously entertained.

Hence, though the worship of ancestors occurs
among races in the stage of Totemism, it long survives,
and may be regarded as characterising Idolatry; which
is really a higher religion, and generally indicates a
more advanced mental condition than the worship of
animals or of the heavenly bodies. At first sight the
reverse would appear to be the case: most would regard the sun as a far grander deity than any in human
form. As a matter of fact, however, this is not so, and
worship is generally, though not invariably, associated
with a lower idea of the Deity than is the case with
Idolatry.

---

[1] *History of Man,* vol. iv. p. 310.

Indeed. the very circumstances which to our minds almost render the sun worthy of deification are precisely those which made sun-worship comparatively a rare form of religion amongst the lower races of savages.

Again, in the lowest religions, man does not form to himself any definite conception of Deity. If we enquire in what sense a savage regards a tree or a serpent as a deity, we are putting to ourselves a question which the savage does not think of asking. But when religion acquired a more intellectual character—when it included faith as well as feeling, belief as well as mystery—man first conceived the Deity as a being like himself in form, character, and attributes, only wiser and more powerful. This is one reason why the deities in this stage are anthropomorphous.

Another is the fact that the gradually increasing power of chiefs and kings has familiarised the mind with the existence of a power greater than any which had been previously conceived. Thus, in Western Africa, the slave trade having added considerably to the wealth and consequently to the power of the chiefs or kings, they maintained much state, and insisted upon being treated with servile homage. No man was allowed to eat with them, or to approach them excepting on his knees with an appearance of fear, which no doubt was in many cases sufficiently well-founded.

These marks of respect so much resembled adoration, that 'the individuals' of the lower classes are 'persuaded that his (the king's) power is not confined ' to the earth.'

[1] Proyart's History of Loango, Pinkerton, vol. xvi. p. 577. See also Bosman, &c. cit., pp. 488, 491. Ast-ley's Collection of Voyages, vol. iii. pp. 70, 223, 226.

Battel mentions that the king of Loango 'is honoured
' among them as though he were a god.'[1] He is so holy
that no one is allowed to see him eat or drink. The
tyrants of Natal, says Casalis, 'exacted almost divine
' homage.'[2]

In Peru the Ynca Uiraccocha was adored as a god
even during his life, 'though he wished to teach the
' Indians not to worship him.'[3]

In Madagascar, also, the reigning sovereign was regarded almost as a god.[4]

In New Zealand, says Hale,[5] 'the great warrior
' chief, Hongi, claimed for himself the title of a god,
' and was so called by his followers. At the Society
' Islands, Tamatoa, the last heathen king of Raitea, was
' worshipped as a divinity. At the Marquesas there are,
' on every island, several men who are termed atua, or
' gods, who receive the same adoration, and are believed
' to possess the same powers, as other deities.

.     .     .     .     .     .     .     .

' At Depeyster's group, the westernmost cluster of
' Polynesia, we were visited by a chief, who announced
' himself as the atua or god of the islands, and was ac-
' knowledged as such by the other natives.'

The king and queen of Tahiti were regarded as so
sacred that nothing once used by them, not even the
sounds forming their names, could be used for any
ordinary purpose.[6] The language of the court was
characterised by the most ridiculous adulation. The

[1] Pinkerton's Travels, vol. xvi. p. 330.
[2] The Basutos, p. 219.
[3] Garcilasso de la Vega, vol. ii. p. 07.
[4] Sibree, Madagascar and its People, p. 315.
[5] U.S. Expl. Exped. p. 21.
[6] Ellis' Polynesian Researches, vol. ii. pp. 348, 360.

king's ' houses were called the aarai, the clouds of
' heaven ; anunnua, the rainbow, was the name of the
' canoe in which he voyaged; his voice was called
' thunder ; the glare of the torches in his dwelling was
' denominated lightning; and when the people saw
' them in the evening, as they passed near his abode,
' instead of saying the torches were burning in the
' palace, they would observe that the lightning was
' flashing in the clouds of heaven.'

Man-worship would not, indeed, be long confined to
the dead. In many cases it extends to the living also.
Indeed, the savage who worships an animal or a tree,
would see no absurdity in worshipping a man. His
chief is, in his eyes, almost as powerful, if not more so,
than his deity. Yet man-worship does not prevail in
altogether uncivilised communities, because the chiefs,
associating constantly with their followers, lack that
mystery which religion requires, and which nocturnal
animals so eminently possess. As, however, civilisation
progresses, and the chiefs separate themselves more and
more from their subjects, this ceases to be the case, and
man-worship becomes an important element of religion.

The worship of a great chief seems quite as natural
to man as that of an idol. ' Why,' said a Mongol [1] to
Friar Ascelin, ' since you Christians make no scruple to
' adore sticks and stones, why do you refuse to do the
' same honour to Bayoth Noy, whom the Khan hath
' ordered to be adored in the same manner as he is
' himself?'

' Tuikilakila,[2] the chief of Somosomo, offered Mr.

---

[1] Astley, vol. iv. p. 551.  [2] Erskine's Western Pacific, p. 240.

' Hunt a preferment of the same sort. " If you die
' " first," said he, " I shall make you my god." In fact
' there appears to be no certain line of demarcation
' between departed spirits and gods, nor between gods
' and living men, for many of the priests and old chiefs
' are considered as sacred persons, and not a few of
' them will also claim to themselves the right of divinity.
' " I am a god," Tuikilakila would sometimes say; and
' he believed it too. They were not merely the words of
' his lips; he believed he was something above a mere
' man.'

This worship is, however, almost always accompanied by a belief in higher beings. We have already
seen that the New Zealanders and some other nations
have almost entirely abandoned the worship of animals,
&c., without as yet realising the higher stage of Idolatry,
owing probably in great measure to their political condition. In other cases where Shamanism has not so
effectually replaced Totemism, the establishment of
monarchical government with its usual pomp and ceremonial, led to a much more organised worship of the old
gods. Of this the serpent-worship in Western Africa
and the sun-worship in Peru, are striking examples.

I do not therefore wonder that white men should
have been so often taken for deities. This was the case
with Captain Cook in the Pacific, with Lander in
Western Africa,[1] and, as already mentioned, Mrs. Thomson was regarded by the North Australians as a spirit,
though she lived with them for some years. In the
Voyage of Sir Francis Drake[2] it is mentioned that some

---

[1] See *antè*, p. 251.                  Southern Indians, p. 392. Stevens,
[2] Jones,   Antiquities  of  the   Flint Chips, pp. 318, 319.

of the North American Indians brought ' feathers and
' bags of *Tobah* for presents, or rather indeed for sacri-
' fices, upon this persuasion that we were gods.'

Mr. Hale tells us that the natives of Oatufu and
other islands thought that these ' came from above, in
' the sky, and were divinities.' [1]

It seems at first sight hard to understand how men
can be regarded as immortal. Yet even this belief has
been entertained in various countries.

Merolla tells us [2] that in his time the wizards of
Congo were called Scinghili, that is to say Gods of the
Earth. The head of them is styled ' Ganga Chitorne,
' being reputed God of all the Earth.' ' He further
' asserts that his body is not capable of suffering a
' natural death; and, therefore, to confirm his adorers in
' that opinion, whenever he finds his end approaching,
' either through age or disease, he calls for such a one of
' his disciples as he designs to succeed him, and pre-
' tends to communicate to him his great powers: and
' afterwards in public (where this tragedy is always
' acted) he commands him to tie a halter about his neck
' and to strangle himself therewith, or else to take a
' club and knock him down dead. This command being
' once pronounced, is soon executed, and the wizard
' thereby sent a martyr to the devil. The reason that
' this is done in public, is to make known the successor
' ordained by the last breath of the predecessor, and to
' show that it has the same power of producing ruin,
' and the like. If this office were not thus continually

[1] U.S. Expl. Exp., pp. 159, 160.    [2] Pinkerton, vol. xvi. p. 226, *et*
See also Gerland, Anthr. de Natur-    *seq.*
völker, vol. vi. p. 607.

' filled, the inhabitants say that the earth would soon
' become barren, and mankind consequently perish.   In
' my time, one of these magicians was cast into the sea,
' another into a river, a mother and her son put to
' death, and many others banished by our order, as has
' been said.'

So also the Great Lama of Thibet is regarded as immortal; though his spirit occasionally passes from one
earthly tenement to another.

These, then, are the lowest intellectual stages
through which religion has passed.   It is no part of my
plan to describe the various religious beliefs of the
higher races.   I have, however, stopped short sooner
perhaps than I should otherwise have done, because the
worship of personified principles, such as Fear, Love,
Hope, &c., could not have been treated apart from that
of the Phallus or Lingam with which it was so intimately associated in Greece, India, Mexico, and elsewhere; and which, though at first modest and pure, as
all religions are in their origin, led to such abominable
practices, that it is one of the most painful chapters in
human history.

I will now, therefore, pass on to some points intimately connected with religion, but which could not be
conveniently treated in the earlier part of this work.

There is no difficulty in understanding that when
once the idea of Spiritual Beings had become habitual
—when once man had come to regard them as exer-
cising an important influence, whether for good or evil
—he would endeavour to secure their assistance and
support.   Before a war he would try to propitiate them
by promising a share of the spoil after victory; and fear,

even if no higher motive, would ensure the performance of his promise.

We, no doubt, regard, and justly regard, sacrifices as unnecessary. 'I will take no bullock,' says David,[1] 'out of thine house, nor he-goat out of thy folds.' This sentiment, however, was far in advance of its time, and even Solomon felt that sacrifices, in the then condition of the Jews, were necessary. They form, indeed, a stage through which, in any natural process of development, religion must pass. At first it is supposed that the Spirits actually eat the food offered to them. Soon, however, it would be observed that animals sacrificed did not disappear; and the natural explanation would be that the Spirit ate the spiritual part of the victim, leaving the grosser portion to his devout worshipper. Thus the Limboos, near Darjeeling, eat their sacrifices, dedicating, as they forcibly express it, 'the life-breath 'to the gods, the flesh to ourselves.'[2]

So also, as Sir G. Grey tells us, the New Zealand fairies, when Te Kanawa gave them his jewels, carried off the shadows only, not caring for the earthly substance.[3] In Guinea, according to Bosman, 'the idol 'hath only the blood, because they like the flesh very 'well themselves.'[4] In other cases the idols were smeared with the blood, while the devotees feasted on the flesh. The Ostyaks, when they kill an animal, rub some of the blood on the mouths of their idols. Even this seems at length to be replaced in some cases, as Mr.

[1] Psalm l.
[2] Campbell, in Trans. Etho. Soc., N.S., vol. vii. p. 151.
[3] Polynesian Mythology, p. 294.
[4] Bosman. Pinkerton's Voyages, vol. xvi. p. 531. Astley's Collection of Voyages, vol. ii. p. 97.

Tylor has suggested, by red paint. Thus, the sacred stones in India, as Colonel Forbes Leslie has shown, are frequently ornamented with red.[1] So also in Congo it is customary to daub the fetiches with red every new moon.[2]

Of the great offerings of food among the Feejeeans, says Williams,[3] 'native belief apportions merely the ' soul thereof to the gods, who are described as being ' enormous eaters; the substance is consumed by the ' worshippers.'

In Madagascar 'in almost all cases the worshippers ' seem to have feasted on the flesh.'[4]

Gradually, indeed, it comes to be a necessary portion of the ceremony that the victim should be eaten by those present. Thus, in India,[5] when the sacrifice ' is over, the priest comes out, and distributes part of ' the articles which have been offered to the idols. ' This is received as holy, and is eaten immediately.'

Ellis[6] mentions an indication of this in Tahiti, when human sacrifices prevailed, but cannibalism was abandoned. The priest handed a portion of the victim to the king, 'who raised it to his mouth as if desirous to ' eat it,' but then handed it to an attendant. Among the Redskins,[7] at the feast held when the hunting season begins, the victim 'must be all eaten and nothing ' left.' It is remarkable that among the Algonkins

[1] See, for instance, Early Races of Scotland, vol. ii. p. 464.

[2] See ante, p.

[3] Fiji and the Fijians, vol. i. p. 231. See also p. 223.

[4] Sibree, Madagascar and its People, p. 309.

[5] Dubois, The People of India, p. 401.

[6] Polynesian Researches, vol. ii. p. 214.

[7] Schoolcraft's Indian Tribes, vol. iii. p. 61. Tanner's Narrative, p. 287.

another rule at the same feast is that not a bone of the victim must be broken.[1]

In many cases a curious confusion arises between the victim and the deity, and the former is worshipped before it is sacrificed and eaten. Thus in ancient Egypt, Apis, the victim, was also regarded as the God,[2] and Iphigenia was supposed by some to be the same as Artemis.[3]

In Mexico[4] at a certain period of the year the priest of Quetzalcoatl made an image of the Deity, of meal mixed with infants' blood, and then, after many impressive ceremonies, killed the image by shooting it with an arrow, and tore out the heart, which was eaten by the king, while the rest of the body was distributed among the people, every one of whom was most anxious to procure a piece to eat, however small.

The great yearly sacrifice in honour of Tezcatlipoca was also very remarkable. Some beautiful youth, usually a war captive, was chosen as the victim. For a whole year he was treated and worshipped as a god. When he went out he was attended by a numerous train of pages, and the crowd as he passed prostrated themselves before him, and did him homage as the impersonation of the good Deity. Everything he could wish was provided for him, and at the commencement of the last month four beautiful girls were allotted to him as wives. Finally, when the fatal day arrived, he was placed at the head of a solemn procession, taken to the temple, and after being sacrificed with much cere-

[1] Tanner's Narrative, p. 105.
[2] Cox's Manual of Mythology, p. 213.
[3] Cox's Manual of Mythology, p. 158.
[4] See Müller, Ges. d. Amer. Urr. p. 605. Wüttke, Ges. der Mensch, vol. i. p. 314.

mony and every token of respect, he was eaten by the priests and chiefs.[1]

Again, among the Khonds[2] of Central India human sacrifices prevailed until quite lately. 'A stout stake
' is driven into the soil, and to it the victim is fastened,
' seated, and anointed with ghee, oil, and turmeric,
' decorated with flowers, and *worshipped* during the day
' by the assembly. At nightfall the licentious revelry
' is resumed, and on the third morning the victim gets
' some milk to drink, when the presiding priest implores
' the goddess to shower her blessings on the people,
' that they may increase and multiply, prosperity attend
' their cattle and poultry, fertility their fields, and hap-
' piness to the people generally. The priest recounts
' the origin and advantage of the rite, as previously
' detailed, and concludes by stating that the goddess
' has been obeyed and the people assembled.

.     .     .     .     .     .     .     .     .

' Other softening expressions are recited to excite
' the compassion of the multitude. After the mock
' ceremony, nevertheless, the victim is taken to the
' grove where the sacrifice is to be carried out; and,
' to prevent resistance, the bones of the arms and legs
' are broken, or the victim drugged with opium or
' datura, when the janni wounds his victim with his
' axe. This act is followed up by the crowd; a number
' now press forward to obtain a piece of his flesh, and
' in a moment he is stripped to the bones.'

An almost identical custom prevails among the

[1] Müller, *loc. cit.*, p. 617. Prescott, *loc. cit.*, vol. 1. p. 5. Rites and Laws of the Incas, p. 28.

[2] Dr. Shortt, Trans. Ethn. Soc., N.S., vol. vi. p. 273. Campbell, Wild Tribes of Khondistan, p. 112.

Marimos, a tribe of South Africa much resembling the
Bechuanas. We find amongst them, says Arbousset,
' the practice of human sacrifices on the occasion of a
' ceremony which they call *mesclebso oa mabele*, or *the*
' *boiling of the corn.* They generally select for this
' sacrifice a young man, stout, but of small stature.
' They secure him, it may be by violence, or it may be
' by intoxicating him with *yoala.* They then lead him
' into the fields, and sacrifice him in the midst of the
' fields, according to their own expression, *for seed.*
' His blood, after having been coagulated by the rays
' of the sun, is burned along with the frontal bone, the
' flesh attached to it, and the brain. The ashes are
' then scattered over the lands to fertilise them, and the
' remainder of the body is eaten.'[1]

In some parts of Africa 'eating the fetish' is a
solemn ceremony, by which women swear fidelity to
their husbands, men to their friends. On a marriage in
Issini, the parties ' eat the fetish together, in token of
' friendship, and as an assurance of the woman's fidelity
' to her husband.'[2] In taking an oath also, the same
ceremony is observed. To know, says Loyer, 'the
' truth from any negro, you need only mix something
' in a little water, and, steeping a bit of bread, bid him
' eat or drink that fetish as a sign of the truth. If the
' thing be so, he will do it freely; but if otherwise, he
' will not touch it, believing he should die on the spot
' if he swore falsely. Their way is to rasp or grate a
' little of their fetish in water, or on any edible, and so
' put it in their mouth without swallowing it.'

[1] Tour to the N.E. of the Cape of Good Hope, p. 59.   [2] Loyer, in Astley's Collection of Voyages, vol. ii. pp. 424, 441.

The sacrifices were, as a general rule, not eaten by all indiscriminately. In Feejee they were confined to the old men and priests; women and young men being excluded from any share.

In many cases, the priests gradually established a claim to the whole; a result which could not fail to act as a considerable stimulus to the practice of sacrifice. It also affected the character of the worship. Thus, as Bosman tells us, the priests encouraged offerings to the Serpent rather than to the Sea, because, in the latter case, as he expresses it, 'there happens no remainder to 'be left for them.'

As already mentioned, the feeling which has led to the sacrifice of animals would naturally culminate in that of men. So natural, indeed, does the idea of human sacrifice appear to the human mind in this stage, that we meet with it in various nations all over the world; and it is unjust to regard it, with Prescott,[1] as evidence of fiendish passions: on the contrary, it indicates deep and earnest religious feeling, perverted by an erroneous conception of the Divine character.

Human sacrifices occurred in Guinea,[2] and Burton[3] saw 'at Benin city a young woman lashed to a scaffold- 'ing upon the summit of a tall blasted tree, and being 'devoured by the turkey-buzzards. The people de- 'clared it to be a " fetish " or charm for bringing rain.' I have already mentioned the existence of human sacrifice among the Marimos of South Africa.

Captain Cook describes human sacrifices as prevalent

[1] History of Mexico, vol. i. p. 68.    vol. iii. p. 118.

[3] Abookuta, vol. i. p. 10.

[2] Astley's Collection of Voyages,

among the islanders of the Pacific,[1] and especially in the Sandwich group.[2] He particularly describes[3] the case of a sacrifice offered by Towha, chief of the district of Tettaha, in Tahiti, to propitiate the Deity on the occasion of an expedition against Eimeo (Pl. IV.); and mentions that, during the ceremony, 'a kingfisher, 'making a noise in the trees, Otoo (the king) turned 'to me, saying, "That is the Eatooâ," i.e. Deity.' War captives were frequently sacrificed in Brazil.

In Madagascar human sacrifices seem to have prevailed in the province of Vangaidrano, but not elsewhere.[4]

Various nations in India, besides the Khonds, who have been already mentioned, used to offer up human sacrifices on extraordinary occasions; but so recently as 1865–66 such sacrifices were resorted to in hopes of averting the famine;[5] and even now in some places, though the actual sacrifice is no longer permitted, they make human figures of flour, paste, or clay, and then cut off the heads in honour of their gods;[6] just as the Romans used to throw dolls into the Tiber as a substitute for human sacrifices.

Many cases of human sacrifice are mentioned in ancient history. The Carthaginians, after their defeat of Agathocles, burnt some of their captives as a sacrifice; the Assyrians offered human sacrifices to the god Nergal.

Although resorted to on various critical occasions by the Greeks, human sacrifice appears to have been foreign to the mythology, and opposed to the spirit of

[1] Cook, Voyage to the Pacific, vol. ii. p. 41.
[2] *Loc. cit.*, vol. iii. p. 101.
[3] *Loc. cit.*, vol. ii. p. 30.
[4] Sibree, Madagascar and its People, p. 300.
[5] Hunter, Annals of Rural Bengal, 1868, p. 128.
[6] Dubois, *loc. cit.*, p. 490.

that people. Human sacrifices are connected with a more earnest and melancholy theology. In Roman history they occur far more frequently, and even down to a late date. In the year 46 B.C., Cæsar sacrificed two soldiers on the altar in the Campus Martius.[1] Augustus is said to have sacrificed a maiden named Gregoria.[2] Even Trajan, when Antioch was rebuilt, sacrificed Calliope, and placed her statue in the theatre.[3] Under Commodus, and later emperors, human sacrifices appear to have been more common; and a gladiator appears to have been sacrificed to Jupiter Latialis even in the time of Constantine.[4] Yet these awful rites had been expressly forbidden B.C. 95; and Pliny asserts that in his time they were never openly solemnised.[5]

In Northern Europe human sacrifices were not uncommon. The Yarl of the Orkneys is recorded to have sacrificed the son of the King of Norway to Odin in the year 893.[6] In 993, Hakon Yarl sacrificed his own son to the gods. Domald, King of Sweden, was burnt by his people as a sacrifice to Odin, in consequence of a severe famine.[7] At Upsala was a celebrated temple, round which an eye-witness assured Adam of Bremen that he had seen the corpses of seventy-two victims hanging up at one time.[8]

In Russia, as in Scandinavia, human sacrifices continued down to the introduction of Christianity. In Mexico and Peru they seem to have been peculiarly numerous. Müller[9] has suggested that this may have

[1] Dio, II. R., xliii. 24.
[2] Malalas, Chron., p. 221.
[3] Ibid., p. 275.
[4] Porphyry, De Abstin., ii. 56.
[5] Nat. His, xxx. 1, 12.
[6] Snorre, Heimskringla, vol. ii.
p. 51. Torfæus, His. Rer. Norregicarum, vol. ii. p. 52.
[7] Snorre, vol. i. p. 50.
[8] Adam of Bremen, vol. iv. p. 27.
[9] Geschichte der Americanischen Urreligionen, p. 23.

partly arisen from the fact that these nations were not softened by the possession of domestic animals. Various estimates have been made of the number of human victims annually sacrificed in the Mexican temples. Müller thinks 2,500 is a moderate estimate; and in one year it appears to have exceeded 100,000.

Among the Jews we find a system of animal sacrifices on a great scale, and symbols of human sacrifices, which can, I think, only be understood on the hypothesis that the latter were once usual. The case of Jephtha's daughter is generally looked upon as quite exceptional,[1] but the twenty-eighth and twenty-ninth verses of the twenty-seventh chapter of Leviticus appear to indicate that human sacrifices were at one time habitual among the Jews.

I do not here refer to the human sacrifices at burials, because these are not, strictly speaking, of a religious character, but intended to supply the deceased with wives or slaves in the land of spirits.

The lower savages have no Temples or sacred buildings. Throughout the New World there was no such thing as a temple, excepting among the semi-civilised races of Central America and Peru.

The Stiens of Cambodia 'have neither priest nor 'temples.'[2] We should seek in vain, says Casalis,[3] 'from the extremity of the southern promontory of 'Africa to the country far beyond the banks of the 'Zambesi, for anything like the pagodas of India, the 'maraes of Polynesia, or the fetish huts of Nigritia.'

---

[1] See Kalisch, Commentary on the Old Testament, Lev., pt. i. p. 409.

[2] Mouhot's Travels in the Central Parts of Indo-China, vol. i. p. 250.

[3] The Basutos, p. 237.

The people of Madagascar, as we are informed by
Drury,[1] who resided fifteen years among them, although
they have settled abodes, keep large herds of cattle, and
are diligent agriculturists, 'have no temples, no taber-
' nacles, or groves for the public performance of their
' divine worship; neither have they solemn fasts, or
' festivals, or set days or times; nor priests to do it for
' them.'

The Toorkmans, says Burnes,[2] 'are without
' mosques.' The Micronesians, according to Hale,[3]
' have neither temples, images, nor sacrifices.' The
Khasias[4] 'have no temples.' The same is the case
with the Ostyaks and other savage races of Siberia.[5]

Professor Nilsson was, I believe, the first to point
out that certain races buried the dead in their houses,
and that the chambered tumuli of Northern Europe are
probably copies of the dwellings then used; sometimes
perhaps the actual dwellings themselves. We know
that as the power of chiefs increased, their tombs became
larger and more magnificent; and Mr. Fergusson has
well shown how, in India, the tumulus has developed
into the temple.

In some cases, as, for instance, in India, it is far
from easy to distinguish between a group of stone gods
and a sacred fane. In fact, we may be sure that the
very same stones are by some supposed to be actual
deities, while others more advanced regard them as
sacred only because devoted to religious purposes. Some

[1] Adventures of Robert Drury,
p. 10.

[2] Travels into Bokhara, vol. ii. p.
260.

[3] U.S. Explor. Exped. pp. 77, 84.

[4] Godwin-Austen, Jour. of the
Anthr. Inst., 1871, p. 130.

[5] Muller, Des. de toutes les Nat.
de l'Emp. Russe, Pt. II. p. 105,
Pt. III. p. 141.

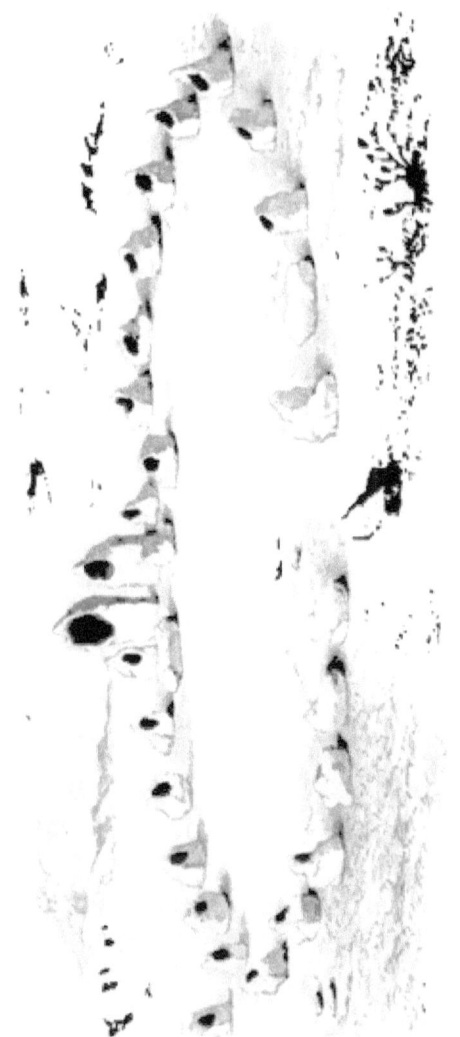

GROUP OF BAKERS STONES IN THE DEMERA

of the ruder Hindostan tribes actually worship upright stones; but Colonel Forbes Leslie regards the sacred stones represented in Pl. III. as a place of worship, rather than as actual deities; and this is at any rate the case with another group similarly painted, which he observed near Andlee, also in the Dekhan, and which is peculiarly interesting from its resemblance to those stone circles of our own country; of which Stonehenge is (see *Frontispiece*) the grandest representative. Fig. 18, p. 248, represents[1] a religious dance as practised by the Redskins of Virginia. Here, also, as already mentioned, we see a sacred circle of stones, differing from those of our own country, and of India, only in having a human head rudely carved on each stone.

The lower races of men have no Priests, properly so called. Many passages, indeed, may be quoted which, at first sight, appear to negative this assertion. If, however, we examine more closely the true functions of these so-called 'priests,' we shall easily satisfy ourselves that the term is a misnomer, and that wizards only are intended. Without temples and sacrifices there cannot be priests.

According to Drury, there were no priests in Madagascar; more recently, however, the guardians of the idols had usurped priestly functions, and even claimed for themselves immunities from legal consequences, akin to the custom of privilege of clergy, which survived until so recently among ourselves.[2]

Even the New Zealanders[3] had 'no regular priest-

---

[1] Mœurs des Sauv. Amér., vol. ii. p. 136.

[2] Sibree, Madagascar and its People, p. 400.

[3] Yate, p. 140.

'hood.' Mr. Gladstone[1] observes that the priest was not, 'as such, a significant personage in Greece at any 'period, nor had the priest of any one place or deity, so 'far as we know, any organic connection with the priest 'of any other; so that if there were priests, yet there 'was not a priesthood.'

Müller again expresses himself in very similar language. 'That there ever was in Greece,' he says, 'a priesthood, strictly speaking, in contradistinction to 'a laity, is a point which, in my opinion, cannot at all 'be established.'[2]

The progress seems to be that at first all men were, in this respect at least, alike. After a while some became more celebrated than others as sorcerers and diviners. These persons gradually associated themselves into a special class or caste, and assumed also the functions of doctors and priests. These qualities by degrees assumed more and more importance. It is, therefore, in some cases, difficult to say whether the 'medicine men,' or 'mystery men,' are doctors or priests. For instance, among the Kaffirs there are certain persons known as 'Isanusi,' 'Intongu,' or, 'Igqira,' which terms, says Mr. Warner,[3] 'I choose 'to translate by the word "priest," in preference to 'that of "doctor," the term generally employed by 'Europeans to designate this class of persons.'

An important part of their duty consists in regulating the weather. 'This,' says Mr. Warner,[4] 'is another 'of the heathenish vanities in which the benighted

---

[1] Juventus Mundi, p. 181.
[2] Scientific System of Mythology, p. 188.
[3] Kaffir Laws and Customs, p. 80.
[4] Ibid., p. 104.

' Kaffirs put their trust. They firmly believe that some
' of their priests have the power to cause it to rain.'

I have already pointed out (*ante*, p. 226) the great
difference between the belief in ghosts and in the immortality of the soul. Some races entirely disbelieve
in the survival of the soul after the death of the body,
and even those which are more advanced, often differ
from us very much in their views; in fact the belief in
a universal, independent, and endless existence is confined to the very highest races of men. The New
Zealanders believe that a man who is eaten as well as
killed, is thus destroyed both soul and body.[1] Even,
however, those who have proper interment are far from
secure of reaching the happy regions in the land of
spirits. The road to these is long and dangerous, and
many a soul perishes by the way.

In the Tonga Islands the chiefs are regarded as immortal, the Tooas or common people as mortal; with
reference to the intermediate class, or Mooas, there is a
difference of opinion.

A friend of Mr. Lang's [2] ' tried long and patiently to
' make a very intelligent docile Australian black under-
' stand his existence without a body, but the black
' never could keep his countenance, and generally made
' an excuse to get away. One day the teacher watched
' and found that he went to have a hearty fit of
' laughter at the absurdity of the idea of a man living
' and going about without arms, legs, or mouth to eat;
' for a long time he could not believe that the gentle-
' man was serious, and when he did realise it, the more

---

[1] Taylor, New Zealand and its
Inhabitants, p. 101.

[2] The Aborigines of Australia, p.
31.

' serious the teacher was the more ludicrous the whole
' affair appeared to the black.'

The resurrection of the body, as preached by the
missionaries,[1] appeared to the Tahitians 'astounding'
and 'incredible;' and 'as the subject was more fre-
' quently brought under their notice in public discourse,
' or in reading the Scriptures, and their minds were
' more attentively exercised upon it in connection with
' their ancestry, themselves, and their descendants, it
' appeared invested with more than ordinary difficulty,
' bordering, to their apprehension, on impossibility.'

Although the Feejeeans believe that almost everything has a spirit, few spirits are immortal: the road to
Mbulu is long, and beset with so many difficulties, that
after all ' few attain to immortality.'[2]

We find a very similar belief also among the Esquimaux[3] and the Kaffirs.[4]

As regards Central India, Colonel Dalton says,[5] ' I
' do not think that the present generation of Kols have
' any notion of a heaven or hell that may not be traced
' to Brahminical or Christian teaching. The old idea
' is that the souls of the dead become "bhoots," spirits,
' but no thought of reward or punishment is connected
' with the change. When a Ho swears, the oath has
' no reference whatever to a future state. He prays
' that if he speak not the truth he may be afflicted in
' this world with the loss of all—health, wealth, wife,

[1] Ellis' Polynesian Researches,
vol. ii. p. 105.

[2] Fiji and the Fijians, vol. i. p.
247. Seemann, Mission to Viti, p.
400.

[3] Cranz's Greenland, p. 259,

quoted in Tylor's Primitive Culture,
vol. ii. p. 20.

[4] Callaway, Amazulu Religion,
p. 355.

[5] Trans. Ethn. Soc., 1807, p. 38.

' children ; that he may sow without reaping, and
' finally may be devoured by a tiger; but he swears
' not by any happiness beyond the grave. He has in
' his primitive state no such hope ; and I believe that
' most Indian aborigines, though they may have some
' vague ideas of continuous existence, will be found
' equally devoid of original notions in regard to the
' judgment to come.'

In his 'Descriptive Ethnology of Bengal' he makes
a similar statement with reference to the Chalikatas,
another of the hill tribes, declaring that they ' utterly
' rejected all notions of a future state. The spirits they
' propitiated were, they declared, mortal like them-
' selves.'[1] The Buihers,[2] Oraons,[3] and Juangs[4] also
held very similar views. Again, 'all enquirers on the
' subject appear to have arrived at the conclusion that
' the Santals have no belief in a future state.'[5]

Among the Micronesians, according to Hale,[6] the
souls of those, 'only those, who are tattooed (being
' chiefly persons of free birth) can expect to reach the
' *Kuinakaki.* All others are intercepted on their way,
' and devoured by a monstrous giantess, called *Baine.*'
Some of the Guinea negroes considered that the soul of
the departed was subjected to an examination as to
their conduct during life, and if found wanting ' his
' god plunges him into the river, where he is drowned,
' and buried in eternal oblivion.'[7]

Even when the spirit is supposed to survive the

[1] Trans. Ethn. Soc., 1867, p. 21.
[2] Des. Ethn of Bengal, p. 133.
[3] Loc. cit., p. 257.
[4] Loc. cit., p. 157.
[5] Loc. cit., p. 218.
[6] U.S. Expl. Exped., p. 90.
[7] Bosman, Pinkerton's Voyages, vol. xvi. p. 401.

body, the condition of souls after death is not at first considered to differ materially from that during life. Heaven is merely a distant part of earth. Thus the ' seats of happiness are represented by some Hindu ' writers to be vast mountains on the north of ' India.' [1]

The Haitians considered that the paradise of the dead was situated in the lovely western valleys of their island. [2]

Again, in Tonga the souls are supposed to go to Bolotoo, a large island to the north-west, well stocked [3] with all kinds of useful and ornamental plants, ' always ' bearing the richest fruits and the most beautiful ' flowers, according to their respective natures ; that ' when these fruits or flowers are plucked, others im- ' mediately occupy their place . . . The island of Bolo- ' too is supposed to be so far off as to render it danger- ' ous for their canoes to attempt going there; and it ' is supposed, moreover, that even if they were to suc- ' ceed· in reaching so far, unless it happened to be the ' particular will of the gods, they would be sure to ' miss it.'

They believe, however, that on one occasion a canoe actually reached Bolotoo. The crew landed, but when they attempted to touch anything, ' they could no more ' lay hold of it than if it had been a shadow.' Conse- quently hunger soon overtook them, and forced them to return, which they fortunately succeeded in doing.

A curious notion, already referred to, is the belief that each man has several souls. It is common to

[1] Dubois, loc. cit., p. 485.          ii. p. 50.
[2] Tylor's Primitive Culture, vol.     [3] Mariner, loc. cit., vol. ii. p. 108.

various parts of America,[1] and exists in Madagascar as well as among the Khonds of Hindostan. It apparently arises from the idea that each pulse is the seat of a different life. It also derives an appearance of probability from the inconsistencies of behaviour to which savages are so prone. The Feejeeans also believed that each man has two spirits.[2] Among the ancient Greeks and Romans there are some indications of the existence of a similar belief.[3]

The belief in a future state, if less elevated than our own, is singularly vivid among some barbarous races. Thus we are told that among the Ancient Britons money was habitually lent on what may strictly be termed 'postobits'—promises to pay in another world, and it is said that the same thing occurs even now in Japan.

A striking instance of undoubting faith is mentioned by Mr. Tylor. A Hindoo thought he had been unfairly deprived of forty rupees, whereupon he cut off his own mother's head, with her full consent, in order that her spirit might haunt and harass the man who had taken the money and those concerned with him.[4]

The Feejeeans believe that 'as they die, such will be 'their condition in another world; hence their desire to 'escape extreme infirmity.'[5] The way to Mbulu, as already mentioned, is long and difficult; many always perish, and no diseased or infirm person could possibly succeed in surmounting all the dangers of the road.

[1] Tertre's History of the Caribby Islands, p. 288. It prevails also in Greenland. Müller, Gen. der Am. Urreligionen, p. 60.
[2] Fiji and the Fijians, vol. i. p. 241.
[3] Lafitau, vol. ii. p. 424.
[4] Primitive Culture, vol. ii. p. 102.
[5] Fiji and the Fijians, vol. i. p. 183.

Hence, as soon as a man feels the approach of old age, he notifies to his children that it is time for him to die. If he neglects to do so, the children after a while take the matter into their own hands. A family consultation is held, a day appointed, and the grave dug. The aged person has his choice of being strangled or buried alive. Mr. Hunt gives the following striking description of such a ceremony once witnessed by him. A young man came to him and invited him to attend his mother's funeral, which was just going to take place. Mr. Hunt accepted the invitation, and joined the procession, but, surprised to see no corpse, he made enquiries, when the young man 'pointed out his mother, ' who was walking along with them, as gay and lively ' as any of those present, and apparently as much ' pleased. Mr. Hunt expressed his surprise to the ' young man, and asked how he could deceive him so ' much by saying his mother was dead, when she was ' alive and well. He said, in reply, that they had made ' her death-feast, and were now going to bury her; ' that she was old, that his brother and himself had ' thought she had lived long enough, and it was time to ' bury her, to which she had willingly assented, and ' they were about it now. He had come to Mr. Hunt ' to ask his prayers, as they did those of the priest.

' He added, that it was from love for his mother ' that he had done so; that, in consequence of the same ' love, they were now going to bury her, and that none ' but themselves could or ought to do such a sacred ' office! Mr. Hunt did all in his power to prevent so ' diabolical an act; but the only reply he received was ' that she was their mother, and they were her children,

' and they ought to put her to death. On reaching the
' grave, the mother sat down, when they all, including
' children, grandchildren, relations, and friends, took an
' affectionate leave of her; a rope, made of twisted
' tapa, was then passed twice around her neck by her
' sons, who took hold of it and strangled her; after
' which she was put in her grave, with the usual
' ceremonies.' [1]

So general was this custom that in one town containing several hundred inhabitants Captain Wilkes did
not see one man over forty years of age, all the old
people having been buried.

For the same reason the Australians in some cases
cut off the right thumb of a dead foe, believing that
being thus ' unable to throw the spear, or to use the
' dowak efficiently, his spirit can do them very little
' injury.' [2] We find also a very similar belief among
some of the negroes.[3]

In Dahome the king sends constant messages to
his deceased father, by messengers who are killed for
the purpose.[4] The same firm belief which leads to this,
reconciles the messengers to their fate. They are well
treated beforehand, and their death, being instantaneous,
is attended with little pain. Hence we are assured that
they are quite cheerful and contented, and scarcely
seem to look on their death as a misfortune.

The North American Indian, as Schoolcraft tells us,
has little dread of death. ' He does not fear to go to a
' land which, all his life long, he has heard abounds in

---

[1] Wilkes' Exploring Expedition, condensed edition, p. 211.

[2] Oldfield, Trans. Ethn. Soc., N.S., vol. III. p. 287.

[3] Wuttke, Gen. der Mensch. vol. I. p. 107.

[4] Burton's Dahome, vol. II. p. 25.

'rewards without punishments.'[1] The Japanese commit suicide for the most trifling causes; and it is said that in China, if a rich man is condemned to death, he can sometimes purchase a willing substitute at a very small expense.

The lower races have no idea of Creation, and even among those somewhat more advanced it is at first very incomplete. Their deities are part of, not the makers of, the world; and even when the idea of creation dawns upon the mind, it is not strictly a creation, but merely the raising of land already existing at the bottom of the original sea.

The Abipones had no theory on the subject; when questioned by Dobritzhoffer,[2] 'My father,' replied Ye-'hoalay readily and frankly, 'our grandfathers, and 'great-grandfathers, were wont to contemplate the earth 'alone, solicitous only to see whether the plain afforded 'grass and water for their horses. They never troubled 'themselves about what went on in the heavens, and 'who was the creator and governor of the stars.'

Father Baegert,[3] in his account of the Californian Indians, says, 'I often asked them whether they had 'never put to themselves the question who might be 'the Creator and Preserver of the sun, moon, stars, and 'other objects of nature, but was always sent home with 'a "vara," which means "no" in their language.'

The Chipewyans[4] thought that the world existed at first in the form of a globe of water, out of which the Great Spirit raised the land. The Lenni Lenape[5] say

[1] Schoolcraft's Indian Tribes, vol. ii. p. 68.
[2] Loc. cit., vol. ii. p. 50.
[3] Loc. cit., p. 300.
[4] Dunn's Oregon, p. 102.
[5] Müller, Gesch. d. Amer. Urr., p. 107.

that Manitu at the beginning swam on the water, and made the earth out of a grain of sand. He then made a man and woman out of a tree. The Mingos and Ottawwaws believe that a rat brought up a grain of sand from the bottom of the water, and thus produced the land. The Crees[1] had no ideas at all as to the origin of the world.

Stuhr, who was, as Müller says, a good observer of such matters, tells us that the Siberians had no idea of a Creator. When Burchell suggested the idea of creation to the Bachapin Kaffirs, they 'asserted that every-' thing made itself, and that trees and herbage grew by 'their own will.'[2] It also appears from Canon Calla-way's researches that the Zulu Kaffirs have no notion of creation. Casalis makes the same statement: all the natives, he says, 'whom we questioned on the ' subject have assured us that it never entered their ' heads that the earth and sky might be the work of an ' Invisible Being.'[3] The same is also the case with the Hottentots.

The Australians, again, had no idea of creation. According to Polynesian mythology, heaven and earth existed from the beginning.[4] The latter, however, was at first covered by water, until Mawe drew up New Zealand by means of an enchanted fish-hook.[5] This fish-hook was made from the jawbone of Muri-ranga-whenna, and is now the cape forming the southern ex-tremity of Hawkes' Bay. The Tongans[6] and Samoans[7]

[1] Franklin's Journey to the Polar Sea, vol. I. p. 143.
[2] Loc. cit., vol. ii. p. 550.
[3] The Basutos, p. 23d.
[4] Polynesian Mythology, p. 1.
Shortland, loc. cit., p. 35.
[5] Ibid., p. 45.
[6] Mariner, loc. cit., vol. I. 284.
[7] Hale, U.S. Exp. Exp. p. 25.

have a very similar tale. Here the islands were drawn up by Tangaloa, 'but, the line accidentally breaking, the 'act was incomplete, and matters were left as they now 'are. They show a hole in the rock, about two feet in 'diameter, which quite perforates it, and in which 'Tangaloa's hook got fixed. It is moreover said that 'Tooitonga had, till within a few years, this very hook 'in his possession.'

As regards Tahiti, Williams [1] observes that the 'origin of the gods, and their priority of existence in 'comparison with the formation of the earth, being a 'matter of uncertainty even among the native priests, 'involves the whole in the greatest obscurity.' Even in Sanskrit there is no word for creation, nor does any such idea appear in the Rigveda, in the Zendavesta, or in Homer.

When the Capuchin missionary Merolla [2] asked the Queen of Singa, in Western Africa, who made the world, she, 'without the least hesitation, readily an-'swered, "My ancestors." "Then," replied the Capu-'chin, "does your Majesty enjoy the whole power of '"your ancestors?" "Yes," answered she, "and '"much more, for over and above what they had, I am '"absolute mistress of the kingdom of Matamba!" A 'remark which shows how little she realised the mean-'ing of the term "Creation."' The negroes in Guinea thought that man was created by a great black spider.[3] The Bongos of Soudan 'have no conception of there being a Creator.'[4] Other negroes, however, have more

[1] Polynesian Researches, vol. ii. p. 191.
[2] Pinkerton's Voyages, vol. xvi.
[3] Ibid, p. 450.
[4] Heart of Africa, vol. ii. p. 306.
p. 305.

just ideas on the subject, probably derived from the missionaries.

The Kumis of Chittagong believe that a certain Deity made the world and the trees and the creeping things, and lastly ' he set to work to make one man and ' one woman, forming their bodies of clay ; but each ' night, on the completion of his work, there came a ' great snake, which, while God was sleeping, devoured ' the two images.'[1]   At length the Deity created a dog, which drove away the snake, and thus the creation of man was accomplished.

We cannot fail also to be struck with the fact that the lower forms of religion are almost independent of Prayer.   To us prayer seems almost a necessary part of religion.   But it evidently involves a belief in the goodness of God, a truth which, as we have seen, is not early recognised.

Of the Hottentots Kolben says, ' It is most certain ' they neither pray to any one of their deities nor utter ' a word to any mortal concerning the condition of their ' souls or a future life.'  . . .  Even those negroes, says Bosman, who have a faint conception of a higher Deity, ' do not pray to him, or offer any sacrifices to ' him; for which they give the following reasons:— ' " God," say they, " is too high exalted above us, and ' " too great to condescend so much as to trouble him- ' " self, or think of mankind." '[2]

The Mandingoes, according to Park, regard the Deity as ' so remote, and of so exalted a nature, that it ' is idle to imagine the feeble supplications of wretched

[1] Lewin's Hill Tracts of Chittagong, p. 90.
[2] Bosman, loc. cit., p. 403.

' mortals can reverse the decrees, and change the pur-
' poses, of unerring Wisdom.' [1]  They, seem, however,
to have little confidence in their own views, and generally
assured Park, in answer to his enquiries about religion
and the immortality of the soul, that 'no man knows
' anything about it.'  'The uncontaminated African,'
says Livingstone, believes that the Great Spirit lives
above the stars, 'but they never pray to him.' [2]
'Neither among the Eskimos nor Tinne,' says Richardson, 'could I ascertain that prayer was ever made to
' the " Kitche Manito," the Great Spirit or " Master of
' " Life." ' [3]   Mr. Prescott, in Schoolcraft's Indian
Tribes, also states that the North American Indians do
not pray to the Great Spirit. [4]  The Caribs considered
that the Good Spirit 'is endued with so great goodness,
' that it does not take any revenge even of its enemies:
' whence it comes that they render it neither honour
' nor adoration.' [5]

According to Metz, the Todas (Neilgherry Hills)
never pray.  Even among the priests, he says, ' the
' only sign of adoration that I have ever seen them
' perform is lifting the right hand to the forehead,
' covering the nose with the thumb, when entering the
' sacred dairy: and the words, "May all be well!" are
' all that I have ever heard them utter in the form of a
' prayer.' [6]

A very different objection to prayer (in the sense of
a request for material benefits) was expressed by Tomo-

---

[1] Park's Travels, vol. L p. 207.    Tribes, vol. iii. p. 220.
[2] Zambesi, p. 147.                 [5] Tertre's History of the Caribby
[3] Richardson's Boat Journey, vol.  Islands, p. 278.
i. p. 44.                            [6] Tribes of the Neilgherries, p.
[4] Prescott, Schoolcraft's Indian   27.

chichi, the Chief of the Yamacraws (North America), to General Oglethorpe;[1] 'that the asking for any par-' ticular blessing looked to him like directing God; and, ' if so, that it must be a very wicked thing. That for ' his part he thought everything that happened in the ' world was as it should be; that God of himself ' would do for every one what was consistent with ' the good of the whole; and that our duty to him was ' to be content with whatever happened in general, and ' thankful for all the good that happened in particular.'

The connection between morality and religion will be considered in a later chapter. Here, I will only observe that the deities of the lower races, being subject to the same passions as man; and in many cases, indeed, themselves monsters of iniquity, regarded crime with indifference, so long as the religious ceremonies and sacrifices in their honour were not neglected. Hence it follows that through all these lower races there is no idea of any being corresponding to Satan. So far, indeed, as their deities are evil they may be so called; but the essential character of Satan is that of the Tempter; hence in the order of succession this idea cannot arise until morality has become connected with religion.

Thus, then, I have endeavoured to trace the gradual development of religion among the lower races of man.

The lower savages regard their deities as scarcely more powerful than themselves; they are evil, not good; they are to be propitiated by sacrifices, not by prayer; they are not creators; they are neither omniscient nor all-powerful; they neither reward the good nor punish the evil; far from conferring immortality

---

[1] Jones, Antiquities of the Southern Indians, p. 421.

on man, they are not even in all cases immortal themselves.

Where the material elements of civilisation developed themselves without any corresponding increase of knowledge, as for instance in Mexico and Peru, a more correct idea of Divine power, without any corresponding enlightenment as to the Divine nature, led to a religion of terror, which finally became a terrible scourge of humanity.

Gradually, however, an increased acquaintance with the laws of nature enlarged the mind of man. He first supposed that the Deity fashioned the earth, raising it out of the water, and preparing it as a dwelling-place for man; and subsequently realised the idea that land and water were alike created by Divine power. After regarding spirits as altogether evil, he rose to a belief in good as well as in evil deities, and, gradually subordinating the latter to the former, worshipped the good spirits alone as gods, the evil sinking to the level of demons. From believing only in ghosts, he came gradually to the recognition of the soul: at length uniting this belief with that in a beneficent and just Being, he connected Morality with Religion, a step, the importance of which it is scarcely possible to overestimate.

Thus we see that as men rise in civilisation, their religion rises with them. The Australians dimly imagine a being, spiteful, malevolent, but weak, and dangerous only in the dark. The Negro's deity is more powerful, but not less hateful—invisible, indeed, but subject to pain, mortal like himself, and liable to be made the slave of man by enchantment. The deities of the South Sea Islanders are, some good, some evil; but, on the whole, more is to be feared from the latter than to be hoped from the former. They fashioned the land, but are not truly creators, for earth and water existed before them. They do not punish the evil, nor reward the good. They watch over the affairs of men; but if, on the one hand, witchcraft has no power over them, neither, on the other, can prayer influence them—they require to share the crops or the booty of their worshippers.

It appears, then, that every increase in science—that is, in positive and ascertained knowledge—brings with it an elevation of religion. Nor is this progress confined to the lower races. Even within the last century, science has purified the religion of Western Europe by rooting out the dark belief in witchcraft, which led to thousands of executions, and hung like a black pall over the Christianity of the middle ages.

The immense service which Science has thus rendered to the cause of Religion and of Humanity, has not hitherto received the recognition which it deserves. Science is still regarded by many excellent, but narrow-minded, persons as hostile to religious truth, while in fact she is only opposed to religious error. No doubt her influence has always been exercised in opposition to those who present contradictory assertions under the excuse of mystery, as well as to all but the highest conceptions of Divine power. The time, however, is approaching when it will be generally perceived that, so far from Science being opposed to Religion, true religion is, without Science, impossible; and if we consider the various aspects of Christianity as understood by dif-

ferent nations, we can hardly fail to see that the
dignity, and therefore the truth, of their religious beliefs, is in direct relation to their knowledge of Science
and of the great physical laws by which our universe
is governed.

# CHAPTER VIII.

## CHARACTER AND MORALS.

THE accounts which we possess of the character of savage races are conflicting and unsatisfactory. In some cases travellers have expressed strong opinions, for which they had obviously no sufficient foundation. Thus the unfortunate La Perouse, who spent only one day on Easter Island, states his belief that the inhabitants 'are as corrupt as the circum-' stances in which they are placed will permit them to ' be.'[1] On the other hand, the Friendly Islanders were so called by Captain Cook on account of the apparent kindness and hospitality with which they received him. Yet, as we now know, this appearance of friendship was entirely hypocritical. The natives endeavoured to lull him into security, with the intention of seizing his ship and massacring the crew; which design a fortunate accident alone prevented them from carrying into effect; yet Captain Cook never had the slightest suspicion of their treachery, or of the danger which he so narrowly escaped.

In some cases the same writer gives accounts at variance with one another. Thus Mr. Ellis,[2] the excellent missionary of the Pacific, states that the moral

[1] La Perouse's Voyage, English edition, vol. ii. p. 327.

[2] Polynesian Researches, vol. ii. p. 26.

character of the Tahitians was 'awfully dark, and
' notwithstanding the apparent mildness of their dispo-
' sition, and the cheerful vivacity of their conversation,
' no portion of the human race was ever, perhaps, sunk
' lower in brutal licentiousness and moral degradation.'
Yet, speaking of this same people, and in the very
same volume, he tells us that these were most anxious
to obtain Bibles: on the day when they were to be distributed the natives came from considerable distances, and
' the place was actually thronged until the copies were
' expended. In their application at our own houses we
' found it impossible to restrain the people, so great
' was their anxiety.' Under these circumstances we
cannot wonder that Captain Cook and other navigators
found in them much to admire as well as to condemn.

The Kalmucks, again, have been very differently
described by different travellers. Pallas, speaking of
their character, says, 'Il m'a paru infiniment meilleur
' que ne l'ont dépeint plusieurs de nos historiens voya-
' geurs. Il est infiniment préférable à celui des autres
' peuples nomades. Les Kalmouks sont affables, hospi-
' taliers et francs; ils aiment à rendre service ; ils sont
' toujours gais et enjoués, ce qui les distingue des
' Kirguis, qui sont beaucoup plus flegmatiques. Telles
' sont leurs bonnes qualités; voici les mauvaises. Ils
' sont sales, paresseux et fort rusés ; ils abusent très-
' souvent de ce dernier défaut.'[1] So also the aboriginal
tribes of India, as pointed out by Mr. Hunter,[2] have
been painted in the blackest colours by some, and
highly praised by others.

[1] Voyages, vol. i. p. 400.
[2] Comparative Dictionary of the    Non-Aryan Languages of India and
High Asia, pp. 5, 9.

Mariner gives an excellent account of the state of manners among the Tongans, and one which well illustrates the difficulty of arriving at correct ideas on such a subject, especially among a people of a different race from ourselves and in a different state of civilisation. He describes them as loyal[1] and pious,[2] obedient children,[3] affectionate parents,[4] kind husbands,[5] modest and faithful wives,[6] and true friends.[7]

On the other hand, they seem to have had little feeling of morality. They 'had no words for justice or ' injustice, for cruelty or humanity.'[8] 'Theft, revenge, ' rape, and murder under many circumstances are not ' held to be crimes.' They had no idea of future rewards and punishments. They saw no harm in seizing ships by treachery and murdering the crews. The men were cruel, treacherous, and revengeful. Marriages were terminable at the whim of the husband,[9] and, excepting in married women, chastity was not regarded as a virtue, though it was thought improper for a woman frequently to change her lover. Yet we are told that, on the whole,[10] this system, although so opposed to our feelings, had ' not the least appearance of any bad effect. ' The women were tender, kind mothers, the children ' well cared for.' Both sexes appeared to be contented and happy in their relations to each other, and 'as to ' domestic quarrels, they were seldom known.' We must not judge them too hardly for their proposed treachery to Captain Cook. Even in Northern Europe

---

[1] *Loc. cit.*, vol. ii. p. 155.
[2] P. 164.
[3] P. 165.
[4] P. 170.
[5] P. 170.
[6] P. 170.
[7] P. 152.
[8] P. 148.
[9] P. 107.
[10] P. 177.

shipwrecks were long considered fair spoil, the strangers being connected with the natives by no civil or family ties, and the idea of natural right not being highly developed.[1]

Lastly, if, in addition to the other sources of difficulty, we remember that of language, we cannot wonder that the characters of savage races have been so differently described by different travellers. We all know how difficult it is to judge an individual, and it must be much more so to judge a nation. In fact, whether any given writer praises or blames a particular race, depends at least as much on the character of the writer as on that of the people.

On the whole, however, I think we may assume that life and property are far less secure in savage than in civilised communities; and though the guilt of a murder or a theft may be very different under different circumstances, to the sufferer the result is much the same.

Mr. Galbraith, who lived for many years, as Indian agent, among the Sioux (North America), thus describes them :[2] They are ' bigoted, barbarous, and exceedingly ' superstitious. They regard most of the vices as ' virtues. Theft, arson, rape, and murder are among ' them regarded as the means of distinction ; and the ' young Indian from childhood is taught to regard ' killing as the highest of virtues. In their dances, and ' at their feasts, the warriors recite their deeds of theft, ' pillage, and slaughter as precious things ; and the ' highest, indeed the only, ambition of a young brave is

<hr>

[1] See Montesquieu, Esprit des Lois, vol. ii. p. 109.
[2] Ethn. Journal, 1869, p. 304.

' to secure " the feather," which is but a record of his
' having murdered or participated in the murder of
' some human being—whether man, woman, or child,
' it is immaterial; and, after he has secured his first
' " feather," appetite is whetted to increase the number
' in his cap, as an Indian brave is estimated by the
' number of his feathers.'

In Tahiti the missionaries considered that 'not less
' than two-thirds of the children were murdered by their
' parents.'¹ Mr. Ellis adds, 'I do not recollect having
' met with a female in the islands during the whole
' period of my residence there, who had been a mother
' while idolatry prevailed, who had not imbrued her
' hands in the blood of her offspring.' Mr. Nott also
makes the same assertion. Girls were more often killed
than boys, because they were of less use in fishing and
in war.

Mr. Wallace maintains that savages act up to their
simple moral code at least as well as we do; but if a
man's simple moral code permits him to rob or murder;
that may be some excuse for him, but it is little consolation to the sufferer.

As a philosophical question, however, the relative
character of different races is less interesting than the
moral condition of the lower races of mankind as a
whole.

Mr. Wallace, in the concluding chapter of his interesting work on the Malay Archipelago, has expressed
the opinion that while civilised communities ' have
' progressed vastly beyond the savage state in intel-
' lectual achievements, we have not advanced equally in

¹ Polynesian Researches, vol. i. pp. 334, 340.

' morals.' Nay, he even goes further: in a perfect social
state, he says, 'every man would have a sufficiently
' well-balanced intellectual organisation to understand
' the moral law in all its details, and would require no
' other motive but the free impulses of his own nature
' to obey that law. Now, it is very remarkable that
' among people in a very low state of civilisation, we
' find some approach to such a perfect social state;'
and he adds, 'it is not too much to say that the mass of
' our populations have not at all advanced beyond the
' savage code of morals, and have in many cases sunk
' below it.'

Far from thinking this true, I should rather be
disposed to say that Man has, perhaps, made more
progress in moral than in either material or intellectual
advancement; for while even the lowest savages have
many material and intellectual attainments, they are, it
seems to me, almost entirely wanting in moral feeling;
though I am aware that the contrary opinion has been
expressed by many eminent authorities.

Thus Lord Kames[1] assumes as an undoubted fact
' that every individual is endued with a sense of right
' and wrong, more or less distinct;' and after admitting that very different views as to morals are held by
different people and different races, he remarks, ' these
' facts tend not to disprove the reality of a common
' sense in morals; they only prove that the moral sense
' has not been equally perfect at all times, nor in all
' countries.'

Hume expresses the same opinion in very decided
language. 'Let a man's insensibility,' he says, 'be ever

---

[1] *History of Man*, vol. ii. p. 0, vol. iv. p. 18.

' so great, he must often be touched with the images of
' right and wrong; and, let his prejudices be ever so
' obstinate, he must observe that others are susceptible
' of like impressions.'[1]  Nay, he even maintains that
' those who have denied the reality of moral distinc-
' tions may be ranked among the disingenuous dispu-
' tants ; nor is it conceivable that any human creature
' could ever seriously believe that all characters and
' actions were alike entitled to the affection and regard
' of every one.'

Locke, on the other hand, questions the existence
of innate principles, and terminates his chapter on the
subject in the following words : 'It is reasonable,' he
says,[2] 'to demand the marks and characters, whereby
' the genuine innate principles may be distinguished
' from others; that so, amidst the great variety of pre-
' tenders, I may be kept from mistakes in so material
' a point as this.  When this is done, I shall be ready
' to embrace such welcome and useful propositions; and
' till then I may with modesty doubt, since I fear
' universal consent, which is the only one produced,
' will scarce prove a sufficient mark to direct my choice,
' and assure me of any innate principles.  From what
' has been said, I think it past doubt that there are no
' practical principles wherein all men agree; and therefore none innate.'

Let us now see what light is thrown on this interesting question by the study of savage life.  Mr.
Wallace draws a charming picture of some small savage
communities which he has visited.  Each man, he says,

---

[1] Hume's Essays, vol. ii. p. 203.
[2] On the Human Understanding, book i. ch. 3, sec. 2.

'scrupulously respects the rights of his fellow, and any
'infraction of those rights rarely or never takes place.
'In such a community all are nearly equal.  There are
'none of those wide distinctions of education and igno-
'rance, wealth and poverty, master and servant, which
'are the product of our civilisation ; there is none of
'that wide-spread division of labour, which, while it
'increases wealth, produces also conflicting interests ;
'there is not that severe competition and struggle for
'existence, or for wealth, which the population of
'civilised countries inevitably creates.'

But does this prove that they are in a high moral
condition?  Does it prove even that they have any
moral sense at all?  Surely not.  For if it does, we
must equally credit rooks and bees, and most other
gregarious animals, with a moral state higher than that
of civilised man.  I would not indeed venture to assert
that the ant or the bee is not possessed of moral feelings, but we are surely not in a position to affirm it.
In the very passage quoted, Mr. Wallace has pointed
out that the inducements to crime are in small communities much less than in populous countries.  The
absence of crime, however, does not constitute virtue,
and, without temptation, mere innocence has no merit.

Moreover, in small communities almost all the members are related to one another, and family affection
puts on the appearance of virtue.  But though parental
and filial affection possess a very moral aspect, they
have a totally different origin and a distinct character.
To do a thing which is right, is by no means the same
as to do it because it is right.

We do not generally attribute moral feelings to

quadrupeds and birds, yet, perhaps, among animals there is no stronger feeling than that of the mother for her offspring. She will submit to any sacrifices for their welfare, and fight against almost any odds for their protection. No follower of Mr. Darwin will be surprised at this, because for generation after generation those mothers in whom this feeling was most strong have had the best chance of rearing their young. It is not, however, moral feeling in the strict sense of the term; and she would, indeed, be a cold-hearted mother who cherished and protected her infant only because it was right to do so.

Family affection and moral feeling have indeed been very generally confused together by travellers, yet there is some direct testimony which appears to show that the moral condition of savages is really much lower than has been usually supposed.

Thus Mr. Dove, speaking of the Tasmanians, asserts that they were entirely without any 'moral views and 'impressions.'

Governor Eyre says of the Australians that, 'having 'no moral sense of what is just and equitable in the 'abstract, their only test of propriety must in such 'cases be, whether they are numerically or physically 'strong enough to brave the vengeance of those whom 'they may have provoked or injured.'[1]

Mr. Ridley tells us[2] that he had very great difficulty in conveying to the nations of Australia any idea of sin, and eventually he could only describe it by the following roundabout expression: 'Nyeane kauungo warawara 'yunani.'

[1] Discoveries in Central Australia, vol. ii. p. 384.
[2] Queensland, p. 442.

'Conscience,' says Burton, 'does not exist in Eastern
'Africa, and "repentance" expresses regret for missed
'opportunities of mortal crime. Robbery constitutes
'an honourable man; murder—the more atrocious the
'midnight crime the better—makes the hero.'[1]

The Yoruba negroes, on the West Coast of Africa,
according to the same author,[2] 'are covetous, cruel, and
'wholly deficient in what the civilised man calls con-
'science;' though it is right to add that some of his
other statements with reference to this tribe seem
opposed to this view.

Mr. Neighbors states that among the Comanches of
Texas 'no individual action is considered a crime, but
'every man acts for himself according to his own judg-
'ment, unless some superior power—for instance, that
'of a popular chief—should exercise authority over him.
'They believe that when they were created the Great
'Spirit gave them the privilege of a free and uncon-
'strained use of their individual faculties.'[3]

The Kacharis, according to Dalton, had, 'in their
'own language no words for sin, for piety, for prayer,
'for repentance.'[4]

Speaking of the Kaffirs, Mr. Casalis, who lived for
twenty-three years in South Africa, says[5] that 'morality
'among these people depends so entirely upon social
'order that all political disorganisation is immediately
'followed by a state of degeneracy, which the re-estab-
'lishment of order alone can rectify.' Thus, then,
although their language contained words signifying

[1] Burton's First Footsteps in
East Africa, p. 170.
[2] Abeokuta, vol. i. p. 303. See
also vol. ii. p. 218.
[3] Schoolcraft's Indian Tribes, vol.
ii. p. 131.
[4] Des. Ethn. of Bengal, p. 85.
[5] The Basutos, p. 300.

most of the virtues, as well as the vices, it would
appear from the above passages that their moral quality
was not clearly recognised.   It must be confessed,
however, that the evidence is not very conclusive, as
Mr. Casalis, even in the same chapter, expresses an
opinion on the point scarcely consistent with that
quoted above.

Similar accounts are given as regards Central Africa.
Thus at Jenna,[1] and in the surrounding districts, 'when-
' ever a town is deprived of its chief, the inhabitants
' acknowledge no law—anarchy, troubles, and confusion
' immediately prevail, and till a successor is appointed
' all labour is at an end.   The stronger oppress the
' weak, and consummate every species of crime, with-
' out being amenable to any tribunal for their actions.
' Private property is no longer respected ; and thus
' before a person arrives to curb its licentiousness, a
' town is not unfrequently reduced from a flourishing
' state of prosperity and of happiness to all the horrors
' of desolation.'   Livingstone mentions[2] a similar custom
among the Banyai, a tribe living on the river Zambesi;
and the same state of things also occurred in the Sandwich Islands.[3]

The Tongans, or Friendly Islanders, had in many
respects made great advances, yet Mariner[4] states that,
' on a strict examination of their language, we discover
' no words essentially expressive of some of the higher
' qualities of human merit: as virtue, justice, humanity;
' nor of the contrary, as vice, injustice, cruelty, &c.;

[1] H. and J. Lander's Niger Expedition, vol. L p. 90.
[2] Travels in South Africa, p. 624.
[3] Gerland. Waitz's Anthr., vol.
vi. p. 203.
[4] Tonga Islands, vol. ii. p. 147.

'They have, indeed, expressions for these ideas, but
'they are equally applicable to other things.  To ex-
'press a virtuous or good man, they would say
' "tangata lillé," a good man, or "tangata loto lillé," a
'man with a good mind; but the word lillé, good (un-
'like our virtuous) is equally applicable to an axe,
'canoe, or anything else; again, they have no word to
'express humanity, mercy, &c., but afa, which rather
'means friendship, and is a word of cordial salutation.'

Mr. Campbell observes that the Soors (one of the
aboriginal tribes of India), ' while described as small,
'mean, and very black, and like the Santals naturally
'harmless, peaceable, and industrious, are also said to
'be without moral sense.' [1]

The South American Indians of the Gran Chaco are
said by the missionaries to 'make no distinction be-
'tween right and wrong, and have therefore neither
'fear nor hope of any present or future punishment or
'reward, nor any mysterious terror of some super-
'natural power, whom they might seek to assuage by
'sacrifices or superstitious rites.' [2]

Indeed, I do not remember a single instance in
which a savage is recorded as having shown any symptoms of remorse; and almost the only case I can call to
mind, in which a man belonging to one of the lower
races has accounted for an act, by saying explicitly that
it was right, was when Mr. Hunt asked a young Fee-
jecan why he had killed his mother. [3]

It is clear that religion, except in very advanced

[1] O. Campbell, The Ethnology     220.
of India, p. 37.                       [2] Wilkes' Voyage, p. 95.
     [3] The Voice of Pity, vol. ix. p.

races, has no moral aspect or influence. The deities are almost invariably regarded as evil.

In Feejee[1] 'the names of the gods indicate their 'characters. Thus, as Williams tells us, Ndauthina 'steals women of rank and beauty by night or torch-'light. Kumbunavanua is the rioter; Mbatimona, the 'brain-eater; Ravuravu, the murderer; Mainatavasara, 'fresh from the cutting-up or slaughter; and a host be-'sides of the same sort.'

In Peru every vice had its own especial deity.'[2]

The character of the Greek gods is familiar to us, and was anything but moral. Such beings would not necessarily reward the good, or punish the evil. Hence, it is not surprising that Socrates saw little connection between ethics and religion, or that Aristotle altogether separated morality from theology. Hence also we cannot be surprised to find that, even when a belief in a future state has dawned on the civilised mind, it is not at first associated with reward or punishment.

The Australians, though they had a vague belief in ghosts, and supposed that after death they become whitemen; that, as they say, 'Fall down blackman, 'jump up whiteman;' have no idea of retribution.[3] The Guinea negroes 'have no idea of future rewards or 'punishments, for the good or ill actions of their past 'life.'[4] Other negro races, however, have more ad-vanced ideas on the subject.

'The Tahitians believe in the immortality of the soul, 'at least its existence in a separate state, and that there

[1] Fiji and the Fijians, vol. i. p. 218.

[2] Garcilasso de la Vega, vol. i. p. 124.

[3] Voyage of the 'Fly,' vol. ii. p. 22.

[4] Bosman, loc. cit. p. 401.

' are two situations of different degrees of happiness,
' somewhat analogous to our heaven and hell: the supe-
' rior situation they call " Tavirua l'erai," the other
' " Tiahoboo "  They do not, however, consider them
' as places of reward and punishment, but as receptacles
' for different classes; the first for their chiefs and
' principal people, the other for those of inferior rank ;
' for they do not suppose that their actions here in
' the least influence their future state, or indeed that
' they come under the cognisance of their deities at
' all.' [1]

In Tonga and at Nukahiva the natives believe that
their chiefs are immortal, but not the common people.[2]
The Tonga people, says Mariner, 'do not indeed
' believe in any future state of rewards and punish-
' ments.' [3]

Williams [4] tells us that ' offences, in Fijian estima-
' tion, are light or grave according to the rank of the
' offender.  Murder by a chief is less heinous than a
' petty larceny committed by a man of low rank.
' Only a few crimes are regarded as serious; e.g., theft,
' adultery, abduction, witchcraft, infringement of a
' tabu, disrespect to a chief, incendiarism, and treason;'
and he elsewhere mentions that the Feejeeans,[5] though
believing in a future existence, ' shut out from it the
' idea of any moral retribution in the shape either of
' reward or punishment.'  In the religion of the Feejeeans, says Seemann, 'there does not seem to be any

[1] See Cook's Voyage round the
World in Hawkesworth's Voyages,
vol. ii. p. 239.
[2] Kliram, vol. iv. p. 351.
[3] Tonga Islands, vol. ii. pp. 147,
18.  Hale, U. S. Exp. Exp. p. 38.
[4] Fiji and the Fijians, vol. i. p.
28.
[5] Ibid. p. 242.

'separation between the abodes of the good and the
'wicked, nothing that corresponds to our heaven and
'hell.'[1] The Sumatrans, according to Marsden, 'had
'some idea of a future life, but not as a state of retribu-
'tion; conceiving immortality to be the lot of a rich
'rather than of a good man. I recollect that an in-
'habitant of one of the islands farther eastwards ob-
'served to me, with great simplicity, that only great
'men went to the skies; how should poor men find
'admittance there?'[2]

In the Island of Bintang,[3] 'the people, having an
'idea of predestination, always conceived present pos-
'session to constitute right, however that possession
'might have been acquired; but yet they made no
'scruple of deposing and murdering their sovereigns,
'and justified their acts by this argument: that the
'fate of concerns so important as the lives of kings was
'in the hands of God, whose vicegerents they were,
'and that if it was not agreable to him, and the conse-
'quence of his will, that they should perish by the dag-
'gers of their subjects, it could not so happen. Thus
'it appears that their religious ideas were just strong
'enough to banish from their minds every moral senti-
'ment.'

The Kookies of Chittagong 'have no idea of hell or
'heaven, or of any punishment for evil deeds, or rewards
'for good actions.'[4] Forsyth also makes a similar
statement as regards the Gónds.[5] According to Bailey,

[1] Seemann's Mission to Viti, p. 400.

[2] Marsden's History of Sumatra, p. 289.

[3] *Ibid.* p. 412.

[4] Rennel, quoted in Lewin's Hill Tracts of Chittagong, p. 110.

[5] Highlands of Central India, p. 145.

again, the Veddahs of Ceylon 'have no idea of a future
'state of rewards and punishments.'[1]

The Hos in Central India 'believe that the souls
'of the dead become "bhoots," spirits, but no thought
'of reward or punishment is connected with the
'change.'[2]

Speaking of South Africa, Kolben[3] says, 'that the
'Hottentots believe the immortality of the soul has
'been shown in a foregoing chapter. But they have
'no notion, that ever I could gather, of rewards and
'punishments after death.'

Chief Commissioner Warner remarks that the Kaffirs
have not 'the slightest knowledge of a future state of
'rewards and punishments, arising out of the moral
'quality of our actions in this life.'[4]

In Dahome, according to Burton,[5] the 'next world
'offers none of those rewards and punishments by
'which, according to the Semitic animist, the balance
'of good and evil in this life is to be struck. He who
'escapes punishment here, is safe hereafter.'

Among the Mexicans[6] and Peruvians,[7] again, the
religion was entirely independent of moral considerations, and in some other parts of America the future
condition is supposed to depend not on conduct but
on rank.[8] In North America 'it is rare,' says Tanner,
'to observe among the Indians any ideas which would

---

[1] Trans. Ethn. Soc. N.S. vol. ii.
p. 300.

[2] Dalton, Trans Ethn. Soc. 1868,
p. 32.

[3] History of the Cape of Good
Hope, vol. i. p. 314.

[4] Maclean's Comprnd. of Kaffir
Laws and Customs, p. 78.

[5] Mission to Dahome, vol. ii. p.
157.

[6] Müller, Ges. der Amer. Urre-
ligion., p. 505.

[7] Ibid. p. 410. But see Prescott,
vol. i. p. 83.

[8] Ibid. p. 130. See also pp. 289,
605.

' lead to the belief that they look upon a future state as
' one of retribution.' [1]

Among the Siberian tribes the deities are supposed
to reward those who conciliate them by worship and
offerings, but to morality they are regarded as indifferent.[2]

The Arabs and Afghans conceive that a broken
oath brings misfortune on the place where it was
uttered.[3]

In fact, I believe that the lower races of men may
be said to be deficient in the idea of Right, though
quite familiar with that of Law. This leads to the
curious, though not illogical, results mentioned in page
389.

That there should be any races of men so deficient
in moral feeling, was altogether opposed to the preconceived ideas with which I commenced the study of
savage life, and I have arrived at the conviction by
slow degrees, and even with reluctance. I have, however, been forced to this conclusion, not only by the
direct statements of travellers, but also by the general
tenor of their remarks, and especially by the remarkable
absence of repentance and remorse among the lower
races of men.

On the whole, then, it appears to me that the moral
feelings deepen with the gradual growth of a race.

External circumstances, no doubt, exercise much
influence on character. We very often see, however,
that the possession of one virtue is counterbalanced by

[1] Tanner's Narrative, p. 309.
[2] Müller, Des. de toutes les Nations de l'Empire de Russe, Pt. III. p. 140.
[3] Klemm, Culturgeschichte, vol. iv. p. 100. Masson, Journeys in Balochistan, &c., vol. ii. p. 268.

some corresponding defect. Thus the North American Indians are brave and generous, but they are also cruel and reckless of life. Moreover, in the early stages of law, motive is never considered ; a fact which shows how little hold morality has, even on communities which have made considerable progress. Some cases which have been quoted as illustrating the contrast between the ideas of virtue entertained by different races seem to prove the absence, rather than the perversity, of sentiment on the subject. I cannot believe, for instance, that theft and murder have ever been really regarded as virtues. In a barbarous state they were, no doubt, means of distinction, and in the absence of moral feelings were regarded with no reprobation. I cannot, however, suppose that they could be considered as 'right,' though they might give rise to a feeling of respect, and even of admiration. So also the Greeks regarded the duplicity of Ulysses as an element in his greatness, but surely not as virtue in itself.

What, then, is the origin of moral feeling? Some regard it as intuitive, as an original instinct implanted in the human mind. Herbert Spencer,[1] on the contrary, maintains that ' moral intuitions are the results of accu- ' mulated experiences of utility; gradually organised ' and inherited, they have come to be quite independent ' of conscious experience. Just in the same way that I ' believe the intuition of space, possessed by any living ' individual, to have arisen from organised and consoli- ' dated experiences of all antecedent individuals, who ' bequeathed to him their slowly-developed nervous or-

---

[1] Bain's Mental and Moral Science, p. 722.

' ganisation: just as I believe that this intuition, requir-
' ing only to be made definite and complete by personal
' experiences, has practically become a form of thought
' apparently quite independent of experience; so do I
' believe that the experiences of utility, organised and
' consolidated through all past generations of the human
' race, have been producing corresponding nervous mo-
' difications, which, by continued transmission and accu-
' mulation, have become in us certain faculties of moral
' intuition—certain emotions responding to right and
' wrong conduct, which have no apparent basis in the
' individual experiences of utility.'

I cannot entirely subscribe to either of these views.
The moral feelings are now, no doubt, intuitive; but if
the lower races of savages have none, they evidently
cannot have been so originally, nor can they be regarded
as natural to man. Neither can I accept the opposite
theory. While entirely agreeing with Mr. Spencer that
' there have been, and still are, developing in the race,
' certain fundamental moral intuitions,' I feel, with Mr.
Hutton, much difficulty in conceiving that, in Mr.
Spencer's words, ' these moral intuitions are the results
' of the accumulated experiences of Utility;' that is to
say, of Utility to the individual. When it is once realised that a given line of conduct would invariably be
useful to the individual, it is at once regarded as ' saga-
' cious' rather than 'virtuous.' Virtue implies temptation; temptation indicates a feeling that a given action
may benefit the individual at the expense of others, or
in defiance of authority. It is evident, indeed, that
feelings acting on generation after generation might
produce a continually deepening conviction, but I fail

to perceive how this explains the difference between 'right' and 'utility.'

Yet utility in one sense has, I think, been naturally and yet unconsciously selected as the basis of morals. Mr. Hutton, if I understand him correctly, doubts this. Honesty, for instance, he says,[1] 'must certainly have 'been associated by our ancestors with many unhappy 'as well as many happy consequences, and we know 'that in ancient Greece dishonesty was openly and 'actually associated with happy consequences, in the 'admiration for the guile and craft of Ulysses.'

This seems to me a good crucial case. Honesty, on their own part, may, indeed, have been, and no doubt was, 'associated by our ancestors with many unhappy 'as well as many happy consequences;' but honesty on the part of others could surely have nothing but happy results. Thus, while the perception that 'Honesty 'is the best policy' was, no doubt, as Mr. Hutton observes, 'long subsequent to the most imperious enun- 'ciation of its sacredness as a duty,' honesty would be recognised as a virtue so soon as men perceived the sacredness of any duty. As soon as contracts were entered into between individuals or states, it became manifestly the interest of each that the other should be honest. Any failure in this respect would naturally be condemned by the sufferer. It is precisely because honesty is sometimes associated with unhappy conse-quences, that it is regarded as a virtue. If it had always been directly advantageous to all parties, it would have been classed as useful, not as right; it would have lacked the essential element which entitles it to rank as a virtue.

[1] *Macmillan's Magazine*, 1869, p. 271.

Or take respect for Age. We find, even in Australia, laws, if I may so term them, appropriating the best of everything to the old men. Naturally the old men lose no opportunity of impressing these injunctions on the young; they praise those who conform, and condemn those who resist. Hence the custom is strictly adhered to. I do not say, that to the Australian mind this presents itself as a sacred duty; but it would, I think, in the course of time have come to be so considered.

For when a race had made some progress in intellectual development, a difference would certainly be felt between those acts which a man was taught to do as conducive to his own direct advantage, and those which were not so, and yet which were enjoined for any other reason. Hence would arise the idea of *right* and *duty*, as distinct from mere utility.

How much more our notions of right depend on the lessons we receive when young than on hereditary ideas, becomes evident, if we consider the different moral codes existing in our own country. Nay, even in the very same individual, two contradictory systems may often be seen side by side in incongruous association.

Lastly, it may be observed that in our own case religion and morality are closely connected together. Yet the sacred character, which forms an integral part in our conception of duty, could not arise until Religion became moral. Nor would this take place until the deities were conceived to be beneficent beings. As soon, however, as this was the case, they would naturally be supposed to regard with approbation all that tended to benefit their worshippers, and to condemn all actions of the opposite character. This step was an immense benefit to mankind, since that dread of the unseen powers which had previously been wasted on the production of mere ceremonies and sacrifices, at once invested the moral feelings with a sacredness, and consequently with a force, which they had not until then possessed.

Authority, then, seems to me the origin, and utility, though not in the manner suggested by Mr. Spencer, the criterion, of virtue. Mr. Hutton, however, in the concluding paragraph of his interesting paper, urges that surely, if this were the case, by this time 'some *one* ' elementary moral law should be as deeply ingrained ' in human practice as the geometrical law that a ' straight line is the shortest way between two points.' I see no such necessity. A child whose parents belong to different nations, with different moral codes, would, I suppose, have the moral feeling deep, and yet might be without any settled ideas as to particular moral duties. And this is in reality our own case. Our ancestors have now for many generations had a feeling that some actions were right and some were wrong, but at different times they have had very different codes of morality. Hence we have a deeply-seated moral feeling, and yet, as any one who has children may satisfy himself, no such decided moral code. Children have a deep feeling of right and wrong, but no such decided or intuitive conviction as to which actions are right and which are wrong.

# CHAPTER IX.

LANGUAGE.

ALTHOUGH it has been at various times stated
that certain savage tribes are entirely without
language, none of these accounts appear to be well
authenticated, and they are à priori extremely improbable.

At any rate, even the lowest races of which we
have any satisfactory account possess a language, imperfect though it may be, and eked out to a great
extent by signs. I do not suppose, however, that this
custom has arisen from the absence of words to represent their ideas, but rather because in all countries inhabited by savages the number of languages is very
great, and hence there is a great advantage in being
able to communicate by signs.

Thus James, in his expedition to the Rocky Mountains, speaking of the Kiawa-Kaskaia Indians, says,
' These nations, although constantly associating toge-
' ther and united under the influence of the Bear-Tooth,
' are yet totally ignorant of each other's language, inso-
' much that it was no uncommon occurrence to see two
' individuals of different nations sitting upon the ground
' and conversing freely by means of the language of
' signs. In the art of thus conveying their ideas they
' were thorough adepts; and their manual display was

D D

'only interrupted at remote intervals by a smile, or by
'the auxiliary of an articulated word of the language
'of the Crow Indians, which to a very limited extent
'passes current among them.'[1]    Fisher,[2] also, speaking
of the Comanches and various surrounding tribes,
says that they have 'a language of signs by which
'all Indians and traders can understand one another;
'and they always make these signs when communicat-
'ing among themselves.    The men, when conversing
'together, in their lodges, sit upon skins, cross-legged
'like a Turk, and speak and make signs in corrobora-
'tion of what they say, with their hands, so that either
'a blind or a deaf man could understand them.    For
'instance, I meet an Indian, and wish to ask him if he
'saw six waggons drawn by horned cattle, with three
'Mexican and three American teamsters, and a man
'mounted on horseback.    I make these signs:—I point
'"you," then to his eyes, meaning "see;" then hold
'up all my fingers on the right hand and the fore finger
'on the left, meaning "six;" then I make two circles by
'bringing the ends of my thumbs and fore fingers to-
'gether, and, holding my two hands out, move my
'wrists in such a way as to indicate waggon wheels
'revolving, meaning "waggons;" then, by making an
'upward motion with each hand from both sides of my
'head, I indicate "horns," signifying horned cattle;
'then by first holding up three fingers, and then by
'placing my extended right hand below my lower lip
'and moving it downward stopping in midway down
'the chest, I indicate "beard," meaning Mexican; and

[1] See James, Expedition to the      [2] Trans. Etbn. Soc. 1869, vol. i
Rocky Mountains, vol. iii. p. 62.      p. 283.

' with three fingers again, and passing my right hand
' from left to right in front of my forehead, I indicate
' "white brow" or "pale face." I then hold up my
' fore finger, meaning one man, and by placing the fore
' finger of my left hand between the fore and second
' finger of my right hand, representing a man astride
' of a horse, and by moving my hands up and down,
' give the motion of a horse galloping with a man on
' his back. I in this way ask the Indian, "You see six
' " waggons, horned cattle, three Mexicans, three
' " Americans, one man on horseback?" If he holds
' up his fore finger and lowers it quickly, as if he was
' pointing at some object on the ground, he means
' " Yes;" if he moves it from side to side, upon the
' principle that people sometimes move their head from
' side to side, he means "No." The time required to
' make these signs would be about the same as if you
' asked the question verbally.' The Bushmen also are
said to intersperse their language with so many signs
that they are unintelligible in the dark, and, when they
want to converse at night, are compelled to collect
round their camp fires. So also Burton tells us that
the Arapahos of North America, 'who possess a very
' scanty vocabulary, can hardly converse with one
' another in the dark; to make a stranger understand
' them they must always repair to the camp fire for
' pow-wow.'[1]

Morgan mentions a case in which a couple who
had been married three years, conversed entirely by
signs; the man being a Blackfoot Indian, the woman an

<hr>

[1] City of the Saints, p. 151.

Ahahnelin, and neither understanding a word of each other's language.[1]

A very interesting account of the sign-language, especially with reference to that used by the deaf and dumb, is contained in Tylor's 'Early History of Man.' But although signs may serve to convey ideas in a manner which would probably surprise those who have not studied this question; still it must be admitted that they are far inferior to the sounds of the voice; which, as already mentioned, are used for this purpose by all the races of men with whom we are acquainted.

Language, as it exists among all but the lowest races, although far from perfect, is yet so rich in terms, and possesses in its grammar so complex an organisation, that we cannot wonder at those who have attributed to it a divine and miraculous origin. Nay, their view may be admitted as correct, but only in that sense in which a ship or a palace may be so termed: they are human in so far as they have been worked out by man; divine, inasmuch as in doing so he has availed himself of the powers which Providence has given him.[2]

M. Renan[3] draws a distinction between the origin of words and that of language, and as regards the latter

---

[1] System of Consanguinity, p. 227.

[2] Lord Monboddo, in combating those who regard language as a revelation, expresses a hope that he will not, on that account, be supposed to 'pay no respect' to the account 'given in our sacred books of the 'origin of our species; but it does not 'belong to me,' he adds, 'as a philo- 'sopher or grammarian, to enquire 'whether such account is to be under- stood allegorically, according to the 'opinions of some divines.' He for- gets, however, that those who regard language as a miracle, do so in the teeth of the express statement in Genesis that God brought the ani- mals 'unto Adam to see what he 'would call them: and whatsoever 'Adam called every living creature, 'that was the name thereof.'

[3] De l'Origine du Langage, p. 16.

says: ' Je persiste donc, après dix ans de nouvelles
' études, à envisager le langage comme formé d'un seul
' coup, et comme sorti instantanément du génie de
' chaque race,' a theory which involves that of the
plurality of human species. No doubt the complexity
and apparent perfection of the grammar among very
low races, is at first sight very surprising ; but we must
remember that the language of children is more regular
than ours. A child says, ' I goed,' ' I comed,' badder,
baddest, &c. Moreover the preservation of a complicated system of grammar among savage tribes shows
that such a system is natural to them, and not merely a
survival from more civilised times. Indeed, we know
that the tendency of civilisation is towards the simplifi-
cation of grammatical forms.

Nor must it by any means be supposed that complexity implies excellence, or even completeness, in a
language. On the contrary, it often arises from a cumbersome mode of supplying some radical defect. Adam
Smith long ago pointed out that the verb 'to be ' is
' the most abstract and metaphysical of all verbs, and
' consequently could by no means be a word of early
' invention.' And he suggests that the absence of this
verb probably led to the intricacy of conjugations.
' When,' he adds, ' it came to be invented, however, as
' it had all the tenses and modes of any other verb, by
' being joined with the passive participle, it was capable
' of supplying the place of the whole passive voice, and
' of rendering this part of their conjugations as simple
' and uniform, as the use of prepositions had rendered
' their declensions.' [1] He goes on to point out that the

[1] Smith's Moral Sentiments, vol. ii. p. 420.

same remarks apply also to the possessive verb ' I have,'
which affected the active voice, as profoundly as ' I am '
influenced the passive; thus these two verbs between
them, when once suggested, enabled mankind to relieve
their memories, and thus unconsciously, but most
effectually, to simplify their grammar.

In English we carry the same principle much further, and not only use the auxiliary verbs ' to have ' and
' to be,' but also several others—as do, did; will, would;
shall, should; can, could; may, might.[1]  Adam Smith
was, however, mistaken in supposing that the verb
' to be ' exists ' in every language;'[2] on the contrary,
the complexity of the North American languages is in a
great measure due to its absence.  The auxiliary verb
' to be ' is entirely absent in most American languages,
and the consequence is that they turn almost all their
adjectives and nouns into verbs, and conjugate them,
through all the tenses, persons, and moods.[3]

Again, the Esquimaux, instead of using adverbs,
conjugate the verb; they have special terminations implying ill, better, rarely, hardly, faithfully, &c.; hence
such a word as aglekkigiartorasuarniarpok, 'he goes
' away hastily and exerts himself to write.'[4]

In other cases the grammatical forms are but few.
The language of Akra and Fantee, according to Wultke,[5]
possesses only six conjunctions, no adverbs or prepositions, only one sex, no comparative, and no passive

[1] Smith's Moral Sentiments, p.
432.
[3] Loc. cit., p. 420.
[4] See Gallatin, Trans. Amer.
Antiq. Soc. vol. ii. p. 170. Hale,

U.S. Exp. Exp. p. 540.
[4] Crantz, His. of Greenland, vol.
I. p. 224.
[5] Ges. der Menschheit, vol. i. p.
158.

mood: that of the Hottentots is said to have contained no auxiliary verbs.[1]

The number of words in the languages of civilised races is no doubt immense. Chinese, for instance, contains 40,000; Todd's edition of Johnson, 58,000; Webster's Dictionary, 70,000; and Flügel's more than 65,000.[2] The great majority of these, however, can be derived from certain original words, or roots which are very few in number. In Chinese there are about 450, Hebrew has been reduced to 500, and Müller doubts whether there are more in Sanskrit. M. D'Orsey even assures us that an ordinary agricultural labourer has not 300 words in his vocabulary.

Professor Max Müller[3] observes, that 'this fact sim-
'plifies immensely the problem of the origin of lan-
'guage. It has taken away all excuse for those rap-
'turous descriptions of language which invariably
'preceded the argument that language must have a
'divine origin. We shall hear no more of that wonder-
'ful instrument which can express all we see, and hear,
'and taste, and touch, and smell; which is the breath-
'ing image of the whole world; which gives form to
'the airy feelings of our souls, and body to the loftiest
'dreams of our imagination; which can arrange in
'accurate perspective the past, the present, and the
'future, and throw over everything the varying hues of
'certainty, of doubt, of contingency.'

This, indeed, is no new view, but was that generally adopted by the philologists of the last century, and is fully borne out by more recent researches.

[1] Lichtenstein, Travels in South Africa, vol. ii. p. 371.
[2] Saturday Review, November 2 1861. Lectures on Language, p. 268.
[3] *Ib.* 350.

In considering the origin of these root-words, we must remember that most of them are very ancient, and much worn by use. This greatly enhances the difficulty of the problem.

Nevertheless, there are several large classes of words with reference to the origin of which there can be no doubt. Many names of animals, such as cuckoo, crow, peewit, &c., are evidently derived from the sounds made by those birds. Every one admits that such words as bang, crack, creak, crush, crash, splash, dash, purr, whizz, hum, &c., have arisen from the attempt to represent sounds characteristic of the object they are intended to designate.[1]

Take, again, the inarticulate human sounds—sob, sigh, moan, groan, laugh, cough, weep, whoop, shriek, yawn.

Or of animals; as cackle, chuckle, gobble, quack, twitter, chirp, coo, hoot, caw, croak, chatter, neigh, whinny, mew, purr, bark, yelp, roar, bellow.

The collision of hard bodies; clap, rap, tap, knap, snap, trap, flap, slap, crack, smack, whack, thwack, pat, bat, batter, beat, butt; and again, clash, flash, plash, splash, smash, dash, crash, bang, clang, twang, ring, ding, din, bump, thump, plump, boom, hum, drum, hiss, rustle, bustle, whistle, whisper, murmur, babble, &c.

So also sounds denoting certain motions and actions; whirr, whizz, puff, fizz, fly, flit, flow, flutter, patter, clatter, crackle, rattle, bubble, guggle, dabble, grabble, draggle, dripple, rush, shoot, shot, shut, &c.

---

[1] Wedgwood, Introduction to Dic. of English Etymology. Farrar, Origin of Language, p. 60. See also Wedgwood's Origin of Language, which I regret I had not read when this chapter was written.

Many words for cutting, and the objects cut, or used for cutting, &c., are obviously of similar origin. Thus we have the sound sh—r with each of the vowels; share, a part cut off; shear, an instrument for cutting; shire, a division of a country; shore, the division between land and sea, or as we use it in Kent, between two fields; a shower, a number of separate particles; again, scissors, scythe, saw, scrape, shard, scale, shale, shell, shield, skull, schist, shatter, scatter, scar, scoop, score, scrape, scratch, scum, scour, scurf, surf, scuttle, sect, shape, sharp, shave, sheaf, shed, shoal, shred, split, splinter, splutter, &c.

Another important class of words is evidently founded on the sounds by which we naturally express our feelings. Thus from Oh! Ah! the instinctive cry of pain, we get woe, væ (Latin), wail, ache, ἄχος, Gr.

From the deep guttural sound ugh, we have ugly, huge, and hug.

From pr, or prut, indicating contempt, or self-conceit, comes proud, pride, &c.

From fie, we have fiend, foe, feud, foul, Latin putris, Fr. puer, filth, fulsome, fear.

From that of smacking the lips we get γλυκύς, dulcis, lick, like, which though originally no doubt applied to things eaten, is now used generally. Turner mentions that on presenting some hatchets to the natives of Tauna, they ' smacked their lips, and made their ' usual *click, click* with the mouth shut, in admiration of ' the fine new hatchets.' [1]

Under these circumstances I cannot but think that we may look upon the words above mentioned as the

---

[1] Nineteen Years in Polynesia, p. 55.

still recognisable descendants of roots which were
onomatopœic in their origin; and I am glad to see that
Professor Max Müller, in his second series of lectures
on language,[1] wishes to be understood as offering no
opposition to this theory, although for the present
'satisfied with considering roots as phonetic types.'

It may be said, and said truly, that other classes of
ideas are not so easily or naturally expressible by corresponding sounds; and that abstract terms seldom have
any such obvious derivation. We must remember,
however, firstly, that abstract terms are wanting in the
lowest languages; and, secondly, that most words are
greatly worn by use, and altered by the difference of
pronunciation. Even among the most advanced races
a few centuries suffice to produce a great change; how,
then, can we expect that any roots (excepting those
which are preserved from material alteration by the
constant suggestion of an obvious fitness) should have
retained their original sound throughout the immense
period which has elapsed since the origin of language?
Moreover, every one who has paid any attention to
children, or schoolboys, must have observed how nicknames, often derived from slight and even fanciful
characteristics, are seized on and soon adopted by
general consent. Hence even if root-words had remained with little alteration, we should still be often
puzzled to account for their origin.

Without, then, supposing with Farrar that all our
root-words have originated from onomatopœia, I believe
that they arose in the same way as the nicknames and
new slang terms of our own day. These we know are

---

[1] Loc. cit. p. 92.

often selected from some similarity of sound, or connection of ideas, often so quaint, fanciful, or far-fetched, that we are unable to recall the true origin even of words which have arisen in our own time. How, then, can we wonder that the derivations of root-words which are thousands of years old should be in so many cases lost, or at least undeterminable with certainty?

Again, the words most frequently required, and especially those used by children, are generally represented by the simplest and easiest sounds, merely because they are the simplest. Thus in Europe we have papa and daddy, mamma, and baby; poupée for a doll; amme for a nurse, &c. Some authorities, indeed, have derived Pater and Papa from a root Pa to cherish, and Mater, Mother, from Ma to make; this derivation is accepted by writers representing the most opposite theories, as for instance by Pictet, Renan, Müller, and even apparently by Farrar.

According to Professor Max Müller, the fact that ' the name father was coined at that early period, shows ' that the father acknowledged the offspring of his wife ' as his own, for thus only had he a right to claim the ' title of father. Father is derived from a root Pa, ' which means, not to beget but to protect, to support, ' to nourish. The father, as genitor, was called in ' Sanskrit ganitár, but as protector and supporter of his ' offspring he was called pitar; hence, in the Veda, ' these two names are used together, in order to express ' the full idea of Father. Thus the poet says :—

> Dyaús me petâ genitâ
> Jovis mei pater genitor
> Ζεὺς ἐμοῦ πατὴρ γενντήρ.

'In a similar manner mâtar, mother, is joined with
'ganitû, genitrix, which shows that the word mâtar
'must soon have lost its etymological meaning, and
'have become an expression of respect and endearment.
'For among the early Arians, mâtar had the sense of
'maker, from Ma, to fashion.'[1]

Now let us see what are the names for father and
mother among some other races, omitting all languages
derived from Sanskrit.[2]

### AFRICA.

| Language | Father | Mother |
|---|---|---|
| Filham | Pepai | Inya [3] |
| Bola (N. W. Africa) | Papa | Ni |
| Sarar | Paba | Ne |
| Pepel | Papa | Nana |
| Diafada | Baba | Na |
| Baga | Bapa | Mana |
| Timne | Pa | Kara |
| Mandenga | Fa | Na |
| Kabunga | " | " |
| Toronka | " | " |
| Dsalunka | " | " |
| Kankanka | " | " |
| Bambara | " | Ba |
| Kono | " | Ndé |
| Vei | " | Ba |
| Soso | Fafa | Nga |
| Kisekise | " | " |
| Tene | Fafa | " |
| Dewoi (Guinea) | Ba | Ma |
| Basa | " | Ne |

[1] Comparative Mythology. Oxford Essays, 1856, p. 14.

[2] When this was written, and the following table was compiled, I had not seen Professor Buschmann's paper on the same subject contained in the Trans. of the Berlin Academy for 1852, and translated by Mr. Clarke in the Proc. of the Philological Soc., vol. vi.

[3] Koelle's Polyglotta Africana.

| Language | Father | Mother |
|---|---|---|
| Gbe | Ba | De |
| Dahome | Da | Noe |
| Mahi | „ also Dadyo | „ |
| Ota | Baba | Iya |
| Egba | „ | „ |
| Idsesa | „ | „ |
| Yoruba | „ | „ |
| Yagba | „ | „ |
| Eki | „ | „ |
| Dsumu | „ | „ |
| Oworo | „ | „ |
| Dsebu | „ | „ |
| Ife | „ | Yeye |
| Ondo | „ | Ye |
| Mose (High Sudan) | Ba | Ma |
| Gurma | „ | Na |
| Sobo (Niger District) | Wawa | Nene |
| Udso | Dada | Ayo |
| Nupe | Nda | Nna |
| Kupa | Dada | Mo |
| Esitako | Da | Na |
| Musu | Nda | Meya |
| Basa | Ba | Nno |
| Opanda | Ada | Onyi |
| Igu | „ | Onya |
| Egbira | „ | „ |
| Buduma (Central Africa) | Bawa | Ya |
| Bornu | Aba | „ |
| Munio | Bawa | „ |
| Nguru | „ | Iya |
| Kanem | Mba | „ |
| Karekaro | Baba | Nana |
| Ngodsin | „ | „ |
| Doai | „ | Aye |
| Basa | Ada | Am |
| Kamuku | Baba | Bina |
| Songo (S. W. Africa) | Papa | Mama |
| Kiriman (S. E. Africa) | Baba | Mwa |
| Bidsogo | „ | Ondsunei |

| Language | Father | Mother |
|---|---|---|
| Wun | Baba | Omsion |
| Gadsaga | ,, | Ma |
| Gura | Da | Nye |
| Banyun | Aba | Aai |
| Nalu | Baba | Nya |
| Bulanda | ,, | Ni |
| Limba | Papa | Na |
| Landoma | ,, | Mama |
| Barba | Baba | Inya |
| Timbuktu | ,, | Nya |
| Bagrmi | Babi | Kuuyun |
| Kadzina | Baba | Ua |
| Timbo | ,, | Nene |
| Salum | ,, | Yuma |
| Goburu | ,, | Inna |
| Kano | ,, | Ina |
| Yala | Ada | Ene |
| Dsarawa | Tada | Nga |
| Koro | Oda | Ma |
| Yasgua | Ada | Ama |
| Kambali | Dada | Omo |
| Soa (Arabic group) | Aba | Aye |
| Wadai | Abba | Omma |
| Malenba | Tata | Mamma [1] |
| Embomma | Tánta | Mama |
| Kaffir | Ubaba | Umame [2] |

## NON-ARYAN NATIONS OF EUROPE AND ASIA. [3]

| Turkish | Baba | Ana |
|---|---|---|
| Georgian | Mama | Deda |
| Mantshu | Ama | Eme |
| Javanese | Bapa | Ibu |
| Malay | ,, | Ma [4] |
| Syami (Thibet) | Dhada | ,, |

[1] Tuckey's Narrative.
[2] Morgan, Systems of Consanguinity.
[3] Hunter, Dic. of Non-Aryan Languages of India, &c.
[4] Crawford's Malay Dictionary and Grammar.

| Language | Father | Mother |
|---|---|---|
| Thibetan | Pha | Ama |
| Serpa (Nepal) | Aba | ,, |
| Murmi | Apa | Amma |
| Pakhya | Babai | Ama |
| Lepcha (Sikkim) | Abo | Amo |
| Bhutani | Appa | Ai |
| Dhimal (N. E. Bengal) | Aba | Ama |
| Kocch | Bap | Ma |
| Garo | Aba | Ama |
| Burman (Burmah) | Ahpa | Ami |
| Mru | Pa | Au |
| Sak | Aba | Anu |
| Talain (Siam) | Ma | Ya |
| Ho (Central India) | Appu | Enga |
| Santhali | Baba | Ayo |
| Uraon ,, | Babe | Ayyo |
| Gayeti ,, | Baba | Dai |
| Khond | Abba | Ayya |
| Tuluva (Southern India) | Amme | Appe |
| Badaga ,, | Appa | Avve |
| Irula ,, | Amma | Avve |
| Cinghalese | Appa | Amma |
| Chinese | Fu | Mu |
| Karen | Pa | Mo [1] |

### ISLANDERS.

| | | |
|---|---|---|
| Kingsmill | Tama | Mama |
| New Zealand | Pa-Matuatana | Matua wahina |
| Tonga Islands | Tamny | Fae |
| Erroob (N. Australia) | Bab | Ama |
| Lewis' Murray Island | Baab | Hammah |

### AUSTRALIA.

| | | |
|---|---|---|
| Jajowrong (N. W. Australia) | Marmook | Barbook |
| Knenkorenwurro ,, | Marmak | Barpanorook |
| Durapper ,, | Marmook | Barbook |

[1] Morgan, Sys. of Consanguinity.

| Language | Father | Mother |
|---|---|---|
| Taungurong          ,, | Warredoo | Barbanook |
| Boraipar (S. Australia) | Murmme | Parppe |
| Murrumbidgee | Kunny | Maruma |
| Western Australia | Mammun | Ngangan |
| Port Lincoln | Pappi | Maitya |

### ESQUIMAUX.

| Language | Father | Mother |
|---|---|---|
| Esquimaux (Hudson's Bay) | Atata | Amama |
| Tshuktchi (Asia) | Atta | ? |

The American languages seem at first sight opposed
to the view here suggested; on close examination, however, this is not the case, since the pronunciation of the
labials is very difficult to many American races.   Thus
La Hontan (who is confirmed by Gallatin [1]) informs us
that the Hurons do not use the labials, and that he
spent four days in attempting without success to teach
a Huron to pronounce b, p, and m.   The Iroquois are
stated not to use labials.   Garcilasso de la Vega tells
us that the Peruvian language wanted the letters b, d,
f, g, s, and x; b, d, f, g, r, and s in Aztec ; [2] and the
Indians of Port au Français, according to M. Lamanon,
made no use of the consonants b, d, f, j, p, v, or x. [3]
Still, even in America we find some cases in which the
sounds for father resemble those so general elsewhere;
thus—

| Language | Father | Mother |
|---|---|---|
| Costanos (N. W. America) | Ah Pah | Ah nah |
| Tahakli          ,, | Apa | ,, |
| Tlatskanai          ,, | Mama | Naa |
| Nasqually          ,, | Baa | Sogo |

---

[1] Trans. Am. Antiq. Soc. vol. i.     vol. i, p. 270.
p. 230.                           [2] Gallatin, *loc. cit.* p. 63.
[3] Wuttke's *Gen. der Mensch.*

| Language | Father | Mother |
|---|---|---|
| Nootka (N. W. America) | Api | Una |
| Athapascans (Canada) | Appa | Unnungeool |
| Omahas (Missouri) | Dadai | Echong |
| Minnetarees | Tantai | Eeka |
| Choctas (Mississippi) | Aunkke | Iskeh |
| Caribs | Baba | Bibi |
| Quichua | Yaya | Mama |
| Uainamben (Amazons) | Pai | Ami |
| Cobeu ,, | Ipaki | Ipako |
| Tucano ,, | Pagui | Maou |
| Tariana ,, | Paica | Naea |
| Baniwa | Padjo | Nadjo |
| Barre | Mbaba | Memi |
| Muysea | Paba | Guuira |

Finding, then, that the easiest sounds which a child
can produce denote father and mother almost all over
the world; remembering that the root ba or pa indicates baby as well as father; that in various parts of
the world the roots 'pa' and 'ma' denote other near
relationships; and observing that in some cases the
usual sounds are reversed; as for instance in Georgian,
where mama stands for father, and dada for mother;
or in Tuluva, where amme is father, and appe mother;
in Chilian, where 'papa' means mother; in Tlatskanai,
where 'mama' stands for father; in Madurese again,
'mama' means father, 'ambu' or 'babu' mother; or
some of the Australian tribes, in which combinations of
the sound mar stand for father, and bar for mother; we
must surely admit that the Sanskrit verb Pa, to protect,
comes from pa, father, and not *vice versâ*.

There are few more interesting studies than the
steps by which our present language has been derived
from these original roots. This subject has been ad-

mirably dealt with by my friend Professor Max Müller
in his 'Lectures on Language,' and, tempting as it
would be to do so, I do not propose to follow him into
that part of the science.  As regards the formation of
the original roots, however, he declines to express any
opinion.  Rejecting what he calls the pooh-pooh and
bow-wow theories[1] (though they are in reality but
one), he observes that 'the theory which is suggested
' to us by an analysis of language carried out according
' to the principles of comparative philology, is the very
' opposite.  We arrive in the end at roots, and every
' one of these expresses a general, not an individual
' idea.'  But the whole question is, How were these roots
chosen?  How did particular things come to be denoted
by particular sounds?

Here, however, Professor Max Müller stops.  Nothing, he admits,[2] 'would be more interesting than to
' know from historical documents the exact process by
' which the first man began to lisp his first words, and
' thus to be rid for ever of all the theories on the origin
' of speech.  But this knowledge is denied us ; and, if
' it had been otherwise, we should probably be quite
' unable to understand those primitive events in the
' history of the human mind.'

Yet in his last chapter he says,[3] 'And now I am
' afraid I have but a few minutes left to explain the
' last question of all in our science, namely, How can
' sound express thought?  How did roots become the
' signs of general ideas?  How was the abstract idea of
' measuring expressed by mâ, the idea of thinking

---

[1] Science of Language, p. 373.        [2] Loc. cit. p. 340.
[3] Loc. cit. p. 380.

' by man?  How did gâ come to mean going, stha
' standing, sad sitting, dâ giving, mar dying, char
' walking, kar doing?  I shall try to answer as briefly
' as possible.  The 400 or 500 roots which remain as
' the constituent elements in different families of lan-
' guage are not interjections, nor are they imitations.
' They are phonetic types produced by a power inherent
' in human nature.  They exist, as Plato would say, by
' nature ; though with Plato we should add that, when
' we say by nature, we mean by the hand of God.
' There is a law which runs through nearly the whole
' of nature, that everything which is struck rings. . . .
' Man, in his primitive and perfect state, was not only
' endowed, like the brute, with the power of expressing
' his sensations by interjections, and his perceptions by
' onomatopœia.  He possessed likewise the faculty of
' giving more articulate expression to the natural con-
' ceptions of his mind.  That faculty was not of his
' making.  It was an instinct, an instinct of the mind
' as irresistible as any other instinct.  So far as lan-
' guage is the production of that instinct, it belongs to
' the realm of nature.'

This answer, though expressed with Professor Max
Müller's usual eloquence, does not carry to my mind
any definite conception.  On the other hand, it appears
to me that at any rate, as regards some roots, we
have, as already pointed out, a satisfactory explanation.
Professor Max Müller,[1] indeed, admits that ' there are
' some names, such as cuckoo, which are clearly formed
' by an imitation of sound.  But,' he adds, 'words of
' this kind are, like artificial flowers, without a root.

[1] Science of Language, p. 343.

'They are sterile, and are unfit to express anything
'beyond the one object which they imitate. If you
'remember the variety of derivatives that could be
'formed from the root spac, to see, you will at once
'perceive the difference between the fabrication of such
'a word as cuckoo, and the true natural growth of
'words.' It has, however, been already shown that
such roots, far from being sterile, are, on the contrary,
very fruitful, and we must remember that savage languages are extremely poor in abstract terms.

Indeed, the vocabularies of the various races are
most interesting from the indications which they afford
with reference to the condition of those by whom they
are used. Thus we get a melancholy idea of the moral
state and family life of tribes which are deficient in
terms of endearment. Colonel Dalton[1] tells us that the
Hos of Central India have no 'endearing epithets.'
The Algonquin language, one of the richest in North
America, contained no verb 'to love,' and when Elliot
translated the Bible into it in 1661, he was obliged to
coin a word for the purpose. The Tinné Indians on
the other side of the Rocky Mountains had no equivalent for 'dear' or 'beloved.' 'I endeavoured,' says
General Lefroy, 'to put this intelligibly to Nanette, by
'supposing such an expression as ma chère femme; ma
'chère fille. When at length she understood it, her
'reply was (with great emphasis), "I' disent jamais ça;
'"i' disent ma femme, ma fille."' The Kalmucks and
some of the South Sea Islanders are said to have had
no word for 'thanks.' Lichtenstein,[2] speaking of the

[1] Trans. Ethn. Soc. N.S. vol. vi. p. 27.
[2] Vol. i. p. 110; vol. ii. p. 40.

Bushmen, mentions it as a remarkable instance of the total absence of civilisation among them that 'they ' have no names, and seem not to feel the want of such ' a means of distinguishing one individual from another.' Pliny [1] makes a similar statement concerning a race in Northern Africa. Freycinet [2] also asserts that some of the Australian tribes did not name their women. I confess that I am inclined to doubt these statements, and to refer the supposed absence of names to the curious superstitions already referred to (*antè*, p. 236), and which make savages so reluctant to communicate their true names to strangers. The Brazilian tribes, according to Spix and Martius, had separate names for the different parts of the body, and for all the different animals and plants with which they were acquainted, but were entirely deficient in such terms as 'colour,' ' tone,' 'sex,' ' genus,' ' spirit,' &c.

Bailey [3] mentions that the language of the Veddahs (Ceylon) 'is very limited. It only contains such ' phrases as are required to describe the most striking ' objects of nature, and those which enter into the daily ' life of the people themselves. So rude and primitive ' is their dialect that the most ordinary objects and ' actions of life are described by quaint periphrases.'

' In Kocch, Bodo, and Dhimal there is not a single ' vernacular word to express matter, spirit, space, ' instinct, reason, consciousness, quantity, degree, or ' the like.' [4] Among the Bongo of Central Africa words for 'abstract ideas, such as spirit, soul, hope, fear,

---

[1] Nat. His., l. v. s. viii.

[2] Vol. ii. p. 749.

[3] Trans. Ethn. Soc. N.S., vol. ii. p. 298; see also p. 300.

[4] Essay on the Kocch, Bodo, and Dhimal Tribes, by R. H. Hodgson, Esq., p. ii. See also Hunter's Annals of Rural Bengal, p. 113.

'appear to be absolutely wanting, but experience
'shows that in this respect other negro tongues are not
'more richly provided.'[1]

According to missionaries the Fuegians had 'no
'abstract terms.' In the North American languages a
term 'sufficiently general to denote an oak-tree is ex-
'ceptional.' Thus, the Choctaw language has names
for the black oak, white oak, and red oak, but none for
an oak, still less for a tree.

The Tasmanians, again, had no general term for a
tree, though they had names for each particular kind;
nor could they express 'qualities such as hard, soft,
'warm, cold, long, short, round,' &c.

Speaking of the Coroados (Brazil), Martius observes
that 'it would be in vain to seek among them words for
'the abstract ideas of plant, animal, and the still more
'abstract notions colour, tone, sex, species, &c.; such a
'generalisation of ideas is found among them only in
'the frequently used infinitive of the verbs to walk, to
'eat, to drink, to dance, to see, to hear, &c. They
'have no conception of the general powers and laws of
'nature, and therefore cannot express them in words.'[2]
It is remarkable that barbarous races are often deficient
in terms denoting colours.

There is, perhaps, no more interesting part of the
study of language than that which concerns the system
of numeration, nor any more striking proof of the low
mental condition of many savage races than the undoubted fact that they are unable to count their own
fingers, even of one hand.

[1] Schweinfurth's Heart of Africa, vol. i. p. 311.

[2] Spix and Martius, Travels in
Brazil, vol. ii. p. 253.

According to Lichtenstein, the Bushmen could not count beyond two. Spix and Martius make the same statement about the Brazilian Wood-Indians. The Cape Yorkers of Australia count as follows:—

| One | Netat. |
|-----|--------|
| Two | Nacs. |
| Three | Nacs-netat. |
| Four | Nacs-nacs. |
| Five | Nacs-nacs-netat. |
| Six | Naca nacs-nacs. |

Speaking of the Lower Murray nations, Mr. Beveridge says, 'Their numerals are confined to two alone, 'viz. "ryup," "politi," the first signifying "one" and 'the second "two." To express five, they say "ryup '"murnangin," or one hand, and to express ten, "politi '"murnangin," or two hands.'[1] Indeed, no Australian can go beyond four, their term for five simply implying a large number. The Dammaras, according to Galton, used no term beyond three. He gives so admirable and at the same time so amusing an account of Dammara difficulties in language and arithmetic that I cannot resist quoting it in full. 'We had,' he says,[2] 'to trust 'to our Dammara guides, whose ideas of time and dis-'tance were most provokingly indistinct; besides this 'they have no comparative in their language, so that 'you cannot say to them, "Which is the longer of the '"two, the next stage or the last one?" but you must 'say, "The last is little; the next is it great?" The 'reply is not, It is a "little longer," or "very much

[1] Trans. of the Il. S. of Victoria, vol. vi. p. 161. Lang Queensland, p. 433.

[2] Galton's Tropical South Africa, p. 213.

' " longer," but simply, " It is so," or " It is not so."
' They have a very poor notion of time.  If you say,
' " Suppose we start at sunrise, where will the sun be
' " when we arrive?" they make the wildest points in the
' sky, though they are something of astronomers, and
' give names to several stars.  They have no way of
' distinguishing days, but reckon by the rainy season,
' or the pig-nut season.  When inquiries are made
' about how many days' journey off a place may be,
' their ignorance of all numerical ideas is very annoying.
' In practice, whatever they may possess in their lan-
' guage, they certainly use no numeral greater than
' three.  When they wish to express four, they take to
' their fingers, which are to them as formidable instru-
' ments of calculation as a sliding rule is to an English
' schoolboy.  They puzzle very much after five, be-
' cause no spare hand remains to grasp and secure the
' fingers that are required for units.  Yet they seldom
' lose oxen; the way in which they discover the loss of
' one is not by the number of the herd being diminished,
' but by the absence of a face they know.  When
' bartering is going on, each sheep must be paid for
' separately.  Thus, suppose two sticks of tobacco to be
' the rate of exchange for one sheep, it would sorely
' puzzle a Damara to take two sheep and give him
' four sticks.  I have done so, and seen a man put two
' of the sticks apart, and take a sight over them at one
' of the sheep he was about to sell.  Having satisfied
' himself that that one was honestly paid for, and finding
' to his surprise that exactly two sticks remained in
' hand to settle the account for the other sheep, he
' would be afflicted with doubts; the transaction seemed

' to come out too "pat" to be correct, and he would
' refer back to the first couple of sticks; and then his
' mind got hazy and confused, and wandered from one
' sheep to the other, and he broke off the transaction
' until two sticks were put into his hand, and one sheep
' driven away, and then the other two sticks given him,
' and the second sheep driven away. When a Dam-
' mara's mind is bent upon number, it is too much
' occupied to dwell upon quantity; thus a heifer is
' bought from a man for ten sticks of tobacco, his large
' hands being both spread out upon the ground, and a
' stick placed upon each finger. He gathers up the
' tobacco, the size of the mass pleases him, and the
' bargain is struck. You then want to buy a second
' heifer; the same process is gone through, but half
' sticks instead of whole sticks are put upon his fingers;
' the man is equally satisfied at the time, but occasion-
' ally finds it out, and complains the next day.

' Once while I watched a Damara floundering
' hopelessly in a calculation on one side of me, I ob-
' served Dinah, my spaniel, equally embarrassed on the
' other. She was overlooking half-a-dozen of her new-
' born puppies, which had been removed two or three
' times from her, and her anxiety was excessive, as she
' tried to find out if they were all present, or if any
' were still missing. She kept puzzling and running
' her eyes over them, backwards and forwards, but
' could not satisfy herself. She evidently had a vague
' notion of counting, but the figure was too large for
' her brain. Taking the two as they stood, dog and
' Damara, the comparison reflected no great honour
' on the man.'

All over the world the fingers are used as counters; and although the numerals of most races are so worn down by use that we can no longer detect their original meaning, there are many savage tribes in which the words used are merely the verbal expressions of the signs used in counting with the fingers.

Of this I have just given one instance. In Labrador 'Tallek,' a hand, means also 'five,' and the term for twenty means hands and feet together.

So also the Esquimaux of Greenland [1] for twenty say 'a man; that is, as many fingers and toes as a man 'has; and then count as many fingers more as are 'above the number; consequently, instead of 100, they 'say five men. But the generality are not such 'learned arithmeticians, and therefore, when the num- 'ber is above twenty, they say "it is innumerable." 'But when they adjoin the thing itself to the number, 'they express many numbers otherwise, as innuit 'pingasut, three men.' So also among the Kolusches the word for twenty is the lika, literally 'one man;' for forty, tach hka, 'two men.' [2]

Speaking of the Ahts, Mr. Sproat [3] says, 'It may be 'noticed that their word for one occurs again in that 'for six and nine, and the word for two is that for 'seven and eight. The Aht Indians count upon their 'fingers. They always count, except where they have 'learnt differently from their contact with civilisation, 'by raising the hands with the palms upwards, and 'extending all the fingers, and bending down each

---

[1] Crantz, His. of Greenland, vol. i. p. 225.    1871, p. 217.
[2] Erman. Zeit. f. Ethnologie,    [3] Scenes and Studies of Savage Life, p. 121.

' finger as it is used for enumeration. They begin
' with the little finger. This little finger, then, is one.
' Now six is five (that is, one whole hand) and one
' more. We can easily see, then, why their word for
' six comprehends the word for one. Again, seven is
' five (one whole hand) and two more—thus their
' word for seven comprehends the word for two.
' Again, when they have bent down the eighth finger,
' the most noticeable feature of the hand is that two
' fingers, that is, a finger and a thumb, remain ex-
' tended. Now the Aht word for eight comprehends
' atlah, the word for two. The reason for this I
' imagine to be as follows:—Eight is ten (or the whole
' hands) wanting two. Again, when the ninth finger
' is down, only one finger is left extended. Their
' word for nine comprehends tsowwauk, the word for
' one. Nine is ten (or two whole hands) wanting
' one.' [1]

The Zamuca and Muysca Indians [2] have a cumbrous,
but interesting, system of numeration. For five they
say, 'hand finished.' For six, 'one of the other hand;'
that is to say, take a finger of the other hand. For ten
they say, 'two hands finished,' or sometimes more simply
' quicha,' that is 'foot.' Eleven is foot-one; twelve,
foot-two; thirteen, foot-three, and so on: twenty is the
feet finished; or in other cases 'Man,' because a man
has ten fingers and ten toes, thus making twenty.

Among the Jaruroes the word for forty is 'noeni-
' pume;' *i.e.* two men, from noeni, two, and canipune,
men.

[1] Scenes and Studies of Savage Life, pp. 121, 122.

[2] Humboldt's Personal Re-searches, vol. II. p. 117.

Speaking of the Guiana natives, Mr. Brett observes[1] that 'another point in which the different nations agree ' is their method of numeration. The first four num- ' bers are represented by simple words, as in the table ' above given. Five is " my one hand," *abar-dakabo* ' in Arawâk. Then comes a repetition, *abar timen*, ' *biam timen*, &c., up to nine. *Biam-dakabo*, " my two ' " hands," is ten. From ten to twenty they use the ' toes (*kuti* or *okuti*), as *abar-kuti-bana*, " eleven" *biam-* ' *kuti bana*, " twelve," &c. They call twenty *abar-loko*, ' one *loko* or man. They then proceed by *men* or ' scores; thus, forty-five is laboriously expressed by ' *biam-loko-abar-dakabo tajeago*, " two men and one ' " hand upon it." For higher numbers they have now ' recourse to our words *hundred* and *thousand*.' So also among the Caribs, the word for 'ten,' Chonnoucabo raim, meant literally 'the fingers of both hands;' and that for 'twenty' was Chonnougouci raim, *i.e.* the fingers and toes.[2]

The Coroados[3] generally count only by the joints of the fingers, consequently only to three. Every greater number they express by the word 'mony.'

According to Dobritzhoffer 'the Guarinics, when ' questioned respecting a thing exceeding four, imme- ' diately reply ndipapahabi, ndipapahai, innumerable.'[4] So also 'the Abipones[5] can only express three numbers ' in proper words: *Íñitára*, one, *Íñoaka*, two, *Íñoaka* ' *yekaini*, three. They make up for the other numbers

---

[1] Brett's Indian Tribes of Guiana, p. 417.

[2] Teriro's History of the Caribby Islands.

[3] Spix and Martius, Travels in Brazil, vol. ii. p. 255.

[4] History of the Abipones, vol. ii. p. 171.

[5] *Loc. cit.* p. 169.

' by various arts ; thus, *geyenk ñatè*, the fingers of an
' emu, which, as it has three in front and one turned
' back, are four, serves to express that number: *nèn-*
' *halek*, a beautiful skin spotted with five different
' colours, is used to signify the number five.' ' *Handim-*
' *begem*, the fingers of one hand, means five; *landin*
' *rihegem*, the fingers of both hands, ten; *landin rihegem*
' *cat gracherhaka anamichirihegem*, the fingers of both
' hands and both feet, twenty.'

Among the Malays and throughout Polynesia the
word for five is *ima, lima,* or *rima*.  In Bali, lima also
means a hand; this is also the case in the Bugis, Mand-
har, and Endé languages ; in the Makasar dialect it is
liman, in Sasak it is ima, in Bima it is rima, in Sem-
bawa it is limang.[1]

In the Mpongwe language ' tyani ' or ' tani ' is five,
' ntyame ' is ' hand.'[2]  The Koossa Kaffirs make little
use of numerals.  Lichtenstein could never discover
that they had any word for eight, few could reckon
beyond ten, and many did not know the names of any
numerals.  Yet if a single animal was missing out of a
herd of several hundred, they observed it immediately.[3]
This, however, as Mr. Galton explains, is merely
because they miss a face they know.  Among the Zulu,
' tatitisupa ' six, means literally ' take the thumb;' *i.e.,*
having used the finger of one hand, take the thumb of
the next.  'The numbers,' says Lichtenstein, ' are
' commonly expressed among the Beetjuans by fingers
' held up, so that the word is rarely spoken ; many are

[1] Raffles's History of Java, Ap-    guage.  1817.
pendix F.                           [3] Lichtenstein, vol. i. p. 280.  See
[2] Grammar of the Mpongwe Lan-    also App.

'even unacquainted with these numerals, and never
'employ anything but the sign. It therefore occasioned
'me no small trouble to learn the numerals, and I could
'by no means arrive at any denomination for the num-
'bers five and nine. Beyond ten even the most learned
'could not reckon, nor could I make out by what signs
'they ever designated these higher numbers.' [1]

Even in our own language the word 'five' has a
similar origin, since it is derived from the Greek πέντε,
which again is evidently connected with the Persian
pendji; now in Persian 'pentcha' means a hand, as
Humboldt has already pointed out. [2]

Hence, no doubt, the prevalence of the decimal system in arithmetic; it has no particular advantage; indeed, either eight or twelve would, in some respects,
have been more convenient; eight, because you can
divide it by two, and then divide the result again by
two; and twelve because it is divisible by six, four,
three, and two. Ten, however, has naturally been
selected, because we have ten fingers.

These examples, then, appear to me very instructive;
we seem as it were to trace up the formation of the
numerals; we perceive the true cause of the decimal
system of notation; and we obtain interesting, if melancholy, evidence of the extent to which the faculty of
thought lies dormant among the lower races of man.

[1] *Loc. cit.* vol. ii. App.
[2] *Personal Researches*, London, 1814, vol. ii. p. 110.

# CHAPTER X.

## LAWS.

THE customs and laws of the lower races, so far as religious and family relations are concerned, have already been discussed. There are, however, some other points of view with reference to which it seems desirable to make some remarks. The progress and development of law is indeed one of the most interesting as well as important sections of human history. It is far less essential, as Goguet [1] truly observes, ' de savoir ' le nombre des dynasties et les noms des souverains ' qui les composoient; mais il est essentiel de connoître ' les loix, les arts, les sciences et les usages d'une nation ' que toute l'antiquité a regardée comme un modèle de ' sagesse et de vertu. Voilà les objets que je me suis ' proposés, et que je vais traiter avec le plus d'exacti- ' tude qu'il me sera possible.' It is, however, impossible thoroughly to understand the laws of the most advanced nations, unless we take into consideration those customs of ruder communities from which they took their origin, by which they are so profoundly influenced.

It is, therefore, very much to be regretted that we are not more thoroughly acquainted with the laws and customs of savage races.

[1] De l'Origine des Loix, des Arts, et des Sciences, vol. i. p. 45.

At the time Goguet published his celebrated work, our knowledge was even more defective than is now the case.

Still I am surprised that with the evidence which was before him, and especially as he was one of the first to point out that much light is thrown by the condition of modern savages on that of our ancestors in times now long gone by,[1] he should have regarded the monarchical form of government as the most ancient and most universally established.[2] 'C'est, sans con-'tredit,' he says, ' le plus anciennement et le plus uni-'versellement établi.'

A more careful consideration of the evidence afforded by the lower races of man would probably have modified his views on some other points. For instance,[3] he observes that 'il n'est pas difficile de faire 'sentir par quelles raisons le gouvernement monarchique 'est le premier dont l'idée a dû se présenter. Il étoit 'plus aisé aux peuples, lorsqu'ils ont pensé à établir 'l'ordre dans la société, de se rassembler sous un seul 'chef, que sous plusieurs: la royauté est d'ailleurs une 'image de l'autorité que les pères avoient originairement

---

[1] M. Goguet remarks that some races, being ignorant of the art of writing, even now, ' pour constater ' leurs ventes, leurs achats, leurs em-' prunts, etc., emploient certains mor-' ceaux de bois entaillés diversement. ' On les coupe en deux : le créancier ' en garde une moitié, et le débiteur ' retient l'autre. Quand la dette ou la ' promesse est acquittée, chacun re-' met le morceau qu'il avoit par devers ' lui ' (p. 20). This method of keep-ing accounts is not confined to savage races. It was practised by the En-glish Government down to the com-mencement of the present century, and I myself possess such a receipt given by the English Government to the East India Company in the year 1770, and duly preserved in the India House until within the last ten years. It represents 24,000£, represented by twenty-four equal notches in a rod of wood.

[2] Loc. cit. vol. i. p. 0.

[3] Loc. cit. p. 10.

' sur leurs enfants: ils étoient dans ces premiers tems
' les chefs et les législateurs de leur famille.'

Whereas, it has been already shown in the earlier
chapters of this work that the family is by no means so
perfectly organised among the lowest races.

Sir G. Grey,[1] speaking of the Australians, truly says
that the ' laws of this people are unfitted for the govern-
' ment of a single isolated family, some of them being
' only adapted for the regulation of an assemblage of
' families; they could, therefore, not have been a series
' of rules given by the first father to his children: again,
' they could not have been rules given by an assembly
' of the first fathers to their children, for there are these
' remarkable features about them, that some are of such
' a nature as to compel those subject to them to remain
' in a state of barbarism.'

Again, Goguet[2] states that ' les loix du mariage ont
' mis un frein à une passion qui n'en voulroit recon-
' noître aucun. Elles ont fait plus: en déterminant les
' degrés de consanguinité qui rendent les alliances illé-
' gitimes, elles ont appris aux hommes à connoître et à
' respecter les droits de la nature,' which is very far
from being the case.  I have already observed that
even Sir Henry Maine would probably have modified
in some points the views expressed in his excellent
work,[3] if he had paid more attention to the manners,
customs, and laws of savages.  But, although the
progress and development of law belong, for the
most part, to a more advanced stage of human society
than that which is the subject of this work, still,

---

[1] Grey's Australia, vol. ii. p. 223.     [2] Ancient Law.
[3] *Loc. cit.*, p. 20.

in one sense, as already mentioned, even the lowest races of savages have laws.

Those who have not devoted much attention to the subject have generally regarded the savage as having one advantage, at least, over civilised man; that, namely, of enjoying an amount of personal freedom greater than that of individuals belonging to more civilised communities.

There cannot be a greater mistake. The savage is nowhere free. All over the world his daily life is regulated by a complicated and often most inconvenient set of customs (as forcible as laws), of quaint prohibitions and privileges; the prohibitions as a general rule applying to the women, and the privileges to the men. Nay, every action of their lives is regulated by numerous rules, none the less stringent because unwritten.

Fashion, says Schweinfurth, ' in the distant wilds ' of Africa, tortures and harasses poor humanity as ' much as in the great prison of civilisation.' [1]

Mr. Lang, speaking of the Australians,[2] tells us that, ' instead of enjoying perfect personal freedom, as ' it would at first appear, they are governed by a code ' of rules and a set of customs which form one of the ' most cruel tyrannies that has ever, perhaps, existed ' on the face of the earth, subjecting not only the will, ' but the property and life of the weak to the dominion ' of the strong. The whole tendency of the system is ' to give everything to the strong and old, to the pre- ' judice of the weak and young, and more particularly ' to the detriment of the women. They have rules by

[1] Heart of Africa, vol. i. p. 410.   Eyre, loc. cit., vol. ii. p. 385.  See
[2] Aborigines of Australia, p. 7.   Note.

' which the best food, the best pieces, the best animals,
' &c., are prohibited to the women and young men, and
' reserved for the old.  The women are generally ap-
' propriated to the old and powerful, some of whom
' possess four to seven wives; while wives are altogether
' denied to young men, unless they have sisters to give
' in exchange, and are strong and courageous enough
' to prevent their sisters from being taken without
' exchange.'

Among the Mbayas of South America the married
women are not allowed to eat beef, capibara, or monkey;
and the girls are forbidden to partake of any meat, or
any fish which is more than a foot long.  ' Les Char-
' treux mêmes n'e sont pas venus à cepoint d'aus-
térité.'[1]

' To believe,' says Sir G. Grey,[2] ' that man in a
' savage state is endowed with freedom, either of
' thought or action, is erroneous in the highest degree.'

In Tahiti,[3] ' the men were allowed to eat the flesh of
' the pig, and of fowls, and a variety of fish, cocoa-nuts,
' and plantains, and whatever was presented as an offer-
' ing to the gods, which the females, on pain of death,
' were forbidden to touch, as it was supposed they would
' pollute them.  The fires on which the men's food was
' cooked were also sacred, and were forbidden to be used
' by the females.  The baskets in which their provisions
' were kept, and the house in which the men ate, were
' also sacred, and prohibited to the females under the
' same cruel penalty; hence the inferior food, both for

[1] Azara's Voy. dans l'Amér. 217.
Meridionale.                    [2] Polynesian Researches, vol. i.
[3] Grey's Australia, vol. ii. p.    p. 222.

' wives, daughters, &c., was cooked at separate fires,
' deposited in distinct baskets, and eaten in lonely
' solitude by the females in little huts erected for the
' purpose.' 'Nothing,' says the Bishop of Wellington,
' can be more mistaken than to represent the New
' Zealanders as a people without law and order. They
' are, and were, the slaves of law, rule, and prece-
' dent.'[1]

The head of a chief was regarded as especially
sacred; and Shortland gives an amusing account of a
case in which an unfortunate child suffered sadly,
because ' no one could for a long time be found of suffi-
' ciently high rank to cut his hair or wash his head.'[2]

If savages pass unnoticed many actions which we
should consider as highly criminal, on the other hand
they strictly forbid others which we should consider
altogether immaterial.

The natives of Russian America, near the Yukon
river, ' have certain superstitions with regard to the
' bones of animals, which they will neither throw on the
' fire nor to the dogs, but save them in their houses or
' *caches*. When they saw us careless in such matters,
' they said it would prevent them from catching or
' shooting successfully. Also, they will not throw away
' their hair or nails just cut short, but save them, hang-
' ing them frequently in packages on the trees.'[3]

The Mongols[4] think it a fault to touch the fire, or
take flesh out of the pot with a knife, or to cleave wood
with a hatchet near the hearth, imagining it takes away

[1] Trans. Ethn. Soc. 1870, p. 307.
[2] Traditions of the New Zealanders, p. 108.
[3] Whymper, Trans. Ethn. Soc.,
N.S., vol. vii. p. 174.
[4] Astley's Coll., vol. iv. p. 648.

the fire's power. It is no less faulty to lean on a whip
or touch arrows with it; to kill young birds; or pour
liquor on the ground: to strike a horse with a bridle ; or
break one bone against another. Mr. Tylor has already
pointed out [1] that almost exactly the same prohibitions
occur in America.

Some savage rules are very sensible. Thus Tanner
states that the Algonkin Indians, when on a war-path,
must not sit upon the naked ground ; but must, at least,
have some grass or bushes under them. They must, if
possible, avoid wetting their feet ; but if they are compelled to wade through a swamp, or to cross a stream,
they must keep their clothes dry, and whip their legs
with bushes or grass when they come out of the water. [2]
For others the reason is not so obvious. Thus, the
small bowls out of which they drink are marked across
the middle ; in going out they must place one side to
their mouth; in returning, the other. The vessels
must also on their return be thrown away or hung up
in a tree.

Hunting tribes generally have well-understood
rules with reference to game. Among the Greenlanders, should a seal escape with a hunter's javelin in
it, and be killed by another man afterwards, it belongs
to the former. But if the seal be struck with the harpoon and bladder, and the string break, the hunter
loses his right. If a man find a seal dead with a harpoon in it, he keeps the seal, but returns the harpoon.
In reindeer hunting, if several hunters strike a deer
together, it belongs to the one whose arrow is nearest

[1] Early History of Man, p. 134.
[2] Tanner's Narrative, p. 123.

the heart. The arrows are all marked, so that no dispute can arise, but since guns have been introduced many quarrels have taken place. Any man who finds a piece of drift-wood (which in the far North is extremely valuable) can appropriate it by placing a stone on it, as a sign that some one has taken possession of it. No other Greenlander will then touch it.

Among the Khonds, hunters in pursuit of game have ' an admitted right to pursue it to any place, either ' within or without their own boundaries, until the ' animal is killed or captured,' but it is also understood that ' the villagers on whose land it may be killed have ' a right to a share of the meat.'[1]

Again, far from being informal or extemporary, the salutations, ceremonies, treaties, and contracts of savages are characterised by the very opposite qualities.

Eyre mentions that in Australia ' in their inter- ' course with each other, natives of different tribes are ' exceedingly punctilious.'[2]

Mariner gives a long account of the elaborate ceremonies practised by the Tongans, and of their ' regard ' for rank.'[3] The king[4] was by no means of the highest rank. The Tooitonga, Veachi, and several other chiefs preceded him. Indeed the name Tooitonga means King of Tonga; the office, however, had come to be wholly of a religious character; the Tooitonga being regarded as descended from the gods, if not a deity himself. He was so sacred that some words were retained for his exclusive use.

[1] Campbell's Wild Tribes of Khondistan, p. 41.
[2] Discoveries in Australia, vol. II. p. 214.
[3] Tonga Islands, vol. ii. pp. 185, 193, 207.
[4] Loc. cit., vol. ii. p. 79.

Below Tooitonga and Veachi came the priests, while civil society was divided into five ranks—the king, the nobles, the Matabooles, the Moous, and the Tooas. The child took the rank of the mother among the nobles, but the Matabooles were succeeded by the eldest son.

Among the Micronesians also distinctions of rank were very strictly observed. Thus in Banabe, one of the Caroline Islands, there were three classes, and we are assured that even in battle 'a person of one class ' never attacked one of another.'[1]

It is curious that the use of the third person in token of respect occurs in Tonga, as well as some other countries. 'Thus the King of Tonga addressing the ' Tooitonga says, " Ho egi Tooitonga;" that is, literally, ' thy Lord Tooitonga, in which the possessive pronoun ' thy, or your, is used instead of my; or, if the word ' egi be translated lordship or chiefship, the term of ' address will be more consistent and similar to ours, ' your lordship, your grace, your majesty. The title, ' ho egi, is never used but in addressing a superior chief, ' or speaking of a god, or in a public speech. Ho egi! ' also means chiefs, as in the commencement of Finow's ' speech.'[2]

In Samoa we are assured that the distinction between the language of ceremony and that of common life is even more marked than in Tonga.[3] Here also the plural is always used in speaking to a superior. Mr. Turner mentions that the first time he was so addressed he felt somewhat hurt, for as he did not know the custom, and happened to be riding, he

[1] Hale's U. S. Expl. Exped. p. 83.
[2] Mariner, vol. ii. p. 142.
[3] Hale's U. S. Expl. Exp. p. 280.

thought the native intended to couple him with his horse.[1]

In Feejee, if by chance a chief slipped or fell, every one of inferior rank was expected immediately to do the same, lest they should appear more careful or skilful than their superior. In such a case, however, the chief was expected to pay handsomely for the compliment.[2]

The Egbas, a negro race of West Africa, who are, says Burton,[3] 'gifted with uncommon loquacity and ' spare time, have invented a variety of salutations and ' counter-salutations applicable to every possible occa- ' sion. For instance, Oji re, did you wake well? ' Akwaro, good morning! Akuasan, good day! Akwale, ' good evening! Akware, to one tired. Akushe, to ' one at work. Akurin (from rin, to walk), to a tra- ' veller. Akule, to one in the house. Akwatijo, after ' a long absence. Akwalejo, to a stranger. Akurajo, ' to one in distress. Akujiko, to one sitting. Akudaro, ' to one standing. Akuta, to one selling. Wolebe (be ' careful), to one met, and so forth. The servile shash- ' tanga or prostration of the Hindus is also a universal ' custom. It is performed in different ways; the most ' general is, after depositing the burden, and clapping ' hands once, twice, or thrice, to go on all-fours, touch ' the ground with the belly and breast, the forehead, ' and both sides of the face successively; kiss the earth, ' half rise up, then pass the left over the right forearm, ' and vice versâ, and finally, after again saluting mother ' Hertha, to stand erect. The inferior prostrates to the

[1] Nineteen Years in Polynesia, p. 340.

[2] Fiji and the Fijians, vol. i. p. 30.

[3] Burton's Abeokuta, vol. i. p. 113.

' superior, the son to the mother, the younger to the
' elder brother, and I have been obliged to correct a
' Moslem boy of the evil practice of assuming a position
' in which man should address none but his Maker.
' The performance usually takes place once a day on
' first meeting, but meetings are so numerous that at
' least one hour out of the twenty-four must thus be
' spent by a man about town.  Equals kneel, or rather
' squat, before one another, and snap the fingers in the
' peculiarly West African way, which seems to differ in
' every tribe.'

Livingstone[1] 'was particularly struck, in passing
' through the village, with the punctiliousness of man-
' ners shown by the Balonda.  The inferiors, on meet-
' ing their superiors in the streets, at once drop on
' their knees and rub dust on their arms and chest.
' They continue the salutation of clapping the hands
' until the great ones have passed.'

In the religious customs of Tahiti,[2] 'however large
' or costly the sacrifices that had been offered, and
' however near its close the most protracted ceremony
' might be, if the priest omitted or misplaced any word
' in the prayers with which it was always accompanied,
' or if his attention was diverted by any means, so that
' the prayer was hai, or broken, the whole was rendered
' unavailable ; he must prepare other victims and repeat
' his prayers over from the commencement.'

In Feejee[3] 'public business is conducted with tedious
' formality.  Old forms are strictly observed and inno-
' vations opposed.  An abundance of measured clapping

[1] Travels in South Africa, p. 289.
[2] Ellis's Polynesian Researches, vol. ii. p. 157.
[3] Williams' Fiji and the Fijians, vol. i. p. 24.

' of hands and subdued exclamations characterise these
' occasions. Whales' teeth and other property are never
' exchanged or presented without the following or simi-
' lar form: "A! woi! woi! woi!   A! woi! woi! woi!!
' "A tabua levu! woi! woi! A mudua, mudua, mudua!"
' (clapping).' But little consideration is required to
show that this is quite natural. In the absence of
writing, evidence of contracts must depend on the
testimony of witnesses, and it is necessary, therefore, to
avoid all haste which might lead to forgetfulness, and
to imprint the ceremony as much as possible on the
minds of those present.

Among the Romans also, an importance was attached
to formalities and expressions, which seems to us most
excessive. 'Celui,' for instance, says Ortolan, 'qui
' dira vignes (vites) parce qu'il plaide sur des vignes,
' au lieu de dire arbores, terme sacramental de la loi,
' perdra son procès.'[1] Under the Emperors, however,
this strictness was considerably relaxed.[2]

Passing on to the question of property, 'La pre-
' mière loi,' says Goguet,[3] 'qu'on aura établie, aura été
' pour assigner et assurer à chaque habitant une certaine
' quantité de terrain. Dans les tems où le labourage
' n'étoit point encore connu, les terres étoient en com-
' mun. Il n'y avoit ni bornes ni limites qui en réglas-
' sent le partage, chacun prenoit sa subsistance où il
' jugeoit à propos. On abandonnoit, on reprenoit suc-
' cessivement les mêmes cantons, suivant qu'ils étoient
' plus ou moins épuisés: cette manière de vivre n'a plus
' été practicable quand l'agriculture a été introduite.

[1] Ortolan's Justinian, vol. I. p.     [2] Loc. cit., p. 354.
510.                                    [3] Loc. cit.

' Il fallut alors distinguer les possessions et prendre les
' mesures nécessaires pour faire jouir chaque citoyen du
' fruit de ses travaux. Il étoit dans l'ordre que celui
' qui avoit semé du grain fût sûr de le recueillir, et ne
' vit pas les autres profiter des peines et des soins qu'il
' s'étoit donnés. De là sont émanées les loix sur la
' propriété des terres, sur la manière de les partager et
' d'en jouir.'

The same view has been taken by other writers. It
does not, however, appear that property in land implies,
or necessarily arose from, agriculture. On the contrary,
it exists even in hunting communities. Usually, indeed,
during the hunting stage, property in land is tribal, not
individual. The North American Indians seem, as a
general rule, to have had no individual property in
land. It appears, therefore, at first sight, remarkable
that among the Australians,[1] who are in most respects
so much lower in the scale, 'every male has some
' portion of land, of which he can always point out the
' exact boundaries. These properties are subdivided
' by a father among his sons during his own lifetime,
' and descend in almost hereditary succession. A man
' can dispose of or barter his lands to others, but a
' female never inherits, nor has primogeniture among
' the sons any peculiar rights or advantages.' Nay,
more than this, there are some tracts of land, peculiarly
rich in gum, &c., over which, at the period when
the gum is in season, numerous families have an acknowledged right, although they are not allowed to
come there at other times.[2] Even the water of the

---

[1] Eyre, Discoveries in Australia,     Grey's Australia, vol. ii. p. 232.
vol. ii. p. 297. See also Lang in     [2] Grey's Australia, vol. ii. p. 298.

rivers is claimed as property by some of the Australian tribes. 'Trespass for the purpose of hunting' is in Australia regarded as a capital offence, and is, when possible, punished with death.[1]

The explanation seems to be that the Redskins depended mainly on the larger game, while the Australians fed on opossums, reptiles, insects, roots, &c. The Redskin, therefore, if land had been divided into individual allotments, might have been starved in the vicinity of abundance; while the Australian could generally obtain food on his own property.

In Polynesia,[2] where cultivation was carefully attended to, as in Tahiti, 'every portion of land has its 'respective owner; and even the distinct trees on the 'land had sometimes different proprietors, and a tree 'and the land it grew on different owners.'

However, even an agricultural condition does not necessarily require *individual* property in land; in the Russian 'Mirs,' or communal villages, moveable property alone was individual, the land was common.[3]

In New Zealand there were three distinct tenures of land:[4] viz., by the tribe, by the family, and by the individual. The common rights of a tribe were often very extensive, and complicated by intermarriages. The eel cuts, also, are strictly preserved as private property. Children, as soon as they were born, had a right to a share of the family property. Shortland, however, states 'that the head of a family had a recognised 'right to dispose of his property among his male off-

[1] *Loc. cit.*, p. 290.
[2] Ellis's Polynesian Researches, vol. ii. p. 362. Dieffenbach, vol. ii. p. 114.
[3] Faucher, in Systems of Land Tenure, p. 362, *et seq.*
[4] Taylor's New Zealand and its Inhabitants, p. 364.

' spring and kinsmen.' [1] Probably on these points the custom was not the same in all the tribes.

In some cases, land was private property for a portion of the year,[2] and belonged to the community for the remainder. Thus our 'Lammas Lands' were so called, because they were private property until Lammas-day (August 1), by which time the crops were supposed to be gathered in; after which period they were subject to common rights of pasturage till the spring. These meadows were seldom manured, and, as the portions assigned were often exceedingly small, it was difficult to retain the exact boundaries during the joint occupation of the land; it was therefore most convenient to make a fresh partition each year.

In some parts of Russia, 'after the expiration of a ' given, but not in all cases of the same, period, separate ' ownerships are extinguished, the land of the village is ' thrown into a mass, and then it is re-distributed among ' the families composing the community, according to ' their number. This re-partition having been effected, ' the rights of families and of individuals are again ' allowed to branch out into various lines, which they ' continue to follow till another period of division comes ' round.' [3] Communal villages, moreover, are by no means confined to Russia, and Sir H. Maine has recently pointed out[4] the many points of similarity between the village communities which still exist in India with the old Teutonic cultivating villages of Germany and England. That a similar state of things

---

[1] Shortland's Traditions, &c., of the New Zealanders, p. 273.

[2] Nasse, On the Agric. Comm. of the Middle Ages. Pub. by the Cobden Club, 1871.

[3] Maine's Ancient Law, p. 207.

[4] Village Communities in the East and West, 1871.

existed in Ireland is indicated in the Brehon laws, on
which we are also promised a volume by Sir H. Maine,
which will no doubt be a most valuable contribution to
our knowledge of this subject.

It is stated to have been a principle of the earliest
Sclavonian laws that the property of families could not
be divided for a perpetuity. Even now, in parts of
Servia, Croatia, and Austrian Sclavonia, the entire
land is cultivated by the villagers, and the produce is
annually divided.

In Peru, also, the land belonged to the State, and
every year a fresh allotment took place, an additional
portion being granted for every child; the amount
allowed for a son being twice as much as for a daughter.[1]

Diodorus Siculus informs us that the Celtiberians
divided their land annually among individuals, to be
cultivated for the use of the public; and that the product was stored up and distributed from time to time
among the necessitous.[2]

It does not necessarily follow that property in land
involves the power of sale. 'We are too apt,' says
Campbell,[3] ' to forget that property in land, as a trans-
' ferable mercantile commodity absolutely owned and
' passing from hand to hand like any chattel, is not an
' ancient institution, but a modern development, reached
' only in a few very advanced countries.' ' It may be

[1] Wuttke's Gea. der Menschheit, vol. i. p. 326; Prescott, vol. i. p. 44. A somewhat different account is given by Polo de Ondegardo, Rites and Laws of the Incas, p. 102.

[2] Lord Kames' History of Man, vol. i. p. 93.

[3] Systems of Land Tenure, p. 151.

' said,' he adds,' ' of all landed tenures in India pre-
' vious to our rule, that they were practically not trans-
' ferable by sale, and that only certain classes of the
' better defined claims were to some extent transferable
' by mortgage.  The seizure and sale of land for private
' debt was wholly and utterly unknown—such an idea
' had never entered into the native imagination.'

Still less does the possession of land necessarily
imply the power of testamentary disposition, and we
find as a matter of fact that the will is a legal process
of very late origin.

In some cases it seems to be held that the title to
property ceases with the life of the owner.  Thus, on
Vanua Levu, one of the Feejee Islands, a chief's death
' is the signal for plunder, the nearest relations rushing
' to the house to appropriate all they can seize belong-
' ing to those who lived there with the deceased.' [2]

I have already mentioned (*ante*, p. 388) the state of
entire lawlessness which exists in parts of Africa and
in some of the Polynesian Islands between the death
of one ruler and the election of his successor.

It is stated that formerly, when a Greenlander died,
if he had no grown-up children, his property was
regarded as having no longer an owner, and every one
took what he chose, or at least what he could get,
without the slightest regard to the wretched widow or
children.[3]

There is, indeed, no more interesting chapter in Sir
H. Maine's work than that on the early history of testa-

---

[1] Systems of Land Tenure, p.
171.
[2] Fiji and the Fijians, vol. i. p.

187.
[3] Crantz's Hist. of Greenland, vol.
i. p. 162.

mentary succession. He points out that the essence of
a will, as now understood, is—firstly, that it should
take effect at death; secondly, that it may be secret;
and thirdly, that it is revocable. Yet in Roman law
wills acquired these characteristics but slowly and
gradually, and in the earlier stages of civilisation wills
were generally unknown.

In Athens, the power of willing was introduced by
Solon; only, however, in cases when a person died
childless. The barbarians on the north of the Roman
empire were, says Maine,[1] 'confessedly strangers to any
' such conception as that of a Will. The best authori-
' ties agree that there is no trace of it in those parts of
' their written codes which comprise the customs prac-
' tised by them in their original seats, and in their
' subsequent settlement on the edge of the Roman
' Empire.'

And again, in studying the ancient German laws,
' one result has invariably disclosed itself—that the
' ancient nucleus of the code contains no trace of a
' will.'[2]

The Hindoos were also entire strangers to the will.[3]

It is therefore very remarkable that in Australia ' a
' father divides his land during his lifetime, fairly ap-
' portioning it amongst his several sons, and at as early
' an age as fourteen or fifteen they can point out the
' portion which they are eventually to inherit. If the
' males of a family become extinct, the male children
' of the daughters inherit their grandfather's land.'[4]

[1] *Loc. cit.*, p. 172.
[2] *Loc cit.*, p. 106.
[3] Maine's Ancient Law, p. 193.

Campbell in Systems of Land
Tenure, p. 177.
[4] Eyre's Australia, vol. ii. p. 290.

Again, in Tahiti, the system of willing was (I presume when there were no children) in full force,[1] ' not
' only with reference to land, but to any other kind of
' property. Unacquainted with letters, they could not
' leave a written will; but, during a season of illness,
' those possessing property frequently called together
' the members of the family or confidential friends,
' and to them gave directions for the disposal of their
' effects after their decease. This was considered a
' kind of sacred charge, and was usually executed with
' fidelity.'

For the modern will, however, we are mainly indebted to the Romans. At first, indeed, even Roman
wills, if so they may be called, were neither secret,
deferred, nor revocable. On the contrary, they were
made in public, before not less than five witnesses;
they took effect at once, and were irrevocable. Hence
it is probable that they were only made just before death.

It seems likely that the power of willing was confined to those who had no natural heirs; such was certainly the case in Athens. So also in Rome the will
does not seem to have been used as a means of disinheriting, or of effecting an equal distribution of the
property.

Under these circumstances it appears at first sight
remarkable that the Romans should have regarded forfeiture of testamentary privileges as one of the greatest
misfortunes, and should have regarded as a bitter curse
the wish that a man might die intestate. The explanation of this seems to lie in the ideas of family relationship. Children being slaves, and as such incapable of

---

[1] Ellis' Polynesian Researches, vol. ii. p. 362.

holding property,[1] it would naturally be the wish of the father to emancipate his favourite sons; but as soon as this was effected they ceased to belong to the family, and could not consequently inherit as heirs at law. On the death of a Roman citizen, in the absence of a will, the property descended to the unemancipated children, and after them to the nearest grade of the agnatic kindred. Hence the same feeling which induced a Roman to emancipate his sons impelled him also to make a will, for, if he did not, emancipation involved disinheritance.

The turning point in the history of the Roman will appears to have been the period at which the presence of the true heir was dispensed with when the will was made. When this was first sanctioned does not seem to be exactly known, but it was permitted in the time of Gaius, who lived during the reigns of the Antonines; at this period also wills had become revocable,[2] and even in the time of Hadrian a testament was rendered invalid when a 'posthumus suus' arose, i.e. when a child was born after the will was made.[3]

In the absence of wills, the interests of the children were in some cases secured by customs resembling those of the Russian village communities, or 'Mirs,' in which children have a right to their share as soon as they are born. Nor are such rights confined to communal properties. In some countries the children have a vested right to a portion of their father's estate. Here, therefore, in the absence of children, the will is replaced by adoption, the importance attached to which

---

[1] Maine's Ancient Law, p. 180.
[2] Tomkins' and Lemon's Commentaries of Gaius, com. 11, &c.
[3] Loc. cit., com. 11, &c. cxliii.
cxliv.

is, as I have already mentioned, one of the reasons for the inaccuracy of thought among the lower races on the subject of relationship.

Among the Hindoos, 'the instant a son is born' he ' acquires a vested right in his father's property, which ' cannot be sold without recognition of his joint-owner- ' ship. On the son's attaining full age, he can some- ' times compel a partition of the estate, even against ' the consent of the parent; and, should the parent ' acquiesce, one son can always have a partition even ' against the will of the others. On such partition ' taking place, the father has no advantage over his ' children, except that he has two of the shares instead ' of one. The ancient law of the German tribes was ' exceedingly similar. The Allod or domain of the ' family was the joint property of the father and his ' sons.' According to ancient German law, also, children were co-proprietors with their father, and the family endowment could not be parted with except by general consent.

This probably explains the remarkable custom that in many parts of Polynesia the son was considered of higher rank than the father; and that even in some cases—as, for instance, in the Marquesas, and in Tahiti—the king abdicated as soon as a son was born to him ; and landowners under similar circumstances lost the fee-simple of their land, and became mere trustees for the infant possessors.[2]

The Basutos have a strict system of primogeniture,

---

[1] Maine's Ancient Law, p. 228.  Waitz' Anthr. vol. vi. pp. 210, 215,
[2] Ellis' Polynesian Researches,  219.
vol. ii. pp. 340, 347; Oerland

and, even during the father's life, the eldest son has considerable power both over the property and the younger chidren.[1]

The same system, in combination with inheritance through females, is also in full force in Feejee, where it is known as Vasu. The word means a nephew or niece, ' but becomes a title of office in the case of the ' male, who in some localities has the extraordinary ' privilege of appropriating whatever he chooses belong- ' ing to his uncle, or those under his uncle's power.'[2] This is one of the most remarkable parts of Feejee despotism. ' However high a chief may be, if he has ' a nephew he has a master,' and resistance is rarely thought of. Thakonauto, while at war with his uncle, actually supplied himself with ammunition from his enemies' stores.

Perhaps also the curious custom of naming the father after the child may have originated from some such regulation. Thus in Australia,[3] when a man's eldest child is named, the father takes ' the name of the ' child, Kadlitpinna, the father of Kadli; the mother is ' called Kadlingangki, the mother of Kadli, from ' ngangki, a female or woman.' This custom seems very general throughout the continent. Among the Bechuanas of South Africa ' the parents take the name ' of the child.' Mrs. Livingstone's eldest boy being ' named Robert, she was, after his birth, always called ' Ma-Robert,' the mother of Robert.[4] In Madagascar also parents often take the name of their eldest child.[5]

[1] Casalis' Basutos, p. 170.
[2] Fiji and the Fijians, vol. i. p. 34.
[3] Eyre, loc. cit. vol. ii. p. 325.
[4] Livingstone's Travels in South Africa, p. 120.
[5] Sibree's Madagascar and its People, p. 108.

In America we find the same habit.[1] Thus 'with
'the Kutchin the father takes his name from his son or
'daughter, not the son from the father, as with us.
'The father's name is formed by the addition of the
'word "tee" to the end of the son's name; for instance,
'Que-cch-et may have a son and call him Sah-neu.
'The father is now called Sah-neu-tee, and the former
'name of Que-cch-et is forgotten.'

In Sumatra 'the father,'[2] in many parts of the coun-
'try, particularly in Passum-mah, is distinguished by
'the name of his first child, as "Pa-Ladin," or "Pa-
'"Rindu" (Pa for bapa, signifying "the father of"),
'and loses, in this acquired, his own proper name.
'This is a singular custom, and surely less conformable
'to the order of nature than that which names the son
'after the father. There it is not usual to give them a
'galar on their marriage, as with the Rejangs, among
'whom the filio-nymic is not so common, though some-
'times adopted, and occasionally joined with the galar,
'as Radin-pa-Chirano. The women never change the
'name given them at the time of their birth; yet fre-
'quently they are called through courtesy, from their
'eldest child, "Ma si ano," the mother of such an one;
'but rather as a polite description than a name.'

As a general rule property descends to the eldest
son, or is divided between all; but Duhalde mentions
that among the Tartars the youngest son inherits the
property, because the elder ones as they reach manhood
leave the paternal tent, and take with them the quantity

[1] Jones, Smithsonian Report, 1800, p. 326.    [2] Marsden's History of Sumatra, p. 286.

of cattle which their father chooses to give them. Arbousset mentions that, according to Kaffir law, the successor to a chief must be chosen from among the younger sons, the two eldest being ineligible.[1] In Northern Australia, according to Macgillivray,[2] both sexes share alike, but the youngest child receives the largest portion. Dr. Anderson also states that the youngest son inherits among the Shans and Kakhyens of Western Yunan.[3] A similar custom exists among the Mrus of the Arrawak hills,[4] and prevailed even in some districts of our own country, under the name of Borough English.[5]

There are also cases, as, for instance, among the Hindoos, in which the rule of primogeniture is followed as regards office or power politically, but not with reference to property.

The Singphos[6] ' have a peculiar custom. The eldest
' takes the landed estate with the titles, the youngest
' the personalities; the intermediate brethren, when any
' exist, are excluded from all participation, and remain
' in attendance on the chief or head of the family as
' during the lifetime of their father.'

Among the lower races of men the chiefs scarcely take any cognisance of offences, unless they relate to such things as directly concern, or are supposed to concern, the interests of the community generally. As regards private injuries, every one must protect or

[1] Tour to the N.E. of the Cape of Good Hope, p. 140.
[2] Voyage of H.M.S. Rattlesnake, vol. ii. p. 28.
[3] Expedition to Western Yunan, pp. 117, 131.
[4] Lewin's Hill Tracts of Chittagong, p. 104.
[5] Wren Hoskyns in Customs of Land Tenure, p. 104.
[6] Dalton's Des. Ethn. of Bengal, p. 13.

avenge himself. The administration of justice, says Du Tertre,[1] 'among the Caribbians is not exercised by 'the captain, nor by any magistrate; but, as it is among 'the Tapinambous, he who thinks himself injured gets 'such satisfaction of his adversary as he thinks fit, 'according as his passion dictates to him or his strength 'permits him. The public does not concern itself at all 'in the punishment of criminals ; and if any one among 'them suffers an injury or affront, without endeavour-'ing to revenge himself, he is slighted by all the rest 'and accounted a coward and a person of no esteem.'

In Ancient Greece there were no officers whose duty it was to prosecute criminals.[2] Even in the case of murder, the State did not take the initiative ; this was left to the family of the sufferer, nor was the accused placed under arrest until he was found guilty. Hence the criminal usually fled as soon as he found himself likely to be condemned.

Among the North American Indians,[3] if a man was murdered, 'the family of the deceased only have the 'right of taking satisfaction ; they collect, consult, and 'decree. The rulers of a town or of the nation have 'nothing to do or say in the business.' Indeed, it would seem that the object of legal regulations was at first not so much to punish the offender as to restrain and mitigate the vengeance inflicted by the aggrieved party.

The amount of legal revenge, if I may so call it, is

[1] History of the Caribby Islands, p. 310. Labat also makes a very similar statement, Voyage aux Isles de Amérique, vol. ii. p. 83. Azara, Voy. dans l'Amér. Mér. vol. ii. p. 16.

[2] Goguet, vol. ii. p. 60.

[3] Trans. Amer. Antiq. Soc. vol. i. p. 281.

often strictly regulated, even where we should least
expect to find such limitations. Thus, in Western Australia,[1] crimes 'may be compounded by the criminal
'appearing and committing himself to the ordeal of
'having spears thrown at him by all such persons as
'conceive themselves to have been aggrieved, or by
'permitting spears to be thrust through certain parts
'of his body; such as through the thigh, or the calf of
'the leg, or under the arm. The part which is to be
'pierced by a spear is fixed for all common crimes, and
'a native who has incurred this penalty sometimes
'quietly holds out his leg for the injured party to
'thrust his spear through.' So strictly is the amount
of punishment limited that if, in inflicting such spear
wounds, a man, either through carelessness or from any
other cause, exceeded the recognised limits—if, for
instance, he wounded the femoral artery—he would
in his turn become liable to punishment. This custom
does not appear to exist in South Australia, but it also
occurs in New South Wales.[2]

Such cases as these seem to me to throw great light
on the origin of the idea of property. Possession de
facto needs, of course, no explanation. When, however,
any rules were laid down regulating the amount or
mode of vengeance which might be taken in revenge for
disturbance ; or when the chief thought it worth while
himself to settle disputes about possession, and thus,
while increasing his own dignity, to check quarrels
which might be injurious to the general interests of the

---

[1] Sir G. Grey's Australia, vol. ii.
p. 243.

[2] Eyre's Exp. into Central Australia, vol. ii. p. 380.

tribe, the natural effect would be to develop the idea of mere possession into that of property.

Since, then, crimes were at first regarded merely as personal matters, in which the aggressor and the victim alone were interested, and with which society was not concerned, any crime, even murder, might be atoned for by the payment of such a sum of money as satisfied the representatives of the murdered man. This payment was proportioned to the injury done, and had no relation to the crime as a crime. Hence, as the injury was the same whether the death was accidental or designed, so also was the penalty. Hence our word 'pay,' which comes from the Latin 'pacare,' to appease or pacify.

Among the Kaffirs,[1] 'the law makes no distinc- 'tion between a murder from malice or forethought, 'or from one committed on the impulse of the 'moment or in revenge for the blood of a relative. 'A man is punished for taking the law into his own 'hands, and in no case is he justified in doing so, even 'in a case of retaliation.' On the other hand, 'the law ': does not appear to demand compensation for what is ': clearly proved to be a purely accidental injury to 'property, although it will do so in accidental injuries 'to the *persons* of individuals if the injury is of a 'serious nature, as the latter would come under the 'head of criminal cases, and therefore could only be 'overlooked or the fine remitted by the chief himself.'[2]

The Romans, on the contrary, based any claim for compensation on the existence of a 'culpa;' and hence

---

[1] Kaffir Laws and Customs, p. 110. See also p. 99.     [2] *Ibid.* p. 97. See also p. 113.

laid down that where there had been no 'culpa,' no
action for reparation could lie. This led to very inconvenient consequences. Thus, as Lord Kames[1] has
pointed out, 'Labeo scribit, si cum vi ventorum navis
'impulsa esset in funes anchorarum alterius, et nautæ
'funes præcidissent ; si, nullo alio modo, nisi præcisis
'funibus, explicare se potuit, nullam actionem dandam;'
b. 29, § 3, *ad leg. Aquil.* 'Quod dicitur damnum in-
'juria datum Aquilia persequi sic erit accipiendum, ut
'videatur damnum injuria datum quod cum damno
'injuriam attulerit; nisi magna vi cogente, fuerit fac-
'tum. Ut Celsus scribit circa eum, qui incendii arcendi
'gratia vicinas ædes intercidit: et sive pervenit ignis,
'sive antea extinctus est, extimat legis Aquiliæ actionem
'cessare.' b. 49, § 1, eod. In English thus : In the
opinion of Labeo, if a ship is driven by the violence of
a tempest among the anchor-ropes of another ship and
the sailors cut the ropes, having no other means of
getting free, there is no action competent. The Aquilian law must be understood to apply only to such
damage as carries the idea of an injury along with it,
unless such injury has not been wilfully done, but from
necessity. 'Thus Celsus puts the case of a person who,
'to stop the progress of a fire, pulls down his neigh-
'bour's house ; and whether the fire had reached that
'house which is pulled down, or was extinguished
'before it got to it, in neither case, he thinks, will an
'action be competent from the Aquilian law.'

It would, however, appear that, even in Roman law,
the opposite and more usual principle originally prevailed. This is indicated, for instance, by the great

[1] History of Man, vol. iv. p. 34.

difference in the penalties imposed by ancient laws on offenders caught in the act, and those only detected after considerable delay.    In the old Roman law, as in that of some other countries, thieves were divided into manifest and non-manifest.    The manifest thief who was caught in the act, or at any rate with the stolen goods still in his possession, became, according to the law of the twelve tables, the slave of the person robbed, or, if he was already a slave, was put to death. The non-manifest thief, on the other hand, was only liable to return double the value of the goods he had stolen.    Subsequently, the very severe punishment in the case of the manifest thief was mitigated, but he was still forced to pay four times the value of what he had stolen, or twice as much as the non-manifest thief.

The same principle was followed by the North American Indians.[1]    Again, in the German and Anglo-Saxon codes, a thief caught in the act might be killed on the spot.    Thus the law followed the old principles of private vengeance, and in settling the amount of punishment took as a guide the measure of revenge likely to be taken by an aggrieved person under the circumstances of the case.[2]

In the South Sea Islands, according to Williams,[3] cases of theft were seldom brought before the king or chiefs, but the people avenged their own injuries.    The rights of retaliation, however, had almost a legal force, for 'although the party thus plundered them, they ' would not attempt to prevent the seizure: had they

---

[1] Trans. Amer. Antiq. Soc. vol. i. p. 285.

[2] See Maine, loc. cit. p. 378.

[3] Polynesian Researches, vol. ii. p. 300, 372.

'done so, the population of the district would    no
'assisted those who, according to the established on-
'tom, were thus punishing the aggressors.   Such has
'the usual method resorted to for punishing the pevis
'thefts committed among themselves.'

So also as regards personal injuries.   Among the
Anglo-Saxons the 'wergild,' or fine for injuries, was
evidently a substitute for personal vengeance.   Every
part of the body had a recognised value, even the teeth,
nails, and hair.   Nay, the value assigned to the latter
was proportionately very high ; the loss of the beard
being estimated at twenty shillings, while the breaking
of a thigh was only fixed at twelve.   In other cases
also the effect on personal appearance seems to have
carried great weight, for the loss of a front tooth was
estimated at six shillings, while the fracture of a rib
was only fixed at three.   In the case of a slave, the
fine was paid to the owner.

The amount varied according to the rank of the
person injured.   All society below the royal family and
the Ealdorman was divided into three classes ;   the
Tywhind man, or Ceorl, was estimated at 200 shillings
according to the laws of Mercia; the Sixhind man at
600 shillings, while the death of a royal thane was
estimated at 1,200 shillings.[1]

In Ireland a composition or fine was admitted for
murder 'instead of capital punishment; and this was
'divided, as in other countries, between the kindred of
'the slain and the judge,'[2] down to a comparatively
late period.

---

[1] Hume, p. 74.  Hallam, Cons.        [2] Hallam, loc. cit. vol. iii. pp. 341,
Hist. of England, vol. i. p. 272.            357.

Among the Hill tribes of North Aracan, 'all offences
'or injuries are remedied by fine,' the amount of which
is fixed by long custom, and always rigorously demanded.[1]

Among the Kirghiz the family of a murdered man
are at liberty to compound with the murderer for a certain payment in horses, &c.  A woman or a child
count for half as much as a man.  There is also a
scale of compensation for injuries; 100 sheep for a
thumb, 20 for a little finger, and so on.[2]

So also among the Kaffirs,[3] 'as banishment, im-
'prisonment, and corporal punishment are all unknown
'in Kaffir jurisprudence, the property of the people
'constitutes the great fund out of which the debts of
'justice are paid.'  The fines, however, thus levied,
were paid to the chief.[4]  The principle is, that a
man's goods are his own property, but his person is the
property of the chief.  A man who is injured therefore, however severely, derives no benefit from the fine.
Their proverb is, 'No man can eat his own blood.'

The severity of early codes, and the uniformity in
the amounts of punishment which characterises them,
is probably due to the same cause.  An individual who
felt himself aggrieved would not weigh very philoso-
phically the amount of punishment which he was
entitled to inflict; and no doubt when in any community some chief, in advance of his time, endeavoured
to substitute public law for private vengeance, his
object would be to induce those who had cause of com-

[1] St. John, Journ. Anthrop. Institute, 1872, p. 240.
[2] Des. de toutes les Nat. de
l'Emp. de Russe, Tt. I. p. 148.
[3] Kaffir Laws and Customs, p.
38.
[4] Ibid. p. 35.

plaint to apply to the law for redress, rather than to
avenge themselves; which of course would not be the
case if the penalty allotted by the law was much less
than that which custom would allow them to inflict for
themselves.

Subsequently, when punishment was substituted for
pecuniary compensation, the same rule was at first
applied, and the distinction of intention was overlooked.
Nay, so long had the importance of intention been
disregarded, that although it is now recognised in our
criminal courts, yet, as Mr. Bain points out,[1] 'a moral
' stigma is still attached to intellectual error by many
' people, and even by men of cultivation.'

In this, as in so many of our other ideas and tastes,
we are still influenced by the condition of our ancestors
in bygone ages.  What that condition was I have in
this work attempted to indicate, believing as I do that
the earlier mental stages through which the human race
has passed are illustrated by the condition of existing,
or recent, savages.  The history of the human race has,
I feel satisfied, on the whole been one of progress.  I
do not of course mean to say that every race is necessarily advancing: on the contrary, most of the lower
ones are almost stationary ; and there are, no doubt,
cases in which nations have fallen back; but it seems
an almost invariable rule that such races are dying out,
while those which are stationary in condition are stationary in numbers also; on the other hand, improving
nations increase in numbers, so that they always en-
croach on less progressive races.

In conclusion, then, while I do not mean for a mo-

[1] *Mental and Moral Science*, p. 718.

ment to deny that there are cases in which nations have retrograded, I regard these as exceptional instances. The facts and arguments mentioned in this work afford, I think, strong grounds for the following conclusions, namely:—

That existing savages are not the descendants of civilised ancestors.

That the primitive condition of man was one of utter barbarism.

That from this condition several races have independently raised themselves.

These views follow, I think, from strictly scientific considerations. We shall not be the less inclined to adopt them on account of the cheering prospects which they hold out for the future.

In the closing chapter of 'Prehistoric Times,' while fully admitting the charms of savage life, I have endeavoured to point out the immense advantages which we enjoy. Here I will only add that if the past history of man has been one of deterioration, we have but a groundless expectation of future improvement: on the other hand, if the past has been one of progress, we may fairly hope that the future will be so too; that the blessings of civilisation will not only be extended to other countries and to other nations, but that even in our own land they will be rendered more general and more equable ; so that we shall not see before us always, as now, countrymen of our own living, in our very midst, a life worse than that of a savage ; neither enjoying the rough advantages and real, though rude, pleasures of savage life, nor yet availing themselves of the far higher and more noble opportunities which lie within the reach of civilised Man.

# APPENDIX.

## ON THE PRIMITIVE CONDITION OF MAN.

### PART I.

BEING THE SUBSTANCE OF A PAPER READ BEFORE THE BRITISH
ASSOCIATION AT DUNDEE.

SIDE by side with the different opinions as to the origin of
man, there are two opposite views with reference to the
primitive condition of the first men, or first beings worthy to
be so called. Many writers have considered that man was at
first a mere savage, and that the course of history has on the
whole been a progress towards civilisation; though at times —
and at some times for centuries — some races have been
stationary, or even have retrograded. Other authors, of no
less eminence, have taken a diametrically opposite view. According to them, man was, from the commencement, pretty
much what he is at present; if possible, even more ignorant
of the arts and sciences than now, but with mental qualities
not inferior to our own. Savages they consider to be the degenerate descendants of far superior ancestors. Of the recent
supporters of this theory, the late Archbishop of Dublin was
amongst the most eminent.

Dr. Whately enunciates his opinions in the following
words:[1]—

'We have no reason to believe that any community ever
'did or ever can emerge, unassisted by external helps, from a
'state of utter barbarism unto anything that can be called

[1] Whately's Political Economy, p. 68.

H H

' civilisation.' ' Man has not emerged from the savage state ;
' the progress of any community in civilisation, by its own in-
' ternal means, must always have begun from a condition re-
' moved from that of complete barbarism, out of which it does
' not appear that men ever did or can raise themselves.'

Thus, he adds, ' the ancient Germans, who cultivated corn
' — though their agriculture was probably in a very rude
' state—who not only had numerous herds of cattle, but
' employed the labour of brutes, and even made use of cavalry
' in their wars . . . these cannot with propriety be reckoned
' savages ; or if they are to be so called (for it is not worth
' while to dispute about a word), then I would admit that, in
' this sense, men may advance, and in fact have advanced, by
' their own unassisted efforts, from the savage to the civilised
' state.'  This limitation of the term ' savage ' to the very
lowest representatives of the human race no doubt renders Dr.
Whately's theory more tenable by increasing the difficulty of
bringing forward conclusive evidence against it.   The Archbishop, indeed, expresses himself throughout his argument as
if it would be easy to produce the required evidence in opposition to his theory, supposing that any race of savages ever had
raised themselves to a state of civilisation.   The manner,
however, in which he has treated the case of the Mandans—a
tribe of North American Indians—effectually disposes of this
hypothesis.  This unfortunate people is described as having
been decidedly more civilised than those by which they were
surrounded.   Having, then, no neighbours more advanced than
themselves, they were quoted as furnishing an instance of
savages who had civilised themselves without external aid.   In
answer to this, Archbishop Whately asks—

' 1st.  How do we know that these Mandans were of the same
' race as their neighbours ? '

' 2ndly.  How do we know that theirs is not the original level
' from which the other tribes have fallen ? '

' 3rdly and lastly.  Supposing that the Mandans did emerge
' from the savage state, how do we know that this may not
' have been through the aid of some strangers coming among
' them—like the Manco-Capac of Peru—from some more civi-
' lised country, perhaps long before the days of Columbus ? '

Supposing, however, for a moment, and for the sake of argument, that the Mandans, or any other race, were originally savages, and had civilised themselves, it would still be manifestly—from the very nature of the case—impossible to bring forward the kind of evidence demanded by Dr. Whately. No doubt he ' may confidently affirm that we find no one *recorded* ' instance of a tribe of savages, properly so styled, rising into ' a civilised state without instruction and assistance from a ' people already civilised.' Starting with the proviso that savages, properly so styled, are ignorant of letters, and laying it down as a condition that no civilised example should be placed before them, the existence of any such record is an impossibility: its very presence would destroy its value. In another passage, Archbishop Whately says, indeed, ' If man ' generally, or some particular race, be capable of self-civilisa- ' tion, in either case it may be expected that some record, or ' tradition, or monument of the actual occurrence of such an ' event should be found.' So far from this, the existence of any such record would, according to the very hypothesis itself, be impossible. Traditions are short-lived and untrustworthy. A ' monument ' which could prove the actual occurrence of a race capable of self-civilisation I confess myself unable to conceive. What kind of a monument would the Archbishop accept as proving that the people by whom it was made had been originally savage? that they had raised themselves, and had never been influenced by strangers of a superior race?

But, says Archbishop Whately, ' We have accounts of ' various savage tribes, in different parts of the globe, who ' have been visited from time to time at considerable intervals, ' but have had no settled intercourse with civilised people, and ' who appear to continue, as far as can be ascertained, in the ' same uncultivated condition ; ' and he adduces one case, that of the New Zealanders, who ' seem to have been in quite as ' advanced a state when Tasman discovered the country in ' 1642 as they were when Cook visited it one hundred and ' twenty-seven years after.' We have been accustomed to see around us an improvement so rapid that we forget how short a period a century is in the history of the human race. Even taking the ordinary chronology, it is evident, that if in 6,000

years a given race has only progressed from a state of utter
savagery to the condition of the Australian, we could not
expect to find much change in one more century.  Many a
fishing village, even on our own coast, is in very nearly the
same condition as it was one hundred and twenty-seven years
ago.  Moreover, I might fairly answer that, according to
Whately's own definition of a savage state, the New Zealanders
would certainly be excluded.  They cultivated the ground,
they had domestic animals, they constructed elaborate fortifi-
cations and made excellent canoes, and were certainly not in a
state of utter barbarism.  Or I might argue that a short visit,
like that of Tasman, could give little insight into the true
condition of a people.  I am, however, the less disposed to
question the statement made by Archbishop Whately, because
the fact that many races are now practically stationary is, in
reality, an argument against the theory of degradation, and
not against that of progress.  Civilised races are, I believe,
the descendants of ancestors who were once in a state of barbarism.  On the contrary, argue our opponents, savages are
the descendants of civilised nations, and have sunk to their
present condition.  But Archbishop Whately admits that the
civilised races are still rising, while the savages are stationary ;
and, oddly enough, seems to regard this as an argument in
support of the very untenable proposition, that the difference
between the two is due, not to the progress of the one set of
races—a progress which everyone admits—but to the degradation of those whom he himself maintains to be stationary.
The delusion is natural, and like that which everyone must
have sometimes experienced in looking out of a train in
motion, when the woods and fields seem to be flying from us,
whereas we know that in reality we are moving and they are
stationary.

But it is argued, ' If man, when first created, was left, like
' the brutes, to the unaided exercise of those natural powers of
' body and mind which are common to the European and to
' the New Hollander, how comes it that the European is not
' now in the condition of the New Hollander?'  The answer
to this is, I think, the following :—In the first place, Australia
possesses neither cereals nor any animals which can be domes-

ticated with advantage; and in the second, we find even in the
same family—among children of the same parents—the most
opposite dispositions; in the same nation there are families of
high character, and others in which every member is more or
less criminal. But in this case, as in the last, the Archbishop's
argument, if good at all, is good against his own view. It is
like an Australian boomerang, which recoils upon its owner.
The Archbishop believed in the unity of the human race, and
argued that man was originally civilised (in a certain sense).
'How comes it, then,' I might ask him, 'that the New
'Hollander is not now in the condition of the European?' In
another passage, Archbishop Whately quotes, with approbation, a passage from President Smith, of the College of New
Jersey, who says that man, 'cast out an orphan of nature,
'naked and helpless, into the savage forest, must have perished
'before he could have learned how to supply his most imme-
'diate and urgent wants. Supposing him to have been created,
'or to have started into being one knows not how, in the full
'strength of his bodily powers, how long must it have been
'before he could have known the proper use of his limbs, or
'how to apply them to climb the tree!' &c. &c. Exactly the
same, however, might be said of the gorilla or the chimpanzee,
which certainly are not the degraded descendants of civilised
ancestors.

Having thus very briefly considered the arguments brought
forward by Archbishop Whately, I will proceed to state, also
very briefly, some facts which, I think, support the view here
advocated.

Firstly, I will endeavour to show that there are indications
of progress even among savages.

Secondly, that among the most civilised nations there are
traces of original barbarism.

The Archbishop supposes that men were, from the beginning,
herdsmen and cultivators. We know, however, that the
Australians, North and South Americans, and several other
more or less savage races, living in countries eminently suited
to our domestic animals and to the cultivation of cereals, were
yet entirely ignorant both of the one and the other. It is, I
think, improbable that any race of men who had once been

agriculturists and herdsmen should entirely abandon pursuits so easy and advantageous; and it is still more unlikely that, if we accept Usher's very limited chronology, all tradition of such a change should be lost. Moreover, even if in the course of time the descendants of the present colonists in (say) America or Australia were to fall into such a state of barbarism, still herds of wild cattle, descended from those imported, would probably continue to live in those countries; and even if these were exterminated, their skeletons would testify to their previous existence; whereas, we know that not a single bone of the ox or of the domestic sheep has been found either in Australia or in America. The same argument applies to the horse, since the fossil of South America did not belong to the same species as our domestic race. So, again, in the case of plants. We do not know that any of our cultivated cereals would survive in a wild state, though it is highly probable that, perhaps in a modified form, they would do so. But there are many other plants which follow in the train of man, and by which the botany of South America, Australia, and New Zealand has been almost as profoundly modified as their ethnology has been by the arrival of the white man. The Maoris have a melancholy proverb, that the Maoris disappear before the white man, just as the white man's rat destroys the native rat, the European fly drives away the native fly, and the clover kills the New Zealand fern.

A very interesting paper on this subject, by Dr. Hooker, whose authority no one will question, is contained in the 'Natural History Review' for 1864:—' In Australia and New 'Zealand,' he says, 'for instance, the noisy train of English 'emigration is not more surely doing its work than the stealthy 'tide of English weeds, which are creeping over the surface of 'the waste, cultivated, and virgin soil, in annually increasing 'numbers of genera, species, and individuals. Apropos of 'this subject, a correspondent, W. T. Locke Travers, Esq., 'F.L.S., a most active New Zealand botanist, writing from 'Canterbury, says, " You would be surprised at the rapid '" spread of European and foreign plants in this country. All '" along the sides of the main lines of road through the plains, '" a *Polygonum* (*aviculare*), called cow-grass, grows most

‘ " luxuriantly, the roots sometimes two feet in depth, and the
‘ " plants spreading over an area from four to five feet in
‘ " diameter.   The dock (*Rumex obtusifolius* or *R. crispus*) is
‘ " to be found in every river-bed, extending into the valleys
‘ " of the mountain-rivers, until these become mere torrents.
‘ " The sow-thistle is spread all over the country, growing
‘ " luxuriantly nearly up to 6,000 feet.   The watercress in-
‘ " creases in our still rivers to such an extent as to threaten
‘ " to choke them altogether." '   The cardoon of the Argentine
Republics is another remarkable instance of the same fact.
We may therefore safely assume that if Australia, New
Zealand, or South America had ever been peopled by a race of
herdsmen and agriculturists, the fauna and flora of those
countries would almost inevitably have given evidence of the
fact, and differed much from the condition in which they were
discovered.

We may also assert, as a general proposition, that no
weapons or implements of metal have ever been found in
any country inhabited by savages wholly ignorant of metallurgy.   A still stronger case is afforded by pottery.   Pottery
is very indestructible ; when used at all, it is always abundant,
and it possesses two qualities—those, namely, of being easy to
break and yet difficult to destroy, which render it very valuable
in an archæological point of view.   Moreover it is, in most
cases, associated with burials.   It is therefore a very significant fact, that no fragment of pottery has ever been found in
Australia, New Zealand, or the Polynesian Islands.   It seems
to me extremely improbable that an art so easy and so useful
should ever have been lost by any race of men.   Moreover,
this argument applies to several other arts and instruments.   I
will mention only two, though several others might be brought
forward.   The art of spinning and the use of the bow are
quite unknown to many races of savages, and yet would
hardly be likely to have been abandoned, when once known.
The absence of architectural remains in these countries is
another argument.   Archbishop Whately, indeed, claims this
as being in his favour ; but the absence of monuments in a
country is surely indicative of barbarism, and not of civilisation.

The mental condition of savages also seems to me to speak

strongly against the 'degrading' theory. Not only do the religions of the lower races appear to be indigenous, but, as already shown[1]—according to many trustworthy witnesses, merchants, philosophers, naval men, and missionaries alike—there are many races of men who are altogether destitute of a religion. The cases are, perhaps, less numerous than they are asserted to be; but some of them rest on good evidence. Yet I feel it difficult to believe that any people who once possessed any belief which can fairly be called a religion would ever entirely lose it. Religion appeals so strongly to the hopes and fears of men, it takes so deep a hold on most minds, in its higher forms it is so great a consolation in times of sorrow and sickness, that I can hardly think any nation would ever abandon it altogether. Moreover, it produces a race of men who are interested in maintaining its influence and authority. If, therefore, we find a race which is now practically without religion, I cannot but assume that it has always been so.

The character of the religious belief of savage races, as I have elsewhere[2] attempted to show, points strongly to the same conclusion. I am glad to find that so acute a reasoner as Mr. Bagehot is satisfied by the evidence which has been brought forward on this point. 'Clearly,' he says,[3] 'if all 'early men unanimously, or even much the greater number 'of early men, had a religion *without* omens, no religion, or 'scarcely a religion anywhere in the world, could have come 'into existence *with* omens.'

It seems also impossible to understand how races which have retained the idea of a heaven should have lost that of a hell, supposing they had ever possessed one.

I will now proceed to mention a few cases in which some improvement does appear to have taken place, though, as a general rule, it may be observed that the contact of two races tends to depress rather than to raise the lower one. According to Macgillivray, the Australians of Port Essington, who, like all their fellow-countrymen, had formerly bark-canoes only, have now completely abandoned them for others hollowed out of the trunk of a tree, which they buy from the Malays,

---

The inhabitants of the Andaman Islands have recently introduced outriggers. The Bachapins, when visited by Burchell, had just commenced working iron. According to Burton, the Wajiji negroes have recently learned to make brass. In Tahiti, when visited by Captain Cook, the largest morai, or burial-place, was that erected for the then reigning queen. The Tahitians, also, had then very recently abandoned the habit of cannibalism.

The natives of Celebes, whose bamboo houses are very liable to be blown down, have discovered that if they fix some crooked timbers in the sides of the house it is less likely to fall. Accordingly they chop 'the crookedest they can find, but they 'do not know the rationale of the contrivance, and have not 'hit on the idea that straight poles fixed slanting would have 'the same effect in making the structure rigid.'[1]

Sha-gwaw-koo-sink, an Ottawwaw, who lived at the beginning of this century, first introduced the cultivation of corn among the Ojibbeways.[2] Moreover, there are certain facts which speak for themselves. Some of the American races cultivated the potato. Now, the potato is an American plant, and we have here, therefore, clear evidence of a step in advance made by these tribes. Again, the Peruvians had domesticated the llama. Those who believe in the diversity of species of men may argue that the Peruvians had domestic llamas from the beginning. Archbishop Whately, however, would not take this line. He would, I am sure, admit that the first settlers in Peru had no llamas, nor, indeed, any other domestic animal, excepting, probably, the dog. The bark-cloth of the Polynesians is another case in point. Another very strong case is the boomerang of the Australians. This weapon is known to no other race of men.[3] We cannot look on it as a relic of primeval civilisation, or it would not now be confined to one race only. The Australians cannot have learnt it from any civilised visitors, for the same reason. It is, therefore, as it seems to me, exactly the case we want, and a clear proof of

[1] Wallace's Malay Archipelago, quoted in Tylor's Primitive Culture, vol. i. p. 66.

[2] Tanner's Narrative, p. 180.

[3] With one doubtful exception. The ancient Egyptians used a curved stick to throw at birds, 'but in no instance 'had it the round shape and flight of the 'Australian boomerang.' Wilkinson's Ancient Egyptians, vol. i. p. 235.

a step in advance—a small one, indeed, but still a step made
by a people whom Archbishop Whately would certainly admit
to be true savages. The Cherokees afford a remarkable instance
of progress, and indeed—alone among the North American
hunting races—have really become agriculturists. As long ago
as 1825, with a population of 14,000, they possessed 2,923
ploughs, 7,683 horses, 22,500 black cattle, 46,700 pigs, and
2,566 sheep. They had 49 mills, 69 blacksmiths' shops, 762
looms, and 2,486 spinning-wheels. They kept slaves, having
captured several hundred negroes in Carolina. Nay,
one of them, a man of the name of Sequoyah, invented a
system of letters which, as far as the Cherokee language is
concerned, is better than ours. Cherokee contains twelve consonants and five vowels, with a nasal sound ' ung.' Thus, com-
bining each of the twelve consonants with each of the six vowels,
and adding the vowels which occur singly, but omitting any
sign for ' mung,' as that sound does not occur in Cherokee, he
required seventy-seven characters, to which he added eight—
representing the sounds s, ka, hna, nah, ta, te, ti, tla—making,
altogether, eighty-five characters. The alphabet, as already
mentioned, is superior to ours. The characters are indeed
more numerous, but, when once learnt, the pupil can read at
once. It is said that a boy can learn to read Cherokee, when
thus expressed, in a few weeks ; while, if ordinary letters were
used, two years would be required. Obviously, however, this
alphabet is not applicable to other languages.

The rude substitutes for writing found among other tribes
—the wampum of the North American Indians, the picture-
writing and quippu of Central America—must also be regarded
as of native origin. In the case of the system of letters
invented by Mohammed Doalu, a negro of the Vei country,
in West Africa, the idea was no doubt borrowed from the
missionaries, although it was worked out independently. In
other cases, however, I think this cannot be. Take that
of the Mexicans. Even if we suppose that they were descended from a primitively civilised race, and had gradually
and completely lost both the use and tradition of letters
—to my mind, a most improbable hypothesis—still we must
look on their system of picture-writing as being of American

origin. Even if a system of writing by letters could ever
be altogether lost, which I doubt, it certainly would not
be abandoned for that of picture-writing, which is inferior
in every point of view. If the Mexicans had owed their
civilisation, not to their own gradual improvement, but to the
influence of some European visitors, driven by stress of weather
or the pursuit of adventure on to their coasts, we should have
found in their system of writing, and in other respects, unmistakable proofs of such an influence. Although, therefore, we
have no historical proof that the civilisation of America was
indigenous, we have in its very character evidence more satisfactory perhaps than any historical statements would be. The
same argument may be derived from the names used for numbers by savages. I feel great difficulty in supposing that any
race which had learned to count up to ten would ever unlearn
a piece of knowledge so easy and yet so useful. Yet, as has
already been pointed out, few, perhaps none, of those whom
Archbishop Whately would call savages can count so far.

In many cases, where the system of numeration is at present
somewhat more advanced, it bears on it the stamp of native
and recent origin. Among civilised nations the derivations
of the numerals have long since been obscured by the gradual
modification which time effects in all words—especially those
in frequent use, and before the invention of printing. And if
the numerals of savages were relics of a former civilisation, the
waifs and strays saved out of the general wreck, they would
certainly have suffered so much from the wear and tear of
constant use, and their derivations would be obscured or wholly
undiscoverable, instead of which they are often perfectly clear
and obvious, especially among races whose arithmetical attainments are lowest. These numerals, then, are recent, because
they are uncorrupted; and they are indigenous, because they
have an evident meaning in the language of the tribes by whom
they are used.[1]

Again, as I have already pointed out,[2] many savage languages
are entirely deficient in such words as 'colour,' 'tone,' 'tree,'
&c., having names for each kind of colour, every species of

[1] See Chapter IX. This argument would be conclusive were it not that new words are coined from time to time in all languages.   [2] Ch. IX.

tree, but not for the general idea. I can hardly imagine a nation losing such words if it had once possessed them.

Other similar evidence might be extracted from the language of savages; and arguments of this nature are entitled to more weight than statements of travellers, as to the objects found in use among savages. Suppose, for instance, that an early traveller mentioned the absence of some art or knowledge among a race visited by him, and that later ones found the natives in possession of it. Most people would hesitate to receive this as a clear evidence of progress, and rather be disposed to suspect that later travellers, with perhaps better opportunities, had seen what their predecessors had overlooked. This is no hypothetical case. The early Spanish writers assert that the inhabitants of the Ladrone Islands were ignorant of the use of fire. Later travellers, on the contrary, find them perfectly well acquainted with it. They have, therefore, almost unanimously assumed, not that the natives had made a step in advance, but that the Spaniards had made a mistake; and I have not brought this case forward in opposition to the assertions of Whately, because I am inclined to be of this opinion myself. I refer to it here, however, as showing how difficult it would be to obtain satisfactory evidence of material progress among savages, even admitting that such exists. The arguments derived from language, however, are liable to no such suspicions, but tell their own tale, and leave us at liberty to draw our own conclusions.

I will now very briefly refer to certain considerations which seem to show that even the most civilised races were once in a state of barbarism. Not only throughout Europe—not only in Italy and Greece—but even in the so-called cradle of civilisation itself, in Palestine and Syria, in Egypt and in India, the traces of a stone age have been discovered. It may indeed be said that these were only the fragments of those stone knives, &c., which we know were used in religious ceremonies long after metal was in general use for secular purposes. This, indeed, resembles the attempt to account for the presence of elephants' bones in England by supposing that they were the remains of elephants which might have been brought over by the Romans. But why were stone knives used by the Egyptian and Jewish priests? evidently because they had been at one time in general use, and a feeling of respect made the priest reluctant to introduce a new substance into religious ceremonies.

There are, moreover, other considerations; for instance, the gradual improvement in the relation between the sexes, and the development of correct ideas on the subject of relationship, seem to me strongly to point to the same conclusion.

In the publications of the Nova Scotian 'Institute of Na-' tural Science' is an interesting paper, by Mr. Haliburton, on ' The Unity of the Human Race, proved by the universality ' of certain superstitions connected with sneezing.' 'Once ' establish,' he says, ' that a large number of arbitrary customs ' —such as could not have naturally suggested themselves to ' all men at all times—are universally observed, and we arrive ' at the conclusion that they are primitive customs which have ' been inherited from a common source, and, if inherited, that ' they owe their origin to an era anterior to the dispersion of ' the human race.' To justify such a conclusion, the custom must be demonstrably arbitrary. The belief that two and two make four, the decimal system of numeration, and similar coincidences of course prove nothing; but I very much doubt the existence of any universal, or even general, custom of a clearly arbitrary character. The fact is, that many things appear to us arbitrary and strange because we live in a condition so different from that in which they originated. Many things seem natural to a savage which to us appear absurd and unaccountable.

Mr. Haliburton brings forward, as his strongest case, the habit of saying ' God bless you!' or some equivalent expression, when a person sneezes. He shows that this custom, which, I admit, appears to us at first sight both odd and arbitrary, is ancient and widely extended. It is mentioned by Homer, Aristotle, Apuleius, Pliny, and the Jewish rabbis, and has been observed among the Negroes and Kaffirs; in Koordistan, in Florida, in Otaheite, in New Zealand, and the Tonga Islands.

It is not arbitrary, however, and it does not, therefore, come under his rule. A belief in invisible beings is very general among savages; and while they think it unnecessary to account for blessings, they attribute any misfortune to the ill-will of these mysterious beings. Many savages regard disease as a case of possession. In cases of illness they do not suppose that the organs are themselves affected, but that they are being devoured by a god; hence their medicine-men do not try to cure the disease, but to extract the demon. Some tribes have a distinct deity for every ailment. The Australians do not believe in natural death. When a man dies, they take it for granted that he has been destroyed by witchcraft, and the only doubt is, who is the culprit? Now, a people in this state of mind—and we know that almost every race of men is passing, or has passed, through this stage of development—seeing a man sneeze, would naturally, and almost inevitably, suppose that he was attacked and shaken by some invisible being; equally natural is the impulse to appeal for aid to some other invisible being more powerful than the first.

Mr. Haliburton admits that a sneeze is 'an omen of impending 'evil;' but it is more—it is evidence, which to the savage mind would seem conclusive, that the sneezer was possessed by some evil-disposed spirit; evidently, therefore, this case, on which Mr. Haliburton so much relies, is by no means an 'arbitrary 'custom,' and does not, therefore, fulfil the conditions which he himself laid down. He has incidentally brought forward some other instances, most of which labour under the disadvantage of proving too much. Thus, he instances the existence of a festival in honour of the dead, 'at or near the beginning of 'November.' Such a feast is very general; and, as there are many more races holding such a festival than there are months in the year, it is evident that, in several cases, they must be held together. But Mr. Haliburton goes on to say: 'The 'Spaniards were very naturally surprised at finding that, while 'they were celebrating a solemn mass for All Souls on 'November 22, the heathen Peruvians were also holding their 'annual commemoration of the dead.' This curious coincidence would, however, not only prove the existence of such a festival, as he says, 'before the dispersion ' (which Mr. Haliburton evidently looks on as a definite event rather than as a gradual process), but also that the ancestors of the Peruvians were at that epoch sufficiently advanced to form a calendar, and that their descendants were able to keep it unchanged down to the present time. This, however, we know was not the case. Again, Mr. Haliburton says: ' The belief in Scotland and ' equatorial Africa is found to be almost precisely identical re- ' specting there being ghosts, even of the living, who are ex- ' ceedingly troublesome and pugnacious, and can be sometimes ' killed by a silver bullet.' Here we certainly have what seems at first sight to be an arbitrary belief; but if it proves that there was a belief in ghosts of the living before the dispersion, it also proves that silver bullets were then in use. This illus- tration is, I think, a very interesting one; because it shows that similar ideas in distant countries owe their origin, not ' to ' an era before the dispersion of the human race,' but to the fundamental similarity of the human mind. While I do not believe that similar customs in different nations are ' inherited ' from a common source,' or are necessarily primitive, I certainly do see in them an argument for the unity of the human race, which, however (be it remarked), is not necessarily the same thing as the descent from a single pair.

On the other hand, I have attempted to show that ideas, which might at first sight appear arbitrary and unaccountable, arise naturally in very distinct nations as they arrive at a similar stage of progress; and it is necessary, therefore, to be extremely cautious in using such customs or ideas as implying any special connection between different races of men.

---

## PART II. [1]

At the Dundee meeting of the British Association I had the honour of reading a paper ' On the Origin of Civilisation and ' the Primitive Condition of Man,' in answer to certain opinions and arguments brought forward by the late Archbishop of Dublin. The views therein advocated met with little opposi- tion at the time. The then Presidents of the Ethnological and Anthropological Societies both expressed their concurrence

[1] The substance of this was read before the British Association during their meeting at Exeter in 1869.

in the conclusions at which I arrived; and the Memoir was
printed *in extenso* by the Association. It has, however, subsequently been attacked at some length by the Duke of Argyll;[1]
and as the Duke has in some cases strangely misunderstood me,
and in others (I am sure unintentionally) misrepresented my
views—as, moreover, the subject is one of great interest and
importance—I am anxious to make some remarks in reply to
his Grace's criticisms. The Duke has divided his work into
four chapters:—I. Introduction; II. The Origin of Man;
III. and IV. His Primitive Condition.

I did not in my first Memoir, nor do I now, propose to
discuss the subjects dealt with in the first half of the Duke's
'Speculations.' I will only observe that in attacking Professor
Huxley for proposing to unite the Bimana and Quadrumana
in one Order, 'Primates,' the Duke uses a dangerous argument; for if, on account of his great mental superiority over
the Quadrumana, Man forms an Order or even Class by himself, it will be impossible any longer to regard all men as
belonging to one species or even genus. The Duke is in
error when he supposes that 'mental powers and instincts'
afford tests of easy application in other parts of the animal
kingdom. On the contrary, genera with the most different
mental powers and instincts are placed, not only in the same
order, but even in the same family. Thus our most learned
hymenopterologist (Mr Frederick Smith) classes the hive-bee,
the humble-bee, and the parasitic apathus in the same sub-
family of Apidæ. It seems to me, therefore, illogical to separate man zoologically from the other primates on the ground of
his mental superiority, and yet to maintain the specific unity
of the human race, notwithstanding the mental differences
between different races of men.

I do not, however, propose to discuss the origin of man,
and pass on therefore at once to the Duke's third chapter; and
here I congratulate myself at the outset that the result of my
paper has been to satisfy him that ' Whately's argument,'
' though strong at some points, is at others open to assault, and
' that, as a whole, the subject now requires to be differently
' handled, and regarded from a different point of view.' ' I do

---

[1] Good Words: March, April, May, and June, 1868. Also since republished in
a separate form.        [2] *Ibid.*, 1868. p. 156.

'not, therefore,' he adds in a subsequent page,[1] 'agree with
'the late Archbishop of Dublin, that we are entitled to assume
'it as a fact that, as regards the mechanical arts, no savage
'race has ever raised itself.' And again:[2] 'The aid which
'man had from his Creator may possibly have been nothing
'more than the aid of a body and of a mind, so marvellously
'endowed that thought was an instinct and contrivance a
'necessity.'

I feel, however, less satisfaction on this account than would
otherwise have been the case, because it seems to me that,
though the Duke acknowledges the Archbishop's argument to
be untenable, he practically reproduces it with but a slight
alteration and somewhat protected by obscurity. What
Whately called 'instruction' the Duke terms 'instinct;' and
he considers that man had instincts which afforded all that was
necessary as a starting-ground. He admits, however, that
monkeys use stones to break nuts; he might have added that
they throw sticks and stones at intruders. But he says,
'Between these rudiments of intellectual perception and the
'next step (that of adapting and fashioning an instrument for
'a particular purpose) there is a gulf in which lies the whole
'immeasurable distance between man and brutes.' I cannot
agree with the Duke in this opinion; nor indeed does he agree
with himself, for he adds, in the very same page, that—'The
'wielding of a stick is, in all probability, an act equally of
'primitive intuition, and from this to throwing of a stick and
'the use of javelins is an easy and natural transition.'

He continues as follows:—'Simple as these acts are, they
'involve both physical and mental powers which are capable of
'all the developments which we see in the most advanced in-
'dustrial arts. These acts involve the instinctive idea of the
'constancy of natural causes and the capacity of thought,
'which gives men the conviction that what has happened under
'given conditions will, under the same conditions, always occur
'again.' On these, he says, 'as well as on other grounds, I
'have never attached much importance to Whately's argument.'
These are indeed important admissions, and amount to a virtual
abandonment of Whately's position.

[1] Good Words, June, 1868. p. 386.    [2] P. 392.

I I

The Duke blames the Archbishop of Dublin for not having defined the terms 'civilisation' and 'barbarism.' It seems to me that Whately illustrated his meaning better by examples than he could have done by any definition. The Duke does not seem to have felt any practical difficulty from the omission; and it is remarkable that, after all, he himself omits to define the terms, thus being himself guilty of the very omission for which he blames Whately. In truth, it would be impossible in a few words to define the complex organisation which we call civilisation, or to state in a few words how a civilised differs from a barbarous people. Indeed, to define civilisation as it should be is surely as yet impossible, since we are far from having solved the problem how we may best avail ourselves of our opportunities, and enjoy the beautiful world in which we live.

As regards barbarism, the Duke observes: 'All I desire to 'point out here is, that there is no necessary connection 'between a state of mere childhood in respect to knowledge 'and a state of utter barbarism, words which, if they have any 'definite meaning at all, imply the lowest moral as well as the 'lowest intellectual condition.' To every proposition in this remarkable sentence I entirely demur. There is, I think, a very intimate connection between knowledge and civilisation. Knowledge and barbarism cannot coexist—knowledge and civilisation are inseparable.

Again, the words 'utter barbarism' have certainly a very definite signification, but as certainly, I think, not that which the Duke attributes to them. The lowest moral and the lowest intellectual condition are not only, in my opinion, not inseparable, they are not even compatible. Morality implies responsibility, and consequently intelligence. The lower animals are neither moral nor immoral. The lower races of men may be, and are, vicious; but allowances must be made for them. On the contrary (*corruptio optimi, pessima est*), the higher the mental power, the more splendid the intellectual endowment, the deeper is the moral degradation of him who wastes the one and abuses the other.

On the whole, the fair inference seems to be that savages are more innocent, and yet more criminal, than civilised races;

they are by no means in the lowest possible moral condition, nor are they capable of the higher virtues.

In the first part of this paper I laid much stress on the fact that even in the most civilised nations we find traces of early barbarism. The Duke maintains, on the contrary, that these traces afford no proof, or even presumption, that barbarism was the primeval condition of man. He urges that all such customs may have been not primeval, but mediæval; and he continues : ' Yet this assumption runs through all Sir J. Lubbock's argu-' ments. Wherever a brutal or savage custom prevails, it is ' regarded as a sample of the original condition of mankind. ' And this in the teeth of facts which prove that many of such ' customs not only may have been, but must have been, the ' result of corruption.'

Fortunately, it is unnecessary for me to defend myself against this criticism, because in the very next sentence the Duke directly contradicts himself, and shows that I have not done that of which he accuses me. He continues his argument thus :— ' Take cannibalism as one of these. Sir J. Lubbock ' seems to admit that this loathsome practice was not primeval.' Thus, by way of proof that I regard all brutal customs as primeval, he states, and correctly states, that I do not regard cannibalism as primeval. It would be difficult, I think, to find a more curious case of self-contradiction.

The Duke refers particularly to the practice of Bride-catching, which he states ' cannot possibly have been primeval.' He omits, however, to explain why, from his point of view, it could not have been so; and of course, assuming the word ' primeval ' to cover a period of some length, it would have been interesting to know his reasons for this conclusion; in fact, however, it is not a case in point, because, as I have attempted to show, marriage by capture was preceded by a custom still more barbarous. It may, perhaps, however, be as well to state emphatically that all brutal customs are not, in my opinion, primeval. Human sacrifices, for instance, were, I think, certainly not so.

My argument, however, was that there is a definite sequence of habits and ideas ; that certain customs (some brutal, others not so) which we find lingering on in civilised communities are a page of past history, and tell a tale of former barbarism; rather on account of their simplicity than of their brutality, though many of them are brutal enough. Again, no one would go back from letter-writing to the use of the quippu or hieroglyphics; no one would abandon the fire-drill and obtain fire by hand-friction.

Believing, as he does, that the primitive condition of man was one of civilisation, the Duke accounts for the existence of savages by the remark that they are ' mere outcasts of the ' human race,' descendants of weak tribes which were 'driven ' to the woods and rocks.' But until the historical period these ' mere outcasts ' occupied almost the whole of North and South America, all Northern Europe, the greater part of Africa, the great continent of Australia, a large part of Asia, and the beautiful islands of the Pacific. Moreover, until modified by man, the great continents were either in the condition of open plains, such as heaths, downs, prairies, and tundras, or they were mere ' woods and rocks.' Now everything tends to show that mere woods and rocks exercised on the whole a favourable influence. Inhabitants of great plains rarely rose beyond the pastoral stage. In America the most advanced civilisation was attained, not by the occupants of the fertile valleys, not along the banks of the Mississippi or the Amazon, but among the rocks and woods of Mexico and Peru. Scotland itself is a brilliant proof that woods and rocks are compatible with a high state of civilisation.

My idea of the manner in which, and the causes owing to which, man spread over the earth, is very different from that of the Duke. He evidently supposes that new countries have been occupied by weak races, driven there by more powerful tribes. This I believe to be an entirely erroneous notion. Take, for instance, our own island. We are sometimes told that the Celts were driven by the Saxons into Wales and Cornwall. On the contrary, however, we know that Wales and Cornwall were both occupied long before the Saxons landed on our shores. Even as regards the rest of the country, it would not be correct to say that the Celts were driven away; they were either destroyed or absorbed.

The gradual extension of the human race has not, in my

opinion, been effected by force acting on any given race from without, but by internal necessity and the pressure of population; by peaceful, not by hostile force; by prosperity, not by misfortune. I believe that of old, as now, founders of new colonies were men of energy and enterprise, animated by hope and courage, not by fear and despair; that they were, in short, anything but mere outcasts of the human race.

The Duke relies a good deal on the case of America. ' Is ' it not true,' he asks, ' that the lowest and rudest tribes in the ' population of the globe have been found in the furthest ex- ' tremities of its great continents, and in the distant islands ' which would be the last refuge of the victims of violence and ' misfortune? "The New World" is the continent which ' presents the most uninterrupted stretch of habitable land ' from the highest northern to the lowest southern latitude. ' On the extreme north we have the Esquimaux, or Inuit race, ' maintaining human life under conditions of extremest hard- ' ship, even amid the perpetual ice of the Polar seas. And ' what a life it is! Watching at the blow-hole of a seal for ' many hours, in a temperature of 75° below freezing point, is ' the constant work of the Inuit hunter. And when at last ' his prey is struck, it is his luxury to feast upon the raw blood ' and blubber. To civilised man it is hardly possible to con- ' ceive a life so wretched, and in many respects so brutal, as ' the life led by this race during the long-lasting night of the ' Arctic winter.'

To this question I confidently reply, No, it is not true; it is not true as a general proposition that the lowest races are found furthest from the centres of continents; it is not true in the particular case of America. The natives of Brazil, possessing a country of almost unrivalled fertility, surrounded by the most luxuriant vegetation, watered by magnificent rivers, and abounding in animal life, were yet unquestionably lower than the Esquimaux,[1] whom the Duke pities and despises so much.[2] He pities them, indeed, more than I think

---

[1] See Martius, p. 77. Dr. Rae ranks the Esquimaux above the Red Indians. Trans. Ethn. Soc. 1866. Martius was himself at one time of opinion that the Brazilians were degenerate, but his in-

vestigations finally led him to the opposite conclusion. See *Nature*, 1871, pp. 146, 204.

[2] When the Duke states that 'neither an agricultural nor pastoral

the case requires. Our own sportsmen willingly undergo great hardships in pursuit of game ; and hunting in earnest must possess a keen zest which it can never attain when it is a mere sport.

'When we rise,' says Mr. Hill,[1] ' twice or thrice a day ' from a full meal, we cannot be in a right frame either of body ' or mind for the proper enjoyments of the chase. Our slug- ' gish spirits then want the true incentive to action, which ' should be hunger, with the hope before us of filling a craving ' stomach. I could remember once before being for a long ' time dependent upon the gun for food, and feeling a touch of ' the charm of a savage life (for every condition of humanity ' has its good as well as its evil), but never till now did I fully ' comprehend the attachment of the sensitive, not drowsy, ' Indian.'

Esquimaux life, indeed, as painted by our Arctic voyagers, is by no means so miserable as the Duke supposes. Captain Parry, for instance, gives the following picture of an Esquimaux hut :—' In the few opportunities we had in putting their hospi- ' tality to the test, we had every reason to be pleased with ' them. Both as to food and accommodation, the best they had ' were always at our service ; and their attention, both in kind ' and degree, was everything that hospitality and even good ' breeding could dictate. The kindly offices of drying and ' mending our clothes, cooking our provisions and thawing ' snow for our drink, were performed by the women with an ' obliging cheerfulness which we shall not easily forget, and ' which demanded its due share of our admiration and esteem. ' While thus their guest I have passed an evening not only with ' comfort, but with extreme gratification ; for with the women ' working and singing, their husbands quietly mending their ' lines, the children playing before the door, and the pot boiling ' over the blaze of a cheerful lamp, one might well forget for ' the time that an Esquimaux hut was the scene of this do- ' mestic comfort and tranquillity ; and I can safely affirm with ' Cartwright that, while thus lodged beneath their roof, I know

---

' life is possible on the borders of a    Siberia.
' frozen sea,' he forgot for the moment
the inhabitants of Lapland and of    [1] *Travels in Siberia*, vol. ii. p. 288.

'no people whom I would more confidently trust, as respects
'either my person or my property, than the Esquimaux.' Dr.
Rae,' who had ample means of judging, tells us that the
Eastern Esquimaux 'are sober, steady, and faithful. . . .
'Provident to their own property, and careful of that of others
'when under their charge. . . . Socially they are a lively,
'cheerful, and chatty people, fond of associating with each
'other and with strangers, with whom they soon become on
'friendly terms, if kindly treated. . . . In their domestic
'relations they are exemplary. The man is an obedient son,
'a good husband, and a kind father. . . . The children
'when young are docile. . . . The girls have their dolls,
'in making dresses and shoes for which they amuse and employ
'themselves. The boys have miniature bows, arrows, and
'spears. . . . When grown up they are dutiful to their
'parents. . . . Orphan children are readily adopted and
'well cared for until they are able to provide for themselves.'
He concludes by saying, 'the more I saw of the Esquimaux
'the higher was the opinion I formed of them.'

Again, Hooper [2] thus describes a visit to an Asiatic Esquimaux belonging to the Tuski race: 'Upon reaching Mooldoo-
'yah's habitation, we found Captain Moore installed at his
'ease, with every provision made for comfort and convenience.
'Water and venison were suspended over the lamps in prepa-
'ration for dinner; skins nicely arranged for couches, and the
'hangings raised to admit the cool air; our baggage was
'bestowed around us with care and in quiet, and we were free
'to take our own way of enjoying such unobtrusive hospitality
'without a crowd of eager gazers watching us like lions at
'feed; nor were we troubled by importunate begging such as
'detracted from the dignity of Metns's station, which was
'undoubtedly high in the tribe.'

I know no sufficient reason for supposing that the Esquimaux were ever more advanced than they are now. The Duke,
indeed, considers that before they were 'driven by wars and
'migrations' (a somewhat curious expression) they 'may have
'been nomads living on their flocks and herds;' and he states
broadly that 'the rigours of the region they now inhabit have

[1] Trans. Eth. Soc. 1856, p. 128.　　　[2] The Tents of the Tuski, p. 102.

'reduced these people to the condition in which we now see
'them;' a conclusion for which I know no reason, particularly
as the Tinné and other Indians living to the south of the Esquimaux are ruder and more barbarous.

It is my belief that the great continents were already occupied by a widespread though sparse population when man was
no more advanced than the lowest savages of to-day; and
although I am far from believing that the various degrees of
civilisation which now occur can be altogether accounted for by
the external circumstances as they at present exist, still these
circumstances seem to me to throw much light on the very
different amount of progress which has been attained by different races.

In referring to the backwardness of the aboriginal Australians, I had observed that New Holland contained 'neither
'cereals nor any animals which could be domesticated with
'advantage;' upon which the Duke remarks that 'Sir John
'Lubbock urges in reply to Whately that the low condition of
'Australian savages affords no proof whatever that they could
'not raise themselves, because the materials of improvement
'are wanting in that country, which affords no cereals nor
'animals capable of useful domestication. But Sir J. Lubbock
'does not perceive that the same argument which shows how
'improvement could not possibly be attained, shows also how
'degradation could not possibly be avoided. If with the few
'resources of the country it was impossible for savages to rise,
'it follows that with those same resources it would be impossible
'for a half-civilised race not to fall. And as in this case again,
'unless we are to suppose a separate Adam and Eve for Van
'Diemen's Land, its natives must originally have come from
'countries where both corn and cattle were to be had; it
'follows that the low condition of these natives is much more
'likely to have been the result of degradation than of primeval
'barbarism.'

But my argument was that a half-civilised race would have
brought other resources with them. The dog was, I think,
certainly introduced into that country by man, who would
probably have brought with him other domestic animals also if
he had possessed any. The same argument applies to plants;

the Polynesians carried the sweet potato and the yam, as well
as the dog, with them from island to island; and even if the
first settlers in Australia happened to have been without them,
and without the means of acquiring them, they would certainly
have found some native plants which would have been worth
the trouble of cultivation, if they had already attained to the
agricultural stage.

This argument applies with even more force to pottery; if
the first settlers in Australia were acquainted with this art, I
can see no reason why they should suddenly and completely
have lost it.

The Duke, indeed, appears to maintain that the natives of
Van Diemen's Land (whom he evidently regards as belonging
to the same race as the Australians and Polynesians, from both
of which they are entirely distinct) ‘ must have originally come
‘ from countries where both corn and cattle were to be had,’
still ‘ degradation could not possibly be avoided.’ This seems
to be the natural inference from the Duke's language, and
suggests a very gloomy future for our Australian fellow-
countrymen. The position is, however, so manifestly untenable, when once put into plain language, that I think it
unnecessary to dwell longer on this part of the subject. Even
the Duke himself will hardly maintain that our colonists must
fall back because the natives did not improve. Yet he extends
and generalises this argument in a subsequent paragraph,
saying, ‘ There is hardly a single fact quoted by Sir J. Lubbock
‘ in favour of his own theory which, when viewed in connection
‘ with the same indisputable principles, does not tell against
‘ that theory rather than in its favour.’ So far from being
‘ indisputable,’ the principle that when savages remained
savages, civilised settlers must descend to the same level,
appears to me entirely erroneous. On reading the above
passage, however, I passed on with much interest to see which
of my facts I had so strangely misread.

The great majority of facts connected with savage life have
no perceptible bearing on the question, and I must therefore
have been not only very stupid, but also singularly unfortunate, if of all those quoted by me in support of my argument
‘ there was hardly a single one ’ which, read aright, was not

merely irrelevant, but actually told against me.  In support of
his statement the Duke gives three illustrations, but it is remarkable that not one of these three cases was referred to by
me in the present discussion, or in favour of the theory now
under discussion.  If all the facts on which I relied told against
me, it is curious that the Duke should not give an instance.
The three illustrations which he quotes from my ' Prehistoric
' Times ' seem to me irrelevant; but, as the Duke thinks otherwise, it will be worth while to see how he uses them, and to
inquire whether they give any real support to his argument.
As already mentioned, they are three in number.

' Sir J. Lubbock,' he says, ' reminds us that in a cave on
' the north-west coast (of Australia) tolerable figures of sharks,
' porpoises, turtles, lizards, canoes, and some quadrupeds, &c.,
' were found, and yet that the present natives of the country
' where they were found were utterly incapable of realising
' the most artistic vivid representations, and ascribe the
' drawings in the cave to diabolical agency.'  This proves
nothing, because the Australian tribes differ much in their
artistic condition ; some of them still make rude drawings like
those above described.

Secondly, he says, ' Sir J. Lubbock quotes the testimony
' of Cook, in respect to the Tasmanians, that they had no
' canoes.  Yet their ancestors could not have reached the island
' by walking on the sea.'  This argument would equally prove
that the Kangaroo and the Echidna must have had civilised
ancestors; they inhabit both Australia and Tasmania, and it
would have been impossible for *their* ancestors to have passed
from the one to the other ' by walking on the sea.'  The Duke,
though admitting the antiquity of man, does not, I think, appreciate the geological changes which have taken place during the
human period.

The only other case which he quotes is that of the highland
Esquimaux, who had no weapons nor any idea of war.  The
Duke's comment is as follows :—' No wonder, poor people !
' They had been driven into regions where no stronger race
' could desire to follow them.  But that the fathers had once
' known what war and violence meant there is no more con-
' clusive proof than the dwelling-place of their children.'  It

is perhaps natural that the head of a great Highland Clan should regard with pity a people who, having ' once known ' what war and violence meant,' have no longer any neighbours to pillage or to fight ; but a Lowlander can hardly be expected seriously to regard such a change as one calculated to excite pity, or as any evidence of degradation.

In my first paper I deduced an argument from the condition of religion among the different races of man, a part of the subject which has since been admirably dealt with by Mr. Tylor in a lecture at the Royal Institution. The use of flint for sacrificial purposes long after the introduction of metal seemed to me a good case of what Mr. Tylor has aptly called ' Survival.' So also is the method of obtaining fire. The Brahman will not use ordinary fire for sacred purposes ; he does not even obtain a fresh spark from flint and steel, but reverts to, or rather continues, the old way of obtaining it, by friction with a wooden drill, one Brahman pulling the thong backwards and forwards while the other watches to catch the sacred spark.

I also referred to the non-existence of religion among certain savage races, and, as the Duke correctly observes, I argued that this was probably their primitive condition, because it is difficult to believe that a people which had once possessed a religion would ever entirely lose it.[1]

This argument filled the Duke with ' astonishment.' Surely, he says, ' if there is one fact more certain than another in ' respect to the nature of man, it is that he is capable of losing ' religious knowledge, of ceasing to believe in religious truth, ' and of falling away from religious duty. If by " religion " ' is meant the existence merely of some impressions of powers ' invisible and supernatural, even this, we know, can not only ' be lost, but be scornfully disavowed by men who are highly ' civilised.' Yet in the very same page the Duke goes on to say, ' The most cruel and savage customs in the world are ' the direct effect of its " religions." And if men could drop ' religions when they would, or if they could even form the wish ' to get rid of those which sit like a nightmare on their life,

---

[1] It is rarely unnecessary to explain that I did not intend to question the possibility of a change in, but a total loss of, religion.

'there would be many more nations without a "religion"
'than there are found to be.  But religions can neither be put
'on nor cast off like garments, according to their utility, or
'according to their beauty, or according to their power of com-
'forting.'

With this I entirely agree.  Man can no more voluntarily
abandon or change the articles of his religious creed than he
can make one hair black or white, or add one cubit to his stature.  I do not deny that there may be exceptional cases of
intellectual men entirely devoid of religion; but if the Duke
means to say that men who are highly civilised habitually or
frequently lose and scornfully disavow religion, I can only say
that I should adopt such an opinion with difficulty and regret.
There is, so far as I know, no evidence on record which would
justify such an opinion, and, as far as my private experience
goes, I at least have met with no such tendency.   It is indeed
true that from the times of Socrates downwards men in advance of their age have disavowed particular dogmas and particular myths; but the Duke of Argyll would, I am sure, not
confuse a desire for reformation with the scornful disavowal of
religion as a whole.   Some philosophers may object to prayers
for rain, but they are foremost in denouncing the folly of witchcraft; they may regard matter as aboriginal, but they would
never suppose with the Redskin that land was created while
water existed from the beginning, nor does anyone now believe with the South Sea Islanders that the Peerage are immortal, but that commoners have no souls.   If, indeed, there
is 'one fact more certain than another in respect to the nature
'of man,' I should have considered it to be the gradual diffusion
of religious light, and of nobler conceptions as to the nature
of God.

The lowest savages have no idea of a deity at all.   Those
slightly more advanced regard him as an enemy to be dreaded,
but who may be resisted with a fair prospect of success, who
may be cheated by the cunning and defied by the strong.  Thus
the natives of the Nicobar Islands endeavour to terrify their
deity by scarecrows, and the negro beats his Fetich if his
prayers are not granted.   As tribes advance in civilisation
their deities advance in dignity, but their power is still

limited; one governs the sea, another the land; one reigns over the plains, another among the mountains. The most powerful are vindictive, cruel, and unjust. They require humiliating ceremonies and bloody sacrifices. But few races have arrived at the conception of an omnipotent and beneficent Deity.

One of the lowest forms of religion is that presented by the Australians, which consists of a mere unreasoning belief in the existence of mysterious beings. The native who has in his sleep a nightmare or a dream does not doubt the reality of that which passes; and as the beings by whom he is visited in his sleep are unseen by his friends and relations, he regards them as invisible.

In Fetichism this feeling is more methodised. The negro, by means of witchcraft, endeavours to make a slave of his deity. Thus Fetichism is almost the opposite of Religion; it stands towards it in the same relation as Alchemy to Chemistry, or Astrology to Astronomy; and shows how fundamentally our idea of a deity differs from that which presents itself to the savage. The negro does not hesitate to punish a refractory Fetich, and hides it in his waistcloth if he does not wish it to know what is going on. Aladdin's lamp is, in fact, a well-known illustration of a Fetich.

A further stage, and the superiority of the higher deities is more fully recognised. Everything is worshipped indiscriminately—animals, plants, and even inanimate objects. In endeavouring to account for the worship of animals, we must remember that names are very frequently taken from them. The children and followers of a man called the Bear or the Lion would make that a tribal name. Hence the animal itself would be first respected, at last worshipped. This form of religion can be shown to have existed, at one time or another, almost all over the world.

' The Totem,' says Schoolcraft, ' is a symbol of the name of ' the progenitor—generally some quadruped, or bird, or other ' object in the animal kingdom, which stands, if we may so ex' press it, as the surname of the family. It is always some ' animated object, and seldom or never derived from the inani' mate class of nature. Its significant importance is derived

'from the fact that individuals unhesitatingly trace their
'lineage from it. But whatever names they may be called
'during their life-time, it is the totem, and not their personal
'name, that is recorded on the tomb or "adjedating" that
'marks the place of burial. Families are thus traced when
'expanded into bands or tribes, the multiplication of which, in
'North America, has been very great, and has decreased, in
'like ratio, the labours of the ethnologist.' Totemism, however, is by no means confined to America. In Central India
'the Moondah "Enidhi," or Oraon "Minijrar," or eel tribe,
'will not kill or eat that fish. The Hawk, Crow, or Heron
'tribes, will not kill or eat those birds. Livingstone, quoted in
'Latham, tells us that the subtribes of Bitshaunas (or Bechu-
'anas) are similarly named after certain animals, and a tribe
'never eats the animal from which it is named, using the term
'" ila," hate or dread, in reference to killing it.' [1]

Traces, indeed, of Totemism, more or less distinct, are
widely distributed, and often connected with marriage prohibitions.

As regards inanimate objects, we must remember that the
savage accounts for all action and movement by life; hence a
watch is to him alive. This being taken in conjunction with
the feeling that anything unusual is 'great medicine,' leads to
the worship of any remarkable inanimate object. Mr. Fergusson has recently attempted to show the special prevalence of
Tree and Serpent worship. He might, I believe, have made
out as strong a case for many other objects. It seems clear
that the objects worshipped in this stage are neither to be regarded as emblems, nor are they personified. Inanimate objects have spirits as well as men; hence, when the wives and
slaves are sacrificed, the weapons are also broken in the grave,
so that the spirits of the latter, as well as of the former, may
accompany their master to the other world.

The gradually increasing power of chiefs and priests led to
Anthropomorphism, with its sacrifices, temples, and priests, &c.
To this stage belongs idolatry, which must by no means be re-
garded as the lowest state of religion. The writer of ' The

' Wisdom of Solomon,' [1] indeed, long ago pointed out how it
was connected with monarchical power—

' When men could not honour in presence, because they dwelt
' far off, they took the counterfeit of his visage from far, and
' made an express image of a king, whom they honoured, to
' the end that by this, their forwardness, they might flatter him
' that was absent, as if he were present.

' Also the singular diligence of the artificer did help to set
' forward the ignorant to more superstition.

' For he, peradventure willing to please one in authority,
' forced all his skill to make the resemblance of the best
' fashion.

' And so the multitude, allured by the grace of the work,
' took him now for a God which a little before was but
' honoured as a man.'

The worship of principles may be regarded as a still further
stage in the natural development of religion.

It is important to observe that each stage of religion is
superimposed on the preceding, and that bygone beliefs linger
on among the children and the ignorant. Thus witchcraft is
still believed in by the ignorant, and fairy tales flourish in the
nursery.

It certainly appears to me that the gradual development of
religious ideas among the lower races of men is a fair argument in opposition to the view that savages are degenerate
descendants of civilised ancestors. Archbishop Whately would
admit the connection between these different phases of religious
belief; but I think he would find it very difficult to show any
process of natural degradation and decay which could explain
the quaint errors and opinions of the lower races of men, or to
account for the lingering belief in witchcraft, and other absur-
dities, &c., in civilised races, excepting by some such train of
reasoning as that which I have endeavoured to sketch.

There is another case in this memoir wherein the Duke,
although generally a fair opponent, brings forward an unsup-
portable accusation. He criticises severely the ' Four Ages,'
generally admitted by archæologists, especially referring to the
terms ' Palæolithic ' and ' Neolithic,' which are used to denote
the two earlier.

---

[1] Wisdom, xiv. 17.

I have no wish to take to myself in particular the blame which the Duke impartially extends to archæologists in general, but, having suggested the two terms in question, I will simply place side by side the passage in which they first appeared and the Duke's criticism, and confidently ask whether there is any foundation for the sweeping accusation made by the noble Duke.

The Duke says : ' For here ' I must observe that Archæo- ' logists are using language on ' this subject which, if not po- ' sitively erroneous, requires, ' at least, more rigorous de- ' finitions and limitations of ' meaning than they are dis- ' posed to attend to.    They ' talk of an Old Stone Age ' (Palæolithic), and of a Newer ' Stone Age (Neolithic), and ' of a Bronze Age, and of an ' Iron Age.    Now, there is no ' proof whatever that such ' Ages ever existed in the ' world.    It may be true, and ' it probably is true, that most ' nations in the progress of the ' Arts have passed through ' the stages of using stone for ' implements before they were ' acquainted with the use of ' metals.    Even this, however, ' may not be true of all na- ' tions.    In Africa there ap- ' pear to be no traces of any ' time when the natives were ' not acquainted with the use ' of iron; and I am informed ' by Sir Samuel Baker that ' iron ore is so common in

My words, when proposing the terms, were as follows :— ' From the careful study of ' the remains which have come ' down to us, it would appear ' that the prehistoric archæo- ' logy may be divided into ' four great epochs. ' Firstly, that of Drift, when ' man shared the possession of ' Europe with the mammoth, ' the cave-bear, the woolly- ' haired rhinoceros, and other ' extinct animals.    This we ' may call the " Palæolithic " ' period. ' Secondly, the latter or po- ' lished Stone Age; a period ' characterised by beautiful ' weapons    and    instruments ' made of flint and other kinds ' of stone, in which, however, ' we find no trace of the know- ' ledge of any metal, excepting ' gold, which seems to have ' been sometimes used for or- ' naments.    This we may call ' the Neolithic period. ' Thirdly, the Bronze Age, ' in which bronze was used for ' arms and cutting instruments ' of all kinds.

'Africa, and of a kind so
'easily reducible by heat, that
'its use might well be disco-
'vered by the rudest tribes,
'who were in the habit of
'lighting fires. Then again
'it is to be remembered that
'there are some countries in
'the world where stone is as
'rare and difficult to get as
'metals.

'The great alluvial plains
'of Mesopotamia are a case in
'point. Accordingly we know
'from the remains of the first
'Chaldean monarchy that a
'very high civilisation in the
'arts of agriculture and of
'commerce coexisted with the
'use of stone implements of a
'very rude character. This
'fact proves that rude stone
'implements are not necessa-
'rily any proof whatever of
'a really barbarous condition.
'And even if it were true that
'the use of stone has in all
'cases preceded the use of
'metals, it is quite certain
'that the same age which was
'an Age of Stone in one part
'of the world was an Age of
'Metal in the other. As re-
'gards the Eskimo and the
'South Sea Islanders, we are
'now, or were very recently,
'living in a Stone Age.'

'Fourthly, the Iron Age, in
'which that metal had super-
'seded bronze for arms, axes,
'knives, &c.; bronze, how-
'ever, still being in common
'use for ornaments, and fre-
'quently also for the handles
'of swords and other arms, but
'never for the blades.

'Stone weapons, however,
'of many kinds were still in use
'during the Age of Bronze,
'and even during that of Iron.
'So that the mere presence of a
'few stone implements is not in
'itself sufficient evidence that
'any given " find " belongs to
'the Stone Age.

'In order to prevent mis-
'apprehension, it may be as
'well to state at once that I
'only apply this classification
'to Europe, though in all pro-
'bability it might also be ex-
'tended to the neighbouring
'parts of Asia and Africa.
'As regards other civilised
'countries, China and Japan
'for instance, we, as yet, know
'nothing of their prehistoric
'archæology. It is evident,
'also, that some nations, such
'as the Fuegians, Andama-
'ners, &c., are even now only
'in an Age of Stone.'

I have therefore actually pointed out those very limitations,
the omission of which the Duke condemns.

K K

I will now bring forward one or two additional reasons in support of my view. There is a considerable body of evidence tending to show that the offspring produced by crossing different varieties tends to revert to the type from which these varieties are descended. Thus Tegetmeier states that ' a cross ' between two non-sitting varieties (of the common fowl) almost ' invariably produces a mongrel that becomes broody, and sits ' with remarkable steadiness.' Mr. Darwin gives several cases in which such hybrids or mongrels are singularly wild and un- tameable, the mule being a familiar instance. Messrs. Boitard and Corbié state that, when they crossed certain breeds of pigeons, they invariably got some young ones coloured like the wild *C. livia.* Mr. Darwin repeated these experiments, and found the statement fully confirmed.

So, again, the same is the case with fowls. The original of the domestic fowl was of a reddish colour, but thousands of the Black Spanish and the white silk fowls might be bred without a single red feather appearing; yet Mr. Darwin found that on crossing them he immediately obtained specimens with red feathers. Similar results have been obtained with ducks, rabbits, and cattle. Mules also have not unfrequently barred legs. It is unnecessary to give these cases in detail, because Mr. Darwin's work on ' Animals and Plants under Domestica- ' tion ' is in the hands of every naturalist.

Applying the same test to man, Mr. Darwin observes that crossed races of men are singularly savage and degraded. ' Many years ago,' he says, ' I was struck by the fact that in ' South America men of complicated descent between Negroes, ' Indians, and Spaniards, seldom had, whatever the cause might ' be, a good expression. Livingstone remarks that "it is un- ' " accountable why half-castes are so much more cruel than the ' " Portuguese, but such is undoubtedly the case." A native ' remarked to Livingstone—"God made white men, and God ' " black men, but the devil made half-castes!" When two ' races, both low in the scale, are crossed, the progeny seems to ' be eminently bad. Thus the noble-hearted Humboldt, who ' felt none of that prejudice against the inferior races now so ' current in England, speaks in strong terms of the bad and ' savage disposition of Zambas, or half-castes between Indians

'and Negroes, and this conclusion has been arrived at by
'various observers. From these facts we may perhaps infer
'that the degraded state of so many half-castes is in part due
'to a reversion to a primitive and savage condition, induced by
'the act of crossing, as well as to the unfavourable moral con-
'ditions under which they generally exist.'

I confess, however, that I am not sure how far this may not
be accounted for by the unfortunate circumstances in which
half-breeds are generally placed. The half-breeds between
the Hudson's Bay Company's servants and the native women,
being well treated and looked after, appear to be a creditable
and well-behaved set.[1]

I would also call particular attention to the remarkable
similarity between the mental characteristics of savages and
those of children. 'The Abipones,' says Dobritzhoffer,[2] 'when
'they are unable to comprehend anything at first sight, soon
'grow weary of examining it, and cry "orqueenàm?" what
'is it after all? Sometimes the Guaranies, when completely
'puzzled, knit their brows and cry "tupã oiquaã," God knows
'what it is. Since they possess such small reasoning powers,
'and have so little inclination to exert them, it is no wonder
'that they are neither able nor willing to argue one thing from
'another.'

Richardson says of the Dogrib Indians, 'that however high
'the reward they expected to receive on reaching their desti-
'nation, they could not be depended on to carry letters. A
'slight difficulty, the prospect of a banquet on venison, or a
'sudden impulse to visit some friend, were sufficient to turn
'them aside for an indefinite length of time.'[3] Le Vaillant[4]
also observes of the Namaquas, that they closely resembled
children in their great curiosity.

M. Bourien,[5] speaking of the wild tribes in the Malayan
Peninsula, says that an 'inconstant humour, fickle and erratic,
'together with a mixture of fear, timidity, and diffidence, lies
'at the bottom of their character; they seem always to think

[1] Dunn's Oregon Territory, p. 147.
[2] His. of the Abipones, vol. ii. p. 69.
[3] Arctic Expedition, vol. ii. p. 23.
[4] Travels in Africa, 1776, vol. iii. p. 12.
[5] Trans. Ethn. Soc. N. S. vol. iii. p. 76.

' that they would be better in any other place than in the one
' they occupy at the time. Like children, their actions seem
' to be rarely guided by reflection, and they almost always act
' impulsively.' The tears of the South Sea Islanders, ' like
' those of children, were always ready to express any passion
' that was strongly excited, and, like those of children, they
' also appeared to be forgotten as soon as shed.' [1]

The Kutchin Indians of North-West America, according
to Morgan, ' give vent to injured feelings, as well as physical
' pain, by crying, a practice shared equally by the males and
' females, and by the old as well as the young.'

At Tahiti, Captain Cook mentions that Oberea, the Queen,
and Tootahah, one of the principal chiefs, amused themselves
with two large dolls. D'Urville tells us that a New Zealand
chief, Tauvarya by name, ' cried like a child because the sailors
' spoilt his favourite cloak by powdering it with flour.' [2]
Williams [3] mentions that in Feejee not only the women, but even
the men give vent to their feelings by crying. Burton even
says that among East Africans the men cried more frequently
than the women. [4]

The Negro Kings of Western Africa, ' from Gelele to Ru-
' manika of Karaqwah, are delighted with children's toys,
' gutta-percha faces, Noah's Arks; in fact, what would be most
' acceptable to a child of eight—which the Negro is.' [5]

Not only do savages closely resemble children in their
general character, but a curious similarity exists between them
in many small points. For instance, the tendency to reduplication, which is so characteristic of children, prevails remarkably
also amongst savages. The first 1000 words in Richardson's
dictionary (down to allege), contain only three, namely, adsci-
titious, adventitious, agitator, and even in these it is reduced
to a minimum. There is not a single word like *ahi ahi*,
evening; *ake ake*, eternal; *oki oki*, a bird; *aniwaniwa*, the
rainbow; *anga anga*, agreement; *ungi ungi*, abroad; *aro aro*,
in front; *aru aru*, to woo; *ati ati*, to drive out; *awa awa*, a
valley; or *awanga wanga*, hope, words of a class which abound
in savage languages.

[1] Cook's first Voyage, p. 103.
[2] Vol. ii. p. 308.   See also Yate's New Zealand, p. 101.
[3] Fiji and the Fijians, vol. ii. p. 121.
[4] Lake Regions, p. 332.
[5] Burton's Dahome, vol. i. p. 326.

The first 1000 words in a French dictionary I found to contain only two reduplications, namely, anana and assassin, both of which are derived from a lower race, and cannot, strictly speaking, be regarded as French.

Again 1000 German words, taking for variety the letters C and D, contain six cases, namely, *Cacadu* (cockatoo), *Cacau*, *Cocon* (cocoon), *Cocosbaum*, a cocoa-tree, *Cocosnuss*, cocoa-nut, and *dagegen*, of which again all but the last are foreign.

Lastly, the first 1000 Greek words contained only two reduplications, one of which is ἀβαρβαρος.

For comparison with the above I have examined the vocabularies of the following eighteen tribes, and the results are given in the following table:—

| Languages | Number of words examined | Number of redu- plications | Propor- tion per mil. | |
|---|---|---|---|---|
| Europe — | | | | |
| English . . . | 1000 | 3 | 3 | |
| French . . . | 1000 | 2 | 2 | Both foreign. |
| German . . . | 1000 | 6 | 6 | All but one foreign. |
| Greek . . . | 1000 | 2 | 2 | One being ἀβαρβαρος. |
| Africa — | | | | |
| Beetjuan . . . | 189 | 7 | 37 | Lichtenstein. |
| Bosjesman . . | 129 | 5 | 38 | „ |
| Namaqua Hottentot . | 1000 | 75 | 75 | H. Tindall. |
| Mpongwe . . | 1264 | 76 | 60 | Snowden and Prall. |
| Folap . . . | 204 | 28 | 137 | Koelle. |
| Mbalon . . . | 267 | 27 | 100 | „ |
| America — | | | | |
| Makah . . . | 1011 | 80 | 79 | Smithsonian Contribu- tions, 1869. |
| Darien Indians . . | 184 | 13 | 70 | Trans. Eth. Soc. vol. vi. |
| Ojibwa . . . | 283 | 21 | 74 | Schoolcraft. |
| Tupy Brazil . . | 1000 | 66 | 66 | Gonsalves Dias. |
| Negroid — | | | | |
| Brumer Island . . | 214 | 37 | 170 | Macgillivray. |
| Redscar Bay . . | 125 | 10 | 80 | „ |
| Louisiade . . . | 138 | 22 | 160 | „ |
| Erroob . . . | 513 | 23 | 45 | Jukes. |
| Lewis Murray Island . | 506 | 19 | 38 | „ |
| Australia — | | | | |
| Kowrarega . . . | 720 | 28 | 38 | Macgillivray. |
| Polynesia — | | | | |
| Tonga . . . | 1000 | 166 | 166 | Mariner. |
| New Zealand . . | 1300 | 220 | 160 | Dieffenbach. |

For African languages I have examined the Beetjuan and Bosjesman dialects, given by Lichtenstein in his 'Travels in

'Southern Africa;' the Namaqua Hottentot, as given by Tindall in his 'Grammar and Vocabulary of the Namaqua 'Hottentot;' the Mpongwe of the Gaboon, from the Grammar of the Mpongwe language published by Snowden and Prall of New York; and lastly the Fulup and Mbofon languages, from Koelle's 'Polyglotta Africana.' For America, the Makah dialect, given by Mr Swan in the Smithsonian Contributions for 1869; the Ojibwa vocabulary, given in Schoolcraft's 'Indian Tribes;' the Darien vocabulary, from the 6th vol. N.S. of the Ethnological Society's Transactions; and the Tupy vocabulary, given in A. Gonsalvez Dias's 'Diccionaria 'da Lingua Tupy, chamada lingua geral dos indigenas do 'Brazil.' To these I have added the languages spoken on Brumer Island, at Redscar Bay, Kowrarega, and at the Louisiade, as collected by Macgillivray in the 'Voyage of the 'Rattlesnake;' and the dialects of Erroob and Lewis Murray Island, from Jukes's 'Voyage of the Fly.' Lastly, for Polynesia, the Tongan dictionary, given by Mariner, and that of New Zealand by Dieffenbach.

The result is, that while in the four European languages we get about two reduplications in 1000 words, in the savage ones the number varies from thirty-eight to 170, being from twenty to eighty times as many in proportion.

In the Polynesian and Feejee Islands they are particularly numerous; thus, in Feejee, such names as Somosomo, Rakiraki, Raviravi, Lumaluma are numerous. Perhaps the most familiar New Zealand words are meremere, patoo patoo, and kivi kivi. So generally, however, is reduplication a characteristic of savage tongues, that it even gave rise to the term 'barbarous.'

The love of pets is very strongly developed among savages. Many instances have been given by Mr. Galton in his Memoir on the 'Domestication of Animals.'[1]

Among minor indications may be mentioned the use of the rattle. Originally a sacred and mysterious instrument, as it is still among some of the Siberian Red-skin and Brazilian[2] tribes, it has with us degenerated into a child's toy. Thus

[1] Trans. Ethn. Soc. vol. iii. p. 122.
[2] Martius, Von dem Rechtszustande unter den Ur.-Brasilieus, p. 34.

Dobritzhoffer tells us, the Abipones at a certain season of the
year worshipped the Pleiades. The ceremony consisted in a
feast accompanied with dancing and music, alternating with
praises of the stars, during which the principal priestess 'who
' conducts the festive ceremonies, dances at intervals, rattling
' a gourd full of hardish fruit-seeds to musical time, and
' whirling round to the right with one foot, and to the left with
' another, without ever removing from one spot, or in the
' least varying her motions.' [1] Spix and Martius [2] thus describe
a Coroado chief:—In the middle of the assembly, and nearest
to the pot, stood 'the chief, who, by his strength, cunning, and
' courage, had obtained some command over them, and had re-
' ceived from Marlier the title of Captain. In his right hand
' he held the maracá, the above-mentioned castanet, which
' they call gringerina, and rattled with it, beating time with
' his right foot.' 'The Congo Negroes had a great wooden
' rattle, upon which they took their oaths.' [3] The rattle also is
very important among the Indians of North America.[4] When
any person is sick, the sorcerer or medicine-man brings his
sacred rattle and shakes it over him. This, says Prescott, ' is
' the principal catholicon for all diseases.' Catlin [5] also describes
the 'rattle' as being of great importance. Some tribes have
a sacred drum closely resembling that of the Lapps.[6] When
an Indian is ill, the magician, says Carver,[7] 'sits by the
' patient day and night, rattling in his ears a gourd-shell filled
' with dried beans, called a chichicoué.'

Klemm [8] also remarks on the great significance attached to
the rattle throughout America, and Staad even thought that it
was worshipped as a divinity.[9]

Schoolcraft [10] also gives a figure of Oshkabaiwis, the Redskin
medical chief, ' holding in his hand the magic rattle,' which is
indeed the usual emblem of authority in the American picto-

[1] Dobritzhoffer, vol. ii. p. 65. See
also p. 72.

[2] Travels in Brazil. London, 1824,
vol. ii. p. 234.

[3] Astley's Coll. of Voyages, vol. iii.
p. 233.

[4] Prescott in Schoolcraft's Indian
Tribes, vol. ii. pp. 179, 180.

[5] American Indians, vol. i. pp. 37.
40. 163, &c.

[6] Catlin, &c. cit. p. 40.

[7] Travels, p. 385.

[8] Culturgeschichte, vol. ii. p. 172.

[9] Mœurs des Sauvages américains,
vol. ii. p. 297.

[10] Indian Tribes, Pt. III. pp. 490,
492.

graphs. I know no case of a savage infant using the rattle as a plaything.

Tossing half-pence, as dice, again, which used to be a sacred and solemn mode of consulting the oracles, is now a mere game for children.

So again the doll is a hybrid between the baby and the fetich, and, exhibiting the contradictory characters of its parents, becomes singularly unintelligible to grown-up people. Mr. Tylor has pointed out other illustrations of this argument, and I would refer those who feel interested in this part of the subject to his excellent work.

Dancing is another case in point. With us it is a mere amusement. Among savages it is an important, and, in some cases, religious ceremony. 'If,' says Robertson,[1] 'any inter-'course be necessary between two American tribes, the ambas-'sadors of the one approach in a solemn dance, and present the 'calumet or emblem of peace ; the sachems of the other receive 'it with the same ceremony. If war is denounced against an 'enemy, it is by a dance, expressive of the resentment which 'they feel, and of the vengeance which they meditate. If the 'wrath of their gods is to be appeased, or their beneficence to 'be celebrated, if they rejoice at a birth of a child, or mourn 'the death of a friend, they have dances appropriated to each 'of these situations, and suited to the different sentiments with 'which they are then animated. If a person is indisposed, a 'dance is prescribed as the most effectual means of restoring 'him to health ; and if he himself cannot endure the fatigue of 'such an exercise, the physician or conjuror performs it in his 'name, as if the virtue of his activity could be transferred to 'his patient.'

But it is unnecessary to multiply illustrations. Every one who has read much on the subject will admit the truth of the statement. · It explains the capricious treatment which so many white men have received from savage potentates; how they have been alternately petted and ill-treated, at one time loaded with the best of everything, at another neglected or put to death.

Robertson's America, bk. iv. p. 133.

The close resemblance existing in ideas, language, habits, and character between savages and children, though generally admitted, has usually been disposed of in a passing sentence, and regarded rather as a curious accident than as an important truth. Yet from several points of view it possesses a high interest. Better understood, it might have saved us many national misfortunes, from the loss of Captain Cook down to the Abyssinian war. It has also a direct bearing on the present discussion.

The opinion is rapidly gaining ground among naturalists, that the development of the individual is an epitome of that of the species, a conclusion which, if fully borne out, will evidently prove most instructive. Already many facts are on record which render it, to say the least, highly probable. Birds of the same genus, or of closely allied genera, which, when mature, differ much in colour, are often very similar when young. The young of the Lion and the Puma are often striped, and fœtal whales have teeth. Leidy has shown that the milk-teeth of the genus *Equus* resemble the permanent teeth of *Anchitherium*, while the milk-teeth of *Anchitherium* again approximate to the dental system of *Merychippus*.[1] Rütimeyer, while calling attention to this interesting observation, adds that the milk-teeth of *Equus caballus* in the same way, and still more those of *E. fossilis*, resemble the permanent teeth of *Hipparion*.[2]

Agassiz, according to Darwin, regards it as a ‘law of nature,’ that the young states of each species and group resemble older forms of the same group; and Darwin himself says,[3] that ‘in ‘two or more groups of animals, however much they may at ‘first differ from each other in structure and habits, if they ‘pass through closely similar embryonic stages, we may feel ‘almost assured that they have descended from the same parent ‘form, and are therefore closely related.’ So also Mr. Herbert Spencer says,[4] ‘Each organism exhibits within a short

[1] Proc. Acad. Nat. Soc. Philadelphia, 1858, p. 28.

[2] Beiträge zur Kenntniss der fossilen Pferde. Basle, 1863.

[3] Origin of Species, 4th edition. p. 532.

[4] Principles of Biology, vol. i. p. 348.

'space of time, a series of changes which, when supposed to
'occupy a period indefinitely great, and to go on in various
'ways instead of one way, give us a tolerably clear conception
'of organic evolution in general.'

It may be said that this argument involves the acceptance
of the Darwinian hypothesis; this would, however, be a mistake; the objection might indeed be tenable if men belonged
to different species, but it cannot fairly be urged by those who
regard all mankind as descended from common ancestors; and,
in fact, it is strongly held by Agassiz, one of Mr. Darwin's
most uncompromising opponents. Regarded from this point
of view, the similarity existing between savages and children
assumes a singular importance and becomes almost conclusive
as regards the question now at issue.

The Duke ends his work with the expression of a belief
that man, ' even in his most civilised condition, is capable of de-
' gradation, that his knowledge may decay, and that his religion
' may be lost.' That this is true of individuals, I do not of
course deny; that it holds good with the human race, I cannot
believe.[1]   Far more true, far more noble, as it seems to me,
are the concluding passages of Lord Dunraven's opening address to the Cambrian Archæological Association, ' that if we
' look back through the entire period of the past history of
' man, as exhibited in the result of archæological investigation,
' we can scarcely fail to perceive that the whole exhibits one
' grand scheme of progression, which, notwithstanding partial
' periods of decline, has for its end the ever-increasing civilisa-
' tion of man, and the gradual development of his higher facul-
' ties, and for its object the continual manifestation of the de-
' sign, the power, the wisdom, and the goodness of Almighty
' God.'

[1] The Duke appears to consider that
the first men, though deficient in
knowledge of the mechanical arts, were
morally and intellectually superior, or
at least equal, to those of the present
day; and it is remarkable that, sup-
porting such a view, he should regard
himself as a champion of orthodoxy.
Adam is, on the contrary, represented
to us in Genesis not only as naked, and
subsequently clothed with leaves, but as
unable to resist the most trivial temptation, and as entertaining very gross and
anthropomorphic conceptions of the
Deity. In fact in all three characteristics—in his mode of life, in his moral
condition, and in his intellectual conceptions—Adam was a typical Savage.

I confess therefore that, after giving the arguments of the Duke of Argyll my most attentive and candid consideration, I see no reason to adopt his melancholy conclusion, but I remain persuaded that the past history of man has, on the whole, been one of progress, and that, in looking forward to the future, we are justified in doing so with confidence and with hope.

# NOTES.

## PAGE 70.

### *Position of Women in Australia.*[1]

'FŒMIN.E sese per totam pene vitam prostituunt. Apud
' plurimas tribus juventutem utriusque sexus sine discrimine
' concumbere in usu est. Si juvenis forte indigenorum cœtum
' quendam in castris manentem advenial, ubi quævis sit puella
' innupta, mos est, nocte veniente et cubantibus omnibus,
' illam ex loco exsurgere et juvenem accidentem cum illo per
' noctem manere, unde in sedem propriam ante diem redit. Cui
' fœmina sit, eam amicis libenter præbet; si in itinere sit, uxori
' in castris manenti aliquis supplet illi vices. Advenis ex
' longinquo accidentibus fœminas ad tempus dare hospitis esse
' boni judicatur. Viduis et fœminis jam senescentibus sæpe in
' id traditis, quandoque etiam invitis et insciis cognatis, adole-
' scentes utuntur. Puellæ teneræ a decimo primum anno, et
' pueri a decimo tertio vel quarto, inter se miscentur. Seniori-
' bus mos est, si forte gentium plurium castra appropinquant,
' viros noctu hinc inde transeuntes, uxoribus alienis uti et in
' sua castra ex utraque parte mane redire.

' Temporibus quinetiam certis, machina quædam ex ligno
' ad formam ovi facta, sacra et mystica, nam fœminas aspicere
' haud licitum, decem plus minus uncias longa et circa quatuor
' lata, insculpta ac figuris diversis ornata, et ultimam perforata
' partem ad longam (plerumque e crinibus humanis textam)
' inserendam chordam cui nomen "Moo yumkarr," extra castra
' in gyrum versata, stridore magno e percusso ære facto, liber-

[1] Eyre's Discoveries, &c, vol. ii. p. 320.

' tatem coeundi juventuti esse tum concessam omnibus indicat.
' Parentes sæpe infantum, viri uxorum quæstum corporum
' faciunt. In urbe Adelaide panis præmio parvi aut paucorum
' denariorum meretrices fieri eas libenter cogunt. Facile potest
' intelligi, amorem inter nuptos vix posse esse grandem, quum
' omnia quæ ad fœminas attinent, hominum arbitrio ordinentur
' et tanta sexuum societati laxitas, et adolescentes quibus ita
' multæ ardoris explendi dantur occasiones, haud magnopere
' uxores, nisi ut servos, desideraturos.'

### Page 89.

#### *Adoption.*

' Adjiciendum et hoc, quod post evectionem ad Deos, Juno,
' Jovis suasu, filium sibi Herculem adoptavit, et omne deinceps
' tempus materna ipsum benevolentia complexa fuerit. Illam
' adoptionem hoc modo factam perhibent: Juno lectum in-
' gressa, Herculem corpori suo admotum, ut verum imitaretur
' partum, subter vestes ad terram demisit. Quem in hoc
' usque tempus adoptionis ritum barbari observant.' '

### Page 117.

#### *Expiation for Marriage.*

The passage in St. Augustin is as follows:—

' Sed quid hoc dicam, cum ibi sit et Priapus nimius
' masculus, super cujus immanissimum et turpissimum fasci-
' num sedere nova nupta jubeatur, more honestissimo et religio-
' sissimo matronarum.' '

In his description of Babylonian customs, Herodotus says:'

Ὁ δὲ δὴ αἴσχιστος τῶν νόμων ἐστὶ τοῖσι Βαβυλωνίοισι ὅδε·
δεῖ πᾶσαν γυναῖκα ἐπιχωρίην ἱζομένην ἐς ἱρὸν Ἀφροδίτης, ἅπαξ ἐν
τῇ ζόῃ μιχθῆναι ἀνδρὶ ξείνῳ. Πολλαὶ δὲ καὶ οὐκ ἀξιεύμεναι ἀνα-
μίσγεσθαι τῇσι ἄλλῃσι, οἷα πλούτῳ ὑπερφρονέουσαι, ἐπὶ ζευγέων ἐν
καμάρῃσι ἐλάσασαι, πρὸς τὸ ἱρὸν ἑστᾶσι· θεραπηίη δέ σφι ὄπισθεν
ἔπεται πολλή. αἱ δὲ πλεῦνες ποιεῦσι ὧδε· ἐν τεμένεϊ Ἀφροδίτης

---

' Diodorus, iv. 39.       ' Civit. Dei, vi. 9.       ' Clio I. 199.

κατέαται, στέφανον περὶ τῇσι κεφαλῇσι ἔχουσαι θώμιγγος, πολλαὶ
γυναῖκες· αἱ μὲν γὰρ προσέρχονται, αἱ δὲ ἀπέρχονται· σχοινοτενέες
δὲ διέξοδοι πάντα τρόπον ὁδῶν ἔχουσι διὰ τῶν γυναικῶν, δι' ὧν
οἱ ξεῖνοι διεξιόντες ἐκλέγονται. ἔνθα ἐπεὰν ἵζηται γυνή, οὐ πρότερον
ἀπαλλάσσεται ἐς τὰ οἰκία, ἢ τίς οἱ ξείνων ἀργύριον ἐμβαλὼν ἐς τὰ
γούνατα, μιχθῇ ἔξω τοῦ ἱροῦ· ἐμβαλόντα δὲ δεῖ εἰπεῖν τοσόνδε·
Ἐπικαλέω τοι τὴν θεὸν Μύλιττα. Μύλιττα δὲ καλέουσι τὴν
Ἀφροδίτην Ἀσσύριοι· τὸ δὲ ἀργύριον μέγαθός ἐστι ὅσον ὦν· οὐ
γὰρ μὴ ἀπώσηται· οὐ γάρ οἱ θέμις ἐστί· γίνεται γὰρ ἱρὸν τοῦτο τὸ
ἀργύριον· τῷ δὲ πρώτῳ ἐμβαλόντι ἕπεται, οὐδὲ ἀποδοκιμᾷ οὐδένα·
ἐπεὰν δὲ μιχθῇ ἀποσιωσαμένη τῇ θεῷ ἀπολλάσσεται ἐς τὰ οἰκία,
καὶ τἀπὸ τούτου οὐκ οὕτω μέγα τί οἱ δώσεις ὥς μιν λάμψεαι.
ὅσαι μέν νυν εἰδεός τε ἐπαμμέναι εἰσὶ καὶ μεγάθεος, ταχὺ ἀπαλλάσ-
σονται· ὅσαι δὲ ἄμορφοι αὐτέων εἰσί, χρόνον πολλὸν προσμένουσι
οὐ δυνάμεναι τὸν νόμον ἐκπλῆσαι· καὶ γὰρ τριέτεα καὶ τετραέτεα
μετεξέτεραι χρόνον μένουσι. ἐνιαχῇ δὲ καὶ τῆς Κύπρου ἐστὶ
παραπλήσιος τούτῳ νόμος.

Mela[1] tells us that among the Auzilea, another Æthiopian
tribe, 'Feminis solemne est, nocte, qua nubunt, omnium
'stupro patere, qui cum munere advenerint: et tum, cum
'plurimis concubuisse, maximum decus; in reliquum pudicitia
'insignis est.'

Speaking of the Nasamonians, Herodotus observes:

πρῶτον δὲ γαμέοντος Νασαμῶνος ἀνδρὸς, νόμος ἐστὶ τὴν νύμφην
νυκτὶ τῇ πρώτῃ διὰ πάντων διεξελθεῖν τῶν δαιτυμόνων μισγομένην·
τῶν δὲ ὡς ἕκαστός οἱ μιχθῇ, διδοῖ δῶρον, τὸ ἂν ἔχῃ φερόμενος ἐξ
οἴκου.[2]

Diodorus[3] also gives a very similar account of marriage in
the Balearic Islands.

## PAGE 111.

### The Character of Helen.

The character and position of Helen has not, I think, been
as yet correctly appreciated. Mr. Gladstone truly observes[4]
that 'No one forming his estimate of Helen from Homer only

[1] Mela, i. 8.  
[2] Malpomene, iv. 172.  
[3] Diodorus, v. 18.  
[4] Juventus Mundi, p. 507.

' could fall into the gross error of looking upon her as a type
' of depraved character ;' but even he has, I think, hardly done
justice.   He continues as follows :—

   ' Her fall once incurred, she finds herself bound by the
' iron chain of circumstance, from which she can obtain no
' extrication.   But to the world, beneath whose standard of
' morality she has sunk, she makes at least this reparation, that
' the sharp condemnation of herself is ever in her mouth, and
' that she does not seek to throw off the burden of her shame
' on her more guilty partner.   Nay, more than this, her self-
' debasing and self-renouncing humility come nearer, perhaps,
' than any other heathen example to the type of Christian
' penitence.'

   Other writers have felt the same difficulty.   Maclaurin, for
instance, says: [1] ' What is most astonishing of all is, that they
' (the Trojans) did not restore her upon the death of Paris,
' but married her to his brother Deiphobus.   Here Chrysostom
' argues, and with great plausibility, that this is perfectly in-
' credible, upon the supposition that Paris had possessed him-
' self of her by a crime.'

   We must, however, judge Helen by the customs of the
time, and it has been clearly shown that among the lower races
of man, marriage by capture was a recognised custom.   Hers
seems to me a case of this kind.   It will be observed that she
is always spoken of as Paris' wife.   Thus, speaking of Paris,
she says—

     Would that a better man had called me wife ; [2]

and again —

     Godlike Paris claims me as his wife.[3]

Paris himself speaks of her as his wife—

     Yet hath my wife, e'en now, with soothing words
     Urged me to join the battle.[4]

   So also Hector, though he regarded Paris with great contempt, and reproached him in strong language, addresses him
as married.

[1] Dissertation to prove that Troy was
not taken by the Greeks.   By John
Maclaurin, Esq.

[2] VI. 402.   Lord Derby's Trans.
[3] L. c. xxiv. 892.
[4] VI. 391.

Thou wretched Paris, though in form so fair,
Thou slave of woman, manhood's counterfeit!
Would I thou had'st ne'er been born, or died at least
Unwedded! [1]

and speaks to Helen with kindness and affection; as, for instance, in the VIth Book he says:

Though kind thy wish, yet, Helen, ask me not
To sit or rest; I cannot yield to thee,
For burns e'en now my soul to aid our friends,
Who feel my loss, and sorely need my arm.
But thou thy husband rouse, and let him speed,
That he may find me still within the walls. [2]

The aged Priam, even when grieving over the fatal war, is careful to assure Helen that he does not complain of her:

Not thee I blame,
But to the Gods I owe this woful war. [3]

These were no exceptional cases. On the contrary, in her touching lament over Hector's corpse, Helen says:

Hector, of all my brethren dearest thou!
True, Godlike Paris claims me as his wife,
Who bore me hither—would I then had died!
But twenty years have pass'd since here I came.
And left my native land; yet ne'er from thee
I heard one scornful, one degrading word;
And when from others I have borne reproach,
Thy brothers, sisters, or thy brothers' wives,
Or mother (for thy sire was over kind
E'en as a father), thou hast check'd them still
With tender feeling, and with gentle words.
For thee I weep, and for myself no less;
For, through the breadth of Troy, none love me now,
None kindly look on me, but all abhor.
Weeping she spoke, and with her wept the crowd.

Even in that hour of sorrow, the people pitied, but did not upbraid her. It is true that she reproaches herself; not, however, apparently for her marriage with Paris, but on account of the misfortunes which she had been the means of bringing on Troy.

I dwell on these considerations, because unless we realise the fact that marriage by capture was a recognised form of

[1] III. 43.   [2] VI. 410.   [3] L. c. iii. 195.

I. L

matrimony, involving, according to the ideas of the time, no disgrace, at any rate to the woman, it seems to me that we cannot understand the character of Helen, or properly appreciate the ' Iliad' itself. If Helen was a faithless wife, an abandoned and guilty wretch, the terms in which she is described by Homer would be, to say the least, misplaced: he would have condoned vice when clad in the garb of beauty.

Yet his treatment of Venus shows how little likely he was so to err, and we must, I think, on the whole, conclude that according to the ideas of the time Helen was legally married to Paris, and was guilty of no crime.

## PAGE 344.

### *The Multiplicity of Rules in Australia.*

It seems at first sight remarkable that a race so low as the Australians should have such stringent laws and apparently complex rules. In fact, however, they are merely customs to which antiquity has gradually given the force of law; and it is obvious that when a race has long remained stationary we may naturally expect to find many customs thus crystallised, as it were, by age.

# INDEX.

LONDON: PRINTED BY
SPOTTISWOODE AND CO., NEW-STREET SQUARE
AND PARLIAMENT STREET

39 PATERNOSTER ROW, E.C.
LONDON, *August* 1875.

# GENERAL LIST OF WORKS

### PUBLISHED BY

## MESSRS. LONGMANS, GREEN, AND CO.

## HISTORY, POLITICS, HISTORICAL MEMOIRS, &c.

*Journal of the Reigns of King George the Fourth and King William the Fourth.*

*By the late Charles Cavendish Fulke Greville, Esq.*

*Edited by Henry Reeve, Esq.*

*Fifth Edition.* 3 vols. 8vo. *price* 36s.

*The Life of Napoleon III. derived from State Records, Unpublished Family Correspondence, and Personal Testimony.*

*By Blanchard Jerrold.*

*Four Vols. 8vo. with numerous Portraits and Facsimiles.* VOLS. I. and II. *price* 18s. *each.*

\*₄\* Vols. *III. and IV. are in preparation.*

A

Recollections and Sugges-
tions, 1813–1873.
By John Earl Russell, K.G.
New Edition, revised and enlarged. 8vo. 16s.

Introductory Lectures on
Modern History delivered
in Lent Term 1842 ; with
the Inaugural Lecture de-
livered in December 1841.
By the late Rev. Thomas
Arnold, D.D.
8vo. price 7s. 6d.

On Parliamentary Go-
vernment in England: its
Origin, Development, and
Practical Operation.
By Alpheus Todd.
2 vols. 8vo. £1. 17s.

The Constitutional His-
tory of England since the
Accession of George III.
1760–1870.
By Sir Thomas Erskine
May, K.C.B.
Fourth Edition. 3 vols. crown 8vo. 18s.

Democracy in Europe;
a History.
By Sir Thomas Erskine
May, K.C.B.
2 vols. 8vo.    [In the press.

The History of England
from the Fall of Wolsey to
the Defeat of the Spanish
Armada.
By J. A. Froude, M.A.
CABINET EDITION, 12 vols. cr. 8vo. £3. 12s.
LIBRARY EDITION, 12 vols. 8vo. £8. 18s.

The English in Ireland
in the Eighteenth Century.
By J. A. Froude, M.A.
3 vols. 8vo. £2. 8s.

The History of England
from the Accession of
James II.
By Lord Macaulay.
STUDENT'S EDITION, 2 vols. cr. 8vo. 12s.
PEOPLE'S EDITION, 4 vols. cr. 8vo. 16s.
CABINET EDITION, 8 vols. post 8vo. 48s.
LIBRARY EDITION, 5 vols. 8vo. £4.

Critical and Historical
Essays contributed to the
Edinburgh Review.
By the Right Hon. Lord
Macaulay.
Cheap Edition, authorised and complete,
crown 8vo. 3s. 6d.

STUDENT'S EDITION, crown 8vo. 6s.
PEOPLE'S EDITION, 2 vols. crown 8vo. 8s.
CABINET EDITION, 4 vols. 24s.
LIBRARY EDITION, 3 vols. 8vo. 36s.

Lord Macaulay's Works.
Complete and uniform Li-
brary Edition.
Edited by his Sister, Lady
Trevelyan.
8 vols. 8vo. with Portrait, £5. 5s.

Lectures on the History
of England from the Ear-
liest Times to the Death of
King Edward II.
By W. Longman, F.S.A.
Maps and Illustrations.  8vo. 15s.

The History of the Life
and Times of Edward III.
By W. Longman, F.S.A.
With 9 Maps, 8 Plates, and 16 Woodcuts.
2 vols. 8vo. 28s.

*History of England* under the Duke of Buckingham and Charles the First, 1624–1628.
By S. Rawson Gardiner, late Student of Ch. Ch.
2 vols. 8vo. with two Maps, 24s.

*History of Civilization in* England and France, Spain and Scotland.
By Henry Thomas Buckle.
3 vols. crown 8vo. 24s.

*A Student's Manual of* the History of India from the Earliest Period to the Present.
By Col. Meadows Taylor, M.R.A.S.
Second Thousand. Cr. 8vo. Maps, 7s. 6d.

*Studies from Genoese* History.
By Colonel G. B. Malleson, C.S.I. Guardian to His Highness the Maharájá of Mysore.
Crown 8vo. 10s. 6d.

*The Native States of* India in Subsidiary Alliance with the British Government; an Historical Sketch. With a Notice of the Mediatized and Minor States.
By Colonel G. B. Malleson, C.S.I. Guardian to His Highness the Maharájá of Mysore.
With 6 Coloured Maps, 8vo. price 15s.

*The History of India* from the Earliest Period to the close of Lord Dalhousie's Administration.
By John Clark Marshman.
3 vols. crown 8vo. 22s. 6d.

*Indian Polity; a View of* the System of Administration in India.
By Lieut.-Colonel George Chesney.
Second Edition, revised, with Map. 8vo. 21s.

*Waterloo Lectures;* a Study of the Campaign of 1815.
By Colonel Charles C. Chesney, R.E.
Third Edition. 8vo. with Map, 10s. 6d.

*Essays in Modern Mili-* tary Biography.
By Colonel Charles C. Chesney, R.E.
8vo. 12s. 6d.

*The Imperial and Colo-* nial Constitutions of the Britannic Empire, including Indian Institutions.
By Sir E. Creasy, M.A.
With 6 Maps. 8vo. 15s.

*The Oxford Reformers—* John Colet, Erasmus, and Thomas More; being a History of their Fellow-Work.
By Frederic Seebohm.
Second Edition. 8vo. 14s.

The New Reformation, a Narrative of the Old Catholic Movement, from 1870 to the Present Time; with an Historical Introduction.
By Theodorus.
8vo. price 12s.

The Mythology of the Aryan Nations.
By Geo. W. Cox, M.A. late Scholar of Trinity College, Oxford.
2 vols. 8vo. 28s.

A History of Greece.
By the Rev. Geo. W. Cox, M.A. late Scholar of Trinity College, Oxford.
Vols. I. and II. 8vo. Maps, 36s.

A School History of Greece to the Death of Alexander the Great.
By the Rev. George W. Cox, M.A. late Scholar of Trinity College, Oxford; Author of 'The Aryan Mythology' &c.
1 vol. crown 8vo. [In the press.

The History of the Peloponnesian War, by Thucydides.
Translated by Richd. Crawley, Fellow of Worcester College, Oxford.
8vo. 21s.

The Tale of the Great Persian War, from the Histories of Herodotus.
By Rev. G. W. Cox, M.A.
Fcp. 8vo. 3s. 6d.

Greek History from Themistocles to Alexander, in a Series of Lives from Plutarch.
Revised and arranged by A. H. Clough.
Fcp. 8vo. Woodcuts, 6s.

General History of Rome from the Foundation of the City to the Fall of Augustulus, B.C. 753—A.D. 476.
By the Very Rev. C. Merivale, D.D. Dean of Ely.
With 5 Maps, crown 8vo. 7s. 6d.

History of the Romans under the Empire.
By Dean Merivale, D.D.
8 vols. post 8vo. 48s.

The Fall of the Roman Republic; a Short History of the Last Century of the Commonwealth.
By Dean Merivale, D.D.
12mo. 7s. 6d.

The Sixth Oriental Monarchy; or the Geography, History, and Antiquities of Parthia. Collected and Illustrated from Ancient and Modern sources.

By Geo. Rawlinson, M.A.
With Maps and Illustrations.  8vo. 16s.

The Seventh Great Oriental Monarchy; or, a History of the Sassanians: with Notices Geographical and Antiquarian.

By Geo. Rawlinson, M.A.
8vo. with Maps and Illustrations.
[In the press.

Encyclopædia of Chronology, Historical and Biographical; comprising the Dates of all the Great Events of History, including Treaties, Alliances, Wars, Battles, &c. Incidents in the Lives of Eminent Men, Scientific and Geographical Discoveries, Mechanical Inventions, and Social, Domestic, and Economical Improvements.

By B. B. Woodward, B.A. and W. L. R. Cates.
8vo. 42s.

The History of Rome.
By Wilhelm Ihne.
Vols. I. and II. 8vo. 30s.  Vols. III. and IV. in preparation.

History of European Morals from Augustus to Charlemagne.
By W. E. H. Lecky, M.A.
2 vols. 8vo. 28s.

History of the Rise and Influence of the Spirit of Rationalism in Europe.
By W. E. H. Lecky, M.A.
Cabinet Edition, 2 vols. crown 8vo. 16s.

Introduction to the Science of Religion: Four Lectures delivered at the Royal Institution; with two Essays on False Analogies and the Philosophy of Mythology.
By F. Max Müller, M.A.
Crown 8vo. 10s. 6d.

The Stoics, Epicureans, and Sceptics.
Translated from the German of Dr. E. Zeller, by Oswald J. Reichel, M.A.
Crown 8vo. 14s.

Socrates and the Socratic Schools.
Translated from the German of Dr. E. Zeller, by the Rev. O. J. Reichel, M.A.
Crown 8vo. 8s. 6d.

*Sketch of the History of the Church of England to the Revolution of 1688.*
By T. V. Short, D.D. sometime Bishop of St. Asaph.
New Edition. Crown 8vo. 7s. 6d.

*The Historical Geography of Europe.*
By E. A. Freeman, D.C.L.
8vo. Maps. [In the press.

*Essays on the History of the Christian Religion.*
By John Earl Russell, K.G.
Fcp. 8vo. 3s. 6d.

*The Student's Manual of Ancient History: containing the Political History, Geographical Position, and Social State of the Principal Nations of Antiquity.*
By W. Cooke Taylor, LL.D.
Crown 8vo. 7s. 6d.

*The Student's Manual of Modern History: containing the Rise and Progress of the Principal European Nations, their Political History, and the Changes in their Social Condition.*
By W. Cooke Taylor, LL.D.
Crown 8vo. 7s. 6d.

*The History of Philosophy, from Thales to Comte.*
By George Henry Lewes.
Fourth Edition, 2 vols. 8vo. 32s.

*The Crusades.*
By the Rev. G. W. Cox, M.A.
Fcp. 8vo. with Map, 2s. 6d.

*The Era of the Protestant Revolution.*
By F. Seebohm, Author of 'The Oxford Reformers.'
With 4 Maps and 12 Diagrams. Fcp. 8vo. 2s. 6d.

*The Thirty Years' War, 1618–1648.*
By Samuel Rawson Gardiner.
Fcp. 8vo. with Maps, 2s. 6d.

*The Houses of Lancaster and York; with the Conquest and Loss of France.*
By James Gairdner.
Fcp. 8vo. with Map, 2s. 6d.

*Edward the Third.*
By the Rev. W. Warburton, M.A.
Fcp. 8vo. with Maps, 2s. 6d.

## BIOGRAPHICAL WORKS.

**Autobiography.**
By John Stuart Mill.
8vo. 7s. 6d.

**The Life and Letters of Lord Macaulay.**
By his Nephew, G. Otto Trevelyan, M.P. for the Hawick District of Burghs.
2 vols. 8vo.    [In the press.

**Admiral Sir Edward Codrington,** a Memoir of his Life; with Selections from his Private and Official Correspondence.
Abridged from the larger work, and edited by his Daughter, Lady Bourchier.
With Portrait, Maps, &c. crown 8vo. price 7s. 6d.

**Life and Letters of Gilbert Elliot, First Earl of Minto,** from 1751 to 1806, when his Public Life in Europe was closed by his Appointment to the Vice-Royalty of India.
Edited by the Countess of Minto.
3 vols. post 8vo. 31s. 6d.

**Recollections of Past Life.**
By Sir Henry Holland, Bart. M.D. F.R.S.
Third Edition. Post 8vo. 10s. 6d.

**Isaac Casaubon,** 1559-1614.
By Mark Pattison, Rector of Lincoln College, Oxford.
8vo. price 18s.

**The Memoirs of Sir John Reresby, of Thrybergh, Bart. M.P. for York, &c.** 1634-1689.
Written by Himself. Edited from the Original Manuscript by James J. Cartwright, M.A. Cantab. of H.M. Public Record Office.
8vo. price 21s.

**Biographical and Critical Essays,** reprinted from Reviews, with Additions and Corrections.
By A. Hayward, Q.C.
Second Series, 2 vols. 8vo. 28s. Third Series, 1 vol. 8vo. 14s.

**The Life of Isambard Kingdom Brunel,** Civil Engineer.
By I. Brunel, B.C.L.
With Portrait, Plates, and Woodcuts. 8vo. 21s.

**Lord George Bentinck;** a Political Biography.
By the Right Hon. B. Disraeli, M.P.
New Edition. Crown 8vo. 6s.

*The Life and Letters of
the Rev. Sydney Smith.
Edited by his Daughter,
Lady Holland, and
Mrs. Austin.*
Crown 8vo. 2s. 6d. sewed; 3s. 6d. cloth.

*Essays in Ecclesiastical
Biography.
By the Right Hon. Sir J.
Stephen, LL.D.*
Cabinet Edition. Crown 8vo. 7s. 6d.

*Leaders of Public Opi-
nion in Ireland; Swift,
Flood, Grattan, O'Connell.
By W. E. H. Lecky, M.A.*
Crown 8vo. 7s. 6d.

*Dictionary of General
Biography; containing
Concise Memoirs and No-
tices of the most Eminent
Persons of all Ages and
Countries.
By W. L. R. Cates.*
New Edition, 8vo. 25s. Supplement, 4s. 6d.

*Life of the Duke of
Wellington.
By the Rev. G. R. Gleig,
M.A.*
Crown 8vo. with Portrait, 5s.

*Felix Mendelssohn's
Letters from Italy and
Switzerland, and Letters
from 1833 to 1847. Trans-
lated by Lady Wallace.*
With Portrait. 2 vols. crown 8vo. 5s. each.

*The Rise of Great Fami-
lies; other Essays and
Stories.
By Sir Bernard Burke,
C.B. LL.D.*
Crown 8vo. 12s. 6d.

*Memoirs of Sir Henry
Havelock, K.C.B.
By John Clark Marshman.*
Crown 8vo. 3s. 6d.

*Vicissitudes of Families.
By Sir Bernard Burke,
C.B.*
2 vols. crown 8vo. 21s.

## MENTAL and POLITICAL PHILOSOPHY.

*Comte's System of Posi-
tive Polity, or Treatise upon
Sociology.
Translated from the Paris
Edition of 1851–1854,
and furnished with Ana-
lytical Tables of Contents.
In Four Volumes, each
forming in some degree an
independent Treatise:—*
Vol. I. General View of Positivism and
Introductory Principles. Translated by

J. H. Bridges, M.B. *formerly Fellow of Oriel
College, Oxford.* 8vo. price 21s.

Vol. II. The Social Statics, or the Abstract Laws of Human Order. Translated
by Frederic Harrison, M.A.    [In Oct.

Vol. III. The Social Dynamics, or the
General Laws of Human Progress (the Philosophy of History). Translated by E. S.
Beesly, M.A. Professor of History in University College, London. 8vo.    [In Dec.

Vol. IV. The Synthesis of the Future of
Mankind. Translated by Richard Congreve,
M.D., and an Appendix, containing the
Author's Minor Treatises, translated by
H. D. Hutton, M.A. Barrister-at-Law.
8vo.    [Early in 1876.

Order and Progress:
Part I. Thoughts on Go-
vernment; Part II. Stu-
dies of Political Crises.
By Frederic Harrison,
M.A. of Lincoln's Inn.
8vo. 14s.

Essays, Political, Social,
and Religious.
By Richd. Congreve, M.A.
8vo. 18s.

Essays, Critical and
Biographical, contributed
to the Edinburgh Review.
By Henry Rogers.
New Edition. 2 vols. crown 8vo. 12s.

Essays on some Theolo-
gical Controversies of the
Time, contributed chiefly
to the Edinburgh Review.
By Henry Rogers.
New Edition. Crown 8vo. 6s.

Democracy in America.
By Alexis de Tocqueville.
Translated by Henry
Reeve, Esq.
New Edition. 2 vols. crown 8vo. 16s.

On Representative Go-
vernment.
By John Stuart Mill.
Fourth Edition, crown 8vo. 2s.

On Liberty.
By John Stuart Mill.
Post 8vo. 7s. 6d. crown 8vo. 1s. 4d.

Principles of Political
Economy.
By John Stuart Mill.
2 vols. 8vo. 30s. or 1 vol. crown 8vo. 5s.

Essays on some Unsettled
Questions of Political Eco-
nomy.
By John Stuart Mill.
Second Edition. 8vo. 6s. 6d.

Utilitarianism.
By John Stuart Mill.
Fourth Edition. 8vo. 5s.

A System of Logic,
Ratiocinative and Induc-
tive. By John Stuart Mill.
Eighth Edition. 2 vols. 8vo. 25s.

The Subjection of Women.
By John Stuart Mill.
New Edition. Post 8vo. 5s.

Examination of Sir
William Hamilton's Phi-
losophy, and of the principal Philosophical Questions
discussed in his Writings.
By John Stuart Mill.
Fourth Edition. 8vo. 16s.

Dissertations and Dis-
cussions.
By John Stuart Mill.
Second Edition. 3 vols. 8vo. 36s. Vol. IV.
(completion) price 10s. 6d.

B

*Analysis of the Pheno-*
*mena of the Human Mind.*
*By James Mill.    New*
*Edition,   with   Notes,*
*Illustrative and Critical.*
2 vols. 8vo. 28s.

*A   Systematic   View   of*
*the   Science   of   Jurispru-*
*dence.*
*By Sheldon Amos, M.A.*
8vo. 18s.

*A Primer of the English*
*Constitution   and   Govern-*
*ment.*
*By Sheldon Amos, M.A.*
Second Edition.   Crown 8vo. 6s.

*Principles of Economical*
*Philosophy.*
*By H. D. Macleod, M.A.*
*Barrister-at-Law.*
Second Edition, in 2 vols. Vol. I. 8vo. 15s.
Vol. II. Part I. price 12s.

*The Institutes of Jus-*
*tinian; with English In-*
*troduction,   Translation,*
*and Notes.*
*By T. C. Sandars, M.A.*
Fifth Edition.   8vo. 18s.

*Lord Bacon's Works,*
*Collected and Edited by R.*
*L. Ellis, M.A. J. Sped-*
*ding, M.A. and D. D.*
*Heath.*
New and Cheaper Edition.   7 vols. 8vo.
£3. 13s. 6d.

*Letters   and   Life   of*
*Francis Bacon, including*
*all his Occasional Works.*
*Collected and edited, with*
*a   Commentary,   by   J.*
*Spedding.*
7 vols. 8vo. £4. 4s.

*The Nicomachean Ethics*
*of Aristotle.  Newly trans-*
*lated into English.*
*By R. Williams, B.A.*
8vo. 12s.

*The Politics of Aristotle;*
*Greek Text, with English*
*Notes.*
*By Richard Congreve, M.A.*
New Edition, revised.   8vo. 18s.

*The Ethics of Aristotle;*
*with Essays and Notes.*
*By Sir A. Grant, Bart.*
*M.A. L.L.D.*
Third Edition.   2 vols. 8vo. price 32s.

*Bacon's   Essays,   with*
*Annotations.*
*By R. Whately, D.D.*
New Edition.   8vo. 10s. 6d.

*Picture   Logic;   an   At-*
*tempt   to   Popularise   the*
*Science of Reasoning by the*
*combination of Humorous*
*Pictures with Examples of*
*Reasoning taken from Daily*
*Life.*
*By A. Swinbourne, B.A.*
With Woodcut Illustrations from Drawings
by the Author.   Fcp. 8vo. price 5s.

*Elements of Logic.*
By R. Whately, D.D.
New Edition. 8vo. 10s. 6d. cr. 8vo. 4s. 6d.

*Elements of Rhetoric.*
By R. Whately, D.D.
New Edition. 8vo. 10s. 6d. cr. 8vo. 4s. 6d.

*An Outline of the Necessary Laws of Thought: a Treatise on Pure and Applied Logic.*
By the Most Rev. W. Thomson, D.D. Archbishop of York.
Ninth Thousand. Crown 8vo. 5s. 6d.

*An Introduction to Mental Philosophy, on the Inductive Method.*
By J. D. Morell, LL.D.
8vo. 12s.

*Elements of Psychology,* containing the Analysis of the Intellectual Powers.
By J. D. Morell, LL.D.
Post 8vo. 7s. 6d.

*The Secret of Hegel:* being the Hegelian System in Origin, Principle, Form, and Matter.
By J. H. Stirling, LL.D.
2 vols. 8vo. 28s.

*Sir William Hamilton;* being the Philosophy of Perception: an Analysis.
By J. H. Stirling, LL.D.
8vo. 5s.

*Ueberweg's System of Logic, and History of Logical Doctrines.*
Translated, with Notes and Appendices, by T. M. Lindsay, M.A. F.R.S.E.
8vo. 16s.

*The Senses and the Intellect.*
By A. Bain, LL.D. Prof. of Logic, Univ. Aberdeen.
8vo. 15s.

*Mental and Moral Science; a Compendium of Psychology and Ethics.*
By A. Bain, LL.D.
Third Edition. Crown 8vo. 10s. 6d. Or separately: Part I. Mental Science, 6s. 6d. Part II. Moral Science, 4s. 6d.

*The Philosophy of Necessity; or, Natural Law as applicable to Mental, Moral, and Social Science.*
By Charles Bray.
Second Edition. 8vo. 9s.

*Hume's Treatise on Human Nature.*
Edited, with Notes, &c. by T. H. Green, M.A. and the Rev. T. H. Grose, M.A.
2 vols. 8vo. 28s.

*Hume's Essays Moral, Political, and Literary.*
By the same Editors.
2 vols. 8vo. 28s.

*\*\** The above form a complete and uniform Edition of HUME's Philosophical Works.

## MISCELLANEOUS & CRITICAL WORKS.

**Miscellaneous and Post-humous Works of the late Henry Thomas Buckle.** Edited, with a Biographical Notice, by Helen Taylor.
3 vols. 8vo. £2. 12s. 6d.

**Short Studies on Great Subjects.** By J. A. Froude, M.A. formerly Fellow of Exeter College, Oxford.
CABINET EDITION, 2 vols. crown 8vo. 12s.
LIBRARY EDITION, 2 vols. 8vo. 24s.

**Lord Macaulay's Miscellaneous Writings.**
LIBRARY EDITION, 2 vols. 8vo. Portrait, 21s.
PEOPLE'S EDITION, 1 vol. cr. 8vo. 4s. 6d.

**Lord Macaulay's Miscellaneous Writings and Speeches.**
Students' Edition. Crown 8vo. 6s.

**Speeches of the Right Hon. Lord Macaulay, corrected by Himself.**
People's Edition. Crown 8vo. 3s. 6d.

**Lord Macaulay's Speeches on Parliamentary Reform in 1831 and 1832.**
16mo. 1s.

**Manual of English Literature, Historical and Critical.** By Thomas Arnold, M.A.
New Edition. Crown 8vo. 7s. 6d.

**The Rev. Sydney Smith's Essays contributed to the Edinburgh Review.**
Authorised Edition, complete in One Volume.
Crown 8vo. 2s. 6d. sewed, or 3s. 6d. cloth.

**The Rev. Sydney Smith's Miscellaneous Works.**
Crown 8vo. 6s.

**The Wit and Wisdom of the Rev. Sydney Smith.**
Crown 8vo. 3s. 6d.

**The Miscellaneous Works of Thomas Arnold, D.D. Late Head Master of Rugby School and Regius Professor of Modern History in the Univ. of Oxford.**
8vo. 7s. 6d.

**Realities of Irish Life.** By W. Steuart Trench.
Cr. 8vo. 2s. 6d. sewed, or 3s. 6d. cloth.

**Lectures on the Science of Language.** By F. Max Müller, M.A. &c.
Eighth Edition. 2 vols. crown 8vo. 16s.

**Chips from a German Workshop; being Essays on the Science of Religion, and on Mythology, Traditions, and Customs.** By F. Max Müller, M.A. &c.
3 vols. 8vo. £2.

Southey's Doctor, complete in One Volume.
Edited by Rev. J. W. Warter, B.D.
Square crown 8vo. 12s. 6d.

Families of Speech.
Four Lectures delivered at the Royal Institution.
By F. W. Farrar, D.D.
New Edition. Crown 8vo. 3s. 6d.

Chapters on Language.
By F. W. Farrar, D.D. F.R.S.
New Edition. Crown 8vo. 5s.

A Budget of Paradoxes.
By Augustus De Morgan, F.R.A.S.
Reprinted, with Author's Additions, from the Athenæum. 8vo. 15s.

Apparitions; a Narrative of Facts.
By the Rev. B. W. Savile, M.A. Author of 'The Truth of the Bible' &c.
Crown 8vo. price 4s. 6d.

Miscellaneous Writings of John Conington, M.A.
Edited by J. A. Symonds, M.A. With a Memoir by H. J. S. Smith, M.A.
2 vols. 8vo. 28s.

Recreations of a Country Parson.
By A. K. H. B.
Two Series, 3s. 6d. each.

Landscapes, Churches, and Moralities.
By A. K. H. B.
Crown 8vo. 3s. 6d.

Seaside Musings on Sundays and Weekdays.
By A. K. H. B.
Crown 8vo. 3s. 6d.

Changed Aspects of Unchanged Truths.
By A. K. H. B.
Crown 8vo. 3s. 6d.

Counsel and Comfort from a City Pulpit.
By A. K. H. B.
Crown 8vo. 3s. 6d.

Lessons of Middle Age.
By A. K. H. B.
Crown 8vo. 3s. 6d.

Leisure Hours in Town.
By A. K. H. B.
Crown 8vo. 3s. 6d.

The Autumn Holidays of a Country Parson.
By A. K. H. B.
Crown 8vo. 3s. 6d.

Sunday Afternoons at the Parish Church of a Scottish University City.
By A. K. H. B.
Crown 8vo. 3s. 6d.

The Commonplace Philosopher in Town and Country.
By A. K. H. B.
Crown 8vo. 3s. 6d.

Present-Day Thoughts.
By A. K. H. B.
Crown 8vo. 3s. 6d.

Critical Essays of a Country Parson.
By A. K. H. B.
Crown 8vo. 3s. 6d.

The Graver Thoughts of a Country Parson.
By A. K. H. B.
Two Series, 3s. 6d. each.

## DICTIONARIES and OTHER BOOKS of REFERENCE.

A Dictionary of the English Language.
By R. G. Latham, M.A. M.D. Founded on the Dictionary of Dr. S. Johnson, as edited by the Rev. H. J. Todd, with numerous Emendations and Additions.
4 vols. 4to. £7.

Thesaurus of English Words and Phrases, classified and arranged so as to facilitate the expression of Ideas, and assist in Literary Composition.
By P. M. Roget, M.D.
Crown 8vo. 10s. 6d.

English Synonymes.
By E. J. Whately. Edited by Archbishop Whately.
Fifth Edition. Fcp. 8vo. 3s.

Handbook of the English Language. For the use of Students of the Universities and the Higher Classes in Schools.
By R. G. Latham, M.A. M.D. &c. late Fellow of King's College, Cambridge; late Professor of English in Univ. Coll. Lond.
The Ninth Edition.    Crown 8vo. 6s.

A Practical Dictionary of the French and English Languages.
By Léon Contanseau, many years French Examiner for Military and Civil Appointments, &c.
Post 8vo. 10s. 6d.

Contanseau's Pocket Dictionary, French and English, abridged from the Practical Dictionary, by the Author.
Square 18mo. 3s. 6d.

*New Practical Dictionary of the German Language; German - English and English-German.*
By Rev. W. L. Blackley, M.A. and Dr. C. M. Friedländer.
Post 8vo. 7s. 6d.

*A Dictionary of Roman and Greek Antiquities. With 2,000 Woodcuts from Ancient Originals, illustrative of the Arts and Life of the Greeks and Romans.*
By Anthony Rich, B.A.
Third Edition. Crown 8vo. 7s. 6d.

*The Mastery of Languages; or, the Art of Speaking Foreign Tongues Idiomatically.*
By Thomas Prendergast.
Second Edition. 8vo. 6s.

*A Practical English Dictionary.*
By John T. White, D.D. Oxon. and T. C. Donkin, M.A.
1 vol. post 8vo. uniform with Contanseau's Practical French Dictionary.
[In the press.

*A Latin-English Dictionary.*
By John T. White, D.D. Oxon. and J. E. Riddle, M.A. Oxon.
Third Edition, revised. 2 vols. 4to. 42s.

*White's College Latin-English Dictionary; abridged from the Parent Work for the use of University Students.*
Medium 8vo. 18s.

*A Latin-English Dictionary adapted for the use of Middle-Class Schools.*
By John T. White, D.D. Oxon.
Square fcp. 8vo. 3s.

*White's Junior Student's Complete Latin - English and English-Latin Dictionary.*
Square 12mo. 12s.
Separately { ENGLISH-LATIN, 5s. 6d.
{ LATIN-ENGLISH, 7s. 6d.

*A Greek-English Lexicon.*
By H. G. Liddell, D.D. Dean of Christchurch, and R. Scott, D.D. Dean of Rochester.
Sixth Edition. Crown 4to. 36s.

*A Lexicon, Greek and English, abridged for Schools from Liddell and Scott's Greek - English Lexicon.*
Fourteenth Edition. Square 12mo. 7s. 6d.

*An English-Greek Lexicon, containing all the Greek Words used by Writers of good authority.*
By C. D. Yonge, B.A.
New Edition. 4to. 21s.

C. D. Yonge's New Lexicon, English and Greek, abridged from his larger Lexicon.

Square 12mo. 8s. 6d.

M'Culloch's Dictionary, Practical, Theoretical, and Historical, of Commerce and Commercial Navigation.

Edited by H. G. Reid.

8vo. 63s.

A General Dictionary of Geography, Descriptive, Physical, Statistical, and Historical; forming a complete Gazetteer of the World.

By A. Keith Johnston, F.R.S.E.

New Edition, thoroughly revised. [In the press.

The Public Schools Manual of Modern Geography. Forming a Companion to 'The Public Schools Atlas of Modern Geography'

By Rev. G. Butler, M.A. [In the press.

The Public Schools Atlas of Modern Geography. In 31 Maps, exhibiting clearly the more important Physical Features of the Countries delineated.

Edited, with Introduction, by Rev. G. Butler, M.A.

Imperial quarto, 3s. 6d. sewed; 5s. cloth.

The Public Schools Atlas of Ancient Geography. Edited, with an Introduction on the Study of Ancient Geography, by the Rev. G. Butler, M.A.

Imperial Quarto.    [In the press.

---

## ASTRONOMY and METEOROLOGY.

The Universe and the Coming Transits: Researches into and New Views respecting the Constitution of the Heavens.

By R. A. Proctor, B.A.

With 22 Charts and 22 Diagrams. 8vo. 16s.

Saturn and its System.

By R. A. Proctor, B.A.

8vo. with 14 Plates, 14s.

The Transits of Venus; A Popular Account of Past and Coming Transits, from the first observed by Horrocks A.D. 1639 to the Transit of A.D. 2012.

By R. A. Proctor, B.A.

With 20 Plates (12 Coloured) and 27 Woodcuts.    Crown 8vo. 8s. 6d.

*Essays on Astronomy.*
A Series of Papers on
Planets and Meteors, the
Sun and Sun-surrounding
Space, Stars and Star
Cloudlets.
By R. A. Proctor, B.A.
With 10 Plates and 24 Woodcuts. 8vo. 12s.

*The Moon; her Motions,*
Aspect, Scenery, and Phy-
sical Condition.
By R. A. Proctor, B.A.
With Plates, Charts, Woodcuts, and Lunar
Photographs. Crown 8vo. 15s.

*The Sun; Ruler, Light,*
Fire, and Life of the Pla-
netary System.
By R. A. Proctor, B.A.
Second Edition. Plates and Woodcuts. Cr.
8vo. 14s.

*The Orbs Around Us; a*
Series of Familiar Essays
on the Moon and Planets,
Meteors and Comets, the
Sun and Coloured Pairs of
Suns.
By R. A. Proctor, B.A.
Second Edition, with Chart and 4 Diagrams.
Crown 8vo. 7s. 6d.

*Other Worlds than Ours;*
The Plurality of Worlds
Studied under the Light
of Recent Scientific Re-
searches.
By R. A. Proctor, B.A.
Third Edition, with 14 Illustrations. Cr.
8vo. 10s. 6d.

*Brinkley's Astronomy.*
Revised and partly re-writ-
ten, with Additional Chap-
ters, and an Appendix of
Questions for Examination.
By John W. Stubbs, D.D.
and F. Brunnow, Ph.D.
With 49 Diagrams. Crown 8vo. 6s.

*Outlines of Astronomy.*
By Sir J. F. W. Herschel,
Bart. M.A.
Latest Edition, with Plates and Diagrams.
Square crown 8vo. 12s.

*A New Star Atlas, for*
the Library, the School, and
the Observatory, in 12 Circular Maps (with 2 Index
Plates).
By R. A. Proctor, B.A.
Crown 8vo. 5s.

*Celestial Objects for Com-*
mon Telescopes.
By T. W. Webb, M.A.
F.R.A.S.
New Edition, with Map of the Moon and
Woodcuts. Crown 8vo. 7s. 6d.

*Larger Star Atlas, for the*
Library, in Twelve Cir-
cular Maps, photolitho-
graphed by A. Brothers,
F.R.A.S. With 2 Index
Plates and a Letterpress
Introduction.
By R. A. Proctor, B.A.
Second Edition. Small folio, 25s.

C

Dove's Law of Storms, considered in connexion with the ordinary Movements of the Atmosphere.
Translated by R. H. Scott, M.A.
8vo. 10s. 6d.

Air and Rain; the Beginnings of a Chemical Climatology.
By R. A. Smith, F.R.S.
8vo. 24s.

Air and its Relations to Life, 1774–1874. Being, with some Additions, a Course of Lectures delivered at the Royal Institution of Great Britain in the Summer of 1874.
By Walter Noel Hartley, F.C.S. Demonstrator of Chemistry at King's College, London.
1 vol. small 8vo. with Illustratations.
[Nearly ready.

Magnetism and Deviation of the Compass. For the use of Students in Navigation and Science Schools.
By J. Merrifield, LL.D.
18mo. 1s. 6d.

Nautical Surveying, an Introduction to the Practical and Theoretical Study of.
By J. K. Laughton, M.A.
Small 8vo. 6s.

Schellen's Spectrum Analysis, in its Application to Terrestrial Substances and the Physical Constitution of the Heavenly Bodies.
Translated by Jane and C. Lassell; edited, with Notes, by W. Huggins, LL.D. F.R.S.
With 13 Plates and 223 Woodcuts. 8vo. 28s.

# NATURAL HISTORY and PHYSICAL SCIENCE.

The Correlation of Physical Forces.
By the Hon. Sir W. R. Grove, F.R.S. &c.
Sixth Edition, with other Contributions to Science. 8vo. 15s.

Professor Helmholtz' Popular Lectures on Scientific Subjects.
Translated by E. Atkinson, F.C.S.
With many Illustrative Wood Engravings.
8vo. 12s. 6d.

*Ganot's Natural Philosophy for General Readers and Young Persons; a Course of Physics divested of Mathematical Formulæ and expressed in the language of daily life.*
  *Translated by E. Atkinson, F.C.S.*
Second Edition, with 2 Plates and 429 Woodcuts. Crown 8vo. 7s. 6d.

*Ganot's Elementary Treatise on Physics, Experimental and Applied, for the use of Colleges and Schools.*
  *Translated and edited by E. Atkinson, F.C.S.*
New Edition, with a Coloured Plate and 726 Woodcuts. Post 8vo. 15s.

*Weinhold's Introduction to Experimental Physics, Theoretical and Practical; including Directions for Constructing Physical Apparatus and for Making Experiments.*
  *Translated by B. Loewy, F.R.A.S. With a Preface by G. C. Foster, F.R.S.*
With 3 Coloured Plates and 404 Woodcuts. 8vo. price 31s. 6d.

*Principles of Animal Mechanics.*
  *By the Rev. S. Haughton, F.R.S.*
Second Edition. 8vo. 21s.

*Text-Books of Science, Mechanical and Physical, adapted for the use of Artisans and of Students in Public and other Schools. (The first Ten edited by T. M. Goodeve, M.A. Lecturer on Applied Science at the Royal School of Mines; the remainder edited by C. W. Merrifield, F.R.S. an Examiner in the Department of Public Education.)*
  Small 8vo. Woodcuts.

Edited by T. M. Goodeve, M.A.
Anderson's *Strength of Materials*, 3s. 6d.
Bloxam's *Metals*, 3s. 6d.
Goodeve's *Mechanics*, 3s. 6d.
———— *Mechanism*, 3s. 6d.
Griffin's *Algebra & Trigonometry*, 3s. 6d.
  *Notes on the same, with Solutions*, 3s. 6d.
Jenkin's *Electricity & Magnetism*, 3s. 6d.
Maxwell's *Theory of Heat*, 3s. 6d.
Merrifield's *Technical Arithmetic*, 3s. 6d.
  *Key*, 3s. 6d.
Miller's *Inorganic Chemistry*, 3s. 6d.
Shelley's *Workshop Appliances*, 3s. 6d.
Watson's *Plane & Solid Geometry*, 3s. 6d.

Edited by C. W. Merrifield, F.R.S.
Armstrong's *Organic Chemistry*, 3s. 6d.
Thorpe's *Quantitative Analysis*, 4s. 6d.
Thorpe and Muir's *Qualitative Analysis*, 3s. 6d.

*Fragments of Science.*
  *By John Tyndall, F.R.S.*
  New Edition, in the press.

*Address delivered before the British Association assembled at Belfast.*
  *By John Tyndall, F.R.S. President.*
8th Thousand, with New Preface and the Manchester Address. 8vo. price 4s. 6d.

*Heat a Mode of Motion.*
By *John Tyndall, F.R.S.*
Fifth Edition, Plate and Woodcuts.
Crown 8vo. 10s. 6d.

*Sound.*
By *John Tyndall, F.R.S.*
Third Edition, including Recent Researches
on Fog-Signalling; Portrait and Woodcuts. Crown 8vo. 10s. 6d.

*Researches on Diamag-
netism and Magne-Crystal-
lic Action; including Dia-
magnetic Polarity.*
By *John Tyndall, F.R.S.*
With 6 Plates and many Woodcuts. 8vo. 14s.

*Contributions to Mole-
cular Physics in the do-
main of Radiant Heat.*
By *John Tyndall, F.R.S.*
With 2 Plates and 31 Woodcuts. 8vo. 16s.

*Six Lectures on Light,
delivered in America in
1872 and 1873.*
By *John Tyndall, F.R.S.*
Second Edition, with Portrait, Plate, and
59 Diagrams. Crown 8vo. 7s. 6d.

*Notes of a Course of Nine
Lectures on Light, delivered
at the Royal Institution.*
By *John Tyndall, F.R.S.*
Crown 8vo. 1s. sewed, or 1s. 6d. cloth.

*Notes of a Course of
Seven Lectures on Electri-
cal Phenomena and Theo-
ries, delivered at the Royal
Institution.*
By *John Tyndall, F.R.S.*
Crown 8vo. 1s. sewed, or 1s. 6d. cloth.

*A Treatise on Magne-
tism, General and Terres-
trial.*
By *H. Lloyd, D.D. D.C.L.*
8vo. price 10s. 6d.

*Elementary Treatise on
the Wave-Theory of Light.*
By *H. Lloyd, D.D. D.C.L.*
Third Edition. 8vo. 10s. 6d.

*An Elementary Exposi-
tion of the Doctrine of
Energy.*
By *D. D. Heath, M.A.*
Post 8vo. 4s. 6d.

*The Comparative Ana-
tomy and Physiology of the
Vertebrate Animals.*
By *Richard Owen, F.R.S.*
With 1,472 Woodcuts. 3 vols. 8vo. £3. 13s. 6d.

*Sir H. Holland's Frag-
mentary Papers on Science
and other subjects.*
Edited by the Rev. *J. Holland.*
8vo. price 14s.

*Light Science for Lei-
sure Hours; Familiar Es-
says on Scientific Subjects,
Natural Phenomena, &c.*
By *R. A. Proctor, B.A.*
First and Second Series. 2 vols. crown 8vo.
7s. 6d. each.

*Kirby and Spence's In-
troduction to Entomology,
or Elements of the Natural
History of Insects.*
Crown 8vo. 5s.

Strange Dwellings; a Description of the Habitations of Animals, abridged from 'Homes without Hands.'
By Rev. J. G. Wood, M.A.
With Frontispiece and 60 Woodcuts. Crown 8vo. 7s. 6d.

Homes without Hands; a Description of the Habitations of Animals, classed according to their Principle of Construction.
By Rev. J. G. Wood, M.A.
With about 140 Vignettes on Wood. 8vo. 14s.

Out of Doors; a Selection of Original Articles on Practical Natural History.
By Rev. J. G. Wood, M.A.
With 6 Illustrations from Original Designs engraved on Wood. Crown 8vo. 7s. 6d.

The Polar World : a Popular Description of Man and Nature in the Arctic and Antarctic Regions of the Globe.
By Dr. G. Hartwig.
With Chromoxylographs, Maps, and Woodcuts. 8vo. 10s. 6d.

The Sea and its Living Wonders.
By Dr. G. Hartwig.
Fourth Edition, enlarged. 8vo. with many Illustrations, 10s. 6d.

The Tropical World.
By Dr. G. Hartwig.
With about 200 Illustrations. 8vo. 10s. 6d.

The Subterranean World.
By Dr. G. Hartwig.
With Maps and Woodcuts. 8vo. 10s. 6d.

The Aerial World; a Popular Account of the Phenomena and Life of the Atmosphere.
By Dr. George Hartwig.
With Map, 8 Chromoxylographs, and 60 Woodcuts. 8vo. price 21s.

Game Preservers and Bird Preservers, or ' Which are our Friends?'
By George Francis Morant, late Captain 12th Royal Lancers & Major Cape Mounted Riflemen.
Crown 8vo. price 5s.

A Familiar History of Birds.
By E. Stanley, D.D. late Ld. Bishop of Norwich.
Fcp. 8vo. with Woodcuts, 3s. 6d.

Insects at Home; a Popular Account of British Insects, their Structure Habits, and Transformations.
By Rev. J. G. Wood, M.A.
With upwards of 700 Woodcuts. 8vo. 21s.

Insects Abroad; being a Popular Account of Foreign Insects, their Structure, Habits, and Transformations.
By Rev. J. G. Wood, M.A.
With upwards of 700 Woodcuts. 8vo. 21s.

**Rocks Classified and De-scribed.**
By B. Von Cotta.
English Edition, by P. H. Lawrence (with English, German, and French Syno-nyms), revised by the Author. Post 8vo. 14s.

**Heer's Primæval World of Switzerland.**
Translated by W. S. Dal-las, F.L.S. and edited by James Heywood, M.A. F.R.S.
2 vols. 8vo. with numerous Illustrations. [In the press.

**The Origin of Civilisa-tion, and the Primitive Condition of Man; Men-tal and Social Condition of Savages.**
By Sir J. Lubbock, Bart. M.P. F.R.S.
Third Edition, with 25 Woodcuts. 8vo. 18s.

**The Native Races of the Pacific States of North America.**
By Hubert Howe Bancroft.
Vol. I. Wild Tribes, their Manners and Customs; with 6 Maps. 8vo. 25s.
Vol. II. Native Races of the Pacific States. 25s.
*⁎* To be completed early in the year 1876, in Three more Volumes—
Vol. III. Mythology and Languages of both Savage and Civilised Nations.
Vol. IV. Antiquities and Architectural Remains.
Vol. V. Aboriginal History and Migra-tions; Index to the Entire Work.

**The Ancient Stone Im-plements, Weapons, and Or-naments of Great Britain.**
By John Evans, F.R.S.
With 2 Plates and 476 Woodcuts. 8vo. 2s.

**The Elements of Botany for Families and Schools.**
Eleventh Edition, revised by Thomas Moore, F.L.S.
Fcp. 8vo. with 154 Woodcuts. 2s. 6.

**Bible Animals; a De-scription of every Living Creature mentioned in the Scriptures, from the Ape to the Coral.**
By Rev. J. G. Wood, M.A.
With about 100 Vignettes on Wood. 8vo. 21s.

**The Rose Amateur's Guide.**
By Thomas Rivers.
Tenth Edition. Fcp. 8vo. 4s.

**A Dictionary of Science, Literature, and Art.**
Re-edited by the late W. T. Brande (the Author) and Rev. G. W. Cox, M.A.
New Edition, revised. 3 vols. medium 8vo. 63s.

**On the Sensations of Tone, as a Physiological Basis for the Theory of Music.**
By H. Helmholtz, Pro-fessor of Physiology in the University of Berlin.
Translated by A. J. Ellis, F.R.S.
8vo. 36s.

The *History of Modern Music*, a Course of Lectures delivered at the Royal Institution of Great Britain.
By *John Hullah*, Professor of Vocal Music in Queen's College and Bedford College, and Organist of Charterhouse.
*New Edition, 1 vol. post 8vo. [In the press.*

The *Treasury of Botany*, or Popular Dictionary of the Vegetable Kingdom; with which is incorporated a Glossary of Botanical Terms.
Edited by *J. Lindley*, F.R.S. and *T. Moore*, F.L.S.
*With 274 Woodcuts and 20 Steel Plates. Two Parts, f.p. 8vo. 12s.*

A *General System of Descriptive and Analytical Botany.*
Translated from the French of *Le Maout* and *Decaisne*, by Mrs. *Hooker*. Edited and arranged according to the English Botanical System, by *J. D. Hooker*, M.D. &c. Director of the Royal Botanic Gardens, Kew.
*With 5,500 Woodcuts. Imperial 8vo. 52s. 6d.*

*London's Encyclopædia of Plants*; comprising the Specific Character, Description, Culture, History, &c. of all the Plants found in Great Britain.
*With upwards of 12,000 Woodcuts. 8vo. 42s.*

*Handbook of Hardy Trees, Shrubs, and Herbaceous Plants*; containing Descriptions &c. of the Best Species in Cultivation; with Cultural Details, Comparative Hardiness, suitability for particular positions, &c. Based on the French Work of Decaisne and Naudin, and including the 720 Original Woodcut Illustrations.
By *W. B. Hemsley*.
*Medium 8vo. 21s.*

*Forest Trees and Woodland Scenery*, as described in Ancient and Modern Poets.
By *William Menzies*, Deputy Surveyor of Windsor Forest and Parks, &c.
*In One Volume, imperial 4to. with Twenty Plates, Coloured in facsimile of the original drawings, price £5. 5s.
[Preparing for publication.*

## CHEMISTRY and PHYSIOLOGY.

Miller's Elements of Chemistry, Theoretical and Practical.
Re-edited, with Additions, by H. Macleod, F.C.S.

3 vols. 8vo. £3.

PART I. CHEMICAL PHYSICS, 15s.
PART II. INORGANIC CHEMISTRY, 21s.
PART III. ORGANIC CHEMISTRY, New Edition in the press.

A Dictionary of Chemistry and the Allied Branches of other Sciences.
By Henry Watts, F.C.S. assisted by eminent Scientific and Practical Chemists.

6 vols. medium 8vo. £8. 14s. 6d.

Second Supplement to Watts's Dictionary of Chemistry, completing the Record of Discovery to the year 1873.

8vo. price 42s.

Select Methods in Chemical Analysis, chiefly Inorganic.
By Wm. Crookes, F.R.S.
With 22 Woodcuts. Crown 8vo. 12s. 6d.

Todd and Bowman's Physiological Anatomy, and Physiology of Man.
Vol. II. with numerous Illustrations, 25s.
Vol. I. New Edition by Dr. LIONEL S. BEALE, F.R.S. Parts I. and II. in 8vo. price 7s. 6d. each.

Health in the House, Twenty-five Lectures on Elementary Physiology in its Application to the Daily Wants of Man and Animals.
By Mrs. C. M. Buckton.
Crown 8vo. Woodcuts, 2s.

Outlines of Physiology, Human and Comparative.
By J. Marshall, F.R.C.S. Surgeon to the University College Hospital.
2 vols. cr. 8vo. with 122 Woodcuts, 32s.

---

## The FINE ARTS and ILLUSTRATED EDITIONS.

Poems.
By William B. Scott.

I. Ballads and Tales.  II. Studies from Nature.  III. Sonnets &c.
Illustrated by Seventeen Etchings by L. Alma Tadema and William B. Scott.
Crown 8vo. 15s.

Half-hour Lectures on the History and Practice of the Fine and Ornamental Arts.
By W. B. Scott.
Third Edition, with 50 Woodcuts. Crown 8vo. 8s. 6d.

*In Fairyland; Pictures from the Elf-World. By Richard Doyle. With a Poem by W. Allingham.*

With 16 coloured Plates, containing 36 Designs. Second Edition, folio, 15s.

*A Dictionary of Artists of the English School: Painters, Sculptors, Architects, Engravers, and Ornamentists; with Notices of their Lives and Works. By Samuel Redgrave.*

8vo. 16s.

*The New Testament, illustrated with Wood Engravings after the Early Masters, chiefly of the Italian School.*

Crown 4to. 63s.

*Lord Macaulay's Lays of Ancient Rome. With 90 Illustrations on Wood from Drawings by G. Scharf.*

Fcp. 4to. 21s.

*Miniature Edition, with Scharf's 90 Illustrations reduced in Lithography.*

Imp. 16mo. 10s. 6d.

*Moore's Lalla Rookh, Tenniel's Edition, with 68 Wood Engravings.*

Fcp. 4to. 21s.

*Moore's Irish Melodies, Maclise's Edition, with 161 Steel Plates.*

Super royal 8vo. 31s. 6d.

*Sacred and Legendary Art. By Mrs. Jameson.*

6 vols. square crown 8vo. price £5. 15s. 6d. as follows:—

*Legends of the Saints and Martyrs.*

New Edition, with 19 Etchings and 187 Woodcuts. 2 vols. 31s. 6d.

*Legends of the Monastic Orders.*

New Edition, with 11 Etchings and 88 Woodcuts. 1 vol. 21s.

*Legends of the Madonna.*

New Edition, with 27 Etchings and 165 Woodcuts. 1 vol. 21s.

*The History of Our Lord, with that of his Types and Precursors. Completed by Lady Eastlake.*

Revised Edition, with 13 Etchings and 281 Woodcuts. 2 vols. 42s.

D

## The USEFUL ARTS, MANUFACTURES, &c.

*Industrial Chemistry; a Manual for Manufacturers and for Colleges or Technical Schools. Being a Translation of Professors Stohmann and Engler's German Edition of Payen's 'Précis de Chimie Industrielle,' by Dr. J. D. Barry. Edited, and supplemented with Chapters on the Chemistry of the Metals, by B. H. Paul, Ph.D.*
8vo. with Plates and Woodcuts.
[In the press.

*Gwilt's Encyclopædia of Architecture, with above 1,600 Woodcuts.*
*Fifth Edition, with Alterations and Additions, by Wyatt Papworth.*
8vo. 52s. 6d.

*The Three Cathedrals dedicated to St. Paul in London; their History from the Foundation of the First Building in the Sixth Century to the Proposals for the Adornment of the Present Cathedral.*
*By W. Longman, F.S.A.*
With numerous Illustrations. Square crown 8vo. 21s.

*Lathes and Turning, Simple, Mechanical, and Ornamental.*
*By W. Henry Northcott.*
With 240 Illustrations. 8vo. 18s.

*Hints on Household Taste in Furniture, Upholstery, and other Details.*
*By Charles L. Eastlake, Architect.*
New Edition, with about 90 Illustrations. Square crown 8vo. 14s.

*Handbook of Practical Telegraphy.*
*By R. S. Culley, Memb. Inst. C.E. Engineer-in-Chief of Telegraphs to the Post-Office.*
Sixth Edition, Plates & Woodcuts. 8vo. 16s.

*Principles of Mechanism, for the use of Students in the Universities, and for Engineering Students.*
*By R. Willis, M.A. F.R.S. Professor in the University of Cambridge.*
Second Edition, with 374 Woodcuts. 8vo. 18s.

*Perspective; or, the Art of Drawing what one Sees: for the Use of those Sketching from Nature.*
*By Lieut. W. H. Collins, R.E. F.R.A.S.*
With 37 Woodcuts. Crown 8vo. 5s.

*Encyclopædia of Civil Engineering, Historical, Theoretical, and Practical.*
*By E. Cresy, C.E.*
With above 3,000 Woodcuts. 8vo. 42s.

*A Treatise on the Steam Engine*, in its various applications to Mines, Mills, Steam Navigation, Railways and Agriculture.

By *J. Bourne, C.E.*

With Portrait, 37 Plates, and 546 Woodcuts. 4to. 42s.

*Catechism of the Steam Engine*, in its various Applications.

By *John Bourne, C.E.*

New Edition, with 89 Woodcuts. Fcp. 8vo. 6s.

*Handbook of the Steam Engine.*

By *J. Bourne, C.E.* forming a KEY to the Author's Catechism of the Steam Engine.

With 67 Woodcuts. Fcp. 8vo. 9s.

*Recent Improvements in the Steam Engine.*

By *J. Bourne, C.E.*

With 124 Woodcuts. Fcp. 8vo. 6s.

*Lowndes's Engineer's Handbook;* explaining the Principles which should guide the Young Engineer in the Construction of Machinery.

Post 8vo. 5s.

*Ure's Dictionary of Arts, Manufactures, and Mines.* Seventh Edition, re-written and greatly enlarged by R. Hunt, F.R.S. assisted by numerous Contributors.

With 2,100 Woodcuts. 3 vols. medium 8vo. price £5. 5s.

*Practical Treatise on Metallurgy.* Adapted from the last German Edition of Professor Kerl's Metallurgy by W. Crookes, F.R.S. &c. and E. Röhrig, Ph.D.

3 vols. 8vo. with 625 Woodcuts. £4. 19s.

*Treatise on Mills and Millwork.*

By *Sir W. Fairbairn, Bt.*

With 18 Plates and 322 Woodcuts. 2 vols. 8vo. 32s.

*Useful Information for Engineers.*

By *Sir W. Fairbairn, Bt.*

With many Plates and Woodcuts. 3 vols. crown 8vo. 31s. 6d.

*The Application of Cast and Wrought Iron to Building Purposes.*

By *Sir W. Fairbairn, Bt.*

With 6 Plates and 118 Woodcuts. 8vo. 16s.

*Practical Handbook of Dyeing and Calico-Printing.*

By *W. Crookes, F.R.S. &c.*

With numerous Illustrations and Specimens of Dyed Textile Fabrics. 8vo. 42s.

Occasional Papers on Subjects connected with Civil Engineering, Gunnery, and Naval Architecture.
By Michael Scott, Memb. Inst. C.E. & of Inst. N.A.
2 vols. 8vo. with Plates, 42s.

Mitchell's Manual of Practical Assaying.
Fourth Edition, revised, with the Recent Discoveries incorporated, by W. Crookes, F.R.S.
8vo. Woodcuts, 31s. 6d.

Loudon's Encyclopædia of Gardening; comprising the Theory and Practice of Horticulture, Floriculture, Arboriculture, and Landscape Gardening.
With 1,000 Woodcuts. 8vo. 21s.

Loudon's Encyclopædia of Agriculture; comprising the Laying-out, Improvement, and Management of Landed Property, and the Cultivation and Economy of the Productions of Agriculture.
With 1,100 Woodcuts. 8vo. 21s.

## RELIGIOUS and MORAL WORKS.

An Exposition of the 39 Articles, Historical and Doctrinal.
By E. H. Browne, D.D. Bishop of Winchester.
New Edition. 8vo. 16s.

Historical Lectures on the Life of Our Lord Jesus Christ.
By C. J. Ellicott, D.D.
Fifth Edition. 8vo. 12s.

An Introduction to the Theology of the Church of England, in an Exposition of the 39 Articles. By Rev. T. P. Boultbee, LL.D.
Fcp. 8vo. 6s.

Three Essays on Religion: Nature; the Utility of Religion; Theism.
By John Stuart Mill.
Second Edition. 8vo. price 10s. 6d.

Sermons Chiefly on the Interpretation of Scripture.
By the late Rev. Thomas Arnold, D.D.
8vo. price 7s. 6d.

Sermons preached in the Chapel of Rugby School; with an Address before Confirmation.
By the late Rev. Thomas Arnold, D.D.
Fcp. 8vo. price 3s. 6d.

*Christian Life, its Course, its Hindrances, and its Helps; Sermons preached mostly in the Chapel of Rugby School.*
By the late Rev. Thomas Arnold, D.D.
8vo. 7s. 6d.

*Christian Life, its Hopes, its Fears, and its Close; Sermons preached mostly in the Chapel of Rugby School.*
By the late Rev. Thomas Arnold, D.D.
8vo. 7s. 6d.

*Synonyms of the Old Testament, their Bearing on Christian Faith and Practice.*
By Rev. R. B. Girdlestone.
8vo. 15s.

*The Primitive and Catholic Faith in Relation to the Church of England.*
By the Rev. B. W. Savile, M.A. Rector of Shillingford, Exeter; Author of 'The Truth of the Bible' &c.
8vo. price 7s.

*Reasons of Faith; or, the Order of the Christian Argument Developed and Explained.*
By Rev. G. S. Drew, M.A.
Second Edition Fcp. 8vo. 6s.

*The Eclipse of Faith; or a Visit to a Religious Sceptic.*
By Henry Rogers.
Latest Edition. Fcp. 8vo. 5s.

*Defence of the Eclipse of Faith.*
By Henry Rogers.
Latest Edition. Fcp. 8vo. 3s. 6d.

*A Critical and Grammatical Commentary on St. Paul's Epistles.*
By C. J. Ellicott, D.D.
8vo. Galatians, 8s. 6d. Ephesians, 8s. 6d. Pastoral Epistles, 10s. 6d. Philippians, Colossians, & Philemon, 10s. 6d. Thessalonians, 7s. 6d.

*The Life and Epistles of St. Paul.*
By Rev. W. J. Conybeare, M.A. and Very Rev. J. S. Howson, D.D.

LIBRARY EDITION, with all the Original Illustrations, Maps, Landscapes on Steel, Woodcuts, &c. 2 vols. 4to. 42s.

INTERMEDIATE EDITION, with a Selection of Maps, Plates, and Woodcuts. 2 vols. square crown 8vo. 21s.

STUDENT'S EDITION, revised and condensed, with 46 Illustrations and Maps. 1 vol. crown 8vo. 9s.

*An Examination into the Doctrine and Practice of Confession.*
By the Rev. W. E. Jelf, B.D.
8vo. price 7s. 6d.

*Fasting Communion, how Binding in England by the Canons. With the testimony of the Early Fathers. An Historical Essay.*

By the Rev. H. T. Kingdon, M.A.

Second Edition. 8vo. 10s. 6d.

*Evidence of the Truth of the Christian Religion derived from the Literal Fulfilment of Prophecy.*

By Alexander Keith, D.D.

40th Edition, with numerous Plates. Square 8vo. 12s. 6d. or in post 8vo. with 5 Plates, 6s.

*Historical and Critical Commentary on the Old Testament; with a New Translation.*

By M. M. Kalisch, Ph.D.

Vol. I. Genesis, 8vo. 18s. or adapted for the General Reader, 12s. Vol. II. Exodus, 15s. or adapted for the General Reader, 12s. Vol. III. Leviticus, Part I. 15s. or adapted for the General Reader, 8s. Vol. IV. Leviticus, Part II. 15s. or adapted for the General Reader, 8s.

*The History and Literature of the Israelites, according to the Old Testament and the Apocrypha.*

By C. De Rothschild and A. De Rothschild.

Second Edition. 2 vols. crown 8vo. 12s. 6d. Abridged Edition, in 1 vol. fcp. 8vo. 3s. 6d.

*Ewald's History of Israel.*

Translated from the German by J. E. Carpenter, M.A. with Preface by R. Martineau, M.A.

5 vols. 8vo. 63s.

*The Types of Genesis, briefly considered as revealing the Development of Human Nature.*

By Andrew Jukes.

Third Edition. Crown 8vo. 7s. 6d.

*The Second Death and the Restitution of all Things; with some Preliminary Remarks on the Nature and Inspiration of Holy Scripture. (A Letter to a Friend.)*

By Andrew Jukes.

Fourth Edition. Crown 8vo. 3s. 6d.

*Commentary on Epistle to the Romans.*

By Rev. W. A. O'Conor.

Crown 8vo. 3s. 6d.

*A Commentary on the Gospel of St. John.*

By Rev. W. A. O'Conor.

Crown 8vo. 10s. 6d.

*The Epistle to the Hebrews; with Analytical Introduction and Notes.*

By Rev. W. A. O'Conor.

Crown 8vo. 4s. 6d.

Thoughts for the Age.
By Elizabeth M. Sewell.
New Edition.  Fcp. 8vo. 3s. 6d.

Passing Thoughts on Religion.
By Elizabeth M. Sewell.
Fcp. 8vo. 3s. 6d.

Preparation for the Holy Communion; the Devotions chiefly from the works of Jeremy Taylor.
By Elizabeth M. Sewell.
32mo. 3s.

Bishop Jeremy Taylor's Entire Works; with Life by Bishop Heber.
Revised and corrected by the Rev. C. P. Eden.
10 vols. £5 5s.

Hymns of Praise and Prayer.
Collected and edited by Rev. J. Martineau, LL.D.
Crown 8vo. 4s. 6d.  32mo. 1s. 6d.

Spiritual Songs for the Sundays and Holidays throughout the Year.
By J. S. B. Monsell, LL.D.
9th Thousand.  Fcp. 8vo. 5s  18mo. 2s.

Lyra Germanica; Hymns translated from the German by Miss C. Winkworth.
Fcp. 8vo. 5s.

Endeavours after the Christian Life; Discourses.
By Rev. J. Martineau, LL.D.
Fifth Edition.  Crown 8vo. 7s. 6d.

Lectures on the Pentateuch & the Moabite Stone; with Appendices.
By J. W. Colenso, D.D. Bishop of Natal.
8vo. 12s.

Supernatural Religion; an Inquiry into the Reality of Divine Revelation.
Fifth Edition.  2 vols. 8vo. 24s.

The Pentateuch and Book of Joshua Critically Examined.
By J. W. Colenso, D.D. Bishop of Natal.
Crown 8vo. 6s.

The New Bible Commentary, by Bishops and other Clergy of the Anglican Church, critically examined by the Rt. Rev. J. W. Colenso, D.D. Bishop of Natal.
8vo. 25s.

## TRAVELS, VOYAGES, &c.

**Italian Alps; Sketches in the Mountains of Ticino, Lombardy, the Trentino, and Venetia.**

By Douglas W. Freshfield, Editor of 'The Alpine Journal.'

*Square crown 8vo. Illustrations. 15s.*

**Here and There in the Alps.**

By the Hon. Frederica Plunket.

*With Vignette-title. Post 8vo. 6s. 6d.*

**The Valleys of Tirol; their Traditions and Customs, and How to Visit them.**

By Miss R. H. Busk.

*With Frontispiece and 3 Maps. Crown 8vo. 12s. 6d.*

**Two Years in Fiji, a Descriptive Narrative of a Residence in the Fijian Group of Islands; with some Account of the Fortunes of Foreign Settlers and Colonists up to the time of British Annexation.**

By Litton Forbes, M.D. L.R.C.P. F.R.G.S. late Medical Officer to the German Consulate, Apia, Navigator Islands.

*Crown 8vo. 8s. 6d.*

**Eight Years in Ceylon.**

By Sir Samuel W. Baker, M.A. F.R.G.S.

*New Edition, with Illustrations engraved on Wood by G. Pearson. Crown 8vo. Price 7s. 6d.*

**The Rifle and the Hound in Ceylon.**

By Sir Samuel W. Baker, M.A. F.R.G.S.

*New Edition, with Illustrations engraved on Wood by G. Pearson. Crown 8vo. Price 7s. 6d.*

**Meeting the Sun; a Journey all round the World through Egypt, China, Japan, and California.**

By William Simpson, F.R.G.S.

*With Heliotypes and Woodcuts. 8vo. 24s.*

**The Dolomite Mountains. Excursions through Tyrol, Carinthia, Carniola, and Friuli.**

By J. Gilbert and G. C. Churchill, F.R.G.S.

*With Illustrations. Sq. cr. 8vo. 21s.*

**The Alpine Club Map of the Chain of Mont Blanc, from an actual Survey in 1863–1864.**

By A. Adams-Reilly, F.R.G.S. M.A.C.

*In Chromolithography, on extra stout drawing paper 10s. or mounted on canvas in a folding case, 12s. 6d.*

The Alpine Club Map
of the Valpelline, the Val
Tournanche, and the South-
ern Valleys of the Chain of
Monte Rosa, from actual
Survey.
By A. Adams-Reilly,
F.R.G.S. M.A.C.
Price 6s. on extra Stout Drawing Paper, or
7s. 6d. mounted in a Folding Case.

Untrodden Peaks and
Unfrequented Valleys; a
Midsummer Ramble among
the Dolomites.
By Amelia B. Edwards.
With numerous Illustrations.  8vo. 21s.

The Alpine Club Map
of Switzerland, with parts
of the Neighbouring Coun-
tries, on the scale of Four
Miles to an Inch.
Edited by R. C. Nichols,
F.S.A. F.R.G.S.
In Four Sheets, in Portfolio, price 42s.
coloured, or 34s. uncoloured.

The Alpine Guide.
By John Ball, M.R.I.A.
late President of the
Alpine Club.
Post 8vo. with Maps and other Illustrations.

Eastern Alps.
Price 10s. 6d.

Central Alps, including
all the Oberland District.
Price 7s. 6d.

Western Alps, including
Mont Blanc, Monte Rosa,
Zermatt, &c.
Price 6s. 6d.

Introduction on Alpine
Travelling in general, and
on the Geology of the Alps.
Price 1s. Either of the Three Volumes or Parts
of the 'Alpine Guide' may be had with
this Introduction prefixed, 1s. extra.
The 'Alpine Guide' may also be had
in Ten separate Parts, or districts, price
2s. 6d. each.

Guide to the Pyrenees, for
the use of Mountaineers.
By Charles Packe.
Second Edition, with Maps &c. and Appendix.  Crown 8vo. 7s. 6d.

How to See Norway;
embodying the Experience
of Six Summer Tours in
that Country.
By J. R. Campbell.
With Map and 5 Woodcuts, fcp. 8vo. 5s.

Visits to Remarkable
Places, and Scenes illus-
trative of striking Passages
in English History and
Poetry.
By William Howitt.
2 vols. 8vo. Woodcuts, 25s.

## WORKS of FICTION.

*Whispers from Fairy-land.*

By the Rt. Hon. E. H. Knatchbull - Hugessen, M.P. Author of 'Stories for my Children,' &c.

With 9 Illustrations from Original De-si as engraved on Wood by G. Pear-s. Crown 8vo. price 6s.

*Lady Willoughby's Diary during the Reign of Charles the First, the Protectorate, and the Restoration.*

Crown 8vo. 7s. 6d.

*The Folk-Lore of Rome, collected by Word of Mouth from the People.*

By Miss R. H. Busk.

Crown 8vo. 12s. 6d.

*Becker's Gallus; or Roman Scenes of the Time of Augustus.*

Post 8vo. 7s. 6d.

*Becker's Charicles: Illustrative of Private Life of the Ancient Greeks.*

Post 8vo. 7s. 6d.

*Tales of the Teutonic Lands.*

By Rev. G. W. Cox, M.A. and E. H. Jones.

Crown 8vo. 10s. 6d.

*Tales of Ancient Greece.*

By the Rev. G. W. Cox, M.A.

Crown 8vo. 6s. 6d.

*The Modern Novelist's Library.*

Atherstone Priory, 2s. boards; 2s. 6d. cloth.
Mlle. Mori, 2s. boards; 2s. 6d. cloth.
The Burgomaster's Family, 2s. and 2s. 6d.
MELVILLE'S Digby Grand, 2s. and 2s. 6d.
——— Gladiators, 2s. and 2s. 6d.
——— Good for Nothing, 2s. & 2s. 6d.
——— Holmby House, 2s. and 2s. 6d.
——— Interpreter, 2s. and 2s. 6d.
——— Kate Coventry, 2s. and 2s. 6d.
——— Queen's Maries, 2s. and 2s. 6d.
——— General Bounce, 2s. and 2s. 6d.
TROLLOPE'S Warden, 1s. 6d. and 2s.
——— Barchester Towers, 2s. & 2s. 6d.
BRAMLEY-MOORE'S Six Sisters of the Valleys, 2s. boards; 2s. 6d. cloth.

*Novels and Tales.*

By the Right Hon. Benjamin Disraeli, M.P.

Cabinet Editions, complete in Ten Volumes, crown 8vo. 6s. each, as follows :—

Lothair, 6s.                    Venetia, 6s.
Coningsby, 6s.              Alroy, Ixion, &c. 6s.
Sybil, 6s.                       Young Duke, &c. 6s.
Tancred, 6s.                 Vivian Grey, 6s.
    Henrietta Temple, 6s.
    Contarini Fleming, &c. 6s.

*Stories and Tales.*

By Elizabeth M. Sewell, Author of 'The Child's First History of Rome,' 'Principles of Education,' &c. Cabinet Edition, in Ten Volumes :—

Amy Herbert, 2s. 6d. | Ivors, 2s. 6d.
Gertrude, 2s. 6d.       | Katharine Ashton,
Earl's Daughter,       |     2s. 6d.
    2s. 6d.                    | Margaret Percival,
Experience of Life,   |     3s. 6d.
    2s. 6d.                    | Laneton Parsonage,
Cleve Hall, 2s. 6d.   |     3s. 6d.
         Ursula, 3s. 6d.

## POETRY and THE DRAMA.

Ballads and Lyrics of Old France; with other Poems.
By A. Lang.
Square fcp. 8vo. 5s.

Moore's Lalla Rookh, Tenniel's Edition, with 68 Wood Engravings.
Fcp. 4to. 21s.

Moore's Irish Melodies, Maclise's Edition, with 161 Steel Plates.
Super-royal 8vo. 31s. 6d.

Miniature Edition of Moore's Irish Melodies, with Maclise's 161 Illustrations reduced in Lithography.
Imp. 16mo. 10s. 6d.

Milton's Lycidas and Epitaphium Damonis.
Edited, with Notes and Introduction, by C. S. Jerram, M.A.
Crown 8vo. 2s. 6d.

Lays of Ancient Rome; with Ivry and the Armada.
By the Right Hon. Lord Macaulay.
16mo. 3s. 6d.

Lord Macaulay's Lays of Ancient Rome. With 90 Illustrations on Wood from Drawings by G. Scharf.
F. p. 4to. 21s.

Miniature Edition of Lord Macaulay's Lays of Ancient Rome, with Scharf's 90 Illustrations reduced in Lithography.
Imp. 16mo. 10s. 6d.

Horatii Opera, Library Edition, with English Notes, Marginal References and various Readings.
Edited by Rev. J. E. Yonge.
8vo. 21s.

Southey's Poetical Works with the Author's last Corrections and Additions.
Medium 8vo. with Portrait, 14s.

Poems by Jean Ingelow.
2 vols. Fcp. 8vo. 10s.
FIRST SERIES, containing 'Divided,' 'The Star's Monument,' &c. 16th Thousand. Fcp. 8vo. 5s.
SECOND SERIES, 'A Story of Doom,' 'Gladys and her Island,' &c. 5th Thousand. Fcp. 8vo. 5s.

Poems by Jean Ingelow.
First Series, with nearly 100 Woodcut Illustrations.
Fcp. 4to. 21s.

*Bowdler's Family Shak-speare, cheaper Genuine Edition.*

Complete in 1 vol. medium 8vo. large type, with 36 Woodcut Illustrations, 14s. or in 6 vols. fcp. 8vo. price 21s.

*The Æneid of Virgil Translated into English Verse.*

*By J. Conington, M.A.*

Crown 8vo. 9s.

## RURAL SPORTS, HORSE and CATTLE MANAGEMENT, &c.

*Down the Road; or, Reminiscences of a Gentle-man Coachman.*

*By C. T. S. Birch Rey-nardson.*

Second Edition, with 12 Coloured Illustra-tions from Paintings by H. Alken. Medium 8vo. price 21s.

*Blaine's Encyclopædia of Rural Sports; Complete Accounts, Historical, Prac-tical, and Descriptive, of Hunting, Shooting, Fish-ing, Racing, &c.*

With above 600 Woodcuts (20 from Designs by JOHN LEECH). 8vo. 21s.

*A Book on Angling: a Treatise on the Art of Angling in every branch, including full Illustrated Lists of Salmon Flies.*

*By Francis Francis.*

Post 8vo. Portrait and Plates, 15s.

*Wilcocks's Sea-Fisher-man: comprising the Chief Methods of Hook and Line Fishing, a glance at Nets, and remarks on Boats and Boating.*

New Edition, with 80 Woodcuts. Post 8vo. 12s. 6d.

*The Ox, his Diseases and their Treatment; with an Essay on Parturition in the Cow.*

*By J. R. Dobson, Memb. R.C.V.S.*

Crown 8vo. with Illustrations 7s. 6d.

*Youatt on the Horse. Revised and enlarged by W. Watson, M.R.C.V.S.*

8vo. Woodcuts, 12s. 6d.

*Youatt's Work on the Dog, revised and enlarged.*

8vo. Woodcuts, 6s.

*Horses and Stables.*

*By Colonel F. Fitzwygram, XV. the King's Hussars.*

With 24 Plates of Illustrations. 8vo. 10s. 6d.

*The Dog in Health and Disease.*

*By Stonehenge.*

With 73 Wood Engravings. Square crown 8vo. 7s. 6d.

*The Greyhound.*

*By Stonehenge.*

Revised Edition, with 25 Portraits of Grey-hounds, &c. Square crown 8vo. 15s.

Stables and Stable Fittings.
By W. Miles, Esq.
Imp. 8vo. with 13 Plates, 15s.

The Horse's Foot, and how to keep it Sound.
By W. Miles, Esq.
Ninth Edition. Imp. 8vo. Woodcuts, 12s. 6d.

A Plain Treatise on Horse-shoeing.
By W. Miles, Esq.
Sixth Edition. Post 8vo. Woodcuts, 2s. 6d.

Remarks on Horses' Teeth, addressed to Purchasers.
By W. Miles, Esq.
Post 8vo. 1s. 6d.

The Fly-Fisher's Entomology.
By Alfred Ronalds.
With 20 coloured Plates. 8vo. 14s.

The Dead Shot, or Sportsman's Complete Guide.
By Marksman.
Fcp. 8vo. with Plates, 5s.

## WORKS of UTILITY and GENERAL INFORMATION.

Maunder's Treasury of Knowledge and Library of Reference; comprising an English Dictionary and Grammar, Universal Gazetteer, Classical Dictionary, Chronology, Law Dictionary, Synopsis of the Peerage, Useful Tables, &c.
Fcp. 8vo. 6s.

Maunder's Biographical Treasury.
Latest Edition, reconstructed and partly rewritten, with about 1,000 additional Memoirs, by W. L. R. Cates.
Fcp. 8vo. 6s.

Maunder's Scientific and Literary Treasury; a Popular Encyclopædia of Science, Literature, and Art.
New Edition, in part rewritten, with above 1,000 new articles, by J. Y. Johnson.
Fcp. 8vo. 6s.

Maunder's Treasury of Geography, Physical, Historical, Descriptive, and Political.
Edited by W. Hughes, F.R.G.S.
With 7 Maps and 16 Plates. Fcp. 8vo. 6s.

Maunder's Historical Treasury; General Introductory Outlines of Universal History, and a Series of Separate Histories.

Revised by the Rev. G. W. Cox, M.A.

Fcp. 8vo. 6s.

Maunder's Treasury of Natural History; or Popular Dictionary of Zoology.

Revised and corrected Edition. Fcp. 8vo. with 900 Woodcuts, 6s.

The Treasury of Bible Knowledge; being a Dictionary of the Books, Persons, Places, Events, and other Matters of which mention is made in Holy Scripture.

By Rev. J. Ayre, M.A.

With Maps, 15 Plates, and numerous Woodcuts. Fcp. 8vo. 6s.

Collieries and Colliers: a Handbook of the Law and Leading Cases relating thereto.

By J. C. Fowler.

Third Edition. Fcp. 8vo. 7s. 6d.

The Theory and Practice of Banking.

By H. D. Macleod, M.A.

Second Edition. 2 vols. 8vo. 30s.

Modern Cookery for Private Families, reduced to a System of Easy Practice in a Series of carefully-tested Receipts.

By Eliza Acton.

With 8 Plates & 150 Woodcuts. Fcp. 8vo. 6s.

A Practical Treatise on Brewing; with Formulæ for Public Brewers, and Instructions for Private Families.

By W. Black.

Fifth Edition. 8vo. 10s. 6d.

Three Hundred Original Chess Problems and Studies.

By Jas. Pierce, M.A. and W. T. Pierce.

With many Diagrams. Sq. fcp. 8vo. 7s. 6d. Supplement, price 3s.

The Theory of the Modern Scientific Game of Whist.

By W. Pole, F.R.S.

Seventh Edition. Fcp. 8vo. 2s. 6d.

The Cabinet Lawyer; a Popular Digest of the Laws of England, Civil, Criminal, and Constitutional.

Twenty-fourth Edition, corrected and extended. Fcp. 8vo. 9s.

**Pewtner's Comprehensive Specifier; a Guide to the Practical Specification of every kind of Building-Artificer's Work.**
Edited by W. Young.
Crown 8vo. 6s.

**Protection from Fire and Thieves. Including the Construction of Locks, Safes, Strong-Room, and Fire-proof Buildings; Burglary, and the Means of Preventing it; Fire, its Detection, Prevention, and Extinction; &c.**
By G. H. Chubb, Assoc. Inst. C.E.
With 32 Woodcuts. Cr. 8vo. 5s.

**Chess Openings.**
By F. W. Longman, Balliol College, Oxford.
Second Edition, revised. Fcp. 8vo. 2s. 6d.

**Hints to Mothers on the Management of their Health during the Period of Pregnancy and in the Lying-in Room.**
By Thomas Bull, M.D.
Fcp. 8vo. 5s.

**The Maternal Management of Children in Health and Disease.**
By Thomas Bull, M.D.
Fcp. 8vo. 5s.

# INDEX.

F

www.ingramcontent.com/pod-product-compliance
Lightning Source LLC
Chambersburg PA
CBHW021934110726
47901CB00003B/832